His Queen

Elvendon Book Two

Rosie Lynch

November 2025

For my daughter, Melissa, for encouraging me finish Kaitlin
and Keltor's story

Table of Contents

Chapter One
Earth, the New World

The warmth of the sun on her face roused Kaitlin from unconsciousness. She squinted, her eyelids fluttering against the brightness, struggling to open them fully. Attempting to move, she became aware of Keltor's arm draped heavily over her waist. Panic gripped her for a moment, but as she pressed closely to him, she felt the gentle rise and fall of his breathing. Relief washed through her, calming her nerves.

"Keltor," she whispered, sensing him stir beside her.

His arm shifted, and his hand reached out to find her. "Kaitlin," he responded urgently, his voice trembling with relief as he realised she was alive. He grasped her firmly, unwilling to let go.

Kaitlin's eyes finally opened a little, and she managed to turn her head towards him. She noticed he, too, was struggling to open his eyes.

"Kaitlin are you okay?" he asked, with concern in his voice, and squinting back at her.

"Yes," Kaitlin breathed, her voice trembling with uncertainty, "at least I think so." She swallowed, her brow furrowing as the enormity of their survival pressed in on her. "Oh my god, why aren't we dead?" The words slipped out, laced with disbelief and a faint note of guilt. Relief mixed with confusion in her chest— she was grateful, achingly so, but the question gnawed at her, refusing to loosen its grip. The last image lodged in her mind was of holding Keltor tightly, bracing for the end, then the sudden cocooning of a force field. After that—nothing but void.

Keltor sat up, blinking as he forced his eyes open and took stock of their surroundings. They found themselves in the centre of a vast, grassy field. Ahead, a dense forest beckoned, while more fields stretched out behind them. Breathing in deeply, Keltor noted the freshness of the air—it was earthy and clean, a stark contrast to what he remembered.

As Kaitlin stirred beside him and sat up, Keltor instinctively pulled her into his arms, holding her close. His hand gently rose to her cheek, offering comfort and reassurance.

"We did it, Kitcat," he said with a relieved smile.

"Yes, we did," Kaitlin replied, matching his smile as she gazed into his deep blue eyes. She leaned into his touch, savouring the moment.

"I love you so much, Kitcat," Keltor whispered, before leaning in to kiss her.

Kaitlin closed her eyes, her heart fluttering with happiness at his touch. She ran her fingers through his hair as their kiss deepened, overwhelmed by a sense of gratitude and joy—never had she felt so glad to be alive.

When their kiss ended, they pressed their noses together briefly, sharing a quiet moment before turning their attention outward to survey the unfamiliar landscape. It was clear—they were no longer on the hill where they had released Star.

Keltor took Kaitlin's hand, steadying her as they both rose to their feet. Instantly, a wave of dizziness swept over them, and they wobbled unsteadily, struggling to maintain their balance.

"Are you okay?" Keltor asked, concern etched into his features as he looked at her.

"Yeah, I think so, my legs feel a little weak," Kaitlin replied, her voice tinged with fatigue. She bent over, bracing herself with both hands on her knees, taking a moment to steady her breath.

"Me too. How long do you think we've been out for, and how did we get down here?" Keltor wondered aloud, glancing over at Kaitlin as she straightened up. He reached out again, his fingers finding hers, and she squeezed his hand tightly, drawing comfort from his presence.

"I don't know, a day or so perhaps. I think it was Star—she put a force field around us and saved us. Maybe she dropped us here," Kaitlin said, her words uncertain but hopeful.

"Maybe," Keltor responded absently, his gaze drifting ahead as he tried to make sense of their new surroundings. He inhaled deeply and let the breath out slowly, gathering his resolve. "Come on, let's go for a walk and see if we can figure out where we are."

As they began to move forward, Kaitlin's steps faltered with a lingering sense of dread. "Do you think everyone is dead?" she asked, her voice thick with regret.

Keltor shook his head, determination firm in his expression. "No, the prophecy said there would be survivors," he assured her. Without warning, he stopped, pulling Kaitlin to a sudden halt beside him.

"What is it?" Kaitlin asked, her voice trembling with fear at Keltor's sudden stop.

He offered a reassuring smile, squeezing her hand gently. "It's okay, look—over there," he said, gesturing towards the edge of the woodland with his free hand.

Kaitlin's eyes followed the direction he indicated. Relief and wonder mingled on her face as she took in the sight. "It's a deer," she whispered, glancing back at Keltor before returning her gaze to the animal.

"See? We're not alone. Mother Nature has still provided food for the survivors," Keltor observed, his tone hopeful.

But Kaitlin shook her head quickly, her brow furrowing. "I don't want to eat it," she replied, the idea of harming another living creature too much to bear in that moment.

Keltor's expression softened. "I wasn't suggesting we did. Look over there," he added, pointing once more—this time towards the edge of the treeline.

"Wild garlic?" Kaitlin said, surprise colouring her words as she spotted the fresh, green leaves growing nearby.

Keltor nodded in confirmation. "Yes, and chickweed as well, by the look of it," he said, surveying the undergrowth.

Kaitlin's brow knitted in confusion. "But it's July. Why would there be fresh garlic in July?" she wondered aloud, finding the situation strange and out of season.

He shrugged as they moved closer to the patch of greenery. "There's young nettles as well," Kaitlin noted, observing the vibrant new growth among the wild plants. "It's like spring."

"It's unusual for sure, but perhaps it has something to do with what happened," Keltor suggested thoughtfully. "Like a regrowth of everything or something."

"Hmm, maybe," Kaitlin agreed, casting her gaze over the lush foliage, still trying to make sense of the changes in their world.

"At least it's something to eat, let's gather some as we walk," Keltor suggested, his voice breaking the hush beneath the ancient trees as he gently released Kaitlin's hand. He shrugged off his cloak, the soft fabric brushing against a bed of emerald moss speckled with dew and twisted it deftly until it formed a makeshift sack. The scent of damp earth and wild garlic drifted up around them, familiar yet strangely comforting amidst their uncertainty.

Kaitlin managed a small, genuine smile, her cheeks still flushed from nerves. "Clever," she remarked, her voice low and warm, trying to anchor herself in his resourcefulness.

"It's an old woodsman trick," he replied with a mischievous glint in his eye, glancing up at her as stray shafts of sunlight filtered through the thick green canopy, dappling his face in patterns of gold and shadow. Together, they crouched and began to fill the cloak-sack with crisp leaves and pungent garlic, their fingers brushing through dew-wet stalks. Kaitlin's heart thudded in her chest—a heavy drum of anxiety beneath the gentle forest sounds: the distant call of a wood pigeon, the sharp scent of crushed grass underfoot, the cool brush of a breeze that carried the faint sweetness of the forest.

As they worked, Kaitlin's shoulders tensed, and she glanced at Keltor, needing reassurance. "How do we get home? I mean, what if the portal's not there anymore?" Her voice trembled, betraying her fear even as she tried to keep it steady.

Keltor paused, his hands full of wild greens, and offered her a lopsided smile—brave, but uncertain. "I don't see why it wouldn't be," he said, though his tone was tinged with doubt. Then something flickered in his memory. "The map, do you still have it?" he asked, urgency sharpening his words.

Kaitlin's hand flew to her dress, fingers searching the folds with growing alarm. Her pulse quickened as she fumbled. "No, I haven't got it. Hey, wait a minute, didn't you have it last?" Her brow creased, panic making her words spill out faster than she intended.

Keltor's hand shot to his shirt. "Did I?" For a heartbeat, uncertainty clouded his features—then relief washed over him as he felt the familiar crinkle in his pocket. "Oh, yeah, sorry," he said with a sheepish grin, pulling out the map.

He dropped his cloak to the leafy ground, and together they bent over the faded parchment. The green, earthy light played across their faces as they traced the lines, realising with a jolt that they were at least twenty miles from where they'd released Star. The knowledge settled like a stone in Kaitlin's stomach. She glanced upward, longing and grief twisting in her chest as she thought of Star's clear, sweet notes of her song—how she was going to miss her. The loss was raw, a dull ache in her heart, and she wrapped her arms around herself, shivering despite the warmth of the sunbeams.

Keltor's finger traced a trembling line across the map. "That's weird," he muttered, frowning as he studied it.

"What is?" Kaitlin leaned in, her breath catching, desperate for some measure of hope.

He hesitated. "The portal we came from in the Eccleston forest—it's gone. I can't see it."

Kaitlin's voice softened as she spoke, her worry etched in her expression. "What about the one to Elvendon?" she asked, looking to Keltor for reassurance.

Keltor unfolded the map further, hands trembling just slightly. He scanned the worn parchment, then let out a shaky breath. "It's still there," he said softly, relief blooming across his features.

8

"Oh, thank God," Kaitlin whispered, her shoulders relaxing as she let herself breathe again. Relief softened her features, and she stood quietly for a moment, drawing in slow, steady breaths, feeling herself regain composure after the tension of the past few minutes.

Keltor managed a crooked smile, doing his best to lift the mood. "The portal is another twenty miles or so away. We should reach it tomorrow, if we walk quickly."

Kaitlin nodded, but uncertainty gnawed at her. The weight of what lay ahead pressed in, making her words falter as she tried to focus on the path rather than the fear swirling in her chest.

After a pause, Kaitlin's voice trembled with a fresh concern. "What about the bodies?" She glanced at Keltor, anxiety flickering in her eyes.

Keltor turned towards her, brow furrowing. "Bodies?" he echoed, confusion momentarily clouding his expression.

"Yes, Aragon and his men," Kaitlin explained, her voice barely above a whisper. "If we go straight to Elvendon, we won't be able to... well, you know, get rid of them."

Keltor ran a hand through his hair, a grimace passing over his face. "Damn, I'd forgotten about them. But honestly, no one's out looking for us—they don't even know about the portal from Eccleston Forest. There's no way anyone will find them."

He tried to sound reassuring, though doubt lingered around the edges of his words. "When we get home, we'll go back there first, before facing your father."

"What do we tell my father?" Kaitlin asked, her voice laced with worry as she looked searchingly at Keltor.

Keltor met her gaze, hesitating before answering. "That he didn't make it, and he died saving you here on Earth," he said quietly, uncertainty flickering in his eyes.

Kaitlin frowned, her concern deepening. "Do you think he will believe us?"

"He may," Keltor replied, "but I don't know about King Iwein." Doubt coloured his words, and Kaitlin's anxiety grew.

She sighed softly. "That's what I'm afraid of."

Keltor admitted, "Kaitlin, I hadn't thought this far ahead. I mean, we didn't exactly plan on killing him and his men, and to be honest, I didn't think we were going to survive this."

"I know," Kaitlin murmured, her tone gentle as she stepped closer and wrapped her arms around his neck. "But we did. Despite everything, we made it, and I guess whatever is to come, we face together."

Keltor's lips brushed hers, kissing her gently, passionately, and with such love that Kaitlin knew, deep in her heart, they could survive anything. His hand moved up through her hair, his eyes lingering on her face, filled with tenderness.

"We should get going," he said, as his hand moved down her face and then his finger brushed across her lips. She nodded and kissed him.

Keltor closed his eyes, his heart fluttering with emotion, as if a thousand butterflies were whirling inside him. Kaitlin was his entire world, and he felt profoundly grateful for the chance to spend his life with her, whether their time together was long or short. Every day in her presence felt wonderful.

As they walked together, Kaitlin asked, "What time do you think it is?"

Keltor glanced up at the sun and replied, "Around two, I would think. We have at least eight hours of daylight left." He carefully folded the map and handed it to her, and she tucked it away inside her dress. They continued their way, side by side.

After a while, Kaitlin remarked on the unusual stillness and quiet. "There are no aeroplanes, no traffic noise. It's so strange— it's like being in Elvendon."

Keltor nodded in agreement. "I know. Earth has returned to how it was hundreds of years ago. Let's hope those who survived have learnt their lesson," he said, sounding somewhat despondent.

But Kaitlin was less optimistic. "I doubt it. I can guarantee you that wherever these settlements exist, sooner or later someone will take charge, crave more power, and seek to take over others' lands. It's simply part of human nature."

Keltor found the thought saddening and drew his arm around her shoulders. "That's sad," he said softly.

"I know," she agreed, and together they walked on in silence, comforted by each other's presence.

"You know Elvendon has stayed the same for centuries. We have modernised a little, you know, with hot water, toilets and so on." Keltor's voice was thoughtful as he shook his head, a hint of concern in his eyes. "I would hate to see it turn into what Earth used to be, with concrete buildings, cars and motorways." He paused, glancing all around them, taking in the natural beauty that surrounded them, before looking back at Kaitlin. "This is beautiful, the humans are so lucky they had you."

"And you," Kaitlin replied softly. "I couldn't have done it on my own."

Without hesitation, Keltor pulled her into his arms, holding her close. His presence was reassuring, a silent promise that she would never have to face anything alone. "I will always be here for you, and when we get back home, we shall face your father together," he assured her.

She nodded in agreement, but a cold shudder ran down her body at the thought of telling her father. The uncertainty ahead weighed on her, yet Keltor's support gave her the courage to keep moving forward.

"Come on, let's go," he said gently, taking her hand once more in his. Together, they continued their journey, walking for another five hours as the terrain gradually shifted—slipping out of the evergreen forest and descending into a valley.

As they drew nearer to what appeared to be an orchard, Kaitlin's curiosity was piqued. "Blossoms why are there blossoms?" she asked, her gaze taking in the delicate, colourful display.

Keltor considered her question thoughtfully. "It must be something Star did. I don't understand what else it could be. I'm beginning to think the reset has sent this world into a regrowth of some kind." His words hinted at a mysterious transformation that was unfolding around them.

"It's beautiful," Kaitlin remarked, enchanted by the scene. As they walked beneath the arching branches, magical wisps of pink and white apple blossoms floated gently down, swirling around them like snow and carpeting their path as they followed the valley further down.

Before long, Keltor noticed the dimming light. "It's getting dark already," he observed, a note of concern in his voice. "I would have thought we had at least another three hours, but the sun is low and setting."

Kaitlin immediately sensed his unease. "What does that mean, do you think something's wrong?" she asked, glancing up at the changing sky.

He shook his head, uncertain. "I don't know, maybe. It might have something to do with the sonic boom, or perhaps it's just later than I thought. This sun sits differently to ours; I may have just misread it. Either way we should look for shelter, preferably near some water."

Heeding Keltor's advice, they continued, their eyes scanning the landscape as dusk approached. Eventually, they came upon a steep incline leading into a narrow gorge.

"Look," Keltor said, pointing into the valley below. Kaitlin followed the direction of his finger and saw, at the bottom, a pool of water—a promising place to rest for the night.

"Come on, this looks okay for the night. Be careful, it's quite steep," he warned, and he turned sideways and began to shimmy down the incline. Kaitlin hitched up her dress and followed cautiously behind him.

"Wow, it's beautiful," Kaitlin remarked as they reached the bottom.

In amongst the trees was a small, sheltered pool, being fed from a stream. A waterfall poured gently over the edge of the gorge and splashed on the rocks below. The orange and fiery red of the setting sun filtered through the trees and reflected on the surface of the water.

"This will do us," Keltor called to her when he found a sheltered area underneath a tree that was a perfectly suitable place to spend the night.

Kaitlin shrugged off her cloak and rucksack, letting them fall to the ground, while Keltor placed his beside hers. Together, they walked to the edge of the pool.

"It's like home," Keltor remarked, casting her a glance. "Only on a smaller scale, and there's more nettles."

"And junk," Kaitlin added, nodding towards some debris. He looked at her as she pointed. "Obviously, mother nature missed cleaning up this bit," she said with a chuckle.

"Or...," Keltor began, removing his boots and socks, rolling up his trousers, and stepping into the cool water, "she left it for us to use." As he waded in, he pulled up his sleeve and fished out the offending item—a stainless-steel saucepan. He rinsed it thoroughly and filled it with fresh water from the pool.

"Do you fancy some dinner?" he asked.

Kaitlin nodded. "Yes, actually, I'm quite hungry."

"Well, don't just stand there, go and gather some wood then, and get a move on, it'll be dark soon," he teased.

She playfully shoved him before heading off to gather firewood. Once she had collected enough, she stacked the wood neatly into a pile and began to build the fire. Raising her hand, she uttered, "*Ignis*," and the fire sprang to life.

Keltor approached, putting his arm around her. "Hey, you did that without using your wand," he observed.

Together, they watched the flames as they grew. Kaitlin glanced at him, her eyes crinkling with a smile. "I didn't even realise," she admitted. "I just did it."

"Your magic is getting stronger," Keltor said.

"Yes, I think it has something to do with Star. I know she's gone, but I still feel like I have a connection to her, or to an energy source. And what about you?" She turned to face him as his hand came to rest on her shoulder.

"Me?"

"Yes, Mr Wizard," she said with a grin.

13

"Oh, yeah, to be fair it was the same as you, it just kind of happened instinctively."

"So, you admit it now, that you're a wizard?"

"Yeah, I guess," Keltor replied, lifting his hand gently to Kaitlin's face. "I admit it, I'm a wizard." He leaned in, closed his eyes, and kissed her. In that moment, nothing in any world could compare to how wonderful she made him feel—he was the happiest man alive.

"I love you," he said softly.

"I love you too," she replied. With a teasing glint in her eye, she added, "So, Protector, are you going to cook me something or not?"

"Yeah, okay, your highness," he replied with an exaggerated bow. "But it might be a bit of a meagre broth though."

"Anything would be fantastic," Kaitlin said, her stomach grumbling in anticipation.

Keltor walked to his cloak, retrieved the foraged goods, and dropped them all into the water before placing the pan on the fire. He settled down next to the flames, watching Kaitlin as she paddled in the water. His heart swelled with love, reflecting on how he once thought he would spend the rest of his life heartbroken, watching her from afar as nothing but her protector and the King's servant.

"I really fancy a cuppa," he yelled to her as she moved through the stream.

"Me too," she called back.

"Can't you magic me one?" he asked.

She looked up at him and replied, "Sorry, I'm not that good a witch yet. Can't you magic one, Mr Wizard?"

"Syronic witch," he yelled back. "And no, unfortunately."

Kaitlin laughed, then spotted movement in the water. She held her long hair back with her hands and leaned closer to see what it was.

"Keltor," she called, glancing up to him and then back to the water.

"What?" he asked, seeing her wave her hand at him. He jumped up, grabbed his sword, and hurried down to her.

"You don't need a sword," she whispered.

"Why are you whispering?" he asked.

"Look, by the rock, what are they?" she asked.

Still holding his sword, Keltor waded carefully into the water until he was beside her. "Crayfish," he said.

"You can eat crayfish, can't you?" Kaitlin asked, glancing at him. He nodded.

"You don't object to eating these?" he asked, remembering her earlier reluctance to kill a deer.

As her stomach rumbled, she shook her head. "No, I don't. How do we…"

His sword pinned the crayfish down to the bottom. "Catch it," she finished, watching his gloating face as he bent and picked it up.

"It's still snapping," Kaitlin said warily, tightening her grip on the crayfish. Its shell was slick and cold, its legs twitching between her fingers in a way that made her shiver.

"It will, but it's only its nerves," Keltor replied. "Here, hold it—there's more over there.

"Where am I supposed to put it?" she asked, recoiling slightly as she took hold of the crayfish. The creature's shell was slick and cold, and its legs twitched between her fingers, sending an involuntary shiver up her arm. Although wary of its snapping claws, she kept her grip firm, not wanting to drop it back into the water.

He gave a nonchalant shrug and returned his attention to the water. The cool, fresh stream lapped against his legs as he moved swiftly, expertly pinning another crayfish to the riverbed.

Kaitlin scooped up some material from her dress and deftly dropped the crayfish into its folds, using the fabric as an impromptu bowl. As she held it steady, Keltor tossed in another crayfish, then another, until, within minutes, he had managed to catch six sizeable specimens. The pair then made their way back

15

to the crackling warmth of the fire, Keltor remarking confidently, "These are going to taste so good."

Kaitlin carefully dropped all six crayfish into the boiling saucepan, along with the garlic and chickweed they had gathered. Once the ingredients were combined, she sat down beside the fire, allowing the mixture to simmer as they both waited for their meal to cook.

"I'm so hungry," Kaitlin remarked, her stomach rumbling audibly. "I feel like I haven't eaten for months."

"Me too, they should be ready now," Keltor replied, unable to hide his impatience. He shifted to his knees and reached out to remove the pan from the fire, only to recoil immediately as he realised the handle was far too hot to touch.

"I'll do it," Kaitlin offered. Using the fabric of her dress as a makeshift oven mitt, she gripped the handle and successfully moved the pan off the flames.

"Thanks. You know, I didn't think about how we'd eat this broth. The crayfish we can manage with our hands, but..." Keltor trailed off, glancing around for a solution.

"That's a point," Kaitlin agreed, scanning their surroundings. Suddenly, a grin spread across her face, and she let out an impromptu laugh.

"What?" Keltor asked, smiling at her reaction.

"Look over there, we must have missed them earlier." With her back to him, Kaitlin walked to the water's edge. She appeared to be rinsing something in the stream, her movements hidden from his view.

After a moment, she straightened and turned back to him, holding her find aloft. "Look, cups," she announced, triumphantly displaying two chipped but serviceable cups. "No way, that's mad," he replied as he took one from her.

"They're a little chipped but they'll do," Kaitlin remarked as she sat back down beside Keltor. He took her cup, dipped it carefully into the steaming broth, and handed it to her with a satisfied nod.

"Practically a feast," she said, smiling as she accepted the cup and selected a crayfish from him. Together, they savoured the meal, finding the crayfish remarkably delicious. They ate every edible part, not leaving a morsel behind. By the time they had finished, darkness had settled around them, the warmth of the evening lingering as the moon rose, casting a gentle light through the canopy above.

The waterfall pounded gently in the background, and after they'd eaten, Kaitlin stood abruptly and announced, "I'm going brave a quick dip in that waterfall and freshen up," and she bounded to her feet with confidence.

"Great, so I get to do the cooking and the washing up," Keltor grumbled in mock protest, his tone light and teasing. "Anyone would think you're a princess or something," he added, continuing to mutter as she walked away.

"Yep," Kaitlin replied over her shoulder, her tone playful as she made her way towards the water. "One whole dirty pan and two cups. Not that we are going to actually use them again," she called back, her voice fading as she hurried off to the water's edge.

Keltor watched her go, a smirk playing on his lips. He gathered up the two cups, placed them into the pan, and tucked the whole lot beneath a nearby bush, hiding them from view before turning his attention elsewhere.

Kaitlin plunged her hand under the water coming over the edge of the small gorge and she gave a shudder, as it was chillingly cold. She took off her dresses and threw them over a branch and then stepped underneath the water. It was hardly a pounding shower, but it was refreshing.

Opening her mouth, she drank the water. It was hard not to think about what had happened, but in a way, it felt like they were on holiday. It was only a couple of weeks ago when she had been in her shower at home in Surrey, oblivious along with billions of other people as to what was about to descend upon the world.

She knew they were lucky to be alive, and she was convinced Star had saved them. Kaitlin was sad for those who had died, but

17

she was glad they had not, as now she had more time to spend with Keltor, and she gave a hearty sigh.

"That was a big sigh," Keltor remarked, his gaze lingering on Kaitlin as he took in her beauty. In that quiet moment, he felt an unexpected surge of power, a spark of magic that seemed to leap towards her, connecting them in ways he could not fully comprehend.

Kaitlin glanced back over her shoulder, her eyes widening in surprise as she saw Keltor standing behind her. The cool night air brushed against her skin, heightening her senses as she stared at him, the silence punctuated only by the sound of her quickening breath. Moonlight danced across Keltor's body, casting shifting shadows that added a mysterious allure to the scene.

With a playful arch of her eyebrow, Kaitlin broke the silence. "Don't you knock?" she asked, her tone teasing as she met his gaze.

Keltor shook his head, a gentle smile playing on his lips, and stepped beneath the stream of water. The coolness enveloped them both, heightening every sensation. With a tender motion, he turned Kaitlin around to face him, drawing her in until his body pressed warmly against hers. He leaned down and kissed her, their connection deepening beneath the rush of the water.

As his fingers traced delicately down the length of her spine, Kaitlin shivered with delight, each touch sending a wave of anticipation through her. The world around them faded away, leaving only the intimacy of the moment and the bond that grew ever stronger between them.

As their lips parted, Kaitlin leaned in closer, her voice barely above a whisper as she confessed, "I feel like Adam and Eve." The words hung in the air, intimate and laden with meaning.

Keltor's brow furrowed in confusion. "Adam and who?" he asked, his gaze roaming appreciatively over her, clearly unfamiliar with the reference.

A faint smile tugged at Kaitlin's lips, and she gave a small shake of her head. "Adam and—oh, never mind," she murmured, brushing off the explanation. Her hands found their way to his back, fingers curling with gentle urgency as she drew him closer once again, her heart pounding with anticipation.

After their kiss ended, Kaitlin looked deeply into Keltor's eyes, but her expression grew troubled as an anxious thought crept in. She hesitated before speaking, concern edging her voice.

"Keltor, what will we do when we get back to Elvendon?" she asked, her gaze searching his face for reassurance.

Keltor reached out, gently stroking her cheek with the back of his fingers. "What do you mean?" he replied softly.

Kaitlin took a steadying breath. "Well, us being together," she clarified, her worries clearly weighing on her mind.

Without hesitation, Keltor pulled her closer, pressing her firmly against his chest. His words were gentle but resolute. "I told you, we will tell your father we are together," he whispered, his eyes locked with hers, full of affection.

"I know," Kaitlin replied, her voice barely above a whisper, "but what if my father says no? What will we do?" Her apprehension was clear, her uncertainty about the future looming large. "You know what he's like, and he is a powerful man, Keltor."

Keltor shook his head, unconcerned, and let out a soft laugh. Wrapping his arms around her, he hugged her tightly and placed a gentle kiss on the top of her head.

"You worry too much," he said, his tone light, trying to dispel her fears. "I will tell him that I, Keltor Dracon, am a wizard, and that I intend to bond with his daughter whether he likes it or not. If we can't stay at the palace, I'll build us a house in the forest. We'll make our own happily ever after," he promised, smiling warmly at her.

"Keltor," she whispered, her heart pounding in her chest, excitement threatening to burst forth. "Are you asking me to be your wife?" Her voice trembled with barely contained joy.

He stepped back and nodded, a smile lighting his face.

Taking her hand, he pressed a gentle kiss to her knuckles, lifting his eyes to meet hers. "Kaitlin Elvendon, *Ille carnor hel eni herves*," he whispered, his words soft and tender in the language

19

of dragona. Her eyes sparkled with joy as her heart raced—he was offering her his heart.

Keltor smiled, his eyes filled with warmth and devotion. *"Keltor Dracon, erama eh ille,"* she murmured, the words rich with meaning as she gave him hers. His lips found hers, gentle but assured, sealing the promise he had just spoken. He reached up, his hand sliding through her hair to rest at the back of her head, holding her close as the moment lingered in the night's embrace.

When they parted, Kaitlin laughed—a sound bright and clear, full of relief and happiness. She threw her head back, allowing the cool water to cascade across her face, washing away any remnants of doubt. In this simple, joyful act, her spirit seemed lighter, the weight of their uncertain future momentarily forgotten.

Keltor pressed gentle kisses along Kaitlin's neck and throat, his lips trailing across her shoulders. Each touch was filled with tenderness, expressing the depth of his feelings. Kaitlin, overwhelmed with relief and gratitude, closed her eyes for a moment and allowed herself to truly savour the sensation of being alive and safe in his arms. Every breath she took felt lighter, as though the weight of all her worries had melted away, leaving behind only the warmth and security of Keltor's embrace. In that instant, she was fully present, her fears momentarily forgotten, held steady by the unwavering comfort he offered. The gentle rise and fall of his chest beneath her cheek reassured her that, for now, they were together and nothing else mattered.

Taking her hand, Keltor guided her from the water's edge. She quickly gathered up her clothes, and together they made their way back to the warmth of the fire. There, they spread out their cloaks, creating a comforting space where they could be together.

As they lay side by side, Keltor whispered softly, "I love you," his fingers brushing through her damp hair with affection.

"I love you, Keltor Dracon," Kaitlin replied in a voice rich with emotion, and their lips met in a tender kiss, sealing their promise to one another.

Chapter Two

Return to Elvendon

As the sun rose, its warmth trickled across Keltor's face waking him. He yawned and then stretched as his eyes began to adjust to the daylight. Above him, sunlight glistened through the gaps in the branches of a tree, rippling over their bodies as they lay beneath it.

The weather was fair and quite warm. Keltor turned onto his side and propped himself up with his elbow. For a while, he just watched her sleep. He was in awe of her, of what she had done, how she a fought to save this Earth from its doom. None of the survivors on Earth would ever know what she had done, who she was, and how close they had come to losing this whole planet to the darkness. He gave a sigh; he was so unbelievably happy they had survived, and that he was going to be able to spend the rest of his life with her.

"Morning, sleepy," Keltor said softly as Kaitlin's eyes fluttered open. She blinked against the gentle light filtering through the trees and smiled back at him, her expression full of affection and contentment.

A soft breeze stirred, sending a few strands of her hair drifting across her face. Keltor reached out, his touch tender as he brushed the wayward locks aside. His hand lingered, tracing gently down the side of her soft cheek. With a quiet intimacy, he leaned forward, their connection deepened in the peaceful stillness of the new day.

"*Enl boscara Molarnera,*" Keltor whispered softly in dragona, his eyes filled with affection as he leant forward and kissed

Kaitlin. The meaning of his words—my beautiful princess—resonated deeply with her. She lifted her hand to the side of his face, closing her eyes and savouring both the tenderness of his kiss and the warmth of his words. When he gently released her, he smiled reassuringly at her.

"Ready to go home?" he asked quietly.

Kaitlin nodded, though her heart was heavy with worry. Keltor's eagerness to return to Elvendon stemmed from his longing to see his family again. For Kaitlin, however, the thought of going home brought a wave of anxiety. She was concerned about her father, King Severon of Elvendon, uncertain how he would react upon learning about her relationship with Keltor. The prospect of revealing their bond filled her with apprehension. Moreover, she wondered how King Iwein would respond to the devastating news that his first-born son—the heir to the throne of Aranstream—was dead. The uncertainty of their homecoming weighed heavily on her mind, casting a shadow over the path ahead.

Keltor sprang to his feet, stretching his arms high above his head and holding the pose for a minute or two to loosen his muscles. Afterwards, he began to stroll down towards the water's edge, taking in the serenity of the morning.

"Looks like it's going to be a nice day," he remarked, glancing back over his shoulder towards Kaitlin.

"Yes, it does," she replied, rising to her feet and beginning to straighten her clothes. She ran her fingers through her long blonde hair, attempting to tidy it, but ultimately chose to plait it into a single braid that hung over her shoulder. Fastening her cloak securely, she looked across at Keltor, who was now crouched by the water. Seeing him give an exaggerated shiver as he splashed cold water onto his face made her smile. They had endured so much together, and she couldn't imagine her life without him—nor did she ever want to.

Keltor sensed Kaitlin's gaze upon him—a subtle, magical tingling that ran through his body, alerting him to her attention.

Rising to his feet, he crossed the short distance back to her, his movements gentle and purposeful.

"Are you ready?" he asked quietly, bending to pick up his cloak from the ground. He shook it briskly, dusting off any debris, before draping it over his shoulders. The familiar weight of the cloak seemed to ground him, signalling that it was truly time to move on.

Kaitlin nodded in reply, her eyes meeting his as she reached out to take his offered hand. Their fingers intertwined, a silent reassurance passing between them—a reminder of all they had endured and the uncertain journey still ahead.

As they stood together, Kaitlin was acutely aware of how much the world had changed. Visions had haunted her dreams: buildings and roads dissolving, entire towns and cities swallowed back into the earth. She was certain these images came from Star, sent purposefully to show her how the planet had reclaimed itself—how Star had taken back possession of her world. This knowledge settled over her, mingling with both sorrow for what was lost and hope for what might yet come.

As they walked together, Keltor noticed a change in Kaitlin's demeanour. She had grown unusually quiet, her thoughts clearly troubled. Concerned, he glanced over and gently asked, "What's up?"

Kaitlin's response was subdued, her sigh heavy with emotion. "Oh, I don't know," she admitted, her voice betraying her despondency. She tried to make sense of her feelings, explaining, "I know Star had to do what she did in order to save the planet, but it just seems weird to think we are on Earth, it's so quiet and desolate."

Seeing a tear slip down Kaitlin's cheek, Keltor stopped their progress and faced her, his voice soft with concern. "Hey. What's wrong?"

Kaitlin's sorrow deepened as she confessed, "I suppose it's just kind of hit me; all those millions of people who have died. I mean the chaos, the fear, and the panic they must have all felt." She paused, recollecting a moment from before their departure. "I did send a text message to one of my oldest friends before we left the farm, warning him, whether he listened or not, I don't know. He lived in Somerset, so I told him to take his family to Wookey Hole, and to get deep into the caves."

Keltor sought to reassure her, asking gently, "Would he be the type to believe?"

Kaitlin nodded, recalling their families shared histories. "Yes, I think so, his mum was friends with mine, so, thinking about it now, he was probably the son of a witch."

Keltor offered comfort, his words steady and encouraging. "Then he's probably okay Kaitlin. If he were from a family of witches, they would have known what was coming, and they would have had a sanctuary somewhere and used their magic for protection."

Kaitlin drew a deep breath and released it slowly. His reassurance seemed to settle her unease. "You're probably right," she replied, trying to find solace in his words.

Keltor drew Kaitlin closer, wrapping his arm around her shoulder as they continued along the path together. The quiet companionship between them offered a brief reprieve from the weight of recent events.

Curiosity edged into Kaitlin's voice as she asked, "How far do you think it is to the portal?"

Keltor glanced ahead, considering their progress. "We're actually not that far away now, an hour or so I would say."

As they pressed on, the remains of Esimae's house soon came into view. What had once been a charming little home now lay in ruins—the roof completely gone, straw and splintered timbers strewn across the ground, and the belongings inside torn to shreds and scattered amongst the trees.

Kaitlin's voice was tinged with sadness as she took in the destruction. "It's such a shame. It was such a beautiful little house. I'm glad she decided to go back to Elvendon, I don't think she would have survived this."

Keltor nodded in agreement. "No, I don't think she would have either. Come on, let's go," he urged, his tone gentle but eager to continue towards home.

The path to the portal was treacherous, covered with fallen trees that forced them to climb and clamber over the debris to make their way through. Despite the obstacles, they pressed on determinedly.

Eventually, they reached a clearing. Standing together, Keltor raised his hand and summoned a wave of magical light. He no longer needed the sparkling magical dust; having embraced his identity as a wizard, his power was now strong enough to open the portal unaided. He reached for Kaitlin's hand, and she took it willingly.

"Home," he said softly. Kaitlin managed a small, if somewhat unenthusiastic, smile in response.

"Hey, it will be alright, Kitcat," Keltor reassured her with a gentle smile and a squeeze of her hand. She nodded, drawing comfort from his words, and together they stepped into the swirling mist, passing through the portal to Elvendon.

Opening her eyes, Kaitlin inhaled deeply, savouring the sensation—they were home. Elvendon's distinctive fragrance, a sweet blend of the ancient trees and the invigorating freshness of the air, washed over her. The scent instantly transported her back to her childhood, to the first time she had set foot in this magical realm at just five years old, when everything in life seemed so much simpler.

As they stood together, Keltor broke the silence. "We're going to have to go around the outskirt of Elvendon in order to get back on the trail to the cave," he explained, quickening their pace by gently pulling Kaitlin along. "I'm not sure whether we should go home first and pick up some supplies; we haven't got any food left."

Kaitlin considered the risks. "Do you think we can get to yours without being seen? If anyone recognises me, we'll never get back to clear up the mess."

Keltor's brow furrowed with concern. "That's what worries me. I'll be alright, I'm used to foraging for food, but what about you? I can catch a rabbit or something, if you'd eat it."

She tried to reassure him. "Don't worry about me, I'll be fine; we managed last night, didn't we?"

Keltor slipped his arm around her shoulder, and Kaitlin leaned into him, grateful for his warmth and presence. He attempted to lighten the mood. "What's that saying the humans have? You can take the princess out of the castle, but you can't take the girl out of the forest. No, wait, that's not right. You can take the girl out of the forest, but you can't take the princess out of the castle, no wait, that's—"

Kaitlin burst out laughing, interrupting him. "Keltor, you're a nut," she teased, playfully slapping his chest with her hand.

He clutched his chest in mock outrage. "Ouch," he protested, feigning injury.

She shook her head in amusement, laughter still lingering between them.

Keltor grinned. "Yeah, well, you know what I mean. You're no ordinary princess, Kaitlin."

"I should hope not. I'd hate to be ordinary."

"No chance of that," he murmured under his breath.

She gave him a playful shove. "Hey!"

He laughed, unable to hide his delight at her reaction.

Turning serious, Keltor confirmed their decision. "So, seriously now, we've decided then—we go around the city and straight to the cave."

"Yes, I think so," Kaitlin agreed. A mischievous glint appeared in her eyes. "Besides, it means we get a few more days to ourselves before the shit hits the fan, so to speak."

Keltor paused, and for a moment Kaitlin wondered if he was about to scold her for her choice of words. Instead, to her surprise, he leaned in and kissed her.

As he drew away, Kaitlin looked up at him, curiosity in her eyes. "What was that for?" she asked softly.

26

He gazed back at her, his expression gentle. "You know, I would leave everything to be with you, if that's what it takes for us to be together."

Kaitlin shook her head earnestly. "Keltor, I didn't mean I wouldn't go back. I'm frightened of what my father and King Iwein will do when they find out Aragon is dead, but I would never expect you to leave your family. I know how much they mean to you."

He nodded in agreement. "Yes, I love my family, but they'd be alright without me around. Kitcat, you are my world, and I couldn't exist in it without you."

He wrapped his arms around her, and she instinctively buried her face against his chest, seeking comfort in his embrace.

"Nor I you," she whispered, holding him tightly.

Keltor drew back slightly, just enough to look into her face. "Whatever happens next, we stay together, all right? We won't let anyone separate us."

Kaitlin gave a determined nod. "Agreed."

He kissed her again, sealing their promise.

"Right, let's go, we should get to the brow of the valley in about half an hour, and from there we can wait it out until dark, and then follow the valley around the village, and pick up the trail to the Forest of Time." Keltor took Kaitlin's hand, and together they pressed on, weaving their way through the ancient forest of oak and ash. The woods were thick with shadows, the late afternoon light filtering through the branches above as they moved quietly, alert to every sound.

After some time, they reached the brow of a hill overlooking the valley of Elvendon. The last light of day was fading, and the shadows grew longer as dusk settled in. They paused at the crest, gazing down upon the village below. What they saw rooted them to the spot, hearts pounding in disbelief. The scene before them was one of devastation; the village was in ruins. Houses were charred, gardens torn apart, and the entire settlement appeared shattered and lifeless.

Kaitlin, overwhelmed by shock, instinctively raised her hands to her mouth. At the same moment, Keltor pulled her into his arms, holding her tightly as he struggled to process the sight. His lips trembled as he fought to hold back tears.

"Kaitlin, what the hell has happened to my village?" he managed to say at last, his voice thick with emotion. The shock left him almost speechless.

In a whisper, Kaitlin replied, "It looks like it's been attacked."

Desperation surged through Keltor as he cried out for his family. Releasing Kaitlin, he seized her hand and urged her forward, determined to reach his home and find out what had become of his loved ones. "Come on," he pleaded, his fear and anguish driving him on.

But a sudden, chilling sense of foreboding swept over Kaitlin. Her eyes darted anxiously towards the deepening shadows, unease gripping her heart. Abruptly, she halted, pulling Keltor to a stop beside her.

"Kaitlin, what is it? Come on, I want to get home, we can sort out Aragon later," Keltor insisted, impatience and worry colouring his tone as he attempted to pull away from her grasp.

Kaitlin shook her head, her grip on his arm tightening with urgency. "No, it's not that," she replied, her voice low and urgent. "We can't go down there, not yet. Someone's coming, we need to hide, now!"

Confusion flickered across Keltor's face. "Hide, why?" he asked, frowning at her.

"I've got a really bad vibe," Kaitlin barked, yanking him hard and practically dragging him back into the cover of the trees. "Get down!" she urged in a frantic whisper, pulling him down and concealing them within the dense shrubbery.

Ten men emerged from the trees, passing just a few feet from their hidden position. Keltor's brow furrowed as he recognised their dark blue and red uniforms. "Aranstream," he whispered under his breath, the realisation dawning on him. He turned to Kaitlin and whispered, "Why are there soldiers from Aranstream here in Elvendon?"

Kaitlin met his gaze, her voice tense with apprehension. "Keltor, I've got a bad feeling about this. Do you think they've found Aragon?"

"But how, it's only been a couple of days or so," he whispered.

Placing his arm around her and holding her close to him, they watched the soldiers head down the hill towards the village. "How could they have found him and attacked Elvendon in just two days. Where is our army?"

When they were sure it was safe, they stood and moved outside the cover of the trees.

Her fingers gently entwined with his, he glanced at her and then squeezed them tightly.

Worry etched across Kaitlin's face as she voiced her fears. "You don't think Aragon could have survived," she said anxiously, recalling the threat he had posed to Elvendon.

Keltor shook his head, his tone resolute. "No, he was definitely dead, I'm sure he was."

Undeterred, Kaitlin pressed on, her mind racing with possibilities. "What about his brother, Keion?" she suggested. "Both brothers were involved in the plan to take over Elvendon."

Keltor paused, considering her words. After a moment, he spoke with determination. "Kaitlin, we have go down. I must know if my family are safe."

Kaitlin nodded in agreement, but caution coloured her reply. "Okay, but I think we should wait until it is completely dark," she advised. "It will not do us or them any favours if we get caught."

Accepting her suggestion, Keltor nodded firmly. Together, they retreated to the shelter of the trees, settling beneath the spreading branches of a large oak. Leaning against its sturdy trunk, they waited, tense and silent, for the sun to set.

Kaitlin's concern resurfaced as the shadows lengthened. "Keltor, what if they attacked Elvendon while we were gone?" she asked, her voice hushed with worry.

Keltor met Kaitlin's gaze, his uncertainty clear. "We've only been on Earth a few days. I don't understand how he would know

Aragon was dead already," he admitted, matching her confusion and apprehension.

Kaitlin pressed on, her grip tightening on his arm. "No, I mean as soon as we left for Star. Remember what Aragon said, King Iwein was in on the plan too and he was already at the Palace for my birthday." Her anxiety was evident. "I am really worried about my father, and my sister."

Keltor let out a sigh, his impatience overtaking his caution. "Come on, let's go, it's dark enough, I can't wait any longer," he urged, quickly getting to his feet and reaching down to help her up.

Kaitlin took his hand, allowing him to pull her to her feet. Together, they moved cautiously down the hill and entered the village, keeping to the shadows for safety. As they slipped through the silent streets, it became clear that something was very wrong; not a single soldier crossed their path, and the entire village was eerily quiet.

"Where is everyone?" Keltor whispered, the silence unsettling him as much as the darkness.

"It's like there's a curfew or something," Kaitlin whispered back, her voice barely audible.

Sticking close to the buildings and carefully avoiding the shifting light cast by the moon as it faded in and out behind clouds, they navigated the narrow, winding streets towards Keltor's home. As they approached, Kaitlin gasped, her distress clear. The house, like so many others in the village, was in disrepair; the once-beautiful garden was trampled, and the front door had been crudely re-hinged after having been forced open.

Keltor's anxiety grew, the tension visible in his posture as they drew nearer. "We'll go around the back," he suggested quietly, determined to be cautious.

Holding tightly to Kaitlin's hand, Keltor led her around to the back door, only to discover that it, too, had been hastily repaired and re-hinged. He reached for the handle and tried to turn it, but it refused to budge—it was locked.

30

"Let me try," Kaitlin whispered, and Keltor stepped aside, allowing her access. Raising her hand towards the stubborn lock, she focused her growing magical ability—no longer dependent on her wand as she once was. In a low, careful voice, she intoned, "*Aperta ianua.*" Almost immediately, the lock gave a soft click, the mechanism releasing under her spell.

Without hesitation, Keltor grasped the handle and swung the door open. Together, they slipped quietly into the darkness of the kitchen, their nerves taut as they listened for any sound.

Inside, Sharelle Dracon rose abruptly from her chair by the fire, startled by the sudden intrusion. Grabbing a small lantern for light and snatching a fire poker from the hearth, she held the heavy metal rod defensively before her as she left the living room, her footsteps quick and wary. She moved towards the kitchen, ready to confront whoever had just entered her home.

"Mum," Keltor said, his relief evident as he recognised her in the dim light.

At the sight of her son, Sharelle gasped, her voice trembling with shock. "Keltor!" she cried, immediately dowsing the lantern and plunging the kitchen back into darkness. Her eyes wide with disbelief, she stared at him, trying to make sense of his sudden appearance.

"Mum, what's going on, what's happened to the village?" Keltor pressed, the urgency clear in his voice.

Still reeling from the shock, Sharelle hurried past her son, dropping the poker and lantern onto the kitchen table. She quickly re-locked the back door, her movements hurried and anxious, as if fearful that someone might have followed them.

Spinning back towards Keltor, she peered at him through the gloom. "Keltor, by the stars, is that really you?" she repeated, her voice filled with relief. Rushing to him, she threw her arms around her son and hugged him so tightly that Keltor could scarcely breathe.

"Mum, please..." he pleaded, gently pulling himself free. "What's happened?"

Sharelle looked at him with tears in her eyes. "Keltor, my darling son, I thought you were dead. Where have you been?" she wept. She reached out to Kaitlin, who took her hand, and drew her in, sweeping both into a trembling embrace. "I thought you were both dead," she managed, fighting back another sob.

"Dead? Why would you think that? And what's happened to the house, and to the village?" Keltor asked, his worry intensifying.

Sharelle glanced anxiously at the kitchen window before urging them quietly, "Come into the living room. There are too many eyes that may see you in here."

They trailed after Sharelle through the darkness and into the living room. Immediately in front of them, a fire crackled warmly, its glow mingling with the scattered light of a few candles placed thoughtfully around the room. Sharelle hurried to the window and drew the curtains closed, shutting out the world beyond. Although the light remained dim, it was enough for Keltor to see how much his mother had changed; the beauty that usually shone from her now seemed dulled by exhaustion and worry.

Without warning, she seized Keltor once more and pulled him into a tight embrace. "I can't believe you're here," she whispered, her hands gently lifting to caress his face, her voice trembling as she tried to contain her tears.

"Mum, please, tell me what the hell is going on?" Keltor pleaded as she finally let go of him. He could hear the desperation in his own voice.

"Sit down," Sharelle instructed, gesturing towards the large sofa situated before the fire. "Where have you been? We were told you both died."

"Been?" Keltor echoed, glancing at Kaitlin for reassurance. "It's only been a couple of weeks, Mum. We've been on the quest for the Star, you know that."

Sharelle looked at him with a confused frown and shook her head in disbelief. "No, Keltor, it's been eight months since you both left. Elvendon has fallen. Four weeks after you left, King Iwein sent men to search for you and his son. A week later,

Aranstream's army attacked and overpowered us. Your brother was taken as a prisoner, along with all the other able men of Elvendon." She paused, a tear slipping down her cheek as she wiped it away. "Anna is being forced to work at the castle as a maid."

Keltor stared at Kaitlin, his face etched with disbelief. "Eight months? How the hell can it be eight months?" he demanded, turning to her, unable to accept what he was hearing.

Kaitlin's worry grew as she struggled to process the news. Her voice quivered as she asked, "What happened to my father?"

Sharelle, her expression pained, reached for Kaitlin's hands and held them gently between her own. "Oh, my darling, I'm so sorry, I... I don't know how to tell you this, but, but the King... your father." She paused, rubbing Kaitlin's hands with her thumbs as she searched for the words. "I really am so sorry to have to tell you this," she said softly, "but King Iwein killed your father."

The words hit Kaitlin with the force of a blow. Her lip trembled as she tried to speak. "What... my father's dead?" she finally managed, her voice barely above a whisper.

Sharelle nodded solemnly, confirming the terrible truth. "And my sister...?" Kaitlin asked, her voice breaking, tears streaming down her cheeks as she waited for an answer.

Sharelle shook her head; her face etched with sorrow. "I'm so sorry, your sister, she's gone too," she confirmed.

Kaitlin's heart seemed to stop as she tried to take in the words. "No, no, that can't be right. Keltor," she said, turning to him, desperate for comfort. "How can it be, we've only been gone a couple of weeks. I mean, I, I haven't even met her yet, she can't be dead, she just can't!"

Keltor wrapped his arm around her, drawing her close. She leaned against him, seeking comfort, and he pressed a sorrowful kiss to the top of her head, holding her tightly for a moment.

"Dead... how can they both be dead," she mumbled, the reality refusing to sink in. It made no sense; they had only been gone a short time, not eight months. Kaitlin trembled, wiping her tears away as confusion and grief overwhelmed her. "But how... why, I don't understand?" she asked, her voice trembling with anguish.

"It all happened so fast," Sharelle began to explain. "One day, late in the afternoon the village was suddenly attacked by Aranstream soldiers, they burned the homes of those who fought back. We were told by Prince Keion that they had captured the King and your sister." She stopped as she really didn't want to tell this poor child how her family had died.

"Mum?" Keltor pressed, his tone insistent as he sought clarification.

"Please, Sharelle, tell me what happened to my father and sister," Kaitlin begged, although she knew whatever it was his mother was struggling to tell her was going to be distressing.

Sharelle's voice faltered as she struggled to find the right words. "There is no easy way to say this," she managed, shaking her head with a heavy sorrow. Her gaze shifted to her son. "Keltor," she said quietly, her eyes silently imploring him to offer Kaitlin support during this difficult moment.

Understanding his mother's unspoken request, Keltor gently wrapped his arms around Kaitlin, drawing her close in a protective embrace. Kaitlin looked to him for a fleeting moment, seeking reassurance in his presence, before turning her tear-stained eyes back to Sharelle, bracing herself for the painful truth that was about to be revealed.

His mother took in a deep breath and looked Kaitlin in the eyes. For a moment, she seemed to search for the right words, her expression shadowed with sorrow and the weight of what she was about to reveal. The silence in the room grew heavier, anticipation and dread mingling as she prepared herself to speak the truth that Kaitlin so desperately needed, yet feared, to hear. "They publicly executed your father and sister in the village square. King Iwein beheaded your father himself, and.... And."

Sharelle's expression grew even more sorrowful as she continued, her voice almost a whisper. "Prince Keion did the same to your sister." Her words hung heavily in the air, confirming that Kaitlin's sister had met the same tragic fate as her father. The pain

34

was palpable, and the room was filled with a sense of loss and devastation, as the reality of what had happened settled over them all.

Kaitlin closed her eyes and collapsed against Keltor's chest, overcome by sobs. He held her gently, whispering, "Kitcat, I am so sorry," as he placed a tender kiss on the top of her head. His hand moved softly through her hair, pulling her closer, offering what comfort he could as her body trembled in his arms.

Through his own tears, Keltor glanced at his mother, silently seeking solace. Sharelle, moved by the pain she saw in both Kaitlin and Keltor, mouthed, "I'm so sorry," to her son, her expression heavy with empathy and regret.

Keltor responded to his mother's silent apology with a sorrowful smile and a gentle, understanding nod, acknowledging both her grief and her support as they shared the burden of loss together.

"Mum?" Keltor pressed, his voice insistent, yearning for clarity as dread settled in his chest.

Sharelle continued, her tone heavy with sorrow, "That's when Elvendon surrendered to King Iwein. There was no point in continuing with the fight if the King and his only heir were gone. There was no one left to lead the people or the army." She turned her gaze to Kaitlin; her expression filled with regret. "Kaitlin, I'm so sorry, truly I am."

Rising to her feet, Sharelle looked down at her son. "I can't tell you how happy I am that you are both still alive." Reaching out, she gently ruffled Keltor's hair, letting her hand rest there for a moment. Although her heart ached for Kaitlin, a note of joy resonated within her at the sight of her son alive and well.

For months, Sharelle had mourned Keltor, unable to face the thought of clearing out his room. She had left everything untouched, spending long hours surrounded by his belongings, breathing in the lingering scent on his clothes. The pain of his absence had nearly broken her, compounded by the loss of her other children, who had also been taken from her.

Finally, Sharelle offered, "I'll give you a few minutes, I'll go and make some tea," and gave Keltor a sorrowful smile before leaving the room.

He gave a gentle nod, watching her as she walked back towards the kitchen. For Keltor, just like his mother, making tea was always their way of dealing with hardship and sorrow.

"Keltor, this is all our fault; how can it be eight months since we left?" Kaitlin wept, the pain in her voice mingling with frustration and anger. "If we had been here... if we hadn't killed Aragon." Her heart ached with regret and anguish.

Keltor reached out to comfort her. "I know, Kitcat, I know. Star must have done something to us, she must have put us in stasis to protect us while she repaired the Earth, and you know we had no choice but to kill Aragon—it was him or us." His tone was gentle but resolute, reassuring her that their actions, though tragic, were necessary.

Kaitlin's grief deepened as she cried, "I hadn't even met her, my sister?" The loss was compounded by never having known the sibling she now mourned.

Keltor drew her closer, his voice soft with empathy. "I know, my love, I'm so sorry." He let out a deep sigh, thinking of his own sister—at least he knew she was still alive, even if enslaved in the palace. The thought brought him a bittersweet sense of relief.

Kaitlin pulled back from his embrace and gazed up into his blue eyes. He raised his hand to her cheek, gently brushing away her tears with his thumb. She closed her eyes, pained, as he leant in and pressed a tender kiss to her lips, offering silent comfort in their shared grief.

As their lips parted, Keltor rested his forehead gently against Kaitlin's, and for a quiet moment, neither spoke. The simple touch of his skin against hers brought Kaitlin immense comfort; she wished he would never let her go.

Sensing his mother's presence in the room, Keltor turned to find her watching them, a tea tray balanced in her hands. He released Kaitlin, rose to his feet, and took the tray from his mother, placing it carefully on the coffee table.

Kaitlin wiped away her tears with the cuff of her sleeve, sniffing quietly as she settled herself back into the sofa.

Breaking the silence, Keltor turned to his mother. "Mum, Kaitlin and I are together now," he explained, reaching for the teapot. "A lot has happened to us since we left, even though to us it only feels like a couple of weeks."

His mother sat down in her armchair, her eyes never leaving Keltor as he poured tea into three delicate blue china cups.

Her voice trembled as she spoke. "Keltor," she said, her lip quivering. "They said you killed Prince Aragon."

Keltor drew in a deep breath before nodding. "Yes, I did," he admitted, and then offered Kaitlin a cup of tea.

"We both did," Kaitlin added, taking the tea from Keltor with a slightly shaking hand.

Sharelle's voice was strained with disbelief. "Why? King Iwein said this was why they attacked Elvendon, that it was an act of war."

Keltor shook his head emphatically. "No, that's not true. He was planning an attack all along. That's why I..." He paused, glancing at Kaitlin before correcting himself. "We killed Aragon. He was going to take Kaitlin and seize the Kingdom once they returned to Elvendon. He only accompanied us to try and harness the power of the Star for himself, and then to use it against Elvendon. He wanted to prevent us from saving Earth."

Sharelle's eyes widened. "They said you failed, that Earth has gone, and you had both been killed by the Shadowmen."

Keltor shook his head again. "No, we didn't fail. Earth has been saved. I mean, millions of humans have died, but the planet is safe. Mum, he would have killed us. He attacked Kaitlin; we really had no choice. It was either him or us."

She looked between her son and Kaitlin, her expression torn with grief and confusion.

"She is a princess of the elves, son."

"I know, but we love each other, and it was only together that we were able to release Star and save the Earth," Keltor replied firmly.

Kaitlin sniffled, wiping her eyes with her sleeve once more. "Sharelle, your son is an incredibly powerful wizard. I couldn't have done it without him."

Keltor, sensing a shift in his mother's demeanour, edged forward on his seat. Sharelle's voice was barely above a whisper as she admitted, "I had guessed as much."

With a mixture of surprise and frustration, Keltor pressed her for clarity. "You knew all along that I may have been a wizard?" His voice rose slightly, betraying his agitation. Sharelle lifted her eyes to meet his, her expression pained. "Yes. It is what I had feared the most," she responded, her words heavy with regret.

Keltor's frustration grew. "Why? Mum, I have been hiding it from you my entire life. You told me when I was little that if anyone had magic apart from an Elder or a royal, they would be killed. From the age of twelve I grew up terrified of someone finding out. If you had told me, helped me, I could have worked with the King, and we may have been able to prevent all of this." His voice was tight; the weight of years spent in secrecy evident.

Sharelle's face fell as she revealed her deepest fear. "Keltor, your father died working for the King. I didn't want the same happening to you."

Keltor leaned forward, his brow furrowed and his gaze intense. "Are you telling me dad was a wizard?" he asked, each word measured and deliberate as he fought to control his anger. Sharelle nodded, lowering her head in shame for having concealed the truth for so long.

Keltor cursed quietly, running his fingers through his hair as the realisation dawned on him. Suddenly, the dragon Kailan's words echoed in his mind: '*You have a strong magical bloodline on your father's side.*' Kaitlin, sensing his turmoil, squeezed his knee in support and offered him a sympathetic look.

With emotion rising, Keltor confided, "Mum, for years I grew up trying to hold my powers back, trying to pretend they were not real. I was too scared to show you, to show anyone." Overwhelmed, he rose to his feet, anger surging within him.

Sharelle's confession was raw. "It frightened me, Keltor," she admitted, staring up at him. His anger boiled over. "Frightened you? How the hell do you think I felt!" he shouted, his voice echoing in the room. "Knowing I could do things like this?"

Turning towards his mother, Keltor tilted his head and muttered a few words. A flash of white light travelled down his body, and in an instant, Mr Thomas—Kaitlin's 'boss'—stood before Sharelle. Kaitlin gasped, startled by the sudden transformation, still shaking from the shock of everything that had transpired. "And that I couldn't tell anyone!" Keltor complained, his frustration clear.

Overwhelmed, Sharelle recoiled in her chair, tears streaming down her face as she looked at her son with a mix of fear and astonishment. Keltor quickly returned to his own form.

"And now, since I have embraced my powers, I can do things like this," he declared. With a wave of his hand, a surge of angry energy sent a chair soaring across the room, crashing to the floor. Kaitlin, alarmed by his display, grabbed his hand urgently, her eyes pleading for calm as she looked up at his fuming face.

"Keltor, that's enough," Kaitlin whispered forcefully. Her eyes caught his, and as he looked down at her, at the pain held within her eyes, he closed his briefly and took a breath. He opened his eyes. His mother was sobbing uncontrollably, her head buried in her hands.

Keltor's heart sank as he tried to steady his emotions, inhaling deeply to regain control. The overwhelming revelation that his mother had always suspected he might be a wizard—and the shock of discovering his father had been one—left him reeling. Realising he had let his frustration get the better of him, Keltor knelt before Sharelle, his hand trembling ever so slightly as he gently placed it on her knee.

"Mum, I'm sorry," he said quietly. "I didn't mean to frighten you. It's just... everything that's happened to me, all the things I can do—it's so much to comprehend."

Sharelle, still sniffling, looked up at her son, her eyes red from crying. She shook her head, her voice wavering with emotion.

"No, Keltor," she replied, her tone full of regret. "I'm the one who should apologise. You're right—I should never have tried to hide your true self, especially not from you, or our family."

Keltor's voice trembled with emotion as he turned to his mother. "Mum, without my magic, Kaitlin and I wouldn't have been able to release Star and save Earth, and I've spoken to and understood a dragon." His words lingered in the air, heavy with significance.

Sharelle's tearful eyes lifted to meet his, suddenly filled with curiosity and wonder. "A dragon? How—where have you seen a dragon?" she asked, her voice wavering between disbelief and hope.

"To find Star, Kaitlin had to open a portal, and we travelled through it," Keltor explained, "and ended up in Malgar, where we met a dragon called Kailan."

At the mention of Kailan, Sharelle's eyes brightened, a spark of recognition flickering within them—one Keltor had never seen before. Sensing her reaction, Keltor raised an eyebrow, pressing gently, "Mum, do you know this dragon?"

Sharelle took a shaky breath, her voice faltering as she looked at Keltor, tears brimming in her eyes. "Yes, and Keltor, I'm so sorry. I should have told you everything a long time ago, but after your dad died, I just couldn't cope. I still miss him so much, and I feel him in my heart every day. I didn't want to believe in the prophecy," she wept, her shoulders trembling with grief.

Keltor stood up, running an exasperated hand through his hair before sitting down beside his mother. Desperation coloured his tone as he pleaded, "Mum, what prophecy? Please, tell me everything."

Sharelle nodded, composing herself as she prepared to finally reveal the long-held secrets. "Keltor, your father and I—we were both dragon riders for the King of Malgar."

"What?" Keltor exclaimed, releasing her and leaning back on the sofa in disbelief, the news clearly overwhelming him.

Sharelle's expression softened with the memories. "Your father, Forde, was a dragon lord. He, like the King, could speak

40

and understand all dragons. I could only understand my own dragon—her name is Ayver." She managed a small, wistful smile. "I miss her too," she added, wiping her tears away with the back of her hand.

Keltor looked towards Kaitlin, noticing the alarmed expression in her widened eyes. In that moment, he realised that Kailan, the dragon they had encountered, had spoken the truth all along.

Still overwhelmed by the barrage of revelations, Keltor fixed his gaze on his mother, unable to fully comprehend what he had just heard. Disbelief was etched across his face as he finally managed to speak. "Are you serious? You and Dad were dragon riders?"

Sharelle managed a smile, her pride clear in her softened features. "Yes, and bloody good ones too," she said, her voice tinged with fondness for memories long kept hidden. "The King of Malgar, Kainan, sent your father and me back to Elvendon after we bonded, as envoys. That's the reason you have no family here in Elvendon—I left this place over five hundred years ago to live in Malgar."

Keltor stared at her, bewilderment crossing his face as he tried to process the enormity of her words. "You're five hundred years old?" he asked, incredulity colouring his tone.

Sharelle laughed gently, shaking her head at her son's confusion. "No, no. There is so much I need to tell you about our past, and I promise I will explain everything. But it will take some time."

She paused, her gaze drifting as she recalled the struggles faced upon their return. "When we came back to Elvendon, it was already under threat from Aranstream—even then, they were trying to take over the Kingdom. Your father was given a prophecy, one that foretold our son would play a crucial role in saving the world of Earth. So, we chose to stay, and your father became the King's wizard."

Keltor's voice trembled with a mix of frustration and longing as he turned to his mother. "Mum, if you knew all this," he began, "why—why didn't you let me work for the King? Surely, if

41

Aranstream had known there was a wizard at Elvendon, we could have avoided all of this."

Sharelle's composure crumbled, and tears slipped down her cheeks as she tried to find the words. "I'm sorry," she wept, her voice barely more than a whisper. "I—I was so frightened I might lose you, just as I lost your father." Her sorrow was etched deep into her features as she lifted her tear-filled eyes to meet his.

"Keltor, my heart aches for him every single day," she continued, her voice thick with emotion. "There were times I thought about taking you, and your brother and sister, back to Malgar—far away from Elvendon and its dangers. But I couldn't bring myself to return without your dad. It just wouldn't feel right—not without him by my side."

Kaitlin sat quietly, deep in thought as she mulled over what her father had confided in her. After a moment's hesitation, she decided it was time to speak up. "Keltor, my father told me they never found the Wizard's body—your dad's, I mean."

Keltor turned towards her, a pained expression on his face. "Yes, I know. We were told he was... disintegrated."

Shaking her head, Kaitlin pressed on. "That's not what my father said. He told me his men had been attacked. The soldiers, yes, they were partially disintegrated, but there were remains. Yet, they found nothing of the Wizard himself. Only his cloak, his staff, and a pendant."

Sharelle, startled by this revelation, sat up straighter. "A pendant?" she echoed, surprise colouring her voice.

Kaitlin nodded. "Yes, that's what my father said."

Sharelle's eyes widened with astonishment. "Oh, my stars, I always thought it had perished with Forde."

Confused, Keltor turned to his mother. "Mum?"

Taking his hand and squeezing it gently, Sharelle explained, "Keltor, the pendant was given to your father by the Wizard Marton of Malgar. Your father wasn't born a wizard—he was granted the power by Marton and the great spirits from the world beyond. The pendant is what activates his magic. I never knew you would be born a wizard, Keltor. I truly thought you'd need the pendant, just as your father did, to work magic. When it was lost, I believed that was the end of it."

Keltor looked at his mother, hope flickering in his eyes. "Mum, that means dad could still be alive, somewhere," he said, his voice trembling with emotion. His mother, lost in her thoughts, turned slowly towards him as she processed his words.

A tear escaped down her cheek as she replied softly, "I have always felt still connected to him." She paused to wipe her face and then addressed Kaitlin, "Kaitlin, do you know where the pendant is?"

Kaitlin shook her head, uncertainty evident. "No, but I expect it would have been put in the treasury."

Keltor's pain was palpable as he pressed on, "But if dad is alive, where is he? Do you think someone could have captured him, maybe taken him through another portal somewhere? How would we ever know, it's been years?"

His mother could only shake her head. "I don't know, my darling, but if we could get his pendant back—and if we could find him—it would restore his magic."

Keltor shifted the conversation, his determination growing. "Mum where is our army?" he asked, knowing their hopes of reclaiming the kingdom depended on their strength.

With a weary sigh, his mother answered, "King Iwein has them working like slaves to build him a new fancy castle in Aranstream."

Keltor's resolve hardened. "Then we need to free them," he said.

His mother challenged, "Free them, how? There is no one left in Elvendon to fight?"

Keltor shook his head. "No, maybe not in Elvendon, and we don't necessarily need to fight."

She looked at him, confused. "What do you mean?"

Keltor explained, "We just need to let the army know that their princess—" His eyes found hers, "—their Queen," he corrected, "is still alive. It will give them hope and the spirit to fight for their freedom."

Kaitlin met Keltor's gaze as the realisation dawned. "Me," she whispered, reacting to his referral to her as their Queen. As Keltor nodded, she exhaled slowly, weighed down by the enormity of what he was suggesting.

Keltor offered a sorrowful smile. "Yes, Kaitlin, with the King and your sister… gone, you are now the Queen of Elvendon."

Overwhelmed, Kaitlin averted her gaze, her eyes fixed on the ground as she struggled to process the immense responsibility now resting on her shoulders. The prospect of becoming queen left her feeling unprepared and wholly inadequate. She was acutely aware of how little she understood about Elven law, the expectations of the people, or the burdens of royal leadership. The enormity of it all made her feel young, inexperienced, and out of her depth.

Keltor watched her closely, sensing her pain and anxiety. He understood her reluctance—he shared it himself. The role she was being asked to assume meant that their dream of quietly living together in the forest was no longer possible. That life was now beyond their reach.

Their thoughts were interrupted by his mother's sceptical question: "And the two of you are going to do this, alone?" Her raised eyebrow brought Keltor back to the present.

He shook his head firmly. "No. We're going to get help."

Kaitlin looked up at him, uncertainty in her voice. "Who, Keltor?"

"The trolls, or whatever they are now."

"Belrack?" Kaitlin asked, searching his face for reassurance.

Keltor nodded in response.

She hesitated. "I don't know, do you think he would?"

"He owes us, Kaitlin. And don't forget, Aranstream's men attacked them."

Kaitlin frowned. "But how do we know we broke the enchantment?"

"He was starting to turn when we left. There's only one way to find out," Keltor replied. "We can look for Esimae, Uly, and Ren—I'm sure they would help us. With our magic, and Esimae's, we stand a good chance, Kitcat."

"That's if they're still alive," Kaitlin murmured, fear creeping into her voice.

Keltor turned to his mother. "Mum, do you know if the Deodar village is still there, or have they been attacked as well?"

His mother replied, "No, it's still there. They did not fight against King Iwein, but there are Aranstream soldiers there. The Deodar men have also been taken to build the new castle."

Keltor drew his lower lip through his teeth, anxiety etched on his face. He pressed on with his next question. "And what happened to Esendil? Do you know where he is?"

His mother took a deep breath, exhaling slowly. "I don't know. They took him when they first attacked. Anna hasn't been able to find out where he is; she hasn't seen him in our palace. He could be at Aranstream building the castle, or..." She hesitated, pain in her voice. "Keltor, I don't even know if he is still alive."

Keltor frowned deeply, his hand covering his nose and mouth in a moment of despair. At that moment, he felt the gentle reassurance of Kaitlin's touch on his knee. He glanced at her, taking comfort from her presence beside him.

"Keltor, we'll find him," Kaitlin assured him, her voice steady and full of determination.

He managed a nod in response, gathering himself before pushing to his feet. "What about Anna, how is she?" he asked, concern for his sister evident in his tone.

"She's okay. I've seen her as I do work at the palace myself," his mother replied.

Keltor's expression grew serious. "You mustn't let her know we're back, or it will put her in danger," he cautioned. His mother nodded in agreement as she rose to her feet. Though it broke her heart to let Keltor go once more, she understood the necessity.

"I'll pack up some food to keep you going for a while," she offered, making her way to the kitchen. "Are you hungry?" she asked, glancing back at them.

Keltor looked to Kaitlin, who nodded in response. "Yes, a little," he answered.

"Okay, I'll fix you both something to eat before you go," his mother replied, setting about preparing a meal for them.

Keltor then drew Kaitlin into his arms, and for a few moments, they simply held each other in silence, seeking solace in one another. With a heavy sigh, he pressed a gentle kiss to the top of her head before letting her go.

"Are you okay?" he asked softly, cupping her face in his hand.

She leaned into his touch, shaking her head. "No, not really."

"Me neither," he admitted, his voice low. He took her hand, and together they walked into the kitchen.

His mother packed the supplies into an old rucksack. "Thank you," Keltor said gratefully as he did it up.

"Just one more thing," Sharelle said, briefly leaving the kitchen. A few minutes later, she returned holding a book in her hand. "Here, this is yours now. It belonged to your father. Wizard Marton gave it to him when he received his Wizard's power; it's a book of spells of some sort," she explained.

Keltor accepted the old, worn, leather-bound book from his mother. The front cover was embossed with the image of a dragon. As he traced his thumb over the dragon's form, a faint tingle of magic surged through his fingers. Closing his eyes, Keltor could sense the energy of his father lingering within the pages, and as he held the book, that energy intensified.

Suddenly, an image materialised in Keltor's mind. He saw a dark and damp cell or dungeon. Inside, a man crouched in the corner, appearing haggard with a thick beard obscuring his face and heavy iron chains biting into his wrists. The man looked up, his eyes searching the gloom, as if he felt someone watching him.

Keltor gasped loudly, immediately recognising the man's eyes. "Keltor, my son, is that you?" the man spoke, his voice echoing in Keltor's mind.

Choked with emotion, Keltor uttered, "Dad," tears springing to his eyes. Kaitlin, noticing his distress, pulled at his arm, asking anxiously, "Keltor?" But Keltor, caught in the vision, didn't hear her. He called out again, "Dad."

The man smiled through his thick beard. "My son," he said warmly, and then the vision faded. Keltor's mind searched for the man, but he could no longer see him or the cell. Opening his tearful eyes, Keltor returned to the present.

Kaitlin, her hand still resting on his arm, asked, "Keltor, are you okay, what was that all about?"

Wide-eyed, Keltor replied, "I think I just saw my dad." He turned to his mother as she spoke, trying to process what had just happened.

Sharelle asked, uncertain, "What do you mean?"

"When I held his book, Mum, I saw him. It was Dad, I know it was. He's being held prisoner in a cell or dungeon somewhere. He is alive, Mum!" Keltor exclaimed.

Sharelle responded with relief, "By the stars, you must have connected with him through his book. I just knew he wasn't dead."

"Mum, I think he saw me or felt me. He said my name," Keltor said, his eyes shining with hope. "Maybe there is something in this book that will help me connect with him again, so I can find out where he is."

"Keltor, I feel such a fool. If only I had told you who your father was, and given you his book earlier, you may have been able to find him sooner."

"Mum, no," he disagreed, "I don't think I would have connected with him before now. It's only because of Kaitlin that I've embraced who I really am and allowed my true magic to become part of me."

Sharelle let out a sorrowful sigh and said, "I'm so sorry," her voice thick with regret. Determined, she insisted, "Look, I will help you find him." Her words were resolute, unwavering in their intent.

Keltor shook his head, concern etched across his face. "No, it will be too dangerous," he replied, trying to dissuade her from joining the search.

Sharelle met his protest with steady confidence. "Son, I am a King's dragon rider. I might be a little rusty, but I know how to fight—it's not something you forget. When you get your army together, you come back for me, do you understand? I want to fight with you and help find your father."

Keltor implored her, desperation in his gesture, "Mum, please," he pleaded, shaking his head. "I don't want to worry about you when we're in the middle of a fight."

Seeing his doubt, Sharelle interjected, "Wait there a minute." She understood his uncertainty; after all, to him, she was just his plain, ordinary mum, and he had no reason yet to believe in her fighting skills.

Kaitlin looked at him with concern. "Are you okay?" she asked gently.

Keltor glanced over at her, then slipped his arm around her and drew her closer, seeking comfort in her presence. "Yeah, I guess," he replied, though uncertainty lingered in his voice. "Kaitlin, that was a real vision, I'm sure of it. I know that was my dad."

"I believe you, Keltor," Kaitlin said reassuringly. "You totally zoned out then—you didn't hear me at all."

Keltor nodded, still trying to process what had happened. "It was weird," he said slowly. "It was like I was above him, looking down into his cell, but he knew I was there. He looked straight up at me and said my name."

His mother re-entered the room, a long silver elven sword gleaming in her hand. Keltor stared in disbelief. "Bloody hell, where did you get that?" he exclaimed, letting go of Kaitlin and moving towards his mother.

Sharelle shot him a disapproving look at his language but addressed his question. "It's mine. The King of Malgar gave it to me as a bonding gift. You have the one he gave your father."

Keltor's eyes widened in surprise. "The King of Malgar gave you both swords?" He instinctively touched the sword at his hip, glancing at Kaitlin, who smiled encouragingly at him. "I always knew this sword was special. You can see it's a work of art, but a gift from a king?"

Sharelle nodded, her smile tinged with nostalgia. "Yes, he did. The King and I were good friends, once." She straightened with purpose. "Now stand back," she cautioned, gripping the sword with both hands. In a swift, fluid motion, she spun and twisted the blade around her head, so fast that Keltor struggled to follow its movement.

"Wow," Kaitlin breathed, instinctively taking a few steps further back. She grinned at Keltor. "Now I know where you get your skills from."

Keltor couldn't contain his astonishment, his voice edged with awe. "Shit, mum," he exclaimed, his eyes wide with disbelief. "And I always thought it was from dad."

Sharelle, though clearly pleased by his reaction, gave him another admonishing look for his language. Still grinning, she lowered the sword, a proud smile on her face. Keltor returned her grin, albeit a little sheepishly. "Sorry," he murmured. "But honestly, mum, I never would have guessed you could fight like that."

Sharelle's expression softened. "I know, to you I'm just mum, but I've not lost my touch yet. Do you remember when your dad and I used to ride out into the forest at least once a week? We always said we were exercising the horses."

Keltor's memory stirred, a forgotten detail surfacing. "Yeah, you'd always get old Nosy from next door to keep an eye on us," he recalled, a smile playing on his lips.

Sharelle nodded. "That's right. Well, out in the forest, your dad and I would practise our sword fighting. Even though I don't have a sparring partner anymore, I still go out and keep my moves sharp."

Keltor approached her, lifting his hand to gently squeeze her arm. "Mum, I hope it never comes to that, but if it does, I'd be honoured to fight by your side. And when we have the time, I want to hear all about you and dad as Dragon Riders for the King of Malgar."

Sharelle smiled at him warmly. "I will, I promise. Now, sit down and eat. I'm going to hide this away again," she said, lifting her sword once more.

The two of them sat together at the meticulously scrubbed pine kitchen table, where his mother had thoughtfully laid out a simple meal of bread, butter, cheese, and ham. Kaitlin took up the task of slicing the bread, while Keltor spread each slice with butter, and together they assembled cheese and ham sandwiches. The kitchen was shrouded in near darkness, with only a faint glow from the lounge spilling through the open doorway as they ate in silence.

At last, Kaitlin broke the quiet. "Keltor," she said softly. He looked up, pulled from his own wandering thoughts about his father. "I'm scared," she admitted, her voice trembling.

Reaching across the table, Keltor took her hand in his, offering silent reassurance. "I know, so am I. I can't even begin to understand how it's been eight months since we left, let alone everything that's happened here. My dad, and my mum—turns out she's a bloody dragon rider."

A faint smile flickered across Kaitlin's face at his words. She drew in a shaky breath. "And I am so sorry about your dad and sister." Despite her efforts, she could not stop her tears from welling up as she bit her top lip to steady herself.

"Keltor, it's not that," she said at last, her voice barely above a whisper. "I can't be a queen. I mean, I can't lead people; nobody has ever listened to me."

Keltor's chair scraped loudly against the kitchen floor as he pushed it back and stood. He walked over to Kaitlin, gently drawing her head against his stomach and wrapping his arms around her in a comforting embrace. "Kaitlin, you're not going to do this alone, okay? I'm here for you."

She nodded tearfully against him. Releasing her, Keltor crouched down on one knee to meet her gaze.

"Kitcat, I love you so much, I always have, ever since the first day you arrived in Elvendon when you were so little. From that day, you became my very best friend, and I have grown to love you even more every day. Those five years we were parted were like hell for me—torturous, bloody hell," he said, his words drawing a small, sniffling smile from Kaitlin.

"I will never leave your side; I loved you before I ever knew you were a Princess, and I wouldn't care if you weren't. If things were different, and the only way I could be with you would be to leave and go to Earth, I would, but Elvendon needs you, Kaitlin. They need their Queen."

"I know, Keltor, and I wouldn't abandon them. I just don't want to do it on my own."

"You won't have to, Kitcat. I seem to remember asking you to bond with me," he said, grinning. "So, when we can, do you still want to bond with me, even though you're going to be the Queen?"

"Keltor, of course I do. I love you—I wouldn't want anyone else to be my King!"

As he kissed her, Kaitlin felt her broken heart suddenly surge with happiness and hope.

Standing quietly at the doorway, Keltor's mother lifted a hand to her eye and wiped away a tear. Her son was so like his father— caring, compassionate, and protective—and she gave a quiet sigh as she turned and left the pair alone in their moment.

Keltor leaned back in his chair as they finished their meal, the atmosphere in the kitchen settling into thoughtful silence. Kaitlin was the first to break it, her tone searching. "So, what's the plan?"

Keltor considered for a moment before replying, "I suppose our first step is to check if Esimae, Uly, and Ren are still at the Deodar village. If they are, we'll see if they're willing to help us."

Kaitlin's confidence was unwavering. "They'll help us, I know it," she assured him, earning a nod from Keltor. Yet, she pressed further. "And if they're not there?"

"Then we'll move on to the Trolls on our own," Keltor responded, determination in his voice.

Kaitlin's brow furrowed with concern. "That took us a week last time."

Keltor nodded, acknowledging the difficulty. "I know. Still, if we pick up the pace, perhaps we can do it faster this time. Either way, Kaitlin, Elvendon has been like this for eight months. It's better to go slowly and get there safely than to risk being caught or seen."

Kaitlin pondered alternative strategies. "You could cloak yourself," she suggested.

Keltor shook his head. "No, maintaining a cloak drains my power. I can hold a different form for maybe an hour, two at the most, but after that, I'm utterly knackered."

"Okay, can we disguise ourselves some other way? I suppose I could cut my hair short?" Kaitlin offered, searching for a practical solution.

Keltor's response was immediate and adamant. "No, absolutely not," he said, shaking his head. Her hair was precious, not just for its beauty but for its significance. "Kaitlin, I know you grew up on Earth and there's still much for you to learn about Elven traditions, but as a royal, you must not cut your hair. It's simply not done. Also, if you did, it would make you stand out even more among other elven women."

He paused, softening his tone. "Honestly, not many elves actually know what you look like—just King Iwein, the palace staff, and perhaps a few of the Deodars."

"I think we could trust them, don't you, the Deodars I mean?"

"Maybe, but I wouldn't risk our lives on it. Anyway, they all think we're dead so there is no one looking for us as such, my only concern is that all the young elven men have been sent to Aranstream, so I'm more likely to be spotted."

"You could disguise yourself as a woman," she said with a grin.

"Erm, no I don't think so," he said grinning back at her.

"Keltor, Kaitlin," his mum said from the door. They both looked over to her.

"Come on in, and I will tell you as briefly as I can about me and your dad."

Keltor glanced to Kaitlin, and she widened her eyes at him curiously, he looked back at his mother and gave a nod as he rose from his chair.

All three sat down in the living room, and Keltor leaned forward with his arms crossed and elbows on his knees.

"Now, it will all sound a little crazy and it is a shortened version of a very long story," she started, "but it is the truth. Over five hundred years ago when Earth was in the Middle Ages, Albion was ruled by a great King. However, his evil twin brother, Gemini wanted to rule. Gemini harnessed the magic from a dragon and in the short, killed his brother, took his magical sword known as the Twin Sword, and took over Albion. Now back in those times Kaitlin, on Earth there were elves, dwarfs, giants, and people with magic.

Gemini sought to kill them all. He wanted to be the only one who possessed magic. He killed thousands, and many more fled into inner Earth. Gemini split the Twin Sword, the sword he used, the Gameron Sword contained such evil that without the other half, the Deragan Sword balancing the magic, he was able to use it to do unspeakable things. The fallen king's daughter, Princess Starre and her wizard Elrone managed to steal the Deragan Sword, and they used it to create a portal, which took them and many elves, dwarfs, giants and so on to the world of Malgar. Some of those elves also came back here to Elvendon, this is how we knew of Malgar.

Anyway, Princess Starre met and fell in love with King Aranthor of Malgar, and they married. They had two sons, twins. Prince Kainan and Prince Gareion. For many years they had peace, the lands were united, and the King Aranthor gave each race their own lands to make their home.

When the twin boys were in their mid-twenties, Kainan married Arweyn, and all was well. This is when your father and I joined him as dragon riders. Several of us went as envoys from Elvendon to see how things were, and a few of us decided to stay. Your dad was born and raised in Malgar and was already in training when I arrived. Then somehow Gemini found a portal to Malgar, and he invaded. Now, by drinking the blood of his dragon, Gemini had become an immortal, and the only way he could be killed was by uniting the Deragan Sword with the Gameron Sword, thereby joining back the Twin Sword, the only known weapon that can kill an immortal.

The King, Aranthor was killed in the fighting, and in the end the new King, Aranthor's son, Kainan knew he was not powerful enough to be able to defeat Gemini. On discovering a prophecy, the King decided he would put the entire Kingdom to sleep in order that he and the Queen would be reborn with a power greater than Gemini's. And so, it was, the entire Kingdom, including your father and I were put in the magic sleep. They only thing was the King did not realise how long it would take for them to be reborn; it was over five hundred years."

"Mum, this is."

"Crazy? I know son," she interrupted. "And when we have more time I will go into the finer details, but all you need to know is that when the King and Queen re-awoke us, it was then that your father and I got together," she said with a smile. "We had to fight Gemini and his black dragons, with our own dragons, and at one point he almost died, and I thought I had lost him. So, I pretty much declared my love for him then and there and, thankfully, he felt the same way about me."

As Sharelle finished recounting her extraordinary history, Kaitlin could not help but respond, her face lighting up with a gentle smile. "Oh, how beautiful," she said, clearly moved by the story of love, sacrifice and the unbreakable bond between Keltor's parents. The warmth in the room was palpable, and her words hung in the air, a testament to the deep connection and admiration she felt for the tale she had just heard.

"Yeah, it is as I look back, but at the time we were in a major battle with an evil tyrant. After Kainan killed Gemini using the Deragan Sword, your dad and I eventually bonded. Even then it wasn't smooth sailing, we were on our honeymoon when our Kingdom was attacked by Gemini's daughter, Analise, another nasty, evil sorceress.

Anyway, we have no time to go into this story yet, but when the battle was over and Kainan's wizard was dying, he gave your father his power and said he was to go back to Elvendon, and our son would be instrumental in saving Earth in years to come."

Keltor broke the warm silence with a playful grin. "Mum, I had no idea you and dad were so exciting. I thought you guys were the most boring parents on the planet," he teased, his eyes alight with newfound admiration.

54

Sharelle responded with an amused shake of her head, her lips curled in a gentle smile. "Thank you," she replied dryly, clearly entertained by her son's surprise. "You know we probably overcompensated to make ourselves look normal."

"Well, it worked," Keltor affirmed with a chuckle. He stood up and crossed the room to her, the warmth and affection between them evident in every gesture.

"I love you, mum," Keltor said sincerely, embracing her tightly in a moment filled with affection and gratitude.

"I love you, son," Sharelle replied warmly, pressing a gentle kiss to his brow, her face radiating the deep bond they shared.

Standing nearby, Kaitlin felt her heart flutter. The sight of such genuine care between mother and son stirred within her both joy and sorrow—joy at witnessing their closeness, and sorrow as she was reminded of her own loss. She ached for the love she once received from her own mother and Richard, and the emptiness left in their absence weighed heavily on her.

Breaking the emotional silence, Keltor turned to Kaitlin. "We should probably go," he said softly, releasing his mother from the embrace and gently encouraging them onwards.

"Okay," Sharelle conceded, setting about to remove any trace of their presence from the room. Her actions were methodical, driven by an urgent need for secrecy and safety.

As preparations for departure continued, Keltor swung the rucksack onto his back, his movements purposeful. The gravity of the moment was not lost on Sharelle, who reached out to him, her voice tinged with concern. "Keltor, please, please be careful," she implored, wrapping her arms tightly around him in a protective embrace.

He returned her hug, offering a reassuring, "I will, mum." The exchange was tender, underscoring the deep bond between mother and son.

Sharelle then extended her arms towards Kaitlin, her gesture both welcoming and reverent. "You too, Kaitlin, my Queen," she said, bowing her head in respect as she released her. Kaitlin's response was warm and appreciative: "I will and thank you."

With a heavy breath, Sharelle approached the door and unbolted it, the sound echoing in the quiet room. Keltor offered one last promise as he followed Kaitlin out: "Bye mum, we'll be back as soon as we can."

Sharelle replied, her voice filled with love, "Bye my darling, I love you."

"I love you too," Keltor whispered back, his words lingering in the air as he disappeared through the doorway. As Sharelle closed and secured the door behind them, she leaned heavily against it, overcome by emotion. Closing her eyes, she let out a sob as the weight of her feelings broke through.

In a final, heartfelt plea, she whispered to the Spirits, "Please, Spirits, please protect my son, and our new Queen."

Chapter Three

Esimae

Kaitlin and Keltor moved silently through the sleeping village, careful not to draw attention to themselves. Above them, the thick clouds of the night gradually parted, allowing silvery moonlight to filter down. Though the moon was not yet full, its gentle glow provided just enough illumination for them to pick their way along the shadowed paths.

Neither spoke as they made their way forward, each step taken with quiet purpose and caution. Only when they had put a considerable distance between themselves and the village—far enough that even the faintest whisper would not travel back on the wind to an Aranstream soldier—did they allow themselves to speak in hushed tones, confident that they were finally out of earshot.

As they walked quietly side by side, Keltor broke the silence with words weighted by regret. "Kaitlin, this was not what I had hoped for when we survived the rebirth of Earth," he admitted, casting a solemn glance in her direction. "I mean, I wasn't expecting to come back like heroes or anything, but I wasn't expecting to come back eight months later and find our home destroyed."

Kaitlin's reply was gentle, underscored by sadness. "No, me neither," she said, her voice soft and tinged with sorrow.

Keltor hesitated before continuing, his concern for Kaitlin evident. "I'm so sorry about your father and sister; at the time I didn't even think about the repercussions of our actions, I just wanted you safe."

"I know," she said with a gentle smile, slipping her arm through his and leaning into him for comfort. "None of this is our fault, Keltor. There was nothing either of us could have done to change what happened. I didn't choose to be chosen as the Guardian of the Star, just as you didn't choose to become my Protector. These roles were given to us, not something we sought out ourselves."

"Yeah, but you know I would never change that. Even when we're bonded, I'll always be your Protector, Kitcat," Keltor reassured her, his tone gentle yet resolute.

Kaitlin met his gaze, searching his face for the comfort she so often found there. "I know you are," she replied softly. She hesitated, struggling to find the words that could adequately express the tangled emotions inside her. "Keltor, I don't really know how I feel about losing my father and my sister. It was such a shock when your mother told me. The truth is, I didn't really know my sister at all, or my father that well, and honestly, I didn't like him much. Oh god, that sounds awful, doesn't it?"

"No, not really, I understand," Keltor replied quietly. "They were strangers to you. The King was quite a tyrant, and to be honest, Kaitlin, most people feared him. Though, not as much as King Iwein."

Kaitlin took a steadying breath before speaking, her words carrying a gentle conviction. "The thing is, Richard was my dad," she began, her voice softening. "He raised me and loved me, and in my heart, he will always be my dad. Richard was the kindest and most loving man you could ever hope for in a father. Compared to the King, there is simply no contest." Kaitlin's expression darkened as she spoke, her words edged with pain. "The way the King treated my mother was appalling—he used her just so he could have a child. It's just so wrong." She paused, her eyes glistening with unshed tears. "As much as I miss her, I'm glad my mum and Richard are together now, and not here, having to deal with all this shit." The emotion in her voice was unmistakable as she shook her head, struggling to contain the turmoil within her.

"Kaitlin," Keltor chided softly, a gentle reproach in his tone at her choice of language.

She responded with a shrug and a lopsided grin, her light-heartedness cutting through some of the tension between them.

Keltor nudged her playfully with his elbow, prompting a genuine laugh from Kaitlin—a moment of levity amidst the weight of their situation.

Still, her voice carried a note of frustration as she spoke. "It is shit though, Keltor. All this responsibility—it's not what I ever imagined for my life. All I really want is to be with you. I'd be perfectly content if it was just the two of us, living in a little house like Esimae's, tucked away somewhere deep and hidden in the forest."

At her words, Keltor paused, gently pulling Kaitlin to a stop. He reached up, his hand tender as he brushed her hair away from her eyes, his affection clear in the simple gesture.

"Kaitlin, there is nothing I would have liked more than to have that, just you and I together with our happy ever after, but we just can't, not yet anyway. I know you don't want to be, but I also know that you will be an amazing Queen, and you know why?"

Kaitlin shook her head, uncertain.

"Because you are caring, compassionate and you don't take shit from no one," Keltor said, his laughter lightening the moment.

"Keltor!" she replied, laughing with him.

He grinned. "Well, it's true. If anyone can unite these two Kingdoms and bring us peace, it will be you."

Kaitlin's voice grew firm with conviction. "It will be us, Keltor," she insisted, emphasising the partnership between them. He nodded in agreement.

"Yes, Kitcat, it will be us. Just think, we can change so much, we can make Elvendon a better place for everyone, not just the rich and pompous Elders. We can help build free schools, like you have on Earth, and proper healthcare for the poorer families."

Hope flickered in Kaitlin's eyes as she responded, "Yes, you're right Keltor, we can do this, can't we. We don't have to rule it like it used to be."

"Exactly," he agreed. "We can bring a little of the good things from your Earth to Elvendon."

"That's always assuming we make it, of course," Kaitlin said, her voice tightening with a hint of anxiety about the uncertain future.

Keltor met her gaze with quiet confidence. "We will, I promise. With our magic and Esimae's help, we stand a good chance." His words carried a reassuring certainty, as though he could see a path forward where hope still lived.

Determined, Kaitlin pressed on, her resolve clear. "And we'll find your dad."

Keltor nodded, slipping his arm through hers for comfort and support. For a moment, his thoughts drifted to his father, the pain of absence evident. "Yes, we will. As soon as I get the chance, I'll look through his book and see if I can find a spell to help locate him. I still can't believe he's alive. It makes me feel so bad that we never looked for him. Twelve years he's been gone, twelve years living in that hell hole I saw him in."

Kaitlin shook her head, her tone turning gentle yet firm. "Why would you and your mum have looked for him when my father lied and told you he was dead? Why would you doubt your King's word?"

Keltor sighed. "We didn't."

"Exactly," Kaitlin replied, her conviction unwavering. "You have no reason to feel bad about your father. All you need to feel is anger towards those who took him from you and know that we will find him and bring him home."

Keltor gave a sigh, the weight of his memories and guilt pressing down on him. The thought of his father's long absence—twelve years spent in misery and darkness—hung heavily in the space between them. He could not help but feel a deep ache for all the lost time and the pain his father must have endured. Yet, despite the sorrow, he found comfort in Kaitlin's firm reassurance. Her words reminded him that the blame did not lie with him or his mother, but with those who had deceived them. Determined and bolstered by her support, Keltor drew strength from the promise that together, they would do everything in their power to find his father and bring him home.

"Do you remember the first time we met?" Keltor asked.

"How could I ever forget? I saw fairies and an Elf and a whole new magical world that day," Kaitlin replied, grinning at him.

Keltor laughed. "You were so cute."

"You were too," Kaitlin teased, "with your elf ears that were too big for your face because you hadn't grown into them yet."

He laughed, the memory bringing warmth between them.

"Do you remember when I was thirteen? It was the last time I was here, before you said goodbye to me at Elvendon Farm," Kaitlin continued, her voice tinged with sadness. "We were at the lake having a picnic, the sun was setting, and I was just about to go home. You looked at me so intensely."

Keltor smiled and nodded gently, recalling the moment with her.

"It was the first time I realised that I loved you, more than just as a best friend. I thought you were going to kiss me," she admitted.

"I was," he replied, smiling at the memory.

"So, why didn't you?" she asked quietly.

He hesitated before answering, his hand instinctively moving to his chest as the emotions of that day flooded back. "I guess I was scared. I knew then you were the Princess, and that this was going to be the last time we would be together—properly, I mean, as friends. From that evening, I was going to be just your Protector.

You couldn't know who I was or remember all the times we spent together. I felt my heart breaking, like my entire world was about to end. I regretted that decision—not to kiss you—that's why I kissed you in the woods the next day." He smiled at her. "To be honest, I couldn't stop myself. I knew in the back of my mind you wouldn't remember that kiss, but for me—I treasured it for five years."

Kaitlin leaned in against him, comforted by his honesty. "Funny how things turn out. I guess we were always meant to be together."

"Yes, Kitcat, we were," Keltor replied softly.

"Oh my god, do you remember when we sneaked into your bedroom, and your mum heard me giggle, and you shoved me in your wardrobe?" Kaitlin asked, her eyes sparkling with laughter at the memory.

Keltor joined in, his laughter warm and genuine as the recollection came back to him. "That was so funny, I was absolutely terrified she was going to find you."

"When she came in, you started prancing about, pretending you were acting or something in a silly girl's voice," Kaitlin continued, grinning at the absurdity of the situation.

Keltor chuckled again, shaking his head. "Mum thought I'd lost my mind and told me I needed to get out more and make friends."

The two of them carried on walking for another four hours, sharing and reliving stories from their childhood, each memory drawing them closer and filling the journey with warmth and nostalgia. Eventually, they decided to search for a place to take a break.

"How about up there?" Kaitlin suggested, pointing towards a large oak tree. She had always admired the sheer scale of the trees in Elvendon—many were colossal, towering four or five times higher than any oak found on Earth. The branches of this tree were especially broad, forming a natural cradle that promised both safety and comfort, making it an ideal spot to nestle in for a while without worrying about falling out.

Keltor groaned as he followed her gaze upwards. "Kaitlin, you and your darn trees," he muttered, unable to hide his reluctance. She responded with a firm nudge, undeterred.

"Well, it's safer than being down on the ground. Whoever thinks to look up when they're walking by? And it's not even that high," Kaitlin insisted, her tone both practical and encouraging.

Despite his misgivings, Keltor had to concede the point. He groaned again, knowing she was right—this would be the perfect hiding place for a few hours while they rested. "It is that high, in fact, it's terrifyingly high," he replied, his sarcasm masking a genuine hint of unease. Kaitlin simply grinned at him, undaunted.

"But you're right, it's probably the safest place. Go on then, up you go," he said, giving her an encouraging nod towards the tree.

Kaitlin wasted no time. Climbing trees had always come naturally to her, thanks to a childhood spent at Elvendon farm and exploring the surrounding woodlands. With confidence and ease, she scaled the tree, reaching the branches without any difficulty at all.

"Come on then," she called down at him as she reached the top, then settled herself comfortably in the bough of the tree.

"Okay, I'm coming," he yelled back, although just looking up at her made him feel giddy, prompting a hefty sigh.

He glanced back at the ground, realising the need to conceal their tracks. With a sweep of his hand and a touch of magic, the debris on the forest floor began to swirl around him. He moved his hand one way and then another, ensuring any traces of their footprints were hidden. Once satisfied that their location was securely disguised, he stopped, allowing the leaves and debris to settle back down naturally.

Turning towards the tree once more, he readjusted the rucksack on his back, looked up into the leafy canopy, and gave another hefty sigh. Determined, he lifted his leg, grasped the trunk firmly, and began to climb.

"See," Kaitlin said, grinning as Keltor finally managed to pull himself over the edge and into the welcoming embrace of the tree's deep bough. She glanced around with satisfaction. "It's perfect, isn't it? Deep enough so we won't fall out, and high enough that no one will spot us from below."

Keltor, still catching his breath and looking a little uneasy, nodded in reluctant agreement as he nestled close to her. "Yeah, okay," he conceded, wrapping an arm around her shoulders. "But let's not mention falling out, all right?"

Kaitlin laughed softly, leaning into him, the warmth of their closeness comforting after the tense journey. "You're such a chicken," she teased, her tone light and affectionate.

He looked at her, puzzled. "How am I a chicken?"

She chuckled, shaking her head. "Oh, Keltor, it's another one of those human metaphors."

He blinked, still not quite following. "Oh," he said, the word trailing off as he tried to make sense of it, though the expression on his face showed he was still a little lost when it came to human vocabulary.

Kaitlin's laughter bubbled up again. "It means you're a scaredy cat," she explained, unable to keep a straight face as he looked at her as though she'd entirely lost her senses.

"What?" he said, but his confusion melted into a wide grin.

"Nothing," Kaitlin replied, her head shaking gently, a fond smile lingering on her lips as she relaxed beside him.

"It's so beautiful, isn't it?" Kaitlin sighed, shifting the conversation as she gazed upwards through the tree's leafy canopy to the stars twinkling between patches of dark night cloud. She waited for a reply, but when Keltor didn't answer, she turned her head towards him and found him staring at her. Their eyes met, and her heart skipped a beat as his hand reached up, gently resting on her cheek.

"Yes, it is," he replied softly, before leaning in to kiss her.

When their lips parted, his eyes lingered on hers, studying her intently.

She smilcd, teasing, "What?"

"I love you so much, Kitcat," he said, his heart swelling with happiness just from being so close to her.

She whispered back, "I love you too," then, noticing the sudden seriousness in his expression, asked quietly, "Are you okay?"

He smiled warmly. "Yeah, I'm just glad I'm alive and here with you." With that, he reclined back against the sturdy bough of the tree.

Kaitlin watched him for a moment as he gazed up at the stars. Her heart brimmed with love, so much so she thought it might burst. Keltor, catching her gaze, let the moonlight illuminate her face, feeling a silent gratitude for having been saved, for having been granted another day with her.

"Come here," he murmured, lifting his arm invitingly.

She nestled in beside him, and he wrapped his arm around her. Together, they watched the night sky in peaceful silence.

Suddenly, Kaitlin broke the quiet. "Oh, look—a shooting star!" she cried, pointing upwards. "On Earth, if you see a shooting star, your wish is supposed to come true."

"Did you wish?" he asked, turning slightly towards her. She nodded.

"Yes."

"What did you wish for?"

She grinned, turning to meet his gaze. "I can't tell you, or it won't come true." Keltor raised his left eyebrow in a silent question.

"I'm not telling you, Keltor," she said with a playful smirk. "Even if you give me that look."

"What look?"

"Oh, you know the one—the one that says you may think you're not going to tell me, but you are."

He quipped, "I do not have a look that says that at all."

"Hmm, you think," she replied, and he let out a quiet snicker.

"Well, just make sure it's a good one then," he said, settling into the moment.

"It is, I promise."

For a few minutes, they simply lay there, gazing up at the night sky, the gentle sound of owls hooting back and forth echoing through the trees around them.

Kaitlin broke the comfortable silence as they lay beneath the stars. "What's the plan then?" she asked, her voice soft but curious.

Keltor, half asleep from dozing, took a moment to respond. "Hmm," he murmured, not quite ready to leave the realm of dreams.

"Sorry, were you asleep?" Kaitlin asked, a hint of guilt in her tone.

"No, no," Keltor replied quickly, blinking hard to shake off his drowsiness and come fully awake.

Kaitlin pressed on, "When we get to the Deodar village, what's the plan?"

Keltor considered the question for a moment before answering. "I don't know, really. I suppose we'll need to scout the village when we arrive, check for any signs of Aranstream soldiers, find Esimae, and convince her to help us."

Kaitlin didn't seem concerned about Esimae's willingness. "I don't think she'll need much convincing," she said, shifting onto her side and nestling her head against Keltor's chest. "I hope Jaike found her, and she forgave him."

Keltor tried to reassure her. "Why wouldn't she? She clearly still had feelings for him, and it wasn't his fault he got caught by the witches and couldn't meet up with her to go to Earth."

"Yeah, I know," Kaitlin replied, her voice trailing into a yawn. "I just hope she believed him."

"We should get some sleep," Keltor said, barely able to keep his own eyes open.

"Okay, night, Keltor." Kaitlin leaned up and gave him a gentle kiss.

"Night, Kitcat," he replied affectionately, then closed his eyes, letting sleep claim him.

Keltor lay in a deep, unsettled sleep, his mind consumed by dreams of his father. In the dream, he was locked in a desperate fight against Aranstream soldiers, sword clashing fiercely as he struggled to keep them at bay. Meanwhile, Kaitlin was at his father's side, working urgently to release him from his shackles with her magic. The boundary between sleep and wakefulness blurred, and Keltor's senses slowly dragged him towards consciousness. He became aware of a noise—but was it part of his dream or something real?

Gradually, clarity returned. Keltor realised the sound was not a figment of his imagination but was coming from the base of the tree beneath their hiding place. He glanced to his side and saw Kaitlin was still asleep, undisturbed. As thick clouds shifted to reveal the moon, silvery light spilled down, offering a clearer view of their surroundings. Exercising the utmost caution, Keltor carefully peered over the edge of their concealed position.

"Hell," he muttered under his breath as he took in the scene below. A group of Aranstream soldiers had chosen this exact spot to halt for a rest. There were seven of them in total, their figures illuminated by the glow of oil lamps. Each wore the unmistakable Aranstream uniform: grey trousers, blue tunics, sleek silver swords at their sides, and long, dark hair pulled back, secured with silver bands around their heads.

Relief swept through Keltor as he recalled the care he had taken earlier to erase their footprints. Without that careful precaution, he knew they might have already been discovered by the soldiers below. As Kaitlin began to stir beside him, Keltor acted quickly, placing his hand gently yet firmly over her mouth to prevent any accidental noise that might give away their hiding place. Kaitlin's eyes flew open in alarm, but Keltor immediately pressed a finger to his lips, signalling her to remain silent. She nodded in understanding, and he quietly removed his hand.

Keltor then pointed downward, mouthing the words, "Aranstream soldiers." Kaitlin's eyes widened in horror at the realisation, but she gave a silent nod and pressed herself tightly against Keltor. Together, they lay completely still, barely daring to breathe, determined to remain as inconspicuous and silent as possible while the danger loomed just below.

Below, the atmosphere among the soldiers grew tense. Jasen, clearly relishing the grim prospect, declared with a grin, "I like a good execution." Logan reacted with disgust, muttering, "You're sick."

Jasen responded scornfully, "Why, she's a witch, she deserves to burn for what she did."

"No one deserves to burn, especially not alive," Logan snapped.

68

The first soldier stood up, he was older, but stocky, his hair grey and pulled back in a braid which ran the length of his back, around his head a gold band engraved with the King's warding. He looked down at the other, a younger soldier in his twenties, he was attractive, his dark hair scraped back of his face and held back with a band of plain silver. Sat on the ground and leaning against the base of the huge oak tree the young soldier looked up at him.

"You mind your traitorous tongue, Logan," the older man snarled, his hand teetering on the hilt of his sword as he glared down at him.

Logan sprang to his feet with a sudden, sharp movement and took an assertive step towards Jasen, his posture tense and challenging. The commotion immediately drew the attention of the other five soldiers. Three of them, who had been occupied with their meal, paused mid-bite, their eyes shifting warily to the confrontation. The remaining two, previously resting and lost in their own thoughts, straightened and turned to watch the escalating exchange.

Attempting to defuse the situation, one of the soldiers who had been eating slowly removed the stick of dried meat from his mouth and spoke up, his tone weary, "Guys, come on." His words hung in the air, urging calm and hoping to prevent the argument from boiling over into violence.

Logan bristled at the accusation, his tone firm as he addressed Jasen. "I'm no traitor, Jasen. I just don't think what the King has done is right. I'm entitled to my opinion."

Jasen's response was swift and unyielding. "Not if it is against our King," he retorted, his voice laced with loyalty and warning.

Refusing to back down, Logan pressed the issue. "So, you think it is right to kill women? To kill a Princess for no reason? To start an elven war with a clan who have been allies for centuries?"

Jasen's anger flared. "They killed our Prince, they started it," he shouted, his conviction unwavering.

Logan's voice was edged with defiance as he responded, "So, they say." His words hung in the air, prompting one of the other soldiers to pause mid-bite and look over at him, curiosity piqued.

69

"What do you mean by that?" the soldier asked, suspicion in his tone.

Logan met the soldier's gaze, his expression unwavering. "I heard the Prince, and the King had been planning an attack on Elvendon, even before the Prince set out on his quest to find the Star of Elmrock," he explained, his words carefully measured but resolute.

Jasen immediately bristled at the accusation, his voice rising with disbelief and anger. "Bullshit!" he spat. "Where have you heard that traitorous talk?"

Unfazed by Jasen's outburst, Logan shot back, his eyes narrowing. "From a good source," he snarled. "Not everyone in Aranstream agrees with what the King is doing, or what he has done. Some of us have friends and family in Elvendon."

"You watch your tongue, boy," Jasen warned, stepping up to Logan. His presence was imposing, his voice sharp with authority. "You are a King's soldier, and unless you want to end up like the witch Esimae, I suggest you keep your opinions to yourself." The threat was clear, and his loyalty to the King was unwavering.

Hidden nearby, Kaitlin struggled to suppress a gasp as she heard Esimae's name, her hand instinctively flying to her mouth. Keltor, sensing her distress, gently covered her other hand with his in a silent gesture of reassurance.

The first pale hints of dawn crept over the treetops, casting long, cold shadows across the forest floor. The air was thick with tension, heavy with the scents of damp earth and smouldering campfire. Jasen's voice cut through the hush, harsh and commanding. "It's nearly daybreak, it's time to move out, we've got an execution to do, and we are still hours away," he barked. His eyes flashed with anger as he jabbed a finger towards Logan. "And you can light the torch and make that witch burn."

A surge of dread coiled in Logan's chest; his heart hammered against his ribs as he shook his head, eyes dark with fear and defiance. "No, I can't," Logan replied, his voice trembling yet firm. "I won't be part of this. I—I know her. She's saved people, she's no monster."

70

Jasen's patience had worn thin; he lurched forward in a threatening manner, voice hoarse with pent-up fury. "I have just about had enough of you," he yelled, his fists clenched at his sides. Turning abruptly to one of the other soldiers, Jasen snapped, "Restrain him, now." The soldier glanced at Logan, then back at Jasen, his reluctance evident as he hesitated, the tension palpable between them. The harsh snap of twigs underfoot punctuated Jasen's next command. "I am your superior, do as I say, now!" he barked, and the soldier nodded, the sharpness of Jasen's voice cutting through the heavy silence.

Logan extended his wrists, allowing the soldier to bind them tightly and relieve him of his weapons. Despite the restraint, he fixed Jasen with a defiant glare, his resentment simmering beneath the surface. Logan's presence among the Aranstream soldiers was not of his own choosing. He had left the army the previous year after marrying his beloved, settling with her on his aunt's modest farm along the southern border of Elvendon, close to the mysterious Forest of Time.

When the attack was announced, Logan awoke to find his brothers at his doorstep. They had come to summon him back, but when he refused, they forcibly dragged him to Aranstream. Logan's connection to Esimae was personal—she was a trusted family friend, and the thought of harming her was unthinkable.

Three months after his forced return to military service, Logan received distressing news: his wife had nearly suffered a miscarriage. It was Esimae, with her healing potions, who had saved both his wife and their unborn child. The separation from his family weighed heavily on him, and he longed for their safety and comfort. Yet, he understood that if he complied with orders and remained in the army, his wife and unborn child would be protected. This knowledge kept him compliant; despite the mounting threats and duress he faced.

However, the burden had become unbearable. Logan had witnessed countless horrors during the recent months, and now, being commanded to execute Esimae was more than he could

71

bear. His loyalty to his family and his moral conscience left him unable to carry out such a command.

"Move out, now!" Jasen barked, glaring back at him.

The other soldiers responded instantly to Jasen's command. With a sense of urgency, they scrambled to their feet, collecting their gear and weapons. Without hesitation, they fell into line behind their commanding officer, following him into the shadowy depths of the forest. Their movements were brisk and purposeful, driven by the weight of the mission ahead and the unwavering authority in Jasen's tone. The party pressed forward, fading into the dense woodland as the first light of dawn filtered through the trees, leaving only the faint echo of their departure lingering in the chilly morning air.

When they were finally out of earshot, Kaitlin pushed herself up from the security of the bough, her breaths coming in shallow bursts. "Oh my god, Keltor, they're going to kill Esimae!" she whispered, her voice trembling with panic.

Keltor glanced at her, his face set and urgent as he snatched up his rucksack. "I know, I heard him. Come on, we need to go, now," he urged, his tone clipped and low to avoid drawing attention.

Bark scraped against their palms as they slid down the rough trunk, the morning's chill biting into their skin. Overhead, leaves rustled softly, and the distant voices of the soldiers faded into the misty forest air. The ground below was slick with dew, and the sharp scent of earth filled their nostrils as they dropped to the forest floor.

Kaitlin landed, wincing as twigs snapped beneath her boots. "We can't let them kill her, Keltor. She's the only family I have left," she said, her words fractured by a sniffle as she wiped away tears with the back of her hand.

"We won't," Keltor said firmly as he landed beside her, a look of determination flashing in his eyes. "We'll save her somehow. I promise you, Kaitlin. I owe her my life."

XXX

Jasen and his men reached the other soldiers at the Deodar village by mid-morning. The pyre had already been built, and they were all ready for the execution. The mood in the village was sombre. Esimae was well known in the village; she was a healer and had helped and saved many of the villagers in the months she had been living there. She was greatly respected. The Deodars busied themselves so as not to think about what was about to happen. It wasn't that they were cowards, or that they didn't care or want to help Esimae—far from it—but they simply couldn't. Aranstream soldiers had seized most of the able-bodied men to work on the new castle, and the few that remained were either elders or the infirm. Any attempt to intervene would be met with swift punishment from the Aranstream soldiers, who watched the villagers with suspicion, hands never straying far from their weapons.

The Deodars mostly lived up in the trees, their homes perched high in the canopy of the giant oaks. The village spanned throughout the forest, with bridges and walkways connecting each home and weaving the entirety of the settlement together. From their lofty walkways, villagers peered down at the clearing below, their vantage points offering little comfort as they witnessed the grim preparations unfolding at ground level. The elevated homes, usually a symbol of safety and unity, now served only to heighten their sense of helplessness as they looked on, unable to protect one of their own.

At midday, the mournful blare of a horn shattered the uneasy hush, summoning the Deodars to gather at ground level. They did not assemble out of curiosity or desire to witness Esimae's agony, but because they were commanded—forced to bear witness under Aranstream's unyielding edict. Traitors were to be beheaded, but for a witch, the punishment was the pyre. It was a lesson meant for all, adults and children alike.

The courtyard below the tree houses, usually alive with children's laughter, was now filled with sombre faces. Among the Deodars stood a handful of elves, refugees whose homes had been razed in the attack eight months before. The crowd was mostly

73

made up of women clutching infants, small children huddling close, and elders leaning on canes. Many averted their eyes, clutching their children tightly, while others whispered prayers under trembling breaths. Tears shone in some eyes, and a palpable fear rippled through the throng—fear for Esimae, for themselves, for what might come next.

"Make sure she's tied tight, I don't want those witchy hands free," Jasen ordered.

The harsh clatter of rope tightening echoed off the surrounding trees as Esimae was bound to the post atop the pyre, the rough fibres biting into her wrists and ankles, pinning her helplessly above the stacked wood. The scent of wood drifted up from the pyre, mingling with the earthy scent of the forest, and she could feel splinters pressing against her back. Her breathing came fast and shallow, panic fluttering in her chest as she strained against the bonds.

Esimae's voice rang out, unwavering despite the peril she faced. "You'll get your comeuppance," she yelled at Jasen, her words echoing through the tense silence that had fallen over the crowd.

"Yeah, maybe I will, but you'll still be dead," Jasen growled back at Esimae.

If she wasn't such a lady, she would have spat at him, but instead she took a deep breath and held her head high, her long dark curls lifting in the subtle breeze as she stood precariously on a shelf balanced atop the pile of wood. She gazed out over the crowd that had come to witness her execution. Amongst the gathering were many Deodars—her friends and former patients— yet fear kept them from intervening. Esimae held no resentment toward them; she understood their terror. The new King had conscripted most of their young men to labour on his grand castle in Aranstream, leaving the villagers weakened and unable to oppose the occupying soldiers. Nor would she wish them to fight and risk their lives on her behalf; she did not want their blood on her conscience as well.

A silent wish echoed in her heart that her punishment might have been beheading or something swifter—anything but the agony she now faced, the fire soon to sear her flesh. Her eyes drifted across the assembled faces, searching for comfort or hope, and as she glanced to her right, her expression shifted in recognition.

Tears filled Logan's eyes as he looked up at Esimae. Powerless, his hands bound and held firm by an Aranstream soldier, he watched as another soldier removed the ladder from the pyre, making escape impossible. All he could do was lift his shackled hands to his face to wipe away his tears, overwhelmed by helplessness and sorrow.

Esimae offered him a gentle, reassuring smile and nodded her head. "It's okay," she mouthed to him, even as cold tears traced paths down her cheeks. She bore no blame for Logan, responsibility lay with her alone. It was the Aranstream soldiers who had killed her beloved Jaike, and in her grief she had tried to protect him with her magic. Now, in the eyes of the new King, her abilities marked her as a threat—and for that, she would burn as a witch.

A hush fell so suddenly across the courtyard that even the wind seemed to hold its breath; the rustling leaves were stilled, and the crowd's whispers died on trembling lips. Jasen's voice erupted through the silence, harsh and commanding, reverberating off the roots and boards of the Deodar homes above. "This is it, Logan. Your last chance. You light the fire, or she burns anyway." His words lingered in the air like the taste of iron—thick, bitter, and inescapable—making the assembled villagers flinch and shift uneasily.

Logan's heart pounded painfully inside his chest as the rough grip of the soldiers bruised his arms, though he scarcely noticed. His world had narrowed to the post, the pyre, and Esimae standing above the waiting wood. Her dark eyes met his—pleading, yet unflinching—and in that gaze he recalled every gentle kindness she had bestowed upon him and his wife. The distant, frightened cry of a child cut through his thoughts, followed by the creak of strained rope and the shuffling feet of onlookers desperate to look away, but unable to.

Cold sweat slicked Logan's back, the acrid aroma of smoke from Jasen's torch beginning to mingle with the salt of his own tears. Summoning his strength, he managed to speak—his voice ragged and unsteady at first, then growing stronger with resolve. "No," Logan said, his defiance clear despite the tremor in his words. He wrenched against the soldiers' grasp, his knuckles white and his eyes never leaving Esimae's face. "I won't be the hand that harms her. Logan's voice shook with emotion as he pleaded with Jasen. "She's done nothing but heal this village, Jasen—she's saved the lives of so many." The words tumbled from his lips, thick with desperation and grief. He looked around at the crowd, his gaze searching the faces of neighbours who had once turned to Esimae in their hour of need, knowing how often she had eased their suffering or brought loved ones back from the brink. Yet now, fear kept them silent, unable to defend the very woman who had so often defended them. Logan's protest hung in the air, a last attempt to remind the villagers—and Jasen—of all the good Esimae had done, even as the threat of the pyre loomed ever closer.

"Fine, just so you know, there are soldiers on their way to your wife," Jasen hissed, his voice low and venomous as he leaned in close. The words slithered into Logan's ears like poison, and Jasen's icy breath raised goosebumps along Logan's neck before he turned and strode towards the looming pyre. Logan tried to wrench free from the soldiers' iron grip. His heart hammered painfully in his chest, each beat thrumming with panic and helpless fury. Desperation surged within him, churning like a tempest as he shouted, his voice raw and jagged, "You son of a bitch, don't you touch her!" He strained violently against the hands restraining him, his entire body trembling with fear and rage.

xxx

76

Keltor and Kaitlin fought their way through the tightly packed crowd of Deodars. Towering above them the Deodars made perfect cover as they struggled to get closer, weaving between the imposing figures of the forest dwellers and other elves who had managed to reach the front. Desperation surged in Kaitlin's voice as she clung to Keltor's arm, her panic mounting at the sight of her aunt, Esimae, bound to a pole atop the pyre. "Oh my god, oh my god, Keltor, we have to do something," she cried, her grip tightening in fear and helplessness. The question gnawed at her: why wasn't Esimae using her magic to free herself?

Keltor, his gaze sweeping the scene, tried to assess their chances. He counted twenty Aranstream soldiers visible among the villagers, but he knew there could be more hidden within the village. There was no time to investigate further. As he searched for answers, he caught Esimae's eye. She was looking directly at someone and mouthing the words "I know," a silent message that carried a weight of understanding and resignation.

Keltor leaned in close to Kaitlin, his voice a tense whisper as he gripped her arm. "Kaitlin, look over there." He directed her attention to a point beyond the crowd, urgency colouring his words. Kaitlin's gaze followed Keltor's direction and immediately fixed on the sight he indicated. Her breath caught as she recognised Uly and Ren, both of whom were being held tightly by Aranstream soldiers. The soldiers' swords pressed dangerously against their stomachs, a silent but unmistakable warning.

The realisation dawned on Kaitlin, and her frustration bubbled to the surface. "It's Uly and Ren. Oh, shit, that's why she won't use her magic," she exclaimed, understanding at last the reason for Esimae's inaction. Esimae was being forced to submit, unable to use her powers for fear that any attempt to escape or resist would endanger Uly and Ren.

Keltor's sharp eyes continued to scan the scene. Amidst the tense standoff, he noticed something unusual—an Aranstream soldier being held captive as well. Unlike the others, this soldier's composure had broken; tears streamed down his face, betraying his distress.

77

"That's who she's talking to," Keltor murmured, his voice tinged with surprise as the pieces began to fall into place. "Not Uly or Ren." His observation was met with a puzzled look from Kaitlin.

"What?" Kaitlin asked, her brow furrowing as she tried to follow Keltor's train of thought.

Keltor clarified, "That soldier being held next to Uly and Ren— he's talking to Esimae. He knows her." The realisation dawned slowly as Keltor strained to recall the events beneath the tree earlier. He remembered the two soldiers who had been arguing, and now, with growing certainty, he pieced together the identity of the captive. "I think I know who he is," Keltor said, his mind racing as he connected this new revelation to the unfolding drama.

Kaitlin's voice trembled as she pressed Keltor for answers. "Who?" she demanded, confusion furrowing her brow.

"It's that soldier, the one under the tree, the one who was defending Esimae. I think it's Logan, Alana's husband," Keltor replied, anxiety clear in his tone. His eyes darted anxiously across the crowd. "Is she here?" he muttered, scanning the assembly of elves for any sign of Alana.

Kaitlin, equally tense, shook her head as her gaze swept over the gathering. "I can't see her," she answered, her voice quick and worried.

The tension escalated sharply when Kaitlin spotted an Aranstream soldier making his way toward the pyre. She watched in horror as the soldier handed a flaming torch to Jasen, her panic mounting. "Keltor!" she cried out, her alarmed shout drowned in the growing chaos.

"No, no!" Kaitlin gasped, her instincts taking over as she surged forward, desperation written plainly across her face. She was prepared to throw herself into the fray, determined to reach the pyre and prevent the unthinkable from happening—no matter the cost to herself.

Before she could act, Keltor reached out and stopped her, his grip firm yet pleading. "No, they will just kill you," he urged, his voice low but insistent, trying to anchor her against the rising tide of panic.

Kaitlin's reply was fierce, her voice trembling with emotion. "I'm not going to let her burn!" she shot back, unwilling to stand by while Esimae suffered.

"I know, I know, we're not," Keltor assured her quickly, his gaze darting between the captives and the soldiers. "We'll free her, but I need to free Uly, Ren and Logan first. Once we start this fight, we're going to need all the help we can get." His tone carried both urgency and a carefully measured strategy, emphasising the need for caution and coordination.

He then turned to her with a critical question. "Can you use your magic to stop the flames without being seen?"

Kaitlin nodded, her resolve hardening. "Yes, I think so," she replied, determination glinting in her eyes as she prepared to act.

"Okay," he replied. Keltor ducked back behind the Deodars and took a deep breath, quietly beginning to chant under his breath. As he spoke, a shimmer of magical light rippled through his body, cloaking him in its glow. Kaitlin glanced up at the Deodars towering overhead, their heads turned towards the unfolding events, paying no attention to the pair concealed below.

Keltor gave Kaitlin's arm a gentle pat, startling her so much that she nearly screamed. When she turned to look, she was shocked to see that Keltor had assumed the form of Xander, one of Aragon's soldiers whom he had killed.

"Holy shit, Keltor, are you trying to give me a heart attack?" she hissed in a strained whisper, struggling to contain her surprise and keep her composure amid the tension all around them.

"Sorry," Keltor apologised in his own voice, "but it has to be someone I've touched, and he was the first face I thought of."

Kaitlin's reaction was immediate; she stared at Keltor, unease written across her face. "It freaks the hell out of me, Keltor. The last time this happened was with Prince Aragon, when he pretended to be you," she whispered, her voice barely audible amid the surrounding tumult.

"I know," he replied gently. "Look, if you're ever unsure, let's have a signal so you always know it is me."

Kaitlin leaned in, curiosity piqued. "A signal, like what?" she murmured.

In response, Keltor lifted his hand. As he signed, he spoke the words to reinforce the gesture. His left-hand pressed flat against his chest, "I," he said softly. Then, curling his hand into a fist, he declared, "Love." Finally, he pointed with his index finger while keeping his hand to his chest, finishing, "You."

Kaitlin's lips curled into a grin. "Okay, and if you can't speak or move, just wink at me," she suggested, the tension easing slightly between them.

Keltor matched her smile with a nod, the new understanding solidifying their trust amid chaos.

"Be careful," he warned quietly.

"You too," she replied in a low voice. With a final glance between them, Keltor dashed back through the shifting crowds, determined to reach Uly and Ren as quickly as possible.

Kaitlin pulled up the hood of her cloak, steeling herself for what was to come. Drawing the fabric close, she readied her mind and body, eyes locked on the scene ahead. She watched intently as the Aranstream soldier gripped the torch, his posture rigid with duty. He raised his voice, delivering a formal declaration to the assembled crowd, stating the reasons for Esimae's impending execution by fire.

Meanwhile, Keltor moved purposefully towards Logan, recognising the soldier's potential in the fight to come. As he hurried through the throng, he passed another cluster of soldiers gathered near the main hall of the Deodars. The main great hall, a place usually reserved for banquets and special events such as bonding ceremonies, now stood ominously in the background, watched over by seven armed soldiers. Keltor pressed on, his focus unwavering, until he reached the area where Uly, Ren, and Logan were being held—situated at the very front, mere metres from the pyre where Esimae's fate hung in the balance.

With calm determination, Keltor approached the Aranstream soldier restraining Logan. Maintaining an air of authority, he tapped the soldier firmly on the shoulder. "You're wanted at the great hall," Keltor announced, his voice steady and direct, projecting the urgency of an official summons.

The soldier looked at him with disbelief, scoffing at the suggestion. "What now, you're joking? And miss this?" He jerked his head towards the pyre, clearly reluctant to abandon the drama unfolding before the crowd.

"Yes, now," Keltor insisted, reinforcing the urgency in his voice.

The soldier hesitated, clearly torn between his duty and the spectacle before him. With a disgruntled sigh, he relented at last. "Fine..." the soldier muttered, his tone heavy with reluctance. Casting a final, longing glance at the pyre, he relinquished his hold on Logan and turned to make his way towards the great hall, his steps slow and resentful. The crowd barely noticed his departure as the tension in the square continued to mount.

Keltor moved in close to Logan, speaking quietly so as not to draw attention. "Logan," he said, his voice low and urgent.

Logan turned sharply towards him, irritation clear in his tone. "What!" he snapped.

"It's Keltor, Alana's friend," Keltor replied, hoping to jog Logan's memory.

Logan turned to face Keltor fully, confusion evident on his face. "What?" he asked, clearly struggling to understand the situation.

Maintaining a steady voice despite the urgency, Keltor explained, "Look, I'm a wizard, okay? This is just a shape shift—I can't hold it for too long if I'm going to use my magic to get you and Esimae out of here."

Logan, still incredulous, protested, "But you're dead," and tried to pull away, but Keltor's grip on his arm was unyielding.

"Clearly, I'm not, and neither is the Princess. Now, we don't have time for a chat. I need to free Uly and Ren—Kaitlin will try

81

to hold back the fire." Keltor's words were quick, his attention divided between Logan and the urgent rescue ahead.

Upon hearing this, Logan's eyes widened in disbelief. "She is here, the Princess?" he asked, astonished.

"Yes, she is and therefore in danger, so the quicker we get the hell out of here the better!" Keltor whispered, pulling out his knife and beginning to cut through Logan's bindings.

Logan cast a wary glance towards the other soldiers, uncertainty flickering in his eyes. "What's the plan?" he asked, his voice tense.

Keltor responded without hesitation, outlining their course of action. "We need to free Uly and Ren. Kaitlin will do her best to delay the pyre from burning. If Esimae sees they're safe, she'll hopefully use her magic to make an escape."

Logan's concern was evident. "Okay, but there's like twenty soldiers," he pointed out, his tone edged with anxiety.

Keltor offered a sardonic reply. "Yeah, I had noticed," he said dryly. Then, shifting to a more serious note, he pressed Logan for assurance. "What I need to know, Logan, is can you kill them? Do you have my back? I realise some of them may be your friends."

Logan looked around at the soldiers, his expression resolute. "No, they're not. I don't have a problem with that," he replied, shaking his head. There was no camaraderie between him and the others; he had always been an outcast since being forced back into service.

Keltor nodded in approval at Logan's resolute response. "Good. Come on then," he instructed, gripping Logan's arm firmly as they advanced with determined steps towards the place where Uly and Ren were being held captive.

As they approached, Keltor called out to the soldier restraining Uly, "Hey, take this one a minute. I need to question the Deodar."

The soldier, still fixated on the pyre, responded with mild irritation, "What, now?"

"Yes, now, it's important," Keltor insisted, his tone impatient as he cast a hurried glance at the pyre. "Look, just take the traitor, will you?"

With a begrudging huff, the soldier relented, sheathing his sword as Keltor drew his own weapon and pressed it lightly against Uly's stomach—enough to maintain the illusion of hostility.

Uly glared down at Keltor, the anger in his eyes clear as a low, threatening rumble escaped from him. Keltor met his gaze, lowering his voice to a whisper. "Hey, friend," he said gently, looking up at the imposing figure before him.

Uly's frown deepened as he studied Keltor's face, suspicion flickering across his features. "It's me, Keltor," Keltor insisted, hoping to break through Uly's uncertainty.

Still unconvinced, the Deodar shook his head slowly. "I don't understand. You are not he," he replied, doubt etched in his words.

Keltor leaned in, his voice earnest. "Yes, I am. I have shape-shifted, Uly, to get to you and Ren. Kaitlin is here too."

The imposing green figure gazed down at Keltor, uncertainty etched in his features. Keltor spoke quietly, reminding him, "You helped save me, Uly, from the shadowman's poison at Esimae's cottage in Elvendon Forest on Earth." The memory stirred something in Uly, prompting him to ask, "Keltor, is it really you?" His frown deepened, confusion mixing with disbelief. "We were told you and the Princess were dead."

Keltor nodded, his tone resolute. "Yes, I know, well we're not and we're both here to save Esimae." Without further hesitation, he swiftly sliced through the ropes that bound Uly, freeing him at last.

The urgency of the moment mounted as Keltor glanced over to Jasen. His heartbeat raced as he watched Jasen move to set the pyre alight, signalling imminent danger for their companions.

Amid the turmoil and confusion, Ren's anguished cry pierced the air. "No!" she shouted, her voice raw with desperation. She struggled fiercely against the grip of the Aranstream soldier who had taken her captive, her resolve clear in every movement as she fought to break free.

Keltor swung his sword towards her. Ren's eyes locked with his, heart pounding as a surge of terror and fear swept through her.

She saw the blade coming straight at her, gleaming in the uncertain light, and felt her breath catch in her throat. Instinct took over—Ren lifted her hands in front of her, silently pleading for him not to strike, desperation and disbelief mingling in her gaze.

But the soldier merely smiled at Ren, an unsettling expression that made her heart race. The terror in her eyes was quickly overtaken by astonishment as Keltor reacted, slicing deftly through the ropes that held her captive. Ren was suddenly free, her hands falling to her sides, relief mingling with disbelief.

Immediately Keltor turned and drove the blade of the sword through the gut of the unsuspecting Aranstream soldier holding Ren captive. The man gasped. Surprise and fear etched across his unsuspecting face. Keltor took a breath, as he withdrew the sword, and watch as the soldier collapsed dead to the ground.

Uly rushed to Ren. The shock on her face freezing her to the spot. Uly pulled her into an urgent embrace and held her close. "Ren, are you okay?" Uly asked tenderly. His hand lifting to her face.

"Uly,' she Ren in response, holding him tightly, unsure what was going on. "Yes, I'm okay. What's going on?" She glanced warily at the soldier who had freed her.

Uly grinned, excitement in his voice. "It's Keltor, Ren!" Uly cried, "The princess is alive as well."

Ren looked at him not understanding and then turned towards Keltor.

Keltor took a deep breath, pulling on his magic. A ripple of magical light rippled down his body.

"Keltor!" Ren cried in both shock and joy, as Keltor now returned to his own form gave her a smile. Her dark green eyes catching is piercing blue eyes which were smiling back at her.

"Hi Ren," he said as he back swung his sword, catching an Aranstream soldier coming at him from behind right in his gut. The soldier dropped to his knees and then keeled over.

Keltor glanced to Logan. "Ready?" he asked, and Logan nodded as he swept up the fallen soldier's sword and lifted it towards the onslaught of men that was now coming towards them.

XXX

Kaitlin took a steadying breath, whispering words of encouragement to herself. "Come on Kaitlin, you can do this," she murmured, urging her nerves to settle as she tried to focus on recalling the correct spell. She lifted her hands with utmost caution, making sure her movements were subtle and unlikely to attract attention from nearby soldiers. With a quiet voice, she began to utter the spell, *"Beltoria escalali porantaira."*

As the words slipped from her lips, a shimmering magic began to glimmer at her fingertips. The energy, both silent and unseen, surged from her hands and drifted across the space towards the flaming torch held aloft by one of the Aranstream soldiers. The moment the spell contacted the fire, the flame faltered and, within seconds, was snuffed out completely.

Jasen stared down at the torch in his hands, confusion written across his face as he tried to understand why its flame had been extinguished so suddenly. His frustration quickly turned to anger, and he barked a command at an Aranstream soldier nearby.

Jasen, his frustration mounting, shouted, "Get me another torch!" at a nearby Aranstream soldier. Not satisfied with just one, he quickly amended his command. "No, get me four!" The soldier nodded obediently and dashed away to fulfil the urgent request.

Within three minutes, the soldier hurried back, clutching four torches in his hands. Wasting no time, Jasen seized one of the torches from him. He then turned to two other soldiers and issued further instructions. "You, and you," he said, gesturing at the pair. "Take one each and light the pyre from the other sides."

The two soldiers acknowledged the command with a brief nod and promptly collected a torch each, moving swiftly to carry out Jasen's orders.

Kaitlin bit down on her bottom lip as she watched Jasen's actions with mounting anxiety. The number of torches had multiplied—now four in total—and two of them had already disappeared from her view, heightening her sense of dread. Her eyes darted over to Keltor, who, amidst the growing turmoil, had managed to free Logan and Uly. The situation was spiralling into chaos, and panic surged within her as she realised how quickly events were escalating.

Determined not to give in to fear, Kaitlin whispered the incantation again: "*Beltoria escalali porantaira.*" She channelled her magic with urgency, directing another wave of energy towards Jasen's torch. The spell took effect, and, for a second time, the torch's flame was snuffed out. Jasen's frustration boiled over; he muttered a curse and spun around, scanning the crowd of Deodars and elves for the culprit responsible for the extinguished flames.

To avoid detection, Kaitlin quickly shrank back, using the legs of a nearby Deodar as cover. She pressed herself close, doing her best to remain inconspicuous. Meanwhile, the soldier's anger was evident. His suspicions grew, certain now that someone among the crowd was behind the mysterious failure of his torches.

Suddenly, Kaitlin's senses were assaulted by the unmistakable scent of smoke drifting towards her. Alarmed, her eyes snapped open wide as she realised the danger unfolding nearby. Compelled by dread, she abandoned the relative safety of her hiding place, pushing herself forward to get a better look at the situation.

"Oh god, no," Kaitlin cried. Her heart raced as the flames began to climb, swiftly transforming the pyre into a raging inferno. She could only watch in horror as fire devoured the base, its heat radiating outward and consuming the wood with alarming speed.

Jasen cast a wary glance back into the assembled crowd as he crouched to relight his torch from the flickering flames. A gnawing suspicion had taken hold—he was certain that someone among the onlookers was secretly aiding the witch. His gaze swept across the faces, searching for anything out of the ordinary. Suddenly, his eyes landed on a woman shrouded in a hooded cloak, standing apart from the rest. He narrowed his eyes, studying her with mounting suspicion. After a tense moment, he turned away from the crowd and focused once more on the pyre, pressing the newly lit torch to his section of the stacked wood. The fire caught, and orange light leapt up to join the growing inferno.

Esimae's scream pierced the night as the oppressive heat from the flames surged around her, threatening to overwhelm her completely. Fear gripped her, but she refused to surrender to it; despite her desperate will to live, she could not allow her friends to perish because of her choices. The weight of responsibility pressed heavily on her—she knew that her actions had led them to this dire moment.

Uly had tried to restrain her from using magic, sensing the danger, but Esimae's emotions had clouded her judgement. The recent reunion with Jaike had left her raw with emotion, and she was determined not to lose him again, no matter the risk. Now, as the suffocating smoke filled her lungs, her throat burned with every breath. She coughed harshly, struggling to force the acrid air back out.

With her strength waning, Esimae looked desperately towards her friends, seeking some comfort in what felt like her final moments. Amidst the chaos, her eyes caught sight of a disturbance—a glimmer of hope. One of the soldiers appeared to be assisting Uly and Ren, and suddenly, a shimmer of light enveloped him, hinting at a magical intervention amidst the turmoil.

"Keltor?" she whispered, scarcely believing the words that had just escaped her lips. Her heart pounded in her chest, each beat echoing the urgency of the moment.

As Kaitlin scanned the chaos, she saw that Keltor had managed to free Logan, Uly and Ren from their restraints. The sight fuelled her determination—consequences be damned, she would not let Esimae perish in the flames.

Without hesitation, Kaitlin surged to the front of the crowd. She raised her hands high, her resolve unwavering. Summoning all her power, she shouted, "*Pandor, isacar, beltoria*!" Channelling her magic through both hands, she unleashed a powerful wave of energy that surged towards the burning pyre. The spell formed a protective seal over the fire, smothering the flames and preventing them from reaching her aunt.

Esimae immediately felt the surge of magic envelop her. Instinctively, her eyes darted in the direction from which the energy emanated.

"Kaitlin!" she called out, her voice thick with emotion as tears pooled in her eyes. Relief and hope mingled in her expression as she caught sight of her niece amid the chaos.

"Esimae!" Kaitlin cried in return, her hands trembling with the effort of keeping the flames at bay. She fought to maintain the barrier of magic, her determination unwavering. "Free yourself!" she urged, pouring every ounce of strength she had into her plea.

Jasen, completely baffled by the sudden eruption of magic and chaos, felt a surge of fury that reddened his cheeks. The possibility of another witch among them set his anger ablaze. Unable to contain himself, he bellowed, "Get her!" His command was punctuated by spittle that sprayed across the soldiers standing before him as he pointed directly at Kaitlin.

Responding instantly to his order, six soldiers surged forward, charging as one towards Kaitlin. The Deodars in the vicinity, uncertain and alarmed by the unfolding events, instinctively retreated, giving Kaitlin no cover or support. She was left exposed and isolated, standing alone in the open.

With the soldiers rapidly closing in, Kaitlin was forced to withdraw one hand from maintaining the protective barrier against the flames to defend herself. In that moment, the fire on the left side of the pyre flared up again, threatening Esimae with renewed intensity.

With the imminent threat of the advancing soldiers, Kaitlin stood firm, her determination burning brighter than ever. Drawing upon the depth of her magical power, she raised her voice above the commotion and cried out, *"Et magicae virtute, conteret eos!"* A surge of raw energy erupted from her outstretched hands, forming a blazing wave that crashed into the soldiers bearing down on her.

The crowd recoiled in shock as Kaitlin's magic sent the soldiers hurtling through the air. Bodies crashed to the ground just a few feet from where she stood—some soldiers lay motionless, others groaned and struggled to rise, stunned by the force of her spell. The onlookers, gripped by fear and uncertainty, retreated further from Kaitlin. Among them, the Deodars and the handful of elves present kept their distance, gazing at her with wide, apprehensive eyes, unwilling to intervene or draw her attention. Kaitlin's gaze flickered across the frightened faces before returning to Esimae. Esimae offered her a reassuring smile and a nod, silently recognising Kaitlin's bravery and strength amid the chaos.

With a desperate incantation, Esimae cried out, "*Pushna carn,*" and the bindings that held her fast abruptly loosened. Suddenly freed, she let out a scream as her full weight, no longer supported by the pole, caused the wood beneath her to give way. She tumbled helplessly towards the hungry flames below.

Keltor, alerted by her scream, spun around just in time to see her fall. Without hesitation, he let his sword drop and thrust his hands forward in a swift, scooping motion.

"*Teneat!*" he commanded, his voice ringing out above the chaos. Instantly, Esimae's descent was halted, suspended in mid-air by Keltor's magic. Her frightened gaze met his, suspended just above the burning pyre.

Summoning all his strength, Keltor swept his hands sharply to the left. Esimae's body moved with his gesture, pulled away from the fire and deposited safely to the ground.

Esimae landed with a heavy thud, her hands outstretched before her to break the fall. Drawing a shaky breath of relief, she pushed herself up, sweeping her hair away from her face as she gathered her composure.

"Holy shit," Kaitlin cried, her voice trembling with shock at the feat Keltor had just accomplished. Relief flooded through her as she withdrew her wave of magic from the pyre, finally able to breathe again.

"*Conteret!*" Esimae shouted, her voice cutting through the chaos as she thrust her hand towards Keltor. In that instant, Keltor turned to see an Aranstream soldier directly in her line of fire. The soldier was struck by Esimae's spell, propelled violently backwards through the air before landing heavily on the ground.

Without missing a beat, Keltor glanced back at Esimae, offering a brief nod of acknowledgement for her swift intervention. Then, he reclaimed his sword and moved decisively towards the fallen soldier, delivering a fatal stab to the heart to ensure the threat was truly neutralised.

With danger closing in from every side, Keltor and Logan positioned themselves back-to-back, ready to face the oncoming wave of soldiers. They braced for impact, determined to hold their ground.

Meanwhile, Uly and Ren hurried to Esimae, who was still catching her breath after her harrowing escape. Uly crouched beside her, concern etched on his face. "Are you okay?" he asked, offering a steadying hand to help her to her feet.

Esimae nodded gratefully as she stood up. "Yes, thank you, Uly." She quickly turned to Ren, who was already regaining her composure. "Ren, how are you?"

Ren gave a reassuring nod, her voice steady. "All is well."

Without wasting another moment, Esimae fixed her gaze on Uly. "Right, Uly, get Ren out of here now," she instructed firmly, rolling up her sleeves as she prepared herself for the next threat.

Uly hesitated, defiance in his eyes. "No, I will help," he insisted, unwilling to leave them behind.

Esimae scowled at him, determination sharpening her tone. "No, you will take her and get her somewhere safe," she commanded. Despite the urgency, a brief smile crossed her lips as Kaitlin stepped in front of her, ready to face whatever came next together.

"Esimae," Kaitlin gasped, her breath coming in shallow bursts as relief mingled with fear.

Overcome with emotion, Kaitlin's aunt rushed forward, tears streaming down her cheeks. "Oh, my goodness child, I thought you were dead," she sobbed as she enveloped Kaitlin in a fierce hug, her arms wrapped tightly around her niece.

Kaitlin returned the embrace, offering what reassurance she could amid the chaos. "No, thankfully not and I'll tell you all about it another time," she replied, her tone gentle but urgent. "I think we have a more pressing situation."

Jasen stood before them, flanked by five soldiers, each gripping a sword and poised for battle. The tension in the air was palpable as they faced off, the threat of violence hanging heavily between the two sides.

Esimae fixed Uly with an urgent look. "Uly," she pressed, her tone brooking no argument.

With a determined nod, Uly gave his assurance. "I will be back," he promised. Without wasting another second, he grasped Ren's hand firmly and quickly led her away from the immediate danger, intent on getting her to safety as Esimae had commanded.

Jasen glared at them; his tone laced with disdain. "So, two witches," he growled, eyeing both Esimae and Kaitlin with open hostility.

Esimae met his gaze without flinching, her posture unyielding as she readied herself for the confrontation. "Yep," she replied, her voice calm but edged with resolve, signalling her readiness for what was to come.

Kaitlin's stomach churned with anxiety, the grim reality settling over her like a suffocating shroud. She understood all too well that if they did not act, they would be killed by these elves— and worse, if any of their enemies escaped, word could reach King Iwein about her and Keltor. The risk was simply too great to allow any witnesses to survive.

"Get them!" Jasen barked, his command ringing out sharply as he signalled his soldiers to attack.

In that tense instant, Kaitlin felt Esimae's hand clamp firmly around her right hand, offering both guidance and solidarity. Esimae's voice was steady and reassuring as she spoke: "Let me guide you." Kaitlin nodded in response, and almost immediately, she felt a peculiar tingling sensation begin to trickle into her hand—Esimae's magic, seeping into her, readying her for the battle that was about to unfold.

"*Conteret eos!*" Esimae shouted, her voice echoing with power. In that moment, both her and Kaitlin's eyes blazed an

91

intense white, the manifestation of magical energy coursing through them. The sensation was overwhelming, raw power surging within their joined hands as they drew upon their combined strength.

With remarkable coordination, Kaitlin and Esimae raised their free hands in perfect unison. From their palms, a surge of concentrated magical energy burst forth, forming a shockwave that rippled outward with immense force. The wave struck the five soldiers as they advanced, its strength so overwhelming that it sent them flying into the air, suspended for a moment, powerless in the grip of the witches' combined might.

Without hesitation, Kaitlin and Esimae swept their hands downward, channelling their magic to slam the soldiers forcefully onto the ground. The impact was devastating, ending the soldiers' lives instantly as they hit the earth with fatal force.

Kaitlin stared in shock at the devastation she and Esimae had wrought, the lifeless soldiers scattered across the ground a grim testament to their combined power. Her breath came in ragged bursts, each heartbeat pounding so fiercely she thought her chest might give out. She could hardly believe what they had done— wielding magic with such deadly force, taking lives to ensure their own survival. A tremor of fear and guilt coursed through her, mingling with a raw surge of adrenaline.

Esimae released Kaitlin's hand, letting their magical connection dissipate. With deliberate intent, she stepped forward towards Jasen, her posture radiating determination and anger.

"Esimae," Kaitlin called out, her voice tinged with hesitation and concern.

Esimae responded firmly, lifting her left hand in a clear signal for Kaitlin to stay back. "No, child," she said, her words both resolute and protective. "This one is mine."

As Esimae locked eyes with Jasen, a powerful surge of rage swept through her, intensifying the tension in the air and underscoring her unwavering resolve.

Esimae released Kaitlin's hand, their magical connection fading. Without a word, she stepped deliberately towards Jasen, her movements heavy with purpose and anger. The air seemed to thicken around her, and Kaitlin sensed a dangerous resolve radiating from her aunt.

Standing before Jasen, Esimae fixed him with a steely gaze, her voice low and commanding as she began to chant, "*Ego teneo et tibi dominantur.*" At her incantation, Jasen's posture abruptly became rigid, his body now moving beyond his own will, held in place by the force of her magic.

With deliberate precision, Esimae issued her next command: "*Arma tua stillabunt.*" Jasen, struggling internally against the compulsion, found his hand trembling violently as he tried to resist. Yet, despite his efforts, the sword he held slipped from his grasp and clattered to the ground, a clear sign that her enchantment held him firmly in its grip.

Esimae was relentless. She directed him further, her finger making a slight beckoning motion as she spoke, "*Tolle tibi pugionem.*" Powerless to resist, Jasen reached down and drew his dagger from the sheath at his hip, his movements jerky and unnatural, his face contorted in horror at what was unfolding.

Esimae's eyes narrowed with cold determination as she uttered a single command, her voice ringing with lethal authority: "*Mortem.*" The word, heavy with finality, hung in the air between them. Jasen's hand shook as he tried to fight against the invisible force; his face covered in horror as he lifted his own blade to his throat. Esimae clicked her fingers. Jasen immediately swiped the blade across this throat, in one swift sharp movement. Blood spurted out everywhere and he dropped to his knees. He gurgled and choked a few times before finally keeling over to the ground, dead.

Kaitlin shut her eyes tightly and turned her face away, unable to bear the sight unfolding before her. Her heart thudded painfully in her chest, each beat echoing the gravity of the moment. Around them, an oppressive silence seemed to settle, as if the entire Deodar tribe stood frozen, collectively holding its breath in anticipation. Though she knew Jasen deserved the punishment he was about to receive, Kaitlin found herself unwilling to watch the act itself.

"That is for Jaike," Esimae whispered as she leaned over Jasen's body, her voice barely audible yet heavy with meaning. The words caught Kaitlin's attention immediately, and she turned back, her heart dropping at the implication. Was Jaike dead?

"Esimae?" Kaitlin called softly, uncertainty in her voice. Esimae glanced over her shoulder, her expression confirming Kaitlin's fears.

"Is Jaike—?" Kaitlin started, but Esimae simply nodded. A single tear traced its way down her cheek, silent testament to her grief.

"I'm so sorry," Kaitlin said, her voice thick with emotion. She hurried to her aunt's side and wrapped her arms around her in a comforting embrace.

"It's okay, I'm okay," Esimae replied, though the tremor in her voice betrayed her true feelings. She tried to sound reassuring, but the pain lingered beneath the surface. "I had nearly seven wonderful months with him before the Aranstream soldiers found him and tried to take him away. I begged him not to fight, but…" She paused, taking a shaky breath. "There was a struggle, and I used my magic. I was so angry I couldn't stop it, and he was killed trying to stop them taking me."

Kaitlin's voice was gentle as she asked, "How did you end up on the pyre?"

Esimae's gaze dropped as she replied, her words heavy with sorrow. "When he died, I just gave up. What was the point? He died because of me." She paused; her face shadowed with remorse. "King Iwein found out I was a witch and sent Prince Keion here. He gave me an ultimatum: to join the King and use my magic against Elvendon or die. Of course, I refused—there is no way I will join them."

She let out a heavy sigh, the weight of her memories clear. "They held Uly and Ren as hostages so that I did not use my magic on them. Prince Keion rounded up all the male Deodars and had them sent to Aranstream to work on the new castle and decided to make an example of me. Hence the dramatic 'burn the witch'."

Kaitlin's eyes filled with sympathy. "Oh, Esimae, I'm so sorry. I know how happy Jaike was when we freed him from those witches. He loved you so much."

Esimae dabbed the tears from her cheek with the sleeve of her dress. "I know," she whispered. Gathering herself, she added with renewed resolve, "Now, come on, Keltor needs our help."

The soldiers fanned out, steadily advancing in a measured line towards Keltor and Logan. Sensing the imminent threat, both men prepared themselves for the confrontation, bracing for what was to come. Suddenly, one of the soldiers' broke formations, rushing forward with reckless abandon and swinging his sword in a wild arc aimed at them.

Keltor reacted instantly, sidestepping as his boots crunched against the earth, narrowly avoiding the soldier's wild and reckless swing. With practiced skill, he switched his sword to his left hand, the hilt cool, and reassuring in his grip. His right hand shot out, seizing the soldier's arm; he could feel the tense muscles straining beneath his grasp, and the metallic scrape as their weapons nearly collided in the chaos.

Using a sudden surge of force, Keltor drove the soldier back, his movements precise and powerful. He kicked out sharply, knocking the man's legs out from under him and with a swift swipe, toppled him to the ground. Keltor whipped his sword around, gripping the hilt firmly with both hands. With a powerful motion, he drove the weapon straight into the man's chest, his actions decisive and unyielding. Quickly, Keltor cast a glance towards Logan, briefly checking to make sure of his companion's position in the chaos. Satisfied he was okay, he adjusted his grip, giving the sword a subtle jiggle in his hand as he readied himself for the next wave of attackers.

Logan watched Keltor, momentarily transfixed by the sheer speed and skill on display. He had never witnessed anyone move with such agility or confidence before. In that instant, a spark of hope flickered within him—perhaps, just perhaps, they truly stood a chance after all.

The soldiers surged forward in unison, attacking with coordinated aggression. Keltor and Logan responded without hesitation, charging to meet them head-on. Their movements were rapid and forceful; each strike delivered with unyielding determination. The relentless sound of steel colliding filled the clearing, ringing out with each blow and parry.

Keltor moved with astonishing speed, his blade slashing and lunging through the melee. Years of dedicated training had honed his swordsmanship to a level where each movement was instinctive, every reaction a product of discipline and experience. Even before the addition of magic to his abilities, Keltor had been a formidable warrior, and now his prowess was near unmatched.

Beside him, Logan held his ground, expertly blocking the incoming attacks. His actions were swift and fluid, matching the ferocity of the assault. Despite the chaos that surrounded them, Keltor could not help but notice the remarkable skill displayed by the young soldier. Logan fought with a fiery passion, fuelled by anger and something deeper—an urgent need that gave his movements an edge of desperation. This intensity was both impressive and, to Keltor, somewhat concerning.

Together, Keltor and Logan poured their all into the battle, standing firm against what seemed like an endless wave of opponents. Each one was determined to hold their ground, refusing to yield as the onslaught continued unabated.

"Logan!" Keltor yelled, his eyes locking onto the fleeting silhouette of an Aranstream soldier making a desperate dash for freedom. The thick smoke from the burning pyre almost concealed the man's escape, but a sudden flash of sunlight glinting off his sword betrayed him. Logan, catching the urgency in Keltor's gaze, quickly spotted the fleeing soldier heading for the Main Hall. They all knew that if even one soldier escaped, King Iwein would be warned—and that was a risk none of them could afford.

"Will you be okay?" Logan shouted back to Keltor, who stood surrounded by the last nine enemy soldiers. Despite the odds,

Keltor's confidence remained unshaken. He glanced to his right, seeing Kaitlin and Esimae racing to support him.

"Yes, get him! Don't let him get away, Logan!" Keltor commanded, his voice resolute.

Logan ran like the wind; he was faster than the escaping soldier and as he caught up with him, he threw his sword to the ground and with a tackle dive grabbed the man's legs stopping him dead, and they both tumbled to the ground. Logan struggled with the man, he flipped him over, sat on him and pinned him to the ground.

Logan stared down at the man, struggling to catch his breath. "Logan," the man gasped, his eyes wide with fear.

"Rob," Logan replied, and his heart sank. Although Logan didn't consider Rob a friend, he remembered that Rob had at least been kind to him.

"Please, just let me go, I won't say anything, I promise," he begged. Logan's mind scrambled as he thought what to do. He really didn't want to kill him.

Rob could see the battle raging in Logan's eyes as he hovered above him. "Logan, please," he whispered, desperation trembling in his voice.

Logan's grip on the knife tightened, hands shaking ever so slightly. For a moment, he hesitated, caught between duty and mercy. Alarna's face flashed through his mind—her gentle smile, her unwavering trust—and a sickening weight pressed down on his chest. If he let Rob go, Alarna, Keltor, and the Princess would all be at risk. He felt the cold press of metal in his palm and the sticky sweat on his brow, the sounds of distant fighting muffled beneath the rush of his own heartbeat.

Rob's voice cracked as he reached out, seizing Logan's arm, eyes wild with fear. "You don't need to do this."

Logan realised that he simply could not gamble with Alarna's life—nor could he endanger Keltor or the Princess by showing mercy now. The risk was too great; any hesitation could cost them everything. The weight of responsibility pressed upon his shoulders, and he understood that mercy, in this moment, was a luxury he could not afford. "I do," he replied in a whisper. In one swift movement he swiped his blade across Rob's throat.

Logan lingered for a moment, his voice barely audible as he whispered, "I'm sorry." Hand trembling, Logan wiped the sticky, warm blood from his blade onto Rob's uniform, feeling the rough, coarse fabric drag against the metal. The coppery smell rose sharply in the chill air, mingling with the distant clash of steel and the frantic shouts of battle. For a heartbeat, he caught his own reflection in the blade—haunted and pale—before sliding it back into the sheath at his belt, the familiar rasp grounding him in the reality of what he'd done. A knot of guilt twisted in his gut, but there was no time to dwell; the weight of responsibility still pressed on his chest. He dashed across the trampled grass, grabbed his discarded sword, its hilt slick in his grasp, and forced himself to run back to the others, heart pounding with a cold, relentless urgency.

"Kaitlin," Esimae called out, extending her hand towards her niece. Without hesitation, Kaitlin clasped her aunt's hand once more, feeling a surge of reassurance steady her nerves. Together, they began to chant in unison, their voices rising above the chaos.

"*Bitcar tormar*," they intoned, and with a sweeping motion of their free hands, four soldiers were suddenly lifted off their feet. The men shot upwards through the air, propelled backwards by an unseen force, before crashing violently to the ground. As the magical energy flowed through them, both Kaitlin and Esimae's eyes glowed an intense white, a sign of the formidable power they wielded when united.

Together, Esimae and Kaitlin shouted, "*Etoo bacara!*" Magic surged from their outstretched hands, and as both women clenched their fists, an invisible force seized the soldiers. The men's necks twisted sharply, snapping with a sickening crack that echoed above the chaos. The display of power left no confusion—it was their combined will that ended the soldiers' lives.

As Esimae released her grip, Kaitlin swayed unsteadily and took a faltering step backwards. The effort of channelling magic left her utterly spent—her limbs felt heavy and weak, and a wave of dizziness swept over her. She pressed a trembling hand to her forehead, biting back a surge of panic as the world seemed to tilt beneath her feet. Heart pounding, Kaitlin struggled to steady her breath, fighting to keep her composure as the enormity of what she'd done settled over her like a weighted cloak.

Esimae, still breathless from the exertion of magic, reached out a steadying hand to Kaitlin. Her voice was gentle but firm as she offered reassurance. "It will get easier," she promised, giving Kaitlin a moment to collect herself after the overwhelming surge of magical energy they had just unleashed together.

Kaitlin acknowledged Esimae's support with a nod, her composure slowly returning. Together, they turned their attention towards the final five soldiers, who had regrouped nearby, clearly uncertain about their next move in the wake of such a devastating magical assault.

In that tense moment, Keltor hurried over to Kaitlin, concern etched across his face. His eyes flicked from Kaitlin to the lifeless bodies on the ground, the reality of the battle's cost still fresh in his mind. "Are you okay?" he asked urgently, his hand reaching out to comfort her as he tried to make sense of the scene before them. "That was......"

Before he could finish, Kaitlin cut in, her voice tinged with remorse. "I didn't want to kill them," she confessed, the weight of their actions clearly heavy on her heart.

But Keltor quickly offered reassurance, his tone shifting to awe. "No, it's okay, I was going to say that was fricking amazing," he said, a genuine smile breaking through the tension as he tried to lighten the mood and acknowledge the power they had displayed.

"Oh," she sighed relieved. "I know, it was Esimae, when she linked with me the power was incredible."

Kaitlin glanced upwards towards the Deodars, noting that they, along with a handful of elves, had all sought shelter high up in their arboreal homes. She called out to Keltor urgently, "Keltor!"

He responded distractedly with, "What?" his focus still fixed on the soldiers before them, his eyes searching for any sign of their next move.

Undeterred, Kaitlin pressed on, her tone insistent as she pointed towards the trees. "Look," she urged, gesturing upwards. Yet, before Keltor had the chance to follow her gaze, a sudden barrage of arrows rained down from above. The arrows sliced through the air at remarkable speed, whistling past Keltor, Kaitlin, and Esimae. Though none came close enough to threaten their heads, instinct took over, and all three immediately ducked in reflex, seeking cover from the unexpected onslaught.

The hail of arrows shot down like rapid fire towards the remaining soldiers. The ambush caught them completely off guard; their attention had been entirely fixed on Keltor and the witches, leaving them unprepared for the assault from above. The force of the arrows sent their bodies jolting and recoiling as they staggered backwards under the sudden attack. Though some of the soldiers' armour offered a degree of protection, the Deodars proved to be expert markswomen. Arrows protruded gruesomely from their faces—eyes and cheeks alike pierced with deadly precision, making them resemble grotesque pin cushions.

"Shit!" Kaitlin exclaimed, her gaze snapping upwards towards the Deodars in shock and disbelief at the devastating efficiency of their strike. Their arrows were twice the size of a normal arrow, and within a minute, all the soldiers were dead. Keltor looked up at the Deodars, noticing that they were all women, except for Uly. He lifted a hand to them in gratitude. "Thank you," he said, and Uly bowed his head in acceptance.

Logan emerged from the lingering haze, his sword drawn and ready for whatever threat might arise. As he stepped forward, Keltor's gaze shot upwards towards the Deodars perched high above in the trees, a surge of panic coursing through him as he realised the imminent danger. "No!" he shouted, his voice cutting through the air as a fresh volley of arrows was loosed from above, all aimed directly at Logan.

Clad in an Aranstream uniform, Logan had been mistaken for an enemy soldier by the Deodars, prompting their swift and deadly response. In a flash, Keltor reacted, conjuring a burst of magic from his hand that struck the incoming arrows, deflecting them away from Logan's path. Instinctively, Logan ducked, raising his hands protectively over his head as the arrows whistled past, narrowly missing him.

At the sight of Keltor's magic and his urgent command, the Deodars quickly understood their mistake and lowered their bows, halting any further attack. Uly, one of the Deodars, glanced down at Keltor, his face twisted in a grimace of apology. "Sorry!" he called out from his vantage point, clearly unsettled by the near miss.

Keltor waved off the apology, his tone reassuring. "It's okay," he replied. He knew it was an honest mistake—there was no way for the Deodars to know that Logan was an ally, not a foe.

Logan glanced up and slowly rose to his feet. He looked to the Deodar's and seeing they had lowered their bows he hurried approach as he took in the scene before him: the ground was littered with soldiers, enormous arrows pinning their bodies in place.

"Thank you," Logan said, closing the distance to Keltor, his heart still pounding from the close call. Relief flickered across his face as he processed how narrowly he had avoided death at the hands of the Deodars' arrows.

"It's okay," Keltor replied with a reassuring smile and a deep, relieved breath. The thought of having to share tragic news with Logan's wife, Alarna—his dearest friend—was something he was grateful to have avoided.

Logan's gaze shifted from Keltor to the aftermath surrounding them. The shock was clear in his voice as he questioned, "They did this?" The reputation of the Deodars as a peaceful race was well established, and Logan had never known them to resort to violence before.

"Yes," Keltor answered simply, confirming the grim reality.

Logan let out a quiet exclamation, muttering "Hell" under his breath. He moved past the fallen soldiers, taking in the scene, and came to stand beside Keltor, the weight of the moment settling silently between them.

"Did you get him?" Keltor asked, his tone serious. Logan nodded in confirmation.

"Yes, he's dead."

"Good," Keltor replied. At that moment, he felt Kaitlin's hand slip into his, drawing his attention. He turned to see her standing at his side, her other hand seeking reassurance as she gripped his arm.

Concern clear in his voice, Keltor asked, "Are you okay?" Kaitlin responded with a nod, her hand holding on tightly.

"Your highness," Logan said, dropping to one knee in front of Kaitlin, his voice tinged with formality and uncertainty. Kaitlin blinked, awkwardness clear in her posture as she tucked a stray lock of hair behind her ear.

Kaitlin gave a small, uneasy laugh. "You really don't have to call me that—it's just Kaitlin." Her words were gentle yet carried an undercurrent of discomfort at the formality Logan had used.

Logan hesitated, his gaze shifting to Keltor as if searching for guidance or approval. Keltor met his eyes and gave a subtle nod, silently encouraging Logan to follow Kaitlin's lead.

Taking Keltor's cue, Logan looked up at Kaitlin as he rose to his feet, the formality slipping away from his posture. With a respectful tone, he replied, "As you wish... Kaitlin."

Logan turned to Keltor, urgency written plainly in his posture. His tone was insistent as he spoke, the worry in his voice unmistakable. "Keltor, I need to go. I must get to Alarna; they've sent soldiers to get her." The gravity of the situation was evident in every word he uttered.

Keltor's expression shifted in an instant. The smile that had briefly softened his features disappeared, replaced by a look of alarm and concern. He pressed Logan for clarification, his voice tight with worry. "What do you mean, she's not in the village?"

Logan explained, "No, she's back home, at my aunt's farmhouse. Jasen, the man Esimae killed, he said he sent soldiers to get Alarna. I need to go, now." His tone was insistent, underscoring the gravity of the situation. "Keltor," he added with anguish. "She's eight months with child."

Without hesitation, Keltor responded, "I'll come with you." He then turned to Kaitlin, preparing her for their imminent departure.

"Go, I'll be fine," Kaitlin insisted, her determination clear. She wanted Keltor to know she could handle herself in his absence.

"Kaitlin, it won't be safe for the Deodars to stay here. King Iwein is bound to send men when those soldiers don't report in. He will kill them all and burn this village to make an example of them," Keltor said with concern.

Kaitlin glanced upwards, her gaze falling on the Deodars who still lined the walkways above them. Worry etched across her face as she realised the danger they all faced.

"You're right. Esimae," Kaitlin called to her aunt.

Esimae walked over to join them. She turned to Keltor, opening her arms to him. For a moment, Keltor was taken aback; the last time they had met, although she had saved his life, he knew that, because he was an elf, Esimae hadn't always been so keen on him.

"Esimae," he replied, accepting her embrace. The contact was brief but sincere.

"Thank you," Esimae whispered, her voice tinged with genuine gratitude. "For saving me." She released him and stepped back, a gentle smile softening her features.

Keltor felt a warmth spread through his chest at her words, the old tension between them easing ever so slightly. "Now we are even," Keltor said with a grin, and Esimae nodded in agreement, a smile lighting her features. The moment of camaraderie was interrupted by Logan's impatient prompt.

"Keltor," Logan urged, his tone pressing the urgency of their mission.

Turning to him, Keltor nodded. "Okay," he said, glancing at Logan before addressing Esimae again. "Esimae, it's not safe for them to stay here. Can you convince the Deodars to leave the village and take them to the Eccleston Forest? Kaitlin knows the way. They can stay hidden in the witches' fortress until it's safe to return. I need to go with Logan; Alarna is in danger."

Esimae looked up at the Deodars, her concern evident. After a moment's consideration, she nodded. "Yes, they will know it's not safe after what they did."

Relieved, Keltor turned to Kaitlin. He gently took her hand and pressed it to his chest, his eyes searching hers. "Are you sure you'll be okay, if I go?" he asked, his voice low and filled with worry.

Kaitlin nodded firmly, determination set in her features. "I'll be fine," she assured him, her voice steady. Glancing towards her aunt, she added with a reassuring smile, "Besides, I have Esimae." Despite her confident words, concern flickered in her eyes as she turned back to Keltor. "Just be careful," she implored, her tone gentle but insistent, emphasising the worry she felt for his safety as he prepared to leave.

"I will, and we will meet you on the road. We shouldn't be too long. Just keep your wits about you, in case any more soldiers arrive," Keltor said, his voice carrying a note of reassurance, though it was clear he was trying to calm not just Kaitlin but himself as well. He wanted her to know that he would not be far behind, and that he was mindful of the dangers that might still linger nearby.

"We'll be fine," Kaitlin assured him, her voice unwavering and calm, determined to put his worries at ease.

Keltor raised his hand gently to her face, his expression earnest and brimming with emotion. He held her gaze for a moment, letting the depth of his feelings show. "I love you," he murmured softly, his words laden with meaning, then leaned in and pressed his lips to hers in a tender kiss.

"I love you," Kaitlin replied, her voice barely above a whisper, echoing his sentiment as they parted, the connection between them lingering in the space that remained.

With a reluctant, heavy sigh, Keltor forced himself to step back, torn between his desire to stay and the responsibility calling him away. He glanced towards Logan, his resolve hardening. "Let's go," he said, signalling that it was time to leave. Logan, already prepared, wasted no time and together they turned from the village, running off towards their uncertain mission, determination driving them forward.

Chapter Four

Kaitlin and Esimae

Kaitlin watched with a heavy heart as Keltor disappeared into the smoke, her concern for him growing with every moment he was out of sight. Already, she felt a deep ache in her chest at their separation; the thought of anything happening to him was almost unbearable. Her gaze lingered in the direction he had gone, unwilling to let go just yet. However, determined not to succumb to her anxiety, she gave herself a small shake and turned her attention to Esimae.

"Come on, we need to hurry before any more Aranstream soldiers turn up," Kaitlin urged, her tone insistent as she placed a reassuring hand on her aunt's arm.

Esimae, attentive to her niece's distress, responded with gentle concern. "You need to tell me what happened to you both," she said, linking her arm with Kaitlin's as they began walking towards the rope ladder at the base of the tree houses.

"I will, once we're on the road," Kaitlin promised, pausing at the foot of the ladder. Esimae slipped her arm free, and the young Queen grasped the rungs, preparing to climb up to the tree houses above.

As Esimae prepared to climb the ladder, a woman's voice called out from behind her. Pausing, she turned to see an elven woman approaching, her mid-forties marked by a braid of blonde and brown hair and a face etched with lines of worry and exhaustion.

"Shona," Esimae greeted her warmly, stepping back down from the ladder. Shona's face crumpled with emotion, tears welling in her eyes as she apologised, her arms reaching out for an embrace. "I'm so sorry I couldn't do anything to help you," she said desperately.

Esimae accepted Shona's embrace, offering reassurance as she gently patted her friend's back. "Hey, it's okay, I didn't expect you to, not against King Iwein and his men. It was my fault, Shona; I shouldn't have used my magic."

Shona held Esimae close, whispering, "I'm so glad you're okay," before releasing her.

"Thank you. Shona, we need to leave here as soon as we can. When the King finds out what's happened, he will kill everyone. Can you tell the other elves they can only take what they can carry?" Esimae urged, her tone serious.

Shona's expression clouded with concern. "Where are we going to go?" she asked, her frown deepening.

Esimae replied honestly, "I'm not sure to be honest. Kaitlin and Keltor have a plan. All I know is that it's over the bridge towards the Eccleston Forest, so it's going to be a long walk. Just take the bare essentials."

"Okay, I will let them all know," Shona agreed. The women shared another brief embrace before Shona turned to carry out the urgent instructions.

Esimae climbed the ladder after Kaitlin, reaching the top where Kaitlin paused and asked, "Who was that?"

"My friend, Shona," Esimae explained. "She lost her husband in the battle and wandered into the camp about three months ago. She's been helping me administer medicine to the sick and injured." As Kaitlin nodded in understanding, she glanced down to see Shona now speaking with the other elven women, sharing the plan to evacuate the village as instructed.

Esimae made her way over to Uly, but before she could speak, he addressed her first. "I know, we need to leave. I have already told them to collect a few belongings they can carry, but where shall we go?"

107

Kaitlin stepped forward, offering reassurance. "There is a place, beyond the ridge, deep into the Eccleston Forest where they can stay until this is over."

Uly's concern was evident as he replied, "But there are evil witches in there. It is forbidden."

"No, not anymore. Just a few imps, maybe, but I can handle them," Kaitlin responded confidently. "Keltor and I killed the witches a few days— I mean eight months ago," she added with a weary sigh. "King Iwein will never think to look there for the same reason as you just said. He doesn't know they're dead, and I don't think even he will risk releasing those witches into Elvendon."

Uly agreed, though some worry lingered in his tone. "Yes, okay, this sounds good. I'm worried though about Ren travelling. She doesn't have long left now."

Kaitlin, puzzled, asked, "Left for what?"

With a proud smile, Uly replied, "She is with child."

"Oh my god, Uly, that's fantastic!" Kaitlin exclaimed, lifting her hand to her forehead and then offering it to him. Uly mirrored the gesture, and their hands met briefly in a respectful touch—a traditional Deodar gesture of congratulations.

"Thank you. Although in these times, it's less than ideal," Uly added, his pride mingled with the uncertainty that now hung over them all.

Esimae's expression clouded with regret. "Yes, well, I didn't exactly help the situation," she admitted, her voice tinged with guilt.

Uly was quick to reassure her. "Esimae, it was not your fault," he said firmly, his tone gentle but resolute.

She shook her head, unable to accept his words so easily. "Yes, Uly, it was. I used my magic, and I put you both in danger. I'm sorry for that," she apologised, her remorse clear.

But Uly would not allow her to shoulder the blame alone. "No, Esimae, you did what you thought was right, you were trying to save Jaike. Ren and I would never blame you, you are our family," he replied, his words carrying the warmth and solidarity of their bond. Esimae let out a weary sigh and bowed her head to him in a gesture of respect and gratitude, which Uly reciprocated solemnly.

"Come on," Esimae urged, "unfortunately we have the grim task of putting all these bodies onto the pyre. We can't leave them here to rot," Esimae said, and she returned to the ladder.

Kaitlin climbed down after Esimae, with Uly bringing up the rear. As she drew nearer to the bodies, a wave of nausea swept over her. Just weeks before, she had lived a 'normal' life on Earth, blissfully unaware that other worlds even existed. Now, that previous life felt impossibly remote; memories of afternoons at the art gallery and laughter with friends seemed like fragments from another person's story.

Confronted with the grim reality before her, Kaitlin struggled to reconcile who she had been with who she was now. Staring at the bodies—men whose lives she had taken—she realised how much her world had changed. At only nineteen, she bore the crown of the Elves, her new identity both astonishing and overwhelming. Each step she took towards the pyre made the weight of her responsibilities feel heavier, and she could not help but wonder if she would ever truly become accustomed to this life, or even if she wished to.

Esimae approached Kaitlin gently, placing a supportive hand on her back. Sensing the younger woman's turmoil, she asked, "Are you okay?" Kaitlin nodded, but her eyes lingered on the floor, her lips pressed into a thin line as if searching for words she couldn't find. "Yeah, it's just so much to take in. I mean, I killed these men, I took their lives. What if they have families and children?" Kaitlin said.

Esimae's tone was gentle but firm as she tried to comfort Kaitlin. "Honey, it's the path they chose. By becoming soldiers, they understood the risks—they knew they might die for their cause." She paused, her gaze steady on Kaitlin. "It's important to remember, Elvendon didn't start this conflict. Aranstream attacked us first, and they have taken the lives of many of our people. You mustn't feel guilty about what's happened, all right?"

Kaitlin nodded in response, though her expression revealed lingering doubt and uncertainty, suggesting she was not wholly convinced by Esimae's reassurance.

Esimae approached Kaitlin gently, placing a steadying hand on her back. The scent of charred wood and the distant, muffled sobs of villagers hung in the air. Kaitlin stood rigid, her hands trembling ever so slightly, the cold seeping through her skin despite the fire's glow. Her gaze flitted across the fallen soldiers, then dropped to the mud at her boots, her breaths shallow and uneven.

Esimae regarded Kaitlin with sombre honesty, her expression grave. "Kaitlin, before this is over, I'm afraid you will most probably have to kill a lot more," she said, her voice heavy with the weight of experience. The reality of war had settled in around them, and her words reflected the harsh truth that lay ahead.

Kaitlin's face contorted with discomfort as she responded, her voice barely above a whisper. "Oh, Esimae, don't," she said, a shudder rippling through her. "The whole thing makes me feel sick. I just wish there were a way we can resolve this without anyone else dying." The words hung heavily in the air, laden with the weight of her sorrow and revulsion. Kaitlin's gaze shifted away, unable to meet Esimae's eyes, as the enormity of the situation pressed down on her shoulders. The burden of loss, and the horror of the violence she had witnessed—and taken part in— seemed almost too much to bear. Her longing for a peaceful solution was clear, a desperate hope against the grim reality that surrounded them.

Esimae's expression grew even more serious as she fixed her gaze on Kaitlin, her eyes unwavering and filled with solemn understanding. "Kaitlin, so do I, believe me," she said quietly, her words heavy with sorrow and shared pain. "But King Iwein is a tyrant and a psychopath. He will never give the throne of the elves back to you. You need to understand that a battle is inevitable, and many more lives will be lost along the way."

Kaitlin stood by, watching as Uly bent down and lifted the limp body of one of the fallen soldiers. With a laboured effort, he carried it over and cast it onto the growing pyre. The sight sent a tremor through Kaitlin; she could not suppress a violent shudder. The grim reality of their task pressed in upon her, each movement a stark reminder of the horrors they had endured and the burdens now resting heavily on her shoulders.

Esimae's voice was laced with a quiet bitterness as she spoke, her eyes fixed on the smouldering pyre. "They were going to burn me alive," she said, her tone unwavering. "At least these soldiers had a fighting chance, which is more than I can say for myself, your father, and your sister."

Her words hung in the heavy air, the memory of her own ordeal sharp and unyielding. The contrast between the fates of the fallen soldiers and those of her own family was stark—while the soldiers had perished in battle, Esimae, her father, and her sister had faced execution, denied even the dignity of defending themselves. The injustice of it all pressed on Kaitlin, deepening the weight of her responsibilities and the sorrow she felt for all that had been lost.

Kaitlin bit down on her lower lip. She knew she had to toughen up, and as she glanced across at the villagers as they began to assemble, she took in a deep breath. These people were now her responsibility. "Okay, I know you're right, Esimae. I will toughen up, I promise," she said quietly. Her voice wavered as she admitted, "It's just this whole time-delay thing, it's really screwing with my head. It really does feel like just a couple of weeks since I last saw you." A shadow crossed her face as she added, "And I wish mum was here."

Esimae let out a heavy sigh, her empathy clear in the heaviness of her response. "I know you do. I wish she was too," she replied softly. After a moment, her concern deepened. "Do you know what happened to you both?" Esimae asked, her tone gentle but searching.

Kaitlin hesitated before answering, her words tentative. "We think Star put us in some kind of stasis while she repaired the Earth." The explanation hung in the air, confusion and uncertainty reflected in Esimae's furrowed brow as she tried to comprehend the implications.

Kaitlin spoke softly, her gaze drifting upwards as she recalled her encounter. "The Star of Elmrock turned out to be a powerful entity from the Source. She was female, and I connected with her so strongly. To be honest, I really miss her, but I think I can still feel some connection to her, or to the Source."

Esimae looked at Kaitlin, curiosity written across her face. "What do you mean by the Source?" she asked.

Kaitlin took a steadying breath, her response thoughtful. "It's where we get our powers from, our magic. There is a great world of spirits, or gods, or whatever you want to call them. Look, I'm not religious, I never have been, but this place exists, these people, entities or whatever you want to call them are real. She has shown me, and she has guided and helped me with my magic.

Esimae, Keltor and I woke up thinking it had only just happened, and to be honest we really hadn't expected to survive. I mean there were a few things that were odd, like the season seemed to have changed, but we thought it was just part of Earth's healing process."

Esimae regarded Kaitlin with a look of lingering disbelief before finally voicing her thoughts. "What happened to Keltor, that magic he used to get me off the pyre; I'm sorry I didn't take you seriously back at the cottage, about him using magic, but it just seemed so improbable."

Kaitlin offered a reassuring smile, understanding the difficulty in accepting such a truth. "It's okay, it's all hard to believe. Keltor is a wizard, Esimae. He has full-blown wizard's power and, trust me, I've seen him in action—he's incredible," she said, her pride in him unmistakable.

Esimae's brow creased in confusion. "A wizard? But how? It doesn't make sense for an Elf to be a wizard."

"He's not pure elf," Kaitlin explained gently. "His dad is human—he was the last wizard of Elvendon, but he went missing about ten years ago. In fact, Keltor thinks he's connected to his father through his magic book."

Esimae's eyes widened in astonishment. "What, my god, what on earth is going on?"

Kaitlin nodded, acknowledging the strangeness of it all. "I know, it's all crazy, but trust me, Esimae, Keltor is powerful. And together, he and I—we will take back Elvendon."

Esimae's expression turned serious as she posed her next question. "And what happened with Aragon?" she asked, her tone laced with concern. "I mean, Jaike said you killed him, and he said you told him King Iwein had planned to attack Elvendon before you even left on the quest."

Kaitlin let out a weary sigh, nodding in acknowledgment of the gravity of the events. "We did," she admitted, her voice steady but sombre, "but only because he was going to kill us. Aragon confessed to me that his father had planned the attack on Elvendon months before we ever set out for the Star. It was all premeditated."

Kaitlin's expression grew sombre as she continued, her voice steady but edged with emotion. "Aragon wanted to harness the power of Star for himself. When he realised he couldn't, he turned on me—he attacked, and then he tried to kill both of us. Together, Keltor and I had no choice but to fight back. In the end, we killed Aragon."

She paused, her eyes meeting Esimae's. "Believe me, Esimae, we pleaded with him to stop. We begged him to stand down, but he simply refused, and in his desperation, he tried to destroy the Star with his magic. We could not allow that to happen. I had to protect Earth from the shadowmen."

Esimae regarded Kaitlin with a mixture of concern and admiration. "I can see you have developed your magic immensely since I last saw you," she observed.

Kaitlin responded with a gentle smile, her confidence clear. "Yes, I have, and Esimae," she added softly, "Keltor and I are together now—properly together. When the time comes, he will be my King."

Esimae looked into the eyes of her niece, she gave a smile and a nod. "I had thought as much when I saw you together. Tell me everything as we walk, and we can go over some spells and enchantments that will help you as well."

Kaitlin turned to her aunt; her voice filled with gratitude. "Thank you, and I'm so glad you're still here with me," she said, before wrapping her arms around Esimae in a warm embrace.

Esimae chuckled softly, returning the hug. "Me too. Did you see my cottage at all?" she enquired, a hint of curiosity in her tone.

Kaitlin replied apologetically, "Yeah, sorry it's been destroyed, so it was a good job you came through the portal back to Elvendon. Both Keltor and I don't think you would have survived if you had been inside."

Esimae nodded, her expression thoughtful. "I still didn't want to, not really. Anyway, I have no intention of going back to Earth now, I was just curious, that's all." Pausing beneath a ladder, she added, "Just one minute—I need to pop into my hut and grab a few bits."

Kaitlin watched Esimae climb the ladder and hurry into a hut high up among the trees. As she waited, Kaitlin glanced around at the deodars gathering, looking expectantly towards her, ready for her guidance. The prospect of leading others filled her with uncertainty; she had spent much of her life quietly in the background, and the idea of commanding people made her uneasy.

Her attention was drawn upwards by the sound of movement, and she saw her aunt descending the ladder. Esimae jumped down from the last rung, carrying a large sack slung over her back and holding a basket with a lid firmly clasped in her hands.

Kaitlin frowned in confusion. What's in the basket?" Kaitlin asked.

"Meow," came the reply, muffled but persistent.

"Shush, stop your complaining or you can walk," Esimae said sternly, pushing down the basket lid to quieten the noise.

Realising what was inside, Kaitlin's hand reached towards the lid with excitement. "Oh my god, is that Magic?" she exclaimed, only to have Esimae gently bat her hand away.

"Yes," Esimae replied, "and he is as grumpy as hell, so I wouldn't put your hand in there just yet."

Kaitlin couldn't help but coo at the sight of Magic's paw poking out from beneath the lid. "Oh, little cutie," she said affectionately.

Esimae shook her head, tapping the basket lid with her finger. "No, I told you what's going on, just behave, Magic," she admonished.

Kaitlin looked at Esimae with an amused grin. "Does he understand you?" she asked, her curiosity piqued by the exchange between her aunt and the cat.

Esimae responded without hesitation, her tone matter-of-fact. "Of course, he is a witch's cat, we talk all the time." She gave the basket another firm pat, ensuring Magic stayed put. Without missing a beat, Esimae's expression turned serious as she addressed the gathered deodars. "Now come on, we need to help these people get the hell out of here before King Iwein or the Prince turn up and slaughter us all."

Chapter Five
Keltor and Logan

"Can't you do your magic thing?" Logan asked urgently, glancing at Keltor as they crouched low behind the dense shrubbery. They had reached the farmhouse quickly, having sprinted most of the way, and now paused to assess the situation unfolding before them.

Keltor peered intently at the farmhouse, his mind racing. "Okay, let me think," he replied, his voice low and tense. Although he still wasn't entirely sure how his magic worked—having largely relied on intuition so far—he had noticed it was gradually becoming easier to use with practice.

Scanning the area, Keltor's eyes landed on a cluster of old barrels piled up to the left of the building. He quickly counted eleven soldiers stationed around the farmhouse, their presence making the situation more perilous.

Among the soldiers, one had a firm grip on a woman's arm. She stood out in a blue dress, her long dark hair pulled back, though a few loose strands framed her face delicately.

"Is that your aunt?" Keltor whispered, shooting a quick glance at Logan.

Logan nodded. "Yes, I know you were probably expecting an older lady, but my grandmother had her later in life. She's thirty-seven, I think."

Keltor looked back at the woman and commented quietly, "She looks more like your sister."

"What are they doing?" Logan growled in frustration as he watched the soldier dragging his aunt back inside the farmhouse, two more soldiers following close behind. His hands clenched at his sides, and his eyes burned with worry and anger.

"I don't like to think," Keltor replied with a shake of his head. Another soldier was holding Alarna, there was one beside him, and three more were just watching and waiting.

It was the soldier holding Alarna at knifepoint that troubled Keltor most. If they were to have any chance of rescuing her safely, that threat had to be eliminated first. His eyes narrowed as he calculated the risk, understanding that any hesitation could cost them dearly.

Logan, his nerves taut, urged urgency. "We need to move now," he insisted, shifting back on his knees and preparing himself to spring into action. His determination was clear—he would not wait a moment longer while his family was in danger.

Keltor, however, remained focused on the bigger picture. "Yes, but we must take them all down. No one can survive to get word back to the King, okay?" he replied quietly. If even one soldier escaped, the consequences could be dire for everyone involved.

Logan nodded firmly, signalling that he was prepared for what was to come. He unsheathed his sword, its blade glinting faintly in the dim light, to demonstrate his readiness for action. "I have no issues with that," he stated, his voice steady despite the turmoil he felt. He cast a glance at Keltor before turning his gaze back to his wife, his expression clouding with worry and despair as he watched her situation unfold.

"Good," Keltor replied, outlining the next stage of their plan. "I'm going to use my magic to knock over those barrels." Both men shifted, rising onto their knees to get a better view of their targets. "That should hopefully distract them long enough for me to hit the one holding Alarna with my knife."

Logan, still watching the scene with tense anticipation, turned to Keltor. "You can hit him from this distance?" he asked, doubt flickering in his eyes.

"Yes, no problem," Keltor answered with quiet confidence.

"Okay," he replied, and he raised an eyebrow briefly. Although he was concerned about him missing and hitting his wife, he knew he had to trust him.

Keltor leaned in, outlining the next crucial step of their rescue. "Then I need you to charge in and make as much noise as possible, so they all turn to look at you." His words were low but intense, underscoring the risk and need for precise timing.

Logan nodded, determination etched across his face. "I'll do my best to draw their attention—just don't miss," he replied, his voice carrying both resolve and concern. The plan depended on Keltor's accuracy and Logan's ability to create a strong enough diversion.

With the strategy clear, Keltor clarified their roles. "I will take the other soldier near Alarna and then the other three inside, can you manage the rest outside?" The division of responsibilities was stark; each man knew what was at stake and what was required.

"Yes, let's do it," Logan urged, a nervous gesture betraying his anxiety as he drew his lip through his bottom teeth. His gaze flicked to Alarna, who was screaming and struggling desperately against her captor, calling out for her aunt in anguish.

Both men rose to a half crouch, readying themselves for action. Keltor moved to his left while Logan shifted to the right, edging quietly through the trees towards the house. Their approach was tense, every movement measured.

Stopping in their tracks, both men pressed themselves against the trunk of a sturdy tree, keeping out of sight. Keltor silently withdrew his knife, gripping it tightly in his right hand, ready for action. With his left hand, he raised it in preparation, his eyes meeting Logan's. Logan responded with a firm nod, signalling his readiness for the next phase of their plan.

Keltor's eyes flickered with a sharp, white light as he unleashed a surge of magic towards the pile of barrels stacked nearby. The magical force struck with precision, sending the barrels crashing to the ground with a thunderous noise. The sudden commotion startled the guards, causing them to turn their attention towards the source of the disturbance.

The guard who held Alarna momentarily eased the knife from her throat, his attention suddenly drawn to the thunderous commotion. In that fleeting instant, Keltor recognised his opportunity. With practised precision, he stepped out from his cover and hurled his knife with remarkable force; the blade sliced through the air, impossibly fast, closing the distance between them in a heartbeat.

"Don't move, Alarna," Keltor pleaded under his breath. He kept his eyes fixed on the spinning knife, urgency propelling him forward as he sprinted towards her.

Logan sprang from his hiding place among the trees, sprinting at full speed towards the cluster of soldiers from the opposite direction. In an effort to draw their attention, he bellowed, "Hey, you bastards!" while brandishing his sword defiantly in the air. His outburst had the intended effect: the three remaining soldiers, alerted by the sudden noise, immediately turned towards him, drew their swords, and charged in his direction.

Alarna screamed as the soldier suddenly released her, her voice echoing across the farmstead in a desperate, anguished cry. Freed from her captor's grip, she stumbled backwards in shock, her eyes wide as she struggled to comprehend where the knife, that was now embedded in the soldier's throat, came from.

Before Alarna could even register what had happened, Keltor was in front of her. He grabbed the handle of his knife, his eyes raging, as he sliced it to the right, almost decapitating the soldier. The soldier's eyes bulged from his face, his hands grabbing around his throat, blood spurting through his fingers as he crashed to the floor. Keltor watched him for a moment until the man stopped breathing. He then spun towards Alarna; his concern etched across his face. "Alarna, are you okay?" he asked, his voice low but urgent.

For a moment, Alarna's eyes remained wide, her mind struggling to catch up with events. Recognition dawned slowly as she stared at Keltor, tears welling up in her eyes. "Keltor?" she sobbed, unable to contain her disbelief and relief.

119

Keltor managed a swift, reassuring smile. "Hi!" he greeted, taking a steadying breath.

Confusion and shock battled in Alarna's expression as she hesitated, her voice trembling. "Keltor? Is it really you?" The reality of his presence, alive and here, was almost too much to believe.

"Yes," he replied, his hand lifting gently to her arm, offering a comforting touch that confirmed his presence. The moment was deeply reassuring for Alarna, a tangible sign that Keltor was truly there. Yet, amidst the urgency of their situation, there was no time to linger. His expression hardened, and his tone became urgent. "But you need to run, Alarna, now!" he commanded, not allowing her a chance to absorb what had happened.

At that moment, Alarna caught sight of an Aranstream soldier bearing down on them. Panic flooded her features, and she nodded quickly. Without another word, she turned, gathered up her dress, and dashed towards the safety of the trees.

Quickly withdrawing his sword, Keltor thrust it at the Aranstream soldier. Their blades met with a resounding clang, the sound of metal striking metal echoing across the farmstead, a stark testament to the ferocity of the battle unfolding.

Logan's heart surged with relief as he caught sight of his wife fleeing towards the safety of the trees. Fuelled by both passion and hatred, Logan wielded his sword with wild abandon, facing off against three Aranstream soldiers simultaneously.

Keltor responded with swift and deadly precision, executing a powerful quarter turn and launching himself into a controlled flip. His sword arced sideways, finding its mark in the side of the approaching Aranstream soldier. The impact forced a sharp cry from the man, who immediately dropped to his knees, overwhelmed by the sudden and brutal attack.

Without hesitation, Keltor spun on his heel to face his wounded foe. Raising his sword high, he brought it down with unyielding force, the heavy blade severing the man's head in a single, decisive blow.

Keltor cast a quick glance towards the house, noting with mounting concern that no soldiers had yet emerged. He was acutely aware that Logan's aunt was still inside, and that she was likely in grave danger. Even as he finished off his immediate adversary, Keltor's attention was drawn to Logan, who was struggling nearby, locked in combat with another Aranstream soldier.

Keltor quickly seized his knife, lifting it with practised precision. Taking careful aim, he hurled the blade towards the fray. While Logan saw the flash of steel cutting through the air, the Aranstream soldier engaged with him remained unaware of the imminent threat. The knife struck its target squarely between the man's shoulder blades, the force of the blow driving him to his knees before he collapsed to the ground.

Logan glanced towards Keltor, giving him a brief nod of thanks. Keltor returned the gesture and swiftly made his way to the front door of the farmhouse. Pressing his back against the wall, he paused for a moment to steady his breath. With careful deliberation, he pushed the door open a little wider and peered inside, scanning for any sign of danger. The way appeared clear. Without delay, Keltor stepped through the doorway, entering the main living area. The room was deserted; no one was present.

Suddenly, a woman's scream reverberated throughout the house, sharp and desperate. Keltor's expression twisted with anger, and he wasted no time. He hurried toward the rear of the house, drawn by the distressing sound. As he moved, he caught sight of movement in a distant room. Through the doorway, he saw two soldiers laughing and jeering, while another held Logan's aunt pinned down on a bed.

Keltor's anger exploded through every vein in his body, propelling him into action. With a surge of fury, he kicked the door fully open, the force so tremendous that it nearly tore the hinges from the frame.

Keltor snapped his left hand towards the man pinned on the bed. With a swift gesture, magic surged from his palm. The soldier shot upwards, limbs flailing in stunned confusion, then crashed into the far wall. The impact left a deep indentation in the plaster, and he crumpled to the floor, motionless.

As panic seized the remaining soldiers, they hastily drew their swords, spinning around to confront Keltor. One of them shouted, voice trembling with a mixture of fear and bravado, "Who the hell are you?"

Keltor glared at the soldiers, his fury evident in every line of his face. Without hesitation, he bellowed, "The man who's going to kill you!" His voice rang out, sharp and commanding, echoing through the tense air of the room. The declaration left no doubt as to his deadly intent, and for a moment, the soldiers faltered, uncertainty flickering in their eyes as they registered the true danger they now faced.

"Like hell," one screamed back at him. The soldier charged towards Keltor.

Keltor reacted instantly, his sword flashing in a swift, controlled arc. In a single, fluid movement, he knocked the weapon from the soldier's grasp, leaving his opponent momentarily stunned and defenceless. The soldier staggered backwards, eyes wide with shock, unable to recover before Keltor took a hurried step towards the soldier and drove his sword into his stomach. Keltor whipped his sword back out and the man dropped, his body bouncing off the end of the bed as it fell to the floor. Keltor's eyes blazed with determination as he turned to face the other "Your next," Keltor said, gesturing to the remaining soldier to step forward.

The soldiers, his voice raised in a desperate cry, hurled himself over his fallen comrade and rushed at Keltor. Reacting swiftly, Keltor sidestepped the assault, evading the charge with calculated precision. The soldier skidded to a halt and spun back to face him, determined not to let Keltor slip away.

Keltor braced himself, his senses heightened, when he caught the soldier's eyes flickering momentarily to the left. Following the man's gaze, Keltor spotted the soldier he had previously thrown from the bed. That man was now struggling, slowly and unsteadily, to get back on his feet.

122

Keltor's heart pounded as he readied himself, sweat beading on his brow. He felt a surge of adrenaline as he unleashed his magic, determination hardening his features. With a blast of magic, he hit the soldier in the chest sending him crashing back down to the floor, this time dead.

In that same moment, the final soldier, desperate to escape, made a dash towards the open bedroom doorway. Sensing the attempt, Keltor reacted swiftly. Sword drawn, he scrambled across the bed in pursuit, determination etched across his face as he closed the distance between them. As Keltor closed in on his target, he suddenly noticed Logan at the front door, forcing him to stop abruptly. Anger covered Logan face, and he glared at the man impaled on the end of his sword. The man's eyes bulged from their sockets. The soldier, drew in a final, desperate breath. His grip slackened and his sword slipped from his hand, clattering loudly against the stone floor. With the last of his strength gone, he slumped forward, his weight collapsing onto Logan's outstretched blade.

Logan's voice faltered, his concern unmistakable as he peered anxiously past Keltor. The lines of worry deepened across his brow, his gaze filled with hope and apprehension. "Is my aunt okay?" he asked, his eyes scanning Keltor's face, searching for any sign of reassurance that she was unharmed.

Keltor met Logan's anxious gaze, responding in a steady voice. "She's in the bedroom," he said, casting a quick glance over his shoulder towards where he had last seen Logan's aunt. Turning back, he continued, "They were attacking her, but I think she's okay. I got there in time," he assured, his words carrying a quiet confidence meant to offer Logan the reassurance he so desperately sought.

Logan kicked the dead soldier off his sword, the body slamming to the floor with a heavy thud. Without hesitation, he wiped the blood from his blade, using the soldier's own jacket to clean it. His movements were brisk and efficient, betraying both urgency and the tension still lingering in the aftermath of the fight. After sheathing his sword at his belt, Logan walked toward Keltor, pausing to touch his arm and meet his gaze. 'Thank you,' he said softly, his voice heavy with relief. Logan's voice was quick and reassuring as he spoke. "Alarna's okay, she's outside. I told her to wait in the trees until it was safe." The tension in the room eased slightly at his words, a subtle relief passing over both Logan and Keltor.

Keltor nodded in understanding. "I'll go and get her," he replied, determination evident in his tone. Logan acknowledged him with a brief nod before turning away and continuing into the bedroom to check on his aunt.

"Aunt Seline," Logan called with urgency, as he entered the bedroom. He stopped abruptly at the devastation in the room. There was blood, and bodies scattered everywhere. His aunt was lying on the bed. "Logan?" she wept as she recognised his voice and she slowly uncurled from her foetal position. Her long dark hair was stuck to her face; with trembling hands she swept it from her sodden eyes to look at him.

Logan approached his aunt with gentle concern, his voice barely above a whisper. "Hey," he said softly, settling himself beside her on the edge of the bed. Reaching out, he placed a comforting hand on her arm, his touch filled with tenderness.

He looked into her tear-stained face, his expression earnest as he asked, "Are you okay?" The question lingered in the quiet aftermath of the chaos, his eyes searching hers for any sign of distress.

She nodded, tears still streaming down her cheeks, and replied in a shaky voice, "Yes." The relief in her words was evident, though her emotions remained raw. Still clutching his arm, she managed to ask, her voice thick with worry, "Is Alarna okay?" Her red-rimmed eyes searched Logan's face, desperate for reassurance.

A wave of relief washed over Logan as he answered, his voice steady and reassuring. "She's fine," he said, the tension easing from his posture. He pulled his aunt into a comforting embrace, holding her tightly as relief and gratitude overcame them both.

124

Keltor stepped out of the house, a sense of relief washing over him as he took in a deep breath of the fresh air. His gaze immediately fell upon Alarna, who was cautiously hiding behind the treeline. The moment their eyes met, Alarna cried out his name in disbelief and hurried towards him.

Without hesitation, Keltor moved to meet her, embracing her as best he could despite the considerable size of her pregnant belly. Tears streamed down Alarna's face as she clung to him, her emotions overwhelming. "Oh, my goodness, I can't believe you're alive!" she sobbed, her voice thick with relief and astonishment. "Where the hell did you come from?"

Keltor offered a gentle, reassuring smile, his own relief evident. "It's a long story," he replied, his tone carrying both exhaustion and gratitude. "We ran into Logan at the Deodar settlement."

Still holding onto him, Alarna looked up with concern and asked, "And the Princess?"

"Kaitlin's okay," Keltor assured her, his voice steady. "She is taking the Deodars somewhere safe."

A wave of relief swept over Alarna, and she let out a hefty sigh. "Oh, thank goodness," she said, the tension in her shoulders easing. Suddenly, a look of panic flashed across her face as she asked, "Logan's aunt?" She turned anxiously towards the house.

"She's okay, Logan's with her," Keltor replied gently, hoping to reassure her further.

Alarna closed her eyes for a moment, overcome with emotion. "By the spirits," she breathed, "I'm so glad to see you both." She let her head rest back against his chest, drawing comfort from his presence. "When I heard you were both dead, my heart just broke. It's been so awful these past months, Keltor."

Keltor held her close, understanding the pain in her words. "I know, and I'm sorry," he said softly. "Believe me, Kaitlin and I had no idea what was going on. We've basically been held in a magical stasis for the last eight months."

Alarna pulled away slightly, her brows knitted in confusion. "Stasis? What do you mean?"

Keltor met her gaze, his expression earnest as he explained. "The entity we released to save the Earth put Kaitlin and me into a deep sleep for eight months. We had no idea so much time had passed until we came back to Elvendon."

Alarna shook her head in disbelief, struggling to comprehend everything she had just heard. "That's just crazy," she managed, her mind reeling from the revelation. Suddenly, a memory struck her, and her expression shifted to one of alarm. "Keltor, Esimae!" she exclaimed, turning quickly to peer down the road leading away from her farm. "They were going to burn her today for being a witch."

Keltor reached out, placing a comforting hand on her arm. "It's okay, don't worry, we got there in time. Esimae's fine, she's with Kaitlin," he assured her, his tone gentle and reassuring.

Relief flooded Alarna's features, and she let out a grateful sigh. "Oh, thank the spirits," she breathed, visibly relaxing as the tension left her shoulders.

Keltor's eyes softened as he looked at Alarna, his gaze settling on her growing belly. "I'm so glad to see you, Alarna, and your bump!" he said warmly, reaching out to place his hand gently on her stomach.

A broad grin spread across Alarna's face as she looked up at him, her hand moving to rest atop his. "It's not long now," she replied, her smile bright with anticipation.

Keltor's expression was filled with genuine affection as he met her eyes. "You will make a great mother," he told her sincerely, and, glancing towards the house, he added, "and Logan will be an amazing father. He loves you very much."

Alarna looked at Keltor with a smile, releasing his hand from hers. "I know," she said softly. After a brief pause, she asked, "And what of you and the Princess?"

Keltor's heart swelled at her question, and he gently removed his hand from her stomach. There was a noticeable brightness in his eyes.

Alarna caught the change instantly. "I can already tell, just by the way your eyes have suddenly glowed. You are together now?"

He nodded, happiness evident in his voice. "Yes, we are, Alarna, and I can't tell you how happy that makes me. She is my life." To emphasise his words, Keltor placed his hands over his heart.

A wide smile spread across Alarna's face. "Keltor, I'm so happy for you. I guess we both got our wishes."

Keltor returned her smile. "I guess we did, and we need to fight to keep hold of them," he added with quiet determination.

Just then, he noticed movement and turned to see Logan emerging from the cottage, his aunt walking alongside him.

Alarna excused herself as she spotted her husband and aunt. She let go of Keltor's arm and hurried over to them.

Approaching her aunt, Alarna asked with concern, "Are you okay?"

Her aunt smiled warmly. "Yes, darling, thanks to Keltor," she replied, offering Keltor a grateful smile as he walked towards them.

Logan let out a deep sigh as he drew Alarna into a warm embrace. "I have missed you so much," he confessed, holding her close. His hand gently moved to rest on her bump, his fingers tracing the gentle curve. "You've grown so much since I last saw you. Is everything okay?" he asked, his tone full of concern.

Alarna responded with reassurance, nestling her head against his shoulder as she clung tightly to him. "Yes, the baby is fine," she replied softly, her arms wrapped securely around him.

Keltor, noticing the intimacy of their reunion and aware of the grim task that lay ahead, made a practical suggestion. "Logan, why don't you take the ladies away for a little while and I will clear up," he offered, raising an eyebrow at Logan as he subtly referenced the presence of the dead bodies that needed to be dealt with.

Understanding at once, Logan nodded in gratitude. "Oh right, yes, thank you Keltor," he said appreciatively. Alarna lifted her head from Logan's chest, and he took her hand in his, ready to lead her away.

"We'll go over to the stables and check on the animals," Logan suggested, guiding Alarna gently. As she passed Keltor, Alarna reached out with her free hand and rubbed his arm affectionately, a silent gesture of thanks and reassurance before following Logan towards the stables.

Keltor's gaze lingered on Alarna as she walked away, her hand entwined with Logan's, with his aunt accompanying them on the left. A profound sense of relief washed over him, knowing they had arrived in time to prevent any harm befalling Alarna. The thought of her being attacked—or worse, killed—by the Aranstream soldiers was unbearable, and he doubted he could ever have forgiven himself if such a tragedy had occurred.

Keltor waited patiently until Alarna, Logan, and his aunt had disappeared from sight. Once sure he was alone, he turned his attention to the unpleasant duty that awaited him. With a deep breath, he steeled himself and set about removing the bodies of the Aranstream soldiers. Gripping each lifeless form firmly beneath the armpits, he dragged them one by one to the edge of the tree line. There, he let them drop, their weight heavy and unyielding, before returning to retrieve the next. The repetitive work was both physically demanding and emotionally draining, but Keltor pressed on, determined to spare the others from witnessing the grisly aftermath.

He grimaced, muttering under his breath, "Where am I supposed to hide all of you?" Eyes darting from the lifeless bodies to the silent trees standing sentinel around him, a surge of unease twisted in his chest. Unwilling to risk the telltale smoke of a fire—knowing it could summon unwanted scouts to the farm—he pressed deeper into the woods, uncertainty gnawing at him with each step. After about ten tense minutes, relief flickered as he stumbled upon a natural hollow in the earth, thick with ferns and bracken. Its bowl-like shape offered the perfect concealment, promising the secrecy he so desperately needed. The weight of what he was about to do settled on his shoulders, but at least here, the bodies could be hidden from prying eyes.

"Perfect," he said, and he made his way back to Alarna's farmhouse. By the time he finished dragging each one through the trees and dumping their bodies in the ravine he was quite exhausted. It was warm; the sky was almost cloudless and there was hardly any breeze to cool and refresh him.

Keltor made his way back inside the house, his movements weary but purposeful. Crossing the threshold, he walked directly to Logan's aunt's bedroom and paused in the doorway, surveying the scene before him. The events of the day weighed heavily on him, yet he knew the task was not yet complete and that the room needed his attention before the others could return.

Suppressing a surge of frustration, Keltor set about clearing the grisly evidence, determined to erase any sign of the violence that had taken place. He methodically opened the windows to let in the fresh air, fetched rags and a mop, and began scrubbing away at the floor, focusing on the stubborn smears that marred the wooden boards. Each pass of the mop brought with it the faint, metallic tang of blood, but Keltor worked doggedly, his hands steady even as his mind churned with thoughts of what could have happened had they arrived too late. As he worked, the rhythmic scrape and swish of his efforts filled the otherwise silent house, an oddly reassuring reminder that, for now at least, the danger had passed.

A sudden noise from behind made Keltor spin around, alert and ready for anything. Logan stood in the doorway, lifting his hands in a friendly greeting to dispel any tension. "Hey," he said, his tone light, "just checking to see how it's going."

Relief crossed Keltor's face as he realised it was only Logan. "Oh, hi. Yeah, all done," he confirmed, glancing back at the now-clean room. "They can come back in if they want."

Logan approached, gratitude evident in his expression. "Thank you for doing that," he said sincerely.

Setting the mop down, Keltor replied, "No problem. Alarna means a lot to me too." He paused, then added with emphasis, "Like a sister, I mean." Keltor wanted to make it clear to Logan that his feelings for Alarna were purely familial, in case Logan harboured any doubts regarding his intentions towards Logan's wife.

"Yes, I know, she has told me all about you, and your relationship. I'm fine with it, honestly."

"Good," Keltor said, as he squeezed the mop in the bucket. "Well, that should do." He picked up the bucket.

"Here, I'll do that," Logan offered, holding his hand out for the bucket.

"Thanks," Keltor said, giving him the bucket to empty.

"Keltor, Alarna and I have been chatting. She said you are betrothed to the Princess, is that right?"

Keltor leant on the mop, and he nodded with a smile.

"Yeah, we are, although technically she is now the Queen of Elvendon," he said with a grin.

Logan's eyes widened in realisation.

"Yes, of course she is, I'd didn't think... Look Keltor, I want you to know, that I may have been born to Aranstream, but I swear on an oath to fight alongside you and the Queen for Elvendon. I no longer serve King Iwein of Aranstream."

"Thank you, Logan," he said, and he patted the man's arm. "Both Kaitlin and I are glad to have you on board."

"Keltor, I don't think we should leave Alarna and my aunt here. Prince Keion will send more men when they don't report back from the Deodar settlement. They will come here; I know they will."

"Yes, you're right, I'd been thinking about that as well. It's probably best if we take them with us and meet up with Kaitlin, they can stay with the Deodars in the witches' place until it's safe to come home."

"Great, thanks. I will go and tell them." Logan turned about, taking the bucket, and headed outside to inform the others of the plan.

As Logan shared the news, his aunt voiced her concerns. "What about my animals?" she asked, worried about their well-being during their absence.

Logan responded reassuringly, "We shall have to let them free for now." However, his aunt was not convinced. "But who will feed them?" she complained.

Trying to comfort her, Logan explained, "Aunt, pigs will feed themselves."

She persisted, "And my horse and goat!"

Logan considered the situation. "Well, I suppose we could take the goat with us."

"Fine, but what about Ed?" his aunt pressed.

Logan looked towards the house, determined to find a solution. "I'll go and check," he told her, hurrying back inside.

Inside, Logan consulted with Keltor about the possibility of bringing the horse. Keltor shook his head, explaining, "Sorry we can't take a horse. We must cross the ravine via a really narrow rope bridge, and to take a horse will add another three days to the journey to get around it."

Logan acknowledged the difficulty. "She's not going to like that," he replied.

Keltor agreed, "No, but she can't stay here either. The horse will be fine, just tell her to set him free. There is plenty of pasture around, and if she leaves the stable open and food lying about, he should be fine."

Logan turned his attention to the matter of the soldiers' horses. "What about the soldiers' horses?" he asked, seeking a practical solution for their transportation dilemma.

Keltor paused to consider their options carefully. "Do you think Alarna can ride?" he asked. "If she can, we'll take four and cut the rest loose. We can ride them as far as the ravine and then let them go. It will save us time; we may even catch up with Kaitlin by then. They'll only be a few hours ahead of us."

Logan was optimistic about the proposal. "Okay, she should be fine, if we take it steady, or we could use the cart and just leave it at the ravine."

Keltor agreed with this approach. "See what she wants to do," he replied, leaving the decision open based on Alarna's preference and comfort.

Logan weighed up the practicalities of their journey, considering the best way to transport their belongings. "Thinking about it, a cart would actually be the better option," he remarked, aware of his Aunt Seline's determination to bring the goat along. He added with a wry smile, "Aunt Seline wants to take the goat. Plus, you know how women are with their things."

Keltor grimaced at the thought, clearly not thrilled by the prospect of additional burdens. Despite his reluctance, Logan stood firm. "Look, she's leaving everything else behind. I can't stop her from bringing the bloody goat."

After a brief pause, Keltor conceded. "Fine, but whatever they decide to bring, we'll have to carry it over the ravine and then on our backs for the remainder of the journey. It's a good two days' walk after that, so make sure it's only the essentials."

Logan nodded in agreement. "I will," he promised, before heading back to Alarna and his aunt to start gathering and preparing what they needed for the trip.

Logan approached his aunt gently, breaking the difficult news. "Sorry, we can't take Ed," he explained. "We must cross a narrow ravine, and he wouldn't be able to go over it. Keltor said to leave the stable open, put out lots of food and hay, and he will be fine. We shouldn't be more than a month."

His aunt was taken aback by the duration. "A month, oh my goodness!" she exclaimed, anxiety evident in her voice.

Alarna, ever compassionate, placed a reassuring hand on the older woman's arm. "The animals will be fine," she comforted, her tone gentle. "Come on, we should go and get a few belongings and pack some food for the journey."

Logan did his best to ease the worry, offering practical guidance. "Around three days should be enough," he informed her, and Alarna nodded in agreement, ready to help prepare for the trip.

Thoughtful of her situation, Alarna spoke up. "I need to take a few things for the baby. At this rate, I will be giving birth there."

Logan, feeling the weight of their circumstances, apologised sincerely. "I'm sorry," he said, pulling her close.

Alarna met his apology with warmth and optimism. "It's okay, a baby must be born somewhere. As long as I have a few essentials, it will be fine."

He kissed her, their shared resolve strengthening them for the journey ahead. The connection between them was palpable, a silent assurance that whatever lay ahead, they would face it together.

"I love you," he said, his voice earnest and steady.

"I love you too," she replied, before heading off with her aunt back to the house, determination evident in her stride.

Logan made his way to the barn, intent on readying the cart for their journey. He approached two of the soldiers' horses, speaking softly to reassure them. "Easy," he said, gently patting their necks to calm any nerves.

He reached for a bag of cob nuts, attaching them around the horses' ears so that they could munch contentedly. Once they were settled, he proceeded to tack them to the cart, ensuring everything was secure for the trip ahead.

Next, Logan untied three of the other horses. With a gentle slap on their backsides, he encouraged them, "Go on, off you go." The horses responded, neighing softly before trotting off, their freedom granted.

Two horses remained, growing a little skittish in the commotion. "Whoa, not you two," Logan said, taking hold of their reins and guiding them towards the barn. He tied them securely to a stall and offered each a bag of nuts, helping them settle down as the preparations continued.

As Logan entered the house, he found Keltor assisting Alarna with packing some food into a holdall, making sure they would have enough supplies for the journey. Logan, aware of the risks associated with being recognised, announced, "I'm just going to change out of this uniform. I don't want anyone thinking I'm still an Aranstream soldier," and made his way past them towards the stairs.

Alarna, needing to complete her preparations, turned to Keltor. "Are you okay to finish this?" she asked. Keltor paused, glancing at Logan as he disappeared up the stairs, then assured her with a warm smile, "Of course, go." Alarna nodded in appreciation and quickly moved towards the bedroom.

Once inside, she called out, "Logan," before hurrying into their room. The relief and disbelief at seeing him were clear. "I can't believe you're here," she said, emotion in her voice. Logan immediately pulled her into his arms, his concern for her and the baby evident. "My love, I've been so worried about you, never a moment has gone by without me thinking of you and the little one," he confessed, his hand resting protectively on her bump. Almost as if on cue, the baby kicked, making Logan laugh.

"Did you feel him?" Alarna asked, her excitement obvious. Logan nodded, replying, "I did," with a broad grin. He then teased, "You said, him, do you think it's a boy then?" She laughed, "Of course, he'll be a big ox like you. I mean he already kicks like a mule." Their shared laughter brought a brief respite from their troubles.

Logan held her even tighter. "I have missed you so much." Alarna echoed his feelings, "And I you. I can't believe Keltor is here, and alive. You are okay with him being here?" she asked, seeking reassurance.

Logan replied supportively, "Of course, I said as much. I know you are like brother and sister to each other, and I'm only too pleased to have him as a friend. He saved all of us, Alarna. At least now there is hope for our child's future, and he or she will not have to live as a slave to Aranstream. Now, quickly grab what you need, we must go."

Prompted by Logan's words, Alarna hurried to her wardrobe, gathering a few items of clothing for herself and some essentials for the baby, just in case he arrived before they returned home. "Okay, I'm ready," she announced, placing her bag onto the bed.

Logan immediately offered to carry it. "Let me take it," he said, reaching for her bag. She thanked him, and together they made their way back downstairs, ready to face whatever lay ahead.

"All ready?" Keltor asked, his impatience evident as he eagerly awaited their departure. The thought of leaving Kaitlin alone for such an extended period weighed heavily on his mind, making him anxious to be on their way.

"Yes, we're ready," Logan replied, offering reassurance. As he spoke, he glanced towards the door, just as his aunt entered the room, signalling it was time to move.

Without further delay, Keltor urged them on, leading the group out of the farmhouse and towards the waiting horses. Logan assisted Alarna and his aunt, helping them up onto the front seat of the cart. The goat, already tethered in the back, watched the proceedings with mild interest. Logan placed Alarna's belongings carefully in the rear of the cart, ensuring they were beyond the goat's reach, knowing full well the animal's tendency to chew through almost anything.

Logan turned to Alarna, his voice gentle but filled with concern. "Will you be okay?" he asked, watching her closely for any sign of discomfort.

Alarna managed a reassuring smile, doing her best to settle herself comfortably for the journey ahead. "Yes, I'm fine," she replied, her determination clear as she adjusted her position in the cart.

Logan, satisfied with her response, nodded and walked over to the other horse, preparing for their departure. His aunt, taking command of the cart, gathered the reins in her hands, ready to lead the way. Meanwhile, Keltor and Logan mounted their horses, each man checking their gear and offering final glances to ensure everything and everyone was in place.

With everyone prepared, Keltor gave the command to set off. "Let's go," he called out, his voice steady and resolute. Taking the reins, he steered his horse sharply to the left, leading the way towards the road. The group moved forward together, a shared sense of purpose uniting them as they began their journey.

They rode at a gentle pace, far slower than Keltor would have preferred. He felt an undeniable urge to press on, but he understood the need to proceed with caution for Alarna's well-being. Despite his outward composure, Keltor's mind was preoccupied with thoughts of Kaitlin. He regretted having left her behind, the responsibility for her safety weighing heavily on him. Protecting Kaitlin was his duty, and being separated from her made him feel as though he was failing in that role.

Chapter Six

Reunited

There were roughly a hundred people travelling in Kaitlin's procession. This large number made it extremely difficult to keep everyone concealed, and Kaitlin could only hope that as they moved through the Forest of Time, they would not encounter any Aranstream soldiers so far from their usual patrols. The women of the tribe had armed themselves with bows and arrows, prepared to defend the group if necessary. At the front of the procession, Uly and Ren walked alongside Kaitlin and Esimae, leading the way. At the rear, the few Elves who had sought refuge in Deodar Village kept watch, providing a sense of security for those bringing up the back.

As they walked, Kaitlin's anxiety was evident. "This is just insane," she groaned, her eyes constantly scanning the trees surrounding them for any sign of danger. "Soldiers could be hiding anywhere in these trees."

Her aunt, walking beside her, replied with calm reassurance. "I know, honey, but what choice do we have? We've got to get these people to safety."

"Just going over the bridge is going to be risky," Kaitlin admitted, her voice tinged with apprehension. "I nearly died when I got pushed over the top by someone who panicked. If it weren't for Keltor's quick reaction, I would have plummeted to the bottom." She glanced back, concern evident in her eyes as she watched the Deodars and their families, especially the many young children travelling with them.

Kaitlin's thoughts drifted to Keltor as she walked alongside her aunt. Concern coloured her voice as she spoke. "I just hope Keltor gets to the bridge the same time as us. Although he's really scared of heights and I know he hated this bridge," she said, turning to her aunt for reassurance.

As the procession wound its way through the forest, Esimae glanced over at Kaitlin, concern etched on her face. "Is there no other way?" she asked, her voice quiet yet hopeful.

Kaitlin shook her head, though a hint of uncertainty remained. "No, well, yes, there is. Keltor said there is, but it will add another two or three days onto our journey," she replied, her brow furrowed. "And to be honest, I don't think that's a good idea with this many people in tow."

A gentle, affectionate smile spread across Esimae's face as she looked at her niece, her pride unmistakable. "You know I'm really proud of you, Kaitlin," she said, her voice warm and sincere. "You've come so far from the girl who found my cottage to save her Protector." Kaitlin met her gaze, a flicker of nerves causing her to let out a soft, uneasy chuckle.

"To be honest, Esimae, I don't think that girl exists anymore," Kaitlin admitted, recalling the frightened version of herself who had once sought Keltor's witch.

Her aunt's hand reached out, gently resting on Kaitlin's arm in a gesture of comfort. "No, she's still there, with her heart of gold, and passion for kindness to help others," Esimae reassured her.

Kaitlin's expression grew sombre. "Esimae, I've killed people."

Esimae nodded, her voice calm and understanding. "Yes, so have I, but that doesn't change who you are deep down. It was only to save others, and they were killers and tyrants, not good-hearted people."

"I know, still, it's not something I had imagined I would be doing with my life."

Her aunt's question came gently: "Would you change it, and go back to your life before?"

Kaitlin's response was immediate and unwavering. "No."

Her aunt seemed surprised by the certainty. "Wow, that was a quick response."

Kaitlin stopped walking and turned to face her aunt. "If I went back to how it was before, I wouldn't have Keltor, and I can't imagine my life without him now. In fact, I can honestly say that if something happens to him, it will kill me too."

Her aunt began to protest. "Kaitlin—"

But Kaitlin insisted, her voice urgent and full of conviction. "No, Esimae, I mean it, my heart belongs to him, and so does my life. We are so connected that even now, when we are apart, it hurts so much. If, God forbid, he gets killed on this quest, I will not be able to go on and save these people and be their Queen."

Her aunt's shock was evident. "Kaitlin, I'm shocked."

"Why? Esimae, you don't seem to understand what we've been through together. Without him, I would have no heart to love these people, I would have no love to give anyone."

Her aunt's concern deepened. "I don't think you would be like that."

Kaitlin pressed her point. "Really? Have you seen Maleficent?"

Her aunt looked confused. "What, the Disney movie?"

"Yes."

"Yeah, of course. Not strictly accurate of course about the fae folk, but…"

"Yeah, well that would be me, bitter, mean, and I would most probably turn dark. That's of course if I didn't kill myself first."

Her aunt's reaction was immediate and fierce. "Kaitlin, stop! That's enough child," she said, raising her voice. "Seriously, enough. You take those thoughts out of your head right now. Don't you dare even consider such a thing; I understand you love that elf. I get it, really, I do, but you have so much to do. Look at them."

Her aunt turned Kaitlin around to look at the people following behind them. "They need you; they need the Queen of Elvendon. You cannot think only about yourself, not anymore, you have responsibilities whether you like it or not. Whether you have him or not. What do you think Keltor would say if he heard what you just said?"

Kaitlin looked away from her aunt and let out a heavy sigh. "He'd go mad at me."

"Exactly," Esimae responded firmly. "He understands sacrifice, my god child. His entire life has been devoted to protecting you. He would give his life for you, for his Queen. And yet you speak of ending it all—if you did, what would his sacrifice have been for? What would his life have meant? Don't ever forget that. In the days ahead, more people will risk their lives to see you back on the throne. This isn't just about you anymore; it's about what is best for the people of Elvendon. And the fact that I, of all people, am saying this about elves should mean something to you."

Tears welled in Kaitlin's eyes, the significance of her aunt's words hitting home, especially knowing Esimae's feelings towards elves. "I'm sorry, I just suddenly feel so overwhelmed," she admitted, wiping her eyes on the back of her hand. "I've lost so many people in the last few months, and I miss my mum." She drew in a deep breath. "To me, it's only been a couple of months since I lost her, and it still really hurts."

"I know, I know," Esimae soothed, patting Kaitlin's arm gently. "You're only just nineteen, and your life has changed beyond anything you could have imagined. That's partly our fault—your mother and I should have told you the truth about who you really were much earlier, but we thought you'd be safer not knowing. That was wrong. Kaitlin, you can do so much good in the world. And remember, Keltor is the best there is, or he wouldn't have been chosen to protect you. Now he has magic as well, and I'm here to help you too."

"I'm so sorry, I feel such a child," Kaitlin sniffled, wiping her nose with her cloak's sleeve. She took a steadying breath, trying to compose herself. "Please, don't tell him what I said," she pleaded.

"It's okay, I promise I won't say anything," Esimae reassured her. "But you must promise me that you'll never even consider or think like that again." She pulled Kaitlin into a comforting hug.

"We will get through this, all of us, together. Just believe in yourself, Kaitlin. You know Keltor does."

"I know he does, and I promise," she sniffled, "it's just, well he's so much stronger than me, I just feel such a total mess when he's not around."

"No, you're just a normal teenager in a very not normal situation. You've just saved Earth from destruction, saved me from being burned alive, lost your mother, sister and father, within weeks of each other, and goodness knows what else you've been through these past weeks. Come on, we can talk about things when we camp later, I'm sure it will help you," she offered, and she took up her hand and pulled her back into a fast walk.

"Thank you," Kaitlin said, offering her aunt a grateful smile that spoke volumes about her appreciation for the comfort she'd received.

Her aunt squeezed Kaitlin's hand gently and looked at her with warmth. "Look," she said softly, "I know I'm not your mum, but I am here for you, honey." Her words were sincere, a reminder that Kaitlin was not alone, even amid her grief and confusion.

Just then, a small face emerged from the basket nearby—a cat meowed, its presence both unexpected and oddly reassuring.

Her aunt smiled. "And Magic said he is here for you too."

Kaitlin couldn't help but laugh, the tension easing slightly. "Well, thank you, Magic," she said, acknowledging the comfort offered by both her aunt and the loyal feline companion.

XXX

As dusk settled and the darkness began to envelop the landscape, Keltor finally spotted the others in the distance, making their way across the bridge. The sight of that dreadful bridge made his stomach churn with anxiety; he loathed the thought of having to cross it himself. The group was large, and Keltor reflected on how fortunate they had been to get this far without being detected by Aranstream soldiers.

Upon their approach, a contingent of female deodars stood guard, their bows drawn and arrows nocked, ready to defend against any threat. The tension was palpable, but Uly stepped forward, raising a hand in a calming gesture. He addressed one of the archers directly, urging her to lower her weapon. "It's okay, they are with us," he assured her. "Go and tell the princess Keltor is here." The woman, trusting his word, immediately relaxed her stance, lowered her bow, and hurried off across the bridge to relay the message.

Uly then turned his attention to Keltor, greeting him as he took hold of Keltor's horse by the halter. "Uly," Keltor responded, acknowledging him while his gaze drifted over the remaining members of their group still waiting on the near side of the ridge.

"Where is she?" Keltor asked as he dismounted, concern evident in his voice.

Uly pointed across the bridge. "On the other side, organising the camp for the night," he replied.

"Good, let's get the rest over this bridge before it gets too dark," Keltor instructed, and he began to unbuckle the saddle off the horse. Uly gave a nod, turned about, and began waving his hand to usher the rest over the bridge.

"Go on, off you go," Keltor instructed, giving the horse a firm smack on its hindquarters. The animal let out a whinny and began to trot away, only to stop a short distance ahead where it started to graze on the wild plants growing nearby.

"Suit yourself," Keltor muttered, making his way over to the wagon. He deposited the saddle and reins into the back, clearing the way for what needed to be done next. Looking to Logan, he gave a brisk order. "Okay, let's get going as quick as we can," he said, gesturing towards the rear of the wagon.

Logan followed suit, releasing his own horse and allowing it to wander off into the dusk. He then turned his attention to untying his aunt's horse from the wagon, working quickly yet carefully. Suddenly, his aunt called out in distress.

"Wait!" she cried, scrambling down from the wagon to reach her horse. "Let me say goodbye to him first," she pleaded, hurrying over to the animal.

"Sure," Logan replied, stepping aside to give her space. He then moved to assist Alarna in getting down from the wagon, supporting her as her feet touched the ground. Alarna, observing the scene, spoke quietly to Logan.

"She's very upset about leaving him," Alarna remarked, her voice laced with sympathy. Logan gently patted her stomach and exhaled, concern etched on his face.

"I know, but what choice do we have? We can't take him with us. Keltor's right, the horse will be fine. He'll find his way home and he will be there when we return," he replied, attempting to reassure both Alarna and him as well.

Alarna hesitated, her worries lingering. "Do you really think we will, return home I mean?" she asked as they began to gather their belongings from the back of the wagon.

"Yes, of course I do. Keltor and the Princess will see to that, they will defeat King Iwein, and we will get Elvendon back. You'll see," Logan answered, trying to bolster her spirits.

Alarna glanced down, her hand resting on her stomach. "I hope so. I don't want our baby to grow up in Aranstream, not like it is now, I mean."

"No, neither do I. Now come on, we need to get going," Logan said, determination in his voice. He swung her bag over his shoulder and carefully lifted the goat from the back of the wagon, readying them to move on.

Logan approached his aunt, who was overcome with emotion, tears streaming down her face. He tried to comfort her, handing her the rope attached to the goat. "Here, don't worry, he'll be fine," he reassured, passing the tether over. She accepted it with trembling hands; uncertainty etched in her features.

"I hope so," she replied softly, before turning away. She shouldered her bag, determination replacing her sorrow as she prepared to cross the bridge.

Keltor then called out to Logan for assistance. "Logan, give me a hand will you," he asked, heading toward the wagon. Logan, curious, dropped Alarna's bag and joined him. "What are you doing?" he queried.

Keltor replied with purpose. "Pushing this over the ravine, I don't want to give away any indication people have crossed the bridge."

Logan glanced toward his aunt, but she was already making her way across the bridge, unaware of the fate awaiting her wagon. "Okay," Logan agreed, understanding the necessity.

Working together, the two men shoved the wagon to the edge of the ravine. "Ready?" Keltor asked. Logan nodded in response. "Push," Keltor instructed, and together they heaved the wagon over the precipice. Logan leaned over, watching as the wagon crashed to the bottom, splintering into pieces, while Keltor chose not to look.

With their task complete, Keltor gave the final instruction. "Okay, let's go," he said, and the two prepared to follow the others, the last to cross the bridge.

Logan was the first to make his way across the bridge, moving carefully but with determination. Keltor waited behind, watching until Logan was nearly at the other side before he turned his attention back to where the crowd had gathered earlier. The signs of many people passing through were clear and unmistakable, footprints and disturbed earth marking their route.

Raising his hands, Keltor began to chant softly. As his voice wove through the air, he moved his hands in swirling and sweeping motions, drawing upon his magic. Gradually, the loose debris, dirt, and leaves on the ground responded, lifting and shifting at his command. He guided them with deliberate movements, spreading the natural cover back across the path to obscure any evidence of their passage. The forest floor slowly returned to its undisturbed state, the tracks and marks left by the group fading from sight.

After several minutes of concentration, Keltor finished his work. The debris and foliage settled, blending seamlessly into the landscape once more. With dusk giving way to night, his vision was limited, but he felt confident that he had concealed their trail well enough to avoid detection.

Task complete, Keltor turned to face the bridge. A sense of unease churned in his stomach as he gripped the rope handrail, memories of Kaitlin's near fall haunting him. Keeping his head down, he hurried across, determined to put the ordeal behind him.

Kaitlin's eyes widened with a surge of excitement as she watched Keltor approach across the bridge. His head was bowed, his attention fixed on the boards beneath his feet while his hands grasped the rope handrail with a determined grip on each cautious step. She recognised his discomfort with heights, and though tempted to smile at his nervousness, she instead rested her hand gently on the wooden post supporting the rope, waiting eagerly for his arrival.

"Keltor," she called out as he drew nearer.

At the sound of her voice, Keltor glanced up, and a grin spread across his face as the tension visibly melted away upon seeing her silhouette waiting for him. "Hey," he replied, quickening his pace until he reached her.

Relief flooded Kaitlin's expression as he arrived. "Oh, thank God you're okay," she exclaimed, stepping into his embrace. His arms wrapped around her securely, and her head settled against his chest, where she could feel the rapid beat of his heart—a clear sign of the fear he had battled while crossing the bridge. She lifted her head to look at him, and as their eyes met, Keltor reached out to cup her cheek, pressing his lips tenderly to hers. The touch sent a tremor through her, the worries and anxieties that had plagued her dissolving in that moment.

Keltor's hand drifted from her cheek, fingers threading through her long hair and tracing down her back as he drew her even closer. "I love you, Kitcat," he whispered softly, his words lingering as their lips parted.

"I love you, I'm so glad you're back," Kaitlin murmured, her words brushing against his mouth. They kissed again, this time with a deep and passionate intensity.

"I would say get a room, but you know, we're in a forest," Esimae interjected sarcastically, breaking the intimacy between Keltor and Kaitlin. Her dry remark cut through the tenderness of their embrace, prompting them to pull away from one another. They opened their eyes, sharing a look before Keltor's lips curled into a smirk and Kaitlin responded with a broad grin, the moment between them lightened by Esimae's presence.

Keltor acknowledged her with a slight bow of his head. "Esimae," he greeted respectfully, stepping back from Kaitlin.

Esimae eyed him with her usual brusque demeanour. "So, you made it back alive then," she remarked, her tone matter-of-fact.

"Yep," Keltor replied, spreading his arms wide as if to demonstrate his undiminished health and presence.

Without missing a beat, Esimae continued, her tone sharp. "Good, come on, your help is needed in camp." Without waiting for a response, she turned on her heel and strode back into the trees, her commanding presence leaving little room for argument.

Watching her disappear, Keltor glanced back at Kaitlin, a wry smile on his face. "She still doesn't like me," he said quietly.

Kaitlin squeezed his hand reassuringly. "Yeah, she does, she loves you, but she would never admit it. Come on," she urged gently, lacing her fingers through his. With that, they followed after Esimae, hand in hand, ready to rejoin the rest of their group.

A perimeter watch had already been established, and several fires flickered, casting light across the clearing nestled within the trees. The fires were a necessary risk, given the sheer number of people who needed feeding and warmth. On this side of the ravine, there was little concern about encountering Aranstream soldiers, as the area was outside both the elven territories and those claimed by Aranstream or Elvendon.

As Keltor and Kaitlin entered the camp hand in hand, Keltor took note of the well-arranged sleeping spaces and the meals cooking over the fires. "You've done a great job," he remarked, genuinely impressed by the organisation evident throughout the camp.

Kaitlin shook her head, correcting him gently. "Nothing to do with me, I'm afraid; it was Ren. She's had everyone organised from the start. Her people truly respect her, but I'm worried she's pushing herself too hard, given her condition. Perhaps you could persuade her to take a break and rest, since neither Uly nor I have managed to convince her."

Keltor nodded, his expression thoughtful. "I can try, although I doubt very much that she'll listen to me; she doesn't know me that well."

As they approached their area within the camp, Kaitlin changed the subject. "Anyway, what happened at the cottage?" she asked, concern evident in her voice.

Keltor's gaze drifted across the camp to where Logan's aunt sat by the fire, gently stroking her goat. Kaitlin followed his line of sight and asked, "That's Logan's aunt?"

"Yes," Keltor confirmed, giving a brief nod as his gaze lingered on the woman by the fire, her gentle movements as she stroked the goat betraying a quiet resilience.

Kaitlin glanced between Keltor and the figure across the camp, a puzzled expression on her face. "I thought it was his sister or something," she admitted, her voice tinged with surprise as she tried to reconcile her assumption with the truth now revealed.

Keltor explained further, "Yeah, I did too, but she's the youngest in her family. Her mother had her late, according to Logan. When we arrived, she was being attacked by Aranstream soldiers."

Kaitlin's eyebrows rose in concern. "You don't mean?"

Keltor nodded solemnly. "Hmm. Had we not got there when we did, that poor woman..." He sighed and shook his head. "Anyway, let's just say they won't be bothering any other women anymore. None of them will be."

Kaitlin's attention turned to Alarna, scanning the crowd for her. "And Alarna, her and the baby? I haven't seen her yet."

"They're both fine," Keltor assured her, then placed his arm around Kaitlin and drew her closer.

Kaitlin's vulnerability surfaced as she admitted, "Keltor, I'm not going to lie, all this, it's really hard to deal with."

"Hey, come on, let's sit down," Keltor suggested, indicating a fallen tree nearby. Kaitlin joined him, and together they settled onto the log. As they sat, Kaitlin's gaze drifted towards the Deodars, her attention caught by the few elves among them as they prepared to rest for the night. The gentle bustle of the camp provided a backdrop to her swirling thoughts.

Turning to Keltor, uncertainty clouded Kaitlin's expression. "I don't know if I can do this," she confided, her voice barely above a whisper, searching Keltor's deep blue eyes for any sign of reassurance. In response, Keltor offered her a gentle smile, a silent gesture of unwavering support.

"Yes, you can, you just need to believe in yourself, Kaitlin," he encouraged quietly. "Look, you didn't think you could do the quest, but we did—we saved Earth. Come on, how many people can say that? You saved an entire world; I am pretty sure we can save Elvendon."

Kaitlin's resolve wavered, her vulnerability evident as she answered, "Yes, if you're with me, but Keltor, what if something happens to you?" Her eyes dropped to the ground, her voice trembling. "I couldn't bear it."

Keltor gently placed his hand under her chin, guiding her to meet his gaze once more. "I'm not going to leave you, I promise," he reassured her. His thumb softly brushed her bottom lip, causing her lips to part slightly.

"I just want us to be together, and to be safe," Kaitlin whispered, her hopes laid bare.

"We will be, I promise. We will get back Elvendon, you will sit on the throne as their Queen, and…" Keltor's words trailed off as he leaned in, his mouth drawing closer to hers.

Kaitlin took a steadying breath and closed her eyes, surrendering to the moment as his lips met hers.

"You will be my wife." Keltor's kiss was passionate and beautiful—so deeply felt that Kaitlin knew, in her heart, everything would be all right.

148

As their lips parted, Kaitlin whispered softly, "I'm sorry. It's just been one hell of a couple of days. It's hard to get my head around it all." Her voice was tinged with exhaustion and disbelief, the weight of recent events evident in her words.

Keltor offered a reassuring smile, slipping his arm around her shoulders to provide comfort. "I know," he replied gently. "And unfortunately, there will be many more bad days before the good ones can start, but they will, I promise." His optimism was quiet but steady, a hopeful anchor amid chaos.

Drawing her closer, Keltor added with a soft chuckle, "Soon, Kitcat, me and you will be together just chilling, drinking wine and watching the clouds." The familiar, earthly phrase made Kaitlin laugh, lightening the mood and reminding her of simpler times.

"I look forward to that day," she responded, snuggling into him as comfort and companionship soothed her nerves.

"Yeah, me too," Keltor agreed, his voice carrying a touch of wry humour that lightened the heaviness in the air. Though he attempted to mask it, the underlying uncertainty about what the future held was unmistakable. In that moment, his gentle jest was a subtle acknowledgment of the challenges they faced, as well as a quiet reassurance that, despite everything, they would face them together.

For a short while, they remained seated together, letting silence settle around them. The gentle hum of the camp's evening bustle provided a peaceful backdrop as they watched the world carry on, grounded by each other's presence.

Alarna approached with a friendly invitation, asking, "Hey, can we join you? We've brought dinner." Kaitlin, who had been quietly nodding off against Keltor, opened her eyes to greet them warmly.

"Hi, of course," Kaitlin replied, shifting with Keltor to make room on the log for Alarna and Logan.

Alarna smiled and responded with a grateful "Thank you," before curtsying politely upon sitting down.

Seeing this, Kaitlin gently asked, "Please, don't do that."

149

Alarna hesitated, explaining, "But you're the Queen."

With a reassuring smile, Kaitlin insisted, "I know, but please, you don't have to. We're friends."

Alarna nodded in understanding, her smile growing warmer.

Keltor accepted a bowl of stew from Logan and thanked him with a nod. The group settled in, and Alarna commented on the day's events as she blew on her bowl of stew to cool it.

"Well, that was a day," she remarked.

"Yeah, I'll say," Kaitlin agreed, sharing a look with Alarna. Both women laughed, the tension of the day giving way to a moment of camaraderie and relief.

As the group settled around the fire, Logan and Keltor struck up an easy conversation, their laughter drawing a gentle smile from Kaitlin. The warmth of the gathering was a welcome relief after the day's long events.

Kaitlin turned her attention to Alarna, her gaze softening as she nodded towards Alarna's baby bump. "So, how long left?" she asked, curiosity and encouragement in her tone.

Alarna let out a small sigh, replying, "About a month, although to be fair I am ready for it to come out now, I feel so enormous!"

Kaitlin shook her head, her voice warm and reassuring. "No, you look so radiant, it obviously suits you being pregnant."

"Thank you. It was touch and go at the early stages, but Esimae saved me and my baby. She is quite amazing," Alarna replied, gratitude evident in her expression.

Kaitlin glanced at Alarna, then looked across to her aunt, Esimae, who was tending to a nearby family. Pride was evident in her voice as she said, "Yes, she is. She's my aunt, you know."

Alarna's eyes widened in surprise. "Really? Oh, my goodness, I didn't know. She never mentioned it." She glanced over at Esimae thoughtfully. "I suppose it would have put her in danger if Aranstream knew she was related to the royals."

"Yeah, I guess so," Kaitlin replied, considering the situation. "Although she was my mother's sister, so I'm not sure if that counts in their eyes." She hesitated for a moment before continuing, her tone more reflective. "I didn't know her growing up, though I wish I had. I only found her by chance when Keltor was poisoned by a shadow demon back on Earth. Keltor knew about Esimae and her powers, and honestly, he wouldn't have survived without her."

Kaitlin's gaze softened as she admitted, "I wish I had that kind of knowledge. Esimae has promised to teach me, though. My mum was a witch too, but I never knew it while she was alive—she kept this whole world a secret from me."

Alarna looked at Kaitlin, genuine surprise in her eyes. "I didn't realise you were a witch," she said, her voice tinged with wonder.

Kaitlin gave a small laugh. "Really? Keltor didn't tell you?"

Alarna shook her head. "No, how long has he known?"

"Since I was thirteen," Kaitlin replied, her expression thoughtful.

"I suppose he was sworn to secrecy," Alarna mused.

Kaitlin glanced over at Keltor, catching his gaze. He met her eyes and offered a reassuring smile, which she returned.

"Yeah, I guess so," she said quietly. "I'm still learning what I can do, magically speaking. Obviously, I have powers—being a royal and all. You knew that?"

Alarna nodded in acknowledgement.

"Esimae is a really powerful witch," Kaitlin went on, her voice filled with admiration. "As I discovered this morning, we combined our magic to fight the Aranstream soldiers. It was incredible, and honestly, a little frightening."

Alarna reached out and gently touched Kaitlin's arm, offering a quiet reassurance. "It'll work out," she said, her voice steady and encouraging.

Kaitlin's response was tinged with uncertainty. "I hope so. I just don't want anyone else dying because of me."

Alarna turned as much as she could to face Kaitlin, her expression earnest. "Look," she began, "things are different in our world compared to Earth. People here are fiercely loyal to their King or Queen. If they believe in them, they're willing to make sacrifices—even lay down their lives. You can't stop them from choosing that for you."

Kaitlin lowered her gaze, her voice soft. "I just don't feel important enough. My last boyfriend—and I use that word loosely—thought I was so useless. I couldn't even cook a meal to his satisfaction."

Alarna let out a soft laugh, shaking her head.

"What?" Kaitlin asked, her tone light and clearly entertained by Alarna's reaction to her story.

A gentle smile played on Alarna's lips as she replied, "He sounds like a jerk."

Kaitlin rolled her eyes, her agreement obvious. "Yeah, he was."

Alarna offered Kaitlin a reassuring smile. "There you go then, don't put yourself down." As she spoke, she placed a gentle hand on Kaitlin's chest. "Inside of you is a powerful Elven Queen just waiting to emerge, and she will, I know she will."

Gratitude shone in Kaitlin's eyes as she responded, "Thank you." Reaching out, her hand rested affectionately on Alarna's bump, the bond between them quietly deepening.

A warm curiosity entered Kaitlin's voice. "So, do you have a name yet for this little one?"

Alarna shook her head, a hint of amusement in her tone. "No, not yet. We can't agree. Logan is convinced it is a boy, and to be honest, the way it is always kicking me, it probably is."

"Are you ready to get some sleep?" Logan asked as he stood and turned towards Alarna.

"Yes, I'm always ready for some sleep," she replied, extending her hand towards him. Logan took her hand and gently helped her to her feet.

Kaitlin, moved by their earlier conversation, stood as well and gave Alarna a spontaneous, heartfelt hug. "Thank you, for what you said. It's really helped," she whispered softly.

Alarna responded with a brief, understanding touch on Kaitlin's upper arm, her support evident in the gesture.

"Good night," both Alarna and Logan said in unison as they readied themselves to leave.

"Good night," Keltor and Kaitlin replied together, each heading off in their own direction for the evening.

As they made their way towards the area of the camp where they would be sleeping for the night, Keltor glanced over at Kaitlin, curiosity in his voice. "What was that all about?" he asked.

Kaitlin gave a small, dismissive smile. "Oh, nothing, just girly talk, you know."

Keltor looked unconvinced as he unrolled his bedroll and lay down. "No, not really," he replied, waiting for her to elaborate.

She hesitated only a moment before answering. "Babies," she said simply, as she set out her own bedroll beside his and lay down next to him.

He nodded in understanding. "Ah right."

A chill crept into the air, and Kaitlin shivered, pulling her cloak a little tighter around herself as she gazed up at the night sky. "It's getting cold," she remarked.

Keltor reached out, his voice gentle. "Come here," he offered, opening his arms to her. Without hesitation, she rolled into his embrace, and he wrapped his arms securely around her, their bodies pressed close together for warmth and comfort.

They lay quietly for a moment, gazing upwards. "The stars are bright tonight," Keltor observed softly.

"Yes, they are beautiful. I wonder if she is up there, our Star. I know she wasn't technically a star, but she is mother earth, the universe, everything," Kaitlin mused, her voice tinged with longing.

Keltor spoke gently near her ear. "Do you miss her?"

Kaitlin turned to face him, her eyes reflecting the starlight. "Yes, is that crazy to miss a voice in your head?"

He shook his head slightly, offering reassurance. "Nah, not in this world. I'm sure she is still around, watching out for us."

"I hope so," Kaitlin replied quietly, a soft yawn escaping as the day's fatigue caught up with her.

Keltor pressed a gentle kiss to the top of her head. "We'd best get some sleep; we've another long day tomorrow. Goodnight, Kitcat," he whispered affectionately.

She snuggled in closer, her voice a soft murmur. "Night, Keltor."

Chapter Seven
Keltor's Surprise

Kaitlin awoke with a start, immediately aware that Keltor was no longer lying beside her. The space where he had been empty, and a subtle restlessness crept through her. Rising quietly, she surveyed their resting place, but there was no indication of where he might have gone. Driven by a growing sense of unease, Kaitlin slipped from her bedroll and began to wander the camp in silence, her steps careful not to disturb the tranquillity of early morning.

The first light of dawn had just crept over the horizon, casting a gentle glow across the peaceful camp. Most were still lost in sleep, wrapped in quiet dreams, while a few early risers moved about with quiet purpose. As Kaitlin passed these figures, each greeted her with a respectful nod, and she returned their greetings softly. "Morning," she answered each time, pausing to ask, "Have you seen Keltor?" Despite her hopes, every person she encountered shook their head, each unable to offer any clues to his whereabouts.

Continuing her search, Kaitlin made her way to the far side of the camp. Here, she found Alarna seated upon the same log where they had all gathered for dinner the previous evening. Approaching, Kaitlin called out, "Morning, have you seen Keltor?"

Alarna glanced up and offered a small smile. "Morning. He's over there, with Logan," she replied, pointing through a break in the trees.

Following the direction of Alarna's hand, Kaitlin's gaze found Keltor and Logan in a nearby clearing, engaged in sparring. The dawn's first golden rays stretched through the trees, illuminating the pair as they moved with focused energy. The sun's light danced across the damp ground, and the air was crisp with lingering morning dew.

Kaitlin slipped off her cloak and draped it across the log before settling beside Alarna, her attention fixed on the scene before her.

Alarna glanced over, her voice gentle. "Did you sleep okay?"

"Yes, I went out like a light," Kaitlin replied softly, though her eyes remained on Keltor.

In the clearing, Keltor sparred with Logan, his bare chest gleaming beneath the rising sun. His muscles flexed with each movement, abs taut as he swung his sword, the clash of steel ringing out against Logan's blade. Kaitlin's gaze lingered on him, her breath coming a little quicker as she watched. There was something magical about the way he moved—an almost otherworldly aura surrounded him, a universal power that seemed to draw her in, captivating her entirely, as if she were a moth drawn irresistibly to a flame.

Alarna watched Kaitlin closely, her expression softening as she observed the intensity in Kaitlin's gaze. After a quiet moment, she spoke, a gentle smile spreading across her face. "You really love him, don't you?"

Kaitlin, momentarily startled by the question, tore her eyes away from Keltor and glanced at Alarna. "What?" she asked, her voice tinged with surprise, before her attention drifted instinctively back to Keltor.

Alarna repeated herself, her voice calm and kind. "I said, you really love him."

With effort, Kaitlin drew her gaze away from Keltor once more to meet Alarna's eyes. "Yes, I do," she admitted quietly. Then, unable to resist, she looked back towards Keltor in the clearing. "With every part of my being."

Kaitlin shifted to face Alarna, her expression growing earnest. "You know, when I found out that Keltor was betrothed to you, I was overwhelmed with jealousy. It felt as though my heart had been torn from my chest—I just wanted to shrivel up and disappear. After my mother died, when Keltor came to me, I had

155

no recollection of him at all. All I had was a childish drawing of an elf boy I thought I'd met in my aunt's woods. Did you know that as a child, I used to come here, to Elvendon, and play with him?"

Alarna stared at her in surprise, shaking her head in disbelief. "What? No, I had no idea."

Kaitlin let out a small laugh. "Yes, the first time I visited Elvendon, I was five years old. We used to have amazing adventures together. There was one time he almost drowned—he got his foot caught in a giant clam shell, and I had to use a knife to pry it open. It was something he'd taught me to do, just as he'd taught me how to hold my breath for a long time."

Alarna listened, a puzzled yet amused smile spreading across her face as Kaitlin continued. "When I was thirteen, Keltor wiped my memories of him and of Elvendon. That was when he became my Protector. During his training, he didn't know it would be me—not when we were children. My memories of him only returned when we crossed that very bridge we just came over. He thought I was going to die, and he called me by my old nickname, Kitcat. It was like a bolt of lightning to my heart. I looked up at those beautiful blue eyes of his, and suddenly, I knew exactly who he was." She brushed away a tear as the memories washed over her.

"And then, it hurt all over again, knowing I couldn't be with him. The very first moment I saw him in that solicitor's office back on Earth, I just knew I loved him, even though I remembered nothing of our past. When he brought me to my father here in Elvendon, and I met Prince Aragon on my birthday, Keltor foolishly thought I should be bonded to a prince and live in a castle. Keltor never understood—all I ever wanted was to be with him. I would have been content to live in a shed, so long as we could be together."

Alarna's eyes widened as she listened to Kaitlin's revelation. "Kaitlin, I had no idea," she admitted, genuine surprise colouring her voice. "He never said anything, and Keltor and I have been friends since we were little."

Kaitlin offered a sly grin, her gaze sliding back to Keltor in the clearing. "I know, he hid me well," she replied. Her eyes lingered on him, admiration clear in her expression. "I mean, just look at him. He's so powerful, yet there's a grace to his movements—he's simply beautiful to watch."

Alarna couldn't help but laugh at Kaitlin's earnestness. Kaitlin caught the sound and turned, smiling. "What?" she asked, amusement in her voice.

Alarna raised her shoulders in a light shrug. "He just looks like a brother to me. I just don't see what you see, and that's a good thing, right? Clearly, you and he were meant to be together, as me and Logan are."

Reaching over, Kaitlin placed her hand gently over Alarna's. "Yes, we are. If nothing else in this crazy world, we have them."

"Yes, we do," Alarna agreed warmly. Together, they turned their attention back to the sparring duo, quietly watching as Keltor and Logan continued their training in the clearing.

Keltor lunged forward with speed and power, his movements precise and controlled. Logan met his attacks with skill, proving himself a competent opponent. Still, it was clear that Keltor possessed the upper hand—his experience and training made each strike confident and calculated. Despite Logan's best efforts, he struggled to keep pace, his stamina waning against Keltor's relentless energy.

At last, Logan's grip faltered, and his sword slipped from his hand. "Damn," he muttered, frustration edging his voice. He glanced at Keltor, then gestured towards his impressive build. "Where the hell do you get your strength from? I mean, I can see where you get your strength," he said, alluding to Keltor's muscular physique, "but seriously, I can't keep up anymore." Drawing in a deep breath, Logan planted the tip of his sword on the ground for support.

Keltor offered a reassuring smile. "It's from years of training," he explained. "You did great though."

Logan shook his head, unconvinced. "Yeah, whatever, you're not even out of breath."

Keltor laughed, the sound light and untroubled. "Nope, that was just a bit of practice, didn't even break much of a sweat." With that, he strode over to where his shirt lay on the ground, bending to pick it up and giving it a casual shake.

Logan slid his sword back into its sheath, managing a wry smile. "Thanks for making me feel better," he quipped, his tone laced with good-natured sarcasm.

"Well, remember I also have a touch of magic to help me along," Keltor said with a faint smile. He raised his hand as if to silence Logan before he could interject. "Not that I used it then, but it's there if I need it."

Logan offered an appreciative nod. "Either way, you're pretty impressive, and thanks, for looking out for Alarna."

Pulling his shirt on, Keltor approached Logan and extended his hand. Logan took it, and Keltor pulled him into a shoulder-to-shoulder embrace.

"She is as a sister to me. I will always look out for her, and for you and the nipper when he or she is born."

"He. I'm pretty sure it's a boy," Logan replied, a grin spreading across his face.

"Boy? Well, there's a fifty-fifty chance," Keltor replied, sheathing his sword with an easy motion.

Logan glanced at Keltor, curiosity flickering in his eyes. "What about you and the Queen? Do you think you'll ever have a family of your own?"

Keltor let out a warm laugh. "Perhaps one day, yes. But first we need to get bonded—and, of course, win back Elvendon. There's a lot to sort out before we can think about starting a family."

As they walked side by side towards the camp, Logan nudged Keltor, a mischievous grin on his face. "Well, why don't you get bonded now?"

Keltor raised an eyebrow. "Now? That's easier said than done. We'd need an elder to perform the ceremony."

Logan's expression grew more serious as he spoke. "Actually, I know of an elder who managed to escape the castle when it fell. He's hiding out not far from here—I could go and bring him back?"

Keltor shook his head, his tone firm yet gentle. "No, it's too risky, we should stay together. It's only a day and a half until we must split. Kaitlin and I need to go to the trolls, or whatever they are now, we need to get their help. Esimae will take you and the tribe to the Eccleston Forest."

Logan insisted, trying to reassure him. "Keltor, I promise, you won't even know I'm gone. We can arrange it, as a surprise for Kaitlin, Alarna will help, he's the elder that bonded us. When the castle fell, he took refuge on this side of the gorge as he didn't think King Iwein would travel this far."

As Keltor looked through the trees, he saw Kaitlin waving. He returned the gesture, a smile spreading across his face. He couldn't deny that the thought of being bonded with her was truly wonderful.

"Wouldn't she want a proper bonding ceremony, you know, the dress, flowers, a big party?" Keltor asked, uncertainty flickering in his voice as he considered the traditions, he'd always imagined for such a momentous occasion.

Logan shook his head, an amused smile on his face. "Seriously, I've known her for only a day, and even I know she doesn't need all that. All she needs is you." His words were gentle but firm, reassuring Keltor that Kaitlin's happiness lay not in grand gestures, but in their union itself.

Still, another concern lingered for Keltor. "And it would be legal? Who's the elder?" he queried, wanting to ensure everything was done properly.

Logan nodded confidently. "Yes, it's legal," he assured him, then added, "His name is Elder Marlow."

A genuine grin broke across Keltor's face. "I know him," he replied, feeling a bit more at ease. "I suppose we could always have a fancy celebration once we've taken back Elvendon. My mum will be well annoyed if she misses out on my bonding ceremony." The thought of involving his family brought a wistful smile, yet the reality of their current situation weighed heavily.

Logan's tone grew softer, more earnest. "Keltor, what's more important to you?"

Keltor didn't hesitate. "Kaitlin, of course."

"So, what's the issue then?" Logan pressed, encouraging his friend to look past tradition and fear.

Keltor hesitated, grappling with his desire to do things right. "None, I guess, but should I tell her—or at least ask her if that's what she wants?"

Logan regarded him with understanding and certainty. "You know that's all she wants. Life's too short, Keltor. None of us know what's around the corner. Why wait?"

As the words settled, Keltor smiled quietly, lost in thought. He pondered for a moment, then nodded, resolve growing within him.

Keltor took a deep breath, his determination evident. "Okay, let's do it. But only if there is no risk of being caught or spotted, understand, her safety is more important than us being bonded." His priorities were clear; Kaitlin's wellbeing would always come first.

Logan nodded in agreement, promising, "Of course, I swear no one will even know I've gone. Well, except Alarna—I'll have to tell her."

Without wasting another moment, Keltor reached into his back pocket and produced a map. He glanced over at Kaitlin, who was currently speaking with Alarna, making sure that she remained unaware for now.

"Quick," Keltor whispered, pulling Logan with him behind a massive oak tree. He unfolded the map and pointed to a spot. "Look," he said, indicating a lake on the parchment. "We've stopped here before. There's a huge lake, and a clearing where we can camp. It's only about six hours from here and I know the way. Take the map and meet us there. I'll make an excuse for stopping before dusk."

Logan grinned, accepting the map with enthusiasm. "Okay, sounds like a plan," he replied, his confidence infectious.

A wave of excitement surged through Keltor as he returned the grin. The thought of finally bonding with Kaitlin filled him with happiness—a dream he had cherished all his life, one he had long assumed would never come true. Now, with the plan set in motion, he could barely contain his joy; at last, his dream was on the verge of becoming reality.

The two re-emerged from behind the great oak just as Logan tucked the map away in his pocket. As they approached, Keltor caught Kaitlin's eye and offered her a warm smile, his heart fluttering with anticipation for what was about to unfold.

"Hi, good match?" Kaitlin asked as they joined the group.

"Yeah, well, it was for him," Logan replied with a playful groan, settling down beside Alarna. She leaned into him, and Logan wrapped his arm gently around her shoulders.

"He was great," Keltor added, praising Logan's effort. "A little more training and he'll get there."

Alarna smiled as she watched the camaraderie between them. "I'm glad you two get along. I knew you would," she remarked, observing as Keltor put his arm around Kaitlin, drawing her closer to him.

Logan cleared his throat, gaining the attention of both Keltor and Kaitlin. "Actually, Keltor, Kaitlin, there's something Alarna and I would like to ask of you."

"What's that, Logan?" Kaitlin inquired curiously.

Taking Alarna's hand in his, Logan explained, "We would like to ask if you would become guardians for our baby when he is born."

"Or she," Alarna interjected with a smile.

Logan grinned at her. "Or she," he agreed warmly.

Keltor glanced at Kaitlin, who nodded eagerly in response. "We'd love to, thank you—it's an honour," Keltor said sincerely.

They stood and exchanged heartfelt hugs, sealing their new bond and the trust placed in them by their friends.

"Shall we go and get some breakfast?" Keltor suggested as his stomach let out a rumble, drawing attention to the growing activity in the main camp. He nodded towards the hubbub, inviting everyone to join him.

"Sounds like a great idea, I'm so hungry," Alarna responded enthusiastically. With that, she and Logan took the lead, heading towards the centre of camp in search of food.

As they walked, Kaitlin leaned closer to Keltor, lowering her voice. "Keltor, what exactly does that mean?" she asked, referring to the earlier conversation.

"I think you call them godparents on Earth," Keltor replied, clarifying the term for her.

Realising her momentary confusion, Kaitlin quickly apologised. "Oh, right, sorry—that was silly of me. Yes, of course, that makes sense." She paused, then added with a smile, "I'm glad Alarna likes me. We get on well—she's so easy to talk to."

Kaitlin smiled, nodding in agreement. "Yeah, she is. I knew you would get along." She glanced ahead at Alarna, feeling reassured by their easy connection. "Logan's alright too, and he adores Alarna. I guess we're going to get some baby-sitting duties in the future."

Keltor chuckled at the thought. "That will be fun."

"They're kind of family really, aren't they?" Kaitlin observed, her tone warm and thoughtful.

"Yes, they are," Keltor replied, his gaze drifting towards Logan. He couldn't help but smile to himself, reflecting on the pleasant surprise that lay ahead for all of them.

As they approached the fire, Kaitlin greeted Ren warmly. "Good morning, Ren," she said, offering a friendly smile.

Ren returned the greeting, her voice gentle as she replied, "Morning." With a small nod, she asked, "Breakfast?"

"Yes, thank you. Hey, I can do it myself," Kaitlin protested lightly when Ren knelt to pick up a bowl for her.

But Ren insisted, her tone respectful yet firm. "My Queen, it's an honour to serve you." She took the ladle and carefully served up some porridge for Kaitlin.

"Ren, really you don't have to call me that. Anyway, shouldn't you be resting in your condition, not waiting on everyone?"

Kaitlin said as she accepted the bowl. "Thank you," she added sincerely.

Ren shook her head, her determination clear. "No, I cannot, I would rather keep myself busy. I'm lucky I have Uly here with me, they do not have their partners," she said, nodding towards the women nearby.

Kaitlin gently laid a hand on Ren's arm, meeting her gaze. "I know, and I promise, Keltor and I will free them."

Ren gave a grateful nod. "I know you will, my Queen, and that's why I serve you breakfast. You must keep up your strength. Your importance is greater than mine."

Kaitlin shook her head, refusing to accept the distinction. "No, Ren, you are all important. Especially the little one inside you." She gave Ren a reassuring look, and Ren nodded in understanding.

"Have you eaten yet?" Kaitlin asked, noticing Ren's fatigue. Ren shook her head. "Now, let me finish here, you go and eat," Kaitlin insisted, raising a finger to silence any protest.

"Thank you," Ren replied with a respectful nod. She ladled herself some porridge before going to sit down, finally allowing herself a moment to rest and eat.

Kaitlin ate her breakfast as she continued to serve the others, aware that, as Queen, tradition dictated it was not her place to wait on anyone. Yet, to her, the true essence of being a Queen was to serve her people, not simply to be served by them. When the last person in line had been given their meal, she poured herself a mug of coffee and made her way over to where Keltor, Logan, and Alarna were sitting.

"Hey," she greeted as she sat down beside Keltor.

"Hi, all done?" he asked, to which she nodded in response. Keltor did not question her actions; he understood that Kaitlin was never one to follow the rigid traditions expected of a Queen. She was too grounded in her Earthly values, and he regarded this as a positive quality. They both knew that when the day finally came to reclaim Elvendon, it would be reborn as a new kind of Kingdom—one where every individual was valued equally, regardless of status or gender.

Within the hour, the group was once again moving along the trail. Logan, under the guise of going ahead to hunt, quietly slipped away to fetch the elder, making sure Kaitlin remained unaware of his true intentions. The forest they travelled through was dense, with shafts of mottled sunlight occasionally breaking through the thick canopy overhead. The party wound their way through ferns and low-lying shrubs, while the air was alive with the sound of birdsong echoing from deep within the foliage. The earthy aroma of soil, trees, and wildflowers surrounded them, grounding their senses in the natural world.

By mid-afternoon, one of the Deodar scouts returned to the group. Keltor had previously sent the scouts ahead, instructing them to investigate the clearing near the lake and ensure it was safe, as part of his broader plan. The scout approached Keltor and reported, "Keltor, we have secured the clearing, and the others are starting to set up the camp."

"Great, thank you," Keltor responded, his tone appreciative. "Can you let the others know we'll be stopping early?" The Deodar nodded, then turned and went back along the trail to inform the rest of the tribe of their early stop.

Kaitlin glanced at her wrist, an old habit lingering from her life on Earth, as if to check the time on a watch that was no longer there. She turned to Keltor, curiosity in her voice. "We're stopping early?" she asked, seeking confirmation.

Keltor nodded, his tone practical yet considerate. "Yes. The children are weary, and I thought if we halt now and allow them some time to play while it's still light, it will do everyone good. We can set off again at daybreak to make up for the lost time."

Kaitlin accepted the plan. "Oh, okay," she replied, looking back at the tribe trailing behind them. She couldn't help but notice that fatigue was etched into their faces; it was clear they all needed the rest as much as the children did.

It was a large, circular clearing that the Deodar scout had discovered, perfectly concealed amongst the trees. Kaitlin dropped her pack onto the ground, relief spreading through her limbs. Truthfully, it was not only the children who were grateful for a chance to rest; her feet ached from the journey. She recalled walking on weekends with her mum in the woodlands near her home, but nothing compared to the epic treks she had endured since their return to Elvendon.

As she looked around, a wave of familiarity swept over her. She reached out and pulled Keltor's arm as he was moving a log out of the way. "Hey," she called to him.

He stopped and looked at her. "Yes?"

"Is this where we stopped before, with Aragon, when you know…" Her sentence trailed off as nausea surged within her, recalling the moment Aragon had tried to harm her.

Keltor's expression shifted as guilt flickered across his face. He had not considered that this place might bring back such painful memories for her. "Kaitlin," he began, gently lifting his hand to her arm. "I'm so sorry, yes, it is. I didn't even think…"

She cut him off with a shake of her head. "It's okay," she reassured him, even as a group of children darted past, laughing and playing a game of chase. Their joy was infectious, easing the tension between them.

"Do you want to move on further?" he asked, his voice full of genuine concern for her feelings.

"No, no," she replied, raising her hand. "I'm fine, really. It just hit me for a moment, that's all. Look at the kids." She nodded towards the children who were now playing tag around the camp. "They really need this break. Besides, there's that wonderful lake not too far away, and I could really do with a dip in the water."

"Okay, if you're sure. I'm so sorry I didn't…"

Before he could finish, she kissed him. The unexpected gesture drew a small groan from him, and he lifted his hand to her face, holding her gently as he returned the kiss.

When they broke apart, she smiled at him. "Well, I guess that's one way to shut me up," he said, grinning.

"I guess," she replied, her gaze meeting his. "But honestly, I'm fine, so don't worry. Come on, let's get this place cleared up."

Keltor gently rubbed Kaitlin's arm in a gesture of affection before agreeing to continue with the task at hand. He turned his attention back to moving the log, while Kaitlin set about tidying the area, clearing away debris such as sticks, acorns and other detritus. Around her, others began to gather materials and build a fire in preparation for cooking.

As Kaitlin worked, a woman's voice called out from behind. Turning, she saw Shona approaching. "Oh, hi Shona," Kaitlin greeted her.

Shona offered her assistance, indicating the area Kaitlin was clearing. "Can I help?" she asked.

"Sure," Kaitlin replied with a smile, welcoming the company. The woman joined her, both sweeping the ground—Kaitlin with a makeshift broom crafted from sticks and brush.

"Thank you," Kaitlin said, pausing for a moment.

Shona looked up, puzzled. "For what, my Lady?"

"For being so kind to my aunt. She told me how you tried to help her when Jaike was killed."

Shona stopped sweeping, her expression sombre. "Oh. Well, I wasn't much use to be honest. Those soldiers still killed him."

"Hey, you tried, that's the point, and she is so grateful," Kaitlin replied softly.

Shona managed a small smile and resumed her sweeping beside Kaitlin.

While they worked, Alarna approached, her tone light but with an edge of exhaustion. "Kaitlin, can you come with me? Logan says there is a lake just beyond those trees. I could really do with a dip in the water—my back is killing me."

Shona offered to finish the job. "It's okay, my Lady, I will finish up here."

"Okay, thank you, Shona. I will then. I must stink in these clothes now. I'll just let Keltor know where we're going, I don't want him to worry," Kaitlin replied, grateful for the help.

Alarna watched her with a hidden grin as Kaitlin made her way to find Keltor, who was busy chopping wood for the fires.

"Hey," Keltor greeted as she approached.

"Alarna and I are going down to the lake for a quick dip, just to freshen up, you know," Kaitlin explained.

166

Keltor stopped his chopping. "Okay, be careful, there are scouts on the other side of the lake so bear that in mind if you, well you know, strip off."

Kaitlin grinned at his warning. "Okay, I will, no nakedness in the lake. See you later." She gave him a quick kiss, lifted her hand in farewell, and walked away to join Alarna.

Keltor watched as Kaitlin joined Alarna, noting Alarna's quick, knowing wink in his direction. The gesture made his heart flutter in anticipation of what was to come. As the two women walked away together, Keltor lifted his hand towards two deodar scouts standing nearby, signalling them to discreetly follow and keep an eye on Kaitlin. The scouts nodded in silent understanding; he had already spoken to them earlier, asking for their assistance in watching over her while he attended to other matters. They were familiar with his plan and willing to help without hesitation.

Just then, Keltor heard someone call his name. Turning, he saw Logan had returned. "Is he here?" Keltor asked expectantly.

Logan confirmed with a simple "Yes," gesturing over his shoulder. "Come on, we'll go and have a quick dip in the river upstream. Uly and Ren are taking care of things here."

Relieved, Keltor agreed, "Okay," and paused to place a grateful hand on Logan's arm. "Thank you," he added sincerely.

Logan offered a reassuring smile. "No problem."

As they reached the waterfront, Kaitlin spotted her aunt standing nearby. "Hi, Esimae, you've come for a dip too?" she called out, moving to join her at the water's edge.

Esimae flashed a small smile in reply. "Yes, well, you know, I feel gross," she admitted, her tone light but sincere.

Kaitlin glanced over to Alarna, then back to her aunt, a flicker of curiosity in her eyes. "Is there something I don't know about?" she asked, unable to hide her suspicion at the slightly odd atmosphere.

Feigning innocence, Esimae responded, "No, why?" She looked at Kaitlin with wide, untroubled eyes.

"I don't know, you're all acting a bit weird," Kaitlin pressed, glancing once more at Alarna before returning her attention to her aunt.

Esimae gestured broadly towards the idyllic scene—the towering mountains and dense trees that framed the lake, their shadows stretching over the clear, blue water. "Why, because we all want to wash in this wonderful lake?" she replied, a hint of amusement in her voice. The ground was scattered with bright flowers, their scent sweetening the fresh air.

Kaitlin nodded, a grin spreading across her face. "No, I get it, it's beautiful here, and to be fair, we are probably all stinky. Come on, let's get in." With that, she unclipped her cloak and let it fall to the ground. She slipped off her overdress, carefully tucking her mother's wand inside the hood of her cloak to keep it safe.

"Damn, this is really cold," Kaitlin squealed as she waded into the lake. Her white underdress clung to her as she ventured deeper, the water biting against her skin.

Behind her, Alarna struggled to keep up. "Hang on, wait, I can't move as quickly as you," she protested. "He's kicking like crazy; I don't think he likes cold water!"

"I'm so sorry," Kaitlin apologised, realising her oversight and immediately turning back towards Alarna. "I totally forgot about bump!" she exclaimed, concern in her voice.

Moving carefully, Kaitlin took hold of Alarna's hands, steadying her as they both waded deeper into the cool lake, the water swirling around them. As they ventured further, Kaitlin's eyes widened in surprise and fascination.

"Oh my god, look at your bump!" she cried, captivated by the sight of Alarna's stomach shifting visibly from one side to the other beneath the surface of the water.

Alarna shuddered slightly, a mix of discomfort and amazement on her face. "Oh, that feels horrid, he's turning over. Here, feel him," she said quickly, grabbing Kaitlin's hand and placing it gently on her abdomen, inviting her to share in the extraordinary sensation.

Kaitlin recoiled, her face a picture of disbelief. "Eww, no, that's so weird!" she cried out, unable to tear her eyes away as Alarna's stomach flattened noticeably on one side while a pronounced bump pushed out on the other.

Alarna let out a laugh, her finger prodding gently at her belly. "I think that's his bum," she said, her voice tinged with amusement as she felt the pronounced shape beneath her hand.

Kaitlin, still fascinated by the spectacle, hovered her palm over the shifting bump. "That baby needs to come out!" she exclaimed, shaking her head in disbelief. As she pressed her hand lightly against the moving stomach, her eyes widened. "He's kicking," she announced, excitement colouring her voice. Without hesitation, she called out to her aunt, "Hey, Esimae, come and feel this!" inviting her to share in the remarkable moment.

Esimae hesitated, her expression serious as she responded, "Erm, no thanks. I don't have children for a reason. I can't think of anything worse than having something growing inside of me." Without waiting for a reply, she dipped under the surface of the lake, letting the water close over her head. When she resurfaced, she briskly wiped the droplets from her eyes, her face revealing nothing more on the subject.

"Oh, Esimae, it's amazing. There's a whole little person in here, it's such a miracle of life," Kaitlin said softly, her eyes filled with wonder as she addressed Esimae.

Unexpectedly, tears welled up in Alarna's eyes and began to spill down her cheeks.

Startled by the sudden change, Kaitlin reached out gently and placed her hand on Alarna's upper arm. "Hey, oh my god, what's the matter, did I say something wrong?" she asked with genuine concern.

Alarna shook her head and waved her hand dismissively, attempting to collect herself. "No, no," she assured Kaitlin, her voice trembling. "It's just my emotions; they're up and down all the time. That was just so beautiful, what you said."

Relief washed over Kaitlin, and she let out a quiet breath, grateful she hadn't upset her friend.

169

After a brief pause, Kaitlin smiled and continued, "You know, this is just what I needed, to wash away all that horror from the last few days. And I know, before you say anything, Esimae, that there is more to come. But for now, can we just take this moment? Right now, life is beautiful."

As Esimae ducked under the water, Alarna caught her eye and they both burst into laughter, the easy camaraderie between them clear. Little did she know, the evening was about to become even more special for her.

After spending about an hour swimming and playing in the water, the three made their way to the bank and settled down, basking in the lingering warmth of the sun as they dried off. The sunlight danced on the water's surface, adding to the tranquil atmosphere.

"I'm glad Keltor wanted to stop so early, and we got to do this, it's been fun," Kaitlin remarked, appreciation evident in her tone.

Alarna nodded in agreement. "Yeah, it has. It was for the kids mostly, he said they were tired."

Thoughtful, Kaitlin added, "I suppose it must be so hard for them to understand what's going on, where all their fathers, and grandfathers have gone." She settled back, letting the sunshine wash over her. "I will be happy when they are all safe in the Eccleston Forest." With that, she closed her eyes, content in the moment of respite.

"Hey, look what I picked," Alarna said about twenty minutes or so later, rousing Kaitlin from her light doze. Kaitlin sat up, raising her hand to shield her eyes from the dazzling sunlight, and squinted at Alarna, who was silhouetted against the bright sky with the sun behind her.

In Alarna's hand was a bunch of freshly picked flowers. Alarna settled herself on a nearby rock next to Kaitlin, her expression cheerful yet thoughtful.

"Where's Esimae?" Kaitlin asked, glancing around.

"She went back," Alarna replied. "Something about sorting dinner. It's a bit early, but I think she's had enough of baby talk."

Kaitlin nodded in understanding. "Oh, right."

Alarna glanced down at the flowers still in her hands, then looked back at Kaitlin, a tentative smile on her lips. "Hey, do you want to make some headbands out of these flowers?" she asked, her eyes brightening at the thought. "I used to do it all the time with Mum, but since she passed…" Her voice trailed off, and for a moment, the joy of the idea was tinged with sadness as the memory of her mother surfaced, bittersweet and lingering.

"Yes, of course," Kaitlin responded eagerly, sitting up straighter. "Mum and I used to make these too. She had an amazing garden full of flowers. These blue ones are gorgeous," she added, selecting a few from Alarna's bundle and inhaling their sweet fragrance. "I don't recognise this flower though. I don't think we had these back on Earth."

"It's called a bluestar. Do you miss your Earth?" Alarna asked, settling down beside Kaitlin.

Kaitlin paused, her gaze lingering on the flowers. "A little, I miss my mum more."

Alarna nodded, her expression tinged with sadness as she gently rubbed her bump. "Yeah, me too. I'm sad she will never know this little guy." She smiled softly, then amended, "Or girl."

With empathy, Kaitlin reached out, placing her hand briefly on Alarna's arm—a quiet gesture of understanding and shared feeling.

"If you like," Kaitlin said thoughtfully, "I could stay with you when you have the baby. I know you'll probably want your aunt there, but…"

"Yes, yes, I would love you to," Alarna interrupted quickly, her relief evident. "That is, if you really want to."

"Of course I do, I wouldn't have offered otherwise," Kaitlin insisted, her tone warm and reassuring.

Alarna gave a small laugh. "Logan's aunt is rather squeamish, you wouldn't think so, would you? She's helped birth so many animals, but when it comes to human babies…" Alarna shook her head, a smile tugging at her lips. "She's already said she doesn't really want to be there for the birth unless I was desperate."

171

"Okay, then I'll be your birthing partner," Kaitlin agreed with a supportive nod.

"Thank you," Alarna replied, her voice softening. "To be honest, I'm a little scared about the whole thing. I just hope he or she doesn't come too early. I need to keep the little one in there until you've taken back Elvendon."

Kaitlin nodded in agreement, offering a reassuring smile.

"Don't worry, we will," she said. "If you want, you and Logan can come and stay at the castle until the little one is born."

"I'd like that," Alarna said, her eyes brightening. "I do miss Elvendon. Logan's aunt is wonderful, but at the end of the day, it's still her farm and her ways."

"In that case, why don't you both move back to Elvendon? You can stay at the castle if you want. My god, it's big enough, and if you don't want to be in there, I'm sure we can find you a house in the village."

Alarna grinned and nodded at the idea. "I would have to ask Logan and make sure his aunt would be okay. I mean, it's not like her farm is that far away. We could still help her out if she needed us."

"Alarna, I'm the Queen, I'm sure I could find her a farmhand to help her if she needs it."

Alarna's gratitude was clear as she replied, "Thank you."

Changing the subject, Kaitlin lifted her flower hairpiece. "Now, what do you think?"

"Oh wow, it looks beautiful," Alarna complimented, her eyes lighting up as she admired the flower hairpiece. "Here, let me put it in your hair," she offered eagerly.

"Okay, thanks." Kaitlin responded, spinning around so that her back was to Alarna. Alarna gently began to weave Kaitlin's hair through the delicate flower headpiece, her hands working carefully.

"This is really nice," Kaitlin remarked, glancing over her shoulder with a warm smile. "You know, doing girlie things—I haven't done this for a very long time."

"Me too, it's been fun. Now turn around and let me see," Alarna replied, stepping back to admire her handiwork.

Kaitlin spun around to her.

"Wow, that looks amazing, it's so beautiful, just like you," Alarna said, her admiration evident as she gazed at Kaitlin. "Keltor is a very lucky man."

"Stop it," Kaitlin mumbled, embarrassed by the compliment. "Now, turn around and let me put yours in."

Alarna turned around, giving Kaitlin the opportunity to gently weave the flowers through her hair. Kaitlin's hands moved with care and precision as she arranged the blooms, ensuring each one was perfectly positioned amongst Alarna's locks. When she finished, Kaitlin stepped back to admire her handiwork, her eyes bright with satisfaction.

"There, all done. It looks so pretty," Kaitlin remarked, lifting and positioning a final strand of Alarna's hair with a delicate touch.

Alarna reached up, her fingers gently brushing the flowers now woven into her hair. She turned to Kaitlin with a warm, appreciative smile. "Thank you," she said, her voice soft but sincere, clearly touched by Kaitlin's thoughtful gesture.

Kaitlin smiled back, a sense of contentment settling over her. "This was fun," she admitted, the smile lingering on her lips. For a while, she'd been able to forget her worries—those precious, carefree moments had felt priceless.

Reluctantly, Kaitlin glanced around and picked up her cloak and wand. "But, I suppose we should be getting back," she announced, her tone betraying her reluctance to let the moment end. As she prepared herself, a sudden realisation struck her. "Hey, where's my dress gone?" she asked, scanning the area with a puzzled expression.

"The deodars took them, to wash them," Alarna lied.

"What are we supposed to wear, I can't go back in my underdress, Keltor would have a fit?" Kaitlin said.

"It's okay, look the Deodar's left these," Alarna said, picking up a couple of dresses laying on the rocks.

"These are far too fancy," Kaitlin complained as she looked at the blue and white dresses. "I mean, they're beautiful," she remarked picking up the blue dress. "I think this one is for you," she said as she checked the size against her body.

"Oh, thanks," Alarna said with a grin. "Just put it on Kaitlin, it's only for an hour or so until our clothes dry, besides, you know how the deodars love making beautiful dresses, they probably don't think much of it."

"Yeah, well," she muttered as she put the long white gown on. "Wow, this is gorgeous, look how it sits just on my shoulders, it's so floaty." She spun around and the dress swirled about her. "It sparkles too, how the hell do they do it, I mean where do they get the fabric from, they live in the middle of a forest?"

"I've no idea, it's a closely guarded secret," Alarna replied as she pulled the blue dress over her head. "Well, that only just fits," she complained as she forced it over her bump.

"Oh, you look beautiful," Kaitlin said, grinning at her. "Come on we'd best head back, I have to say I'm going to feel ridiculous going back into camp looking like this, they're all going to think I am a right big-headed queen."

Alarna laughed.

"No, they won't, come on. No leave it in, please for me," Alarna begged as Kaitlin went to undo the flowers from her hair.

"Really?"

"Yes, please, I want to show Logan."

"Okay, I guess," Kaitlin mumbled, and she picked up her cloak, took her wand and tucked it inside the top of her dress, and held the cloak over her arm as they walked.

As they headed toward camp, Kaitlin shook her head in disbelief. "I mean, where did they even have them stored? They're only carrying backpacks."

Alarna smiled, "They are very proud of their work, Kaitlin. They probably didn't want to leave them behind."

"Alarna!" Kaitlin called out, her tone laced with concern as they entered the camp. She glanced around, anxiety growing.

"Where the hell is everyone? Oh my god, don't tell me they were attacked, and I've been sunning myself like I was on holiday!"

Alarna quickly tried to reassure her. "No, calm down, it's fine," she said gently. "Look, I can't tell you more, just that you must come with me," she added, holding out her hand encouragingly. "Drop your cloak over there, you don't need it for now."

Kaitlin's confusion turned to alarm as she pressed for answers. "Alarna, what the hell is going on?"

"I promise, it's a good thing, please just trust me, I don't want to spoil the surprise," Alarna replied, determination in her voice.

"Surprise, oh god, what's he done?" Kaitlin muttered, suspicion evident as she eyed her friend.

Alarna pleaded once more, extending her hand. "Please."

"Fine, but whatever it is, I'm going to kill Keltor later," she muttered as she threw her cloak onto a log. She took Alarna's hand and allowed her to lead her towards the other side of the camp.

Xxx

Keltor paced anxiously up and down, his mind swirling with doubt. "This was a mistake," he muttered, wringing his hands. "She hates surprises—she's going to go crazy at me."

Logan tried to reassure him, "Hey, stop it, it's fine. Esimae said she was in a great mood after her swim."

Keltor shook his head, unconvinced. "Yeah, until she finds out I've done all this, and she hasn't got a castle bonding." He gestured towards the makeshift altar he had fashioned out of tree branches, now decorated with flowers gathered from the riverbank. Behind them, the deodars and elves waited patiently, seated on fallen logs arranged in a rough circle at the centre of the clearing.

Panic threatened to overwhelm him. "Shit, no, no… I shouldn't have done it," he whispered, shaking his head. "What if it doesn't work? What if the bonding doesn't take? Then what—does that mean it's over between us?"

Logan offered calm reassurance, "No, it just means the timing wasn't right."

"Exactly," Keltor said, his tone tense as he turned to face his friend. "I should have waited, Logan, until all this was over. What the hell was I thinking!"

Logan looked at him steadily. "Keltor, we might not make it to the end. Take this moment for what it is—now, in this time."

Keltor let out a shaky breath. "Oh, by the spirits, I am so nervous. I think I'd rather fight a damn ogre than go through this torturous wait."

Logan grinned, trying to lighten the mood. "Now, come on, where's that warrior I know?" He reached out, stopping Keltor's pacing to adjust the clip at his throat and fuss with his cloak.

"Long gone, I think," Keltor muttered in reply, prompting Logan to laugh.

"She's coming," Esimae called down the aisle, her voice carrying a note of anticipation that seemed to reverberate through the clearing. Instantly, Keltor's anxiety intensified. "Oh, hell," he muttered, glancing nervously at Elder Marlow, who stood beneath the makeshift altar. The elder, noting Keltor's unease, caught his words and regarded him with a calm, searching gaze.

"You do want to bond with the Queen?" Elder Marlow asked, seeking reassurance and clarity amidst the rising tension.

Keltor's response was immediate, his conviction clear despite his nerves. "Of course I do, more than anything in this universe. I'm just nervous, that's all, in case she doesn't want to do this now, at this time." His admission hung in the air, honest and vulnerable.

The elder's question was gentle but firm. "Do you want to stop?"

Keltor shook his head resolutely. "No, Elder Marlow, let's just see how it goes." Drawing a deep breath, he steadied himself and waited. Whatever her response, he knew it would all have been worth the effort.

Xxx

"Alarna, what the hell," Kaitlin protested, coming to a halt as Alarna began fussing with her hair.

"I want you to look perfect," Alarna whispered, offering a reassuring smile.

Kaitlin's confusion deepened. "Perfect for what?" she asked, her brow arching in question.

"You did mean what you said, didn't you, about Keltor?"

"Mean, I don't understand?"

"When you said you would be with him anywhere, and that you didn't need a fancy castle."

"Yes, of course I did. Alarna, what the hell is going on?" Kaitlin pressed, her voice meaningful and her brow furrowing.

"He's waiting for you, that's all you need to know. I will walk with you, and if you really don't want to, he will understand, okay."

Kaitlin's anxiety grew. "Alarna, what has he done?"

Alarna's reply was gentle. "Only something that will fill your heart with joy, I'm sure. Now come on, we're going."

Taking Kaitlin's hand, Alarna led her forward through vines that draped across a walkway between the trees.

Kaitlin's eyes widened in amazement at the vivid blue and pink flowers decorating the vines, their petals scattered across the ground like a soft carpet beneath her feet. It was beautiful, but she still wondered what it was all for.

Emerging from the trees into a clearing, Kaitlin saw the tribe gathered, sitting as quiet as mice, their eyes fixed upon her. Excitement twisted with nerves in her stomach, forming anxious knots.

Her gaze then travelled down the aisle to an altar, beautifully adorned with riverbank flowers, forest ferns and greenery. Candles were lit and dotted here and there, casting a gentle glow. It was the most beautiful sight she had ever seen.

Keltor swallowed back his nerves, and he turned to look at her. Instantly his eyes fell on the beautiful glow of magic that surrounded her, and as she caught his eyes her aura changed to a

177

rainbow of colour. His heart swelled with such love that he knew he had made the right decision.

Kaitlin's eyes fell on Keltor. He appeared nervous yet exuded a quiet strength. His striking blue eyes met hers, causing her heart to swell with love as she realised the significance of what he had arranged. At the altar stood a man she recognised as an elder from the palace, confirming the gravity of the moment. It was hard to believe that Keltor had orchestrated a bonding ceremony, and all this amid the turmoil of an elven battle.

Taking a tentative step forward, Kaitlin's eyes widened, meeting Keltor's gaze. A gentle smile played on his lips, which she returned, fighting the urge to let out a nervous giggle. She walked towards him, ignoring the smiles and bowing heads from the gathered tribe, her focus fixed solely on Keltor.

As she reached his side, she took in his appearance: he looked undeniably handsome. His long, blonde hair was swept back, accentuating the intensity of his gaze. His cloak was neatly fastened at his throat, one side draped back over his shoulder to reveal the sword at his hip.

In a quiet voice, Kaitlin addressed him. "Keltor," she said gently, "What have you done?"

Keltor looked at Kaitlin with unwavering affection. "I want to bond with you, Kitcat, here and now in this forest, with our friends as witnesses. That is, if you will have me?"

Overcome with emotion, Kaitlin gasped in disbelief, her words a mixture of awe and delight. "Oh my god, yes! I can't believe you did all this without me knowing. It's so beautiful and enchanting, but I haven't prepared anything," she whispered to him.

Keltor gently took her hand, his grip reassuring. "Neither have I. Let's just wing it, shall we?" he replied with a playful grin. Kaitlin couldn't help but chuckle at his light-heartedness.

A sudden thought struck her, and she glanced towards her aunt. "And Esimae, she was alright with this?" she asked, seeking reassurance. Her aunt, seated to her left, smiled warmly at her.

"Yes, she helped organise everything, along with Alarna, and Logan found us an Elder, so it's all legal," Keltor explained, nodding towards the man who stood waiting in front of them.

Kaitlin's eyes widened as she took in the scene. "And they all knew?" she asked, her gaze sweeping over the audience seated in anticipation of her response.

Keltor nodded, a wide grin spreading across his face. "I don't believe it," Kaitlin admitted nervously.

"And they are waiting for your answer, my Queen," Keltor added with a respectful dip of his head.

Turning to face their friends and family, Kaitlin saw that everyone had risen to their feet in unison. "Thank you, all of you," she addressed them sincerely. Then, turning back to Keltor, she spoke with conviction. "And yes," she declared, "I will bond with Keltor. Nothing would make me happier than to be his wife."

As soon as Kaitlin gave her answer, the Deodars began to clap, their applause slow and rhythmic. Kaitlin raised an eyebrow at the unfamiliar gesture.

"It's a traditional Deodar thing," Keltor quickly explained, "wishing us good luck."

"Oh, okay," Kaitlin replied, feeling the warmth of their support.

After a minute, the clapping ceased, and the Deodars bowed to her before returning to their seats.

Keltor looked towards Kaitlin and asked softly, "Shall we do this?"

With a wide, genuine grin, Kaitlin replied, "Most definitely." The excitement between them was palpable as he took her hand, and together, they turned to face the front. Keltor cast a quick glance to his right, catching Logan's eye. He mouthed an enthusiastic "Yes!" while his hand clenched into a euphoric fist. Logan responded with a laugh and a nod of encouragement.

Turning their attention back to the front, the Elder approached and positioned himself before them. Bowing down on one knee to Kaitlin, he began, "Firstly, I must say how thankful to the spirits I was when I heard from Logan that you were still alive, and that

179

our queen was back to save Elvendon. To be given the honour of bonding the queen in marriage, I am forever grateful."

Kaitlin glanced up at Keltor, her face illuminated by a blissful smile. Elder Marlow then rose to his feet, preparing to commence the ceremony.

"Tonight, our ceremony will be short, and to the point," he announced. "Tonight, there is not the usual flamboyance and festivities of a royal wedding, which can go on for many hours. Keltor has asked for a simple, dare I say, romantic ceremony, with just you, their friends, and family to bear witness. Let us begin."

Keltor glanced at Kaitlin once more, offering a reassuring squeeze of her hand as they readied themselves for the ceremony to begin.

The Elder spoke solemnly, his voice carrying through the gathered friends and family. "As we gather here today, deep within the Forest of Time, we ask the spirits of our ancestors to come forward. May they grant their consent and blessing to Kaitlin and Keltor, offering them a true bonding and joining their souls as one." The Elder then stepped towards them with a gentle nod.

"Keltor, please take Kaitlin's hand," he requested.

Keltor nodded in acknowledgement. He released Kaitlin's right hand, then gently took her left in his own, holding it firmly but tenderly.

Turning to Keltor, the Elder asked, "Do you have words you wish to say to Kaitlin?"

Keltor nodded again, then turned to face her, his gaze locking with hers. As he looked into her deep green eyes, a wave of overwhelming love washed over him, threatening to leave him speechless. He took a steadying breath, gathering his thoughts.

"Kaitlin, I don't have anything prepared, but I don't need to. Since the very first day you arrived in Elvendon, when you were just five years old, you stole my heart. Even as a boy, I felt my love for you grow with each passing year. You are the keeper of my heart and soul. Without you, I am nothing; with you, I am the most powerful man in the world. I vow to love, honour, and protect you for all eternity. My love for you goes beyond words, beyond the universe and the stars themselves. All I want in this world is for you to become my wife."

Keltor's beautiful blue eyes drew Kaitlin in, and she felt her soul begin to entwine with his as he spoke.

With emotion trembling in her voice, Kaitlin responded, "Keltor, words cannot express how much you mean to me. Everything we have endured together—from our childhood adventures, to saving Earth, to the heartbreaking loss of my family—has only deepened my love for you." She paused for a moment, steadying herself as she fought back tears, her lips pursed in determination.

Feeling the gentle reassurance of Keltor's grip, Kaitlin found comfort in his touch. She gazed at him, her voice trembling with emotion as she began to speak her heart.

"Keltor, you have always stood by me, offering protection and unwavering love. I love you more than life itself—a life I cannot imagine without you. You are my everything: my world, my universe, my love. My heart belongs to you and will always remain yours. You are my best friend, my soul mate, my lover."

Keltor smiled softly at her, and Kaitlin felt her heart racing with emotion. She continued, her words sincere and full of devotion.

"All I desire is your love, and to offer you mine, as husband and wife."

Moved by her words, Keltor brought her hand to his lips and kissed it tenderly, taking in the moment as his eyes closed briefly. When he opened them, Kaitlin returned his smile, and together they turned their attention back to the Elder.

"Are you ready?" the Elder asked, his tone gentle.

Both Keltor and Kaitlin nodded, though Kaitlin felt a flicker of uncertainty about what would happen next. She glanced over to Esimae, noticing her tears, and a smile touched Kaitlin's lips at the sight.

With a solemn air, the Elder stepped back, signalling the beginning of the next stage of the ceremony. Raising his voice with gravity befitting the occasion, he pronounced, "By the power

181

bestowed in me as an Elder of Elvendon, I ask that the spirits and guides watch over this couple, to guide and protect them, and bless them with children. Come forth and make claim that these two here before me are blessed with a true bonding from the spirits."

As the Elder spoke, the atmosphere shifted. The air surrounding the couple began to swirl, forming a small, whirling vortex like a dust devil. Kaitlin glanced anxiously at Keltor, her nerves evident in her eyes. Sensing her unease, Keltor leaned in and whispered in a soothing tone, "It's okay." He held firmly onto the top of her left hand, his grip offering comfort and reassurance. "Whatever happens, we stay together, forever."

Bolstered by his words, Kaitlin gave him a determined nod. In her heart, she knew that even if the spirits did not grant their blessing, nothing would make her leave him. Their bond was unbreakable, regardless of the outcome.

The swirling wind intensified, moving upwards along their bodies until it reached their arms, before travelling down towards their hands. Kaitlin felt a gentle magic trickling through her, causing her hand to tingle with an unfamiliar but not unpleasant sensation. Watching anxiously, she saw a mist begin to form, swirling between their joined hands as the ceremony progressed.

Keltor held his breath, silently pleading with the spirits for their union to be recognised as a true bonding. Although he knew deep within that they were destined for each other, doubts lingered in his mind—she was a Queen, and he merely her Protector.

Suddenly, Keltor felt the magic coursing down his arm towards his hand. The swirling wind enveloped their hands, drawing them closer together. He glanced at Kaitlin, and she met his gaze, both feeling the intensity of the moment.

Without warning, the magical mist dissipated. Keltor anxiously looked down at their fingers, only to release a tremendous sigh of relief. There, tattooed on their ring fingers, appeared the mark of a true spiritual bonding: a swirling circular knot symbolising the union of two souls into one, with delicate branches resembling those of a tree extending down their fingers.

Overcome with relief, Kaitlin laughed and turned towards Keltor. "Is that it, does that mean it worked?" she asked, her voice filled with hope.

"Yes, my love, it does," Keltor replied, his face alight with joy. He swept her into his arms, holding her close as Kaitlin wrapped her arms around his neck, one hand resting gently on his back.

"I love you," she whispered softly, her lips brushing his earlobe.

"I love you, Kitcat," he murmured in return, squeezing her tightly in his embrace.

The Elder stepped forward, his presence commanding the attention of all gathered. "It has been confirmed," he announced solemnly. "The spirits have agreed to this bonding. In their eyes, they are now as one—husband and wife."

At this proclamation, Esimae could not contain her excitement. "Yes!" she screamed joyfully as an eruption of sparkling lights exploded into the air above them, reminiscent of a vibrant fireworks display. The sudden burst startled Kaitlin, who exclaimed, "Esimae!" as she and the onlookers jumped in surprise.

Esimae, ever exuberant, quickly reassured them, her hands raised in a calming gesture. "It's okay," she called out. "It's contained—no-one can see from the outside." With the crowd's fears eased, she clapped her hands together in delight, her happiness unrestrained.

Keltor, sharing in the light-heartedness, laughed and remarked, "I bet she's been waiting to do that all day!" Kaitlin joined in his laughter, adding, "She's hysterical," the joy of the moment infectious among those present.

However, the Elder soon interrupted their laughter, drawing their attention back to the ceremony. With measured movements, he reached down to a sack resting at his feet. "There is also something else that I must do while I'm here," he said, his tone returning to formality.

At this, Esimae brought her dazzling display of sparkles to an end and quietly returned to her seat. As she settled, her eyes lingered on Uly and Ren, a fleeting look of concern passing across her features. The Elder offered a word of gratitude in her direction, and Esimae acknowledged him with a nod. Their silent exchange signalled to all those present that the ceremony was moving on to the next significant moment.

The Elder then addressed the assembly. "As you know, with the untimely murder of our King, his daughter, Princess Kaitlin, is now our rightful queen." Bowing his head respectfully towards Kaitlin, he received a warm, appreciative smile in response. He continued, "However, she has not yet been given that authority in the eyes of elven law."

Keltor, unable to contain his concern, interjected, "What do you mean?" His brow furrowed with worry as he spoke.

"By law, she must be crowned as the new Queen," the Elder explained, his tone solemn.

Keltor began to reply, but the Elder raised his hand, gently silencing him before he could speak further. "I, Elder Marlow, have that power of authority," he clarified. "However, due to the fact that King Iwein has taken the crown of Elvendon, and the short notice to which I was brought here, I had to improvise."

The Elder carefully reached into the sack and lifted out a crown, beautifully woven from the flora and fauna of the forest. He held it aloft for all to see, explaining, "There are no rules to say that the crown must be made of gold and jewels, only that it is blessed by the spirits. It is a simple process, and if my Princess is willing, we can do this now."

Kaitlin turned to Keltor, seeking reassurance. He offered her a supportive nod and stepped back, granting her space for the momentous occasion. Accepting the invitation, Kaitlin replied, "Okay, yes."

As the Elder requested, Kaitlin gathered the folds of her silken dress, the fabric shimmering with a faint luminescence, and knelt before him at the very heart of the ancient glade. The air itself seemed to grow hushed, as if the forest was holding its breath. The Elder began to chant, his voice reverberating with a timbre older than memory: "*Elarma, otswan neraspar.*" With each syllable, the surrounding trees stirred and a gentle breeze, glittering with motes of light, danced through the leaves, weaving strands of silver through Kaitlin's hair.

The Elder lifted the crown, its woven flowers glistening with sparkles that caught the moonlight and sprayed tiny rainbows through the air. As he gently placed it upon Kaitlin's brow, the ritual phrase echoed once more, *"Elarma, otswan neraspar."* Instantly, the crown blazed with a supernatural radiance, petals unfurling anew and vines weaving tighter as if responding to an unseen hand. Soft, ethereal music whispered through the glen, and the very earth beneath Kaitlin's knees pulsed with living energy. The mystical glow bathed her and all those present, the light streaming outward to touch every soul, binding them together in this enchanted moment. The ceremony shimmered with an otherworldly wonder, marking the dawn of Kaitlin's reign and forever entwining her fate with the spirit of Elvendon.

As the Elder gently placed the crown upon Kaitlin's head, she became acutely aware of the magic awakening within it. A shimmering ripple of light descended, enveloping her entirely, sending a surge of energy – or was it power? – coursing through every nerve in her body. The sensation compelled her eyes to close and her posture to straighten, and she drew in a deep, steadying breath as the transformation took hold.

The Elder knelt before her, his voice gentle as he spoke. "Open your eyes, my Queen." Obediently, Kaitlin opened her eyes to meet the Elder's gaze, finding him smiling warmly at her. He extended his hand, and together they rose to their feet. After helping her stand, the Elder stepped back, releasing her hand with a gesture of respect.

With solemn authority, the Elder proclaimed, "With the power from the spirits, and our ancestors, I proclaim that Princess Kaitlin is now our new Queen of Elvendon."

The weight of the moment pressed upon Kaitlin as she inhaled sharply, the enormity of her new role settling in. No longer merely a teenager from South London, she was now Queen of the Elves, and the realisation struck her that she would need to mature quickly to shoulder this responsibility.

185

Her eyes found Keltor, and she saw tears glistening in his eyes – tears filled with pride and love so intense it nearly overwhelmed her. Moved beyond words, Kaitlin gave an involuntary sob, the emotional significance of her coronation resonating within her heart.

"Wait, please, I have not finished," the Elder announced, reaching into the bag and retrieving a second crown. With deliberate solemnity, he turned to the assembly and declared, "As we are here to celebrate a true bonding, one confirmed by the spirits and our ancestors, I now ask Keltor to step forward."

Keltor, surprised by the request, hesitated. The Elder gestured reassuringly to the space beside Kaitlin, inviting him closer. "As you have bonded with our Queen, and that bond has been confirmed, it is my honour to crown you as the new King of Elvendon."

Though initially surprised by the Elder's request, Keltor shook his head and responded with quiet resolve, "That's not why I bonded with Kaitlin."

The Elder offered reassurance, his tone gentle and knowing. "No, I know, and so do the spirits. If it had not been a true bonding, they would have discerned your true intentions."

Kaitlin turned to Keltor, her eyes full of understanding and certainty. "Keltor," she said softly, reaching out to him, "it's okay. This is what's meant to happen, I know it is." Her words, tender and sincere, provided him with the comfort he needed.

Meeting her gaze, Keltor felt his heart tremble with the depth of love he held for her. He nodded, acceptance shining in his eyes, and took her offered hand.

The Elder then addressed him formally. "Please, Keltor Dracon, kneel before me."

At Kaitlin's gentle release, Keltor let go of her hand. With a composed gesture, he swept the other side of his cloak behind his shoulders and knelt beside her, ready to accept the honour that awaited him.

The Elder raised his voice so all assembled could hear. "Now, let it be known that the Queen holds the final say in all matters of

Elvendon. She is the first ruler, and her King stands as her aid. The King, in turn, is granted the same rightful power of authority as the Queen with respect to their subjects, and it is expected that the people of Elvendon will heed his commands as they would hers.

However, should the Queen pass, the throne will not pass to the King but to a child born of the Queen herself. This child shall ascend to the throne upon reaching the age of maturity, and until that time, the King may guide and support the young heir. If, however, the King were to father an illegitimate child with another woman, that child would have no right to the throne and would be excluded from the royal court.

As Keltor is not of royal blood, it is decreed that no sibling or other family member of his may be granted a royal title. Instead, they may choose to accept the title of Lord or Lady, should they so wish. The law is clear and guided by the spirits.

The Elder turned to Keltor, his tone gentle yet resolute. "If you are accepting of this, Keltor, and of our law and the law of the spirits, then we may proceed."

Keltor, understanding the gravity of what was being asked, nodded in solemn agreement. "Yes, of course, I agree," he confirmed.

The Elder began the ancient rite, his voice resonant as he intoned, "*Elarma, otswan neraspar.*" As the sacred words floated through the twilight air, silvery motes of light rose from the moss-carpeted earth and gathered above Keltor's head. Shafts of moonlight filtered down between towering trunks and leafy canopies, and with every syllable, the forest seemed to deepen its hush. With reverent grace, the Elder lowered the crown, and as it hovered for a breathless moment, radiant runes shimmered and danced along its golden rim, scattering prismatic patterns across the ferns and undergrowth.

The chant echoed: "*Elarma, otswan neraspar.*" At that instant, the crown sparked to life, suffused with a celestial glow that swelled and spilled out in a cascade of luminous energy. As the diadem settled onto Keltor's brow, a rippling wave of light swept through his body, briefly illuminating the veins of his hands and

187

the hem of his cloak with iridescent fire. The ancient oaks seemed to whisper in chorus, a faint melody of ethereal voices rising from roots and branches—the spirits and ancestors of Elvendon welcoming their new sovereign.

The Elder's eyes glistened with awe as he proclaimed, voice ringing with both authority and wonder, "With the power from the spirits, and our ancestors, I proclaim that Keltor Dracon is now our new King. Please, Keltor, rise."

Keltor rose to his feet, his movements steady and dignified. As he stood, Kaitlin's eyes shimmered with tears of love and pride. She quickly reached for his hand, holding it tightly in hers. He returned her gesture with a gentle, reassuring smile, his sharp blue eyes meeting hers and conveying a silent promise of unity and devotion.

The Elder's voice rang out, addressing those gathered for the ceremony. "Please, those of you who have been honoured in witnessing this evening's events, stand for the new King and Queen of Elvendon."

Responding to the Elder's call, the assembled crowd rose to their feet in unison. Applause echoed throughout the sacred clearing, and among the cheers, Logan's loud whistle pierced the air. Catching sight of his friend, Keltor grinned in acknowledgement, a spark of camaraderie lighting his features.

As the applause continued, the Elder stepped forward. With solemn reverence, he knelt on one knee before Kaitlin and Keltor, declaring, "I proclaim my loyalty and devotion to our new Queen and King of Elvendon."

"I proclaim my loyalty and devotion to our new Queen and King of Elvendon," the crowd behind them echoed in unison. At these words, Keltor and Kaitlin turned to face the assembly. Kaitlin's eyes widened in astonishment as she beheld the entire deodar tribe, the elves, and even her aunt, all kneeling and bowing in a gesture of respect to her and Keltor.

The moment was almost overwhelming, and though Kaitlin struggled to find her voice, she knew she must respond. Gathering herself, she spoke, "Thank you, all of you, and as your Queen, and

Keltor, your King, we promise you, we will take back our Kingdom of Elvendon."

As her words resonated through the clearing, the crowd rose to their feet, applause breaking out in a slow and steady rhythm. Keltor gave Kaitlin's hand a reassuring squeeze, and she glanced at him, sharing a smile filled with hope and resolve. When the applause faded, the Elder stepped forward once more, drawing their attention back to him.

The Elder's eyes sparkled with delight as he exclaimed, "Now, I believe, there is the matter of a small party to attend?" His words lifted the tension in the air, prompting Kaitlin and Keltor to share a laugh of pure relief, the weight of the ceremony momentarily forgotten.

Just then, Esimae's voice rang out, "Kaitlin," drawing her attention. Kaitlin spun around, her face alight with amazement and joy. "Oh my god, Esimae, what the hell just happened?" she exclaimed, her laughter bubbling up as her aunt swept her into a warm embrace.

Esimae smiled fondly at her niece, answering with gentle humour, "Nothing much, you just got bonded, and are now officially a Queen."

Turning to Keltor, Esimae's eyes twinkled mischievously. "You know, I always did like you," she said, punctuating her words with a playful wink.

Keltor's grin was broad and genuine as he replied, "Yeah, I know, Esimae." He stepped forward, returning Esimae's embrace, their camaraderie evident to all watching.

"Congratulations!" Alarna cheered as she hurried over to Kaitlin and Keltor, her face bright with delight. Logan, grinning broadly, chimed in, "Yes, congratulations to you both. See, you doubter." His teasing tone was unmistakable.

Kaitlin looked at him, perplexed. Sensing her confusion, Logan explained, "He wasn't certain that you would be happy we had done this without telling you."

With a warm smile, Kaitlin reassured them, "Well, I am, and I'm grateful to all of you that conspired against me."

189

Alarna laughed, her eyes twinkling. "It was great fun, I have to say." Suddenly, she winced and placed a hand gently on her bump. "Ouch, you little—" she muttered, half-amused, half-exasperated.

Concerned, Kaitlin asked, "Kicking again?"

Alarna nodded, her expression softening. "Yes, I think he's hungry. I'd best go and eat something."

Logan, ever quick with a quip, teased her, "Ah, see, you said he. You're coming around to the fact that I know it's a boy." He wrapped an arm around Alarna's shoulders affectionately.

"Oh shush," she retorted, rolling her eyes but unable to hide a fond smile. She bowed her head respectfully to Kaitlin.

Kaitlin nodded back at Alarna, watching fondly as she and Logan made their way out. A warm smile lingered on Kaitlin's face. "I love those two, they're so funny together," she remarked, her eyes following the pair.

Keltor chuckled in agreement. "Yeah, me too," he replied, sharing in her affection for their friends.

Suddenly, a thought occurred to Kaitlin, and she looked up at Keltor, a hint of playful concern in her voice. "Hey, I just had a thought, we missed out a part of the ceremony," she said, realising something had been overlooked.

Keltor looked at her, uncertain. "What part?" he asked, genuinely unsure of what she meant.

"The best part, when you're supposed to kiss the bride," Kaitlin explained, a teasing smile appearing on her lips.

Keltor let out a laugh, the sparkle in his eyes matching hers. "Oh yeah, well I had best make up for it now then, my wife," he declared. Before she could offer a witty retort, he pulled her gently into his arms and kissed her.

As they kissed, the twigs and flowers woven into their ceremonial crowns became tangled, causing them both to laugh. "Hang on," Keltor said with amusement as he carefully untangled them.

Kaitlin grinned as they separated. "We can't keep these on," she said, removing her crown and holding it with a smile for Keltor.

"Whoa," Keltor said, staring intently at Kaitlin's forehead.

"What is it?" she asked, reaching up to touch the spot in question.

Keltor gently guided her hand to the area. "There's a mark, an Elvendon symbol, embedded right there." He pressed her finger softly against the raised mark.

"What the hell," Kaitlin murmured, running her fingers over the unfamiliar raised shape.

Keltor examined it closely. "I mean, it's not massive, only about an inch," he said, still studying the mark.

Kaitlin glanced at Keltor thoughtfully before making a sudden request. "Take yours off," she said, her tone unexpectedly serious.

Keltor blinked in confusion. "What?" he asked, uncertain what she meant.

"Your crown, take it off," Kaitlin clarified, gesturing towards the ceremonial headpiece.

Obliging, Keltor reached up and removed his crown, mirroring Kaitlin's earlier action. As soon as he did, Kaitlin's eyes widened with realisation. "Ooh, you have it too," she observed, reaching out and lightly touching his forehead where the mark appeared.

"No," Keltor replied, his fingers moving to the spot as she withdrew hers. He frowned, feeling the unfamiliar raised shape beneath his skin. "What is it?" he asked, his curiosity piqued and concern clear in his voice.

The Elder approached, offering assistance. "Shall I relieve you of those?" he asked as he drew alongside them, referring to the ceremonial crowns. "I appreciate they're not quite as stunning as the real things, but once you take back Elvendon we can hold another ceremony with the real crowns, if you want to, that is."

Kaitlin responded with gratitude, handing her crown over. "No, it was so kind of you to do this at such short notice, thank you." Her attention, however, quickly shifted to the marks on their foreheads. "What are these marks on our foreheads?" she questioned.

The Elder explained, "They are your Royal signatures, so even without your crown, everyone will know who you are."

191

Kaitlin's reaction was immediate and worried. "Oh shit," she mumbled, prompting a gentle admonishment from Keltor. "Kitcat," he said.

"Sorry, but that's not going to help us, is it?" Kaitlin continued, voicing her concern. "How are we going to hide or blend in with a big fat target on our heads as to who we are?"

Keltor addressed the Elder, seeking a solution. "Can we hide them, magically I mean?" he asked.

The Elder responded to Keltor's query with pragmatic wit. "Well, yes, I guess if you knew a wizard," he said, one eyebrow raised in amusement.

Kaitlin, lowering her voice conspiratorially, hinted that a solution might already be at hand. "Well, I might know one," she murmured, a sly smile glinting in her eyes as she glanced at Keltor. Their eyes met, and Keltor returned her smile, sharing in the unspoken understanding between them.

Turning his attention back to the Elder, Keltor offered his thanks. "Okay, we've got this, thank you, for everything, and for coming out here for the ceremony, and the crowning. Please, if you're hungry, we have a few extras at dinner this evening. Just through there," he said, gesturing back through the archway between the trees.

The Elder nodded appreciatively. "Yes, thank you kindly, I believe I will stop the night, and Logan has offered to escort me back to my hiding place in the morning." Taking both crowns, he placed them safely in his sack before making his way towards the main camp.

"So, can you do it?" Kaitlin asked, her tone laced with both hope and apprehension.

Keltor nodded confidently. "Yeah, I can do a concealment spell. Just give me a minute to find it." He closed his eyes for a moment, gathering his focus. "Yep, I know it. I'm sure you can do it as well, just in case for any reason we get separated and it appears again."

He then lifted a finger, pointing purposefully at her forehead as he prepared to cast the spell. Instinctively, Kaitlin reached out and grabbed his arm, her nerves getting the better of her.

"You are sure you know what you're doing? You're not going to blast out my brain or something?" she asked, only half-joking.

"No," Keltor replied, though he couldn't resist frowning and pretending to consider her question more seriously. The moment lingered, and Kaitlin quickly realised he was teasing her.

"So not funny," she muttered, shaking her head at his joke.

Keltor grinned at her, the tension easing between them. "Okay. Ready?"

She nodded, bracing herself for the magic to come.

"*Ilumara concealmar polsarma*," Keltor intoned, his voice steady as he focused on the spell. Kaitlin felt a fleeting warmth spread across her forehead before the sensation vanished.

"Did it work?" she asked, seeking reassurance.

Keltor looked at Kaitlin with an encouraging smile. "Yes, now do you want to try on me?" he asked, his tone gentle.

Kaitlin considered this for a moment, her eyes narrowing thoughtfully. "Hmm," she mused. After a brief pause, she nodded in agreement. "Okay."

She lifted her hand, steadying herself as she directed her finger towards the mark on Keltor's forehead. Focusing intently, she spoke the incantation, "*Ilumara concealmar polsarma*."

Keltor's brow creased as he felt the comforting warmth of her magic begin to work, gradually erasing the mark from his skin.

"Okay?" he asked, seeking reassurance that the spell had been successful.

Kaitlin smiled and nodded. "Yep, we're good." Her relief and pride were evident in her voice. She then hooked her arm through his, her eyes bright with anticipation. "Come on, I'm hungry, let's go and celebrate, my husband," she said, grinning up at him as they prepared to rejoin their companions.

As they made their way back through the graceful arch of trees and entered the camp, a wave of applause greeted them. Both the tribe and the elves rose to their feet, clapping in honour of their arrival. Kaitlin, feeling a warm blush creep across her cheeks, held onto Keltor's arm more tightly. A laugh escaped her lips as she took in the scene before them. "Oh my god, this is madness," she said, her voice full of disbelief and delight.

Spread out before them was a feast fit for royalty. A wild boar turned slowly over the fire, its aroma wafting through the air. Nearby, fresh salmon, caught from the lake, was laid out alongside generous portions of green leaves and a bounty of foraged delicacies. The abundance and care evident in the spread surprised Kaitlin, especially given all the challenges they had recently faced.

Uly stepped forward to greet them, offering a respectful bow. "My Queen," he addressed Kaitlin formally, then turned to Keltor with a broad grin. "And my King." Keltor responded by playfully slapping Uly's arm in a gesture of camaraderie. "Your feast awaits you," Uly announced, before stepping aside to let them pass.

Still marvelling at the preparations, Kaitlin turned to Keltor. "Keltor, this is incredible. How have they managed to do all this for us, with everything that's going on?" she asked, her voice edged with wonder.

Keltor smiled and replied, "Because, for today, we live for the moment, and this moment is the most wonderful in all of time." He looked at Kaitlin, and as their eyes met, she nodded in agreement. He added reassuringly, "And don't worry, we have scouts out and about, keeping an eye."

The mood in the camp was lifted by the sound of music; one of the deodar women began to play her lute, the melody drifting through the gathering. Before long, everyone was up and dancing, the tensions of the elven war momentarily set aside as they celebrated with Kaitlin and Keltor. If there was one thing the deodars excelled at, it was throwing a celebration.

The feast that evening was nothing short of delightful, with everyone enjoying generous helpings of wild boar which proved to be a particular favourite amongst the group. Laughter and the joyful sounds of children playing filled the camp, a welcome change after two tense days where quiet and caution had been necessary. The renewed sense of freedom and merriment brought hope to Kaitlin, who found herself daring to believe that she and Keltor might truly be able to rise to the challenges before them. The extraordinary events of the day still seemed almost unreal, their lives having been changed so swiftly and dramatically.

As night gently descended over the valley and crept into the surrounding forest, a tranquil calm settled upon the encampment. The evening gradually drew to a close, with people beginning to find their places for the night. Kaitlin found herself seated on a log positioned close to the fire, quietly observing the scene. She watched as Keltor engaged in lively conversation and playful banter with Logan, their laughter mingling with the night air. Nearby, Alarna rested against the sturdy trunk of a tree, her exhaustion evident as she struggled to stay awake. The night itself was serene and still, the heavens above clear and adorned with a shimmering blanket of stars, providing a peaceful end to an eventful day.

As Kaitlin sat quietly, she gazed down at the bonding mark on her finger. With the thumb of her other hand, she gently traced the intricate design. The mark reminded her of a Celtic knot tree, its delicate branches weaving and curling around and down her finger, symbolising the deep connection she now shared with Keltor.

Suddenly, a woman's voice broke through her thoughts. Kaitlin looked up to see her aunt, Esimae, standing nearby, a lantern casting a pool of warm light around her. Esimae smiled softly.

"Oh, hey Esimae," Kaitlin greeted her, returning the smile. She gestured to the space beside her on the log. "Did you want to sit?"

Esimae shook her head. "No, no, I'm going to hit the hay so to speak. Are you okay now?" she asked, her voice gentle with concern.

"Me?" Kaitlin replied, a hint of surprise in her tone.

"Yes, you know, after what we talked about this morning," Esimae clarified.

Kaitlin felt a flush of embarrassment, but she managed a reassuring smile. "Oh, that. Yes," she answered. "I'm good, thank you. Don't worry, I'm ready to be the Queen. I totally understand what I need to do, and I'm prepared for it. Whether I'm going to be any good at it is another question, but I'm going to give it a damn good go."

"Good girl. Well, if you need to talk, just come and find me, anytime about anything, okay?" Esimae assured Kaitlin, her voice warm with encouragement.

Kaitlin nodded in response, a grateful smile appearing on her face.

"And thank you," Kaitlin added softly.

Esimae looked at her with a curious expression. "For what?" she asked.

"For not being cross at me bonding with Keltor."

Esimae shook her head gently. "Why would I be cross?" she replied.

Kaitlin hesitated, then explained, "Well, I wasn't sure how you felt about him."

"Honey, I know in the beginning I was a bit off with him, but that was only because of what I thought Jaike had done to me. Over the last few days, I have seen how much he loves you, and to be honest, I must admit I was wrong."

"Wrong?" Kaitlin asked, surprised.

Esimae nodded, glancing towards Keltor, who was still engaged in cheerful banter with Logan. "Yes, when I said that he was just your Protector. He is far more than that, this I can see now. You were both destined to be together, and I was foolish to try and stop it."

Kaitlin rose to her feet, her gratitude evident. "No, you were just looking out for me, and I appreciate everything you have done for me, and for Keltor."

Esimae smiled wryly. "Yes, well, just don't tell him I said I was wrong, okay?" she said, her tone playful.

"I won't," Kaitlin replied, matching her aunt's smile.

Esimae's expression became gentle once more. "Anyway, I came here to tell you that we've sorted you out a private place for you for tonight."

Kaitlin looked at her in surprise. "What, why?"

Esimae's eyes sparkled mischievously. "Well, you know, it is your bonding night," she said, smiling with a twinkle in her eye.

Kaitlin felt her cheeks flush with embarrassment. "Esimae," she murmured, clearly feeling awkward.

Her aunt responded with a gentle laugh. "Come on, let me show you. It's totally private and safe, so don't worry about anyone prying."

Rolling her eyes at her aunt's motherly tone, Kaitlin picked up the lantern resting by her feet and followed Esimae through the trees. The pair walked beneath the arched branches, travelling along the path to the place where Kaitlin and Keltor had once bonded. Esimae continued ahead for several more minutes, until they reached the base of a small, rocky gully.

"Come on, through here," Esimae said, raising her lantern in front of them. "Isn't it beautiful? Ren discovered it while scouting."

Esimae drew back a curtain of vines, revealing a small cave hidden behind them. A wave of nostalgia swept over Kaitlin as she recognised the intimate setting, reminiscent of the first time she and Keltor had been together.

The cave's interior glowed softly with candlelight. Though it was smaller than the cave they had stayed in before, the bedrolls and packs laid neatly on the ground created a cosy atmosphere.

Spotting a bottle, Kaitlin asked, "What's that?"

"It's wine," Esimae explained with a smile. "One of the deodars had a couple of bottles, can you believe it? So, Ren managed to acquire one."

Kaitlin laughed warmly. "Oh god, love her."

Esimae returned her smile. "Will it do? It's not quite the Ritz, but you know, it's private."

Kaitlin's gratitude was clear. "Esimae, it's perfect, thank you so much."

"Great, shall I get Keltor?" Esimae offered.

"No, I'll go and get him. I want to say goodnight to Alarna and Logan first."

197

"Okay," her aunt replied, and Kaitlin followed her back out of the cave and towards their camp.

"Good night, honey," Esimae said as they parted.

"Good night, Esimae, and thank you," Kaitlin answered.

It was astonishing to Kaitlin how meticulously everything had been arranged, right down to their wedding night. The care and consideration shown by everyone for both her and Keltor deeply moved her, filling her with gratitude. Yet, alongside this warmth, she felt a pang of regret for her earlier behaviour, recognising how childish she had been.

As she approached, Keltor greeted her warmly. "Hey, there you are," he remarked, noting how Alarna was so tired she was nearly asleep on her feet. He opened his arms, and Kaitlin nestled gratefully into his embrace.

"Good night and thank you so much for what you have done for us today. Really, I couldn't have imagined or planned a more perfect day," Kaitlin said, her voice filled with heartfelt appreciation. She hugged and kissed both Alarna and Logan on the cheek, expressing her thanks.

Logan returned her sentiment with a cheerful grin and a respectful dip of his head. "You're welcome; it was a great day. Good night, your highnesses," he replied. Keltor nodded in acknowledgement, and Alarna, weary from the day's excitement, bade them goodnight. Logan gently guided his wife back towards their sleeping area, his arm around her as the camp settled into a peaceful night.

"Right, ready for bed?" Keltor asked.

"Well, not quite," she replied holding on to her secret smile.

"Why, what you got planned," he asked.

"Come on, this lot have thought of everything even down to our wedding night."

Keltor glanced at Kaitlin with a gentle smile. "Right, ready for bed?" he asked, his tone light and expectant.

Kaitlin, however, was not quite ready to settle for the night. She clung onto a secretive smile, her excitement shimmering in her eyes. "Well, not quite," she replied, hinting at something special yet to come.

Curious, Keltor tilted his head, trying to read her intentions. "Why, what have you got planned?" he asked, sensing her playful mood.

Kaitlin grinned, her anticipation infectious. "Come on, this lot have thought of everything—even down to our wedding night."

Surprise flickered across Keltor's face, his eyes wide with amazement. "Our bonding night—we're getting a bonding night?" he exclaimed, clearly thrilled by the prospect.

"Yes, we are. Come on," Kaitlin replied, her grin growing wider. She took his hand, holding her lantern in the other, and gently pulled him back through the archway of trees. The soft glow illuminated their path as they moved together, leaving the bustle of the camp behind.

As they walked, Keltor's curiosity deepened. "Where are we going?" he asked, glancing around as they passed the spot where they had bonded earlier that day and continued onward, venturing out the other side.

With an animated sparkle in her eyes, Kaitlin turned to face him, walking backwards as she spoke. "Do you remember our first night together, in the cave?" she asked, her words filled with nostalgia and affection.

Keltor grinned, the memory clearly dear to him. "You really have to ask me that question?" he replied, his tone warm and playful.

"Well," Kaitlin continued, "it appears Ren has found us our own little cave in which to spend our wedding night—alone and away from everyone."

In disbelief, Keltor quickened his pace to catch up with her. "You're kidding?" he questioned eagerly.

"Nope," Kaitlin replied, stopping to pull back a vine that veiled the cave's entrance.

"Good job I had a bath then," Keltor remarked, leaning a hand on the entrance, his humour lightening the moment.

"Yeah, me too," Kaitlin agreed, sharing in his laughter.

"Well, go on then, wife, in you go," Keltor teased playfully, giving Kaitlin a gentle smack on the backside. She let out a mock holler, "Keltor!" but her protest quickly dissolved into laughter as she stepped inside the cosy cave, her spirits clearly lifted by his light-hearted jest.

"This is very cosy," Keltor remarked as he stooped to enter the cave. His fingers brushed the walls, which shimmered and sparkled in the gentle candlelight.

"I know it's a small space, but it's just for us, and we are finally alone," Kaitlin replied, her eyes shining with contentment.

Keltor leaned down towards her, raising his hand to cup her cheek tenderly. "I can't think of anywhere I would rather be, than here in this cave with my Queen." As he kissed her, they both knelt, and his arms wrapped securely around her, pulling her close into his embrace.

As their lips parted, Kaitlin whispered, "Keltor."

"Yes, Kitcat?" he responded softly, sweeping a stray lock of hair away from her eyes.

"Thank you."

"For what?" he asked, his gaze never leaving hers.

"For today. It was the most romantic and wonderful day." She took a deep breath, her chest rising and falling as she met his eyes.

He smiled gently. "I just wanted to make it special for you. I was really worried you would be cross and want the fancy wedding at the castle."

She shook her head firmly. "No, no. That's the last thing I would have wanted. What you did was just perfect—in the forest with our friends. It was enchanting and beautiful, and I know it must have been hard for you without your family witnessing it."

Keltor's voice was steady and full of warmth. "If it had just been the two of us, I would still be the happiest man alive. We can celebrate with them when all this is over, and you are sitting on that throne in Elvendon castle."

"With you, my King, beside me," she added with a smile, and he nodded in agreement.

"I will always be by your side, Kitcat. I love you so much."

200

Before she could respond, his lips found hers once more, and she groaned softly, overwhelmed by the depth of passion she felt from him.

Chapter Eight
The Trolls

Kaitlin was the first to awaken. She gently lifted her head and glanced over at Keltor, who was still peacefully asleep. Reaching out, she placed her hand firmly on his chest, feeling the steady rise and fall of his breath. Happiness filled her, and memories of the wonderful day before brought a warm smile to her face. She instinctively snuggled closer to him, savouring the comfort of his presence.

"Morning," Keltor greeted softly as he opened his eyes and found her watching him.

"Morning," Kaitlin replied, returning his smile. He wrapped his arms around her, pulling her into a tight embrace that left her feeling cherished and safe.

Kaitlin sighed with contentment, basking in the warmth of his skin against hers. In that moment, there was nowhere else she would rather be than nestled in his arms.

"Sleep well?" Keltor asked, his gaze lingering on hers, his heart brimming with joy.

"I did," she whispered in response.

He looked at her with wonder. "I can't believe you're my wife," he murmured, gently brushing a stray strand of hair from her eyes. "I never, ever thought this would happen. I was convinced that, because you're a princess, all I could ever be is your protector. I thought I would have to live with a broken heart for the rest of my life."

Kaitlin's hand rose to his shoulder, her fingers tracing lightly across it as she drew a deep breath.

"You know, I was terrified when I found out my father had made a deal with Aragon to marry me. As dreadful as it would have been to marry him, all I could think about was that it meant I could never be with you. Even if things had turned out differently and we hadn't had to kill Aragon, I still could never have married him. Keltor, I would have given everything up and run away with you if that was the only way we could be together."

Without a word, Keltor lowered his head towards Kaitlin, his hand rising gently to her cheek. Kaitlin closed her eyes in anticipation, and he kissed her tenderly.

"We were meant to be together, Kitcat. Right from the day we were born, the universe entwined our souls by sending those fairies to bring us together."

Kaitlin smiled, curiosity lighting her features. "You knew about the fairies?"

He nodded. "Yeah, I wasn't out hunting that morning, I was led by the fae to meet you. Because of my magic and trying to keep it a secret from everyone, I kept my distance from the other kids when I was younger in case they found out. Even Alarna didn't know, and I remember wishing to the spirits for a best friend. Although, to be honest, at first, I was a bit shocked you were a girl, that's why I hesitated behind the tree for a moment—I was deciding whether I wanted a girl as a best friend."

Kaitlin laughed at his confession.

He continued, "It made perfect sense, as you didn't know anyone in Elvendon, I could just be myself. I didn't have to worry about magic or the King finding out there was something odd about me."

"Keltor, I can't believe you've never told me this," Kaitlin said, moving into his arms as he kissed the top of her head.

He held her close. "I suppose with everything going on I didn't really think about it, until now. If it hadn't been for those fairies, we might not be together today. You know, I have never seen them since." Keltor looked down at her, waiting until she met his gaze. "I could never have imagined that first meeting in the forest would lead to this. That I would find my soul mate, my best friend, and love her with all my heart and my entire being."

"Keltor," she sighed softly, "I can't even put into words how much I love you; my greatest fear is losing you in this war." At the thought, her heart shuddered with sadness.

Keltor gently brushed his thumb across Kaitlin's cheek, his voice soft but resolute. "Hey," he said, "I'm not going to leave you. I promise we will survive this, I just know we will."

Kaitlin let out a quiet sigh, clinging to the peacefulness of the moment. "I really don't want to get up," she admitted, her voice barely above a whisper. "I could spend the entire day here, with you like this."

A faint smile tugged at Keltor's lips as he replied, "Me too, but I suppose we'd better. The fact no one has come for us yet means it must still be early, but the camp will be waking up soon and we should be there."

"Yeah, I guess," she breathed, reluctant to let go of the comfort they shared.

Keltor reached out and gently lifted her chin, guiding her gaze to meet his. He gave her the most wonderful smile before leaning in to kiss her, sealing his promise with a tender embrace.

The air was crisp and cool that morning as they emerged from the small cave. Kaitlin gave a slight shudder, pulling her cloak tighter around herself to ward off the chill. A light mist danced across the forest floor, while sunlight glistened through the tops of the trees, its rays reaching down and promising to burn away the haze, heralding the arrival of a beautiful day.

Kaitlin's eyes took in the tranquil scene, and she breathed deeply, savouring the earthy freshness of the morning. As Keltor slipped his hand into hers, he offered her a gentle smile. "It's beautiful, isn't it?" she asked, and he nodded in agreement as he looked at her.

"Worth fighting for?" he questioned quietly. Turning to face him, Kaitlin took up his other hand, her thumbs gently rubbing over his knuckles. "Yes, worth fighting for," she replied, meeting the deep blueness of his eyes. She closed her eyes as he leaned in to kiss her, feeling that, in that moment, her world could not have been more perfect.

As they walked into camp, they found it alive with activity. Fires had been stoked, and pots were already cooking porridge, filling the air with the comforting aroma of breakfast.

As Keltor and Kaitlin approached the campfire, Logan greeted them with a broad grin and a quick nod of his head. "Morning, your highnesses," he said cheerfully. He and Alarna were seated on a log near the fire, each with a bowl of steaming porridge in hand.

Keltor returned the grin. "Morning," he replied.

Alarna looked up, offering, "Breakfast?" Kaitlin's stomach rumbled in response, and she nodded eagerly. "Yeah, I'm starving," Kaitlin replied as she crouched down, picking up the ladle and serving porridge into two bowls from the stack on the ground.

With a mischievous glint in his eye, Logan remarked, "It was a good night then," raising an eyebrow at Keltor. Alarna, clearly embarrassed by his comment, immediately elbowed him sharply in the chest. "Logan, you can't ask that!" she whispered, her tone disapproving.

Keltor merely smirked at Logan, who ducked his head, stifling a laugh. "Yeah, it was," Keltor admitted as he crouched beside Kaitlin. She turned to look at him, curiosity in her eyes. "In fact," he continued, "it was one of the best of my life."

Kaitlin raised an eyebrow and pursed her lips, teasing, "One of the best?" She waited expectantly for his answer. Leaning in close, Keltor whispered softly in her ear, "The first cave was the best, and it always will be." Kaitlin smiled affectionately and pressed her cheek gently against his in response.

Their moment was interrupted by Logan, who called out playfully, "Hey, your highnesses, your porridge is getting cold." Keltor caught Logan's eye and grinned, then he and Kaitlin stood and walked over to join the others on the log. Kaitlin sat down beside Alarna, with Keltor taking the spot on her other side.

Alarna leaned in and apologised in a whisper, "Sorry, he's such a jerk sometimes." Kaitlin shrugged off the comment, replying softly, "It's fine, really." She lowered her voice further, a playful smile tugging at her lips, "And, I did have a really good night," she confided, raising an eyebrow at Alarna.

After breakfast, the group set about tidying the camp. The logs they had used for sitting around the fire were returned to their original places, and the fires were carefully dismantled to remove any sign of their presence. As the others finished, Kaitlin remained close to Keltor, quietly observing him. She watched with admiration as he used his magic to gather up the remnants scattered across the forest floor, lifting twigs and leaves into the air and letting them drift back down. The hope was that this subtle magic would help conceal their tracks from any wandering Aranstream soldiers.

The party then set off, pressing deeper into the forest. Their progress was slow and demanding over the course of the next day. The morning sun shone brightly, unimpeded by clouds, and dappled light filtered through the outstretched branches of oak and ash trees. The terrain was challenging, with deadwood strewn across the ground, tangled among the gnarled roots. Despite the hardship, the forest was alive with the cheerful sounds of birdsong overhead, and the day itself was undeniably beautiful.

By midday, the party reached the designated point where Keltor and Kaitlin would separate from the rest to begin their journey towards the trolls. The mood was a mixture of determination and underlying concern as farewells were exchanged.

Kaitlin embraced her aunt tightly, offering reassurance. "We shouldn't be more than a day or so," she said, her tone both confident and comforting. Keltor expanded on their plan for the benefit of the group: "We're kind of going in the same direction, just a slight detour. Hopefully, we'll reach the trolls by sunset, make the arrangements that evening, and get back to you all by late afternoon the next day."

He continued, mapping out their movements with careful precision. "By then, you should have reached the narrow ridge,

and we'll be with you before we go into the Eccleston forest."
Turning to Logan, Keltor gave a firm instruction, "Logan, please,
keep a good watch, especially on the children, ahead of you and
to the rear. As you get nearer to the forest, it's not just Aranstream
soldiers you need to watch for – there are unknown creatures that
live in that forest."

Logan responded with confidence, tapping Keltor's arm in a
gesture of camaraderie. "Don't worry, we'll be okay," he assured
him.

With a final word, Keltor nodded. "Good, stay safe." He placed
a protective hand on Kaitlin's back and guided her away, marking
the moment the two groups set out on their separate paths.

As Kaitlin and Keltor moved further away from the rest of the
party, worry crept into Kaitlin's voice. "They will be okay, won't
they?" she asked anxiously.

Keltor offered reassurance, sounding confident as he answered,
"Yeah, I'm sure they'll be fine. It's really unlikely that Aranstream
soldiers will be out this far. Anyway, Logan's a good soldier – he
knows the drill."

Though comforted, Kaitlin pressed on, "Yeah, I guess. So do
we have a plan?" She slipped her arm through his as they walked,
searching his face for answers.

Keltor glanced at her, then explained quietly, "Well, kind of.
We need to gather a strong band of men—" He paused as Kaitlin
squeezed his arm, prompting him to add with a grin, "—and
women. An elite force, if you like, to take down Aranstream castle
first. My plan is still to break into the encampment and find
Commander Talbot. Once he knows you're alive, he'll rally the
men, and we'll break out our army."

Kaitlin's tone shifted, a touch of sarcasm colouring her words.
"And what will I be doing while you're risking your life breaking
into Aranstream?"

Keltor stopped, forcing her to halt as well. His voice was firm.
"Kaitlin, we must keep you safe. I know you want to come with
me and fight at Aranstream, but you can't. Once we have been to
the trolls and then settled the Deodars into the witches' fortress,

we'll head back to Elvendon, collect Mum, and then I will take you all to the outlander's cottage in the forest."

Kaitlin shook her head in immediate refusal. "No."

Surprised, Keltor asked, "What do you mean, no?"

Determined, Kaitlin replied, "Keltor, I'm not sitting waiting for you in a cottage in the forest. I will come with you to Aranstream."

He protested, concern etched in his features. "Kaitlin, no, you need to stay safe."

She met his gaze, resolute. "Yes, I know that, but I also need to help. Keltor, you keep saying I need to be their Queen—then let me help fight. I have my magic, I can help."

Keltor opened his mouth to argue, but Kaitlin raised her hand, silencing him. "I promise I'll keep back when you go into the encampment; I'll find a place to hide. There must be some abandoned houses or farms nearby, I'll be fine. I cannot and will not sit waiting for you. What if something goes wrong? What if Commander Talbot is dead and you can't get out? I couldn't bear it."

Keltor let out a heavy sigh, his reluctance evident. He didn't want to give in to Kaitlin, but he recognised her stubbornness. As Queen of Elvendon and their first ruler, she had earned her place. Although he knew she would never use her status to override him in matters of combat or strategy, he understood he owed her the opportunity to contribute.

"All right," he conceded, "if, and only if, I can find a safe house on the outskirts of Aranstream. If we arrive and there isn't anywhere suitable, I'm taking you straight to the cottage in the forest."

Kaitlin paused, considering his words carefully, before finally nodding her agreement. "Agreed," she replied, her resolve clear.

The hours slipped quietly by as morning gradually surrendered to the afternoon, and the afternoon in turn faded into dusk. Eventually, they emerged from the thick cover of the forest, stepping cautiously into the open. Ahead, an expansive field opened before them, its long spring grasses swaying gently in the evening breeze. The tranquil sound of flowing water drifted towards them, a clear indication that they had reached the river at last. Across the rippling water, a great mountain rose sharply, its imposing form silhouetted against the darkening sky—the very mountain rumoured to be the home of the trolls.

They walked purposefully towards the riverbank, planning to follow the river's course for another mile before crossing at the bridge further upstream. Suddenly, Keltor came to an abrupt halt, his body tense with alertness.

"What is it?" Kaitlin asked, her voice barely above a whisper, as she felt his grip tighten on her arm, holding her back from moving forward.

"Shh," Keltor cautioned urgently, scanning the forest behind them with sharp, anxious eyes. His heartbeat thundered in his chest, a surge of panic taking hold.

Keltor's voice cut through the tension, urging Kaitlin to act quickly. "Get down, now!" he whispered, gripping her arm tightly and pulling her harshly into the shelter of the long grass. Kaitlin's eyes widened in horror as she realised what he had heard—a group of Aranstream soldiers on horseback appeared in the distance.

"Move backwards, slowly," Keltor instructed in a low voice, his tone urgent. "Keep low to the ground. I don't think they saw us."

With careful, deliberate movements, they began to crawl through the thick grass, edging away from the danger and towards the river. Kaitlin could feel her heart pounding so fiercely she feared it might give them away. Only when their feet touched the muddy riverbank did they stop.

Keltor glanced at her apologetically. "I'm sorry," he whispered, "but we need to go in."

Bracing herself, Kaitlin slid into the freezing water. She hastily pressed her dress down, allowing the weight of the water to help her sink beneath the surface. Together, they moved quietly towards the dense reeds lining the bank, Keltor pulling her close as they submerged themselves as much as possible, leaving only their faces exposed and hidden among the reeds.

Moments later, a procession of roughly fifty men, led by King Iwein, thundered past on horseback, oblivious to the two fugitives concealed at the water's edge.

The water was icy cold, running straight down from the mountains, and Kaitlin couldn't help but shiver violently against its chill. Keltor, sensing her discomfort, gently stroked her arm with his thumb to soothe her as he held her securely in the reeds.

Peering through the dense greenery, Kaitlin whispered, her voice tinged with confusion and fear, "What the hell are they all doing over here?"

Keltor's brow furrowed as he replied in a low voice, "I don't know, but this is really bad."

Concern flickered in Kaitlin's eyes as she asked, "Will Esimae and the tribe be safe?"

Keltor nodded, reassuring her softly, "I think so. They're heading back towards Elvendon. The pass I told you about is two days in that direction."

Kaitlin's mind raced as she considered the danger. "So, they might go via the Deodar village and see them all gone?"

He agreed quietly, "There's a good chance they will."

Kaitlin exhaled a shaky breath, relief mingling with anxiety. "Thank god we didn't go that way, or we would have run straight into them."

Keltor nodded in silent agreement, his head pressed gently against hers as they remained concealed, listening for any sign that the danger had passed.

Kaitlin suddenly whispered, alarm evident in her voice, and her hand gripped Keltor's tightly. Their eyes widened as they watched a procession of men trailing behind the mounted group. These men were bound together with ropes, each one linked to the next and were being led by soldiers on horseback.

"Who are they?" Kaitlin asked, her whisper trembling with uncertainty.

"I'm not sure. They're not elves—they look human," Keltor replied, his eyes narrowed in confusion.

"They can't possibly be, though, can they?" she pressed, struggling to accept what she saw.

Keltor shook his head, still watching the line of prisoners. "Kaitlin, I really don't know. No one ever crosses over the gorge. The lands stretch for hundreds—maybe thousands—of miles, so perhaps there are other settlements, but we've always stayed within our territory."

"Why would he venture beyond our realms? He isn't powerful enough to challenge another kingdom, surely?" Kaitlin questioned, frowning as she tried to make sense of the scene.

"I wouldn't have thought so," Keltor replied, shaking his head once more.

Kaitlin, curiosity and concern mingling in her expression, tried to raise herself slightly out of the water to get a better look. "What's in that waggon?" she asked.

"No, get down—we can't risk being seen," Keltor cautioned firmly, pulling her back down and holding her securely until the entire procession had passed them by.

"Can we get out now?" Kaitlin asked, turning her head towards Keltor. She was shivering, the cold biting through her wet clothes and chilling her to the bone.

Keltor smiled gently at her but shook his head. "No, just wait a while longer."

"Why, it's freezing," she protested, hugging herself for warmth.

He nodded his head back towards the meadow. "That's why."

Kaitlin followed his gaze and saw six men on horseback riding across the meadow. Her heart raced as she realised the danger was not yet over.

Keltor explained quietly, "He will have scouts riding behind. It's what we would do in Elvendon if the King was out on patrol."

She leaned into him for reassurance, and he pulled her even closer, arms tightening protectively around her.

Worry etched across her face, Kaitlin whispered with concern, "Do you think they found the trolls?"

Keltor gave a heavy sigh, uncertain and anxious about what might happen next.

"I think there is a good chance they have, unfortunately. They would have seen the bridge and investigated, although with any luck they may not have found the entrance to the castle inside the mountain. They may think they just live in those caves."

As another four men on horseback rode by, Keltor turned to Kaitlin with a plan. "Do you think you can swim to the other side, the water is pretty calm here? As we're wet, we might as well get over the river here," he suggested. Kaitlin nodded in agreement, and Keltor released her from his embrace.

Moving cautiously, the pair swam across the width of the river. Once they reached the far bank, they scrambled out quickly, seeking shelter in a cluster of bushes at the edge. Hidden from view, they sat down together, attempting to catch their breath and regain some warmth.

Kaitlin shivered from the chill, prompting Keltor to wrap his arm protectively around her. She leaned into him, grateful for the comfort. "We'll wait another hour and then head off," Keltor said quietly, "just to be on the safe side."

Kaitlin's voice trembled with anxiety as she glanced at Keltor. "Keltor, what do we do if they have attacked the trolls? We won't be able to get their help," she said, her worry evident as she sought reassurance.

Keltor gently stroked her wet hair, offering what comfort he could. "I don't know," he admitted honestly. "I suppose we'll just have to carry on without them. Once we get the Deodars to safety, we'll return, collect my mum, and make our way into the Forest of Time. Remember the old forester I told you about? He hated King Iwein even before all this started. I'm certain he'll give us shelter, and we can use it as a safe house. With any luck, he might know where other Elvendons are hiding, and perhaps they'll be willing to help us."

Kaitlin sighed heavily, clearly overwhelmed. "Honestly, I can't believe any of this is happening. It was difficult enough to accept that I wasn't human, and now we're in the middle of an elven war." She paused, her voice softening as she looked into Keltor's eyes. "I just want it all to be over. I want us to be safe. Keltor, I'm so frightened of something happening to you."

Keltor pressed a gentle kiss to the top of her head, his promise earnest yet weighted with unspoken worry. "Kaitlin, I'll be okay. I promise, I'm not going to leave you—ever." Yet, deep in his heart, the promise lingered with uncertainty, for he knew that if it meant saving her life, he would be willing to sacrifice his own.

As the sun began to sink lower in the sky, casting long shadows across the riverbank, Keltor spoke quietly but firmly. "Come on," he announced, glancing at Kaitlin. "We should be safe to go now."

Both rose from their hiding place, shaking off the chill that clung to their damp clothes. Keltor turned to Kaitlin and said, "Take your cloak off. I'll try and wring out some of the water."

Kaitlin nodded, unclasped her cloak, and handed it over. Keltor took it, twisting the heavy fabric tightly in his hands, squeezing out as much water as possible. The effort sent a trickle of water to the ground, but the cloak remained stubbornly damp.

While Keltor worked on her cloak, Kaitlin pulled her wet hair away from her face, then gripped the hem of her dress and scrunched it up, wringing out the water as best she could. The cool air bit at her skin, but she persevered, determined not to let the discomfort slow her down.

When Keltor finished, he handed the cloak back to Kaitlin. "Here, it's still wet, but at least it's not dripping," he said, offering a small, reassuring smile.

"Thank you," Kaitlin replied gratefully, refastening the cloak around her throat and pulling it close for warmth.

Keltor then repeated the process with his own cloak, wringing it out before draping it over his shoulders once more. He untied his hair, shook it loose, and ran his fingers through it, working out the knots left by their swim across the river.

Kaitlin smiled at Keltor, amusement dancing in her eyes.

"What?" he asked, catching her grin and raising an eyebrow in curiosity.

She shook her head, laughter threatening in her voice. "Nothing. You just reminded me of a shampoo advert."

Keltor stared at her in disbelief and repeated her words with mock sarcasm, "A shampoo advert? Really!"

"Yeah," Kaitlin answered, giggling at the incredulous expression on his face. "You know what a shampoo advert is, right?"

He gave her a look and replied with a touch of indignation as he began tying his hair back into a ponytail, "Of course I do. I've seen human TV."

"When you shook your hair and ran your fingers through it just now," she continued, her tone turning playful and direct as she met his gaze, "that was hot."

Keltor arched his brow, a teasing smile tugging at his lips. "Really?"

"Yes," Kaitlin replied, mirroring his gesture by raising her own eyebrow in return.

Keltor grinned and, with a hint of mischief in his tone, joked, "Do you want me to do it again?"

Kaitlin's laughter bubbled out, ringing across the quiet riverbank. Realising just how loudly she had laughed, she quickly glanced about placing her hand over her mouth, her amusement mingling with a touch of embarrassment at the unexpected volume of her reaction.

"Come on, we should really get going," he said, struggling to maintain a straight face as amusement danced in his eyes. He slipped his arm around Kaitlin's shoulders, drawing her close with a gentle, reassuring gesture.

Kaitlin responded by resting her head on his shoulder, signalling her agreement without words. Together, they set off along the tranquil riverbank, heading steadily towards the imposing silhouette of the Tryadeya mountains rising in the distance.

As they approached the familiar foothills, both were reminded of their first, tense journey to the trolls' camp. Back then, the trolls had been camped both outside and within the caves nestled at the mountain's base. Now, however, there was no sign of life—no makeshift shelters, no lingering traces of the former encampment. The area was empty; the trolls and all evidence of their presence vanished.

"This isn't looking good," Kaitlin remarked as they moved cautiously towards the place where they had previously entered the mountain. Her eyes scanned the terrain, and her voice dropped to a hushed whisper. "If they were still here, wouldn't they have someone on watch?"

"I was thinking the same," Keltor replied, his hand instinctively moving to grip the hilt of his sword. The tension between them was palpable as they continued along the uneven terrain, where tufts of grass occasionally broke through the rocky ground underfoot. The path ahead curved gently, and a small cluster of trees hugged the mountainside to their left, providing the only semblance of cover.

Suddenly, Keltor's hand shot out, pressing against Kaitlin's stomach to stop her in her tracks. "What is it?" Kaitlin asked, concern flickering in her eyes as she glanced at him and then looked ahead once more.

"Movement, ahead of us," he answered quietly, his gaze fixed on the path in front of them.

"Soldiers?" Kaitlin whispered, a surge of fear rising within her.

"No, people," Keltor replied after a moment, quickly surveying their surroundings and realising how exposed they were, with nowhere to hide. Summoning his resolve, he pressed onward, memories of the last time they were at this spot—when the trolls had taken them—flitting through his mind. He pushed those thoughts aside, reminding himself that things were different now. The magic had been working when they left, and whoever was ahead of them was surely no longer a troll, but some form of man or woman.

"Hello," Keltor said in a clear voice, making sure his words carried across the quiet terrain. He deliberately moved his hand away from the hilt of his sword, signalling peace and goodwill.

215

A woman's voice answered from the shadows, her figure just visible behind a large boulder, outlined by the pale moonlight. "Who are you?" she asked, her tone cautious but not unkind.

"My name is Keltor, and this is Kaitlin," he replied, choosing his words with care. "We came to you nine months ago, when you were..." He hesitated, searching for the right way to phrase it. "...trolls."

For a moment, silence hung between them, heavy with memory and uncertainty.

"The Keeper of the Star?" the woman finally called back, her voice revealing a hint of recognition.

"Yes," Kaitlin responded, stepping forward with quiet confidence. "That's right. I gave you dragon's blood, hoping it would restore you to who you truly were."

The woman emerged from the shadows, revealing herself fully. No longer a troll, she stood tall—around six feet five—with a powerful build and striking fiery red hair. Her long blue dress was cinched at the chest with intricate golden thread, a testament to her transformation.

"You saved us," she declared, her gratitude clear as she began to walk towards them.

Kaitlin instinctively reached for Keltor's hand, and he squeezed hers in reassurance, sharing a silent moment of comfort.

"We hoped we had," Kaitlin explained, her voice tinged with both hope and apology. "But we couldn't wait to find out. We had to go and save another world, called Earth."

The woman stopped in front of them, her expression thoughtful and warm, marking the beginning of a new chapter in their journey.

"You saved our children," Ila said, placing her hands over her heart with sincere emotion. As she stepped towards Kaitlin to express her gratitude, Keltor instinctively moved to stand protectively between them, his posture tense and watchful.

Noticing Keltor's caution, Ila paused, her movements gentle and non-threatening. "It's okay, I mean her no harm," she assured, raising her hand in a gesture of peace. "I am Ila, Belrack's partner. I wished merely to express my gratitude."

Keltor signalled for Ila to keep her distance, to which she respectfully acquiesced, stepping back and bowing her head slightly in understanding. "I understand," she said quietly, acknowledging his concern.

Extending her hand towards the path ahead, Ila invited them to follow. "Please, come with me, it's not safe to be outside."

Keltor and Kaitlin pressed on along the mountain path, their footsteps echoing in the quiet. As they rounded a bend, a group of women came into view. These women, all impressively tall like Ila, stood over six foot five. Their long dresses, in shades of green and grey, brushed the ground as they moved. Many wore their fiery red hair tied back and braided neatly down their backs, presenting a unified and striking appearance.

Ila signalled to the women, and at her wave, they lowered their spears, allowing Keltor and Kaitlin to pass. Keltor watched the group closely as they walked by. Although the women appeared friendly, he remained vigilant. Experience had taught him that it only took one individual to pose a threat. While he and Kaitlin were now far more skilled in magic than during their previous visit, his protective instincts were as strong as ever, especially when it came to Kaitlin's safety.

As they ascended the winding path around the barren rocks of the mountain, Keltor broke the silence. "Where is Belrack?" he asked, his tone edged with concern.

Ila came to a halt, pausing for a moment before turning to face him. She took a deep breath, the weight of her answer clear in her expression. "He, and the rest of our men, were taken by King Iwein of Aranstream about six months ago. We haven't seen them since, and we don't even know if they are alive or dead." Her words hung heavily in the air before she turned back and continued leading the way up the path.

The revelation struck Kaitlin hard. She glanced at Keltor, who returned her look with a similar sense of dismay. The uncertainty and gravity of the situation settled between them.

217

"Damn it," Kaitlin muttered as they continued their climb. "Now what are we going to do?"

"I don't know, we'll just have to go on without them. We'll get the Deodars to safety as planned and then head back to Elvendon."

The group did not ascend as high up the mountain as they had on their previous visit. After only fifteen minutes, Ila led them through an arched doorway carved into the mountain's side.

Inside, they navigated a labyrinth of dimly lit corridors and passageways, the darkness broken only by the occasional flaming torch set into the stone walls. Eventually, Ila stopped just inside a vast chamber.

"This is where we were before," Kaitlin remarked, releasing Keltor's hand as she surveyed the familiar space.

Firelight flickered in the bowl-shaped vessels positioned in each corner, casting a warm glow across the room.

"They've repaired the carvings," Keltor whispered, his gaze appreciating the restored details.

"Yes, you're right, Keltor," Ila replied, having overheard him. "It was one of the first things Belrack repaired, as he had been the one who destroyed it in his distress. You see us now as we truly are, a peaceful tribe. We are known as Luskarna's, not those awful, awful trolls," she said, shaking her head as if to banish the memory. "I cannot possibly convey to you both how grateful we are for what you did. For so many years, we were as trolls, and now," she smiled softly, "yes we are mortal, but we are who we were meant to be."

Ila gave a heavy sigh, her expression weighted with sorrow. "Only now, I am without my Belrack, our son and daughter without their father."

"Ila, I'm so sorry," Kaitlin sympathised, moving gently towards her despite Keltor's cautious glance. She placed her hand compassionately on Ila's arm. "Truly I am. All of this has been caused because of who I am."

"You are the Keeper of the Star," Ila said, and Kaitlin shook her head.

"No, well yes I was then, but that's not who I truly am. Ila, I am the Queen of Elvendon, my father was King Severon of Elvendon."

For a moment, Ila remained silent, prompting Kaitlin to step away, uncertain of how Ila was processing the revelation. Ila then spoke, her voice tinged with disbelief, "You are the Queen of Elvendon?"

Kaitlin affirmed her identity with a nod, sensing Keltor's reassuring presence as he moved to stand beside her, equally unsure of Ila's response.

Without hesitation, Ila lowered herself to one knee and bowed her head in deep respect. Kaitlin watched, bewildered, as the other women in the chamber followed suit, each kneeling and bowing their heads before her.

"My Queen," Ila declared solemnly, "We are honoured to be in your presence."

Distressed by their display, Kaitlin pleaded, raising her hands in an urging gesture, "Ila, please get up." She turned to the others, imploring, "All of you, please get up."

Ila rose first, followed by the other women, each returning to their feet.

Once standing, Ila shared sombre news. "My Queen, we heard that your father had been killed by King Iwein of Aranstream."

"Yes, he was," Kaitlin confirmed, still taken aback by the depth of Ila's knowledge. "I didn't think you would know who he was."

"On the contrary, we knew the King well," Ila replied. She explained, "Belrack made a deal with the King of Elvendon many years ago, that we would keep to our side of the valley and protect Elvendon from the beasts."

Curious, Keltor inquired, "Beasts, what beasts?"

"Huge, wolflike creatures," Ila answered, before offering reassurance. She smiled and added, "Do not fear, we have not seen any for at least ten years."

"Is that why the people of Elvendon were never permitted to cross the bridge?" Keltor asked, recalling the tales he'd heard in his youth. "We were always told stories of witches and their monstrous creatures in the Eccleston Forest, warnings meant to keep us away."

"Yes," Ila confirmed, her voice steady. "King Severon's father was the one who banished the witches to the Eccleston Forest, and they have remained there for the past sixty years or so."

With a solemn nod, Kaitlin revealed, "They're not there anymore. We killed them. We had no choice—if we hadn't, they would have killed us."

"They were our enemy as well," Ila acknowledged, her expression one of mutual understanding.

Kaitlin reached out and took Keltor's hand in hers, turning to Ila as she spoke. "Keltor is now my husband, and your new King."

Recognising the significance of this announcement, Ila addressed Keltor with respect, dipping her head. "My King."

Keltor offered her a warm smile. "Thank you, Ila, but Kaitlin is still the boss," he replied with a playful grin. Kaitlin gave him a gentle shove while Ila laughed, the tension in the room easing.

"I can see the spirits matched you well," Ila remarked, her eyes shining with humour.

"Yes, they did," Keltor agreed, glancing lovingly at Kaitlin. "Although, at times, I never believed it would happen."

Turning to Ila, Keltor's tone grew more serious. "Ila, we came here hoping to ask Belrack to help us reclaim Kaitlin's throne, but clearly that isn't going to be possible now."

"No, it's not," she replied sadly, "as I said before, I don't even know if Belrack and the others are still alive. I have heard that King Iwein is building a new castle on the other side of Aranstream, and he is using prisoners to help build it."

"Yes, that is right," Keltor confirmed, his tone resolute.

"We hope they are all still alive," Ila continued, "and that with our size and strength, Belrack and the others are being used by the King as labourers. Perhaps, in time, they may find a way to escape or even be released to return home."

Kaitlin's determination was clear as she addressed Ila. "Ila, our plan is to free all those who have been taken, and to take back our Kingdom."

Ila's voice was laced with concern as she replied, "But how? King Iwein and that prince have ransacked Elvendon. They have taken any able-bodied male prisoner or, even worse, killed them."

Keltor, unwavering in his conviction, responded, "If they are being held, they can be freed. And we intend to free them all, one way or another."

Ila nodded, her support unwavering. "You have our support, anything you need at all," she offered, gesturing towards a set of closed doors. "Please."

Kaitlin and Keltor followed Ila to the double doors. As she opened them, a burst of noise greeted them—fits of giggles and laughter. Inside, children played happily, their joy filling the air.

Ila announced their arrival with gentle pride, "Children, this is the Queen and King of Elvendon. They are our friends."

At her words, the children immediately stopped what they were doing and rose to their feet. Ila bowed, demonstrating the proper etiquette, and the children copied her gesture.

Kaitlin grinned at them warmly, remembering the last time she had seen them—all as stone statues, frozen in time for hundreds of years. It was a relief and a joy to see them full of life once more.

"Continue as you were," Ila encouraged, giving a little wave to a boy and girl at the back of the room, who responded with enthusiastic waves of their own.

"My children," Ila informed them with evident pride.

"They are adorable," Kaitlin remarked sincerely. Ila responded with a gentle nod and a warm smile, her gratitude shining through.

"Come," Ila said, turning to lead the way.

Kaitlin and Keltor followed her out of the room, carefully closing the door behind them. Once outside, Ila paused, emotion colouring her words. "I still cannot thank you enough for giving them back to me. I honestly thought that day would never come, and that we were doomed to live as trolls without our children for an eternity. You will stay with us tonight?"

Kaitlin glanced at Keltor, seeking his opinion. He nodded in agreement.

"Yes, if that's okay. It's too late to make a move back to the others," Keltor replied.

"Excellent. I would like you to meet the other women of our tribe. They too are so grateful to you for their lives and that of their children. Now, would you like to bathe before dinner? You both look like you have been through a rough time," Ila asked, her tone both caring and practical.

Kaitlin felt herself flush, acutely aware of how dishevelled she must look—hardly queenly at all. Instinctively, she swept a wild strand of hair from her face and tucked it behind her ear, though she knew it made little difference to her appearance.

"Yes, please, that would be great," Keltor replied before Kaitlin had a chance too, and she felt his hand slip into hers. She glanced at him and fought back a smirk as his face was still covered with dried mud from their scramble up the riverbank.

Ila gave a respectful dip of her head. "Please follow me," she instructed, before turning and beginning to walk away down the corridor.

Kaitlin pressed herself closer to Keltor, her other hand reaching to grip his arm as they walked. Together, they made their way back through the long, winding corridors. Their footsteps echoed softly as they descended a seemingly endless set of spiral stairs.

"I'm sorry it's such a long walk, but I thought you would prefer the natural baths rather than just hot water in a metal tub. It's worth the walk, I promise," Ila said, her voice full of reassurance as she led the way. "It's not much further."

Despite the warmth and friendliness of their host, Keltor kept a cautious hand resting on the hilt of his sword. The memory of the trolls nearly beating him to death still lingered in his mind, making him wary as they journeyed deeper into the mountain. He also remained mindful that most castles kept their dungeons at the lowest levels, and he had yet to spot an alternative exit beyond the one they had used to enter.

At last, they reached the end of the staircase and continued down yet another corridor, this one lit by the flickering glow of fiery torches. As they passed along the corridor, a few other women greeted Ila with polite dips of their heads.

As they continued their descent, Ila pointed out a significant feature. "Our main kitchen and food store is also down here," she informed them, highlighting the practicality of the castle's layout despite its distance from the upper levels.

Kaitlin glanced around, noting the effort required for daily tasks. "That's one hell of a walk to take food up to the top," she remarked, her tone a mix of surprise and admiration at the challenge the tribe faced.

Ila responded with a warm chuckle, clearly amused. "Let me show you something," she said, pausing before a massive wooden door. With a flourish, she opened it and beckoned them inside. "Come," she said with a wave of her hand.

Keltor instinctively stepped ahead of Kaitlin, his protective instincts still on high alert. "Just in case," he whispered, and Kaitlin gave him a reassuring nod.

As they entered, a wave of heat enveloped them, and the inviting aroma of food filled the air. The kitchen chamber was immense, bustling with activity and the comforting sounds of cooking. Kaitlin could not help but comment, "It smells so good in here," as her stomach gave a grateful rumble.

Ila smiled at the reaction. "Yes, this is the main kitchen. Now let me show you this. It was Belrack's invention," she said, pride evident in her voice.

The room was dominated by a large oak table at its centre, surrounded by shelves stretching from wall to ceiling. These shelves were packed with bottles and jars, each containing a different concoction. A huge fire roared along the length of one wall, providing warmth and a place for cooking, while sinks and cupboards lined another wall, making the space both functional and inviting.

Ila moved to what appeared to be a large cupboard and opened it, revealing a clever mechanism inside. "Now, this saves our legs I can tell you," she said, gesturing towards the device. "You see, we put everything on here and then use this to pull it up to the top."

Her tone conveyed both practicality and a hint of pride in the system's efficiency.

"Oh, it's a dumb waiter," Kaitlin remarked, curiosity prompting her to stick her head inside and look up the shaft. She seemed momentarily transported, recalling familiar technology from her own world.

"A dumb what?" Ila asked, a frown of confusion creasing her brow.

"We had these back on Earth," Kaitlin explained, withdrawing her head from the cupboard. "We called it a dumb waiter. Not so much in modern times, but in the past, rich people used them to send food from the kitchen up to the main house, just like you are."

"Oh, I see," Ila said as she closed the door, still appearing a little puzzled by the name. After a brief pause, she added matter-of-factly, "We just call it a pulley."

Kaitlin considered this for a moment, then nodded in agreement. "Well, yes, I guess that's a much more sensible name," she conceded, a small smile crossing her lips. Meanwhile, Keltor just looked away, trying to hide his amusement at the exchange.

"Anyway, come along, let me show you the gardens." Ila turned smartly and began making her way back towards the kitchen door, her steps purposeful.

Keltor let out a quiet chuckle. "A dumb waiter, seriously?" he mused, still amused by the terminology.

Kaitlin shot him an indignant look. "That's what they were called," she insisted, sounding defensive.

Shaking his head, Keltor grinned. "Humans and their weird words. Why the hell would they call it a dumb waiter? That makes no sense." With a gentle hand resting on her lower back, he guided her out of the door, still clearly entertained by the exchange.

Kaitlin mumbled in response, "I don't know, it's just what it was called," her tone quiet as they walked. Instead of pressing further, Keltor simply chuckled to himself, the conversation lingering in the air between them as they proceeded down the corridor.

224

After a short walk, Ila stopped at another door. Without hesitation, she opened it, revealing an exit that led them outside.

"Wow, this is amazing," Kaitlin exclaimed as they entered an abundant garden bursting with vegetables, herbs, and flowers. The sight was both vibrant and inviting, with greenery stretching out in all directions.

Ila nodded in agreement. "Yes, isn't it wonderful? As you know, when we were trolls, our diet was mostly meat," she said, a shudder passing through her at the memory. "But now we have managed to grow so much. It felt strange at first, especially since we hadn't gardened for decades, but even then, there were wild vegetables and herbs still thriving here. That made it much easier for us to cultivate the land to suit our needs." She gestured towards a gate, and the group followed her through.

Beyond the gate, Ila pointed towards another area. "This is where we keep our animals—goats and chickens. Further back, you'll find the beehives." Kaitlin took in the view, marvelling at the careful arrangement of the animal enclosures and the gardens. Everything was surrounded by the mountain's rocky embrace, creating a sheltered haven, almost like a little oasis. The unique setting gave the gardens, and animal pens a microclimate of their own, protected from the outside elements.

"This is so beautiful, and it's all tucked inside the mountain like a little oasis," Kaitlin remarked, truly impressed by the harmonious blend of nature and shelter.

Ila smiled, her expression warm. "We are very lucky. It is a beautiful place to live, and we have been very fortunate. All this is down to you both—if you hadn't freed us from the curse, we would still be living as those awful trolls."

Kaitlin glanced over at Keltor, who returned her look with a gentle smile. The knowledge that something good had come from the chaos and heartbreak of the past few months brought comfort, and it was heartening to see the positive change reflected in the flourishing mountain sanctuary.

"Right, come on, let's get you in that bath," Ila then announced as she turned and headed back through the garden to the door into the 'castle'.

Keltor closed the garden door behind him, and they followed her back along the corridor, until stopping at another door, she walked inside, and they followed her.

"Wow," Kaitlin remarked as she took in the bathing room. However, it was not truly a room in the conventional sense, but rather a spacious, man-made cave. Candles had been carefully placed within the recessed niches of the grey, chiselled stone walls, casting a soft, warm glow that radiated throughout the cavernous space. In front of them stretched a large pool of water, from which hot steam rose in a gentle mist, drifting upwards and giving the area an inviting, almost ethereal quality. To the left side of the pool, two long spouts jutted out from the rock itself: one continuously poured steaming hot water, while the other delivered cool water, creating a perfect balance for bathing.

"It's a natural hot spring," Ila explained, her voice tinged with pride as she watched them take in the view. "The temperature should be just right for you." She glanced at Kaitlin, seeking reassurance that all was well.

"It's beautiful," Kaitlin replied, her gaze lingering over the gently steaming pool as she nodded appreciatively.

Ila then turned her attention to both Kaitlin and Keltor. "You are happy to bathe together?" she asked, ensuring their comfort.

"Yes, we are," Keltor answered, his tone calm and reassuring.

"Good, it's normal for us to bathe together also," Ila continued, offering a small, understanding smile. "But I know that some races prefer not to mix males and females when bathing. If you leave your clothes outside the door, we'll wash them for you. There are fresh robes for you over there, and I'll make sure that some suitable clothes are sent to your quarters for you to use while your things are being cleaned and dried."

She motioned towards a thick rope disappearing into the wall. "When you're ready, just pull this rope and I'll come to take you to your quarters. Then we'll eat together."

"Thank you, Ila, that's very kind of you," Kaitlin said, her voice full of gratitude.

"You're welcome. Now please, enjoy and relax." With a gentle wave towards the inviting water and a short bow, Ila turned and quietly left the cave, closing the wooden door softly behind her.

Ready?" Keltor asked, anticipation clear in his voice.

"Too bloody right, I can't wait," Kaitlin replied enthusiastically. With that, she unclipped her cloak and removed it.

Keltor dropped the backpack and unbuckled his belt, methodically removing it before laying his sword carefully on the floor. Beside him, Kaitlin began to undress, her boots, trousers and overdress quickly joining Keltor's belongings in a neat heap. She slid her wand into one of her boots, ensuring it was safely tucked away, and then left her clothes in a pile just outside the door, following Ila's instructions.

"Hey, stop staring and get your clothes off," Kaitlin teased Keltor, catching his gaze as he watched her carefully ease herself into the water. Her tone was playful, lightening the moment as she glanced over her shoulder at him.

"I'm not staring," he protested, beginning to remove his clothes.

"Yes, you are," she replied, her response gentle and affirming.

Keltor watched her as she dipped beneath the surface, then emerged, drawing in a breath and sweeping her hair away from her face. In that moment, it seemed to him as though he was witnessing a goddess rising from the water, her movements graceful and ethereal.

"Okay, I am," he admitted quietly, his voice barely above a whisper. The sight brought to mind her birthday in the palace at Elvendon, a memory filled with longing and the fear that he might never be with her again. The emotion in his confession was clear, as those recollections mingled with the present, making the moment all the more profound.

He opened the door, peeked out and then added his clothes to Kaitlin's pile. Keltor opened the door just a crack, glanced outside to check that the coast was clear, and then discreetly placed his clothes on top of Kaitlin's pile, following her lead.

Kaitlin waded a little deeper into the pool, beckoning Keltor to join her. "Come on," she urged, her voice bubbling with excitement. "This is freaking amazing." The heat of the water seemed to melt away any tension, and the gentle echo of her words bounced softly off the stone walls.

"How deep is it?" Keltor asked, glancing warily at the clear, gently rippling surface.

Kaitlin grinned over her shoulder. "Well, I can touch the bottom at the edge, but not in the middle, why?" She stretched out her toes, demonstrating, her arms sweeping through the water for balance. The playful tone in her reply reassured him, her confidence in the pool's safety inviting him to set his concerns aside and join her in the centre.

Keltor dashed forward and, with a burst of energy, leapt into the pool. His enthusiastic jump sent a wave of hot water splashing over Kaitlin, who squealed in surprise.

"Keltor!" she exclaimed, raising her hands to shield her face as droplets rained down on her. She quickly wiped the water from her eyes, but the playful scolding in her voice was softened by the hint of a smile.

Keltor resurfaced, laughter bubbling up as he shook the water from his hair. "Blimey, it's so hot!" he said, still grinning at her reaction.

Kaitlin stretched out, letting her head drop back to float on the surface. "No, it's not. It's just perfect," she replied, her voice content as she let herself drift, enjoying the warmth of the water enveloping her.

Keltor moved through the warm water towards Kaitlin, closing the distance between them. As he reached her, he gently wrapped his arms around her waist, drawing her closer. With a tender gesture, he brushed her long, wet hair to one side, exposing the curve of her neck. Leaning in, he pressed a soft kiss against her skin, savouring the closeness between them.

"Yes, it is perfect," he murmured, his voice low and contented as he nestled up to her, allowing the heat of the water and the intimacy of the moment to envelop them both.

The sensation of Keltor's body pressed closely against hers sent Kaitlin's heart racing. She turned to face him, taking in the sight of his strong, muscular shoulders rising just above the shimmering surface of the water. Reaching out, her hand glided up the length of his arm, tracing the defined muscles before curling around his shoulder. Without hesitation, she hooked her arms around his neck, drawing him even closer.

As Kaitlin pressed herself up against him, Keltor felt an undeniable response within his own body. His chest heaved with each breath, his heart thudding rapidly in his chest. For a brief, suspended moment, they simply gazed into each other's eyes, their connection so deep that words became unnecessary.

"Keltor," she finally whispered, her lips barely brushing against his as she spoke his name. The mere sound of it seemed to hang in the air between them, charged with anticipation. Butterflies fluttered wildly in her stomach and an electric thrill coursed through her, heightening every sensation. Keltor's hand moved gently to the back of her head, his fingers threading softly through her hair, anchoring her in the moment. With his other hand, he traced a delicate line down her arm, his touch feather-light and lingering. As his fingers caressed her skin, a shiver ran the length of her body, her senses alive and attuned to his every movement. He gave her arm a gentle, reassuring squeeze and, in response, her whole body trembled. Their lips met in a kiss— gentle at first, exploring and tender, then deepening with a powerful passion that left her breathless, lost in the intensity of their connection.

"Here?" Kaitlin whispered, her breath catching as their lips parted, the question hanging between them in the humid air.

Keltor smiled at her lovingly. "Why not?" he answered, his expression tender before a hint of concern creased his brow. "Unless you don't want to?" he added, his voice serious and filled with genuine care.

Kaitlin's eyes sparkled as she met his gaze. "You really have to ask me that?" she replied, amusement and desire mingling in her voice. She groaned softly as his lips found hers again, his body pressing against her, drawing her deeper into the embrace.

XXX

Kaitlin slipped on her robe, the fabric settling softly around her as she prepared to leave the warmth of the bath. As she did, Keltor stepped up behind her, his hands gently resting on her shoulders. He leaned in, drawing close, and pressed a tender kiss to her neck.

"I love you," he whispered, his voice warm and sincere, his cheek resting against hers in a moment of quiet intimacy.

A pleasurable shiver ran through Kaitlin's body at his touch. Her heart ached with the wish that they could stay in this peaceful moment a thousand times over, instead of returning to the challenges that awaited them. The thought of leaving, and the uncertainty that hung over their future, filled her with dread—she knew Keltor would fight to the death to protect her, and that frightened her deeply.

Turning to face him, Kaitlin looked into his eyes and replied softly, "I love you." She reached up, her fingers gently caressing the softness of his skin, before she kissed him with all the emotion she felt.

"Come on," Keltor said at last, releasing her from their embrace and reaching for another robe. "We'd better ring that bell."

Kaitlin nodded in agreement, stepping across to the rope and giving it a pull. There was no sound.

"I guess it must ring somewhere else," she remarked, letting go of the rope.

"I guess," Keltor replied as he slipped on his boots.

Kaitlin glanced at him, taking in the sight of him in his robe and boots. "Nice look," she teased with a playful smile.

"You too," Keltor replied with a laugh.

"Do you think it will catch on?" Kaitlin asked, spinning around in her robe, her laughter lightening the atmosphere.

"Nah," Keltor replied, shaking his head, his eyes twinkling with amusement.

There was a knock at the door. When Keltor opened it, he found Ila standing there, greeting them with a warm smile.

"Hi, are you both feeling refreshed?" she asked kindly.

"Yes, thank you Ila, it was lovely," Kaitlin replied appreciatively.

"Fabulous, now follow me and I will take you to your quarters for the night, and you can get dressed for dinner." With that, Ila turned and began to lead the way down the corridor.

Keltor gathered his sword and backpack, and together with Kaitlin, they followed Ila. They walked down the long corridor and retraced their steps to the spiral staircase, ascending all the way back up the way they had previously come down.

As they climbed, Kaitlin groaned, struggling to catch her breath. "Bloody hell, I shall need an oxygen mask by the time I get to the top. Have we gone up even further?"

Keltor chuckled at her comment, while Ila glanced back over her shoulder with a frown. He secretly enjoyed it when Kaitlin used her human expressions—no one else seemed to understand her references, making it almost like a private language between the two of them.

When they finally reached the top of the stairs, Ila guided them along a corridor lined with grey stone walls. Their footsteps echoed softly as she led the way, continuing until she came to a halt before a sturdy wooden door.

Ila paused, turning to face them. "I hope this will be okay for you," she said, her tone both hopeful and apologetic. She opened the door, and immediately a comforting warmth enveloped them, radiating from the fire burning cheerfully in the hearth at the far end of the room.

Stepping inside, Ila added, "We're not used to having guests," as she glanced around the room, ensuring everything was in order.

Kaitlin's face lit up with gratitude. "It's perfect, thank you, Ila," she replied, her eyes drawn to the grand wooden-framed bed dominating the room. The bed was piled high with plump, inviting pillows, thick blankets and a luxurious fur draped across the top. After so long without a proper bed, it seemed almost too good to be true, and Kaitlin could easily imagine herself falling asleep there and then.

"Great, I will give you some time to dress and then come back for you both. Those clothes should fit you okay," Ila said, gesturing towards the neatly folded outfits laid out across the bed.

"Thank you," Keltor responded sincerely, nodding his appreciation.

With a polite bow of her head, Ila left the room, closing the door softly behind her.

Overcome with delight, Kaitlin exclaimed, "Oh my god, a bed," and immediately launched herself onto it, sinking deeply into its softness and relishing the comfort it promised.

Keltor let out a hearty laugh at Kaitlin's antics, then climbed onto the bed beside her. Together, they gazed up at the ceiling above them—a stretch of grey, unyielding stone that felt oddly comforting in its simplicity. Despite the cold appearance of the room's architecture, the plush pillows and thick blankets made the space feel like a sanctuary.

"This is heaven," Kaitlin murmured, her voice muffled as she nestled deeper into the welcoming softness of the pillows. The exhaustion from their journey seemed to melt away in the embrace of the bed, and for a fleeting moment, all worries faded into the background.

"It sure is," Keltor replied, his tone both content and amused. The two of them lay side by side for several peaceful minutes, revelling in the much-needed comfort and warmth. The silence was filled only by the gentle crackling of the fire and the subtle rumble of Kaitlin's stomach, which betrayed her growing hunger.

Breaking the tranquillity, Keltor playfully slapped his hand on Kaitlin. "Come on, we'd better get ready, Ila will be back soon," he said, sitting up and swinging his legs off the bed with a sense of purpose.

Kaitlin let out another groan, reluctant to leave the comfort she had only just found. If it weren't for the insistent protest of her empty stomach, she could have easily stayed curled up there until morning.

Keltor reached for the trousers Ila had laid out on the bed, holding them up against his body to check the fit. He raised his eyebrow in silent assessment; the fabric was a soft linen-like material, and they appeared likely to fit well. With a casual movement, he slipped off his gown, drawing Kaitlin's attention. She smiled, her gaze lingering on the defined muscles of his physique and the intricate tribal tattoo that traced down his arm, swept across his chest, and wrapped around to his back.

He pulled on the white trousers, tightening the ties at the waistband to secure them. The trousers sat comfortably on his hips, accentuating his toned torso. Noticing Kaitlin's eyes on him, Keltor glanced her way and asked, "What?"

Kaitlin, grinning as she lay on her front with her chin resting on her hands, replied, "Nothing, I'm just admiring the view." Keltor smirked in response, then reached for the matching white shirt and slipped it on, completing his outfit.

"It kind of suits you," Kaitlin remarked as she slid off the bed and wandered over to where Keltor stood. Her gaze lingered on him, a hint of playful admiration lighting up her features.

"Hmm, I'm not sure about that," Keltor replied, looking down at the trousers, and then fiddling with the waist band. "They don't feel all that secure." His fingers fumbled with the knot, as he pulled them tight.

"You know you drive me crazy, right?" Kaitlin murmured, her voice slightly breathless as the energy between them intensified, making her heart race. The unspoken tension seemed to charge the air, drawing them even closer together.

"Kitcat," Keltor whispered softly, the affectionate nickname carrying a weight of meaning only they understood.

Kaitlin's eyes fluttered closed in anticipation, and a gentle smile touched her lips. She wasn't left waiting long; Keltor leaned in, his lips finding hers in a lingering, tender kiss. Their arms instinctively wrapped around each other, pulling one another into a tight embrace. For a moment, the world around them faded away, and all that remained was the warmth and connection they shared.

"Come on," Keltor said with a smile as their lips parted, the warmth of their kiss still lingering in the charged air between them. He nodded towards the clothes Ila had left out, his tone gentle but insistent. "You'd better get dressed; Ila will be here any minute."

"Okay," she agreed reluctantly, and as she turned around, Keltor smacked her backside in a playful gesture.

Kaitlin spun around, laughter bubbling from her as she protested, "Hey!"—her tone a mix of indignation and amusement. Keltor simply winked at her, his playful grin never fading. In response, Kaitlin stuck out her tongue at him, the familiar gesture carrying a sense of light-hearted banter between them.

Keltor grabbed his boots and sat on the edge of the bed, slipping his feet into them and methodically fastening each one. Meanwhile, Kaitlin removed her robe, letting it fall aside, and reached for the blue gown that Ila had thoughtfully left out for her. She slid the dress over her shoulders, the fabric settling elegantly into place, then swept her long hair over one shoulder to bare her back.

Kaitlin approached Keltor, her blue gown draping elegantly around her as she walked over. "Can you do the ties up for me please?" she asked, her voice soft with trust and familiarity.

As Keltor began to fasten the ties on Kaitlin's dress, he couldn't resist tracing his finger gently down the length of her back, causing her to squirm and giggle as a trail of goosebumps appeared on her skin.

"Stop it," Kaitlin said, casting a playful glance over her shoulder at Keltor, her laughter bubbling up despite her attempt to sound stern. In response, Keltor mischievously repeated his earlier gesture, prompting another involuntary shudder from her as she giggled. She twisted around again to look at him, catching the broad, cheeky grin spreading across his face.

"Okay," Keltor replied, adopting a comically exaggerated tone that made Kaitlin roll her eyes with a fond smile. Carefully, he finished pulling the ties of Kaitlin's gown, ensuring each knot was secure and comfortable. With a final gentle tug, he made sure the dress sat perfectly on her shoulders, then patted her back approvingly. Their eyes met for a moment, the shared humour and trust between them evident in their expressions. With her dress finally fastened, Kaitlin offered a grateful smile, shaking her hair back so it fell smoothly over her shoulders.

At that moment, a knock sounded at the door, and Keltor crossed the room to open it, revealing Ila standing outside. "Are you ready?" Ila asked, her tone warm and expectant. "Yes, two seconds," Kaitlin replied as she finished tying the lace on her second boot. Jumping to her feet, she joined Keltor at the door, slipped her hand into his, pulled the door closed behind her, and together they followed Ila down the corridor, the flickering glow of torches lighting their path. Their eyes wandered to the newly restored paintings that now gleamed with life, a testament to all they had accomplished. Despite the memories that lingered from their last visit—the pain and near-loss that Keltor had endured—Kaitlin felt a deep sense of relief and joy for the people they had helped. She squeezed his hand in silent support, and he returned her glance with quiet strength. Ila led them into the cathedral room, where the once-forgotten table was now beautifully set and laden with food, the sight of fresh fruit, vegetables, and steaming fare inviting them in. Ila gestured for Kaitlin to take a seat as she pulled out a chair, and with a word of thanks, Kaitlin sat, Keltor beside her, while Ila took her place at the head of the table, joined by three other women.

"Your highnesses, may I introduce Miranda, Elizabet and Morgana," Ila said, gesturing towards the three women who stood nearby. Each of them dipped their heads respectfully to Keltor and Kaitlin, acknowledging their presence with quiet dignity.

Ila offered a gentle smile as she added, "Miranda is my sister."

Keltor and Kaitlin responded in unison, their voices overlapping in a friendly greeting. "Hi," they said, their tone warm and welcoming.

As they settled in, Ila addressed their guests with a hint of anticipation. "Despite what we once were as trolls, we are actually vegetarians now, so I hope you like fish." Her words carried a sense of pride and gentle reassurance, as she carefully lifted the lid from the tureen in the centre of the table.

Both Keltor and Kaitlin nodded eagerly, curiosity and hunger evident in their expressions as they leaned forward to peer into the tureen and see what was being served.

"Great, may I?" Ila asked, raising a ladle filled with steaming fish in a fragrant broth.

"Yes, thank you, Ila," Kaitlin replied, her appetite now fully awakened by the delicious smell of the meal. She quickly lifted her plate towards Ila, grateful for the generous offering.

Ila served a generous portion of the fragrant fish broth to both Keltor and Kaitlin, before helping herself. The remaining women at the table—Miranda, Elizabet and Morgana—waited their turn and then served themselves, each moving with quiet familiarity and ease.

As the meal commenced, Kaitlin glanced towards Ila and ventured a question. "Ila, I hope you don't mind me asking, but you are clearly not elves nor human."

Ila shook her head, an amiable expression on her face. She paused to dab her mouth with a napkin before replying. "No, we are originally from the North. Our tribe migrated down south when the snows became too harsh for us to survive. That was many hundreds of years ago."

Keltor, still marvelling at the revelation, added, "I still can't believe as elves we never knew about you. I mean, we knew not to cross over the valley, and there were stories of the witches. No one ever said anything about a tribe of trolls."

"Yes, but that was only to protect you. As you know Keltor, as trolls we had no real control over what we did, our level of intelligence was minimal, we lived with aggression and thought nothing of ripping a man apart."

Keltor involuntarily shuddered as a vivid memory resurfaced, recalling the harrowing moment when he had been tied to the trees. The distress flickered across his face, and Kaitlin, noticing his discomfort, reached gently across the table, her hand resting lightly on his arm in a gesture of reassurance. He met her gaze briefly, drawing comfort from her presence, before turning his attention back to Ila.

With a steadying breath, Keltor asked, "When did King Iwein take Belrack?"

Ila set down her fork, her expression sombre as she gathered her thoughts. "It was about two moons after you saved us," she replied quietly. "They came in force. Belrack fought valiantly, but in the end, there were simply too many of them. We lost five of our men in the struggle, which has been incredibly hard for us, especially since our tribe is already so small."

She paused; her voice tinged with sadness. "In the end, Belrack surrendered. He couldn't bear to see any more of us die. I was terrified they would execute him on the spot, but instead, they restrained him and the others, then took them all away in waggons. Since then, we've had no word of their fate. We don't even know if they're still alive."

Miranda looked across the table, her voice edged with hope as she asked, "Have you come to help us?"

Keltor met her gaze honestly. "To be truthful, we actually came seeking Belrack's help," he admitted, not wanting to give false expectations.

Kaitlin then took a deep breath and began to recount the ordeal that she and Keltor had endured over the past eight months. She explained how they had believed their absence had only lasted a few days, only to discover so much more time had passed. The story unfolded quietly over dinner, and the table listened with rapt attention, taking in the strange twists of fate that had brought Kaitlin and Keltor back to the tribe at such a desperate time.

As the meal drew to a close, Ila turned to them, concern evident in her expression. "So, what will you do now?" she asked, her tone gentle but searching, as everyone awaited their response.

Keltor spoke with quiet determination, reassuring the group, "Our plan remains the same—to help Kaitlin reclaim her rightful place on the throne. We will find a way, believe me," he said firmly. Turning to address the concerns about their captured allies, he added, "And if Belrack and your men are being held at Aranstream, we will free them. I promise you that."

As the meal came to an end, Ila rose from her seat, and the others followed suit. Keltor and Kaitlin stood as well, ready to take their leave. Kaitlin offered her gratitude, "Thank you for dinner, it was lovely."

Ila responded warmly, "You are very welcome, your highness. I am sorry we're unable to help you further in your quest, but I simply cannot send any of the women with you. None of them are truly fighters, and most have children to care for."

Kaitlin lifted her hand in understanding. "No, it's fine—we wouldn't have expected you to. We will find a way," she said, her voice steady with resolve.

Offering to see them off, Ila said, "I will walk you to your room." She moved around the table and led the way down the corridor.

When they reached the door to their room for the night, Kaitlin turned to Ila. "Thank you," she said sincerely.

"You're welcome," Ila replied, dipping her head respectfully. "Sleep well, and I shall see you in the morning."

"Good night," Keltor and Kaitlin said together, and Keltor opened the door to their room, bringing the evening to a close.

"Are you okay?" Keltor asked quietly, noticing the heavy sigh that escaped Kaitlin. She hesitated before responding, her uncertainty clear. "Yeah, well, I know I said we will find a way, but can we? King Iwein has an entire army, and there is just us and Esimae."

Keltor reached for her hands, offering a gentle squeeze. "Hey, and mum remember," he added, trying to lighten the mood.

Kaitlin let out a small, sarcastic laugh. "Oh, well that makes it fine then."

He met her gaze, his tone steady and encouraging. "I know it's hard, Kitcat, but we will find a way. I just need to get into the camp. Once our army knows you are still alive, they will start to fight back, believe me. I understand you haven't been in Elvendon long enough, but the people are loyal to their Royal family, it is part of being an Elvendon. Despite your father's ways, Elvendon was peaceful, the people were generally happy, and your father was nothing like King Iwein. Yes, he instilled some amount of fear in the people, but that was just to keep them in order; he was never as hard as King Iwein."

Kaitlin frowned, her doubts lingering. "So why would he make my sister marry Prince Keion, if he knew what they were like?"

"To ensure peace, Kaitlin, the same reason he was going to marry you off to Aragon. Let's just get through the next few days, get the Deodars to safety and meet back with mum. We'll head off to the forester's place and take it from there."

She nodded in agreement. "Okay."

"Come on, let's get in this bed," Keltor said with a grin, releasing Kaitlin's hands. The long day had left them both exhausted, and the sight of the freshly made bed was a welcome relief. As they stood together, the comfort and warmth promised by the soft furs seemed to beckon them in, offering a brief respite from their worries.

They moved towards the bed, their clothes already laid out clean and dry, a small luxury after weeks without such comforts. The act of climbing under the covers felt almost ceremonial, marking not just the end of the day but a rare moment of peace amid the chaos surrounding them. Keltor pulled the fur cover over them, and Kaitlin nestled close, the tension in her shoulders finally easing as the comfort of the bed enveloped them both.

She let out a contented sigh as she pulled the fur cover over them, nestling herself close to him. "Oh god, I didn't think a bed could feel so wonderful," she murmured, her voice warm with relief. The simple comfort of the soft furs and the solid mattress beneath them felt almost surreal after so long without such luxuries. As she snuggled in, a sense of safety and peace washed over her, if only for a fleeting moment. The tension that had weighed on her shoulders began to melt away, and in the quiet of the room, surrounded by warmth, she allowed herself to relax fully, savouring a rare moment of tranquillity beside him.

"I don't think we've actually slept in a bed since we left Elvendon, so technically that's over eight months ago," Keltor remarked, the disbelief in his voice mingling with a faint trace of amusement at how much had changed. The simple act of lying in a real bed felt almost foreign, a forgotten luxury after such hardship and uncertainty.

Kaitlin shifted, propping herself up on his chest as she gazed down at him. She was about to comment that, in truth, this was the first time they had ever shared a bed together, but the intent words she found in his eyes made her pause. There was a vulnerability there, a depth of feeling that rendered her momentarily speechless.

"Kitcat," he murmured softly, sensing her hesitation. His eyes searched hers, silently conveying all the things words could not. As if understanding passed wordlessly between them, he closed his eyes just as she leaned down, pressing her lips gently to his in a kiss that spoke of relief, longing, and the profound comfort of being together at last.

Chapter Nine
Keltor's Anguish

Keltor drifted into sleep and soon found himself lost in a dream of extraordinary happiness. Kaitlin was there beside him, and together they lived a simple, contented life in a secluded cottage nestled deep within the forest. In this peaceful vision, they had two children, and the burdens of their real lives—no castle, no royal duties, no titles—were nowhere to be found. The air was calm, their home filled with laughter and warmth, free from the pressures and dangers that usually shadowed their days.

But the dream shifted abruptly. Suddenly, Kaitlin was gone. Panic seized Keltor as he searched frantically for her, running through the tangled undergrowth, his sword clutched tightly in his hand. The forest closed in around him, breath rasping, sweat pouring down his brow as he crashed through the trees, desperate to find her. He tried to call out her name, but his voice failed him—no sound would come, no matter how many times he tried to shout. The silence was suffocating, his anxiety mounting with every step.

The nightmare deepened as he found himself inside a vast, unfamiliar castle. He sprinted down a long corridor that seemed to stretch endlessly before him, only to be swallowed by a labyrinth of tunnels twisting into darkness. Each time he caught a glimpse of Kaitlin, she vanished before he could reach her, disappearing into the shadows and leaving him alone with his fear and desperation.

Keltor awoke abruptly, his heart racing and his body drenched in sweat. The remnants of his nightmare lingered, leaving him shaken and breathless. Instinctively, he turned to look beside him, relief flooding through him as he saw Kaitlin sleeping peacefully. For a moment, he simply watched her, reassured by her presence and calmed by the gentle rhythm of her breathing.

The nightmare had exposed his deepest fear: the terror of losing her. To Keltor, the prospect of being separated from Kaitlin was more unbearable than death itself. He knew this dread was something he could never share with her; he could not bring himself to reveal the true extent of his anxiety and vulnerability. Instead, he concealed his worries behind a smile whenever she glanced his way, determined to protect her from the burden of his fears.

Sitting on the edge of the bed, Keltor gathered his thoughts, steeling himself for the day ahead. Though he was willing to sacrifice everything for Kaitlin—even his own life, if it meant seeing her restored to her rightful place on the throne—he could not help but wish for a different fate. Above all, he longed to remain by her side, never to be parted from her.

Keltor rose quietly, pulling on his trousers and moving with purpose across the room. He retrieved his father's book from his backpack, the weight of unresolved guilt pressing on him as he did so. The memory of his father's long imprisonment gnawed at his conscience, and despite Kaitlin's reassurances that he was not to blame, he could not shake the sense of responsibility for not having searched for his father sooner.

Settling himself cross-legged by the fading embers of the fire, Keltor drew in a deep, steadying breath. He closed the book, placed his palm firmly on its cover, and shut his eyes, hoping for a connection. For several minutes, nothing happened. Discouragement crept in, and he was on the verge of giving up when he suddenly felt a tingling sensation of magic beneath his fingertips. Opening his eyes, he saw his entire hand aglow, the faint light pulsing gently in the darkness. Renewing his focus, Keltor closed his eyes once more, clearing his mind and attempting to open a channel to reach his father.

With unwavering determination, Keltor called out into the silence, his voice steady and filled with hope. "Dad."

In a distant, dark cell, Forde sat up suddenly on the old bench bed, his eyes wide with surprise. Swinging his legs around to the front, he listened, hardly daring to believe what he was experiencing. Over the years, he had grown used to his mind playing tricks on him—an expected consequence of so much solitude. Yet, this time felt altogether different. The presence was stronger, the voice much clearer than before.

"Keltor, son," Forde responded, glancing around the dank cell. A flicker of hope sparked within him as he sensed the authenticity of the moment.

Keltor, sensing his father's awareness, repeated his plea, his voice reaching out across the magical connection. "Dad, please, where are you? Tell me so I can come for you?" His words were urgent, driven by longing and desperation to rescue his father.

The quiet in the room was broken as Kaitlin stirred. Awoken by Keltor's voice, she sat up in bed and called out softly, "Keltor?" Drawing the fur cover around her, she slid from the bed, her concern mounting as she saw him sitting cross-legged on the floor, facing the fire in deep concentration.

"Keltor," Kaitlin whispered, her voice edged with worry as she drew closer to him. She noticed his eyes were closed in deep concentration, his hand resting atop his father's book, which now radiated a soft, ethereal glow. Kneeling beside him on the floor, her concern grew, her gaze fixed on the mysterious light and the intensity on Keltor's face.

At that moment, far away, Forde called out, his voice echoing with longing and hope. "Keltor, son," he said aloud, rising to his feet in the dim confines of his cell.

Desperation crept into Keltor's tone as he pleaded once more, "Dad, where are you?" His voice was urgent, fuelled by the fear that their fragile connection might soon be broken.

From the gloom of his prison, Forde's answer finally came, clear and direct. "Aranstream castle, in the dungeon," he replied, his eyes roving the cold, dark corners of his cell as he spoke.

"Dad, I'm coming to get you," Keltor told him.

Kaitlin held her breath as she realised, he was communicating with his father.

"Keltor, I love you son." Forde said, and a smile beamed across his face. He had no idea how his son was doing this, but he knew it was him, he knew it was not his mad imagination wishing him out of this hell hole. His son was coming for him.

"Dad, I'm sorry," Keltor cried, his voice breaking under the weight of his guilt and sorrow. "I'm sorry we didn't look for you." Tears streamed down his cheeks, each one a testament to the anguish he felt for not having searched for his father sooner. His voice grew more urgent, desperation colouring every word as he called out again, "Dad," longing for a reply. But the magical connection had faded, and there was only silence. Keltor's cries echoed in the quiet room, underscoring the pain of the lost connection and the regret that now overwhelmed him.

"Keltor," his father called, his voice echoing softly through the darkness of his cell. Forde's eyes searched the gloom, desperate for a reply, but only silence greeted him. With a weary sigh, he made his way back to the simple bed in the corner of his prison and sat down heavily. Despite the oppressive cold and the seemingly endless solitude, a smile broke across his face as he allowed his thoughts to drift to his family. He tried to picture what his eldest son, Keltor, might look like now, imagining the changes eleven years would have wrought. He pictured his darling Anna and little Esendil too—both only small children when he had set out on the King's errand. The memory of their tiny faces and the hope of seeing them, along with his beloved wife Sharelle, again one day, was what had kept him clinging to sanity during all the long years of his imprisonment.

Keltor opened his eyes, quietly wiping away the tears that had fallen during his magical connection with his father. Kaitlin, sensing the depth of his pain, reached out and gently placed her hand on his arm, a silent gesture of comfort and support.

"Hey," she murmured softly, offering reassurance through both her words and her touch.

He managed a faint smile in response. "Hey."

Looking into his eyes, Kaitlin ventured, "You were talking to your father?"

Keltor nodded, the weight of what he had just experienced clear in his expression. "Kaitlin," he began, exhaling shakily as the vivid image of his father trapped in the dungeon flashed through his mind, "I could feel him—his pain and his sadness." He pressed his hand to his chest, as though to steady his heart. "I feel so awful that we never searched for him."

She tried to ease his guilt, reminding him gently, "Come on, you know why. My father told you he was dead. It's not your fault, or your mum's."

Keltor shook his head slightly, the news still heavy on his mind. "Kaitlin, he told me where he is. He's in a dungeon cell beneath Aranstream castle."

Shock crossed Kaitlin's face. "What, oh my god, Keltor," she whispered, pulling him into her arms and holding him tightly.

He clung to her, the realisation sinking in. "All this time, he was so close. I just can't believe it. That son of a bitch has kept him locked away in that dungeon for eleven years."

Kaitlin squeezed Keltor's arm, her voice gentle and reassuring. "Hey," she murmured, offering comfort in his moment of turmoil. "I know it's dreadful, what they've done to your father. But you can't change what's already happened. The important thing is you finally know where he is."

Keltor nodded, determination settling in his eyes. He reached up, his fingers softly brushing Kaitlin's cheek as he cradled her face. "And I'm going to go in and get him out," he said resolutely.

She nodded in response, pulling him into a tight embrace. Despite the wave of fear that trembled through her at the thought of Keltor attempting to break into Aranstream castle, she understood he needed to do this.

He held her close and whispered, "Don't worry, I'll be all right. I promise."

Kaitlin's voice was quiet and fierce as she replied in his ear, "You'd better be, husband."

He leaned back, a tender smile crossing his face. "Thank you for understanding," he said warmly. "I know this puts extra pressure on us, but I can't leave him there. I must get him out before we confront the King. If the King or the prince realises I'm alive and that you're with me, they might kill my father."

Her gaze lingered on his, her eyes brimming with both sadness and deep concern, yet beneath it all was an unwavering support for him. In a gentle voice, she acknowledged the burden he carried. "I know," she murmured, her words heavy with understanding but also quiet encouragement.

He shifted, determination evident in his posture. "Come on," he said, prompting her as he began to rise. "Let's get dressed and get out of here. The quicker we get the Deodars to the Eccleston Forest and settled, the quicker we can get all this over with." His resolve was clear; there was no time to waste.

Neither of them paused for breakfast, their focus solely on the urgent task ahead. As they prepared to leave, they waved their farewells to Ila and the rest of the tribe. In that moment, an unexpected wave of fear and anxiety swept through Kaitlin, catching her off guard and leaving her unsettled as they set out on their journey.

As they walked side by side through the shadowy woodland, Keltor noticed Kaitlin had grown quiet. He glanced at her with concern. "Hey, are you okay?" he asked softly, his voice laced with genuine worry.

Kaitlin turned to him, uncertainty flickering in her eyes. "I don't know," she admitted, her brow furrowing. "I have this strange sense of something not being quite right, but I can't quite put my finger on it."

He considered her words, searching for the source of her unease. "What, with Ila?" he suggested, wondering if something had happened with the tribe.

Kaitlin shook her head, dismissing the idea. "No, it's something else," she replied, her tone thoughtful.

"Maybe because we don't have Belrack and his men," Keltor offered, recalling their previous journey and the company they had then.

She shook her head again, more firmly this time. "No, I don't think it's that."

Keltor tried another explanation, a wry smile appearing on his lips. "Deja vu? I mean, we've just done this exact same journey. Although I know in reality it was over eight months ago, it still only feels like a couple of weeks ago to us, and to be fair, it didn't exactly go well."

Kaitlin managed a small smile and nodded, though her gaze drifted warily through the dark, foreboding forest. "Yeah, maybe that's it," she said, but her uneasy expression suggested she remained unconvinced.

They pressed on with determination, making impressive progress as the day wore on. By the time afternoon gradually faded into night, they had covered a considerable distance. Although they could have continued for a few more hours and possibly caught up with the rest of the tribe, Keltor judged that travelling through the forest after dark would be unwise.

Upon spotting a massive oak tree with a curved base, Keltor declared, "This will do us." The tree offered a natural shelter, and he suggested they settle down there for the night. "We can snuggle down in there and catch a few hours' sleep."

Kaitlin, feeling the fatigue of their journey, dropped her pack with a weary sigh. "I preferred the bed," she admitted, her discomfort clear.

"Me too," Keltor agreed, echoing her sentiment. He crouched down, opened his pack and retrieved his bedroll, with Kaitlin following suit. Keltor then cleared away sticks and other debris from the base of the tree, creating a smooth, level spot for them to rest. Together, they unrolled their bedrolls as far into the shelter of the tree as possible and sat down on them.

With their makeshift camp prepared, Keltor's thoughts turned to food. "So, what did Ila give us to eat?" he asked, prompted by his rumbling stomach.

"I am not sure. Let me check," Kaitlin replied, rummaging through her pack. She pulled out the bundle of provisions Ila had given them and examined its contents. "Some bread, goat's cheese, and ooh, this looks nice," she said, her eyes lighting up as she discovered something wrapped inside. "It looks like some kind of cake."

"Let me try," Keltor said, reaching out eagerly. Kaitlin passed him a slice, which he sampled straight away. "It's a honey cake," he announced through a mouthful. "You should try this; it's so good."

Taking his advice, Kaitlin tasted the cake herself and nodded in agreement, finding it delicious. She divided up the bread and cheese, and together they finished their simple meal, washing it down with water from their bottles.

"Come here," he said softly. She shifted closer, allowing him to slip his arm around her. Kaitlin nestled her head against his chest and let out a gentle sigh, comforted by Keltor's presence. Being alone together for another night filled her with happiness, even though they were outdoors, sheltering beneath the old oak tree.

The moonlight filtered through the canopy above, but its glow was too faint to reach them, leaving their little camp in near-complete darkness. Around them, the forest was alive with the sounds of night: the distant hoot of an owl among the branches and the subtle rustling of small animals moving through the undergrowth.

He felt her sigh and asked quietly, "Are you okay?"

"Yes. Knackered though," she replied, her fatigue clear.

"Me too," he agreed. "Let's get a few hours' sleep if we can."

They settled down beside each other. He kissed her goodnight, and Kaitlin pulled her cloak around herself, turning so her back faced him. Keltor draped his arm over her and drew closer, seeking warmth and a sense of security. Although he intended to rest, Keltor kept his sword at his side and remained alert, ready for any danger that might arise during the night.

Although the early morning mist obscured the surroundings, the presence of Kaitlin beside him provided a sense of comfort. Keltor watched her as she slept, smiling contentedly to himself and gently stroking her golden hair. When Kaitlin awoke, it took her a moment to regain her bearings. Keltor placed his hand on her arm, prompting her to look over her shoulder.

"Morning," she said with a smile, her eyes taking in his gorgeous face and his scuffed-up hair as he smiled back at her. She rolled over to face him.

"Morning, my beautiful," he replied, then leaned in to kiss her.

As she opened her eyes after the kiss, she shivered at the dampness in the air. "It's cold," she remarked.

Keltor hugged her, gently rubbing her back to warm her.

"Did you sleep okay?" he asked.

"Yeah, on and off. You?"

"Same, on and off."

Keltor glanced at the growing light and said, "I guess we really should make a move."

"Just five more minutes," Kaitlin pleaded, enjoying the comfort of his embrace.

"Okay, five more minutes," he agreed, drawing her closer.

They lay together quietly, listening to the early morning chorus of birds. As daylight broke, Keltor knew they could not stay any longer.

"Come on," he insisted. "We really should get going and catch up with the others."

"Okay," Kaitlin groaned, reluctantly moving out of his arms and sitting up.

She rubbed the sleep from her eyes, untangled her hair, and braided it.

"Here," Keltor offered, handing her a water bottle.

"Thanks," she replied gratefully, taking a long swig.

Kaitlin glanced at Keltor and said quietly, "I need to, you know," widening her eyes at him in a meaningful way.

He nodded, understanding immediately. "Yeah, me too. Don't go too far," he said, watching as she disappeared into the nearby shrubbery. They each took a moment for themselves, stepping away to find some privacy among the trees.

Once they had both finished, they returned to their small camp and began to pack up their belongings. Rolling up their bedrolls, they tucked them neatly back into their packs, making sure nothing was left behind.

As they set off on the path through the forest, Kaitlin drew in a deep breath and smiled. "I love the smell of the early morning, it reminds me of Elvendon farm," she remarked, savouring the freshness in the air as they walked.

Keltor inhaled deeply as well, taking in the earthy scent. "Yeah, me too. It's so fresh and earthy," he agreed, matching her mood.

Kaitlin looked around at the peacefulness that surrounded them. "And so peaceful, it's hard to imagine there's a war going on," she added, her tone reflective.

Keltor didn't reply but simply nodded in agreement. The tranquillity of the forest reminded him of how things used to be. Before all this, there was nothing he enjoyed more than an early morning walk through the woods, setting out at dawn, perhaps in search of deer, with only the sounds of nature for company.

They made good progress as they travelled through the dense forest, their pace steady and determined. Before long, they caught sight of the Deodar tribe up ahead.

"There they are," Keltor said, pointing towards the valley below. "Look, I can just make out Logan and Alarna at the back."

Kaitlin glanced at him, concern flickering across her face. "I hope everything is okay."

Keltor reassured her, his voice calm. "I'm sure they're all fine, it doesn't look like they've had any trouble from here."

They began their descent down the steep, wooded embankment, moving carefully and side-stepping to keep their footing secure on the slope.

Suddenly, Keltor reached out and grabbed Kaitlin's arm, bringing her to an abrupt halt.

"What is it?" she whispered, her voice barely audible.

He responded quietly, his gaze fixed ahead. "Someone's ahead of us." He gently guided her behind the wide trunk of an oak tree; his hand protectively placed on her stomach to keep her hidden. Peering around the tree, Keltor's eyes scanned their surroundings, searching for any sign of danger. After a tense moment, his expression softened and a smile broke across his face as he relaxed.

"It's okay," he said, letting go of her. Raising his voice, he called out, "Uly, it's us!"

Mere moments later, the tall figure of Uly emerged ahead, flanked by two female deodars. As they approached, Uly bowed respectfully to the pair. "Keltor, my Lady," he greeted them with formality.

Keltor stepped forward eagerly, greeting his friend with a warm display of camaraderie—slapping the palms of their hands together. "It's good to see you, my friend."

"Hi Uly," Kaitlin said, offering a friendly greeting. She also nodded to the two female deodars. "Hi."

As they began to walk together, Keltor asked, "Is everything okay?"

Uly nodded in response. "Yes, fine." However, he glanced around and noticed that they seemed to be alone. "Did they not want to help us, your troll friends?"

With a shake of the head, Keltor explained, "Unfortunately, they weren't there. They've also been taken by the King of Aranstream."

Uly's expression darkened. "This is very grave; indeed, it seems no tribe is safe from Aranstream."

Keltor agreed solemnly, "That is how it seems, my friend."

Within fifteen minutes, they had rejoined the main party. Uly moved on ahead to check on Ren, with the female deodars following close behind.

The morning fog continued to hang heavily over the valley, lending a chill to the air and casting an uneasy atmosphere upon the group. As Keltor and Kaitlin joined Logan and Alarna at the rear of the party, Logan turned to them with a look of concern. "No trolls?" he asked, searching their faces for hope.

Keltor shook his head gravely. "No, they've been captured by King Iwein. Only the women and the elderly have been left behind—just like in the Deodar village. The rest have been taken to Aranstream. Although..." He hesitated, his voice faltering, "whether they are alive or not is unknown."

Logan muttered a curse under his breath, frustration evident in his tone. "Damn it. So, what now?" His gaze shifted to Keltor, seeking answers amid the uncertainty.

Keltor simply shrugged, then outlined his plan. "We're going back to Elvendon to collect my mum and then take her and Esimae to an old forester's cottage I know deep in the Forest of Time. I'm hoping he's still there and will help us—perhaps he'll even have some men who can join us in the fight."

Logan's concern for his family was clear as he asked, "What about me and Alarna?"

Keltor replied thoughtfully, "I think you should stay with her and the Deodars until this is all over. She's in no condition to travel, and it's too risky where we are going."

Logan stood torn, his heart divided between the urge to join the impending fight and his responsibility to stay by Alarna's side. Keltor recognised the internal struggle playing out on Logan's face and gently addressed him. "Hey, it's okay, I know you want to come and help with the fight, but your place is with your wife and baby. We'll be okay."

Logan hesitated, voicing his concern. "Yeah, I guess, I just don't want to let you, or the Queen down."

Keltor offered reassurance, his tone sincere. "You're not, believe me. You two are important to us and I know Kaitlin would want you both safe. Especially Alarna—your baby is due any time and you need to be there for her."

Kaitlin, having overheard their conversation, joined in. "Logan, Keltor's right. I don't want anything happening to you two, especially Alarna."

Alarna, attempting to lighten the moment, responded with a nonchalant smile, her hand resting on her bump. "Oh, I'm okay. Please don't worry about us. If you need Logan to go with you, I understand. I have a few weeks left until the baby is due."

Kaitlin, however, was resolute. "No, no, absolutely not. He needs to be here for you and the baby. Besides, there are all these people to look after and feed—Uly needs all the help he can get," she said, gesturing towards the party of deodars ahead.

Alarna looked to Logan, linking her arm through his. "I guess so. Logan?"

Logan nodded, offering a warm smile to his wife. "I'll stay then." Turning to Keltor, he added, "So, what will you do next, after you've dropped your mum off, I mean?"

"I'm going to break into the encampment where they are holding all our men, but before I do that, I need to get into Aranstream castle first," Keltor stated, his voice calm but resolute.

Logan's brow furrowed in concern. "Into the castle, why?" he asked, struggling to understand. "That's just suicide, the place is full of guards, not to mention Prince Keion."

Kaitlin glanced over at Logan, then turned to Keltor with a frown, clearly uneasy about the plan. She did not like the idea either.

Keltor explained his reasoning quietly. "I believe my father is being held there and has been for the last eleven years or so. King Elvendon told my mother he had been killed on a mission, but I had a vision last night, and my dad was in a cell, and he told me he is in an Aranstream dungeon."

Logan looked momentarily confused. "A vision, what, like a magical thing?" he asked.

"Yes," Keltor replied simply, offering no further details.

Logan hesitated, his words faltering as he saw the tense expression on Keltor's face. Sensing it was best not to press further, he paused, but then an idea struck him.

"I think I may know a way in," Logan offered, his tone tentative.

253

Keltor looked up, curiosity piqued. "A way in? What, to the castle?"

Logan nodded. "When I was little, my father used to tell me stories about the old days, back when the castle was first given to the realm of Aranstream. It belonged to Elvendon originally, but a couple of centuries ago, an Elvendon princess married an Aranstream prince. The castle was a wedding gift from her father."

He continued, "There's a small river that runs beneath the castle, flowing out into the forest. After the castle was expanded to its current size, the entrance to the river was blocked off by a metal grate. In those days, supplies were brought in through this passage, and beneath it lies a trap door that opens into what used to be the wine cellar."

"My father said the servants used that route to bring provisions into the castle, though it's not used any more. Now, that area has become the dungeons. If King Iwein is holding your dad, and you saw cells in your vision, it's likely he's being kept there."

Kaitlin glanced at Keltor, observing the intensity with which he was processing Logan's account. Sensing his internal debate, she gently placed her hand on his arm and prompted him, "Well?"

After a brief pause, Keltor finally spoke, his voice steady but resolute. "I've changed my mind. Before I rescue my father, I think our best option is for me to break into the Aranstream camp where they are holding our army. We need to let them all know that you are still alive, that they have a Queen to fight for, and a chance to get the throne of Elvendon back. If Commander Talbot is there, things will be a lot easier—he will rally the soldiers, and we can make plans to break everyone out. When I know we are ready, I can slip out of the camp and get into the castle to rescue Dad. I will need him out before the men attack the castle, as the Aranstream guards may kill him first, especially if they discover who he is to me." He finished with a weary sigh, the weight of the plan evident in his expression.

Concerned, Kaitlin quietly asked, "Are you okay?"

Keltor gave a small, reassuring nod. "Yeah, I was just thinking of Ese," he replied softly.

Logan, unfamiliar with the name, looked puzzled. "Ese?" he queried.

Alarna stepped in to clarify. "It's his brother," she explained, directing a supportive glance at Keltor. However, before she could say more, Keltor spoke up again, determined to keep the conversation moving forward.

"Yeah, he was taken too, and I'm hoping he will be there, if he is he can help me get into the castle and rescue dad."

Alarna, her concern evident, asked, "What about your sister?"

Keltor gave a reassuring answer. "She's okay as far as I know. She's working at the palace in Elvendon."

Logan, still uncertain, pressed further. "Do you really think you can do this?"

Keltor's response was resolute. "Yes, I do. For a start, they don't know Kaitlin is still alive, so they will not be expecting anyone to oppose King Iwein or fight back. I know there are only a few of us, but that does make it easier for me to slip in and out."

Logan nodded in reluctant agreement. "I guess."

Kaitlin then turned to Keltor. "Keltor, I'm just going ahead to let Esimae know we're back," she said, gently releasing his arm. She turned to Alarna and asked, "Do you want to come?"

Alarna shook her head. "No, it's okay, you go. I'll just plod on here," she replied, rubbing her bump and waving Kaitlin off.

"Okay, I'll be back in a little while," Kaitlin responded, her tone determined yet slightly anxious, before hurrying on ahead. She deftly navigated her way through the line of deodars, elves, and children, each of whom dipped their heads respectfully towards her as she passed. Kaitlin acknowledged their greetings with a nod, her pace unbroken as she made her way to the front of the group, where she finally caught sight of her aunt.

Chapter Ten

Ambush

"Hey," she called out, moving in beside her aunt with relief evident in her voice.

Esimae turned, a wide grin lighting up her face, and for a moment she paused to embrace Kaitlin. "Kaitlin," she greeted warmly. "So, did you convince them to help us?"

Kaitlin let out a weary sigh and shook her head. "No, the men have been taken, the same as the deodars. We're not certain, but if they're still alive, they're probably at the camp in Aranstream."

Esimae's face darkened as they continued walking. "Oh hell," she muttered. "So, what now?"

"Keltor says we just carry on," Kaitlin explained. "After we settle the tribe, we head back, collect his mum, and go on to a woodsman that Keltor knows and wait there. He wants to break into the Aranstream camp and find the Commander of the army. He thinks if he knows I am alive, they will fight with us to get back Elvendon."

Esimae nodded in agreement. "They will, without a doubt," she said, though her tone remained cautious. "Still, it's risky."

Kaitlin nodded, her worry evident. "I know, and I am terrified of something happening to him. That's why I'm going with him."

Esimae's voice was firm as she addressed Kaitlin, her concern unmistakable. "Kaitlin, no, that's just ridiculous," she said forcefully. "You know how important you are. Our whole way of life has already changed beyond recognition, and if something happens to you then it's over. King Iwein will rule and that will be the end of Elvendon forever."

256

Kaitlin met her aunt's gaze, her determination unwavering. "I know, Esimae, but if something happens to him... Well, you know how I feel about that. I'm not going into the camp, I'm just going with him, and then when we get near, I will hide somewhere and wait for him. I must be nearby in case something happens, and he needs me."

Esimae let out a resigned sigh, unable to mask her frustration. "I know it's pointless arguing with you," she replied in exasperation, "but I still think that's foolish. What if you get captured, or worse?"

Kaitlin managed a reassuring smile. "I won't, we'll be careful, we've made it this far, haven't we?"

With a disagreeable shake of her head, Esimae voiced her lingering doubts, her worry for Kaitlin clear despite the conversation drawing to a close.

The dense fog that enveloped the group was gradually beginning to lift, but its lingering presence continued to obscure the hills surrounding them. The limited visibility heightened Keltor's unease, making every step forward feel uncertain and perilous.

Logan, perceptive to the change in Keltor's demeanour, asked quietly, "Are you okay?"

Keltor shook his head, tension evident in his voice. "No, something feels wrong," he replied, his senses on high alert as his eyes scanned the shifting mist for any sign of danger.

Suddenly, Keltor's instincts proved correct. "Arrow!" he shouted, reacting with remarkable speed. He drew his sword and deflected the incoming arrow away from Alarna. "It's an ambush. Take cover!" he warned, ducking swiftly as another arrow zipped past his head.

Logan reacted in an instant, pulling Alarna tightly against him. He positioned his body protectively in front of her, determined to shield her from the deadly hail of arrows now hurtling towards them. The threat, once a distant presence in the fog, was now terrifyingly real. Logan braced himself, focusing solely on keeping Alarna safe as the barrage descended upon their position.

257

Nearby, Keltor swiftly assessed the situation. Judging that his sword would be of little use at such a distance, he made the quick decision to rely on his magical abilities instead. He sheathed his blade and began to move his hands in a deliberate circular motion. Sparks of electrical light crackled and danced between his palms as he concentrated, drawing upon his power. Within moments, Keltor conjured a massive ball of fire and, with a forceful throw, hurled it into the thick fog in the direction from which the arrows originated.

An explosion echoed from within the mist, accompanied by the anguished cries of men caught in its blast. Yet, even as the sounds of the explosion faded, danger remained ever-present. Suddenly, a new volley of arrows came raining down upon them, this time from the other side of the ridge, intensifying the peril faced by the group.

Keltor whipped around, his hands moving with desperate speed as he conjured and hurled fire balls at the attackers. Each fiery projectile exploded through the fog, aimed precisely at the source of the relentless arrows. His focus was shattered for a moment as the elf beside him crumpled lifelessly to the ground, an arrow embedded in his heart. Chaos erupted among the deodars, their terrified screams filling the air as they scattered in all directions, desperately trying to escape the deadly onslaught raining down from the hills above.

Amidst the confusion, Logan drew his sword, determined to defend his wife. He pushed Alarna behind him, taking up a protective stance as the arrows rattled towards them. With swift, practiced movements, he struck at the incoming missiles, deflecting each one away from their vulnerable position. Then, through the haze of battle, Logan caught sight of the archers responsible for the attack.

Logan's voice rang out across the chaos. "Brothers!" he shouted, desperation clear in his tone. "Stop! It's me, Logan." Despite the distance shrouded in fog and battle, Logan had no doubt—he would recognise his four brothers anywhere, even from afar.

For a moment, the relentless hail of arrows targeting Logan and his wife ceased, as if the world itself paused in anticipation. The sudden lull in the onslaught brought a fleeting sense of hope, but it was quickly shattered by a furious accusation from one of Logan's brothers. His voice rang out, cutting through the chaos and fog, "You are a traitor to our King!" The words hung heavily in the air, laden with anger and betrayal, making it painfully clear that the bond of brotherhood was now overshadowed by allegiance to the crown.

"What? No," Logan yelled desperately, his voice cracking with anguish as he pleaded. His hands trembled at his sides, a cold sweat breaking out on his forehead. Memories of laughter and camaraderie with his brothers flickered painfully through his mind, contrasting sharply with the hostility now facing him. "I'm not—please, I want no part of this war, I just want to be with my wife and child. I'm your brother!" he begged, the words tumbling out raw and urgent. As he watched them stand and raise their bows, Logan's heart pounded in his chest. He searched their faces for any sign of mercy, recalling the last time they stood united on the battlefield, fighting shoulder to shoulder. That sense of kinship was gone, replaced by cold anger and bitter accusation, leaving Logan paralysed by the knowledge that the bond of family was no longer enough to protect him.

"Alarna!" he cried out, despair filling his voice as the grim reality of their predicament became clear. Logan turned to face her, aware there was nowhere left for them to run and no means of protection against what was about to unfold. Driven by instinct and love, he threw himself in front of Alarna, using his own body as a shield. Determined to protect her from the torrent of arrows he knew would soon rain down upon them, he braced himself, ready to endure whatever came to ensure her safety.

Logan's voice trembled as he turned to Alarna, his eyes shining with tears that streamed down his cheeks. His words were soft yet resolute, the weight of the moment heavy in every syllable. "I love you, Alarna, and our baby, with all of my heart," he said, his voice breaking as he faced the reality of what was about to unfold. "Remember me always."

Alarna shook her head in anguish, tears coursing down her face as she clung to Logan, unable to accept the finality in his voice. Her sobs filled the air, raw with grief and desperation. "I love you, Logan," she replied, her words choked by sorrow, holding onto him with all the strength she could muster as the world around them threatened to collapse.

"TRAITOR!" Logan's brothers cried out in unison, their voices laden with fury and betrayal. In that instant, they unleashed their arrows, each one aimed with deadly intent.

"Logan, no!" Keltor heard Alarna scream in abject terror.

Keltor glanced urgently over his shoulder just as four arrows hit Logan, penetrating deep into his back. As Logan collapsed, his body fell against Alarna's stomach, forcing her to stagger backward under his sudden weight "Logan!" she screamed hysterically.

"Logan, Alarna!" Keltor shrieked, anguish and fear sharpening his voice. His eyes darted urgently towards the direction from which the deadly arrows had flown, searching through the chaos and fog for the source of the attack on his friends.

The terrified screams of the Deodar children pierced through the chaos of battle, seizing Keltor's attention and drawing his desperate gaze towards them. Amid the relentless barrage of arrows, the children scattered, their small forms weaving frantically through the confusion. Panic-stricken, the adult Deodars, faces etched with fear, did everything within their power to shield and guide the young ones, urging them towards any semblance of safety as arrows continued to rain down from above.

Keltor found himself torn between the desperate urge to rescue his friends and his duty to protect the Deodar children. His heart wavered for a split second; agony etched across his face as he weighed the impossible choice. Instinct, however, took command, compelling his left hand to shoot upwards in a swift, decisive gesture. Without allowing himself the luxury of hesitation, Keltor's voice rang out over the tumult, resolute and urgent as he uttered the incantation, *"Deflecto perforabunt sagisttis!"* The magical command echoed through the chaos, a clear sign of his determination to shield the innocent from harm.

Channelling his magic with a sweeping gesture, Keltor summoned a protective force that surged outward, intercepting the deadly arrows aimed at the children. The shimmering barrier deflected the missiles, shielding the young ones from harm and offering a momentary respite amid the turmoil of battle.

Keltor heard Alarna scream again, her voice cutting through the din of the battle. Instinctively, he spun towards her, only to catch sight of an arrow hurtling directly at him. Reacting in a split second, Keltor threw himself backwards, his body arching almost in half as the arrow-streaked past, just grazing his face. The near miss left a burning sting on his cheek, but he had no time to dwell on it.

He turned back to Alarna, but sudden terrified screams of the children pierced the chaos to his right. More arrows whistled through the air; their deadly points aimed directly at the young ones. Acting swiftly, he called out, *"Deflecto perforabunt sagisttis,"* his voice ringing with urgency as he unleashed another surge of protective magic. The barrier shimmered into existence, intercepting the lethal missiles and shielding the children from harm.

Alarna's whole body trembled with fear as she held the dead body of her husband against her. "Logan!" she wept, shaking him even though she knew he was dead. A thousand memories flashed through her mind—his laughter, their whispered promises—now lost forever. The whistling sound of arrows caught her attention. She looked up and screamed. Without mercy his brothers continued with their ruthless assault. Their aim now firmly on Alarna. With a terrible thud, thud, thud, three arrows pounded into Alarna's chest. She crashed to the ground with Logan's body on top of her.

Keltor's anguished cry pierced the chaos. "Alarna!" he shrieked, his face contorted in a mask of panic and horror. In his desperation, his hands fell to his sides, the protective magic he had summoned for the children dissipating as his attention turned towards Alarna's stricken form.

But Alarna, her voice fraught with urgency and pain, stopped him with a desperate scream. "No!" she cried at Keltor, thrusting her hand out in a futile attempt to halt his movement. "You save those children!"

Keltor spun back towards the terrified Deodar children, his focus sharpening as the threat intensified. With a forceful shout, he summoned his protective magic once more. "*Deflecto perforabunt sagisttis!*" he bellowed, his hands raised high as he unleashed the spell. The arcane shield manifested instantly, intercepting the next flurry of arrows that rained down, turning deadly projectiles aside before they could reach their intended targets.

As the last of the arrows ricocheted harmlessly off his magical barrier, the dense fog that had cloaked the battlefield began to lift. The murky veil thinned, gradually revealing the enemy responsible for the merciless attack. High on the ridge, silhouetted against the clearing sky, Keltor could now make out the forms of approximately ten Aranstream soldiers, their bows still poised for another assault. The sight crystallised the threat they faced, making clear both the source of the deadly arrows and the scale of the danger looming over the Deodar tribe.

Kaitlin and Esimae moved at the head of the tribe, guiding their people forward when the sudden onset of terrified screams shattered the relative calm. Esimae's face paled as she spun around, her voice cutting through the confusion. "What the hell," she cried, alarmed by the commotion.

In that instant, Kaitlin's eyes widened in horror as she caught sight of arrows descending from above, their lethal intent clear. Panic surged through her as she screamed, "Esimae!" desperate to warn her companion of the imminent danger threatening their people.

Without hesitation, Esimae reached out, urgency in her tone. "Give me your hand, now," she commanded, extending her hand towards Kaitlin. Responding instinctively, Kaitlin grasped Esimae's hand, their fingers entwining in solidarity. Together, they raised their free hands, spreading them wide to channel their combined magical power. Their voices joined in a chant, resonating above the chaos: "*Magicae ex fonte, protegat eos dominus!*"

A radiant stream of magic burst forth from their hands, the energy cascading like a shower of stars. The brilliant arc arced above their people, forming a protective barrier that shimmered in the turmoil. As the hail of arrows reached the magical shield, each projectile rebounded harmlessly, thwarted in its deadly purpose by the strength of Kaitlin and Esimae's spell.

"Hold it steady!" Esimae cried, as they dodged the arrows that were now redirected towards them.

Kaitlin screamed as pain shot through her shoulder, stumbling backwards several steps as an arrow struck her. The sudden blow caused her momentarily to lose the magical connection with Esimae, the protective forcefield wavering under the disruption.

Kaitlin let out a sharp cry of pain, her hand instinctively flying up to the arrow embedded in her shoulder. Gritting her teeth against the agony, she snapped off the protruding end and tossed it aside, determination etched across her face. Drawing a deep, steadying breath, she reached for Esimae's hand once more, resolutely re-establishing their magical connection and strengthening the protective barrier around their people.

"I'm okay," she insisted through clenched teeth, forcing a reassuring tone despite the pain. "It's just clipped me – it's not in the bone. You can pull the rest of it out later." Her words were meant to settle any concern and keep Esimae focused on maintaining the spell.

Her aunt gave her a firm nod and put all her concentration back into the forcefield. "We can't hold this for much longer," Esimae gasped as she felt her power draining. Gritting her teeth, she channelled the last reserves of her strength into the shimmering barrier, sweat beading along her brow as the relentless barrage persisted. All around them, the magical shield flickered under the strain, wavering dangerously with each impact. Keltor's presence, his own magic flaring, offered a brief flicker of hope to the panicked tribe as the onslaught continued. Yet with each passing moment, the effort demanded from Kaitlin and Esimae became almost unbearable, their arms trembling from the intensity of the spell. The chaos of the attack, the cries of the Deodar children, and the grim determination in Esimae's eyes all melded into a single, desperate will to protect, even as the world threatened to collapse around them.

As Keltor gazed across at Alarna, a surge of anger welled up inside him. His rage intensified with every passing moment, and the force of his emotions began to manifest physically. Throwing his arms wide to either side, he started to tremble, the sheer power coursing through him making his entire body shake. His eyes blazed with a brilliant white light, betraying the raw magical energy building within.

With deliberate purpose, Keltor stepped forward, one leg bent slightly to anchor himself against the magnitude of the power he was about to unleash. He shouted, "*Et magicae virtute simul, et conteret eos,*" his voice echoing throughout the valley. As he spoke, he lifted his hands smoothly, palms facing outwards, and a colossal bolt of pure energy began to form between them.

In a single, fluid motion, Keltor thrust his hands forward. The bolt of energy shot across the valley with unstoppable force, climbing the hillside where the enemy soldiers were concealed. Upon impact, there was a thunderous explosion—his magic struck the soldiers with devastating effect and blasted apart the very side of the hill that had sheltered them.

Kaitlin and Esimae's magical connection were abruptly severed as both, along with the rest of their party, instinctively ducked in response to the deafening explosion that echoed across the valley. The very ground beneath them trembled, the hillside shuddering violently as debris began to rain down in their direction, threatening to engulf them all.

"Run!" Kaitlin screamed, her voice cutting through the chaos as she rushed towards her companions, frantically waving her arms to urge them into action. "Run, come on, hurry!" she pleaded, panic rising in her chest as she watched the hillside shifting menacingly towards them.

Reacting to her call, the Deodars and the Elves wasted no time; they grabbed their children and fled, sprinting at full speed to escape the oncoming danger. Amid the turmoil, Keltor's gaze darted from the landslide he had unintentionally set in motion to the scattering Deodars, understanding the immediate peril they faced.

With a commanding shout of *"Pitdor nar,"* Keltor raised his hands, magical energy rippling through him as he struggled to harness his power. His entire frame shook with the strain as he channelled his magic towards the advancing landslide, desperately attempting to hold it at bay and buy precious seconds for everyone to escape its deadly path.

As the others rushed past her, Kaitlin pushed her way against the tide, fighting through the fleeing crowd in the opposite direction, her determination fixed on reaching Keltor. "Keltor!" she cried, her eyes locking onto him before darting anxiously back to the moving hillside. The realisation of the immense effort he was exerting struck her, and she muttered breathlessly, "My god, Keltor," fully understanding the risk he was taking for them all.

Meeting Kaitlin's gaze, Keltor called out to her, his voice urgent and strained. "Stop, stay there, I can't hold it any longer!" he warned, his strength faltering as he struggled to contain the landslide that threatened to break free once more.

Kaitlin came to an abrupt halt, her desperation to reach Keltor momentarily overridden by the danger in his voice. She glanced back at the landslide, seeing it beginning to shift and move again, realising that Keltor was at his limit and could no longer hold back the advancing earth. Forced to make a split-second decision, she turned away from him and ran back towards the others, just as the crashing sound of the land filled the gap between her and Keltor, cutting off her path.

In the chaos that followed, Kaitlin's voice rang out as she searched frantically for her companion. "Uly, Uly!" she screamed, dodging through the confusion and turmoil to find him.

Her call was answered a moment later. "Your highness," Uly called out, his voice carrying above the noise. Kaitlin spun around and saw him moving towards her, relief flooding through her as she spotted him amid the disorder.

"Keltor's on the other side, with Alarna and Logan, I need to get to him!" she cried urgently.

Uly looked at the landslide, it was far too unstable to climb, and he looked to the banks of the ravine, searching for a way through.

"There, look," he said pointing, "it's a goat track, we can get over the top of the landslide that way."

"Okay, come on," she urged, and she began to hurry towards the start of the track.

"Kaitlin, wait!" her aunt Esimae screamed at her.

"Esimae, I have to get to them!" Kaitlin shouted back, convinced her aunt was about to try and stop her.

"I know, but you can't go with an arrow hanging out of your shoulder!" Esimae retorted.

Kaitlin glanced at her left shoulder and, amidst all the panic, realised she had not yet registered the pain. "Oh shit, yes, can you pull it out, quickly Esimae?" she pleaded, desperation etched in her voice.

"Yes, but it's going to hurt like hell," Esimae cautioned, her gaze steady as she prepared to remove the arrow.

"I don't care, just hurry, please," Kaitlin pleaded, her desperation clear. Esimae gave a firm nod in response.

"After three," she warned, giving Kaitlin a moment to brace herself. Kaitlin nodded, turning her face away in anticipation.

Kaitlin let out a scream and almost collapsed to the ground from the sudden, intense pain as the arrow was pulled from her shoulder. She fought to steady herself, taking several deep breaths to regain her composure. Through the haze of discomfort, she saw Esimae bring the arrowhead close to her nose and sniff at it.

266

As Kaitlin straightened up, she groaned from the pain and fatigue. "What are you doing?" she asked, her voice strained.

"Checking there is no poison," she replied, and Kaitlin's face looked at her in worry. "It's okay, I can't smell anything. Let me sort that."

"Later, I need to get to them," she insisted, determination clear in her tone as she turned to leave with Uly. Before she could move away, Esimae reached out swiftly and grabbed her other arm, holding her back with a firm grip.

Esimae fixed Kaitlin with a stern look. "What, you want to bleed to death? How is that going to help him?" she growled, her frustration evident. Kaitlin glanced at her shoulder and realised it was bleeding quite heavily.

"Oh god, okay, please just hurry," Kaitlin begged.

Esimae quickly tore a strip from the hem of her white underdress, the fabric ripping with a sharp sound amidst the chaos. Kaitlin opened her mouth to protest, but before she could get the words out, her aunt silenced her with a stern look and a gentle shush.

"This will have to do for now, but you'll need a proper poultice on it as soon as possible," Esimae said, her tone firm and practical. She pressed the makeshift bandage firmly into the wound on Kaitlin's shoulder. Kaitlin couldn't help but wince at the pain, but she managed a grateful nod in response.

Without wasting another moment, Esimae took Kaitlin's other hand and guided it to the wound, making sure she applied steady pressure to slow the bleeding.

"Keep the pressure on it," Esimae instructed Kaitlin, her tone resolute. Kaitlin nodded in response, pressing her hand firmly against the wound in her shoulder as her aunt had shown her. The pain was sharp and persistent, but she focused on following the instruction.

Turning to Uly, Esimae reiterated, "Uly, make sure she keeps pressure on it until the bleeding stops." Uly nodded, understanding the seriousness of the situation and remaining close to Kaitlin to ensure she did not falter.

Gratitude flickered across Kaitlin's face as she turned to her aunt. "Thank you," she said quietly, pushing down hard on her wound to staunch the flow of blood. She looked to Uly, urgency driving her forward. "Uly, let's go," she urged.

As they began to move away, Esimae called after them, her voice full of concern. "Be careful!" she shouted, but Kaitlin's mind was already fixed on reaching Keltor and her friends, her determination overriding everything else.

Once he was certain that she was out of harm's way, Keltor summoned the last reserves of his strength and released the landslide. His arms fell limply to his sides, and he dropped to his knees, utterly spent. The ground beneath him trembled violently, and the roar of the collapsing hillside filled the air. Keltor watched as the earth crashed down, severing the path and blocking her from reaching him. Every muscle in his body shook with exhaustion, the effort having drained him completely. He inhaled sharply, stunned by the magnitude of what he had just accomplished, unable to fathom where the power or knowledge to do so had come from.

He glanced to his left and was met with a gut-wrenching sight—Logan's body was slumped protectively over Alarna. The wave of dread that swept through Keltor was so intense that he had to fight the urge to be sick right there and then. Swallowing down his nausea, he forced himself to move. He scrambled awkwardly to his feet and dashed towards Alarna, his heart hammering with fear and desperation.

"Logan," he begged in desperate hope, even though he knew with four arrows pinned into his back that his friend was most likely dead. "God damn it," he swore, in both anger and sadness as his fears turned into reality, and he laid his dead friend's body to the ground.

Keltor's breath caught in his throat as he took in the scene before him. The full horror of it hit him, and a wave of anguish swept through his body. "Oh no. Alarna!" he sobbed, realising the extent of her wounds—she had been gravely injured, perhaps beyond saving. Consumed by grief, he dropped to his knees beside her, unable to hold back his tears. Alarna lay there motionless, her eyes closed, the life seemingly ebbing from her with every passing moment.

"Alarna," he said again in almost a whisper, and he lifted her head gently from the ground. Her face was covered in blood, and she had four arrows protruding from her chest.

It was so quiet it was almost deafening. No bird song, no wind. Just silence. As if the very valley mourned with them, aware of the life slipping away in their midst. Keltor gently swept his hand through her hair. His heart pounded with helplessness, each breath a silent plea for her to hold on. Alarna's eyes flickered open. "Kel...tor," she struggled to say. "My baby..."

Keltor's heart clenched as he fully grasped the weight of Alarna's words. Logan's selfless act—shielding Alarna with his own body—had saved their unborn child, but at a terrible cost. The realisation that the mother might not survive struck him with unbearable sorrow.

Desperate to comfort her, Keltor tried to soothe her fears. "It's okay, your baby's okay, there's no arrows," he reassured gently, his voice thick with emotion. With trembling hands, he reached out and softly touched her face, his thumb brushing her cheek as he tried to anchor her to life.

Her breath shuddered, so faint he feared it might be her last. As Keltor cradled her head, the truth of her wounds pressed down on him like a weight he could not bear. The valley's silence wrapped around them, punctuated only by Alarna's laboured gasps. He pressed his forehead to hers, desperate to anchor her to life, voice trembling as he whispered, "Hold on, Alarna, please." Yet even as he spoke, her grip on his sleeve slackened, her strength slipping away with every heartbeat.

Keltor stared at the landslide, a wall of earth and debris now irrevocably separating him from Kaitlin. The realisation struck him with cold certainty—no matter how desperately Kaitlin might try, she would never make it in time to help Alarna. Even if she could, it was already too late.

As he knelt beside Alarna, her hand trembled and reached for his sleeve, holding on with the last remnants of her strength. Her voice, barely above a whisper, struggled through the pain: "It was his brothers."

Keltor frowned, confused and desperate to understand. "What?" he asked, worry etched into every word.

Alarna's eyes fluttered, and with a shuddering breath she managed, "Logan's brothers killed him. Keltor. I saw them as I fell." Her words were punctuated by a gasp as each breath became harder to draw.

Alarm rippled through Keltor as he watched her fight for consciousness. "Shh, don't talk, Alarna, please stay with me!" he pleaded, fear tightening his voice as her breathing grew more ragged and laboured.

Alarna's voice was barely audible, each word forced out between laboured breaths. "Take my baby out," she whispered, her tone urgent but weak.

Keltor, straining to understand Alarna's faint words, bent closer, his ear nearly touching her trembling lips. "What?" he asked, voice thick with worry as he struggled to make out her weak utterance.

Tears streamed down Alarna's cheeks as she clung to Keltor, her desperation etched in every trembling word. "My baby, Keltor, deliver him. Take him from me—don't let him die," she pleaded, her voice raw with anguish. The agony in her gaze made Keltor's heart wrench with sorrow and dread.

Keltor's voice broke, thick with anguish. "Alarna, no, I can't," he wept, his words trembling with helplessness. A wave of nausea surged through him at the thought of what she was asking, twisting his stomach with horror. Grief struck him with such force it felt as though his heart was being torn from his chest, leaving him hollow and broken, overwhelmed by sorrow and loss.

"I'm not going to make it, Keltor, please don't let my baby die too," she choked. "Please," she begged, as he gently wiped the blood from her lips.

Keltor's voice broke as grief overwhelmed him, tears streaming unchecked down his cheeks. "I can't," he whispered, his gaze fixed on Alarna, torn apart by the impossible request she had made. The thought of what she was asking left him paralysed by horror and sorrow. Keltor's world narrowed to that single, fragile connection, torn between the unbearable loss and the impossible duty she had pressed upon him, the horror of her plea echoing in the stillness as her eyes fluttered shut once more.

"Alarna, I'm so sorry, I should have protected you both," he sobbed, his words choked by anguish. The sense of helplessness crushed him, knowing nothing he could say or do would erase the pain or undo what had happened.

"No, shh," she murmured, her voice trembling before she was wracked by a violent cough, thick blood spilling from her lips.

"Alarna," Keltor cried out, anguish flooding his voice.

"Keltor," she mumbled, and as he leaned closer, Alarna managed to clutch his forearm, her hand glistening with blood as her eyes flickered open. "You can't save everyone, but you can save my baby. Do it!" she begged. "Don't let him die." She gasped for breath. Keltor sobbed. Watching her slip away was killing him. He could do nothing to stop it. "Make him your ward, promise me!"

Keltor nodded through his tears, his voice trembling with emotion as he made his solemn vow. "I will always protect him, I swear this to you," he promised, his words choked by sobs and the weight of responsibility now resting upon him.

Alarna's hand, slick with blood and trembling, fumbled to her neck. Summoning the last of her strength, she yanked her chain free and pressed it into Keltor's palm. "Give this to him," she whispered, her eyes pleading, "Tell him... his mother and father loved him. So much." The chain, glinting with memories, was a symbol of the love and hope she wished to pass on to her child amid the tragedy unfolding around them.

Keltor's hands shook uncontrollably as he took the chain from Alarna, the cold metal pressing into his palm serving as a stark reminder of the immense responsibility he had just accepted. His heart thundered in his chest, weighed down by fear and the magnitude of the vow he had made to her in her final moments.

Keltor's gaze flickered towards the shimmering barrier that separated him from Kaitlin and Esimae—the only two people who might have been able to save Alarna. The crushing realisation dawned on him with painful clarity: he was the one who had brought the barrier down, sealing their fate and extinguishing the last glimmer of hope. The enormity of his actions pressed down on him, sharp and unforgiving, gnawing at his conscience.

"Alarna, I can't do this," he wept, his voice full of anguish. Pain and guilt twisted inside him, but there was no time for hesitation as reality crashed over him. Alarna, her strength spent, gurgled weakly, "You can... save him... please," her bloodstained hand gripping his shirt for a fleeting moment before falling limp onto his lap.

"Alarna, no, no!" Keltor cried, shaking her as despair threatened to overwhelm him, but she was already gone. "No, no," he repeated, his grief pouring out as he lowered his head, resting it on her bump. In that moment of devastation, he felt a kick. The tiny movement jolted him to action. He drew in a shaky breath and wiped his tears away with the back of his hand. There was no time left to grieve. If this baby was to live, he had to act now.

Keltor, desperate and pressed for time, drew his knife from his belt with trembling hands. He quickly lifted Alarna's dress, preparing himself for the task ahead. Placing one hand gently on her baby bump, he paused for a moment as he felt a small kick— a sign of life amid the tragedy unfolding around him.

Keltor's hands trembled uncontrollably as he hovered over Alarna, the enormity of the moment nearly overwhelming him. Desperation and fear surged through him, threatening to paralyse his every movement. Swallowing hard, he squeezed his eyes shut for a brief instant and whispered, "Spirits, please, please guide me," his voice ragged and pleading as he sought comfort and strength from forces beyond his understanding. The weight of his promise to Alarna—and the fate of the unborn child—hung heavy upon him, driving him to steady his shaking hand in the hope that he might yet save a life, even as another had slipped away.

As he cut vertically and carefully into Alarna's lower abdomen, his stomach retched. He knew she was gone and could feel nothing, but it didn't stop the burning pain in his heart at what he was doing to her. With hands trembling and tears still streaking his face, Keltor gently lifted the hem of Alarna's dress. With care, he draped the fabric over her face.

As Keltor worked, each heartbeat felt like an eternity, his hands guided by desperate hope rather than knowledge. The silence was suffocating until, finally, his fingers found what he sought—a small, fragile head slick with life and possibility.

He coaxed the newborn gently, his trembling hands guided by desperation as he cleared the last of the way. In a rush of relief and dread, the baby slipped free—slick, fragile and silent in Keltor's grasp. Panic surged through him; he swept his finger swiftly around the tiny mouth, clearing away mucus, then turned the infant and rubbed its back with the urgency born of hope and fear.

"Come on, baby, please," he begged urgently. The tension hung heavy in the air until a sharp cry pierced the silence, jolting him into laughter and tears all at once, overwhelmed by the impossible joy that the child was alive.

With careful hands, Keltor severed the last physical ties binding the child to Alarna, his breath trembling as he worked. He cradled the baby close, wiping away the remnants of birth with gentle, reverent motions, his heart pounding with a mixture of sorrow and hope. There was no time to linger; he pressed the baby gently against his chest for warmth and comfort. Bracing himself, Keltor reached for Alarna's bag, searching for anything that might help. On finding a blanket, he gently wrapped the infant securely, he wept as he felt both the weight of joy and loss settle on his shoulders. As he cleaned his hands and the newborn, the world around him seemed to pause, the silence broken only by the soft whimpering of the child.

Keltor gazed at Logan's lifeless form before gently pulling the dress away from Alarna's face, his actions tender and reverent. He

273

carefully used the soft fabric to conceal the open wound, a final gesture of dignity for Alarna. Turning his attention back to Logan, he spoke softly, his voice thick with sorrow and affection. "See Logan, and Alarna," Keltor murmured, acknowledging both. He looked at Logan; the pain of loss etched deeply into his features. "Logan was right, you have a beautiful little boy, and he's just perfect.

"Hey, shh," he whispered softly, as he quietly soothed the crying baby, gently patting the child in a calm and protective manner against his chest.

"I'm so sorry I couldn't save your mum and dad," Keltor wept regretfully, "But don't worry, okay, you will be alright. I'm sure Kaitlin will let you stay with us." He looked at him and smiled and then pulled the baby back tight to his chest for warmth.

Keltor's grip tightened instinctively around his sword as he sensed movement behind him. With the baby still held securely in his other arm, he sprang to his feet, pivoting swiftly in a defensive stance. The sudden rush of adrenaline spurred him into action, and he swung around, ready to confront whatever threat might be approaching from behind.

Kaitlin and Uly stood frozen in place, the shock of the devastating scene before them rendering them speechless. As Kaitlin's gaze met Keltor's, a wave of anguish washed over her, tears streaming down her cheeks as the realisation struck—her friends were gone. The enormity of the loss overwhelmed her, and she broke down, her sobs echoing the grief in her heart.

Keltor, overcome by sorrow, felt as though his heart would cease beating beneath the weight of Kaitlin's pain. Her tear-filled eyes reflected his own despair, and in that moment, his composure shattered. Unable to contain his emotions, he let out a strangled sob and, gripped by a sudden surge of anguish, cast his sword to the ground—a silent gesture of defeat and heartbreak.

Kaitlin rushed to Keltor, immediately pulling both him and the baby close to her chest. She held them tightly, her embrace offering comfort amid overwhelming sorrow. Tears streamed down her face as she pressed her cheek to his, her breath warm against his skin and her gentle touch providing a momentary sense of calm amidst the chaos.

Keltor's tears flowed freely as he pressed his face into Kaitlin's shoulder. "I couldn't save her, Kaitlin," he wept, the words a raw confession of the pain and grief he had been holding inside. In that moment, the depth of his sorrow was laid bare, his anguish shared with the only person who might understand the weight of his loss.

"It's okay, it's okay, shush," Kaitlin soothed gently as she held Keltor, her words offering comfort amid their shared grief. She glanced down at the baby; her eyes filled with tenderness and sorrow.

"It's a boy," Keltor whispered, a fleeting smile illuminating his features as he met Kaitlin's gaze. The brief glimmer of happiness was soon overshadowed by the heaviness of recent events. With a trembling voice, he added, "Alarna wanted me to…," he hesitated, struggling to find the words, "take him out of her," he finished softly, the burden of his actions weighing on him.

Kaitlin's eyes widened in disbelief and understanding. "Oh my god, Keltor," she breathed, her hand reaching up to gently touch his anguished face. Her gesture conveyed both empathy and regret. "We tried to get over to you, but the landslide was too loose, so we had to climb around." Her voice was thick with sorrow, the memory of the chaos still vivid in her mind.

Keltor's tears welled up anew as he replied, his voice breaking. "I did that, I blocked you from getting to her," he admitted, the guilt and pain evident in his tearful confession. The weight of what he had done pressed heavily on his heart, even as Kaitlin remained by his side to share in his grief.

"No, no, you didn't," Kaitlin said softly, her voice firm yet gentle as she tried to comfort Keltor. "You saved us all, Keltor. If you hadn't done what you did, we would have all died. Esimae and I could only hold that barrier for a few more minutes. Do you understand? It's not your fault they died. You saved all of us."

Keltor's pain did not ease, and he replied in a quiet, broken voice, "Not all of us." His gaze dropped to the baby nestled against his chest and then drifted to the still forms of Alarna and Logan.

275

He closed his eyes for a moment, overcome with fresh sorrow, and let out a whimper.

Seeing his anguish, Kaitlin held him even tighter, her arms wrapping securely around him. Her hand moved in slow, soothing circles on his back, a loving gesture meant to offer comfort and reassurance.

Keltor's hand, seeking solace, lifted to rest on Kaitlin's shoulder. As he did so, Kaitlin winced, a fleeting expression of pain momentarily breaking through her efforts to console him.

"What's wrong?" Keltor asked, his voice filled with concern as he noticed Kaitlin wince.

Kaitlin attempted to brush away Keltor's concern, offering a faint, reassuring smile. "Oh, it's nothing," she replied, gently releasing him from her embrace, though there was a telltale tightness in her voice.

Before she could say more, Uly stepped forward, his expression sombre as he revealed the truth. "She was hit by an arrow," he admitted quietly, not wanting to alarm Keltor but unwilling to hide the seriousness of the situation.

Keltor's eyes widened with worry, his concern for Kaitlin overwhelming his own pain. "Are you okay?" he asked, his voice trembling as he reached out, carefully pulling back her cloak to see for himself.

"It's nothing, really, it just nipped me, that's all."

Keltor raised an eyebrow at Kaitlin, his concern for her injury evident. In response, she offered a reassuring smile, determined to ease his worries. "I promise, it will be fine. Esimae will give me a poultice for it later," Kaitlin assured him, her voice gentle yet firm, hoping to dispel any lingering doubts about her well-being.

Turning his attention to the aftermath of the recent ordeal, Keltor addressed Uly, his tone marked by both exhaustion and concern as he wiped his tears away with the back of his hand while gently jiggling the baby in his other arm. "Uly, how are the others? Did we lose many?"

Uly's response was sombre but reassuring. "We lost one of the elders. Some have been injured, but no others died, thanks to you both and Esimae," he said, emphasising the collective effort that had ensured the survival of most of their group.

Keltor nodded towards the lifeless body of an elf nearby, acknowledging the sacrifice made. "Well, and him," he added quietly, honouring the fallen with a respectful gesture.

Uly approached quietly, his steps heavy with the weight of loss. Kneeling beside the still figure, he gently turned the man over and studied his features for a moment. "This man is known as Neal," Uly announced with a subdued voice as he rose to his feet. "He had no family here. I will bury him," he added, his resolve evident in the solemnity of his tone.

Keltor nodded, grateful for Uly's willingness to tend to the deceased. "Okay, thanks Uly," he replied, glancing towards the bodies of Alarna and Logan. With a heavy heart, he turned to Kaitlin. "Kaitlin, will you take him for me? I can't leave them like this—I want to bury them as well," he said, his eyes lingering on the fallen companions.

"Of course," Kaitlin responded softly. She accepted the tiny baby from Keltor, her arms providing a safe and nurturing embrace. Cradling the infant gently, she leaned down and smiled warmly. "Hi," she greeted in a whisper, tenderly pulling back the edge of the blanket to reveal the baby's small, delicate face. "You are very cute," she murmured, her little finger softly stroking his cheek as she offered him comfort.

"Uly, will you help me, please?" Keltor asked, his voice trembling with emotion. The big man gave a silent nod, his face set with determination as he stepped forward to assist.

Meanwhile, Kaitlin paced slowly up and down, the baby cradled protectively against her chest. She rocked him gently, her eyes never straying far from the solemn scene unfolding before her. Uly and Keltor worked together to bury Logan and Alarna, carefully covering their bodies with stones and boulders. The weight of their loss pressed heavily on Kaitlin's heart; she struggled to come to terms with the tragedy that had befallen them. It seemed impossible that her dearest friend could be gone so suddenly—Alarna, who had brought so much warmth and light into her life, was now lost forever in the blink of an eye.

Fighting back tears, Kaitlin pressed her lips together in a determined effort to remain strong. She gazed down at the tiny, vulnerable child in her arms—Alarna's baby, who would never know his mother. The cruel reality struck her: this little soul had become an orphan before he had even taken his first breath in the world. Tenderly, she kissed the top of the baby's head and drew him closer, offering what comfort she could.

Her thoughts turned to Keltor, whose courage in the face of heartbreak had made all the difference. Kaitlin could hardly fathom the strength it must have taken for him to do what he had done for Alarna. She knew it must have broken his heart, yet his bravery had ensured that the baby would have a chance at life—a life that surely would have been lost without his intervention. In that moment, Kaitlin felt a deep sense of gratitude and admiration for Keltor's sacrifice and resolve.

As Keltor placed the final stone over the grave, a deep and sorrowful sigh escaped him. He paused, wiping the tears from his eyes before glancing over to Kaitlin. Seeing her softly speaking to the baby and pacing with gentle patience brought a faint smile to his face, a fleeting moment of solace amid the grief. With a determined breath, he braced his hands on his knees and slowly stood up.

"Keltor, he will need feeding," Kaitlin said, her voice tinged with concern as the baby began to cry, his tiny face scrunched up in distress.

Keltor stooped to retrieve Alarna's backpack, his movements careful and deliberate. "Alarna has a few things in here for the baby," he said, his voice low as he checked the contents, making sure to honour her preparations for her child's wellbeing.

Then, pausing with a thoughtful look, Keltor reached into his pocket. "Oh, can you look after this for me?" he asked gently. "Alarna wanted him to have it. It was her necklace." He pulled out a delicate silver locket and chain, holding it out to Kaitlin. "I don't know what's in it. But she wanted him to have it."

Kaitlin accepted the locket, her fingers brushing over its smooth surface. She opened it carefully and smiled sadly. "It's a tiny portrait of them both," she said softly. Keltor gave her a solemn nod. "I'll wear it, so I don't lose it," Kaitlin assured him, slipping the chain around her neck and fastening it securely.

Uly looked over to Kaitlin and, with a reassuring nod, said, "There are a few nursing mothers in the tribe—I'm sure they will help." His voice was calm and resolute, offering a glimmer of hope and comfort as they considered the baby's needs and the support waiting within their community.

Relief washed over Kaitlin, and she gave Uly a grateful smile. "Oh, thank you, Uly," she said, her gratitude clear in her voice for his practical support and kindness.

Keltor, stepped forward with gentle intent. "Here, can I take him?" he asked, extending his hands with genuine concern, clearly wanting to share the responsibility for the infant's wellbeing and comfort.

"Okay, there you go," Kaitlin replied softly, handing the baby over to Keltor. As Keltor cradled the child, a warm smile spread across his face as he gazed down at the tiny features.

"Kitcat," he began, his tone imbued with earnestness.

Before he could finish his thought, Kaitlin responded with reassuring certainty. "Of course, he will," she said with a smile, intuitively understanding what he was about to ask.

"Thank you, it's just I promised her we would take care of him. I feel responsible for him now," Keltor admitted, his voice weighted with the promise he had made and the responsibility he now bore.

"And we will, I promise," Kaitlin replied with heartfelt conviction. She reached up, her hand gently touching his face, then pressed a tender kiss to his cheek, sealing her promise with a gesture of comfort and solidarity.

"Come on," Kaitlin said softly, encouraging Keltor as she glanced at the baby nestled in his arms. "We need to get him fed. What about a name? I did ask Alarna the other night, but they hadn't chosen one."

279

Keltor looked thoughtful, considering her words. "I don't know. I suppose we could name him Logan, after his father."

She nodded, understanding the significance but also aware of the pain it might bring. "Yes, that's a good idea. How about we call him Logie for short, for now?" Kaitlin suggested gently, hoping to ease any sorrow Keltor might feel at using Logan's name so soon after his loss.

He gave a small, grateful smile. "Yes, yes, that's good." As he spoke, Keltor gazed down at the baby, who had drifted off to sleep against his chest. With a tender motion, he rubbed the little one's back soothingly, a gesture full of quiet affection and new-found responsibility.

Chapter Eleven
Breaking the News

Uly led the way, setting off first as the group climbed back up the side of the embankment. Keltor trailed behind, his gaze fixed on the destruction he had wrought. His heart thudded anxiously against his ribs, the weight of recent events pressing down on him. As they moved, his hand instinctively rose to gently pat the baby, who was tucked securely inside his shirt, nestled close to his chest for warmth and comfort.

Keltor grappled with the enormity of what had transpired. He struggled to reconcile his actions, haunted by the knowledge that he had failed Alarna, leaving her child orphaned. Yet, amid his regret, he reaffirmed his determination to keep his promise: together with Kaitlin, he would care for the baby. He recognised, however, that Alarna's father or Logan's aunt might wish to claim custody. Ultimately, the decision rested with Keltor, for the child was now his ward.

As they navigated the rough terrain of the goat track, Keltor found it difficult to grasp the scale of what he had done. The magic that had poured forth from him was unlike anything he had experienced before—so powerful, so raw. His thoughts turned to his own father. More than ever, Keltor wished to find him, to learn about his father's abilities as a wizard, and to seek guidance in mastering his own newfound powers.

As they nearly reached the other side, Kaitlin's voice trembled with emotion. "How are we going to tell Aunt Seline about poor Alarna and Logan? She's going to be devastated." Tears gathered in her eyes, threatening to spill over as the weight of the loss pressed upon her once more.

"I will tell her," Keltor said firmly, his voice resolute. He recognised that this was his responsibility and did not shy away from it. Glancing down at the baby nestled securely against his chest, he felt the weight of the moment press upon him.

Keltor's voice was quiet but steady as he spoke to Kaitlin, his expression shadowed with grief. "Kaitlin, Alarna told me it was his own brothers that attacked them. Alarna saw them. They knew who they were killing, but it didn't stop them." The weight of this revelation hung in the air; a stark reminder of just how deep the betrayal ran within the family.

Kaitlin drew in a shaky breath, her words barely more than a whisper. "No, how could they be so brutal, I just don't understand what's going on with Aranstream. I thought elves were supposed to be peaceful." Her disbelief and sorrow were clear, the violence shattering her trust in everything she believed about their people.

Keltor's voice was heavy with the weight of history and disappointment. "We are, truly we are. I don't know why but King Iwein is so bitter and twisted, and he has always ruled Aranstream with an iron rod. Fear has been his way of getting the people to do what he wants." He shook his head, his expression sombre as he reflected on the differences between the rulers. "I know your father was not always liked, but he never ruled with brutality. He was hard, and as you know his ways were old fashioned when it came to equality, but compared with King Iwein, he was practically one of your earthly saints."

Kaitlin's anguish was evident as she struggled to comprehend the depths of betrayal. "But to turn brother against brother, that's terrible," she said, her voice wavering. "I just don't understand how they could do that; I mean, how can they kill a pregnant woman. It just breaks my heart." The reality of the danger pressed upon her, and she looked at Keltor with urgency. "Keltor, we need to get these people to safety as fast as we can in case Logan's brothers bring back more men."

His Queen ~ Elvendon Book Two ~ Rosie Lynch

Keltor glanced towards Kaitlin, offering her a reassuring nod. "Once we reach the Eccleston forest they won't find us," he said quietly. "You remember how dense and thorny it is—the horses won't be able to track us through that."

Up ahead, members of the tribe were busy tending to the wounded, their movements purposeful yet subdued by the weight of recent events. Kaitlin's gaze fell upon Esimae, who stood waiting for their arrival, and beside her, Aunt Seline. A wave of apprehension rolled through Kaitlin, her stomach twisting with dread as she took in the scene. She heard Keltor release a heavy sigh beside her, the sound carrying his own anxiety and sorrow. As she glanced at him, she noticed his hand gently rise to caress the baby's head, offering comfort and silent reassurance to the child nestled against his chest.

As they drew closer to the waiting group, Kaitlin glanced uncertainly at Keltor, her voice barely above a whisper. "Are you sure you don't want me to do this?" she asked, concern evident in her tone.

Keltor shook his head firmly. "No, you weren't there. I need to tell her," he replied, his voice steady despite the turmoil within.

Uly stepped forward, offering a quiet word. "I will go and find Ren," he said, before continuing down the path to join the others who had already gathered.

Keltor called after him, his gratitude clear. "Okay, thank you." He then turned his attention back to the task at hand, bracing himself for the difficult conversation ahead.

As they approached, Aunt Seline's eyes immediately found Keltor. Her face was etched with confusion and a deepening sense of dread as she took in the scene before her. "Where's Logan and Alarna?" she demanded, her gaze dropping to the blood staining Keltor's clothes, her alarm growing with every second.

Panic laced her voice as she pressed further, "What's happened, are you injured? Where are they?" The fear in her words was unmistakable, her eyes searching Keltor's face for any sign of hope.

Keltor drew a steadying breath, struggling to keep his composure as his emotions threatened to overwhelm him. "Seline," he began softly, pulling back his cloak to gently reveal the baby. "I'm sorry, but—" He hesitated, glancing at Kaitlin for support as tears threatened to spill once more. "They didn't make it. This is their son, Logie," he finished quietly, turning himself slightly so she could see the child cradled in his arms.

Seline recoiled in disbelief, shaking her head as if to deny the reality of his words. "What! No?" Her voice was choked with anguish. "I don't understand, where are they?" Her confusion and grief hung heavy in the air, the enormity of her loss just beginning to dawn on her.

Kaitlin reached out, her hand trembling slightly as she placed it gently on Seline's upper arm. Her voice was heavy with sorrow as she tried to steady herself. "Seline, I'm so sorry, but…" Kaitlin paused, swallowing hard, the words catching in her throat. "Aranstream soldiers killed them both." She faltered for a moment, struggling to say Keltor's name, the emotion almost too much to bear. "Keltor, Keltor…"

Keltor stepped forward then, his voice raw and earnest as he added, "Seline, I had to take the baby out, or he was going to die." He hesitated, the memory clearly weighing on him. "Alarna begged me to, with her last breath. I'm so sorry." The pain in his words was obvious, his remorse evident in his expression and tone.

"No, no," Aunt Seline mumbled, shaking her head in disbelief. The reality of what had just been shared was almost too much for her to comprehend, and her resistance to the truth was apparent in her trembling voice and rigid posture.

Esimae stared in disbelief, her eyes widening as she took in the sight of the infant nestled in Keltor's arms. She gasped, her hand instinctively flying to her mouth, unable to fully process the shock. The weight of the moment was clear on her face as she looked from the baby to Keltor, tears starting to well in her eyes as the reality of the situation settled around them.

Kaitlin drew Seline close, wrapping her arms around Logan's aunt as she broke down in tears. She held her tightly, offering what comfort she could in the face of such unbearable loss. Seline's sobs racked her body, the grief too much to contain, and Kaitlin simply held her, murmuring soft reassurances, "It's okay," her voice gentle and soothing.

Nearby, Esimae's eyes met Keltor's with a silent, agonised question. She mouthed, barely able to speak, "You took the baby out of her?" Keltor nodded, his expression heavy with sorrow. Esimae's lips pressed together, trembling, as tears gathered in her eyes, the weight of what had happened settling over the group.

Aunt Seline, her voice barely audible and trembling with disbelief, asked, "Can I see them?" The reality that Logan and Alarna were truly gone was almost impossible for her to accept; she felt an intense need to say her final goodbye.

Keltor shook his head gently, sorrow in his eyes. "No, I'm sorry. We had to bury them, on the other side of the landslide." His words hung heavily between them as he tried to offer some comfort. "Seline, I know this is incredibly hard, but we must keep moving. Some of the soldiers escaped, and they could return with reinforcements at any time. We must get the villagers to safety in the Eccleston Forest."

At this, Seline drew herself away from Kaitlin's embrace and wiped the tears from her eyes, trying to compose herself despite the overwhelming grief.

Seline's voice was soft and trembling as she turned to Keltor, her grief momentarily giving way to a desperate hope. "Can I see the baby?" she asked, barely above a whisper.

Keltor responded with gentle understanding. "Of course, do you want to hold him?" His words were offered with care, as if he understood the fragile state of her heart. Aunt Seline nodded, her movements hesitant but determined.

Keltor carefully transferred the baby into her arms. The infant whimpered, a small cry escaping as he felt the loss of Keltor's protective warmth. Sensing the baby's distress, Keltor soothed him softly, "Shh, it's okay little guy, this is your great aunt." His words were calm and reassuring, meant as much for Seline as for the child.

Seline gathered the baby close, her arms wrapping around him protectively. Tears streamed down her face as she rocked back and forth, the weight of her sorrow mixing with the fragile comfort of holding her great-nephew. "Oh, my precious," she whispered, her voice raw with emotion. She looked up at Keltor, gratitude shining through her grief. "I don't know how you did it, but thank you, for not letting him die too."

Keltor met her gaze, a sorrowful smile flickering across his face. "Alarna made him my ward, so I promise you he will be cared for and provided for."

Aunt Seline glanced at him as she gathered the baby in her arms and nodded, her trust in his words evident even through her tears.

Keltor's voice was gentle but carried a weight that made Seline tense, sensing the gravity of his words. He reached out, placing a comforting hand on her arm, his gaze shifting momentarily to the baby before meeting Seline's worried eyes.

"Seline, there is something else, and I'm sorry, but this is going to hurt you," he began softly, his tone filled with compassion and regret. The seriousness in his expression caused Seline to look up at him in alarm, her features drawn with concern as she braced herself for what he was about to say.

With a barely audible voice, she asked, "What is it?" Her words were tinged with anxiety, revealing her fear of the pain that might follow.

Keltor's voice dropped, heavy with sorrow as he delivered the devastating truth. "The men who killed Logan and Alarna were his brothers," he told Seline, his words measured and gentle, knowing the pain they would cause.

Seline recoiled at the revelation, her expression twisting in disbelief and anguish. "What, no!" she cried out, her voice rising in angry defence as she instinctively pulled away from Keltor's comforting touch.

Keltor continued, his own shock and grief clear in his eyes. "Seline, I know how hard this is for you to take in, and believe me,

I am equally shocked," he said, his tone earnest and sincere. "But Alarna told me before she died—she saw them."

Aunt Seline's face crumpled with anguish as she absorbed the devastating revelation. Tears streamed down her cheeks, and her voice trembled as she spoke, "By the stars, I knew those boys were brainwashed by that evil King, but I never thought they would turn on their own blood." Overcome with emotion, she clutched baby Logie tightly to her chest, instinctively drawing him close and rocking him in a protective embrace. The depth of her sorrow was apparent in every movement, her grief interwoven with a fierce determination to shield her great-nephew from further harm.

"I'm so sorry," Keltor repeated, his voice thick with emotion as he gently reached out, his hand rubbing Seline's upper arm in a small gesture of comfort. Before either could say more, Uly and Shona hurried towards them, urgency in their steps.

Uly addressed them quickly, relief breaking through his worry. "Keltor, I've spoken with Ren. She said the baby can take goat's milk—they have special feeding bottles for him."

"Oh, thank goodness, thank you Uly," Kaitlin said gratefully, relief evident in her voice as she acknowledged Uly's help with the baby.

Seline, still cradling baby Logie, looked up and asked softly, "I'll take him, if that's okay?" She waited for permission, her arms already instinctively protective around the infant.

Keltor nodded his agreement, trusting Seline to care for the baby amid their sorrow.

Shona stepped forward, ready to assist. "I'll help her," she offered, reaching for Alana's bag to lighten Seline's burden. As she did so, she gently placed a comforting hand on Kaitlin's arm, a silent gesture of solidarity and empathy.

With genuine concern, Shona said, "Uly told me what happened, I am so sorry." Her words carried the weight of shared grief, and Kaitlin nodded at her gratefully, appreciating the compassion offered in such a difficult moment.

Kaitlin watched quietly as Seline and Shona, now united in their care for baby Logie, followed Uly back to the others, each step marked by the subtle strength of those who carry sorrow but choose to help.

Esimae turned to Keltor with gentle concern and asked, "Are you okay?" At first, Keltor managed a nod, but his composure faltered; the weight of his emotions was evident as he gritted his teeth, struggling to keep them in check.

He lowered his gaze to the ground and spoke quietly, "I should have protected them, but it was her, or the children, and I couldn't just let them die."

Esimae responded with calm honesty, "Yes, maybe you should," which drew a shocked look from Kaitlin. Before Kaitlin could interject, Esimae raised her finger slightly, signalling her to remain silent as she continued. "You are only one man, and you had to make a choice. Believe me, as painful as it is now, you made the right decision to save those children. Walk with me," she requested, motioning towards the others gathered nearby.

Kaitlin quietly slipped her hand into Keltor's, offering silent support. He glanced at her and, despite his sorrow, managed a woeful smile as he squeezed her hand, grateful for the comfort amid the turmoil.

Esimae gestured towards a nearby group of deodar mothers, her voice steady but gentle. "You see all those mothers," she said, pointing to the small gathering anxiously watching over their children. "You saved their babies – six over there, and four more gathered just beyond. Imagine, for a moment, how you would feel if you had to face them and say you chose to save two of your friends instead of ten of their children. I believe that pain would be far greater than what you're feeling now."

Keltor's gaze followed Esimae's hand, settling on the children as they played, laughter briefly cutting through the sorrow hanging over the group. The sight filled him with grief for Alarna and Logan, but also a reluctant understanding. He realised Esimae was right – the burden of such a choice was heavy, but the lives of those children mattered deeply.

"Okay, I get it," Keltor replied quietly, meeting Esimae's eyes, "but it doesn't make it any easier."

Esimae's eyes remained steady on Keltor as she spoke, her words unwavering but gentle. "I know it doesn't," she acknowledged, "but in war difficult choices must be made, and in this case, you made the right one. Hold onto that anger you feel inside now and use it when the time comes against King Iwein, as he is responsible for Alarna and Logan's deaths, not you. You saved their child—hold that joy in your heart, young man. He will have a chance to live and to keep Alarna and Logan's spirits alive."

Keltor took a deep breath, exhaling slowly as he lifted his hand to wipe away the tears on his cheek. The weight of Esimae's words settled over him, bringing a mixture of gratitude and surprise at her compassion. "Thank you, Esimae," he said quietly, his voice thick with emotion.

Esimae gently turned her attention to Kaitlin, her concern evident as she said, "Now, Kaitlin, please let me see to that arrow wound before it gets infected."

Keltor, suddenly reminded of Kaitlin's injury, looked at her with alarm. "Oh, hell, I'd forgotten about that, are you okay?" he asked, turning towards her.

Kaitlin offered a reassuring smile and tried to put him at ease. "Yes, don't worry, it's fine, really," she insisted. "I'll just be a few minutes; will you be okay?"

Keltor nodded in response, the worry still lingering in his eyes. "I'm going to check on Logie," he replied, giving her hand a gentle squeeze before letting go and walking away.

Kaitlin watched Keltor as he left, feeling her heart ache for him; the sadness he carried was almost unbearable.

Noticing Kaitlin's concern, Esimae comforted her, lifting her hand to rub Kaitlin's arm reassuringly. "He will be okay," she said softly.

Kaitlin gazed into the distance, her voice trembling as she struggled to contain her emotions. "I hope so. I can't believe a few days ago we celebrated getting married with them, and now they are both gone. It's just not fair, I really loved them both so much." Her words faltered and she gave a snivel, fighting to hold back tears. "For once in my life I had found true friends. I just thought we would have such great times together once we had taken Elvendon back."

Her aunt gently placed a comforting hand on Kaitlin's shoulder. "I know honey, I know it's not fair. In fact, it's tragic, but I am afraid more people will die before the end of this battle. Come on, let me sort your shoulder out."

Kaitlin nodded and quietly followed her aunt back to where her belongings were resting against a tree, seeking solace and care amidst the sorrow.

Esimae was met with a persistent chorus of mewing from her cat, Magic, who was confined to his basket. She knelt beside him and gently opened the lid. Instantly, Magic poked his head out and greeted her with a plaintive meow. Reaching out, Esimae stroked Magic's head, her voice warm and soothing as she tried to explain. "Okay Magic, I'm sorry, but I had to leave you," she said softly. "We found ourselves in a difficult situation, and although I know you always want to help, it was simply too dangerous for you this time." As she spoke, Magic nuzzled her hand in a gesture of immediate forgiveness, clearly not holding any grudge.

Observing the interaction, Kaitlin found herself unable to stifle a chuckle. To her, it truly seemed as if Magic was scolding Esimae for leaving him behind, his tone and manner unmistakably reproachful despite his swift reconciliation.

"How is it that I am a witch, yet I can't understand him?" Kaitlin asked her aunt, her voice tinged with confusion as she watched Magic, Esimae's cat.

Esimae gave her a knowing smile. "That's because he's my cat, that's why. If you had a familiar of your own, you'd understand each other perfectly." She gently scooped Magic into her arms; he immediately curled into her face, his earlier grievance forgotten. Clearly, he had forgiven her for leaving him behind.

"Okay, go on," Esimae said, setting Magic back on the ground. "Don't go too far, do your business and maybe catch a mouse or something, but be quick—we're leaving in less than ten minutes." Her tone was gentle but firm as she addressed the cat directly.

Magic responded with a meow and darted off into the undergrowth, disappearing from sight.

Watching him go, Kaitlin's concern became evident. "He will come back, won't he?" she asked, her voice carrying a hint of worry.

Esimae offered a reassuring smile as she responded to Kaitlin's concern. "Of course he will, I only put him in the basket because he is too lazy to walk. Anyway, he is a free spirit; if he wants to leave me, that's up to him." She glanced towards the undergrowth where Magic had vanished, noticing the worried look on Kaitlin's face. Softening her tone, Esimae added, "Don't worry, he never would. He has an easy life with me."

Kaitlin returned her smile, comforted by Esimae's gentle confidence.

"Right, sit down and let me look at your shoulder," Esimae said, her voice gentle but firm. Kaitlin lowered herself to the cool, leaf-strewn ground, wincing as the damp earth pressed against her skin and the ache in her shoulder throbbed with each movement. The air was tinged with the scent of moss, and the faint rustle of leaves overhead added to the feeling of vulnerability. Esimae took out the now blood-soaked piece of fabric, her fingers deft yet tender, and carefully peeled it away from the wound. Kaitlin bit her lip, feeling the sting as the air met the raw skin; the sight of the injury made her pulse quicken, fear lingering from the earlier ordeal.

"Yeah, it's fine, you were lucky. I'll just pop a poultice on there to stop any infection," Esimae said, rummaging through her pack for the healing herbs. Relief washed over Kaitlin as her aunt pronounced the wound safe, though her heart still raced from the earlier scare. The promise of care and Esimae's reassuring presence brought a sense of comfort, and Kaitlin found herself breathing a little easier, the tension slowly ebbing away as the soothing aroma of the poultice began to fill the air.

Esimae finished tending to Kaitlin's wound, her touch gentle and deliberate as she secured the poultice over the injured

291

shoulder. With a small, reassuring pat to Kaitlin's arm, she declared, "There, all done."

Kaitlin let out a grateful breath, her fingers moving instinctively to the sore spot. She offered Esimae a heartfelt "Thank you," her voice quiet but sincere, as she gingerly pressed her shoulder, feeling both the ache and the comfort of being cared for. Realising she didn't have a change of dress, Kaitlin fetched her flask, poured a little water into her palm, and tore a strip from her underdress. With quiet determination, she scrubbed gently at the blood, cleaning the area as best she could. The cool water soothed her skin, and although the fabric was rough, she managed to remove most of the stain, her movements purposeful and practical.

Esimae tucked the herbs back into her pack, casting a final, approving glance at Kaitlin's shoulder. "I'm going to check on the others," she said, her voice still gentle. With that, she rose and drifted away through the trees, leaving Kaitlin seated on the mossy ground. The hush of the forest enveloped her, broken only by the distant chatter of birds and the occasional snap of a twig. Kaitlin let her gaze drift towards the deodars, her thoughts swirling with worry for the children playing beneath their sprawling branches. The moment lingered, fragile and quiet, until Keltor's familiar voice cut through the silence, his presence grounding her as she wrestled with the fear that threatened to overwhelm her.

"Penny for them," he said.

She looked up and Keltor stood over her.

"Sorry," she replied.

"Penny for them, your thoughts?" he asked giving her a grin.

She laughed in her sigh at his human words and gave him a nod.

Keltor offered his hand to her, and she took it. He pulled Kaitlin to her feet. He had changed his bloody shirt and was now wearing the one he wore for their bonding ceremony.

"Well, are you going to tell me, you were really lost in your own thoughts then."

"I know, it's nothing." She glanced across to the deodars.

"Kitcat," he pushed, and he pulled an arm around her, and she gave a sigh.

Kaitlin's voice trembled as she finally let her fears surface. "I guess I'm just scared. Scared of letting them all down, scared of them all dying."

Seeing her distress, Keltor gently turned her to face him, his fingers brushing softly through her hair. "I know it's hard. We lost four people today; two we loved very much."

Kaitlin's face fell; grief etched deep for the lives lost. She struggled to hold back the sorrow, but Keltor's steady presence anchored her.

He spoke with gentle reassurance, "Kaitlin, my love, you're not going to let them down, okay? We will take back Elvendon for them, I promise."

Her eyes warmed at his words, a faint smile breaking through the gloom. Keltor's hand moved from her hair to her cheek, his thumb stroking her left cheek with tender affection.

She closed her eyes as he kissed her. Despite the desperation and the heavy weight of her worries, the touch of his lips brought her calm and renewed confidence.

When his eyes met hers after the kiss, Keltor's heart raced wildly. In a quiet whisper, he said, "I love you, always."

Kaitlin echoed softly, "I love you," and for a moment, their foreheads rested together, sharing comfort in their closeness.

"Come on, we need to get moving," Keltor announced as he gently placed his hand on Kaitlin's back, guiding her forward with quiet encouragement.

Kaitlin bent down to retrieve her bag from where it rested against the tree. Nearby, Esimae watched the pair as she gathered her own belongings. A faint smile played on her lips, tinged with a trace of regret. She reflected on her earlier interactions with Keltor—how, when they'd first met, she had been wary and treated him with unnecessary harshness. Now, seeing him more clearly, she realised that as an elf, he was not so bad after all. She shouldered her pack and readied herself to join the others.

"Is Magic back?" Kaitlin asked, pulling Esimae from her thoughts.

Esimae smiled in response. "He's coming," she said, opening the basket in preparation.

Moments later, Magic bounded out from the bushes and leapt straight into the basket. Esimae scolded him lightly as she noticed the half-chewed mouse he had brought back with him. "Really, you didn't have time to eat that before you got back!" she complained, shaking her head as Magic meowed in protest.

Kaitlin couldn't help but laugh at the scene.

"What was that all about?" Keltor asked as the group began to move forward.

Kaitlin explained, "They can understand each other. Apparently, witches can have a familiar—Magic is Esimae's, and only she can truly understand him."

Keltor looked impressed. "Wow, that's cool," he remarked, as he and Kaitlin moved to the front to lead the tribe through the forest.

He glanced at Kaitlin with curiosity. "So, what about you?" he asked.

"Me?" Kaitlin echoed, glancing at Keltor as he nodded encouragingly. She hesitated, considering the question. "I don't know. I never had any pets growing up." Her voice softened as she reflected, a faint smile crossing her lips. "Although, come to think of it, the mare Aragon gave me—Aaleyah—it was almost as if I understood her. It was like she told me her name, that Aaleyah was what she wanted to be called." Kaitlin's expression grew wistful. "I hope she's still at the castle. I really did feel a strong connection to her."

Keltor nodded in understanding. "Yeah, I'm hoping I can find Trewin. I love that horse."

Chapter Twelve
The Witch's Fort

The woods began to grow noticeably darker, their atmosphere turning increasingly foreboding. A chill crept down Kaitlin's spine, causing her to shiver. "I know the witches are not here anymore, but these woods are still so creepy," she whispered. Despite her unease, the group pressed forward, ducking beneath low-hanging branches and carefully weaving their way around dead and fallen limbs that littered the forest floor. Each step felt more cautious, the shadows deepening as they ventured further into the heart of the forest.

Keltor lowered his voice, his tone serious as he explained, "That's why I'm hoping the Aranstream soldiers won't venture out this far. The terrain alone would make it nearly impossible for them—they wouldn't be able to bring their horses through such dense forest and overgrown paths." He glanced around, as if to emphasise the point, before continuing. "Besides, they have no idea that the witches are gone. As far as they know, this place is still dangerous and guarded. That uncertainty should be enough to keep them away, at least for now."

The group continued for another hour, working their way through dense tangles of brambles and thorny bushes. The trees twisted and turned, their roots snaking across the path, threatening to trip anyone not paying close attention. At times, Keltor and Uly were forced to hack a path through the stubborn undergrowth.

Eventually, after a considerable struggle to make their way through the tangled forest, the witch's fort gradually emerged ahead of them. The structure was tucked away deep within the trees, its walls looking even more battered and neglected than any of them had recalled. Vines and brambles had crept up the stone, and sections of the roof sagged under the weight of accumulated moss and debris.

"Wow, that's so overgrown," Kaitlin observed as they drew nearer. Her voice carried a mixture of surprise and sadness at the sight of the once formidable stronghold, now slowly being reclaimed by the relentless advance of nature.

Keltor glanced at the fort, then back at the group. "It's been almost nine months now, and nature is taking it back. Hopefully inside will still be okay," he said, his tone practical but tinged with concern for what they might find within.

Turning to Esimae, Keltor spoke quietly, "Esimae, can you ask the tribe to wait here while Kaitlin and I go and have a look around? I want to make sure there is no one or anything still living here." He cast a wary glance at the darkened windows and crumbling walls, his hand instinctively resting on the hilt of his sword as he prepared to lead the way inside.

Esimae acknowledged Keltor's instructions with a nod and dropped back, allowing Kaitlin and Keltor to continue ahead. As they moved cautiously through the ruins, Kaitlin voiced her worries in a hushed tone, glancing around as she ducked beneath a broken door frame, where the wall had begun to crumble. "Keltor, what about the imps? We don't know what happened to them," she said quietly.

Keltor's expression grew serious. "Yeah, I know. That's why I want to look around first. I don't think they'd cause any harm, but we certainly don't want them anywhere near the children."

Kaitlin looked at him, puzzled as they approached the main double doors. He explained, "According to elven folklore, imps are mischievous creatures. There are tales of them whisking children away to play, but the child doesn't always come back."

Kaitlin's eyes widened as she scanned the area, murmuring, "Hell, really?" Keltor nodded, his vigilance clear as they continued their careful inspection of the fort.

Keltor placed his hand upon the door, its blue paint peeling and flaking beneath his touch. He pressed firmly, but the door refused to move. Determined, he turned and put his back into it; with a forceful shove, the door burst open.

As they stepped into the cavernous room beyond, a chill seemed to pass through Kaitlin, causing a shudder to run down her spine.

"Talk about déjà vu, again," she remarked, her voice betraying a sense of discomfort mingled with familiarity.

"Yeah, I know," Keltor replied, his tone heavy with memories. "A memory I would rather forget, thank you. Come on, let's check through here." Without waiting, he moved ahead through the doorway, intent on their search.

Kaitlin managed a small smile, then hurried to catch up with him, as he stepped into the main room, the same one where she had once been imprisoned by the witches. The sight before her was overwhelming—a chaotic scene of scattered debris, remnants of broken furniture, and grim reminders of the horrors that had taken place within these crumbling walls. She let out an involuntary exclamation; her voice tinged with both shock and a lingering sense of dread. "Oh god, what a mess," she said, taking in the devastation and the haunting memories it stirred.

Keltor's gaze swept over the devastated chamber, his expression grim. "Hmm, we can't let the children see this," he remarked, his voice low and resolute. The sight was distressing although the passage of time had reduced much of the witches' and goblins' remains to decaying fragments, a scattering of bones and skulls still littered the floor, stark reminders of the fort's dark history.

"This will take some time to clear up," Kaitlin announced, placing her hands on her hips as she surveyed the chaos.

Keltor turned to her and pointed at himself. "Hey," he said, a playful glint in his eye. "I'm a wizard, remember?"

Kaitlin smiled, her curiosity piqued. "What are you going to do?" she asked.

297

"Step back over by the back wall and I'll show you," he replied, his tone mysterious. Obediently, Kaitlin walked to the back wall opposite the huge fireplace, eager to see what he had planned.

Keltor paused and took a deep breath as he surveyed the devastated hall. With deliberate intent, he raised his hands and closed his eyes, allowing himself a moment of complete concentration. The more he called upon his magic, the more natural it felt, the energy flowing effortlessly through him. Small sparks of magic flickered and danced between his fingertips, illuminating the gloom with ethereal light.

As he extended his hands outward, the power pulsed through the vast chamber, sending subtle vibrations across the stone walls and scattered debris. Kaitlin felt her heart begin to race, the familiar sensation of magic coursing through her body each time Keltor wielded his power. It thrummed within her, leaving her breathless and unable to resist the magnetic pull towards him.

When Keltor finally opened his eyes, they shone with a brilliant white glow, a clear sign of the potent magic he now controlled. The sight was both awe-inspiring and reassuring, a testament to his growing mastery and confidence in his abilities.

Keltor began to chant, his voice steady and resonant as he intoned, *"Etoora spinconra clearat."* He moved his hands in slow, deliberate circles, conjuring a visible surge of magical energy. At once, the scattered bones, skulls, and remains of the witches and goblins began to lift from the floor, swirling upwards and forming a spiralling vortex that filled the centre of the ruined chamber. The debris rose with remarkable force, resembling a miniature tornado, and Kaitlin watched in awe, recalling how he had used a similar spell in the forest to hide their tracks.

"Etora mentaca!" Keltor commanded, his voice charged with raw authority as he swept his hands in a dramatic arc towards the fireplace. Instantly, the swirling vortex of debris responded, the miniature tornado whirling across the ruined chamber with relentless purpose. Fragments of bone, splinters of wood, and dust-laden memories were swept up, spinning in a cacophonous dance before being hurled into the yawning mouth of the fireplace.

Without pausing, Keltor extended his arm and uttered, "Ignite." A surge of magic burst from his fingertips, and the piled wreckage erupted into a blazing inferno. The fire raged with a ferocity that belied its source, burning white-hot with the unmistakable shimmer of pure magic. Shadows leapt across the walls, chased away by the brilliance, while the heat pulsed through the chamber, cleansing it of its haunted past.

Keltor exhaled heavily, letting his hands drop to his sides. Gradually, the brilliant light faded from his eyes, revealing once more the piercing blue beneath. He stood, chest rising and falling, the lingering energy of the spell crackling in the air around him.

Kaitlin stared at him, eyes wide with astonishment, her breath caught in her throat. "Keltor... that was incredible," she whispered, her voice trembling with awe and something deeper—an emotion she could barely name.

Keltor turned to her, a genuine smile breaking across his face. "You know, I think I rather enjoy being a wizard," he replied, his previous uncertainty replaced with an unmistakable confidence. The air between them thrummed with unspoken words, the exhilaration of magic mingling with a growing intimacy neither could ignore.

Kaitlin crossed the distance between them, her eyes alight with admiration and wonder. As she wrapped her arms around him, she felt the last vestiges of magic still humming beneath his skin—a current that leapt between them, making her shiver with delight. She pressed close, her heartbeat entwining with his, both silently marvelling at the power they had unleashed together, and at the bond that was quietly deepening between them.

"Come on," he said, taking her hand. "Let's check the rest of the building." With cautious steps, they ventured deeper into the silent fort, each echo of their movements stirring dust motes in the pale light. The emptiness settled around them like a blanket, but their search proved thorough room after room revealing nothing but the remnants of a lifelong abandoned. Relief flickered across Keltor's face as he confirmed the absence of imps or other inhabitants, and, with the certainty that the building was secure, they retraced their path to gather the waiting tribe. Soon, warmth and life returned to the old place, the fire crackling in the hearth and the kitchen stove humming with renewed purpose, a fragile sense of safety blooming amid the battered walls as the group settled in for the night.

As they sat together by the warming glow of the fire, Keltor turned to Uly, concern etched on his features. "Uly, will you be okay here?" he asked quietly. The trio—Keltor, Kaitlin, and Esimae—were preparing to leave at first light, determined to reach Elvendon with all possible speed.

Uly, ever loyal and resolute, offered to accompany them on their journey. "Let me come with you," the big man suggested, his voice earnest. However, Keltor shook his head firmly. "No Uly, you need to stay here and protect your tribe and be here for Ren," he replied. His tone was gentle but unwavering.

Keltor reassured Uly, "I'm certain that King Iwein's men will not find you, but we are in the Eccleston forest, and there are creatures and possibly imps in the surrounding area, so don't let the children outside alone," Keltor advised, his voice carrying the weight of responsibility.

Uly met Keltor's gaze and nodded in understanding, his face set with quiet resolve. "I understand," he replied, his voice steady and sincere, accepting the responsibility entrusted to him. The simple words carried the weight of Keltor's faith and the heavy burden of protecting the tribe in uncertain times. With this acknowledgement, Uly committed himself to safeguarding his people and supporting Ren, determined to stand firm in the face of whatever dangers might arise.

"Uly, we don't know how long it will take," Keltor admitted, glancing at Kaitlin, who was busy helping to prepare food for the children. Finally, Keltor's words grew heavy with the uncertainty of their quest. "Uly, if we don't make it back, you will have to consider building a new life for your people here," he said, entrusting Uly with the well-being and future of the tribe.

"Keltor," Uly said, and then he dipped his head and added, "my King. I have no doubt you and the Queen will defeat King Iwein, and yes, you're right, I will stay here and protect my tribe and await the birth of my child."

Chapter Thirteen
Sharelle

As the first light of day crept through the battered windows, Keltor knelt beside little Logie, gathering the infant in his arms for a final embrace. He held him close, whispering softly, "See you, little guy, I'll be back for you, I promise." After pressing a gentle kiss to Logie's brow, Keltor handed him back to Seline, who cradled the baby against her chest with tender protectiveness.

Seline offered Keltor a reassuring smile, her arms wrapped tightly around Logie. "Don't worry, he will be fine," she assured him, her voice calm and steady.

Standing nearby, Shona reached out and placed her hand warmly on Seline's upper arm, her own smile radiating quiet support. Turning to Kaitlin, Shona bowed her head respectfully. "I will help also," she promised, her words a silent pledge of solidarity.

Kaitlin returned the gesture, her face lighting up with gratitude. "Thank you, Shona," she replied, smiling. She bent to give Logie a quick kiss on the top of his head and offered Seline a gentle, affectionate stroke on the arm.

Esimae's voice broke the moment's stillness. "We should go," she urged, her tone brisk yet understanding. "Daylight is breaking, and we have a long way to go."

Keltor nodded in agreement, but before turning to leave, he reached out once more, his little finger brushing softly across Logie's cheek in a final gesture of affection.

Seline stepped forward, meeting their eyes with a steady resolve. "Good luck and may the spirits of our elders be with you," she said, her words carrying both blessing and hope as the group prepared to depart.

With their packs slung over their shoulders and Esimae gently carrying Magic, the group began their trek towards Eccleston forest. The road ahead was long; reaching Elvendon would take them four full days. Although they could move more swiftly without the children, the forest's thorny undergrowth remained a constant obstacle, slowing their progress and demanding caution at every step.

They pressed on for nearly three hours, enveloped in an uneasy silence. None of them dared raise their voices, wary of the possibility that Aranstream soldiers might be lurking nearby, ready to catch the faintest sound.

As they walked, Keltor glanced at Kaitlin, who seemed lost in thought. Gone was the spark in her eyes; instead, her gaze was distant, sombre, and lacking its usual vibrancy. Concerned, Keltor gently asked, "Are you alright?"

Kaitlin managed a smile and nodded in response. Sensing that something was wrong, Keltor placed his arm around her, drawing her closer for comfort. He pressed her further: "No, you're not, tell me."

Kaitlin hesitated, then admitted, "I've had too much time to think, replaying everything and wondering if I could have changed it. I'm worried about leaving them—what if he finds them while we're away and something happens to Logie?" A tear slipped down her cheek as she wiped it away.

Keltor tried to reassure her, his voice gentle. "Hey, it's okay. They won't know about that place, I promise. We wouldn't have known it was there if we hadn't been caught by those witches."

Kaitlin nodded, clinging to his reassurance as they continued their silent journey through the forest.

"I guess. I miss her, you know," Kaitlin said softly, her eyes searching Keltor's face. "Alarna," she clarified, a faint smile flickering as she recalled happier times. "We had such a lovely time at the lake, before we bonded. We'd even agreed that I was going to be her birthing partner when Logie was born. I really thought…" Her words faltered as emotion overcame her, and she wiped away more tears.

Keltor reached out with gentle understanding. "I know, I know," he replied, his tone tender. He paused, stopping her in her tracks. His hand rested lightly on her cheek, offering comfort.

"I miss her too, and Logan. They were good friends, and I know we would have had some great times together in the future, but it wasn't meant to be. I wish I could bring them back, I really do," he said, his voice tinged with sadness.

"I know, and I'm sorry," Kaitlin whispered, shaking her head in regret.

"For what?" Keltor asked quietly.

"For making you relive it. I know you're hurting too."

He gathered her into an embrace, kissing her gently on the head as he fought to hold back his own tears. He missed them deeply, but he understood that her loss was even greater—Kaitlin had lost both her parents and her sister to the elven war, a conflict she'd been forced into without a choice.

"We'll get through it, Kitcat," he whispered tenderly.

"There is no time for that," Esimae whispered urgently, gripping Kaitlin's arm and pulling her close. Her eyes were wide with alarm as she added in a hushed voice, "Soldiers ahead." Without hesitation, Esimae guided Kaitlin behind a screen of thick shrubs, doing her best to keep them hidden from view.

Keltor moved silently ahead, every step careful and deliberate as he crept forward to assess the situation. After observing the path for any signs of danger, he quickly returned and joined Esimae and Kaitlin. Together, all three pressed themselves close behind an ancient oak tree, crouching amidst the dense undergrowth to conceal their presence.

Through the leaves, they could see six Aranstream soldiers standing on the path ahead. The soldiers had stopped a young family— a man, a woman, and their three small children— detaining them with stern faces and drawn weapons.

Kaitlin's concern grew deeper as she observed the frightened family. Worry etched her features as she quietly asked, "What are they doing on this side of the gorge?"

Esimae's voice trembled as she answered Kaitlin's question, tension coiling in every word. "I don't know—maybe they're scouting for people hiding over here," she murmured, her gaze darting anxiously through the shifting shadows. The dappled sunlight danced across her face, but it did nothing to ease the fear tightening in her chest. Kaitlin caught the uncertainty in her aunt's eyes, and a cold dread prickled along her own skin. She felt the forest pressing in around them, the distant cry of a bird abruptly silenced as if the woods themselves were watching and waiting to see what happened next.

Suddenly, a harsh command shattered the stillness. "Move it now," barked a soldier, his sword flashing in the patchy sunlight as he jabbed it into the man's back. The blade's metallic glint sent a shiver through Kaitlin. She watched, heart pounding, as the man stumbled over a raised tree root, his breath coming in ragged gasps. She could hear the crunch of leaves beneath his boots, mingling with the frightened whimpers of the children.

"Please!" his wife screamed, "don't hurt him!"

"Keltor," Kaitlin whispered, her voice low and urgent as she took a tentative step forward. Her aunt, quick to react, reached out and placed a firm hand on Kaitlin's arm, holding her back. "No, it's too risky," she cautioned, fear evident in her tone.

Kaitlin's determination did not waver. "We can't just leave them," she insisted, her gaze flicking anxiously between the frightened family and Keltor. "Keltor?" she said again, her voice pleading for reassurance and action.

Keltor's eyes swept swiftly over the scene. He took stock of the soldiers, counting their weapons and judging their positions. In that tense moment, he weighed his chances, silently calculating whether he could take on all the men and protect those in danger.

"Sam!" the woman screamed at her husband, as one of the men pulled her away from her children, separating her from the others.

Tears streamed down her face as she reached for her children, clear panic rising in her chest.

"No, leave her alone. Rosa!" Sam shouted, in fear and helplessness. He struggled to get back up, but was promptly kicked in the face by one of the soldiers. He cried out as his lip split and blood poured from his mouth. Sam's hands grasped the soft mossy ground beneath, the coldness of the earth sinking into his fingers as he tried to pull himself to his feet. Terror clawed at his chest as he realized how powerless he was to help her.

"Get up," a soldier growled at him, "or watch your children die!" he cursed, lifting his sword toward the youngest child, who looked around three years old, and holding the point at the crying child's throat.

Keltor stood up abruptly, his resolve clear as he declared, "Hell, no." Turning his attention to Kaitlin, he issued a firm instruction. "Stay here," he said, ensuring she understood before he stepped out into the open, his movements deliberate and purposeful.

Kaitlin, unwilling to remain passive, called out to him in a hushed voice, "Keltor!" She made to follow, but Esimae intervened swiftly. Placing a steadying hand on Kaitlin's arm, her aunt spoke in a low, calming tone, "Let him handle it."

Kaitlin's worry was clear as she cast a troubled glance towards her husband, the anxiety deeply etched across her features. The tension in the air was unmistakable, a silent testament to her concern for the endangered family and for Keltor, whose actions now held the fate of all in the balance.

Keltor continued forward, his presence drawing the immediate attention of the soldiers. Four of the men reacted swiftly, unsheathing their swords and forming a united front between Keltor and the frightened family. Their blades glinted menacingly in the uncertain light as they faced him down, prepared for confrontation.

One of the soldiers, taking charge, barked a warning. "Stay where you are," he ordered, his tone firm and unyielding. Keltor, however, showed no sign of intimidation. Ignoring the command, he continued his advance, his gaze fixed on the children who remained huddled together, terror etched on their faces.

"Let those children go," Keltor demanded, his right hand outstretched as he indicated the children. Though he had not yet drawn his weapon, the determination in his posture was unmistakable. The tension in the air was apparent as the soldiers, sensing his resolve, stood their ground.

Once again, the lead soldier repeated his command, his voice rising in authority. "I said stay where you are." The standoff hung in the balance, the threat of violence simmering just beneath the surface as both sides awaited the other's next move.

The soldier, who had initially begun to escort the woman away, redirected her and brought her back to join the others. He threw the woman down at her husband's feet. Sam immediately reached for her and drew her to him protectively. She clung to him, sobbing uncontrollably. Her cries echoed in the tense silence, and his arms tightened around her as if shielding her from the world.

The lead soldier turned to face Keltor, his posture rigid and his expression unwavering. His voice, calm yet commanding, echoed through the tense air as he questioned, "Do you truly intend to challenge all of us?" The gravity of his words underscored the seriousness of the situation, making it clear that he was not to be taken lightly.

Keltor drew in a sharp breath, his chest rising as he steeled himself. Within him, fear and determination clashed, but his resolve did not falter. He met the soldier's unwavering gaze, refusing to show any sign of weakness. With a firm, authoritative tone, he demanded, "Let that child go, now!" The force behind his words left no room for doubt about his intentions.

As he spoke, Keltor channelled his magical energy, focusing it into his right hand. The air around him seemed to hum with the intensity of his power as he maintained a prepared stance, signalling both his readiness and his warning to the soldiers. The confrontation teetered on the edge, each side awaiting the other's next move.

The soldier gripping the child reared back his sword, the steel trembling as he wrestled to keep hold of her. The little girl's frantic attempts to break free sent ripples of terror through Keltor, who watched, heart pounding, as the intent to kill flashed unmistakably across the man's hardened features. Cold panic surged through Keltor's veins, his chest tightening with dread, every heartbeat thudding like a drum in his ears. The sword's edge caught the faint glow of sunlight, casting a pale shimmer across the child's vulnerable throat. Her mother's shriek pierced the air—a raw, desperate sound—as she broke away from her husband's protective arms, reaching out in horror.

Time seemed to slow. Keltor's breath caught painfully in his lungs, the world narrowing to the soldier, the helpless child, and the looming blade. He summoned his magic, drawing it up from the depths of his being, and the air around his outstretched hand began to shimmer with a crystalline, blue-green radiance. A sudden rush of ozone flooded his senses, followed by an icy tingle that danced along his fingertips. With a silent invocation, Keltor unleashed his power—a thread of liquid light snaked from his palm, crackling with energy as it bridged the gap in a heartbeat.

The spell struck the man's hand with a sizzling intensity. Flesh hissed and bubbled away from bone, the soldier's grip melting into ruin as the stench of burnt skin mingled with the sharp tang of magic. The sword tumbled to the earth, clattering in the charged silence, and the man's scream twisted through the night—part agony, part terror. Keltor's entire body vibrated with the aftershock of his own magic, a wave of adrenaline and grim relief surging through him as he locked eyes with the child, promising protection, even as the danger lingered.

The child stood ridged to the spot screaming, her father jumped to his feet, swept her up in his arms and hurried back to her crying mother, who was grasping at her other two children protectively. The family watched in terror as the soldier's charge all at once at Keltor.

Keltor had already withdrawn his sword as they came for him.

As the battle raged, Esimae seized Kaitlin's arm just as she sprang up, intent on rushing to Keltor's aid. "No, you need to keep out of the way!" Esimae shouted, her grip tightening as Kaitlin struggled to break free.

Defiant, Kaitlin retorted, "I'm not letting them kill him!" Her voice rang with desperate determination as she pulled against Esimae's hold.

Esimae's response was sharp, bordering on frantic. "Do you really think he can't take them all on? Look!" she cried, urging Kaitlin to turn her attention back to the fight.

For a moment, Kaitlin hesitated, her gaze snapping towards Keltor. In those few heartbeats she had turned away, he had already felled two of his opponents. The sight steadied her, the urge to rush into danger yielding, if only for a moment, to the realisation of Keltor's prowess. She drew in a slow, calming breath, forcing herself to hold back, torn between her impulse to help and her faith in his strength.

As Keltor withdrew his sword from the stomach of another soldier, a spray of blood erupted, splattering across his shirt and skin. The metallic scent filled the air, mingling with the tension and fear that hung over the glade. Without pause, Keltor spun on his heel, instincts razor-sharp, to confront an adversary approaching from behind. The threat was immediate. Raising his sword with practiced precision, Keltor brought it crashing down against his opponent's blade. The impact was thunderous, the force reverberating through both weapons. The soldier's grip faltered as the jolt shot up his arm, wrenching the sword from his grasp and sending it clattering to the ground.

Keltor's eyes burned with fury as he faced the soldier—the very one who had attempted to drag the woman away into the trees. Without hesitation, Keltor channelled his rage into action. He whipped his sword around his head, the weapon slicing through the air with a sharp, whistling sound. The blade moved in a controlled arc, catching the sunlight and scattering it in fleeting flashes. He shifted his stance, bringing the sword back to the front. Keltor glared at the soldier his face tight with anger as with precision Keltor struck the soldier's neck, decapitating him. The soldier's body dropped to the ground, his head thudding and rolling into the mossy grass. The mother clutched her children tightly, her hands trembling as she turned their faces away from the gruesome sight.

The fifth man began to back away, his movements hesitant and filled with dread. He cast a fearful glance towards the wounded soldier whose hand had been disintegrated by Keltor's spell. The injured man remained on the ground, clutching his ruined, bony hand in agony, the pain etched across his face.

Ready if he needed her, Kaitlin remained on edge, eyes fixed on Keltor as the fight unfolded. Each movement he made sent her heart pounding faster—fear and excitement mingled within her, the rush of adrenaline almost overwhelming. There was something captivating about the way he fought; his power and elegance were undeniable, every motion controlled and commanding. Kaitlin could not help but be enthralled by the sight, torn between her anxiety for his safety and her awe at his skill in battle.

The fifth man stumbled as his foot caught on the body of the wounded soldier lying on the ground. The injured man, desperation etched in his voice, screamed up at him, "Help me!" For a moment, the fleeing soldier looked down at his comrade, their eyes meeting in a brief, silent exchange. But fear triumphed over loyalty. Shaking his head, the fifth man turned away, abandoning the wounded soldier to his fate, and ran.

Keltor raised his sword, his expression set with grim determination. With a swift, practised motion, he hurled the blade through the air. The weapon spun as it flew, the steel glinting in the fractured sunlight that filtered through the trees.

The soldier on the ground watched as Keltor's sword flew over the top of him. His eyes followed its path as the whistle of steel sliced through air before the sickening thud echoed through the glade as it struck the fleeing soldier right between his shoulder blades. The man pitched forwards and fell dead to the ground.

The soldier on the ground turned his gaze back towards Keltor, only to find him looming over him, eyes burning with fury. Keltor glared down, his voice laced with venom as he demanded, "You would kill a child?" The accusation hung in the air, heavy and damning, as Keltor's anger threatened to break through his composure.

The man, desperation etched across his features, scrambled for justification. "We have no choice, the King orders it," he pleaded, his voice trembling. "He wants to get rid of all Elvendons."

Keltor's response was immediate and uncompromising. "You always have a choice," he retorted, his words cutting through the soldier's excuses. Keltor's hand swept emphatically over the carnage and misery surrounding them, his frustration growing ever more evident. He glared at the soldier, voice rising with righteous anger as it rang out across the glade. "Where is he?" Keltor bellowed, the words echoing among the trees. "Your King is not here, is he? You didn't have to attack this family!"

The man simply shook his head, terror etched across his features, unable or unwilling to speak in the face of Keltor's wrath. Keltor, his temper flaring, advanced on him, voice raised in a furious accusation. "How many more Elvendons have you killed? How many children?" he demanded, his words cutting through the tense silence and echoing with both pain and outrage. The question hung heavy in the air, its gravity underscored by the violence and loss already witnessed in the glade.

The man's lip curled, beads of sweat ran down his face, and Keltor knew without a doubt they had killed more and would kill again given the chance.

Keltor strode purposefully over to the soldier who had tried to escape, the crunch of leaves beneath his boots echoing in the tense silence. He reached for his sword, the cold metal slick with blood, and pulled it free from the man's back with a practiced tug. The sharp, metallic tang of blood filled the air, mingling with the earthy scent of the forest floor. Keltor felt no remorse as he retrieved his weapon; his mind was singularly focused on the task ahead, his anger simmering just beneath the surface.

With a calm resolve, Keltor turned and walked back towards the wounded man lying on the forest floor. Each step he took was slow and purposeful, betraying neither haste nor hesitation. As he moved, his eyes flickered briefly to the family, still tightly huddled together a short distance away. Fear was written plainly across their faces, the parents clutching their children close in a desperate bid for reassurance amidst the turmoil.

"Hide their eyes," Keltor warned, his voice taut with urgency. The parents shielded their children's eyes by pressing their faces gently against their chests. For a moment, the glade was filled with the muffled sobs of frightened children.

Fury and rage tore through his body, mingling with a cold sense of purpose that numbed his compassion. Keltor lifted his sword, and ignoring the man's pleas for mercy, and with two hands he plunged it straight into his chest. As the man gasped one last breath, Keltor knelt and whispered for the soldier's ears only.

"Know that you were killed by the new King of Elvendon. The Queen has come to overthrow King Iwein and reclaim our lands for our people." The man's eyes widened at the news, and then as Keltor twisted the blade slowly he shuddered in death and lay still.

Keltor slowly rose to his feet, as he withdrew his sword from the fallen soldier. The weapon glistened with blood, a silent testament to the violence that had just occurred.

As Kaitlin approached, concern evident in her eyes, she paused briefly beside Keltor. "Are you okay?" she asked softly, her gaze lingering on the dead man before turning back to Keltor. She reached out and gently touched his arm, offering a small gesture of comfort amidst the turmoil.

Keltor glanced at her, acknowledging the touch with a brief look. "Yeah, I'm fine. Check they're okay, Kitcat," he replied quietly and nodding towards the trembling family. His voice was low, the fatigue and emotional strain evident. He then knelt, methodically wiping his bloody sword blade on the dead soldier's clothes to clean it, his focus unwavering and practical even in the aftermath of conflict.

"Okay," Kaitlin replied softly, offering a comforting touch as she placed her hand briefly on Keltor's shoulder. Their eyes met for a moment, and she managed a reassuring smile. Keltor returned the gesture, his fatigue momentarily eased. With a gentle squeeze of his shoulder, Kaitlin then turned and made her way towards the family.

Kaitlin knelt beside them, her presence calm and compassionate. The mother, still clinging tightly to her children, looked up at Kaitlin with red-rimmed, tear-filled eyes. Her distress was plain to see; the fear and exhaustion etched into her features.

"Are you okay?" Kaitlin asked in a gentle, soothing voice, striving to offer reassurance.

"Yes. Thank you," the woman replied, her voice trembling with emotion. She sniffled and raised her hand to wipe her nose, her gratitude and relief only just concealing the fear that lingered in her eyes.

Esimae stepped forward to stand beside Kaitlin. "Is anyone hurt?" she asked, her tone gentle but concerned.

Kaitlin looked up, meeting her aunt's gaze. The mixture of fear, sadness, and anger etched on Esimae's face spoke volumes. In that moment, Kaitlin was more certain than ever that King Iwein had to be stopped, no matter the cost.

"No, we're okay, thank you," the woman's husband said politely as he got to his feet. He carefully helped his wife stand, steadying her as she wavered slightly. Their children clung tightly to their parents' legs, seeking comfort and reassurance. The mother and father offered gentle words and soothing touches, doing their utmost to calm the frightened youngsters as the danger around them slowly receded.

"My name is Tom," he stated, "and this is my wife, Rosa."

Tom's gaze lingered on Keltor, curiosity mingled with caution as he watched the man wipe his blade clean and slide it back into its sheath. "Who is that man?" he asked quietly, his voice carrying a tentative note.

Kaitlin noticed Tom's lingering gaze on Keltor and responded with a gentle smile. "My husband," she told him, her voice warm with affection, "and a soldier of Elvendon."

Tom's eyebrows lifted in surprise as he looked back at Keltor, clearly impressed. The way Keltor had moved and fought was unlike anything Tom had witnessed before, leaving him both curious and in awe.

"Thank you, for helping us," Tom said politely. He extended a steadying hand to Rosa, helping her regain her balance in the wake of their ordeal. His considerate actions spoke volumes of his concern for her wellbeing and the hardship they had faced together.

Rosa's grip tightened around her husband as she shuddered, her eyes lingering on the fallen soldiers. "We fled when the King attacked Elvendon and took all the men," she explained, her voice trembling. "For months, we lived in the forest, always moving further and deeper as the soldiers drew closer with each passing day. Eventually, we made the difficult decision to cross the bridge, thinking we would find safety there, as nobody ever dared to venture over it. But we were mistaken. The King's army was already marching through, and his scouts grew ever more persistent. We were on our way to the Deodar village, hoping they would offer us refuge."

Kaitlin shook her head slowly, her expression troubled. "You can't go there; the Deodar's have fled and are in hiding. It's not safe," she said, her voice gentle but firm as she addressed Tom's hopes.

Tom's shoulders sagged with resignation as he absorbed Kaitlin's words. He cast a weary glance at the lifeless soldiers scattered across the forest floor, the harsh reality sinking in. "Nowhere is safe," he replied quietly, his tone edged with despair and a sense of inevitability.

Keltor stepped forward, his presence reassuring amidst the uncertainty. "There is somewhere you can go," he said, his tone measured and calm. "If you walk east for two days, following the course of the river, you'll come upon a mountain range. Concealed within those mountains is a tribe known as the Luskarna."

He paused, ensuring Tom and Rosa were listening closely. "Don't be alarmed when you see them," Keltor continued. "The Luskarna are very tall," he explained his hand lifting in demonstration, "and will most likely greet you armed with spears, but you have nothing to fear from them. When you arrive, ask for Ila and explain that Keltor and Kaitlin sent you. They are friends of ours and will understand. Request shelter from them—they will look after you until it is safe for you to return home."

Tom's eyes glistened with gratitude and a faint glimmer of hope as he looked towards Keltor and Kaitlin. "Thank you," he said sincerely, his voice quiet but earnest. He paused for a moment, his uncertainty evident as his gaze drifted downward, anxiety clouding his expression. "Do you really think will?" he asked, the longing to return home weighing heavily on his mind.

Keltor, momentarily taken aback, furrowed his brow. "Will what?" he replied, prompting Tom to clarify his question.

"Be able to return home," Tom said, his tone soft but resolute.

Keltor's gaze shifted to Kaitlin and then back to Tom. He hesitated, knowing he could not reveal everything – the risks were too great. Still, he offered what reassurance he could. "Yes, I do," Keltor replied, his words calm and steady.

Tom's eyes drifted uneasily to the bodies lying motionless nearby, his stomach twisting with dread. The stillness pressed in around him, broken only by the faint rustle of leaves. He swallowed, throat dry, and gestured with a trembling hand towards the fallen soldiers. "What about them?" he asked, voice low and uncertain, the gravity of their situation weighing on his shoulders.

Keltor's jaw tightened as he surveyed the silent, frozen forms. The chilly air seemed to bite more sharply, and for a moment, he glanced at Tom, sympathy flickering in his eyes before pragmatism reclaimed his features. "We don't have time to bury them," he said bluntly, his words cutting through the heavy hush. "A fire might bring more soldiers here; we'll have to hide the bodies." It was grim, Keltor knew to leave bodies to rot, but time was not on their side, and a fire was just too risky.

Tom gently released his wife, determination settling on his features. "I will help you," he said, his voice steady and resolute. Keltor met his eyes and nodded in silent agreement, a sense of mutual understanding passing between them.

As Tom took hold of the feet of one of the fallen men and Keltor grasped the arms, they began lifting the body together. Tom glanced at Keltor, curiosity etched on his face. "How did you do that?" he asked quietly.

Keltor met Tom's gaze, replying in a measured tone, "I'm a King's guard, so I'm trained to fight. Like you, we hid in the forest after the initial attack."

Tom shook his head gently, his voice lowering. "No, I mean the other thing, with the magic?"

At this, Keltor pressed his lips together, clearly uncomfortable and unsure how much to reveal. He paused, then said, "Look, I can't tell you everything. It's too risky to our plan."

Tom persisted, his eyes brightening. "But that was magic, wasn't it?"

Keltor gave a small, reluctant nod. Tom's face broke into a smile. "You're a wizard?"

But Keltor shook his head firmly, cutting him off. "Tom, I can't, okay," he insisted, his voice tense with the weight of secrets he could not share.

Tom gazed down at the earthy forest floor, a quiet sense of hope flickering within him. Even if Keltor refused to admit it, Tom was convinced that Elvendon had a wizard in their midst. For the first time in what felt like ages, he allowed himself a small, unseen smile—perhaps there was hope after all.

Seeking to move the conversation forward, Tom cleared his throat and asked, "Where are you heading now?"

Keltor's expression hardened with resolve. "To raise an army," he replied simply.

Tom glanced over at Esimae and Kaitlin, his confusion evident. "What, just you and those two women?" he asked, struggling to understand the plan.

Keltor looked at him squarely. "Yes, and we have more men and women helping us. Look, I'd like to tell you more, really, but if you get captured again, I can't trust that you wouldn't tell them about us."

"I wouldn't, believe me," Tom insisted as they walked the body towards a mass of shrubbery.

Keltor met Tom's gaze, his voice blunt, but not unkind. "I know you would like to think you wouldn't, but if they threaten your children, you would. Any parent would, and I don't blame you for that, so it's best you don't know anything." With that, they let the body drop into the bushes and off the main track.

Tom hesitated, searching for the right words to say to Keltor. The weight of the situation made him pause, as if he wished to confide something or ask another question, but uncertainty held him back.

Keltor met Tom's uncertainty with gentle firmness. "Tom, just take care of your family. They're your responsibility, get them to safety and let us worry about the rest, okay." His words conveyed both concern and a clear boundary, emphasising the importance of Tom's duty to protect his loved ones while trusting Keltor and his companions to handle the greater dangers.

Reluctantly, Tom nodded. Though he still yearned for more answers, it was obvious that Keltor would reveal nothing further.

The incident had unfolded over several hours, and as they finally hid the last body, the day had faded into late afternoon.

Tom stepped forward and offered his hand to Keltor. "Good luck," he said sincerely. Keltor accepted the handshake, the simple gesture carrying with it a sense of shared understanding and mutual respect as they readied themselves to go their separate ways.

Tom's wife, standing close by, clutched their three children to her and spoke up with gratitude. "Thank you, all of you," she said, her voice warm and heartfelt, acknowledging the help and protection they had received.

Before they parted, Keltor offered a final word of caution. "Keep safe, and in the woods as much as possible," he urged, his tone serious, making clear the ongoing danger and the importance of remaining hidden.

As Tom began to back away, gathering his youngest child into his arms, he turned once more to Keltor and his companions. "I pray to the spirits that whatever it is you are planning, you are successful," he said earnestly, his words a mixture of hope and farewell as he led his family away into the trees.

"We will be," Kaitlin said firmly, gripping Keltor's hand as she glanced at him. She knew that, although helping these people had delayed their journey, the act of saving lives was far more important in her eyes.

Filled with admiration, Kaitlin leaned closer to Keltor. "You're amazing," she said softly, her sincerity clear as she met his gaze. The intensity in Keltor's blue eyes was unmistakable as he looked back at her.

Keltor's voice was heavy with regret as he admitted, "No, I'm not. I'm a trained killer, Kaitlin. I don't even think about it when I'm in that mode; it's only afterwards that I reflect on who they might have been. If they had families or children, I realise I've just taken away someone's father or husband." His words revealed the deep internal conflict he faced, torn between his instincts as a warrior and the consequences of his actions.

"Keltor, no," Kaitlin said softly, her voice trembling with the weight of his confession. She searched his face, wanting him to see how much she meant her words. "You can't hold all that guilt. Those men made their own choices—they weren't forced to come after Tom's family."

Keltor looked at her, his jaw tense, eyes shadowed with doubt. He remembered the coldness in the men's expressions, the certainty with which they had advanced. "I know, Kaitlin. I told him as much before it ended. He had no regrets, no hesitation. If I hadn't stopped them, they'd have done it again, to someone else, maybe to another family hiding in these woods." The memory clearly haunted him, his voice low.

She reached for his hand, squeezing it tightly. "And that's why you had to do it, Keltor. You did what was needed. If you hadn't, more innocent Elvendons would have suffered. You always try to protect people, even when it hurts you."

Keltor managed a faint smile, but his eyes were still clouded. "Maybe. It's just… I never want to get so used to this that I stop caring. The day I walk away without feeling anything will be the day I've lost myself, Kitcat. I couldn't live with that." He hesitated, eyebrows raised, as if unsure whether he'd ever find peace with the things he'd done.

Kaitlin felt a crushing sadness at what Keltor must be feeling. She reached out gently, her concern evident in her words and the soft touch of her hand. "Hey," she said, stopping him in his tracks. She stole a glance ahead at her aunt, who was still walking on, then looked back up at Keltor, her expression earnest and filled with empathy. "When we take back Elvendon you will never need to kill anyone again, and we will have peace in our Kingdom." Her voice was full of hope as she spoke, trying to lift the weight she sensed in him. The promise hung in the air between them, a vision of the future she wanted so desperately to make real for them both.

Keltor's features softened into a smile at her words. He lifted his hand, brushing aside the stray strands of hair that had escaped her braid, his touch tender and full of affection. "It sounds good, doesn't it, our Kingdom," he whispered, his gaze lingering on hers, searching for reassurance and drawing strength from her belief.

Kaitlin's stomach fluttered with butterflies as she met his eyes, the intensity of his look sending ripples through her entire being. She returned his smile, her voice gentle and full of conviction. "It sure does," she whispered back, her words carrying both comfort and determination. "Worth fighting for," she added, her resolve clear.

Keltor nodded in agreement, silently reaffirming the shared hope he and Kaitlin held for the future, and drawing strength from the deep bond between them. He spoke gently; his words filled with determination and honesty. "Definitely. I'm okay, Kitcat," he assured her as he noticed the concern in her eyes. "I know that, before we reclaim our Kingdom, I'll have to face more battles and take more lives. I've come to terms with that. This war wasn't our choice—Aranstream brought it to us."

Kaitlin responded with newfound confidence, her voice steady despite the weight of her responsibilities. "Good, and believe it or not, I'm okay too. I know I was afraid before—afraid to become the Queen of Elvendon and to have all these lives depending on me—but now I accept who I am. Kaitlin of Earth is long gone. I am Kaitlin, Queen of Elvendon, and wife to Keltor, my King, whom I love with all my heart."

Keltor's expression softened with love, and he whispered, "I love you, Kitcat—my beautiful best friend, wife, and my Queen," before his lips met hers in a gentle, reassuring kiss.

Esimae paused, noticing that the voices of Kaitlin and Keltor had faded behind her. Turning, she saw that the two had stopped, lost in a tender moment together. Her gaze softened as she witnessed their kiss, understanding that, despite the urgency of their journey, they needed these precious few minutes to themselves. Respecting their need for privacy, Esimae quietly turned away and wandered over to a nearby tree. She settled on the ground, opened her basket, and called out, "Hey, do you need a toilet break?"

At her words, Magic's head popped up from the basket. The cat meowed in response and promptly leapt out, disappearing behind the tree. Esimae called after him, "Three minutes!" She chuckled to herself, amused by his meowed complaint as he vanished from sight.

Keltor broke away from their kiss, though his hands remained gently cradling Kaitlin's head. His voice was soft, full of longing and hope. "I can't wait for the day when we finally have peace, when we can spend time together without all the killing, fighting, and constant fear. I miss the old days, when we were just children—swimming in the lake, enjoying picnics in the forest."

Kaitlin smiled affectionately at him, her eyes sparkling with warmth. "You're such a romantic," she teased, before adding playfully, "How about climbing some trees?" Her grin was infectious.

Laughing, Keltor released her face and shook his head, still amused. "Yeah, well, we'll see about that one," he replied, his tone light and teasing.

Their laughter mingled as Keltor slipped his arm around Kaitlin's shoulders, drawing her close. Together, they resumed their walk, side by side, their bond strengthened by shared memories and hope for the future.

As they approached Esimae, Kaitlin greeted her with a warm, "Hey." Esimae rose to her feet and gestured behind the tree, explaining with a grin, "Magic is having a toilet break."

Kaitlin matched her grin and replied, "Okay."

After a short pause, Esimae decided Magic's break had lasted long enough. She called, "That's long enough. Magic!" and opened the lid of her basket. Within a minute, the cat emerged, taking his time as he wandered back towards her. Looking up at Esimae, he let out a meow before leaping into his basket.

Amused, Kaitlin asked, "What did he say?"

Esimae chuckled and replied, "Oh, he's just moaning about all the travelling, ignore him." She closed the basket and strapped it securely to her back. "I'm ready, let's go."

Keltor glanced over at Esimae, his expression thoughtful. "We'll walk for another hour or so and then start searching for somewhere to spend the night," he suggested. "There's no chance we'll reach Elvendon before dark, not after we lost so much time helping Tom and his family."

Sleep came only in brief spells for the three companions. Their rest was light, every sense attuned to the slightest sound—the rustle of leaves or the distant crack of a twig. Despite their vigilance, dawn broke peacefully, the pale morning light seeping softly through the dense canopy above.

They moved quietly as they prepared to set off once more, packing up their few belongings with silent efficiency honed from many days travelling. The chilly, crisp air was tinged with the earthy aromas of moss and damp foliage. All around them, the forest was still save for the muted sound of their own footsteps as they pressed forward, their every movement cautious and deliberate. With watchful eyes, they made their way through the thickening woods, each of them anxious to reach the sanctuary of Keltor's village.

The closer they drew to Elvendon, the greater their caution became. Soldiers patrolled the area in increasing numbers, making it far too risky to attempt entry during daylight. Deciding it was safer to wait, the trio remained hidden within the sheltering forest, passing the last hours before nightfall in quiet rotation—one always awake, the others snatching what rest they could to recover from the exhausting journey.

As dusk gave way to darkness, they finally made their move. Moving unseen, they slipped into the village under cover of night, keeping to the deepest shadows and hugging the sides of houses as they advanced. Their progress was slow and careful, every step calculated to avoid detection. At last, they reached the back of Keltor's cottage, hearts pounding with relief and anticipation, ready to seek refuge within its familiar walls.

Keltor rapped firmly on the door with his fist, and the three companions stood waiting in tense silence for a few minutes. From inside, his mother's voice called out, "Who is it?" through the sturdy wooden door.

Keltor leaned in, whispering, "It's me, Mum."

The sound of bolts sliding back was immediate, and Sharelle cautiously opened the door just enough to peer out. Upon recognising her son, she pulled the door wide, ushering the trio swiftly into the safety of the cottage. Once they were inside, Sharelle closed the door behind them and slid the bolts back into place, ensuring they were secure.

Without hesitation, she moved towards her son and enveloped him in a tight embrace. "Thank the spirits," she breathed, her relief clear as she finally released him from her grasp. Turning to Kaitlin, Sharelle offered a respectful bow of her head and greeted her warmly, "Kaitlin, my queen."

Keltor gestured towards Esimae, introducing her to his mother. "Mum, this is Esimae, Kaitlin's aunt. She's a witch too."

Esimae greeted Sharelle with a friendly "Hi," extending her hand in welcome. Instead of shaking Esimae's hand, Sharelle stepped forward and embraced her, catching Esimae off guard.

After a brief pause, Esimae returned the hug, acknowledging Sharelle's warmth.

No sooner had the introductions finished than Sharelle began firing questions at her son, concern and urgency evident in her voice. "So, what's happened, have you got the trolls on your side, how many men have you rallied?" she asked rapidly, keen to know the latest developments.

Seeing the exhaustion on his companions' faces, Keltor intervened gently. "Mum, please, we're knackered. Can we at least get a cup of tea?" He moved over to the kitchen cupboard and took out some mugs, signalling the need for a moment's respite before answering any questions.

Sharelle hastily realised her lapse in hospitality and gave a small apologetic nod. "Oh, yes, of course, where's my manners, please have a seat at the table," she said, pulling out a sturdy pine chair for Esimae, who accepted it with clear gratitude and settled down wearily. Sharelle then moved across to the lamp sitting on the kitchen side and turned up the wick, filling the room with a warmer glow so that everyone's faces were cast in gentle light and the sense of safety became more tangible.

Meanwhile, Keltor set the mugs carefully on the table, his movements slow with fatigue. Suddenly, Sharelle caught sight of the blood staining her son's clothes, and her composure faltered. She gasped, her face drawn with worry, and stepped quickly towards him. "Are you injured?" she demanded, her voice tight with panic as she scanned him anxiously for any sign of wounds.

Keltor looked down at his stained clothes in response to his mother's worried question, quickly trying to reassure her. "Oh, no, no, it's not my blood," he replied. "Sorry, we had a run-in with some soldiers, and I had to kill them." He spoke with a calm practicality, as if the danger he described was a commonplace matter. Without further fuss, he reached for a tin of his mother's homemade biscuits, opened it, and took one out, biting into it with obvious relish. The taste brought a look of pure satisfaction to his face, his eyes closing briefly in delight. He wasted no time in taking another biscuit, then offered the tin to Kaitlin. She accepted, taking a biscuit for herself and tasting it. The shortbread was so delicately made that it seemed to melt in her mouth, prompting her own sigh of satisfaction. Keltor caught her reaction and smiled, evidently proud of his mother's renowned baking.

"Esimae?" Keltor offered, setting the tin of biscuits in front of her. Esimae declined politely, waving her hand and shaking her head. "No, thank you," she said. Keltor simply shrugged at her response and helped himself to another biscuit.

Sharelle turned her attention to Kaitlin, pulling out a chair and offering it to her. "Kaitlin, please," she said warmly.

"Thank you, can I wash my hands first?" Kaitlin asked, glancing towards the kitchen sink.

"Of course," Sharelle replied with a nod in the direction of the sink, granting her permission.

Kaitlin made her way over to the sink and pumped the tap until water began to flow, the chill of it catching her slightly off guard. She took the soap from the side, working it into a lather before thoroughly rinsing her hands clean. As she finished, she glanced over her shoulder and noticed Keltor approaching.

"I got the look," Keltor said with a grin, acknowledging the silent prompt to wash up himself. Kaitlin let out a quiet chuckle, dried her hands with a towel, and then walked back to the table. She eased herself into the chair, feeling a wave of relief at finally sitting down and resting her tired feet. Spotting the tin of biscuits Keltor had left on the table, she reached out and took another, enjoying the simple comfort it offered.

Once Keltor had finished washing his own hands, Esimae followed suit. She washed her hands carefully, dried them, and then took a seat at the table beside her niece, ready to join the others.

Sharelle re-entered the pantry, her words lingering in the air. "So, tell me what's happened?" she called, before returning with a selection of ham, cheese, bread and butter in her arms. Placing the food on the table, she gestured kindly to Kaitlin, touching her gently on the shoulder. "Help yourself," Sharelle encouraged, before disappearing back into the pantry once more.

"Thank you," Kaitlin responded, raising her voice so Sharelle could hear her from inside. Meanwhile, Keltor took up the task of setting the table, placing plates and knives neatly before each person. He glanced at Kaitlin, asking quietly, "Bread and cheese?" She nodded, watching as he sliced the bread, spread it with butter, and topped it with a generous piece of cheese for her.

Kaitlin accepted the simple meal with gratitude. "Thanks," she said, taking the prepared slice from Keltor and settling more comfortably at the table.

As the others settled in, a soft meow echoed from beneath the table. Sharelle paused in her movements, glancing around the kitchen with a puzzled expression.

"Was that a cat I just heard?" she asked, and scanning the room for the source of the sound.

Kaitlin, already enjoying a bite of her bread, butter, and cheese, nodded in response. "That's Magic," she explained, gesturing towards a basket resting by her aunt's feet. "He's my aunt's cat."

Sharelle's nose wrinkled slightly—she was not overly fond of cats. "You have a cat?" she queried, her tone revealing her uncertainty.

Esimae, noticing Magic's restlessness, interjected politely. "Is it all right if I let him out? He's very well trained, and he's been cooped up in this basket for days."

Sharelle hesitated for a moment, then gave a reluctant nod. "Yes, I suppose that's fine," she agreed, keeping a watchful eye as Esimae gently unfastened the basket lid.

Magic poked his head out, surveying his new surroundings before leaping gracefully from the basket. Spotting the food on the table, he padded closer, tail swishing curiously.

"Does he want some ham?" Sharelle offered, picking up a few slices and preparing to share.

"Yes, please, he'd love some. Thank you," Esimae replied gratefully, watching as Sharelle thoughtfully cut the ham into smaller, manageable pieces.

Sharelle placed the plate on the floor near Magic, who immediately began to eat with evident appreciation.

"There you go," Sharelle said, smiling a little despite herself.

Magic meowed again, contentedly enjoying his treat. Esimae smiled and translated for the group, "He said thank you." Sharelle arched an eyebrow at this, clearly intrigued.

Kaitlin took a sip of hot tea, offered by Keltor, and explained quietly, "My aunt understands the cat. He's her familiar."

Sharelle joined the group at the table, settling herself as Keltor began to recount the recent events. He spoke at length, providing a detailed account of their harrowing encounter with the trolls. The group listened intently as he shared the valuable information, they had managed to obtain about the men who had been taken to Elvendon.

After finishing his account, Keltor turned to his mother, his expression sombre. "Mum, there's something else," he said quietly, standing up from his chair and approaching her. The atmosphere at the table shifted, anticipation and apprehension settling over the group.

Kaitlin's head bowed; she understood what was coming and could already feel tears gathering in her eyes. With a trembling voice, she asked, "What is it?" Her anxiety was clear, instantly recognising that her son was about to share bad news.

Desperate for clarity—and relief—she quickly interjected, "It's not about your brother, is it?" Her heart raced, fear and worry making it shake within her as she awaited Keltor's response.

"No, it's about Alarna," Keltor replied, gently draping his arms over his mother's shoulders in a comforting embrace. His mother, sensing the gravity of his words, lifted her hand to rest it atop his, her eyes searching his face for answers.

"What about her?" she asked, concern evident in her voice. "I haven't heard from her since she left to go off with that Aranstream boy." Her words hung in the air, the memory of Alarna's departure still fresh and unresolved.

Keltor took a steadying breath before continuing. "Well, she married Logan, and we met him and Alarna. They joined us for a while." He paused, gathering his thoughts. "They were expecting a baby; she was eight months pregnant."

His mother caught the subtle shift in his phrasing and interjected, "Was? Why do you keep saying was, did she miscarry?" Her anxiety grew, bracing herself for the worst.

Keltor shook his head, struggling to speak as the weight of the news bore down on both him and his mother. The pain was evident in his eyes, and for a moment, he simply could not find the words.

"No, Mum, it's worse than that," he finally managed, his voice trembling with emotion. "I'm sorry to tell you this, as I know you loved Alarna like a daughter, but—" He hesitated, overcome by grief, and gently removed his arms from around his mother. Raising his hand, he wiped away the tears that had begun to fall.

Sharelle, sensing the gravity of the moment, spoke softly, urging him to continue. "Keltor?" she said quietly, turning to face him, her concern clear.

He took a shaky breath and forced himself to go on. "We were ambushed by Aranstream soldiers, and they were both killed." The words hung in the air, the finality of the loss settling over the group.

Sharelle's face fell, and she shook her head in disbelief. "Oh, no," she murmured, her voice barely audible, overwhelmed by the suddenness of the tragedy.

"I'm sorry, Sharelle," Kaitlin added gently. "I only knew them for a short time, but we all became friends." Her words, though simple, were heartfelt, offering what little comfort she could.

Still trying to process the news, Sharelle wiped her eyes with her hand. "What happened?" she asked, her voice thick with emotion, seeking clarity amid her grief.

"We had to evacuate the Deodar tribe from their village for their safety," Keltor began, his voice heavy with the memory. "Kaitlin and Esimae took charge at the front, guiding the tribe through the thick fog that blanketed the valley that morning. I stayed at the back with Logan and Alarna, making sure no one was left behind."

He paused; the details etched painfully in his mind. "The fog was so dense we could barely see a few hundred yards ahead. Suddenly, out of nowhere, we were ambushed from the top of the

327

valley. The attack was swift and chaotic. In that moment, all I could do was protect the tribe's children. Mum, I had to make an impossible choice—I had to choose between saving Alarna and saving those kids."

Keltor's mother reached for his hand, her voice trembling with empathy. "Keltor, I'm so sorry, that must have been tortuous for you," she whispered, her heart aching for the pain her son had endured.

Keltor's voice wavered as he relived the traumatic events of that fateful day. "It broke my heart, but I had no choice. Alarna insisted I save the children instead of her, and she was right. I couldn't let all those little ones die." His words were laced with sorrow, and he paused, struggling to hold back his tears as the memory of Alarna's final wish surfaced.

With great difficulty, Keltor went on. "I saved her baby, though. Just before she passed, she made me promise, so I did as she wanted. Mum, I took the baby out of her and he survived. He's being looked after by her aunt with the Deodars."

Sharelle, overcome with emotion, exclaimed, "By the spirits, Keltor," as tears streamed down her face. Rising to her feet, she opened her arms to him, offering comfort. Keltor leaned into her embrace, closing his eyes, finding solace in his mother's warmth as she held him close.

"I can't believe you did that. That's incredible, you did the right thing," she agreed, her voice full of conviction as she pressed a gentle kiss to the top of his head. The gesture conveyed both pride and deep affection, offering reassurance in the face of his anguish.

Kaitlin, unable to keep her emotions in check, wiped her running nose with the back of her sleeve and dabbed at her tears. Her bond with Keltor was so profound that she could sense the depth of his pain as if it were her own, her heart aching for the impossible decision he had been forced to make.

Esimae, her emotions mounting as memories of Jaike's loss surfaced, gently interrupted the group's embrace. "Look, we should try and get a few hours' sleep and then head off during the night, it would be safer," she said, her voice steady but distant.

The emotional weight in the room was becoming overwhelming for her, and she knew she needed to focus her mind on the immediate challenge: the fight against Aranstream. For now, she pushed aside her grief, determined to channel her energy into the task ahead.

Recognising the wisdom in Esimae's suggestion, Sharelle quickly agreed. "Yes, of course, you're right," Sharelle said. She then made the arrangements for the night. "Keltor, you can share with me, Kaitlin can have your room, and Esimae can have your sister's room." With practical matters settled, the group began preparing to rest, each person seeking a small measure of peace before the difficult journey that awaited them under the cover of darkness.

"Well, mum, you see the thing is," Keltor began, making his way over to Kaitlin. He gently wrapped his arms around her shoulders, seeking both comfort and solidarity as he prepared to share the news with his mother.

Kaitlin, understanding the significance of what Keltor was about to say, leaned into him in quiet support. She braced herself for the conversation, knowing precisely what Keltor was about to reveal to his mother.

Keltor took a steadying breath and turned to his mother. "Mum," he began, his voice soft but earnest, "Kaitlin and I were bonded a few days ago."

At first, Sharelle struggled to comprehend his words, her mind reeling from this unexpected revelation. "What?" she replied, momentarily unable to take in what he was saying.

Keltor took a steadying breath and turned to his mother, his voice soft but filled with emotion. "Mum, Kaitlin and I were bonded a few days ago. It was a surprise; she didn't know until I had arranged it all." He glanced at Kaitlin, whose eyes shone with warmth, before continuing. "Our friend knew of an elder hiding in the Eccleston forest, and he bonded us."

A gentle smile crossed Keltor's face as he recalled the memory. "It was beautiful, Mum, in the forest with our friends and the Deodar tribe. The elder made Kaitlin the Queen of Elvendon, and, well, he crowned me the King." His eyes met his mother's, searching for understanding and acceptance, the significance of the moment clear in his voice.

She stared at him in silence, momentarily lost for words as she absorbed the news. The significance of what Keltor had just shared lingered heavily in the room. He spoke again, his tone apologetic yet sincere. "Look, I'm sorry, I know you would have wanted to be there and have the whole big ceremony thing, but it just felt right, it was something I needed to do."

He glanced towards his wife, seeking reassurance, and she returned his gaze with a gentle, understanding smile. His worry was evident as he turned back to his mother. "You're not cross, are you?" he asked, his voice betraying a hint of uncertainty at her silence.

At last, she smiled—first at her son, then at Kaitlin. Her expression conveyed both her acceptance and her affection, offering comfort and support in the wake of their revelation.

Sharelle shook her head gently; her voice filled with warmth. "Cross, no, of course not," she assured him, dispelling any worries he might have had. Turning to her son, she spoke with heartfelt affection, "Keltor, I love you. You've grown into the most amazing man—kind, loving—and I'm so proud of you." Her words reflected the pride she felt, mixed with the wisdom gained over years of watching him grow.

She paused, her gaze shifting between Keltor and Kaitlin, silently acknowledging the journey they had undertaken together. The weight of the moment hung in the air as she reflected on her own actions. Sharelle spoke with a gentle candour, her voice steady. "I knew you had a destiny, and I fought against it. It was wrong of me; you are your own person, you both are." Her admission carried both regret and relief, as she recognised the importance of allowing her son and Kaitlin to forge their own path.

With this heartfelt confession, Sharelle extended her arms towards them, offering a silent gesture of understanding and acceptance. Kaitlin rose from her chair and moved to stand beside Keltor, responding to the invitation without hesitation. Together, they stepped into Sharelle's embrace, finding solace and reassurance in the warmth of her acceptance and love. Sharelle held them close, her affection unmistakable. "Welcome to the family," she said softly to Kaitlin, her words sincere and full of kindness. Kaitlin smiled in return, gratitude and relief evident in her expression. "Thank you," she replied, her voice quiet but heartfelt.

Sharelle's smile widened, her voice steady and warm as she addressed them both. "Honestly, it's just perfect. Of course, I would have loved to have been there with you both, but the way life is now, you're right to embrace every day you have together.".

With a gentle laugh, she continued, "Anyway, when your father is back home with us, and all of this is over, we can have a great big party then." A sparkle of amusement lit her eyes. "Although, your father never really liked parties. You know, when we bonded, it was just me and your father, and our King and Queen. We tried to sneak off on our dragons for our honeymoon without all the other dragon riders knowing, but our King and Queen had other ideas. They'd arranged a little party for us." Sharelle's laughter bubbled up at the memory. "Your father was horrified. Even the King's dragon was decorated with flowers, much to the poor dragon's dismay."

"Oh Mum, we really must talk more about the old days. You and Dad had such an incredible life together; I can't believe you've never shared those stories with us before," Keltor said, a wide smile spreading across his face as he looked at his mother.

Sharelle drew in a deep, steadying breath, clearly moved as she tried to keep her emotions in check. "I know," she admitted gently, "I should have celebrated my life with your father and shared those memories with all of you. At the time, though, it was simply too painful to talk about. But once we have him back, I promise we'll tell you everything—prepare yourselves to be well and truly bored with tales of our great adventures."

Keltor's eyes lit up with anticipation. "I can't wait, Mum," he replied, his smile full of warmth and excitement.

331

"Me too," Kaitlin added with a laugh. "I didn't even believe in dragons until we met Kailan."

"You met a dragon?" her aunt interrupted in surprise.

Kaitlin smiled, glancing at her aunt. "Yeah, we did meet a dragon," she confirmed, her tone light but weary. "I'll tell you the whole story later, I promise. But for now, I don't know about you, but I could really do with a few hours' sleep." She stretched, giving a sheepish grin as she sniffed her arm. "And honestly, a shower would probably be a good idea as well."

Sharelle gave her a gentle nod, already rising to clear the table. "Yes, go ahead. Towels are on the shelf," she replied, her voice warm and accommodating as she began tidying up.

"Mum, before that, we should restock supplies—it's a long walk to the woodsman's cottage," her son reminded her, his tone practical yet caring. Sharelle nodded in agreement, understanding the importance of being well-prepared. "Yes, of course," she replied with a nod, "I'll pack something for each of us." Her response was gentle and reassuring, demonstrating her dedication to looking after her family's needs.

After showering, Kaitlin swapped places with Keltor, who then went to take his turn. Feeling the comfort of a familiar space, she headed into his bedroom. Naked, Kaitlin slipped into his bed and pulled the blanket over herself, seeking solace in its warmth. Memories of her last stay surfaced—she recalled sleeping in Anna's bed, longing deeply to be with Keltor. At that time, she believed such happiness was beyond reach, convinced her fate was sealed within the castle. Now, as she lay in Keltor's bed, the difference was profound, a silent testament to how much had changed.

Her eyes lifted to the door as it opened, watching as Keltor walked in with a towel wrapped around his waist. Now that they were bonded, his mother was at ease with them sharing his room, a small but meaningful sign of acceptance. Keltor was still towel drying his hair, the simple domesticity of his movements making the room feel warm and familiar as he approached Kaitlin.

"I can't believe how good it feels to be clean," he remarked with a satisfied sigh, tossing both towels onto the back of his desk chair with casual ease.

"Budge over," he said, his grin infectious as he looked at her. The bed was only a single, but that detail hardly mattered to either of them. In truth, the closer they were, the happier they felt, content in each other's presence and the comfort of their shared space.

Kaitlin nestled herself against Keltor, wrapping her arm gently over him. The scent of his skin, fresh from the shower, was irresistible. Although fatigue tugged at her, the comfort of being so close to him made it impossible for her thoughts to rest. The intimacy of sharing a bed—a simple, ordinary act—became something deeply meaningful in that moment.

She pressed soft kisses to his shoulder, letting her hand trace the familiar lines of his tattoo before it drifted to rest on his stomach. Feeling her warmth and affection, Keltor rolled towards her and pulled her closer, his fingers slipping into her still-damp hair. There was no need for words between them; their connection was strong and natural. He kissed her, cherishing every second they shared. Each day together was a gift, and every opportunity to express their love—more precious still.

xxx

Keltor lay quietly, stroking Kaitlin's hair as she slept peacefully on his chest. For as long as he could remember, he had longed for nights such as this—moments where they could be together, bonded not just by duty but by genuine affection. He had always envisioned a simple life: the two of them living in a cottage nestled deep in the forest, surrounded by a handful of animals and perhaps a small family of their own. The tranquillity and contentment of these dreams brought him solace.

Yet, reality had unfolded in ways he could never have anticipated. He had not foreseen a war with Aranstream, or Kaitlin's true identity as a princess—and now, queen of the elves—nor his own unexpected role as king. These responsibilities brought both privileges and difficulties. Despite the challenges,

Keltor found hope in what they could accomplish together. United, he and Kaitlin could bring about meaningful change in Elvendon. They could aid the families most in need and ensure that every child, regardless of their parents' status, had the opportunity to attend school.

Most importantly, Keltor held a firm conviction about one thing, and he was certain Kaitlin would agree: he would ban forced bonding. He believed that everyone should have the freedom to bond with the one they truly loved, rather than being compelled by their parents' expectations or traditions. In this, he saw the possibility of a brighter, kinder future for their people.

He pressed a gentle kiss to the top of her head before softly trying to wake her. "Hey, my love, we have to get up I'm afraid," he said, his tone tender and regretful.

Kaitlin stirred, blinking her eyes open to the darkness that still lingered outside. She let out a heavy sigh, reluctant to leave the comfort of their bed. "Do we have to?" she complained, her voice muffled as her hand traced his warm chest and she nestled herself even closer to him. "I was having such a lovely dream."

He gave a rueful little smile, understanding her reluctance. "Yes, I'm afraid so. The quicker we break out our men, the quicker we can win this war and give Elvendon back to its people," he reminded her, the sense of duty pulling them both away from their moment of peace.

Still, Kaitlin clung to the hope of a different future. "I can't wait for nights like this," she whispered, "when we can make love all night, and then just lie together in the early hours of the morning, just like this."

"Me too," Keltor murmured, his hand gently lifting to cup Kaitlin's face. She responded by shifting up along his body, her lips seeking his until they kissed, slow and lingering. As their embrace deepened, Keltor's hands drifted through her hair, fingers tangling in the soft strands. His heart beat faster, every touch and caress drawing them closer. He could feel the warmth and connection between them intensify, their bodies naturally responding to each other's affection, the world outside momentarily forgotten.

There was a knock at the door, interrupting the peaceful intimacy of the moment.

"Hey, are you two awake?" Esimae's voice called through the door, her tone light but insistent.

Keltor, with a reluctant sigh, broke away from Kaitlin so she could respond. Their connection lingered in the air, a silent promise to return to each other as soon as possible.

"Yes, we are," Kaitlin replied, her voice carrying a mixture of reluctance and resolve as she answered Esimae's call.

"Okay, just making sure," Esimae called back from the hallway, her voice warm but brisk, ensuring that Keltor and Kaitlin were awake and ready for the day ahead.

Inside the room, Kaitlin glanced at Keltor, a mischievous grin spreading across her face. "We'll be fiv... erm, ten minutes," she replied, her tone playful as she corrected herself, knowing full well that lingering a little longer was inevitable. The moment was charged with intimacy, and as she smiled at him, Keltor leaned in, his lips soon finding hers once again. Their connection, deep and affectionate, lingered as they shared another tender kiss, stealing a moment together before duty called them away.

Fifteen minutes later, both Kaitlin and Keltor were ready, each dressed and prepared for the day ahead. Sharelle, ever considerate, had left a set of clean clothes for Kaitlin in the bathroom. The garments, once belonging to Anna, proved to be a relief for Kaitlin—they were riding clothes, practical and comfortable. She slipped into the trousers and pulled the overdress on over the top, feeling a sense of gratitude for the well-chosen outfit. Finally, she fastened her cloak securely around her shoulders before stepping out to join Keltor in the kitchen.

"There you go, get that down you," Keltor said, handing Kaitlin a steaming mug of tea. He watched her with a warm, encouraging smile as she wrapped her hands around the mug, the comforting heat seeping into her skin.

Kaitlin looked up at him, appreciation lighting her eyes. "You're incredible, you know," she said, her voice soft but sincere as she accepted the tea from him.

Keltor's grin widened, a playful spark in his eyes. "Yeah, I know," he replied, raising his eyebrows at her in an exaggerated double arch, his light-hearted response eliciting a small laugh from Kaitlin. She felt her cheeks flush with embarrassment and quickly took a sip of her tea, hoping to compose herself as her aunt caught her eye, an unmistakable grin spreading across her face before she looked away.

Moments later, Keltor's astonishment broke the comfortable atmosphere. "Holy shit, mum," he exclaimed as his mother entered the kitchen, his surprise evident at her striking appearance.

Sharelle's eyes narrowed at her son's language. "Keltor, don't swear!" she admonished, her tone firm but affectionate.

Keltor offered a sheepish apology but couldn't contain his admiration. "Sorry, but look at you, I know I'm your son, but seriously mum, you look incredible."

Sharelle responded to the attention with a playful spin, showing off her striking attire. She wore her old dragon rider outfit— leather trousers paired with a crisp white overtunic, all held together by a wide leather belt that supported her elven sword. The nostalgic uniform gave her a confident presence, drawing appreciative glances from everyone in the room.

Kaitlin's gaze was drawn to the boots Sharelle wore. Each boot featured side pockets, with a dagger tucked neatly into each one— an impressive touch that caught Kaitlin's eye.

"Thank you, I'm just glad I can still fit in it," Sharelle said, laughter in her voice as she clipped her cloak around her throat.

Curiosity getting the better of her, Kaitlin asked, "Where did you get those boots, and those daggers? I love them."

Sharelle smiled warmly as she answered Kaitlin's question. "Just a little gift from the Queen of Malgar. We were very good friends back then; she designed them herself. I can't tell you how many times those daggers came in handy!" The fondness in her voice showed just how much the boots and daggers meant to her.

Kaitlin's eyes lit up with appreciation. "I bet, I'm going to get myself a pair of those made as soon as I can," she said enthusiastically, clearly inspired by Sharelle's story.

Keltor's gaze shifted, noticing another detail. "Is that a dragon rider clasp?" he asked, pointing towards the ornate fastener on her cloak.

Sharelle nodded, pride evident in her posture. "Yes, it is."

Keltor grinned as he walked over to his mother and embraced her. "It's no wonder dad fell head over heels in love with you," he said, his affection plain in his voice.

Sharelle groaned, a hint of embarrassment colouring her cheeks. "Keltor," she protested, "I'm afraid when he sees me, he will think I've aged."

Kaitlin offered Sharelle a genuine compliment, her smile warm and sincere. "No, Sharelle, you are so beautiful," she said, admiring the way Sharelle's outfit accentuated her hourglass figure and noticing how her long, blonde hair was neatly tied back in a braid. Sharelle accepted the compliment graciously, bowing her head as she replied, "You are too kind, my Queen."

As Sharelle moved to the stove, grabbing the pot to pour herself a mug of tea, Kaitlin leaned into Keltor and whispered, "Keltor, I really wish she wouldn't do that." The formality felt awkward to her, especially now that Sharelle was not just Keltor's mother, but also her own mother-in-law.

Keltor nodded in understanding. "I know, but she's old school," he explained, acknowledging the tradition behind his mother's behaviour.

"It just feels weird, she's your mother, in fact she's, my mother-in-law now," Kaitlin added, glancing over at Sharelle.

Keltor considered her words, then offered, "Oh yeah, I didn't think of it like that." He looked towards his mother and continued, "I'll have a word with her and ask her to stop if that's what you want?"

"Yes, please, thank you," Kaitlin replied, relieved that he understood her feelings.

Kaitlin hefted her pack onto her shoulders, adjusting the straps until it was comfortably in place. She turned to Keltor with a questioning look. "Keltor, you did tell her that we weren't going all the way with her and Esimae, didn't you?" she asked, watching as Sharelle left the kitchen to fetch something from the living room.

Keltor glanced at her, his expression uneasy, clearly reluctant to answer. Kaitlin let out a groan of frustration. "Keltor," she urged him pointedly.

Resigned, Keltor replied, "Okay, I'll go and tell her now," before leaving the kitchen to find Sharelle.

After a couple of minutes had passed, Kaitlin could hear raised voices drifting in from the living room. It was mostly Sharelle's voice, unmistakably passionate and agitated. Kaitlin could easily imagine the content of the argument—Sharelle was likely voicing the same concerns she herself had raised earlier, insisting that it was far too dangerous for Keltor to venture into the encampment alone. At the very least, Kaitlin had managed to persuade Keltor to take her with him as far as they could safely go.

When Keltor returned to the kitchen, his expression was wry. "Well, that went well," he remarked with heavy sarcasm.

Kaitlin arched an eyebrow. "She wasn't impressed, then?"

He shook his head, a rueful smile on his lips. "No, she went absolutely mad at the idea of me going into the encampment by myself."

"So how did you convince her?" Kaitlin asked, her curiosity piqued.

Keltor offered a small shrug and replied, "I used a little bit of magic, and reminded her that I am a wizard. I explained that I can copy anyone's appearance after touching them. Once she realised I could leave the encampment at any time by transforming into a guard, she felt reassured."

Sharelle returned to the kitchen, her voice steady as she asked, "Right, are you all ready?"

"Yep, ready as we'll ever be," replied Keltor, determination clear in his tone as he moved towards the kitchen door. Kaitlin followed closely behind him, with Esimae and Magic trailing after. Sharelle, taking one last look around, closed the door behind them and locked it, sealing the house before their departure.

Moving quietly, the group slipped out of the village under the cover of darkness and entered the vast expanse of Elvendon forest. Their footsteps were cautious and hushed, careful not to draw attention as they pressed deeper into the trees. For several hours, they walked in silence, the only sounds the gentle rustling of leaves and the occasional snap of a twig beneath their feet. As dawn began to break, pale light filtered through the dense canopy, illuminating their path as they finally reached the Forest of Time.

Aware of the potential risk, they made the conscious decision to avoid passing near the Deodar village, choosing instead to venture further west through the forest. The journey continued, the party maintaining their quiet vigilance as they navigated the ancient woodlands. By midday, the group arrived at a fork in the path—the predetermined point where they would part ways and continue their separate missions.

Keltor turned to his mother, concern etched on his face. "Are you sure you understand where to go?" he asked her for the third time, his voice hovering between worry and insistence.

Sharelle let out a soft sigh, the beginnings of a complaint in her tone. "Keltor, I have been navigating the forests long before you were even born. I know where I'm going," she replied, clearly exasperated by his fussing.

He hesitated, then pressed on, unable to hide his anxiety. "I know, I just don't want you to get lost. Now, he's not expecting you, so remember what I said—he will have scouts in the trees, so always look up."

"Yes, I know, son," Sharelle replied, her voice warm but firm. "We will be fine. I'm more worried about you and Kaitlin."

Keltor turned to his mother and Esimae, a sense of resolve in his voice. "Mum, we have our magic, so between us we'll have no trouble with the Aranstream soldiers."

Sharelle, however, cautioned against overconfidence. "Just don't get too complacent, that's all I'm saying. King Iwein is snidey, and the prince is even worse." With a look of concern, she drew both Keltor and Kaitlin into a warm embrace.

Esimae then addressed Kaitlin, her tone gentle yet firm. "Kaitlin, remember what I have always said…."

Kaitlin nodded, finishing the familiar phrase. "My magic is within me."

Esimae smiled and released her from the embrace. "Exactly— and never forget it. I will see you soon."

Keltor lingered for a moment, his gaze following Sharelle and Esimae as they walked away in the opposite direction, each setting out on their own uncertain journey. There was a heaviness in the air as he watched his mother disappear amongst the trees, concern etched on his features.

"She'll be okay," Kaitlin said, her voice attempting to reassure him.

He nodded, though the worry was still evident in his eyes. "I know, they'll reach the cottage by nightfall, but I still can't help worrying."

"Keltor, your mum can kick arse, she'll be fine," Kaitlin replied with confidence.

The seriousness of his mood eased a little, and Keltor looked at her, a smile finally breaking through as he laughed. "Yeah, I guess you're right. It's hard to think of her like that, though—she's always been so placid and calm. I suppose, as a dragon rider, she will have killed people," he admitted, a frown crossing his face as he considered the thought. "That's just… hard to imagine her doing anything like that."

Kaitlin grinned and slipped her arm through his, her tone light. "I know, at least you know where you get your talent from."

"Yeah," he chuckled, his hand brushing her arm in a gesture of affection. "I had no chance really, did I, with Mum and Dad both being dragon riders, and Dad a wizard."

Kaitlin smiled, her tone casual as she explained, "Well, my mum was a witch and my dad an elven King." The words hung between them for a moment, and then their eyes met. Amusement flickered across their faces, and soon both were laughing together, the tension easing as the shared absurdity of her heritage became apparent.

Chapter Fourteen

Forester's Cottage

The rain began to fall, the first drops in weeks. Sharelle drew up the hood of her cloak, shielding herself from the sudden downpour. Normally, she would have welcomed the rain for the sake of her parched garden, but this evening it brought only discomfort. She and Esimae had been walking for hours. Their journey had started with a hint of awkwardness, given Esimae's identity as a witch—relations between elves and witches had always been uneasy. However, after the first hour, Sharelle finally managed to break the ice by asking how Esimae was related to Kaitlin.

In response, Esimae shared Kaitlin's story. She explained that she had not seen Kaitlin for many years, not since the child's early days. It was only that morning that Kaitlin had reappeared, desperate and pleading for Esimae to help save Keltor's life.

Sharelle was taken aback when she discovered just how close Keltor had come to losing his life, something he had never mentioned to her. The realisation that it was Kaitlin who had intervened and saved him left Sharelle momentarily speechless. However, as the initial shock faded, the awkwardness between Sharelle and Esimae lessened, and conversation began to flow with ease. Soon enough, the two women felt as though they had known each other for years, the earlier tensions forgotten as they exchanged stories and laughter.

So engrossed were they in their newfound camaraderie that neither of them paid any heed to their surroundings. Deep in conversation, they unwittingly wandered into the forester's territory, only realising their mistake when it was already too late to turn back.

Unbeknownst to Sharelle and Esimae, a man watched them intently from his concealed position. The steady rainfall masked their lively conversation, making it impossible for him to catch their words, though it was clear they were engrossed in whatever they were discussing. After a moment of observation, the man gave a low whistle—a signal to his companion concealed nearby in the branches of the next tree. The second man responded with a subtle movement, acknowledging the signal. Together, they waited in silence, biding their time until the unsuspecting women were directly beneath their hiding places. Then, in one fluid motion, both men leapt down from the trees, launching their ambush.

As the ambush unfolded, Esimae barely had time to react before a man dropped from the trees above and landed squarely on top of her. The force of his descent knocked her violently forwards, causing her to crash face-first into the muddy ground. In the chaos, the basket she carried—with Magic inside—was flung out of her grasp, tumbling away into the darkness.

The man wasted no time. He pinned Esimae to the forest floor, using his weight and strength to restrain her. For a moment, it seemed she would be overpowered. But Esimae, refusing to be subdued, focused her will and called upon her own magical abilities. With a surge of determination, she channelled her energy and unleashed it upon her attacker. A shockwave of raw magical force burst from her, striking the man with the intensity of a lightning bolt. The impact sent him flying backwards, as if he had been hit by an electric shock, and freed Esimae from his grip.

Sharelle heard the faint crack of a branch just above her—a split second warning. She tried to dodge, but the man crashed down, slamming into her with the weight of a falling boulder. His shoulder knocked the breath from her lungs, and cold mud spattered her face as she hit the ground hard. The damp earth pressed against her cheek, gritty and slick beneath her hands. A sharp ache flared in her hip where it struck a hidden root.

Before she could catch her breath, the man scrambled upright. In the gloom, Sharelle could barely make out his shape—only a shadow looming closer. He lunged, grabbing for her arms, rough fingers tightening around her sleeves. Panic surged, but so did her training. Sharelle jerked her head up, the sudden movement jarring her own skull as she smashed her forehead into his nose. A sharp crack sounded, followed by a muffled grunt.

Sharelle, shaken but resolute, scrambled to her feet as the adrenaline surged through her veins. In a swift, practised motion, she reached down to her boot and drew her knife, the blade glinting even in the dim light beneath the trees. Her grip was steady despite the chaos, ready to defend herself against the attacker. Reacting instantly to the threat, Sharelle twisted her body in mid-air, using her momentum to flip over and land squarely atop her attacker. The force of her landing drove him to the ground, pinning him beneath her weight and leaving him momentarily stunned by her swift and decisive manoeuvre.

The hood of Sharelle's cloak slipped back, exposing her to the relentless rain as it hammered down. Her long golden hair tumbled forward, cascading onto the chest of the man she had just overpowered. Despite the cold droplets streaming across her face, Sharelle paid them no mind. Every fibre of her being was focused on the man pinned beneath her, her attention unwavering and intense. Her hand gripped her knife tightly and she pressed it threateningly against the man's throat.

A fleeting look of panic crossed the man's features as the reality of the situation dawned on him—Sharelle had the upper hand. In stark contrast, Sharelle's expression was one of intense concentration; her gaze remained steady and resolute, betraying none of her inner turmoil. Yet, beneath her calm exterior, her heart thudded violently within her chest.

As she stared down at her adversary, Sharelle's eyes grew wide with astonishment. Recognition struck her hard, and disbelief coloured her voice as she uttered his name. "Frankie?" she managed, her shock unmistakable as she took in the face of the man she had just subdued, unable to comprehend how it could possibly be him beneath her.

"Sharelle Dracon?" the man replied, his breath coming in ragged gasps. His eyes grew wide with recognition as he stared up at her, the shock clearly etched on his face. The coolness of her blade pressed on his Adam's apple.

Sharelle's eyes blazed as she stared down at Frankie, her voice rising in a furious mixture of disbelief and concern. "Frankie! What the hell are you doing attacking women?" she demanded, unable to contain her outrage at the shock of recognising him as her assailant. She pulled the knife away from Frankie's throat. Her gaze lingered on him for a moment, a tumult of emotions flickering across her face. Then, unable to contain the surge of adrenaline and shock, she thumped him hard on the shoulder. "I could have killed you!" she exclaimed in a breathless whisper, the words carrying a mixture of relief and fear. The realisation that she had come dangerously close to ending his life overwhelmed her, leaving her shaken by both the possibility and the narrow escape.

With a swift motion, Sharelle flicked her cloak back over her shoulder, then swung her leg over the man and sprang to her feet. She quickly retreated several paces, putting distance between herself and her former attacker. Her grip on the knife remained firm, every muscle tensed in readiness for another assault.

Esimae, having regained her composure after her own struggle, approached Sharelle and regarded her with a mixture of curiosity and concern. "You know this man?" she asked, her tone cautious as she eyed the figure on the ground.

Sharelle turned back to the man; her expression layered with both familiarity and apprehension. "Yes, he's my neighbour," she stated plainly, addressing the group. Then, looking directly at Frankie, she continued, "I thought you were taken by Aranstream soldiers?"

Frankie shook his head, his features shadowed by recent hardships. "I was, but the group I was with escaped. I've been out here hiding with the rest of them."

His attention shifted as he noticed the aftermath of the struggle. "Is he dead?" he asked, gesturing towards Esimae's attacker who lay motionless on the forest floor.

Esimae, not one to take chances, let out a brief huff and crouched beside the man. She pressed two fingers to his neck, searching for a pulse. After a tense moment, she stood and dusted off her hands. "No, he's still alive," she confirmed. Her voice held a hint of relief, though edged with resignation. "Luckily, as that had not been my intention," she added curtly.

Frankie, still processing the scene, turned to Sharelle with wide-eyed incredulity. "How the hell did you learn to fight like that?" he asked, as he moved over to check on his friend. Sharelle met his gaze, her tone clipped and guarded. "It's a long story," she replied, offering him no further details.

Before Frankie could press further, Esimae interjected, her stance assertive and her eyes narrowed in warning. "Before you ask, I'm a witch," she declared. "And a powerful one too, so no funny business," she added, pointing a finger at him with an air of authority.

Frankie raised his hands defensively, his voice placating. "Hey, I have no quarrel with you," he assured her, backing away slightly.

"Good," Esimae muttered under her breath, her attention shifting to her feline companion. She bent down to check on Magic, who appeared disgruntled but unharmed. "He nearly killed my damn cat," she grumbled, as Magic voiced his displeasure with a sharp, indignant meow, still recovering from being thrown so roughly during the commotion.

Sharelle fixed the man with a piercing look, her tone cold and unwavering. "So, I ask you again, what are you doing out here attacking women?"

The man looked uncomfortable under the scrutiny of both Sharelle and Esimae. "We didn't know you were women," he protested, glancing between them as though searching for understanding.

Neither Sharelle nor Esimae softened their expressions, their eyes hard and unyielding. The man shifted uneasily and rushed to explain himself further. "You had your hoods up, and those cloaks could be for a male or female. With this rain, it was hard to tell," he said hurriedly, trying to justify the misunderstanding. "And you, why are you out here late into the night?"

Sharelle's voice was steady as she replied, "We're heading to the old forester's cottage. I have information I need to give him."

The man's demeanour changed slightly at this revelation. "Oh, in that case, you'd best come with me. That's where I've been hiding out. There are quite a lot of us now, scattered about these woods. The old man has been trying to gather an army to attack the encampment and get our men out."

A low groan broke the tense silence, drawing everyone's attention to the ground. Concern etched deeply on his face, Frankie immediately bent down to assess his friend's condition, his movements filled with worry.

"Mick, are you okay?" Frankie asked, offering his hand to help Mick up. The man on the ground grumbled, "No, I feel like I've been electrocuted," but accepted the gesture, allowing Frankie to pull him to his feet.

Esimae, standing close by with her arms folded protectively across her chest, interjected matter-of-factly, "Yes, well, you were." Her tone was guarded, making it clear she was still wary of the situation.

Mick glanced uncertainly at Esimae and then at Frankie, seeking reassurance. Frankie quickly tried to calm him, saying, "It's okay, they're on our side." Mick, now steady on his feet, ran a hand through his hair—still standing on end from the shock of Esimae's magic—and muttered, "Well, that's good to know."

With the immediate tension eased, the man gave a nod towards the path ahead. "Come on, we're taking them to the cottage," he instructed.

Sharelle and Esimae fell in step behind the two men. As they walked, the rain began to ease, its steady patter fading to a gentle drizzle. Sharelle reached up and lowered the hood of her cloak, allowing herself a better view of the path ahead. In the distance, she caught sight of the faint flicker of lights—signs they were nearing their destination.

Sharelle's eyes lifted, scanning the trees that arched above their route. She had been alert throughout the journey, having spotted the presence of other men in the woods some time ago. Esimae, sensing her scrutiny, followed her gaze into the darkened branches.

"How many?" Esimae asked quietly, her tone cautious.

"Seven," Sharelle replied in a low voice. "All armed with bows. Which I may add are pointing directly at us."

As they drew nearer to the cottage, Esimae leaned in, her voice a whisper. "Do you trust him?"

Sharelle's reply was measured and honest. "Esimae, there are only a few people I trust in this world. My husband, my children, and our queen."

Esimae gave her a playful look. "Not me?"

Sharelle glanced over at her companion. "I don't know you well enough yet, but yes, I'm starting to."

Esimae offered a reassuring smile. "Don't worry about them. I can shield us both if I need to."

Frankie opened the cottage door and stepped inside, with Mick close behind. Cautiously, Sharelle and Esimae followed, entering the warmth of the cottage. The comforting heat from the fire at the back of the room was a welcome relief for their rain-soaked faces. The inviting aroma of coffee filled the air, mingling with the scent of a stew simmering over the fire.

"Wait here," Frankie instructed, before making his way to the back of the room and disappearing through a door.

The women took the opportunity to warm themselves by the fire as they waited. Before long, an older man with a long, wiry grey beard and hair entered the room.

"You are Keltor's mother?" he asked as he approached them.

"Yes, I am," Sharelle replied, tilting her head slightly in curiosity. "And you are?"

"Ben, but you probably just know me as the forester."

Sharelle gave a slow nod, acknowledging the introduction.

"Keltor said you would help, with the fight to get back Elvendon."

"Maybe," Ben responded, picking up three mugs from the side. "Coffee?" he offered. Both women nodded in agreement.

Ben took a cloth, wrapped it around the handle of the enamel coffee pot, and poured the hot coffee into their mugs, which had been warming on a hot plate over the fire.

Ben gestured for Sharelle and Esimae to take a seat by the fire, his tone laced with disbelief as he voiced his thoughts. "I thought Keltor was killed on Earth?" he remarked, the statement hanging in the air.

Sharelle acknowledged his surprise, her voice steady. "So did I until recently, and then he just turned up. Keltor is on his way right now to break out the men from the encampment, and he has the queen with him."

Ben, caught off guard by this revelation, almost spat out his coffee. He lowered his mug, searching Sharelle's face for confirmation. "What queen?" he asked, needing clarity.

Sharelle met his gaze directly. "Kaitlin, the Queen of Elvendon, our queen and Keltor's new wife."

Ben studied Sharelle's expression intently, searching for any sign that she might be joking, but her face remained serious. The weight of her revelation pressed upon him, and he repeated his question, still unable to believe it: "You're serious, Kaitlin is alive?"

He looked from Sharelle to Esimae, his disbelief visible. As the truth finally sank in, a wide grin appeared on his face. "I can't believe it. We still have a queen," he whispered, his voice thick with emotion. The months of uncertainty seemed to ease, if only slightly, as hope began to surface.

Ben considered the impact of the news. "The whole of Elvendon believe she perished on Earth. King Iwein told everyone she was dead." Shaking his head, his astonishment was mixed with a renewed sense of possibility. For the first time in a long while, hope flickered at the edge of the impossible.

Ben took a moment to absorb the enormity of the news, but his brow soon furrowed in confusion. "I'm sorry, did you also say Keltor was her husband?" he asked, his voice tinged with disbelief as he sought clarification.

"Yes," Sharelle replied. "They were bonded by an elder in the forest a few days ago. They bear the mark of a true bonding. The elder crowned Kaitlin the Queen and Keltor her King."

Ben let out a laugh, equal parts incredulous and relieved. "I don't believe this. When we thought all hope was gone, it turns out that we have not only our true heir and Queen of Elvendon, but also a King."

The revelation seemed almost too much to comprehend, yet Ben's spirit lightened. What had seemed impossible mere moments ago was now reality: their lost queen had returned, and with her, a king to stand beside her. In the wake of despair, hope was rekindled—stronger and brighter than before.

Sharelle shifted, her expression growing more serious. "Yes, and there is something else," she said, prompting Ben to arch an inquisitive eyebrow. She leaned in, her voice dropping to a whisper meant only for him. "Both Kaitlin and Keltor—" She hesitated, glancing around to ensure no one was listening. Then, with quiet intensity, she continued, "—possess magic. Keltor is a true wizard, and his powers are incredible. And our Queen, although young and still learning, is already exceptionally powerful."

Ben's eyes widened further, absorbing the significance of Sharelle's revelation. The prospect of their restored royalty was astonishing enough; now, the thought of a king and queen both gifted with magic sent a ripple of hope—and awe—through his heart. If ever Elvendon needed a miracle, perhaps this was it.

Esimae's attention shifted as Mick approached the group, drawing Ben's gaze to him. Ben couldn't help but comment on Mick's dishevelled appearance. "What the hell happened to your hair?" he asked, unable to ignore Mick's hair, which stood up in every direction.

Without missing a beat, Mick glanced at Esimae. He made a half-hearted attempt to flatten his short, dark hair, but it stubbornly sprang straight back up. "Ask the witch," he replied, settling himself beside Ben.

Esimae struggled to suppress a laugh, her eyes flicking upwards just as Ben looked over at her. She felt no need to apologise for Mick's predicament; after all, he had been the one to jump her first.

She allowed herself a brief, mischievous smile before quickly looking away. Despite herself, Esimae found Mick rather endearing—for an elf, at least.

Sharelle fixed her gaze on Mick, her tone steady as she spoke. "You're an Aranstream."

Mick met her look without flinching. "Yeah, and?" he replied, his voice edged with defensiveness.

Sharelle simply shrugged, maintaining her stare. "Just saying."

Mick's expression hardened, but he pressed on, addressing the uncertainty lingering in the group. "Look, there are plenty of us who don't agree with what King Iwein is doing. We never wanted this war. In fact, most of us have family in Elvendon. Me included. My sister married an Elvendon, and now her husband is somewhere in that encampment."

Ben stepped in, his voice resolute as he looked around at the others. "We can trust him," he declared, "without a doubt."

Mick lifted his chin in gratitude towards Ben, a silent acknowledgement of his support.

Ben broke the silence with a question, his tone light in an effort to ease the tension. "So, ladies, what's this plan then?" he asked, glancing between Esimae and the others.

Meanwhile, Mick stood up and made his way to the pot of stew that was gently simmering over the fire. He picked up a bowl, ladled in a generous helping, and grabbed a spoon before returning to Esimae. Pausing in front of her, he hesitated for just a moment before extending the bowl towards her.

Esimae looked up at him. She met his gaze, noticing that his grey eyes were clear and honest. As Mick offered her the bowl,

351

his voice was quiet but genuine. "I'm sorry I jumped you," he said, the apology sincere as he held out the stew.

Esimae reached out, her hands closing around the bowl as both held it for a moment. She drew in a steadying breath, feeling the warmth from the bowl seep into her fingers. Meeting his eyes, she replied softly, "I'm sorry I electrocuted you."

Mick gave her a sincere nod, acknowledging her apology, and released his hold on the bowl, leaving it in her care.

"What's in the basket?" Mick inquired, eyeing the basket Esimae had set on the chair beside her.

Esimae's hand instinctively moved to rest protectively atop the basket. "My cat," she answered quietly, her fingers tightening ever so slightly around the handle.

A genuine smile flickered on Mick's face. "I like cats," he replied, the simple statement carrying a warmth that seemed to ease some of the lingering tension. With that, he turned and walked back over to the pot of stew, preparing another bowl. All the while, Esimae's gaze remained fixed on him, thoughtful and perhaps a touch uncertain.

Mick glanced over at the basket once more, a gentle curiosity in his tone. "Is it a boy?" he asked.

"Yes," Esimae replied, her voice quiet but sure.

Mick's gaze softened further. "Would he like some stew?"

A genuine smile touched Esimae's lips, and she felt her heartbeat quicken unexpectedly. She swallowed, steadying herself, and pushed the flutter of emotions back down. "I expect he would, thank you."

It struck Esimae that she had never before apologised to a man, much less an elf man. The realisation lingered, making her feel both vulnerable and oddly empowered.

From within the basket, Magic let out a soft mew.

"Shh, Magic," Esimae whispered, her tone gentle. "I know he seems nice, and I'll let you out in a minute. Let me just make sure you'll be safe."

Magic mewed again as if in agreement, and Esimae couldn't help but smirk to herself at her cat's timing.

Chapter Fifteen
A Grim Discovery

Kaitlin and Keltor huddled beneath the hoods of their cloaks, the relentless rain drumming on their shoulders and soaking through the fabric. The darkness pressed in around them, making it nearly impossible to see the path ahead. Keltor's concern grew with each passing moment, a gnawing worry that they might not find shelter before night fully claimed the forest.

Just as their hopes began to wane, they stumbled upon what appeared to be an abandoned woodsman's cottage. A faint outline of a small clearing emerged between the trees, with a well off to their right. As they drew closer, Keltor carefully examined the property. There were no lights shining from the wooden cabin, and the outbuildings were empty—no sign of livestock or recent activity.

"This looks like it will do," Keltor said, relief evident in his voice as they approached the weathered structure.

He tested the door handle, finding it unlocked, and entered the cottage with measured caution. Kaitlin stayed close behind, keeping a wary eye on their surroundings. The door opened directly onto a living area that was in disarray, furniture toppled and scattered across the floor. Keltor began to right a couple of chairs that had been knocked over, while Kaitlin moved quietly around the room, taking in the scene. Her eyes drawn to the toppled furniture and scattered belongings. She picked up a candle in a wooden holder, inspecting it with a thoughtful frown, before setting it down carefully on the table. "It looks like there was quite a struggle in here," she observed quietly, her voice edged with concern.

They moved methodically through the small cottage, searching each room in turn. There was only a single bedroom, a compact bathroom, and the kitchen and living area where they had first entered. The search was over quickly, given the modest size of the place.

"We can sleep in here," Keltor suggested, standing just inside the bedroom's doorway.

Kaitlin wrapped her arms around herself, feeling the chill in the air. "It's cold in here, though," she murmured, shivering.

Keltor nodded, understanding her discomfort. "I know, but we can't risk a fire. Even the faintest flicker of light through the window could be seen from a long way off, and woodsmoke would carry far in this weather. At least it's dry, and with some luck, this bad weather will blow over by morning." He shrugged off his sodden cloak and hung it over the back of a chair to dry, and Kaitlin did the same, following his lead.

With a smile in his eyes, he said, "We can just snuggle up to keep warm." Kaitlin smiled back at him, comforted by his gentle humour and steady presence.

"We'll grab a few hours' sleep and head off at first light," Keltor added, his tone reassuring despite the uncertainty that lay ahead.

Kaitlin picked up the pillow from the bed and brought it to her nose, giving it a cautious sniff. To her relief, it did not smell unpleasant; in fact, the entire cabin seemed remarkably well maintained, a testament to the care and affection of its absent owners—whoever and wherever they might be. Quietly, she removed her boots and perched herself on the edge of the bed, taking a moment to absorb their surroundings.

"Do you think King Iwein took the people that lived here?" Kaitlin asked, her voice tinged with worry as she gazed around the room.

"I would say that was a high possibility," Keltor replied, his tone thoughtful. "I can't see any evidence of children, so they were either a young couple just starting out, or an older couple." With that, Keltor began to remove his own boots, loosening his wide leather belt before placing his sword carefully by the side of the bed and sliding his dagger beneath the pillow, ever mindful of the need for caution.

There were thick, green woollen blankets on the bed, and they were clean, so he pulled them to cover the bed. Both, still fully clothed, slipped underneath the covers. Kaitlin snuggled into him, gratefully accepting his warmth as he wrapped his arm around her and gently rubbed her arm to help her feel warmer.

"Better?" he asked softly.

"Mmm, thanks," she replied, leaning against his chest and appreciating his willingness to share his warmth.

"Night, Kitcat," he said, using the familiar nickname with a fondness that brought a small, tired smile to her lips.

She turned her face towards him. "Night," she answered, and he kissed her gently. Settling in, Kaitlin lay on her side with her head resting against his chest. She closed her eyes, letting the steady beat of his heart lull her towards sleep.

For a while, Keltor lay awake, his eyes open and fixed on the darkness above. His fingers moved absent-mindedly along Kaitlin's arm as she rested against him, the gentle motion a silent comfort in the quiet of the night. He tried to keep his mind from dwelling on the uncertainties and dangers that awaited them, forcing himself instead to focus on hope—the hope of a triumphant outcome, of the two of them together in Elvendon castle, living their own version of happily ever after.

Eventually, his eyelids grew heavy, and he drifted into sleep. At first, his dreams were filled with beauty and happiness. But soon, they twisted into nightmare. Alarna was screaming, her stomach torn open, the baby gone from her womb, blood covering her. Not just from her stomach, but pouring down her face, her arms outstretched towards him, pleading, and begging for her child. He woke with a start. Sweat bathed his brow. His heart raced in his chest. His eyes wide he stared back into the darkness, and he took a moment to bring himself back to reality.

He felt Kaitlin stir, and his arm drew her in closer, not for her protection, but for his own. He needed her, her calmness, the steadiness of her breathing as she slept. Only in her presence did the terror recede, replaced by a fragile sense of hope he clung to desperately After a few minutes his heartbeat matched hers, his breathing calm and steady.

Keltor lay awake in the darkness, haunted by his nightmare and too fearful to close his eyes again, lest he find himself drawn back into its terror. Time crept by slowly, and as the first faint light of dawn began to filter through the window, he knew it was time to rouse Kaitlin.

Gently, he reached out and woke her. "Morning," he murmured softly, his voice low so as not to startle her. Kaitlin, still half-asleep, squinted up at him, her eyes bleary with fatigue. For a moment, she wondered if it was truly morning already. "Morning," she replied, her voice thick with sleep.

Keltor's hand moved to brush her hair from her face, a tender gesture that brought a touch of comfort to the quiet room. "We should get going," he whispered, his gaze lingering on her features. Kaitlin nodded in response, understanding the necessity even as she hesitated to leave the warmth of his embrace. With some reluctance, she slipped out of his arms as he released her, preparing herself for the day ahead.

Kaitlin sat up on the edge of the bed, letting out a weary groan as the dregs of sleep clung to her. Keltor, already preparing for the day, glanced over with a teasing smile as he pulled on his boots.

"Still not a morning person," he remarked, his tone light and familiar.

"No," Kaitlin replied, her voice laced with a grumble as she bent down to lace her own boots. "Especially without a mug of tea to get me going."

She finished tying the last lace and looked up to find Keltor standing in front of her, his boots firmly planted on the floor. He smiled down at her, warmth in his eyes.

"Here, have some water," he offered, extending his water bottle towards her.

Kaitlin accepted the bottle with a hint of sarcasm. "Oh, how delicious," she quipped, nonetheless grateful for the gesture. She took a drink, then let out a sigh, the cool water helping to rouse her a little further from her morning haze.

Keltor glanced at Kaitlin and offered, "Breakfast?" as he handed her half of a ham sandwich, one that his mother had thoughtfully prepared for them earlier.

"Yes, thank you," Kaitlin replied, accepting the sandwich gratefully.

She took a hearty bite and, still chewing, remarked with genuine appreciation, "This is really good."

"Yes, it is," Keltor agreed, eating the other half of the sandwich himself.

After finishing her meal, Kaitlin wandered over to the window. She peered outside at the soft glow of the early sunrise and commented, "At least it's stopped raining."

"Come on, let's get going, it looks like it's going to be a better day," Keltor announced, picking up his pack and slinging it over his shoulder with a sense of optimism.

Kaitlin followed him out the door, closing it behind her. The early morning air greeted them as they stepped outside, and she took a moment to adjust to the quiet stillness that lay over the landscape. With Keltor leading the way, the two set off, ready to begin their journey and embrace whatever the day might bring.

As they continued their way through the forest, the cheerful morning chorus of the birds filled the air, echoing from the branches above. The sun climbed steadily higher, its rays slipping through the sprawling canopy of oaks and ash. This created a pattern of dappled light and soft, golden patches that illuminated the path ahead, lending a gentle beauty to their journey.

They walked for several hours, the tranquillity and rhythm of their steps occasionally interrupted by the shifting light and the constant birdsong. Eventually, the forest began to narrow, and they found themselves approaching a ravine. The path became increasingly treacherous, with rocks jutting up beneath their feet and forcing them to pick their way carefully. From time to time, they had to duck beneath low-hanging shrubbery and twisted branches growing out from the ravine walls, making progress slow and careful.

Keltor's unease grew as they advanced. He kept his eyes fixed on the top of the ridge, aware that it would make an ideal spot for an ambush—much like before. "I hope Logan was right about that wine cellar under the castle," he murmured, scanning the ridge warily. The memory of past dangers lingered, making every shadow and sudden movement seem like a potential threat.

"He had no reason to lie to us, Keltor. He wanted rid of King Iwein the same as we do," Kaitlin reminded him, her tone reassuring.

"Yeah, I know. I was just clutching at straws," Keltor admitted, a hint of self-deprecation in his voice.

Kaitlin grinned at him, amused by his candour.

"What?" Keltor asked, a smile forming on his lips in response to her expression.

"You used a metaphor," she pointed out, her eyes sparkling with amusement.

Keltor chuckled as he realised she was right. "Yeah, your human phrases are clearly starting to rub off on me. That was a good one though, right?" he said, giving her a playful wink.

"A very good one," Kaitlin agreed warmly, leaning into him and linking her arm through his.

The birdsong faded, their cheerful melodies dwindling until a tense silence settled over the ravine. Keltor became acutely aware of the growing hush, a prickling sense of foreboding creeping in as the usual sounds of the forest faded away.

He halted, his gaze sweeping the now still surroundings. "Something's wrong," he murmured, unsheathing his sword with a measured, deliberate motion as his unease intensified.

Kaitlin's voice dropped to a whisper, her eyes darting about. "Is someone there?"

"I don't know, but I sense something, and it's not good," Keltor replied, every muscle taut with anticipation.

With practiced caution, Kaitlin mirrored Keltor's actions as she pressed herself against the ravine wall. Together, they edged forward, each movement careful and deliberate, bracing themselves for whatever might lie around the approaching blind bend.

"Hang back a little," Keltor advised, his tone barely more than a breath. Kaitlin nodded in response, her heart rate quickening as anticipation surged through her. She positioned herself defensively, hands poised at her sides, ready to call upon her magic should the need arise.

He proceeded with great caution, edging around the blind corner while systematically scanning both the heights above the ravine and the narrow path ahead. The surroundings appeared devoid of any obvious movement, yet a peculiar creaking sound drew his focus, sharpening his sense of unease.

Kaitlin, ever alert, whispered, "What is it?" Her voice was barely audible, betraying her apprehension.

He glanced at her, arching an eyebrow in response, silently urging her to heed his earlier warning. "I thought I told you to wait back a bit," he muttered, unable to hide his concern.

Kaitlin, undeterred, brushed off his remark with a dismissive flick of her hand. "Yeah, you did, and I did," she asserted, her tone firm.

He couldn't resist teasing her. "What, for like three seconds?" he quipped, the tension between wariness and familiarity lending a nervous energy to the moment.

She screwed up her nose at him in defiance, and he shook his head in dismay. Despite his outward frustration, a reluctant smile crept onto his face as he glanced away, quietly amused by her stubbornness.

"Can you hear that?" he asked, his voice tense as the creaking sound grew louder and more insistent.

"Yes, what is it?" she replied, her brow furrowed with concern.

"I don't know, it's coming from beyond the next bend."

They exchanged uneasy glances, each understanding the unspoken danger that might be lurking ahead.

"Okay," she said at last, determination flickering in her eyes as she pushed her sleeves up.

He watched her with a puzzled expression. "What are you doing?"

"Getting ready," she replied simply.

"For what?"

"A fight. My hands are free so I can use my magic," she explained, her tone matter-of-fact.

"Kaitlin, no. You're going to wait here until I see what it is."

"No, I'm not," she said back in a firm whisper.

"Kaitlin, you're the Queen, I must keep you safe. Can't you just for once wait here?" he begged, looking a little exasperated.

"No," she replied with a gentle shake of her head. She lifted her hand to his face, trailing her fingers across his cheek before tickling him gently under the chin. He hesitated, torn between duty and the warmth of her touch, but her resolve was unmistakable.

"Don't do that!" he exclaimed, pulling his face away in a futile attempt to appear annoyed. Despite his best efforts, a laugh threatened to escape him, betraying the stern facade he tried to maintain.

Unfazed by his protest, she repeated her playful gesture, her fingers teasing him once more.

"For crying out loud, Kaitlin, I'm trying to be serious," he implored, his tone earnest even as her finger traced its way to his neck, provoking another round of gentle tickling.

Keltor let out a resigned sigh, grabbing Kaitlin's hand as she tried to move ahead, barely concealing the laughter that threatened to break through his serious demeanour. "Fine," he conceded, "just please, stay behind me." His tone, though firm, carried a hint of affection as he made his request.

"I will, I promise," Kaitlin replied, determination in her voice. "I'll be your backup."

He shot her a questioning look, raising an eyebrow. "My what?"

"Your backup—someone ready to help, just in case you get caught," she clarified with a reassuring smile.

Keltor straightened, a trace of indignation in his response. "I won't get caught."

"Yes, I know, it's just a saying," she replied quickly, hoping to ease his pride.

He rolled his eyes, exasperated but not truly annoyed. "You are impossible," he muttered, a reluctant smile tugging at his lips.

Kaitlin grinned back at him, undeterred. "I know."

Keltor lifted his sword in both hands, his grip tightening as he cautiously approached the next bend. Every movement was deliberate, the blade poised and ready, reflecting his experience and unwavering focus. His posture radiated confidence, and there was a sense of command in the way he held his weapon, as though nothing could take him by surprise.

Remaining true to her word, Kaitlin held back for a moment, resisting the urge to follow immediately. Although she did not wish to undermine Keltor—after all, he was the one accustomed to danger and skilled in dealing with such moments—she struggled with the idea of letting him face the unknown alone. The thought of waiting, separated from him and powerless to help if something were to go wrong, filled her with dread and anxiety.

As she watched him advance, Kaitlin's heartbeat quickened. There was something about the way Keltor moved with his sword that left her breathless; the confidence and control he exuded sent her heart into a wild, erratic rhythm, underscoring both her concern for his safety and the deep connection she felt towards him.

As Keltor advanced, Kaitlin kept a short distance behind, her nerves on edge. She hesitated for a moment, but as he rounded the corner and vanished from sight, a sudden uneasy feeling twisted in her stomach.

Without warning, Keltor's voice rang out—loud and urgent. "Kaitlin!" he called.

The alarm in his tone jolted her, and she dashed forward, anxiety spiking as she hurried around the bend. "Keltor!" she cried, her voice thick with panic.

She found her husband rooted to the spot, his sword's point resting against the earth. The sight before him was so appalling that it rendered him motionless.

"Oh, my fucking god!" Kaitlin gasped, her hand shooting to her mouth in shock and horror as the full extent of what Keltor had found came into view.

The scene before Keltor was so appalling that he could not bring himself to chastise Kaitlin for her swearing. His heart pounded in his chest, nearly choking him with the intensity of his horror. Nothing in all his years had prepared him for such a nightmare, and the reality of it was nearly impossible to grasp.

The very idea that one elf could inflict this level of cruelty upon another was unthinkable, and his mind reeled in disbelief. As the shock settled into his bones, he realised his hands were trembling uncontrollably. Instinctively, he reached for Kaitlin, seeking her presence as an anchor amid the horror. Ahead, men were strung high above on single posts, their arms stretched and bound overhead. The stench of decay hung heavy in the air, mingling with the distant cawing of circling birds. Most of the bodies were skeletal in appearance, where the birds had pecked away at their flesh. However, on some, you could still make out their facial features. The grisly tableau forced both into a stunned silence, their senses reeling not only from the horror of what they beheld, but from the suffocating closeness of death itself. As Kaitlin reached Keltor's side, her trembling hand instinctively sought his, desperate for reassurance amid such carnage. The realisation of the cruelty behind this atrocity pressed in on them both, as unrelenting and bitter as the fetid air that surrounded them.

Overcome by emotion, tears streamed down Kaitlin's cheeks as she gripped Keltor's waiting hand. Her voice barely more than a choked whisper, she managed to say, "What the hell, why—why would someone do this?" The pain and disbelief in her words hung heavy in the air, echoing the horror that confronted them.

"It has to be King Iwein," Keltor replied, his voice thick with anger as he slid his sword back into its sheath. He stared at the dreadful sight, struggling to comprehend the horror. "I just can't believe what I'm seeing."

Just then, a sudden gust of wind swept through the clearing. Instinctively, both Kaitlin and Keltor raised their hands to shield their noses, the overwhelming stench of decomposing flesh assaulting their senses and forcing them to brace against the sickening air.

"I'm sorry Kaitlin, but we have to carry on through, it's the only way to the split in the river," he told her, and Kaitlin gave a reluctant nod. Lifting their cloaks to cover their faces they walked by another four bodies.

"Keltor, I can't help feeling responsible for this," she said, her voice choked with emotion. She couldn't even look at them anymore, instead with her free hand on his shoulder she looked down to the ground as she followed his lead.

"Kaitlin, you didn't take them from their homes and string them up, King Iwein did. He is the only one responsible for this. None of this is our fault, and no matter what happens we must focus on stopping him and Prince Keion. We must keep going, for them," Keltor murmured, squeezing her hand."

Keltor suddenly stopped walking and abruptly fell silent. He stepped towards one of the bodies, a cold dread seizing him as he stared at the remains of the young man. His stomach clenched and the breath caught in his throat. Recognition struck like a blow. Beneath the swarm of insects and the ruin wrought by crows, he could still trace the shape of the boy he once knew. Marcus's wrists were raw where they'd been tied and nailed to the wood, his feet the same. Half his face was gone, but Keltor—through the horror—remembered the echo of Marcus's laughter tumbling through their childhood summers, the way he'd always managed to coax Esendil into mischief. For a heartbeat, Keltor could almost hear that laughter amid the silence, bright and alive. The memory made the loss all the more unbearable.

Observing Keltor's reaction, Kaitlin immediately sensed that something was gravely amiss. Anxiety tightened in her chest as she watched his every move, each gesture betraying a growing distress that she could not yet comprehend. Unable to bear the tension, she pleaded, her voice edged with fear, "Keltor, what is it?" Her eyes searched his face, desperate for an answer. "Do you know him?"

Keltor met her gaze and nodded, the weight of recognition almost too much to bear. Overwhelmed, he pressed a trembling hand to his forehead before pushing his hair back in a gesture of helplessness. His voice, thick with emotion, finally broke through the silence. "This is Marcus. He is… was… my brother's best friend."

Tears welled in Keltor's eyes as he struggled to process the sight before him. "He and Esendil were inseparable since they were about three; they were always up to something," he said, voice cracking with grief. "What the hell is going on? He's like sixteen, he was just a kid."

Keltor's flesh prickled as a wave of cold dread washed over him. The terrifying realisation of what he might discover sent a shiver through his entire body. He turned anxiously to face the unbroken line of bodies, his heartbeat thundering in his chest as fear took hold. For a moment, the world seemed to close in around him, the silence pressing like a weight. Driven by sudden panic and the overwhelming urgency of the moment, he cried out, his voice ringing out across the clearing, "Is he here?"

Kaitlin, hearing the panic in his cry, rushed to his side, her own breath quickening with anxiety. "Who?" she asked, her voice trembling as she reached for him, desperate to offer comfort but uncertain of what he feared most.

Keltor shook his head repeatedly, denial warring with dread. "No, no… no," he murmured, his entire frame shaking as terror overtook him. Then, his voice rose again, thick with anguish and panic, "My brother, Ese, is he here!" The raw fear and desperation in his tone sent a chill through the clearing, the urgency of his question hanging in the air as both he and Kaitlin braced themselves for what might come next.

"Oh God, Keltor, no…" Kaitlin began, her words faltering as she saw the terror and fury etched across Keltor's face. He paid her no heed, his attention wholly consumed by the dreadful task before him.

Driven by desperation, Keltor moved from one body to the next, calling out in anguish each time he checked. "No, no, it's not him," he repeated with each grim discovery, his relief at each step barely concealing the torment inside.

Kaitlin's heart pounded in her chest, nearly stopping every time Keltor approached another corpse. She realised she wouldn't have recognised Esendil if he were among them—the last memory she had of Keltor's brother was from when she was twelve and he was just a boy of seven or eight. All she could recall was his dark hair, so like their father's.

"He's not here," Keltor wept in relief, as they reached the last of the corpses.

"Come here," Kaitlin urged, opening her arms. Keltor fell into them and sobbed. "I was so scared," he admitted. As she held him, she could feel him trembling beneath her.

"I know," she whispered back, and her hand lifted to his face and cupped his cheek. She rested her forehead against his. "It's okay." She comforted.

"If he'd been here, how the hell would I have told my mother," He wept. "How could he do this...Why kill Marcus, why kill any of them. I don't get it. They don't know we're still alive, the King has won as far as he's concerned. Why kill these kids?"

"I don't know, Keltor," she replied sadly, and she looked back down the line of bodies.

The cold wind whipped through the ruined valley, carrying the suffocating stench of death and decay beneath a shroud of intense silence. Keltor's voice trembled as he spoke, his words edged with fury. "That soldier earlier, he would have killed that little girl if I hadn't have stopped him, and Alarna and Logan, killed by his own brothers. It makes no fucking sense," he swore angrily.

"Hey," Kaitlin said, surprised by his choice of words. She knew how much Keltor despised swearing—his anger must have been overwhelming.

"Sorry," he apologised abruptly, brow furrowing as he looked away. He clenched his fists, struggling to contain the storm of guilt and frustration swirling inside him.

Kaitlin gave him a gentle, understanding smile, her hand lifting to rest on his arm. "You're picking up my bad habits," she teased softly, holding him comfortingly as the oppressive quiet—and the ever-present stench—of the valley pressed in around them.

As Keltor's gaze met hers, the tension visibly eased from his features, and a faint, genuine smile appeared on his lips. He let out a shaky laugh, immediately apologising, "Hell, I'm sorry, I don't even know where that came from."

"Keltor, that's where it came from," she replied, pointing to the line of dead bodies. "I get it, you're angry, swearing is a release, don't worry about it."

He put his arm around her, pulling her close. She rested her head against his chest, and together they stood in silence, finding comfort in each other amidst the devastation.

"I never really understood it, when you told me you only swear when you're angry or scared, but I get it now." Keltor's gaze lingered on Kaitlin's face, searching her features as he felt the soothing effect of her presence wash over him. Her energy calmed the turmoil within him, offering a respite from the grief and confusion that had consumed him. "I won't tell you off for swearing any more. If you want to, my love, you go ahead."

As the tension eased slightly, Kaitlin let out a soft laugh. The sound was gentle, almost fragile, and it quickly faltered as she felt tears begin to well in her eyes. The weight of their shared pain threatened to overwhelm her, but she tried to keep her composure. "Keltor, you are…" Kaitlin began, her voice trembling as emotion caught in her throat.

Noticing her sudden quiet, Keltor pressed her, his voice tender but insistent. "Are what?"

Kaitlin looked up at him, her eyes shining with emotion. "My everything," she replied quietly, her voice trembling with sincerity. Keltor took a heavy breath, his own feelings etched plainly on his face, and gently pressed his forehead against hers, seeking comfort in their closeness.

"And you mine," he whispered back, the words full of depth and meaning. As they slowly drew apart, Kaitlin's gaze drifted back towards the line of bodies lying in the valley, the stark reminder of all they had lost and endured together.

Anger and fury sparked through Keltor as he looked back down at the line of bodies. His hands clenched at his sides, and his whole body trembled with the force of his emotion. Voice low but resolute, he vowed, "I'm going to destroy King Iwein, even if I have to do it with my bare hands." The words hung in the air, thick with promise and pain.

Kaitlin glanced at Keltor, feeling the force of his fury as it radiated from him. His eyes glowed an intense white, his expression darkening as he glowered at the line of corpses strewn before them.

"I know you will," Kaitlin murmured, her voice soft as she lifted her hand to Keltor, gently rubbing his arm in an attempt to soothe the anger that simmered beneath the surface. He glanced at her, taking a deep, steadying breath. Gradually, the intense white in his eyes faded, returning to their normal, piercing blue. With a sense of relief and gratitude, he pulled her into a close embrace.

"Kaitlin, I'm so sorry our lives have turned out like this," Keltor whispered, emotion thick in his voice. "That I took you from your normal life on Earth and dragged you through hell."

Kaitlin turned towards him, looking up into his eyes with unwavering conviction. "There is nowhere I would rather be than with you," she said quietly. "Even if we are in hell, so be it."

His hand rose to her face, fingers gently tracing the path of her tears. "I love you so much, my Queen," he said, his words filled with devotion.

She smiled through her tears, replying softly, "And I you, my King."

Keltor pressed a gentle kiss to her lips, the gesture tender and filled with heartfelt promise. Then, drawing back, he spoke with quiet urgency, "Come on, let's get out of here."

Kaitlin looked at Keltor, uncertainty flickering in her eyes. "Should we cut them down?" she asked, her voice quiet but urgent. The question hung in the air, weighted with the consequences of their decision.

Keltor hesitated, torn between his desire to honour the fallen and the harsh reality of their situation. After a moment of tense silence, he shook his head, regret clear in his expression. "No, we can't," he replied, his tone heavy. "I hate to say it, but for now we'll have to leave them where they are. If we move them, it could give us away."

Kaitlin let out a resigned sigh, her shoulders sagging as she acknowledged the painful necessity in Keltor's words. Though her heart ached at the thought of leaving the fallen unburied, she understood the harsh reality that compelled them to move on. The weight of regret pressed heavily upon her, matching the sorrow she saw reflected in Keltor's eyes. Despite her reluctance, she knew that staying would only put them both in greater danger, and so, suppressing her grief, she prepared herself to follow him away from the scene.

"Come on, let's get the hell out of here," Keltor urged, and he held out his hand to her. She didn't need to be asked twice. Her heart pounded in her chest as she grabbed his hand, relief and fear mingling in her hurried steps.

Chapter Sixteen
Prince Keion

They climbed out of the ravine in silence, the horror of what they had witnessed still churning in their stomachs. Each step was heavy with the weight of recent events, and neither spoke as they pressed on. The oppressive atmosphere seemed to cling to them, making the climb feel even more arduous. Within twenty minutes, they had reached the top.

Ahead of them stretched another forest, its dark canopy looming in the distance and offering little comfort after the ordeal they had just endured. The trees stood tall and close together, their shadows merging to create an almost impenetrable wall of darkness.

As they paused, Kaitlin was suddenly overwhelmed by a wave of nausea, every sense on high alert. She reached out instinctively, gripping Keltor's arm tightly. "Keltor, something's wrong," she said, her voice tense.

He nodded, his blue eyes narrowing as he scanned the treeline ahead. "I feel it too."

Kaitlin followed his gaze. There was movement in the trees ahead, the subtle shifting of shadows betraying the presence of someone—or something—lurking just out of sight. With dread, they realised there was nowhere for them to hide.

"Aranstream?" Kaitlin whispered, her voice tense and uncertain.

"Yes," Keltor replied, his heart dropping as he looked ahead. Just then, a horse and rider appeared on the path before them, followed swiftly by another, and then another. It quickly became clear that they were not alone. With growing alarm, Kaitlin glanced over her shoulder and saw more men advancing on foot from behind. Within moments, they found themselves surrounded, the silent threat encircling them.

"Keltor, what are we going to do?" Kaitlin asked, her panic barely contained as she realised the gravity of their situation.

"They don't know who we are, Kaitlin," Keltor responded, trying to keep his voice calm and steady, hoping to reassure her even as uncertainty gnawed at him.

At that moment, a man on horseback broke away from the front line of soldiers, approaching them with a purposeful stride. Keltor noticed the insignia and immediately tightened his grip on Kaitlin's hand, muttering under his breath, "Oh shit, it's Prince Keion."

He glanced quickly at Kaitlin, concern flickering in his eyes. "Will he recognise you?" he asked, his voice barely above a whisper.

Kaitlin shook her head anxiously; her gaze fixed on the approaching prince. "I don't know—I've never met him before." She swallowed, her uncertainty apparent. "What about you?"

Keltor hesitated for a moment, recalling brief, distant encounters. "I don't think so," he replied quietly. "I mean, I've been in the same room as him before, but I doubt he ever noticed me."

Prince Keion appeared at the head of the group, riding towards them with two other men flanking him on horseback. The trio advanced purposefully, their presence commanding attention and heightening the tension in the air. As they drew closer, Keltor instinctively reached for Kaitlin, pulling her down beside him. He bent his knee and lowered himself, signalling submission while remaining alert to the unfolding situation. The movement was deliberate, intended to show deference without surrendering his readiness to act if necessary.

Kaitlin stared intently at the approaching prince, her voice barely audible as she whispered, "My god, he's so like Aragon. We could kill him... now?" The suggestion hung heavy in the air, a dangerous possibility given the circumstances. Instinctively, she felt Keltor's grip on her hand tighten, the gesture communicating his readiness to act. Both remained perfectly still, every muscle tense, as they weighed the risks and considered their next move.

Prince Keion regarded them coldly from his horse before swinging a leg over and dismounting with practiced ease. He strode towards them, his gaze sharp and appraising. "So, what do we have here?" he asked, his tone carrying a note of authority that left little doubt as to his command of the situation.

He studied Keltor and Kaitlin intently. After a moment, a faint, knowing smile touched his lips. "Elvendon's, by the look of you," he remarked, making no effort to hide his suspicion. His attention then shifted to the sword at Keltor's side, eyes narrowing slightly.

Without hesitation, Prince Keion turned to the soldier on his right. "Disarm him," he ordered, his voice crisp and decisive. The soldier immediately stepped forward, ready to carry out the prince's command.

Keltor lifted his gaze to meet Prince Keion's, his mind racing with memories of the fallen men and, above all, young Marcus. The images filled him with a burning fury, the sense of loss and injustice surging through his veins. The power that came with that rage coiled inside him, gathering in his hands, ready to be unleashed at a moment's notice. He could sense Kaitlin's magic as well—a low, steady pulse radiating from her grip in his. It was unmistakable, the energy from her hand transferring into his own, silent confirmation that she, too, was prepared to strike if the situation demanded it. Both stood poised on the brink, united in their readiness, every instinct urging them to act.

As the sun emerged from behind the clouds, its light caught on something hanging around the prince's neck, causing a sharp glint that immediately drew Keltor's attention. The sight brought a sinking feeling to his chest as he recognised the object—it was his father's amulet.

Keltor reacted swiftly, whispering to Kaitlin with urgency, "Kaitlin, stop, he has my father's amulet around his neck." His words were barely audible, yet laden with significance. He

371

released her hand, a deliberate action to halt the flow of magic building between them, knowing the situation had suddenly become even more precarious.

Kaitlin's response came in a hushed tone, her concern evident. "Oh, god, does that mean his magic will be stronger?" she asked, her voice trembling, as the implications of the prince possessing the amulet became clear to them both.

Keltor's voice was barely more than a breath as he whispered in dragona, "Yes. We can't fight him here. *Du nah enra magi unle carnore esen dosdoraun eil. Et ile forn carnor.*" His words, heavy with meaning, carried a warning that settled like a stone in Kaitlin's chest.

She drew in a trembling breath as his message echoed in her mind, translated and clear: "Do not use magic unless your life depends on it. I will find you." The caution in his tone underscored the danger of their predicament, and the bond between them was evident even in this tense exchange.

Kaitlin's reply was a soft, fearful whisper: *"El et garwein mortocar en?"* Her question—"He's going to take me?"—hung in the air, full of dread and uncertainty about what would come next.

"Erama," he affirmed quietly, his tone resolute—yes. Turning urgently to Kaitlin, he whispered, "Kaitlin, hide your bonding mark, now." Without hesitation, he swiftly traced his own mark with his fingers, expertly concealing it in the same manner they had used to hide their royal insignias in the past. Kaitlin responded immediately, bowing her head and murmuring the necessary spell under her breath as she hurried to cover her own mark.

Keltor slowly rose to his feet, his hands raised in a gesture of surrender. Kaitlin followed his lead, mirroring his movements as they stood side by side. One of the soldiers stepped forward, efficiently relieving Keltor of both his sword and his knife. As the soldier examined the sword more closely, a frown creased his brow, clearly recognising its craftsmanship and quality.

Turning to the prince, the soldier addressed him respectfully. "My Lord," he said, holding out Keltor's sword for inspection. The implication in his tone made it clear that this was no ordinary weapon. The prince took the sword, studying it carefully, before shifting his gaze to Keltor, his eyes assessing him with renewed interest.

"This is rather a fine sword for a peasant," the prince remarked, his gaze fixed intently on Keltor as he addressed him. The weight of the moment hung heavily in the air, with Keltor doing his utmost to conceal any trace of his true identity.

With his head bowed, Keltor replied quietly, "It was my father's, my Lord." He kept his eyes lowered, purposefully avoiding the prince's gaze, each word carefully chosen to maintain his disguise.

The prince regarded Keltor thoughtfully, a hint of doubt in his tone. "Hmm," he murmured, his eyes narrowing as he continued to study Keltor's features. "Have I seen you before? You seem a little familiar," he questioned, searching Keltor's face for any sign of recognition. Then, with a commanding tone, he added, "Look up at me."

Keltor felt every muscle in his body tense as he waited for the prince's response, inwardly pleading that the man would not recognise him from the court at Elvendon. Maintaining a careful composure, he replied, "No, my Lord, I haven't had that honour," his voice measured and polite. He lifted his head, presenting his face as commanded, all the while acutely aware of the risk. Keltor's heart hammered in his chest, but he kept his expression neutral. His gaze shifted, drawn irresistibly to the pendant hanging around the prince's neck, just visible where the prince's shirt opened beneath his collarbone. The amulet seemed to pulse with a hidden power, its magical energy so palpable that Keltor could almost feel it from where he stood. He was uncertain whether the prince truly understood the amulet's significance or how to wield its power, and in that tense moment, Keltor weighed his options, considering whether he should risk everything and make a desperate attempt to seize it.

"Hmm," the prince said again, his voice tinged with suspicion. "You do seem a little familiar." He took another step closer to

Keltor, scrutinising him with narrowed eyes and searching for any sign of recognition.

Suddenly, Kaitlin coughed deliberately, her action designed to break the prince's concentration. She was panicking, afraid that the prince might recall where he had previously seen Keltor. Her distraction worked; the prince's attention shifted from Keltor to Kaitlin, his gaze lingering as he took in the striking presence of Keltor's companion.

Her hands tightened anxiously around the folds of her dress as she kept her gaze fixed on the ground. She noticed the prince's booted feet come to a halt directly in front of her, heightening her unease. Although Kaitlin had never met the prince before, uncertainty gnawed at her—she wondered just how much she resembled her sister, especially given her father's insistence that there was little similarity between them.

The prince, wearing leather gloves, reached out and gently placed his hand beneath her chin, lifting her face to meet his eyes. The moment their eyes locked, a fearful shudder coursed through Kaitlin's body, leaving her feeling exposed and vulnerable beneath his intense scrutiny.

"Well, you are a beauty," the prince remarked, his tongue sliding over his lips as he spoke, his gaze lingering on her with clear intent.

Keltor kept his eyes firmly fixed on the ground, unable to bear witnessing what was unfolding before him. He was keenly aware of Kaitlin's actions, and while a sense of relief washed over him, concern lingered just beneath the surface. Despite their combined strength, he doubted they could successfully challenge Keion while the prince possessed the amulet, and he understood all too well what that implied.

The prince's voice cut through the tension. "Show me your left hand," he commanded.

Kaitlin's hand trembled as she obeyed, lifting it for inspection. The prince grasped her hand firmly, his thumb tracing over her skin with deliberate intent.

"So, you're not bonded," he remarked, addressing Kaitlin directly before turning his attention back to Keltor.

Keltor's eyes rose to meet the prince, and he shook his head swiftly, desperately thinking on his feet. "No, my Lord, she is my sister," he replied, fabricating the lie in the hope of protecting both himself and Kaitlin. He was all too aware that any suspicion from the prince could mean instant death, especially if the prince perceived him as a rival for his prized possession.

The prince seemed satisfied for the moment, muttering, "Hmmm, good," before releasing Kaitlin's hand. His attention shifted, and with an air of authority, he issued his orders. "Take him to the encampment, and put him to work," he commanded, turning his back on them and heading towards his horse. As he mounted, he added, "And search her. She's coming with me."

A soldier stepped forward and began patting her down, his hands roaming with an air of entitlement that made Kaitlin's jaw clench. She shot him a glare, but he only smirked, undeterred.

"What's this, then?" he muttered, fingers probing the bodice of her dress.

"Just fabric," she shot back, shifting away from his touch, her voice tight.

"Keep still," he barked, annoyance sharpening his tone as he reached inside her neckline.

His hand found the concealed object. "Well, well—what have we here? Is this a wand?" He held it up triumphantly, his suspicion morphing into a predatory grin.

A chill raced through Kaitlin; she'd completely forgotten about her wand, and fear fluttered in her chest as the realisation hit.

"No, it's a toasting fork," Kaitlin shot back, voice laced with dry humour and just enough irritation to make her meaning clear. Her eyes held his, unflinching—a touch too bold, perhaps, but she was tired of playing the victim.

The man's brow furrowed, uncertainty flickering across his face. His grip on the wand tightened, knuckles whitening as he looked her up and down. He glanced over his shoulder at his comrades, then back at Kaitlin as if expecting her to sprout wings or fangs at any moment. The tension in his jaw betrayed his suspicion—he didn't want to be the one to make a mistake in front of the prince, especially not with magic in the mix.

"Are you… are you a witch?" he stammered, the word catching in his throat. His voice wavered between fear and accusation, and the hand holding the wand trembled ever so slightly.

Kaitlin raised one perfectly arched eyebrow, a sardonic smile tugging at her lips. "If I were, would I be caught so easily?" she retorted, feigning patience. Her heart thudded, the air between them thick with the earthy scent of churned soil and the metallic tang of coming rain. The soldier's breath came quick and shallow, mingling with the distant clanging of armour.

"My Lord!" the man shouted, turning away from Kaitlin to address the prince directly. At that precise moment, Kaitlin's eyes flashed white as she unleashed her magic. The sudden surge of power was palpable—Keltor sensed it immediately. He glanced swiftly at Kaitlin, then back at the prince, watching closely to see if the prince, too, had felt the magical disturbance.

"What is it?" the prince demanded, manoeuvring his horse to face the soldier, his expression wary and alert.

"This woman is a witch, and I have found her wand!" the soldier proclaimed triumphantly, his voice ringing out over the tense silence.

"A witch!" the prince shouted, his horse shying abruptly to the side at the force of his exclamation. Regaining control of the nervous animal, the prince urged it forward, closing the distance towards the soldier who had made the claim. His wary gaze flickered to Kaitlin as he drew nearer.

Kaitlin, sensing the mounting danger, shook her head in denial and sank to her knees before him. Her voice trembled with urgency and desperation as she pleaded, "My Lord, he lies to you—I am no witch, I am simply a farmer's daughter."

The soldier, clearly unconvinced and eager to press his advantage, scoffed at her denial. "Oh really?" he sneered. "Then what's this I found hidden in your dress?"

"It's a long fork for toasting meat on a fire," Kaitlin explained, her eyes wide, her hands outstretched toward the prince, palms open in a desperate plea.

The soldier, his face flushed with indignation and eyes darting between Kaitlin and the prince, jabbed the fork into the air as if determined to prove his point. "It's not a fork, it's a wand!" he insisted, his voice cracking with a mix of frustration and desperation. A ripple of uneasy laughter passed through the watching soldiers, some exchanging sceptical glances while others leaned in, eager to witness what might unfold. Sunlight glinted off his battered armour, casting elongated shadows across the muddy ground, and for a moment, even the prince's horse seemed to pause, ears pricked as if sensing the tension and absurdity in the air.

"Let me see," the prince commanded, his tone firm and expectant.

Obediently, the soldier approached, clutching the supposed 'wand' and presenting it for inspection. His eyes remained fixed on the object, disbelief etched across his face. "I don't understand, my Lord," he stammered, voice unsteady. "I swear it was a wand when I took it from her dress." As he held up the fork, the sunlight glinted off its prongs, revealing nothing more than an ordinary implement.

The prince eyed the item critically, lips curling in sarcasm. "Well, it looks like a fork to me," he remarked, his gaze lingering on the soldier's trembling hand. With a hint of mockery, he added, "In fairness, I suppose it is an extra-long fork, but it's still a damned fork!"

The soldier, his voice rising with accusation, jabbed the fork in Kaitlin's direction. "She did this—she turned it into a fork!" he shouted, brandishing the object as if it were evidence of some cunning sorcery. "Why would she keep a fork hidden in her dress?" His words hung in the air, laden with suspicion and disbelief.

Kaitlin, her face pale and eyes brimming with tears, shook her head in silent protest. "No, I didn't," she said, her voice breaking with emotion. "It's just a fork. It belonged to my late mother." Her hands trembled as she clutched the object to her chest, desperation etched across her features. "I didn't want anyone to steal it. We have lost everything," she wept, her gaze flickering to the figure she called her brother, silently pleading for understanding.

"Silence," the prince commanded, his voice ringing out with such authority that Kaitlin instinctively bowed her head, avoiding his gaze. His frustration was palpable as he turned his ire on the soldier, his tone laced with scorn. "You stupid man, if you can't even tell the difference between a wand and a fork, what use are you to me!" he bellowed, his words cutting through the tension that hung in the air.

Desperation flashed across the soldier's face as he pleaded for understanding. "My Lord, please, I swear, she must have done something to it," he insisted, his voice trembling as he tried to defend himself in the face of the prince's withering condemnation.

"Do you not think that I would know if magic was being used?" Prince Keion shouted down at the soldier, his voice echoing with indignation and authority. The accusation seemed to sting, and all attention shifted to the prince's towering presence.

Keltor, standing nearby, shot a quick glance at Kaitlin. He was surprised; it appeared that the prince had not detected any trace of magic. That in itself was peculiar, and Keltor's mind raced with uncertainty about what this might mean.

"Yes, my Lord, but maybe she is powerful?" the soldier stammered, his voice faltering as he tried to justify his suspicions.

The prince's anger flared at this suggestion. "What, you think this peasant girl is more powerful than me!" he bellowed, his words dripping with disbelief and disdain as he glared at the hapless soldier.

"No, no, that is not what I meant, my Lord, please!" the soldier pleaded, his tone desperate as he tried to backtrack, terrified of further incurring the prince's wrath.

"I have no further use of you," the prince announced, his tone cold and final.

Kaitlin lifted her eyes, seeking comfort. Her gaze found Keltor's, and for a moment, they shared an understanding, a silent exchange of fear and uncertainty. As they turned their attention back to the prince, a sudden change caught their eyes—the amulet hanging around his neck began to emit an ominous glow, casting a strange light across his features and heightening the tension in the air.

The prince, his patience finally snapped, thrust his hand forward and bellowed, *"Blastera separate!"* Instantly, a jagged bolt of lightning erupted from his palm, arcing across the space with crackling fury. The magic struck the unfortunate man directly in the chest, its force knocking him backwards. The air sizzled with the residual energy of the prince's spell, casting a harsh glare over the faces of all who witnessed the display of power. The prince's authority was now undeniable, his command of magic both intimidating and absolute. The soldier screamed as his whole body became electrified, and he dropped to the ground.

Kaitlin let out a startled scream as the soldier was struck, her senses reeling from the violence and suddenness of the prince's magic. As the unfortunate man collapsed, she saw her wand fall from his hand, clattering onto the ground. For a moment, her eyes met those of the prince, who was grinning with satisfaction as he watched the soldier writhe in agony. He seemed oblivious to the transformation that had occurred—the 'fork' he had mocked now lay on the earth, restored to its true form as a wand.

Kaitlin dropped her hands to the ground, her fingers digging into the cold earth as the soldier began to disintegrate under the overwhelming force of Prince Keion's magic. In that moment, she summoned all her resolve, sending a surge of her own magic through the soil, its energy directed purposefully towards her wand.

Under her breath, she whispered, *"Descray,"* focusing her will as her magic enveloped the wand. The spell smothered it, and within seconds, the wand was utterly destroyed, reduced to nothing by the force of her enchantment.

Kaitlin closed her eyes, a wave of emotion crashing over her as she let out an involuntary sob. She could feel the connection to her wand sever—an ache not for the loss of the wand as a tool, for she understood now that she no longer needed it to channel her magic, but for the deep sentimental bond it represented. The wand had been a cherished gift from her dear mother, and its destruction marked the end of a precious link to her past. The pain of that loss lingered in her heart, mingling with the tumult of fear and uncertainty that filled the air around her.

In that moment, Keltor instinctively reached out for Kaitlin, his concern for her overriding any thought of his own safety. However, a soldier stationed by his side reacted swiftly, lifting his sword and delivering a sharp blow to Keltor's flank. The impact forced Keltor to halt, pain flaring where the sword had struck.

"Stay there," the soldier ordered. Keltor looked up at him with an angry sneer.

The prince glanced at Kaitlin, a smile creeping across his face as he heard her sob. Turning to his men, he declared, "You see, she is just a whimpering woman, not a powerful witch." His words prompted laughter from the assembled soldiers, their amusement echoing his own sense of satisfaction. The prince grinned, evidently pleased with their response. He had made a clear display of his dominance and magical strength, confident that, with the wizard's amulet in his possession, he would certainly be able to detect any magical prowess she might possess. In his eyes, Kaitlin's reaction confirmed his belief that she was powerless, and the authority of his amulet made him more certain of it.

Prince Keion, maintaining his command, issued a curt instruction. "Take her to the castle, see she is bathed and given clean clothes," he ordered, gathering his reins and preparing to depart.

At that moment, Keltor summoned his courage and called out, "My Lord, forgive me, but please may I say goodbye to my sister?" His voice was earnest, betraying the depth of his concern.

The prince let out a dismissive huff but relented with a nod. "You have one minute to say your goodbyes," he replied, granting Keltor a brief reprieve.

"Thank you, my Lord," Keltor responded humbly, his gratitude evident. He glanced at the nearby guard, whose sword was still menacingly pointed at him. The guard, sensing the prince's permission, stepped back and indicated with a nod that Keltor could approach.

Without a moment's hesitation, Keltor sprang to his feet and hurried over to Kaitlin, his heart pounding as he took in the fear so clearly etched upon her face. Reaching her side, he gently bent down to help her rise, his words barely more than a whisper, laden with the weight of everything that had just transpired.

"I'm sorry," he murmured, his apology sincere and his concern for her evident in every syllable.

Kaitlin responded with a gentle shake of her head, her quiet strength shining through despite the circumstances. "It's okay, it's not your fault," she assured him softly, accepting his embrace. For a fleeting moment, the couple clung to one another, drawing solace from the enduring bond they shared, finding comfort in the warmth of each other's arms amidst the turmoil surrounding them.

Kaitlin held tightly to Keltor, her body trembling as she tried to steady her breathing. Leaning in close, she whispered, "He clearly can use the amulet." Her voice was barely audible, yet every word was weighted with dread. The fear of being torn away from Keltor mingled with a deeper anxiety about what awaited them both in the hands of Prince Keion.

Keltor met her gaze with grave understanding. "Yes," he replied, his tone quiet but urgent. "If you need to defend yourself from him, *enra carnore magi*." He spoke the words in Dragona, their secret tongue, ensuring their meaning was clear even if overheard. Kaitlin nodded, understanding his instruction—'use your magic'—and silently braced herself for whatever might come next.

Kaitlin clung to Keltor, her grip fierce and unyielding, as she tried to steady herself amid the chaos and fear surrounding them.

With her voice barely above a whisper, she pressed her forehead to his and murmured, "I'll be okay. Stick to the plan, Keltor. Get our army and save your father. I will be okay." The determination in her tone was unmistakable, even as her trembling hands betrayed her anxiety. She wanted Keltor to know that she had faith in him and their shared mission, urging him to focus on rallying their forces and rescuing his father, rather than risking everything by acting rashly now. Her words, though soft, carried the weight of hope and resolve, offering comfort to them both as they prepared to be torn apart.

Keltor clung to Kaitlin, his arms wrapped around her as if he could shield her from the fate awaiting them both. Fear for her—raw and overwhelming—tightened his hold. In Dragona, their secret tongue, his voice trembled as he whispered, *"Et ile forn carnor, Eh mulare carnor."* The words were heavy with emotion: "I will come for you, I love you." Though time was slipping away, Keltor's promise was as fierce as his fear, a desperate vow that no force would keep him from finding her again.

The prince, growing impatient with the emotional exchange between Keltor and Kaitlin, suddenly shouted, "Enough!" His voice rang out sharply, cutting through the air as he gestured forcefully towards the pair. Without further hesitation, he urged his horse forward, making it clear that their moment together was at an end and signalling for the soldiers to intervene.

Two Aranstream soldiers stepped forward, one seizing Keltor and the other grabbing Kaitlin, their grips firm and unyielding. With practiced efficiency, the soldiers forced the pair apart, wrenching them from each other's embrace. Any attempt at resistance was futile; the soldiers' hold was too strong, and the separation was swift. The brief solace the couple had found in each other was abruptly shattered, leaving Keltor and Kaitlin isolated and vulnerable, their connection severed as the prince's command took precedence over all else.

Kaitlin's voice carried across the distance, trembling but determined. *"Eh mulare carnor,"* she called back, her words resonating with emotion. In their secret tongue, her declaration—

'I love you'—was both a promise and a plea, an echo of the bond that bound her to Keltor even as they were being torn apart. The weight of her words lingered in the air, offering comfort and hope despite the looming threat separating them.

Keltor's heart shattered as he watched Kaitlin being lifted onto a horse by a soldier. Every fibre of his being screamed that he should never have let her accompany him on this dangerous path. He was haunted by the promise he had made never to leave her, and now, against his deepest wishes, he found himself powerless as she was taken by their adversaries.

Tormented by regret, Keltor understood that acting against the prince now would be reckless, especially after witnessing the formidable power of the amulet. Any rash attempt to strike before securing the amulet would only jeopardise their chances. He steeled himself, knowing that his principal focus must be liberating the Elvendon army. Only by freeing them could he hope to reclaim what had been lost and protect those he loved.

Kaitlin cast a lingering glance over her shoulder as they began their journey, her eyes fixed on Keltor. His hands were now securely bound, and he was being led along behind the horses, a stark reminder of how powerless they both were in the face of their captors. Fear gnawed at her—she was forced to admit to herself that she was truly afraid. Even the presence of her magic, once a source of solace and confidence, brought her little comfort now. The knowledge that Prince Keion, much like his brother Aragon, could match her abilities in the arcane arts left her feeling vulnerable and exposed. If Keion was anything like Aragon, then she knew she was in grave danger.

Kaitlin's gaze shifted from Keltor to the prince riding ahead. As she watched him, a surge of anger rose within her, mingling with her fear. The memory of her sister's brutal murder at the prince's hands was still fresh and raw, and she could not forget the cruelty he had displayed. The weight of that memory fuelled her resentment, even as she was forced to follow his command, her fate uncertain and her heart heavy with dread.

The group travelled for several hours, the relentless pace interrupted only by brief stops each hour to allow the prisoners to regain some strength. With every halt, the toll of the journey became more evident—fatigue etched onto the faces of those forced to march and ride under harsh conditions.

Keltor was not the only prisoner forced to walk behind the procession, his movements hampered by restraints and the ever-watchful eyes of the prince's soldiers. As the journey continued, the prince's ranks swelled; he met with his men at designated points along the route, each encounter resulting in the addition of more captured Elvendon men and women to his cohort.

Witnessing this, Kaitlin's sense of dread deepened. The sight of so many innocent people, all at the mercy of their captors, left her feeling physically ill. She knew that if their plan failed, these individuals would remain prisoners—condemned to lives of servitude or, even worse, subject to execution at the hands of King Iwein. The stakes had never felt higher, and the burden of responsibility weighed heavily on her heart.

Soon, the imposing silhouette of Aranstream Castle appeared on the horizon, its cold stone walls looming ever larger as the group altered their route. A wave of dread churned in Kaitlin's stomach, the sight filling her with unease. As they changed direction, she risked a glance over her shoulder and, through a blur of tears, managed to catch one last glimpse of Keltor. The soldiers, intent on keeping the prisoners separated, began to lead the men away from the main group—Keltor among them, pulled in the opposite direction. Desperate, he strained towards her, but the effort caused him to stumble and fall, his figure disappearing from her view as he was dragged roughly onwards.

As they turned direction, Keltor glanced behind him, desperate for one last look at her. He was agonized over whether he had made the right decision by letting her go, and was terrified they had just made the biggest mistake of their lives, but with the prince having the amulet and the strength of the guards with him, what choice did they really have?

Her eyes met his, and in that fleeting moment, Keltor felt his heart quake with a tangled mixture of love and fear for her. The rope binding him jerked suddenly, causing him to stumble. He crashed heavily to the ground, the unforgiving rocks beneath scraping and cutting his arms as he struggled to regain his balance. Unable to right himself, he was dragged along the rugged track, the pain intensifying with every jagged stone that tore at his skin.

Suddenly, a hand reached out from his right. A fellow prisoner grabbed Keltor's arm and hauled him upright, steadying him before he could fall again. Grateful for the unexpected help, Keltor muttered a hurried, "Thank you," as he quickly regained his footing and forced himself back into the exhausting rhythm of the march. He took a moment to glance at his rescuer—a young man, seemingly around his own age, whose presence offered a brief flicker of solidarity amidst the hardship.

"No problem," the young man responded, offering Keltor a brief nod of acknowledgement. As they continued walking, he glanced at Keltor and asked, "Is she your wife?"

Keltor hesitated, uncertain how much he could trust the man who had just helped him. He studied his rescuer, noting the bruised and swollen right eye, the bloodied and battered face, and the strands of long, blonde hair that clung to the gritty wounds. It was clear the man had not surrendered quietly; he had fought against the soldiers and suffered for it.

The young man broke the silence. "They took mine," he said quietly.

Keltor looked at him, confused. "Your?"

"My wife," the man clarified, his voice heavy with grief. "We've only been married a few months." He paused and looked at Keltor again, repeating his earlier question. "So, is she your wife?"

Keltor shook his head.

Keltor hesitated, unsure whether he could trust the young man beside him. "No, she's my sister," he lied, keeping his true relationship to Kaitlin hidden.

The man offered little comfort. "I'm sorry, but you'll probably never see her again. She's pretty, the prince will want her for himself." He looked ahead, resignation in his tone. "This is just such a load of bullshit. If it weren't for that princess killing the prince, none of this would have happened," he muttered bitterly.

Keltor's anger flared at the accusation, and he threw the man an angry glare. "No, she didn't do anything," he retorted sharply, unable to hold back.

The young man raised an eyebrow, clearly sceptical. "What, oh, you're a royalist are you?" he asked, his voice edged with sarcasm.

"I happen to know for a fact that the King had already planned to attack, even before the princess arrived back in Elvendon," Keltor replied, his words clipped and resolute.

The young man eyed Keltor sceptically. "Oh really, and how would you know that?" he asked, his tone thick with sarcasm.

Keltor cast a wary glance around them, ensuring no one else was listening, before lowering his voice. "Because I'm her protector," he snapped back, his anger barely contained. "And I was there."

The man's eyes widened in disbelief. "You were there... holy stars, seriously," he muttered, before flicking his gaze anxiously towards the nearby guards.

"Yes," Keltor confirmed, his voice tense. "And if you want to end this war, get your wife back, and reclaim your home, you'll keep your mouth shut about who I am," he warned, his gaze fierce.

The young man leaned closer, his voice barely above a whisper. "Was that her, that woman, was she the princess?" he asked, his tone full of suspicion.

Keltor maintained his composure and answered with a practised lie. "No," he replied, "I told you, she's, my sister. The princess is in a safe place, hiding. And since King Iwein murdered her father and sister, she is now the Queen of Elvendon."

The man absorbed this revelation with a muttered curse. "Hell," he said under his breath, before pressing on with another question. "So, how did you get captured?"

Keltor hesitated for a moment, then explained briefly, "It's a long story, but in short, I wanted to get into the encampment. It's not entirely the way I had planned, but it is what it is." He then shifted the conversation, seeking to learn more about his companion. "What's your name?" Keltor asked.

"Zeb," he answered, a grin spreading across his face. "So, there is hope then, that we can take back Elvendon?" Zeb's eyes searched Keltor's, the question laden with cautious optimism.

"That depends, Zeb—are you truly prepared to fight for Elvendon and see our Queen restored to her throne?" Keltor asked, his tone grave.

"Too bloody right I am," Zeb replied without hesitation, his voice firm and resolute.

"Good. So, can I rely on your help once we're inside the camp?" Keltor pressed, seeking commitment.

"Yes," Zeb answered, the weight of loss clear in his voice, "those bastards killed my brother."

Keltor looked at him, his expression softening with sympathy. "I'm sorry," he said quietly. "But I promise you, the princess had no knowledge of any of this, and the prince—he was only killed in self-defence, when he attacked us."

Zeb nodded, his expression solemn. "After what I have seen him do these past few months, I can understand that now. What do you want me to do?" he asked, his voice steady with resolve.

Keltor glanced around, lowering his voice so only Zeb could hear. "When we get inside camp, I need to find the head of our army. I believe he is being held there. His name is Commander Talbot. We need to let our men know that the Queen is still alive, but we must do it without King Iwein or Prince Keion finding out."

"I'm in. What's your name?" Zeb asked, his commitment clear.

"Keltor," he replied simply.

"Well, I am glad to meet you, Keltor. What's your plan then, once you find this commander?" Zeb pressed, ready to take action.

Keltor held tightly to his plan, unwilling to risk revealing the details to anyone just yet. He weighed his options carefully, knowing that absolute secrecy was crucial at this stage. Trust, though it was beginning to grow between him and Zeb, had not yet been fully earned. The stakes were too high, and too many lives depended on the success of his mission. With measured restraint, Keltor simply replied, "I'm still working on it," keeping his thoughts guarded while buying himself time to observe, strategize, and act when the moment was right.

Chapter Seventeen
Arrival at the Camp

They arrived at the camp soon after, where Keltor took in the scene before him. Sturdy wooden fences, reinforced with wire, surrounded much of the area, forming a clear boundary that separated the camp from the wilderness beyond. Behind the camp, the mountains rose steeply, a natural barrier looming over the compound. As they drew nearer, Keltor saw that the entrance was guarded by imposing high gates, standing firmly shut and providing an additional layer of security for the enclosed space they were about to enter.

They crossed a wide river over a sturdy bridge, broad enough to allow two wagons to pass side by side with ease. As they moved across, Keltor took careful note of their surroundings. He recognised the river immediately; it was the same one that forked into two distinct branches further downstream. One branch veered towards the city, winding its way through the bustling streets, while the other—a narrower stream—disappeared beneath the castle itself.

Keltor knew that this smaller stream was crucial to his plan. If he was to reach his father undetected, he would need to follow its hidden course beneath the castle walls. As they passed over the bridge, he also observed several small row boats moored at the riverbank nearby. Some of these boats, he noticed, were laden with heavy stones and granite, likely quarried from the surrounding area and transported by water for construction or fortification work.

Four armed guards stood watch at the gate, their presence a clear warning to anyone approaching. As the group arrived, the horses halted, and one of the guards stepped forward to greet the lead rider. With a curt nod, the guard signalled for the gates to be opened. The heavy gates swung wide, granting passage to the convoy. Led by the horseman, Keltor—still bound to the others— was ushered through into the heart of the camp.

As they entered, Keltor's gaze swept across the sprawling encampment before him. Hundreds of tents dotted the landscape, interspersed with waggons and bustling groups of men. Some men laboured, loading waggons with hefty stones, while others hammered away at the rock with sledgehammers, breaking it into manageable pieces. The sounds of work blended with the murmurs of men who paused in their tasks, their attention drawn to the new arrivals. Many scanned the line of prisoners, searching for familiar faces—friends, comrades, perhaps loved ones.

Keltor joined in their search, his eyes alert and hopeful. He scanned the busy camp, looking for any sign of his brother, for Commander Talbot, or for anyone he recognised among the workers and prisoners. Each glance was edged with hope and anxiety, the uncertainty of who he might find—if anyone—heavy upon him as he was led deeper into the camp.

The lead horseman drew his mount to a halt and dismounted with purposeful ease. As he did so, he was greeted by another soldier, whose commanding presence and air of authority suggested he was likely the camp leader. Keltor observed the brief exchange between the two men, noting the subtle gestures and the deference shown by others in their presence, which only reinforced the soldier's position of command.

Without delay, the lead horseman raised his hand, signalling to the rest of the soldiers accompanying the convoy. The gesture was clear: it was time to bring the prisoners forward. Responding to the command, one of the soldiers shouted, "Move, all of you!" His voice rang out across the camp, stern and unyielding, as he gestured forcefully and directed the group to stand in line in front of a large tent that loomed nearby.

Keltor moved into position beside Zeb and the other prisoners, his senses alert to every detail. He watched as a soldier made his way methodically down the line, stopping at each man to cut the bindings from their wrists. When the soldier reached Keltor, he felt the rough rope fall away, and he instinctively rubbed at his wrists, which were left red and sore after being dragged for so long. The relief was immediate, though the sting lingered, a silent testament to the journey they had endured.

The officer in charge paced authoritatively along the line of men, his hands clasped firmly behind his back as he surveyed each face with a stern expression. Coming to a halt, he raised his voice so all could hear. "This is now your home," he declared, his tone leaving no room for doubt or dissent. "You will do as you are instructed—nothing more, nothing less. It is your honour to serve King Iwein of Aranstream."

His eyes narrowed as he brought one hand forward, pointing menacingly along the line. The threat was unmistakable as he continued, "Be warned, if anyone attempts to escape, you will be brought down by our archers, who keep constant watch over you. Furthermore, your entire team will be punished for any such actions."

He paused, allowing the weight of his words to settle, then offered a thin, knowing grin. "If you behave, you will be fed and provided a bed in exchange for your labour. And, of course, your lives—as long as you cause no trouble and work hard."

Keltor maintained a stoic expression, careful not to betray any hint of his thoughts or feelings. His eyes, however, were sharp and observant as he assessed the soldier before him. He noted the man's weaponry with keen attention: a sword hung at his hip, sheathed and secured to a robust leather belt, ready to be drawn at a moment's notice. In addition to the sword, two daggers were visible, their blades housed in leather sheaths that crossed the soldier's chest. The handles of the daggers pointed downwards, while the tips faced upwards, making them easily accessible for a swift draw if needed.

As Keltor continued his careful inspection, he caught sight of a set of large iron keys. These keys were attached securely to the inside of the soldier's leather waistcoat, their metallic sheen glinting faintly whenever the soldier moved. The arrangement suggested both their importance and the need for them to be kept close and protected, likely granting access to critical areas, like the armoury.

"Right, move in line, straight to the back, take a bed, and change into the clothes provided," the man ordered, his tone brisk and unyielding as he pulled open the white cloth flap of the tent. The implication was clear: this tent, sparse and unadorned, would serve as their home for the foreseeable future. Without further discussion, the prisoners shuffled forward in a subdued line, each person moving towards the rear of the tent as instructed. The atmosphere inside was tense, filled with the quiet rustling of fabric as each man located an unclaimed bed. Once in place, they found a set of rough, grey clothing laid out for them and began changing, resigned to the reality of their new circumstances.

Keltor ducked into the large tent, following Zeb along a narrow walkway bordered by roughly twenty beds arranged in two lines. The dim glow of a lantern overhead cast long shadows, illuminating the cramped and austere quarters. Each bed was as basic as the next: constructed from plain wooden planks, topped with a thin straw mattress that offered little in the way of comfort, and accompanied by two grey woollen blankets. The absence of pillows only highlighted the harshness of their new environment. Atop each bed, a neatly folded pile of grey clothing awaited them, signalling the start of their enforced routine and stripping away the last remnants of personal identity.

"These look comfy," Zeb muttered, his voice heavy with sarcasm as he sat down heavily on one of the beds. Keltor responded with an equally sarcastic glance, sharing in the grim humour as they resigned themselves to the unyielding reality of the camp.

The officer stepped forward, his gaze sweeping across the line of weary prisoners. His voice, firm and authoritative, cut through the subdued atmosphere of the tent. "You have one hour to recover from your journey; after that, you'll be assigned your tasks for the afternoon," he announced. With that, he turned sharply on his heel and pulled the tent flap closed behind him, leaving the prisoners to absorb the reality of their new routine.

As men changed into the standard grey tunics and trousers, the atmosphere remained subdued. Sarcastic remarks, like Zeb's about the comfort of the beds, offered fleeting relief from the tension. Keltor's mind drifted to worries about Kaitlin and to the task of conserving his strength for whatever lay ahead. Around him, others processed their fate in their own way—some with stoic silence, others with tears. The passage of time was marked by the slow adjustment to the camp's routine and the muted anticipation of the work that awaited them after their hour of rest.

Keltor settled himself on the hard, unyielding bed, releasing a quiet sigh as he reached for the set of grey camp clothing laid out before him. He changed swiftly, slipping into the tunic and trousers with practiced efficiency. The tunic clung uncomfortably close to his frame, while the trousers, at least, were a reasonable fit, offering a small measure of relief amid the discomfort.

Zeb, stretched out on his own bed with his legs propped up, glanced over. "Are you alright?" he asked, concern evident in his tone even as he tried to make himself comfortable.

"Peachy," Keltor replied dryly, mimicking Zeb's posture as he lay back on the thin mattress. His sarcastic response was met with a confused look from Zeb, who lifted his head, eyebrows raised.

"What?" Zeb queried, bemused by Keltor's choice of words.

Keltor offered a faint smile, weary yet genuine. "Nothing, I'm just knackered," he said. The word slipped out almost unconsciously, a human phrase that drew his thoughts instantly to Kaitlin. The memory brought a bittersweet edge to his exhaustion, lingering quietly as he settled into rest.

"Yeah, me too," Zeb agreed.

Keltor shifted on his bed, rolling onto his side and turning away from Zeb. As he did so, his emotions began to overwhelm him. The weight of his concerns pressed heavily on his mind, particularly his anxiety for Kaitlin. He could not help but wonder what she might be enduring at that very moment, far from him and without his support.

As Keltor lay there, his gaze drifted to the man on the adjacent bed. The man appeared to be in his early thirties, seated with his back towards Keltor, hunched over and crying quietly into his hands. For a moment, Keltor closed his eyes, trying to shut out the scene. He felt reluctant to involve himself in another person's troubles; after all, he had more than enough burdens of his own. What he desperately needed right now was rest—to recover his strength and to figure out a way to find Commander Talbot.

After ten minutes of restless lying, Keltor found himself unable to ignore the man's distress any longer. He opened his eyes, swung his legs off the bed, and quietly approached the figure hunched over on the neighbouring bunk. Gently, he placed a comforting hand on the man's shoulder.

"Hey, are you okay?" Keltor asked, his tone gentle and soft, careful not to startle him.

The man halted his quiet sobs, wiped his nose with the sleeve of his tunic, and cast a sidelong glance at Keltor. His voice shook as he finally spoke.

"They killed my wife," he said, the words barely audible as he turned his gaze away, unable to meet Keltor's eyes.

"I am truly sorry to hear that," Keltor replied with genuine sympathy. He moved around the end of the bed and sat beside the grieving man, offering silent support in the face of such profound loss.

Keltor took a steadying breath and decided to introduce himself, hoping to offer some comfort. "My name is Keltor," he said quietly.

The man hesitated for a moment, glancing at Keltor before returning his gaze to the floor. His voice was barely more than a whisper as he replied, "Mikelle."

Gently, Keltor asked, "Do you want to talk about it?" He kept his tone soft and unthreatening, making it clear there was no pressure. Mikelle simply shrugged, unwilling or unable to say more. "It's okay, I just want to help," Keltor assured him, hoping to provide a safe space for the man's grief.

After a pause, Mikelle looked up, his eyes rimmed red from crying, and wiped them with the back of his hand. The pain in his voice was raw and unfiltered as he spoke. "I just wanted to get them to safety, that's all, and they, they killed her," he sobbed, the words catching in his throat as his grief overwhelmed him.

Mikelle's shoulders shook as he struggled with the magnitude of his grief. He pressed the heels of his hands to his eyes, desperately trying to hold himself together, but the words tumbled out regardless, laden with anguish. "I just don't understand what's happening," he choked, voice raw and barely above a whisper. "Why is the King doing this to us? Why did he have to kill her and let me live?" His gaze dropped to the floor, his whole-body tense with despair. "I don't want to live," he admitted brokenly, "I don't want to be here without her."

Keltor's hand trembled slightly as he reached out, resting it gently on Mikelle's arm. He searched for the right words but found none that could possibly ease the man's suffering. The truth was, he knew that if anything ever happened to Kaitlin, he would be inconsolable—no words could dull the searing pain of such a loss. Even the mere thought of it tightened his chest with sorrow.

Keltor finally managed a few words, his voice quiet but sincere. "If you need anything." He gently released his hold on Mikelle's arm, understanding that sometimes only time and space could offer comfort. With a sense of helplessness, Keltor rose and returned to his bed, glancing back as he did so. Mikelle's eyes followed him briefly, filled with grief and longing for what he had lost, before dropping once more to the ground. Left alone with his sorrow, Mikelle began to cry softly again, the weight of his anguish settling over the quiet space between them.

Keltor rolled onto his side, his gaze settling on Zeb, who lay with his back turned and snoring softly. He let out another heavy sigh, closing his eyes in a vain attempt to find rest. Sleep eluded him, his mind unsettled with a flurry of thoughts that refused to quieten.

The silence of the tent was abruptly shattered as the guard chief stormed in, pulling back the flap with authority. "Up!" he shouted, his voice sharp and commanding, and leaving no room for hesitation.

Keltor jumped in surprise, his instincts driving him to reach for his sword, only to remember with a jolt of dismay that it was no longer at his side. At that same moment, Zeb stirred and rose too, exchanging a tense glance with Keltor as they braced themselves for whatever was coming. The guard's presence commanded immediate attention; the rest of the men in the tent quickly scrambled to their feet, following the unspoken order. Within minutes, everyone had fallen into line, standing at the ready and prepared to file out of the tent as instructed.

Once outside, the head of the guards marched along the line of prisoners with an air of authority. He addressed the assembled men in a booming voice, making his expectations clear. "Each one of you will be given a task, and you will work hard until the sun sets. It is your honour to serve our King," he proclaimed, leaving no room for dissent or hesitation.

To enforce his orders, he signalled to the six waiting guards, who immediately sprang into action. Each guard split off, taking charge of a separate group of men and leading them away in different directions to begin their assigned duties.

"Right, you lot follow me," barked one of the guards, his tone brisk and commanding. At this point, Keltor found himself separated from Zeb and Mikelle, his companions from earlier. In his new group, there were only three other men—all of them young and strong, their faces set with determination and apprehension as they prepared to face whatever tasks awaited them.

They proceeded through the sprawling encampment, weaving between rows of tents and groups of men who were assembling for the day's labour. Along the way, he spotted a handful of familiar faces among the throng. With a subtle shake of his head and a cautious glance, he signalled for silence, imploring them not to acknowledge his presence. The sight of him clearly startled some, their eyes wide in disbelief at seeing him alive and within the camp. This reaction unsettled him, and he could only hope that each would exercise the necessary discretion to keep his identity concealed.

He searched the lines for any sign of his brother, scanning the masses with growing anxiety. Despite the sheer number of Elvendon men—surely numbering in the thousands—his brother remained elusive in the crowd. Yet, he kept looking, determined to find him somewhere amongst the prisoners.

A wave of discouragement swept over him as he walked. How was it, with so many men gathered here, that none had risen in resistance? The answer, he supposed, lay in their sense of hopelessness. Even if they managed to break free and reclaim their liberty, what future awaited them? Their kingdom was leaderless, bereft of a King or Queen to rally behind or to protect them. With a heavy heart, he drew in a deep breath, steeling himself as they left the main body of the camp and made their way towards the quarry where their assigned tasks awaited.

"You are assigned to break rocks," he told Keltor as they arrived, handing him a sledgehammer. "Your task is to break those rocks," he continued, indicating a large pile of hard rock. "Once the wagon arrives, load the broken rocks into it and repeat the process. Understood?"

Keltor grasped the sledgehammer firmly by its handle, feeling the weight of the task ahead. As soon as the guard moved away, he raised the sledgehammer and brought it crashing down onto the surface of the rock, the impact sending shards scattering. He glanced briefly to his left, watching as the guard handed out orders and tools to the other three men in his group before stepping back to supervise their efforts. Keltor continued to raise the sledgehammer and bring it down in steady rhythm, his attention divided between the repetitive work and scanning the area for any sign of Commander Talbot.

After about an hour of relentless hammering, a wagon pulled by a solitary mare rolled to a halt beside him. Sitting in the driver's seat was a man whose face Keltor instantly recognised—a former member of the King of Elvendon's elite guard.

Keltor grinned when the driver stepped down from the wagon and approached, his face shining with a mix of astonishment and relief. The man called out to him—"Keltor"—the name uttered with genuine emotion, as if he could barely believe what he saw.

"I heard some of the men talking, so I needed to see for myself. I thought you were dead," the driver confessed, his voice heavy with the rumours that had rippled through the camp.

Keltor kept his reply hushed and earnest. "That's what most people thought. It's good to see you, Jack. Please, don't reveal my identity." The risk of being recognised was never far from his mind.

Jack nodded, understanding the necessity of secrecy. He stooped to gather a piece of broken rock, joining Keltor in the labour, their reunion marked by quiet solidarity and caution as they worked side by side in the shadow of the quarry.

Keltor glanced at the guard, confirming that he was distracted and not paying attention to their conversation. With his heart pounding in anticipation, he leaned in and quietly voiced the question that weighed heavily on the minds of all who had recognised him. "Is the princess still alive?"

Bending down, Keltor picked up a massive slab of rock and, with considerable effort, heaved it into the back of the wagon. He answered in a low, steady voice, "Yes, she is."

At that assurance, a smile spread across Jack's lips, filled with relief and hope.

"Then there is hope," Jack murmured under his breath, pausing a moment to wipe the sweat from his brow with the sleeve of his shirt. The weight of their conversation lingered in the air, laden with the promise of change.

"Yes, I have a plan in motion," Keltor replied quietly, his voice steady despite the uncertainty of their situation.

Jack's face lit up with a broad grin. "That's the best news I've heard in months," he said, his tone filled with genuine relief. "I never believed you were dead—I kept telling everyone, there's no way you'd let the princess die. You're one of our best, Keltor."

Keltor offered a modest smile. "Thanks, Jack, but believe me, she's saved me more times than I have her." As he spoke, he lifted another heavy slab of rock onto the wagon, his muscles straining with the effort. The bond between them, forged through shared loyalty and hardship, was evident in the quiet understanding that passed between their words.

Taking a moment, Keltor asked in a low but hopeful voice, "I need to see Commander Talbot. Is he still alive? Is he here?"

Jack nodded, bending down beside him. A subtle smile creased his weathered face as he replied, "Yes. I'll bring him on the next run over." With that assurance, a renewed sense of determination settled over them as they continued their work, the seeds of their plan quietly taking root amidst the dust and toil of the quarry.

Jack heaved another heavy boulder into the back of the waggon, pausing only briefly to look at Keltor with a mixture of confusion and urgency. His voice, though low, carried the desperation felt by many who had watched events unfold so rapidly. "What the hell happened, Keltor? One minute you left on the quest, the next we were being overrun by Aranstream soldiers?" he asked, struggling to comprehend how quickly their fortunes had changed.

Keltor let out a heavy breath, the weight of recent events clear on his face. "King Iwein had planned an invasion long before I even brought the Princess back from Earth," he explained, his voice steady but sombre.

Jack's expression shifted instantly to one of shock. Keltor continued, "His plan was for Aragon to take the power of the Star from Kaitlin. When Aragon failed, he turned his aggression on us. So, we killed him."

Keltor then gave Jack a detailed account of all that had transpired on Earth, including how Star had placed them in stasis for eight long months and everything that had occurred leading up to the present moment. He spoke with quiet conviction, ensuring Jack understood the full gravity of the situation.

"So, you see," Keltor finished as he loaded the last rock onto the wagon, "whether we killed Aragon or not, King Iwein was determined to attack Elvendon. That's why he was already in the castle for the Princess's birthday."

Jack shook his head in disbelief. "By the stars," he murmured, the enormity of the revelation settling in. "I will inform the Commander."

Chapter Eighteen
Aranstream Castle

"Face forward," the soldier commanded, his grip tightening around Kaitlin's waist as they rode away from the prisoners. Obeying, Kaitlin turned her gaze away from Keltor. Tears welled up in her eyes, and as she blinked, they traced cold, silent paths down her cheeks. Her heart ached; each beat heavy with sorrow as she fought to suppress the dreadful thoughts swirling in her mind—whispering that this moment might be the last time she ever saw him.

The horse beneath Kaitlin shifted into a brisk trot, jolting her backwards so she collided with the soldier behind her.

"Steady there, sweetheart," the soldier said, his voice laced with amusement. As he spoke, his thumb pressed and rubbed against her stomach, a gesture that was both possessive and unwelcome.

Kaitlin kept her gaze fixed ahead, refusing to look back at the soldier. Despite the overwhelming temptation to lash out—her mind flashed with images of punching him square in the face or driving her elbow sharply into his stomach—she forced herself to remain composed. Now was not the time for open defiance; she needed to maintain the appearance of vulnerability, to play the part of the feeble woman, at least for the moment. Though her fists clenched at her sides and resentment simmered beneath the surface, she held herself in check, knowing that her safety— perhaps even her life—depended on her restraint for now.

The group rode on for another hour, the journey marked by an uneasy silence. Eventually, they arrived at the castle of

Aranstream. Unlike the grand and commanding presence of Elvendon, Aranstream's castle appeared somewhat less formidable. This relative lack of grandeur may have influenced King Iwein's ambition to build a new, more imposing stronghold.

The city itself was encircled by a significant wall, offering a sense of security yet also serving as a reminder of the kingdom's rigid control. As the party approached, the guards stationed at the massive fifteen-foot gates moved promptly to allow them entry, swinging the gates open with practiced deference.

Prince Keion led the way, riding through the gates as the guards bowed deeply. Their eyes lingered on her, scrutinising her features. Instinctively, she pulled her hood up and averted her gaze. While it was unlikely she would be recognised, caution compelled her to remain inconspicuous.

The procession made its way through the city, moving at a steady pace. The streets were eerily quiet, with only a handful of citizens visible. As the prince passed, those few halted whatever they were doing and immediately dropped to their knees in deference, avoiding his gaze and remaining perfectly still until he had gone by. Kaitlin observed the scene with growing resentment. Under her breath, she muttered, "What an ass," reflecting on the prince's blatant arrogance. He rode with an air of absolute authority, his posture rigid and regal, never once acknowledging the people who bowed before him.

It was clear to Kaitlin that the prince revelled in his own self-importance. His behaviour was cold and dismissive, offering neither kindness nor recognition to his subjects. Instead, the citizens appeared deeply intimidated, their faces etched with fear as they cowered in his presence. Kaitlin understood their terror all too well; memories of the valley incident with Keltor lingered in her mind. The oppressive atmosphere made it unmistakable that this kingdom maintained its rule through fear and intimidation, subjugating its people under a regime of terror.

Kaitlin drew in a sharp breath as she noticed a group of young children playing in the road ahead. Despite their presence, the prince showed no intention of slowing his horse, maintaining his unyielding pace. A moment of chaos ensued when a man, who had been busily loading a cart with supplies nearby, spotted the children in danger. With barely a second to spare, he dashed into the street and swept the children up into his arms, narrowly saving them from being trampled beneath the prince's horse.

Even amid his panic, the man instinctively bowed apologetically to the prince, as though he were at fault for the children's play. Witnessing this, Kaitlin felt a surge of anger rise within her. It was painfully evident that even the prince's own people were treated with utter disregard, as if their lives and well-being were of no consequence to him.

Her heart pounded with worry, not only for Keltor and whatever fate awaited him, but for all her people who suffered under the rule of King Iwein. The reality of their oppression was impossible to ignore: these rulers were not merely indifferent, they were tyrannical—cruel dictators who ruled through fear and violence. Silently, Kaitlin prayed to the spirits, hoping desperately that she and Keltor would find a way to overthrow them and bring justice to their people.

They stopped in the courtyard, the prince pulling his horse alongside a box covered in dark blue and red fabric, the colours of Aranstream. A young man rushed over to the prince and took the reins of his horse. He dipped his head as the prince slid off his horse onto the box and stepped down onto the courtyard. Two other soldiers dismounted and followed the prince towards the large oak doors, which had been opened ready for them. The two doormen dropped to their knees as the prince walked by them, and he disappeared into the castle.

"Down you get," the soldier barked, his tone clipped and impatient. Before Kaitlin could brace herself, his hands clamped around her waist and he all but hauled her from the saddle. She tumbled to the hard ground, the jolt rattling through her bones and a sharp ache blossoming where she landed. Humiliation burned in her cheeks as she scrambled to her knees, feeling the sting of gravel pressing against her palms. She shot the soldier a glare, her anger simmering beneath the surface, but he only offered a mocking smirk as he swung down from his horse with a practised ease.

"Get up, the prince will want **you** later," he said with emphasis. Reaching down and grabbing her upper arm, he dragged her back to her feet. His hand pinching her skin with a firm grip. Without another word, the soldier propelled her onward, his grasp unyielding as he led her swiftly across the courtyard. The sharp chill of the afternoon air nipped at her exposed skin, mingling with the sting of humiliation and dread that knotted in her chest. Kaitlin tried to steady herself, forcing her legs to match his hurried stride as they approached the looming entrance. The heavy wooden door creaked open, revealing a dimly lit corridor lined with faded tapestries, their musty scent filling the air as she walked briskly, his hand still firmly on her arm.

Her heart pounded as she struggled to steady her breath. Dread coiled in her stomach at his words. What did he mean, the prince would want her later? A fearful shudder shot down her entire body as she remembered Prince Aragon's attack in the forest. She wouldn't let that happen again. Even if it meant blowing her cover too soon, she was prepared to use her magic to defend herself. She fought to master her rising apprehension as the guard's grip propelled her forward, every step echoing with the memory of past dangers and the threat that lingered in his words. Gritting her teeth, Kaitlin forced herself to focus—she needed to remain alert and remember every detail of their route, knowing her safety and perhaps the fate of the others depended on it. She glanced swiftly at the other women being herded with her, their anxious eyes wide with uncertainty, and resolved that no matter what the prince intended, she would not be caught unprepared. The castle's shadowy corridors closed in around them as they were led away, and a flicker of determination burned within her: if danger arose, she would not hesitate to fight back, even if it meant revealing her true power.

After ten minutes of walking, Kaitlin and the others began to ascend a narrow stone spiral staircase. The steps twisted tightly with every turn, forcing them to move in single file. They climbed steadily, circling upwards for two full floors before finally leaving the confines of the staircase. From there, they continued along another long, dimly lit corridor. The guard marched ahead, maintaining a brisk pace until he came to a halt in front of a heavy wooden door. Without hesitation, he opened it, signalling for them to enter.

The guard ushered them forward briskly. "Come on in, all of you," he ordered, and all six women entered the room, their movements hesitant and subdued. The atmosphere inside was tense, with the women glancing nervously at one another as they stepped across the threshold. At the front, a stern-looking woman awaited them, her expression unreadable as she surveyed the new arrivals. The group instinctively drew closer together, uncertainty etched on their faces as they awaited further instruction.

The guard paused at the threshold and addressed the woman who awaited them. "Six more for you," he announced curtly. The woman, clearly advanced in years, greeted them with a stoic nod. Her grey hair was pulled back tightly, and deep lines etched her face, silent testimony to the many hardships she had endured throughout her life. As the new arrivals took in their surroundings, two additional women entered from a door at the back of the room and moved to stand by the older woman's side.

The guard delivered his orders with a tone of authority, his words brooking no argument. "Clean them up and then put them to work," he commanded, making it clear that there would be no respite for the new arrivals.

The woman responded with a silent nod, bowing her head in acknowledgement of his instructions before turning her attention to the group. The atmosphere remained tense as the reality of their situation set in, each woman realising that any resistance was likely to be futile.

As the guard prepared to leave, he paused and cast a glance over his shoulder at the assembled women. "Oh, and this one," he remarked, gesturing toward Kaitlin, his tone making it clear she was to be singled out. "The prince has specifically requested her. Ensure she is properly prepared to serve during the evening meal."

His words hung in the air, drawing the attention of everyone in the room. A ripple of anxiety passed through the group, the other women exchanging worried glances, while Kaitlin tried to mask the apprehension that surged within her. The instruction left no room for doubt: Kaitlin was to be made ready for the prince's presence, and her role in the coming hours would be of particular interest to those in power.

The woman acknowledged the instruction with a nod before observing the guard's departure as he closed the door behind him. She turned to face the group, her expression measured and her tone even as she addressed them. "Very well," she said, her gaze travelling over each of the women, assessing their bedraggled appearance and the exhaustion etched on their faces. It was clear from her reserved manner that she harboured doubts about the new arrivals, yet she maintained a sense of authority as she prepared to instruct them on what was to come.

Kaitlin observed the woman closely, noting the slender wooden rod gripped in her right hand. A sense of unease prickled at her as she took in the expressions of the other women standing nearby. They ranged in age from their early twenties to their late thirties, yet a uniform look of terror marked each of their faces. Kaitlin exchanged a quick glance with the woman beside her, recognising the fear and uncertainty that bound them all together in this unfamiliar and threatening place.

The older woman stood at the front of the group, her expression calm yet authoritative as she addressed the new arrivals. "My name is Ava," she announced, her voice steady and composed. She gestured towards the door at the back of the room, where two other women, Alena and Rosaline, waited in quiet anticipation.

"Go through there with Alena and Rosaline and take a bath," Ava instructed, clearly accustomed to giving orders. Her tone left no room for hesitation, making it evident that compliance was expected. "I will prepare you some new clothes," she added, indicating that their current dishevelled state would soon be remedied.

With Ava's direction, the women understood what was required of them, and the atmosphere in the room shifted as they prepared to follow her instructions, moving towards the indicated doorway to begin the process of cleaning up and changing into fresh attire.

As the women gathered, a timid voice broke the silence. "What's going to happen to us?" one woman asked, her words trembling with uncertainty and fear. Ava approached her, stopping directly in front of her, her presence both commanding and composed.

Ava addressed the group with clarity and authority. "In accordance with the wishes of the King and the prince, you will each be assigned to duties within the kitchens, as well as tasked with the cleaning of the chambers," she explained. Her tone was firm, leaving no room for doubt or dissent. "Furthermore, you are expected to fulfil any other requests made by Their Highnesses as required."

Her words settled heavily over the group, making clear the reality of their new roles and the expectations placed upon them. The women exchanged anxious glances, the gravity of their situation becoming ever more apparent as they listened to Ava's instructions.

Kaitlin, her frustration boiling over, could no longer hold back her anger. She confronted Ava directly, her voice sharp with emotion. "Why would you do this?" she demanded, seeking an explanation for the woman's harsh actions.

In response, Ava remained composed, meeting Kaitlin's gaze with unwavering calm. Her expression betrayed no hint of regret or uncertainty. "Quite simply, my dear, it is to ensure the safety of myself and my family," Ava replied. Her words were measured, carrying a warning beneath their surface. "I advise you to proceed accordingly if you wish to keep your head." The gravity of her statement left little room for further protest, making it clear that self-preservation was the driving force behind her decisions.

Kaitlin clenched her jaw, doing her utmost to suppress the anger threatening to spill over. The fear in the room was unmistakable. She looked around at the other women, noticing that many were visibly shaken and bore clear signs of mistreatment—bruised cheeks, split lips, and other injuries that could only have come from resisting their captors. The reality that these women had fought back during their abduction was unmistakable, and witnessing their suffering only fuelled her growing resentment. Each new mark of cruelty was another reason for Kaitlin to harbour thoughts of vengeance against King Iwein and Prince Keion, whose orders had led to this grim situation.

Kaitlin followed the women as they moved into an adjoining room. The chamber was dominated by a large stone bath, its surface shimmering with hot water. Wisps of steam curled upwards, filling the air with the calming scent of lavender and herbs. The inviting aroma offered a small measure of comfort, but the tension in the room remained.

"All of you, strip and get in," Ava ordered, her voice cold and her gaze fixed on the murky water ahead. The threat in her tone was unmistakable—refusal was not an option. A heavy silence settled over the room. Fear flickered in Maria's eyes as she hugged her arms protectively around herself, while Ingrid clenched her fists, silently weighing her options and fighting the urge to protest. Beside them, Mora's lip trembled, her mind racing with confusion and indignation as she glanced towards the door, desperate for escape. Each woman was gripped by her own turmoil—some paralysed by terror, others burning with anger or shame. No one moved, their reluctance rooted in the uncertainty of what would happen if they obeyed—or if they dared to resist.

Ava's patience snapped as she raised her voice, her insistence cutting through the tense silence. "Now!" she shouted, making it clear that she would accept no hesitation or argument. Her gaze swept over the group, her authority absolute. "Don't think for one minute that I would not report you for disobedience," she warned, her words carrying the weight of a threat already made. "As I have already told you, me and my ladies value our heads, and we will not be put at risk by those who will not comply."

The severity of her tone left no doubt as to her resolve. Ava's message was unmistakable: compliance was not a matter of negotiation, but of survival—for herself, her attendants, and those now under her command.

Ava lifted the rod in her hand, her intent clear as she prepared to strike one of the women. The atmosphere in the room grew even more charged, fear and tension crackling in the air.

"No!" Kaitlin yelled stepping in front of the woman Ava was about to strike. Kaitlin's heart hammered in her chest as she defensively lifted her arm to protect her face as Ava's rod struck down. Kaitlin winced as the rod struck her forearm leaving a sharp red mark across her skin.

"You dare defy me?" Ava growled at Kaitlin, her voice low and threatening.

Standing her ground, Kaitlin shook her head and responded with as much calm as she could muster. "No, I'm not. We shall do as you ask," she said quietly, showing compliance as she began to undo the ties on the front of her dress. She looked at Ava, her voice pleading, "Just don't hurt them. They're scared; can't you see that!"

The woman drew in a steadying breath and regarded Kaitlin from head to toe, her gaze lingering with a sense of reluctant appraisal. It was clear to her why the prince had singled Kaitlin out—her poise and bearing spoke of noble origins, making her stand out even in these dire circumstances.

Ava, however, showed no patience for hesitation. Her tone was sharp and impatient as she snapped, "Just get in the bath." The command left no room for negotiation, only compliance.

Understanding the situation and hoping to spare the others from further harm, Kaitlin nodded obediently to Ava. She then turned to the rest of the women, her voice gentle but insistent as she tried to offer comfort amid fear. "Please, just do as she asks. We're all girls together, it will be fine, okay?" she said, doing her best to reassure them. She mustered an encouraging smile, hoping to ease their anxiety and foster a sense of solidarity among them.

The women each looked at one another, their faces illuminated by flickering candlelight, uncertainty and fear reflected in their eyes. Knowing that compliance was necessary to avoid further punishment—Ava's command and Kaitlin's plea weighing heavily in the air—they slowly began to remove their clothing. The soft rustle of fabric filled the quiet space, mingling with the palpable tension, as each woman hesitated for just a moment before surrendering to the inevitability of the situation. Cold air brushed against their skin, heightening their vulnerability and drawing them closer together in silent solidarity.

Ava took a deliberate step back from the group, positioning herself beside Alena and Rosaline. With a cautious glance towards Kaitlin, she leaned in and whispered, her voice low and laced with caution, "Watch that one." She nodded subtly in Kaitlin's direction. "She has a strong will." The significance of Ava's warning was not lost on Alena and Rosaline; both women exchanged a knowing look and gave a silent nod, their eyes following Kaitlin closely as she and the other five women made their way towards the vast tub. The quiet agreement hung in the air, underscoring the tension and the need for vigilance as the six women climbed into the huge bath, each movement watched carefully by their overseers.

Kaitlin eased herself into the bath, the warm water lapping gently at her skin. As she settled, a sharp sting radiated from her forearm where the rod had struck, and she instinctively brought her other hand to cradle the mark, trying to soothe the pain.

Beside her, the woman to her left offered a quiet word of gratitude. "Thank you," she said softly, her voice edged with both relief and empathy.

Kaitlin turned to meet the woman's gaze, acknowledging her presence with a gentle look.

"My name's Maria," the woman continued, her tone sincere. "Thank you for what you did. I'm sorry you got hurt with her rod."

"That's okay," Kaitlin replied with a reassuring smile, her voice calm and steady despite the tension that filled the room. She leaned in slightly, making her words as gentle and comforting as possible. "Look, we're all in this together, and for now, it's best for us to comply with what they want. Keep your head down and don't make a fuss or be noticed."

Maria hesitated for a moment, glancing around nervously before edging closer to Kaitlin. Her voice was barely above a whisper as she confided, "Can I tell you something?"

Kaitlin noticed the worried expression on Maria's face and nodded softly, encouraging her to speak. "Of course," she said, her tone inviting and kind.

Maria's fear was evident as she whispered, "I'm scared."

Kaitlin understood the depth of Maria's anxiety and reached out, gently resting her hand on Maria's arm in a gesture of solidarity. "It's okay—we all are," she replied, offering support and reassurance through both her words and her touch.

Maria hesitated, casting a furtive glance towards Ava to ensure she wasn't being watched. Her voice trembling, she leaned closer to Kaitlin and revealed her secret, her words barely more than a whisper. "No, I mean..." she began, pausing to steady herself. "I'm with child. What will he do when I start showing properly? They took my husband to the camp." The weight of her situation pressed down upon her, and her composure faltered. She sniffled, unable to hold back her tears any longer, and quickly lifted her hand from the water to wipe them from her eyes, hoping no one would notice her distress.

Kaitlin's heart ached for Maria. She, too, glanced anxiously in Ava's direction, making sure their conversation remained private. Gently, she offered comfort. "Oh, Maria," she said softly, her voice warm and reassuring. "Don't worry. I promise we will be out of here soon. I can't tell you any more right now, but please, for now, just keep your head down."

Maria nodded silently, her expression reflecting the shared anxiety that hung over them all.

Suddenly, another woman sitting to Kaitlin's left spoke up, her voice trembling with emotion. "I don't want to be here," she confessed, unable to hide her distress. Kaitlin turned to face her, noticing that the woman was about her own age. Tears began to stream down her cheeks as she added, "I'm so scared."

Kaitlin reached out with empathy, her words gentle and reassuring. "Hey, I know you are, we all are, and that's okay. As I said, just do as you're told, and keep your heads down. Help will come soon, I promise."

Another woman interjected, her tone heavy with despair. "Help, what help? There is no one to help us, our King is dead, our armies captured. My husband was taken to the camps, along with my son."

Kaitlin turned to address her, seeking to offer comfort despite the overwhelming circumstances. "Ingrid," she said, acknowledging the woman by name as she prepared to speak.

Ingrid looked at Kaitlin, hope flickering in her eyes. Kaitlin leaned in, her voice low and sincere. "Ingrid, I can't tell you how I know, I just do. Just hang in for another week or so and give them no reason to hurt you, okay."

Ingrid nodded, her silent gesture signalling a fragile acceptance of Kaitlin's words and a faint glimmer of hope amidst the uncertainty.

The fourth woman lowered her shoulders beneath the water and quietly introduced herself. "My name is Kenya," she said, her voice subdued as she tried to find some comfort in the warmth. The fifth woman followed, offering her own introduction. "I'm Elsa," she said simply, her tone betraying a cautious hopefulness. The sixth woman, not wishing to be left out, spoke up as well. "Mora," she declared, her introduction brief but clear.

When it was Kaitlin's turn, she hesitated for a moment, uncertainty flickering across her face. Choosing her words carefully, she replied, "I'm… Elizabeth," deliberately concealing her true identity by using her mother's name. Kaitlin then allowed herself to sink further into the welcoming depths of the bath. Despite the worries that weighed heavily on her mind, she found a small comfort in the warmth of the water and the rare feeling of cleanliness. Still, she remained guarded, reluctant to reveal anything more to the others, wary of saying something she might later regret.

"Out!" Ava commanded abruptly, her voice echoing through the steamy chamber and causing Kaitlin to start. Kaitlin had been lost in thought, partially submerged in the bath, her eyes closed as she pondered Keltor's whereabouts and wellbeing. The sudden interruption snapped her from her reverie. Blinking, she wiped the water from her eyes, focusing on Alena and Rosaline, who now stood by the bath, towels in hand. As each woman stepped out of the water, Alena and Rosaline handed them a towel, allowing them to dry themselves after their brief respite.

Kaitlin wrapped the beige towel securely around her chest and followed the others as they made their way back into the adjoining room. Awaiting them was a rail from which hung the clothing allocated to each woman. The garments consisted of a simple dress and a pair of wooden clogs. Kaitlin reached for her assigned grey smock dress, eyeing it with a mixture of dismay and resignation. The fabric was coarse and unappealing, the style shapeless and unflattering.

After drying herself, Kaitlin slipped into the dress, immediately noticing how baggy it was; the excess material hung awkwardly from her frame, making her appear almost as if she were with child. The rough, scratchy texture of the cloth only added to her discomfort, and she found herself absentmindedly adjusting the neckline as it irritated her skin. Despite these grievances, she resigned herself to wearing it, knowing she had little choice in the matter.

Ava regarded Kaitlin critically, her eyes travelling from head to toe with a measured scrutiny. After a moment's assessment, she gave a thoughtful hum and clicked her fingers in a brisk gesture. At this signal, Alena stepped forward and handed Ava a grey sash that matched the drabness of the dress.

Without hesitation, Ava took hold of the excess fabric of Kaitlin's ill-fitting dress, gathering it at the waist. She wrapped the sash firmly around Kaitlin, cinching it tightly and transforming the shapeless garment into something marginally more presentable.

The gathered material now sat more neatly against Kaitlin's figure, alleviating the tent-like appearance that had previously caused her discomfort.

"Well, that's a little better. It will do for now," Ava remarked, her tone practical and matter-of-fact. Satisfied with the adjustment, she turned her attention to the rest of the group. "Right, all of you follow me, and I will take you to your new stations." Without further delay, she led the way, expecting the women to fall in line behind her as they prepared to head towards their assigned duties.

Kaitlin slipped her feet into the wooden clogs, joining the other five women as they began their walk through the castle. The group moved together down a seemingly endless stone corridor, each step echoing softly against the cold walls. Candlelight flickered in iron sconces along the path, casting long shadows and illuminating the bare, grey stone that surrounded them. A persistent draft flowed down the hallway, and Kaitlin, dressed only in her coarse smock dress with her hair still damp from the bath, felt the chill seep into her bones. She shivered involuntarily, trying to ignore the discomfort as she continued after the others.

They proceeded down the narrow spiral stairs, their footsteps echoing in the confined space, before continuing along another lengthy corridor. The group moved in silence, anticipation and uncertainty hanging thick in the air as they awaited further instructions.

At a junction, Ava paused and turned to Ingrid and Kenya. With a decisive gesture, she indicated that they were to accompany Alena, who had been waiting nearby. "Laundry," Ava announced, her tone leaving no room for question. Alena nodded and opened the heavy oak door, beckoning the two women inside. Ingrid and Kenya exchanged brief glances before following Alena into the room, ready to begin their assigned tasks.

The remaining women continued along the corridor until Ava came to another halt. She looked at Mora and Elsa and addressed them directly. "You two—cleaning duties," she declared. "Go with Rosaline." Rosaline stepped forward, ready to guide them.

She opened another oak door and gestured towards the interior, indicating where they should go. Mora and Elsa glanced at Kaitlin, who offered them a reassuring smile. Mora returned the gesture, and then both women entered the room, prepared to take on their responsibilities.

After another five minutes of walking through the castle's winding corridors, Ava came to a halt in front of yet another imposing oak door. She turned to address Kaitlin and Maria directly, her tone brisk and authoritative.

"You two," Ava announced, fixing them with a steady gaze, "will be assigned to the kitchens this evening."

Her attention then shifted to Kaitlin, and she raised an eyebrow in silent expectation. Sensing the need to clarify her identity, Kaitlin spoke up hesitantly. "Erm, Elizabeth," she said.

Ava nodded in acknowledgement before continuing, "Elizabeth, you will serve at the prince's table tonight. Please ensure you remain presentable and composed throughout the event. Do you understand?"

"Yes," Kaitlin replied, nodding in affirmation, determined to meet the expectations set before her.

Ava led Kaitlin and Maria to the kitchen and paused at the heavy door, turning to address them. "Good, now in you go," she instructed as she opened the door. The two women stepped inside the expansive, bustling kitchen. The warmth from the ovens and stoves washed over Kaitlin, a welcome sensation after the chill of the castle corridors. She felt the heat flood her cheeks, grateful for the change in temperature.

Across the busy room, Ava spotted an older woman, Marnia, likely in her early sixties. Marnia's dark hair, streaked with silver at the temples, was scraped neatly away from her face. Her cheeks were flushed red, whether from exertion or the heat, and she was busy wiping her hands on a cloth as she approached.

"Ava," Marnia greeted her, her tone brisk but not unkind.

"These two are for you," Ava announced, indicating both Kaitlin and Maria. Then, grasping Kaitlin firmly by the upper arm and pulling her forward, she added, "and this one—the prince wants her to serve his meal tonight, so get her trained, fast."

"Absolutely," Marnia replied, her voice clipped and commanding, a sharp nod punctuating the word as though dispatching an order. The lingering scent of freshly baked bread mingled with the tang of onions on the air, and the constant clatter of pans bounced off the stone walls, filling the space with urgency.

Kaitlin's gaze tracked Ava as she swept out of the kitchen, the door swinging shut with a dull thud. Already, the rhythm of the kitchen pressed in on her—bubbling pots, the hiss of roasting meat, and a chorus of hurried footsteps on flagstones.

"Right, you two," Marnia barked, her tone brooking no dissent. She strode towards a mountainous stack of plates and pots, her apron already streaked with flour and grease, the smell of soap rising from the sink. "You—start here," she commanded, pointing at Maria with a quick flick of her wrist, as if assigning a new recruit their post. "Nicola!" she called, her voice slicing through the din. A girl of about sixteen, pale-faced and wide-eyed, hurried over, her hands still damp from rinsing spoons. "Show her what's what. No slacking."

Nicola nodded, eyes lowered and motioned for Maria to follow. Maria's uncertain glance sought Kaitlin's reassurance; Kaitlin mustered a small encouraging smile, though her own nerves hummed beneath the surface.

Marnia's focus swung to Kaitlin, her gaze appraising and sharp. "And you—how's your serving?" she demanded, arms folded, making her presence loom larger than her stature. Kaitlin hesitated, feeling the oppressive warmth and steamy haze of the kitchen prickling at her skin. Her shoulders tensed, betraying her apprehension. "It's… all right, I suppose," she offered, voice wavering between defiance and uncertainty, fingers curling slightly at her sides. The clinking from nearby cutlery seemed to echo her anxiety, and she forced herself to hold Marnia's stare, refusing to appear weak.

Marnia's lips pressed into a thin line, her eyes searching Kaitlin's face for any sign of doubt. The heat, the noise, and the sharp tang of metal in the air made Kaitlin's heart thud faster, but determination flashed in her eyes as she steeled herself for whatever tasks lay ahead.

The woman exhaled audibly, making her impatience clear. "'Okay' is insufficient for our prince; you are expected to achieve excellence," she stated firmly, her tone leaving no room for argument. Her sharp gaze lingered on Kaitlin for a moment longer before she continued, "You have five hours to prepare. Follow me." With that, she turned on her heel, expecting Kaitlin to keep pace as they moved on to the next task.

Kaitlin accompanied Marnia out of the bustling kitchen, the sounds of clattering pans and hurried footsteps fading behind them as they entered the quiet of the corridor. They walked side by side along the lengthy hallway, their footsteps echoing off the stone floor until they arrived before a pair of imposing oak double doors. Marnia grasped one of the heavy doors and pushed it open, leading the way inside. Kaitlin followed close behind, nerves taut as she stepped into the next space.

The room they entered was spacious and grand, clearly reserved for important occasions. Rich red velvet curtains framed a tall, arched window at the far end of the chamber, the fabric drawn back and secured with thick golden cords that glinted in the firelight. At one end of the room, a wide fireplace crackled with a lively fire, casting warmth throughout the space and creating dancing shadows on the walls. Above the mantel, a large and imposing portrait of King Iwein dominated the wall, his regal expression keeping watch over the room. Kaitlin shot a quick, scornful glance at the painting, but made sure Marnia did not notice before she hurried to catch up.

In the centre of the chamber, a long oak table stretched from one end to the other, surrounded by twenty finely crafted chairs, each one ready for a distinguished guest. Marnia moved purposefully around the table, and Kaitlin circled after her, taking in the grandeur and anticipating the tasks that lay ahead.

Kaitlin's heart lurched with sudden fear as her eyes landed on the wall to her right, where an enormous portrait of Prince Keion and Prince Aragon dominated the space. The painting was exquisitely rendered, capturing every detail of the princes' features. For a fleeting moment, she was reminded of how strikingly handsome Prince Aragon had once been, his allure far surpassing that of his brother Keion. It was a poignant realisation—Aragon's outward charm belied the darkness within, but considering what she knew of their father's cruelty, perhaps it was inevitable that Aragon had been shaped into the man he became.

Marnia, noticing Kaitlin's gaze fixed on the portrait, commented in a tone that was almost wistful, "He was handsome, wasn't he, our Prince Aragon?"

Kaitlin simply nodded in response. Despite all his flaws—his arrogance and self-absorption—she couldn't honestly deny Aragon's striking looks.

Marnia's tone then darkened as she continued, "That princess killed him. I'm glad she got what she deserved and died alongside the humans. She wasn't even a true elf, just an inbred half-blood." With a curse under her breath, she strode towards a large side table against the wall.

Kaitlin's eyebrows furrowed in anger as she clenched her hands into fists, a surge of magic sparking within her fingers. She could not contain her frustration any longer.

"She was protecting herself, and her people," Kaitlin snapped back, unable to stop herself from defending herself.

Marnia turned and strode up to Kaitlin, her hand trembling with barely contained fury. Without warning, she slapped Kaitlin sharply across the face, the sound echoing in the cavernous room. "Never, ever speak of her like that. Elvendon and all their heirs are dead. Our King would take your head where you stood if you ever disrespect his sons like that again."

Kaitlin touched her throbbing cheek, the sting of fresh pain radiating beneath her fingertips. Her eyes prickled with tears—not just from the blow, but from stunned disbelief and a surge of humiliation. She tried to steady her breathing, the taste of copper sharp on her tongue as she fought the urge to retaliate. For a heartbeat, all she could hear was the crackling of the fire and her own pulse thudding in her ears. The grandeur of the chamber seemed to close in, the weight of portraits and velvet curtains pressing against her, making her feel small and exposed.

"I'm sorry," Kaitlin managed, her voice barely more than a whisper—uncertain whether she felt fear, shame, or the stirring of defiance. Part of her simmered with anger at the injustice, but self-preservation forced her to mask it.

Marnia, breath quick and uneven, rounded on Kaitlin. For a moment, something vulnerable flickered behind her stern expression, but it was gone in an instant, replaced with steely authority. She glared at Kaitlin, jaw clenched as she tried to control herself.

Marnia snapped, "So, you should be. My girl, if you want to survive to see the next day, just do as you are told like the rest of us. Now come here."

She turned away sharply, but not before Kaitlin glimpsed the storm of grief and bitterness in her eyes—a reminder that Marnia's cruelty was not born solely of malice but also of wounds that would not heal.

Kaitlin walked over to where Marnia stood, ready to listen and learn. Marnia gestured to a nearby cupboard. "In here is all the silver cutlery," she explained with precision. "You must get it exactly right, all level, not a thing out of place."

Demonstrating her expectations, Marnia carefully took the silver cutlery from the cupboard. She moved to the table and began to lay each piece out, ensuring every item was perfectly aligned—nothing was allowed to be even slightly askew.

Once satisfied with the arrangement, Marnia returned to the side table. She opened a small door and retrieved a silver goblet, its surface adorned with gleaming emeralds and rubies. The goblet caught the light, standing out amongst the other items on the table, a clear indicator of its importance and value in the setting.

"Now, this is Prince Keion's goblet. For spirits' sake, do not give him the wrong one," Marnia cautioned, her tone firm and insistent. She gestured for Kaitlin to follow her back to the cupboard, where the precious items were stored securely.

Marnia carefully removed two more goblets from within. She held one up for Kaitlin to see. "This is Prince Aragon's," she explained, setting it down on top of the side cupboard so Kaitlin could observe it closely. "You see the diamond on top?" she asked, pointing to the single distinguishing diamond that sat at the very tip of the handle.

Kaitlin nodded, making sure to commit the detail to memory. The goblets were almost identical, and the presence of the diamond was the only thing that set Prince Aragon's apart from Prince Keion's.

Marnia then retrieved another goblet, more ornate than the rest. "And should you serve our king, this is his. You cannot mistake this one." The King's goblet was unmistakable—its lavish decoration and the array of precious stones made its importance clear. Marnia's instructions were explicit: under no circumstances should the goblets be confused or misplaced.

Kaitlin examined the King's goblet with care. Like the others, it was crafted from silver, but what set it apart was its lavish embellishment—diamonds and emeralds studded its surface, making it the most ornate and unmistakable of all the goblets.

After finishing her demonstration, Marnia returned both Prince Aragon's and the King's goblet to the safety of the cupboard. She then turned her attention back to the table, continuing to lay out the cutlery with meticulous precision. As she worked, she spoke firmly, ensuring Kaitlin understood the gravity of her instructions.

"This is how it is done," Marnia reiterated, her tone leaving no room for doubt. "Never, ever change the arrangement, let anything fall out of line, or permit a speck of dirt to remain on his cutlery. If you do, believe me, you will suffer the consequences."

For the next three hours, Marnia led Kaitlin through a relentless routine of training, moving from one task to the next with little pause. First, she demonstrated the precise way to serve the prince and the other guests, her instructions sharp and unwavering. Then, with a brisk nod, she instructed Kaitlin to practise laying the table—again and again—until absolute perfection was reached. Kaitlin had to lay the table repeatedly, her hands trembling as she worried about making a mistake in front of the prince. Each time Marnia corrected her, Kaitlin felt frustration mounting within her, yet beneath it all, a steely determination began to form; she refused to let herself fail. The hours crawled by, filled with tension and careful repetition, until, at last, Marnia finally judged her efforts sufficient. Only then, with an hour remaining before dinner was due to be served, did Marnia take her back to her chamber, leaving Kaitlin's nerves frayed and her mind swirling with apprehension.

"Now, put this dress on," Marnia ordered Kaitlin, her tone leaving no room for hesitation. Kaitlin picked up the pink dress and turned it over in her hands, examining the unfamiliar and elegant fabric with uncertainty.

"Hurry girl, you need to be ready!" Marnia demanded, her impatience clear as she watched Kaitlin.

Kaitlin slipped off the old grey sack dress and put on the pink one. The gown was long, its bodice cinched tightly around her waist and the neckline plunging farther than she found comfortable, exposing more of herself than she ever wished to reveal. She fidgeted with the dress, tugging at the fabric in a futile attempt to cover herself, her cheeks burning with embarrassment and resentment. She hated how vulnerable she felt, clothed by someone else's expectations and desires.

Marnia's sharp gaze caught her movement. With a swift slap, she knocked Kaitlin's hand away and yanked the dress back down. "Leave it as it is, it's what he likes," she ordered, her tone leaving no room for argument, as always. Marnia had long since made it clear—her instructions were to be obeyed without question or complaint. Whether driven by duty or a hardened sense of survival, she never wavered in enforcing the rules.

Kaitlin swallowed hard, biting back a retort. Resentment simmered beneath the surface—resentment at the situation, at Marnia's unwavering resolve, and, most of all, at her own helplessness. She stood rigid as Marnia fetched a brush from the dressing table, the bristles snagging with each brusque stroke.

Marnia's tone softened as she instructed Kaitlin, "Stand still," yet it remained firmly insistent. Kaitlin obeyed, standing motionless, though anxiety churned within her as she considered what the evening might hold.

Without warning, Marnia pulled Kaitlin's head back and began to brush her hair with harsh, hurried strokes. The discomfort was clear, but there was no time for complaint. After a moment, Marnia declared, "That will have to do, we're out of time. Come on, follow me." She tossed the hairbrush onto the dressing table and strode toward the door, leaving Kaitlin to follow reluctantly, her nerves taut.

Though Kaitlin had mastered the art of arranging the prince's cutlery to perfection, her concerns ran much deeper. It was not the serving that troubled her, but what might be expected of her after the dinner. Determined, she resolved that no matter what transpired, she would not permit Prince Keion to touch or harm her.

Kaitlin followed Marnia back into the banqueting hall, her senses immediately assaulted by the rich aroma of freshly prepared food. Along the side tables, the staff had meticulously arranged a series of tureens and covered silver platters, each one placed with careful precision. Attendants, dressed in immaculate uniforms, stood at attention by the tables, poised and ready to serve at a moment's notice.

Marnia paused beside her, casting a critical eye over the scene before leaning in to remind Kaitlin in a low, firm voice, "Stand by the side of his chair, two steps back, remember." The instruction was clear, and Kaitlin nodded, doing her best to steady her nerves as she prepared to take her place by the prince's seat, determined to remember every detail of her training.

Kaitlin did as she was told and waited anxiously for the prince to arrive. Only moments later, the doors opened to reveal Prince Keion. He was accompanied by six men and two women, all entering the room together. She followed the lead of the others and dropped to her knee. Her heart pounded as she wondered what impression she would make on the prince.

As Prince Keion entered, his attention drifted towards Kaitlin while a servant pulled out his chair. Settling into his seat, he cast her a second, lingering glance, accompanied by a slight, knowing smile. Something about her intrigued him—she was clearly not the typical farmer's daughter she appeared to be. His suspicions were not unfounded; he recalled his father saying that, when Aranstream invaded Elvendon nine months ago, some of the noble women had fled into the forest and vanished without a trace. Now, watching Kaitlin, he grew increasingly convinced that she was one of those elusive noblewomen in hiding.

As the servant pushed Prince Keion's chair in behind him, Kaitlin stood, recalling the precise instructions Marnia had drilled into her. With steady hands, she lifted the jug of wine and poured it into the prince's goblet, ensuring it always remained full. This was her sole purpose at the table—to keep his cup brimming and never let it run dry, regardless of how often he drank. Prince Keion did not acknowledge her presence with so much as a word. Once his meal was served, he focused entirely on eating and drinking, leaving Kaitlin to her silent task. She noticed with growing unease that she had already refilled his goblet four times, and he had only just finished his main course.

Kaitlin stood silently, her ears attuned to the men's conversation as they boasted about their exploits. Their voices, filled with pride, recounted the number of Elvendon captives they had taken and the lives they had ended. Each claim sent a fresh wave of anger and revulsion through her. Her gaze drifted to the knife resting beside Prince Keion's plate, and a dangerous thought flickered in her mind—could she seize it and put an end to his cruelty right here and now?

The idea tempted her, the weight of her hatred for him almost tipping her into action. He was, in her eyes, the embodiment of evil, and the urge to see him dead was nearly overwhelming. Yet, even as the thought took shape, Kaitlin recognised the risks. She knew that any attempt to kill him would almost certainly result in her own demise; escape would be nearly impossible in the chaos that would follow. Reluctantly, she suppressed the impulse, focusing instead on surviving the ordeal, biding her time for a better chance.

Once Prince Keion had finished his meal, he rose deliberately from his seat. Instantly, the men and women seated at the table followed suit, standing in unison. The servants, well-drilled in their roles, immediately dropped to their knees in a sign of respect, Kaitlin among them.

The prince's voice carried across the hall as he announced, "We shall convene to the den." At his words, the men at the table bowed their heads solemnly, acknowledging his instruction.

As Prince Keion stepped away from his chair, his gaze fell upon Kaitlin. He halted mid-step, his expression shifting from one of indifference to a steely hardness, betraying a flicker of curiosity. A faint curl of interest appeared on his upper lip as he studied her closely, taking in her demeanour and the way she held herself among the servants.

Fixing Kaitlin with a cold and unwavering stare, Prince Keion addressed her directly, his authority unmistakable in both tone and manner. "Look up at me, woman," he commanded, his voice leaving no room for hesitation or defiance.

A knot tightened in her stomach as Kaitlin obeyed, raising her eyes to meet the prince's gaze. The first thing she noticed was the amulet that hung conspicuously around his neck. Her attention then shifted to the unsettling expression he wore, a look that sent an involuntary shiver through her body.

Prince Keion caught her reaction, one eyebrow arching with curiosity. Mistaking her discomfort for fear, he smiled, a touch of satisfaction in his expression. As he studied her, his gaze lingered on Kaitlin's eyes—strikingly green, deeper and brighter than any he had encountered before. The colour was unusual; while women from Aranstream typically had dark eyes and those from Elvendon favoured blue, hers were distinctly different. Something about them felt oddly familiar to him, though he could not quite determine why.

Without further explanation, Prince Keion issued his command, his authority clear and unyielding. "You will come with me," he ordered.

Kaitlin rose to her feet and, with deliberate care, followed Prince Keion from the room. Every movement she made was measured and obedient, designed to attract as little attention as possible. Outwardly, she maintained a façade of composure, yet beneath the surface, her mind was a storm of apprehension and fear.

As she trailed behind the prince, her thoughts spun anxiously, never settling. She continually assessed her situation, considering what actions she might take if Prince Keion turned violent. In her mind, she rehearsed how she might defend herself or, in an act of desperation, even attempt to kill him should the need arise. Each possibility was weighed carefully, but every plan seemed fraught with peril.

With every step, Kaitlin's awareness was heightened by the sight of Forde's amulet hanging around the prince's neck. The talisman's presence complicated her thoughts, for she knew it held power and that any plan she formed would have to account for its influence. The urge to snatch it from him burned within her, but she could not ignore the ever-watchful eyes of the servants and guards who surrounded them. The risk was almost insurmountable; a single misstep would almost certainly mean her death.

The gravity of her predicament pressed upon her relentlessly, yet it was this same pressure that stoked her determination. Even as dread threatened to overwhelm her, Kaitlin clung to her resolve, refusing to give in to despair. She knew that her survival depended on patience, vigilance, and the hope that a safer opportunity would eventually present itself.

Kaitlin followed Prince Keion and the other men as they made their way into another room. The space was shrouded in darkness, with only a handful of lanterns suspended from the walls providing dim illumination. The atmosphere felt close and secretive, shadows dancing across the faces present.

Relief washed over Kaitlin when she realised she was not the sole woman in attendance. In total, there were six women present, each one expected to wait on the men throughout the evening. Their roles were clear: to serve, to remain attentive, and to ensure the men's needs were met. Kaitlin took up her duties without hesitation, refilling Prince Keion's goblet—a vessel that had been brought along from the banqueting hall. The men settled in, engaging in lively banter amongst themselves. Laughter and jests filled the air as they gathered around the table, shuffling cards and launching into spirited games. The drinking was incessant, the goblets never allowed to remain empty for long.

Each time Kaitlin approached to replenish the prince's drink, her gaze was inevitably drawn to the amulet hanging around his neck. The urge to seize it never left her, but the opportunity was simply not there. The prince's proximity to his men, and the ever-watchful eyes surrounding them, made any attempt impossible. For now, she could only observe, bide her time, and wait for a safer moment.

The night wore on relentlessly, stretching into the early hours of the morning. Kaitlin, along with the other women present, struggled to stay awake as fatigue pressed heavily upon them. Throughout the evening, the men drank continuously, and by now, four of them had succumbed to exhaustion, passing out where they sat on the couch.

Eventually, Prince Keion announced his intention to retire to his chambers. Kaitlin braced herself, half expecting another command, assuming he might insist she accompany him. However, to her surprise, the prince paid her no attention at all. Ignoring her presence, he staggered out of the room, supported by one of his guards.

Uncertain what to do next, Kaitlin leaned over and whispered to one of the other women in attendance, "What now?"

The woman, barely able to stifle a yawn, headed for the door. "Now we get some sleep," she replied. "You're lucky he enjoys his drink. It leaves him incapable of much, if you get my meaning. I suggest you hurry and leave before he changes his mind." With those words, she quietly exited the room, leaving Kaitlin to follow her advice.

Kaitlin was just about to hurry out of the room when she suddenly remembered the goblet. It was her responsibility, and she knew that if it were to be lost or stolen, the consequences would be severe—she could lose her life instantly. With her heart pounding, she quickly snatched the goblet from the table, all the while keeping a wary eye on the men slumped on the sofa. Their presence was a constant reminder of the dangers lurking in her surroundings.

Clutching the goblet tightly, Kaitlin ran out of the room, making sure to shut the door behind her. As she stepped into the corridor, a voice startled her from the shadows. "Good, you remembered," Marnia said, stepping out of the darkness and causing Kaitlin to jump in fright.

"Oh god, you scared me!" Kaitlin exclaimed, instinctively placing a hand over her heart as she tried to steady herself from the shock.

Unmoved by her reaction, Marnia spoke firmly. "It's late, time for you to return to your chamber," she instructed, making it clear that she expected Kaitlin to follow without delay.

Still clutching the goblet, Kaitlin hurried after her, a question pressing on her mind. "What about the goblet?" she asked, anxious about its fate.

"I shall take it," Marnia replied, reaching out to take the goblet from Kaitlin's hands.

Relieved, Kaitlin handed the goblet over and followed behind as Marnia led her back to her chamber, her thoughts racing with exhaustion and apprehension.

Upon reaching the door to her chamber, Marnia produced a key from her pocket and unlocked it with a quiet click.

Marnia's voice was firm as she gave her instructions. "Get some sleep, you'll be woken at first light," she said, making it clear that there would be no further discussion. Kaitlin nodded her acknowledgement, understanding that rest was not only expected but necessary given the day's events. She stepped quietly into the dimly lit room, moving with care so as not to disturb the other women who were already fast asleep inside. Every effort was made to be as silent as possible, her movements gentle and deliberate, out of respect for her companions' much-needed rest.

The chamber was shrouded in darkness, and Kaitlin chose not to light a lantern, respecting the rest of her companions. Silently, she slipped out of her dress and settled herself between the cold, starchy sheets. Exhaustion overwhelmed her, and she had no strength left to reflect on the day's events. Within moments, Kaitlin drifted into a deep and much-needed sleep.

Marnia paused outside the chamber door, her mind occupied by the words she had just overheard from the woman she believed was called Elizabeth—"oh my god." The phrase lingered with her, prompting a moment of contemplation. Elves, she reminded herself, did not have gods, but she understood humans did. This small detail unsettled her, raising the critical question of whether this Elizabeth might truly be human.

She considered informing the prince of her suspicions, weighing the consequences of being mistaken. If Elizabeth's words were merely a repetition of something she had picked up from someone in Elvendon, and Marnia reported incorrectly, the prince's wrath could be fatal; she might face execution for providing false information. The risk was significant, and Marnia's apprehension grew as she stood, her palm resting gently against the oak door.

After a brief, thoughtful pause, Marnia lightly tapped the door, signalling the end of her deliberation. She resolved not to act hastily but instead to observe Elizabeth—more closely. Marnia decided she would vigilantly watch for any further signs of human behaviour before making any accusations or taking the matter to the prince.

Chapter Nineteen
Reunion of Brothers

Keltor and his brother, Esendil, spotted each other at the very same moment. Esendil's eyes grew wide, and his heart began to race—there could be no doubt that the man speaking to Jack was his brother, the very brother he had believed to be dead. Esendil had been certain his brother, who had served as the Princess's protector, had been lost forever.

Troubled by disbelief, Esendil frowned and closed his eyes for a few seconds, as if hoping that when he opened them again, the vision would remain. He looked once more, and as the man met his gaze, Esendil felt an overwhelming urge to shout out and leap for joy. It truly was his brother. He took an eager step forward, ready to call out his brother's name, but in that instant, his brother raised a finger to his lips and shook his head, cautioning Esendil to remain silent.

Esendil's heart raced at the impossible sight before him. Though he forced himself to return his gaze to the ground and resume his labour, the powerful surge of emotion threatened to undo him. Relief and disbelief warred inside him—Keltor, the brother he had mourned, was truly alive. For so long, Esendil's hope had been battered by loss; the news of Keltor and the princess's supposed deaths on Earth had left him hollow, his heart barely daring to wish for a miracle.

Yet, in the grim shadow of Aranstream's invasion, it was hope that clung stubbornly to his spirit. Each day in captivity, as stone dust choked the air and guards barked orders, Esendil's heart held fast to a slender thread of possibility. Even when his best friend was taken away nearly a month ago for resisting, and uncertainty pressed on him like a weight, some part of him continued to believe that freedom, or reunion, was not entirely lost. Now, seeing Keltor was proof that hope, though buried, had survived in his heart all along.

Esendil had kept his head down, trying to be invisible to the guards as much as possible. He'd seen the beatings handed out to those who opposed or fought back, he wanted to keep his head and his face so he just quietly got on with his tasks, just praying to the spirits that freedom would come one day. He gave a sigh and then sneaked another look, but Keltor was gone, a wave of concern flooded him, and his eyes searched the area, but he couldn't see him.

As Esendil continued his work, a voice spoke quietly from behind him, instructing, "Keep working and don't look at me." The words were delivered with caution, prompting Esendil to tense, but the familiarity in the tone stirred something within him.

Unable to contain his rising excitement, Esendil asked in a hushed, urgent whisper, "Keltor, is that really you?" The question trembled with hope, and his heart pounded in his chest as he awaited the reply.

"Hey Ese, yes it's me, little brother," came the gentle confirmation. The relief and joy in Keltor's voice was unmistakable, though tempered by the need for discretion. The brothers' reunion, so long hoped for, was finally at hand, though for now it had to remain hidden, shaped by the dangers surrounding them.

Keltor's heart brimmed with joy at the sight of his brother. Every instinct urged him to embrace Esendil, to ruffle his hair as he had always done to tease him, to revel openly in the relief of finding him alive and well. Yet, mindful of the ever-watchful eyes around them, Keltor restrained himself, determined not to draw unwanted attention to their reunion.

With a voice thick with emotion, Esendil spoke first, his words tinged with disbelief and the lingering ache of loss. "I thought you were dead. Mum said you'd died!"

Keltor nodded gently, understanding the pain his absence had caused. "I know, Ese. It's a long story, but we made it."

Esendil stole a quick glance at his brother, unable to resist the urge despite the risks. Keltor responded with a subtle lift of his eyebrow, a silent acknowledgement of Esendil's curiosity. In that fleeting moment, Keltor took in Esendil's appearance—the resemblance to their father was striking. Esendil's long, dark hair framed his face, and his slender build was just as Keltor remembered. Yet, as Esendil hefted the sledgehammer and brought it down with controlled force, Keltor couldn't help but notice the difference in his younger brother. There was a new strength in Esendil's arms, a testament to the hardships he had endured during their time apart.

Breaking the silence, Esendil asked quietly, "The princess?"

Keltor replied in a low voice, "She's alive, Ese. I was with her when we were captured, but they haven't realised who she is."

Esendil's voice was barely audible as he spoke, the weight of recent events hanging heavy in the air. "You know the King is dead?" he asked, the significance of the news clear in his tone.

Keltor gave a quiet nod of confirmation. "Yes," he replied, his own voice subdued. "I've seen mum."

A surge of emotion threatened to overwhelm Esendil as he fought the urge to turn and face his brother directly, anxious for any news about their mother. "Mum? Is she okay?" he inquired, his concern evident.

"She's fine," Keltor reassured him gently. "She is worried sick about you though."

A small smile flickered across Esendil's face as memories of his mother surfaced, bringing a moment of comfort amid the tension.

The thought of his sister quickly followed. "And our sister?" he asked, his voice laced with hope and uncertainty.

Keltor offered what comfort he could. "Mum said Anna is fine and working in Elvendon Castle for King Iwein."

"Bastard," Esendil muttered under his breath, his frustration evident as he brought the sledgehammer down with renewed

431

force. The harsh impact reverberated through the ground, a physical manifestation of his simmering anger and the tension in the air.

"Hey, it's okay. We've got a plan to take back Elvendon." Keltor's voice was steady, a quiet reassurance threaded through his words as he tried to ease the tension between them. He offered Esendil a brief, meaningful look, signalling the importance of secrecy and trust in these uncertain times.

Esendil, wary but desperate for hope, risked a quick glance at his brother. The unspoken understanding passed between them, a silent pact amid their captivity. Despite the danger, the possibility of reclaiming Elvendon sparked a glimmer of determination in Esendil's eyes, providing a momentary respite from the heaviness that surrounded them. A mixture of hope and disbelief as he spoke, his voice trembling slightly. "For real, you're going to get us out of here?" he asked, searching Keltor's face for reassurance.

Keltor nodded in response, the determination clear in his expression. He hesitated for a moment, biting his lower lip as he weighed whether to share the news about his best friend with Esendil. After a brief pause, he drew in a quiet breath and made the difficult decision to keep that information to himself for the time being. Keltor resolved that once they were safely away from this place, he would tell his brother the sad news.

Keltor glanced around cautiously before lowering his voice. "Which unit are you in?" he asked, referring to the numbering of the accommodation tents that dotted the camp.

Esendil, gripping the sledgehammer with both hands, replied, "Twenty-seven, at the back of the camp." As he spoke, he brought the sledgehammer down again, sending a deep vibration through the ground, a physical assertion of his presence and determination.

Keltor leaned in closer, his voice low and urgent. "Okay, look, no one must know we're brothers," he cautioned, his tone serious. "If they find out who I am, it will put you at risk." He glanced around, keeping a careful watch on the guards to ensure their conversation remained private. Satisfied that no one was paying attention, he continued, "I'll come tonight to tell you what's going on."

With that, Keltor began to walk away but paused, casting one last look over his shoulder to confirm they were still unnoticed. He called softly, using a familiar nickname, "Ese."

Esendil turned to meet his brother's gaze, and Keltor offered him a reassuring smile—a fleeting moment of warmth and understanding between them amid the tension and uncertainty of their captivity.

Keltor, keeping his voice low and urgent. "Dad's alive, I've found him. He's in a dungeon in Aranstream castle."

Shock surged through Esendil at his brother's words. He spun towards Keltor, his voice rising with disbelief. "What, are you freaking kidding me!"

Keltor immediately glanced at the guards, anxiety flaring in his eyes. "Shhh," he warned, his tone tense as he checked to ensure no one overheard them. "No, I'm not kidding. I'll explain everything tonight, but for now, just know this—I'm going to get him out, and I need your help."

Esendil nodded, his gaze dropping to the ground as he tried to process everything that had just been revealed. The tension in his body eased, and after a moment, he let out a small laugh—a sound that carried the weight of shock, relief, and happiness all at once. For the first time in a long while, hope flickered in his eyes.

"I'll see you later," Keltor said quietly, reassuring his brother with a final glance before moving back to his assigned area. Without wasting any time, he picked up a shovel and began the arduous task of digging and lifting granite into the waiting cart, slipping seamlessly back into the rhythm of work.

Esendil took a steadying breath. He hefted the sledgehammer, then brought it crashing down with even more force than before. Relief flooded through him—after everything, they had survived. For a moment, nothing else mattered. His brother was alive. His father was alive. A grin spread across his face; this was the best day he could remember.

Keltor stepped aside as the cart next to him rumbled away, its wheels grinding over the rough ground. Another horse and cart soon took its place, drawing up alongside him to receive the next load of granite. As he prepared to resume his work, a gruff voice rasped from behind him, breaking through the din of the quarry.

"Glad to see you're still alive, Protector."

Keltor glanced over his shoulder, recognising the voice of Commander Talbot. The Commander's face was badly swollen, a bruise spreading beneath one eye—a clear sign he'd recently suffered a brutal encounter.

"Commander," Keltor greeted, turning to face him. "It's good to see you, although you look..."

"Like I've been dragged through a battlefield," Talbot finished, managing a wry smile. He dabbed gingerly at the bruises, his gaze flickering briefly towards the guards' head. "Some of the guards here are very keen on reminding us who's in charge."

Keltor answered with a concerned nod, fully grasping the unspoken warning conveyed by Commander Talbot's glance. The atmosphere between them was tense, each man aware of the dangers that lurked nearby. Keltor discreetly looked past the Commander, checking on the head of the guards, who thankfully had his back turned and appeared to be paying them no attention.

Talbot tried to reassure Keltor, speaking in a low voice, "Don't worry about it, I can handle them." His words held a mixture of bravado and genuine concern, as he urged Keltor to share what he knew. "Please, Keltor, tell me, is the princess..." Talbot hesitated, the question hanging heavy in the air.

Keltor understood the depth of the Commander's anxiety and quietly finished the question for him. "Alive?" he asked, meeting Talbot's apprehensive gaze. The Commander nodded in response, hope and fear mingling in his expression as he awaited Keltor's answer.

Keltor offered a reassuring smile. "Yes, she is alive—and there's more. She has been crowned by an Elder of Elvendon."

The Commander's face lit up with unmistakable joy. "She's been crowned?" he repeated, seeking confirmation.

Keltor nodded, his voice low but steady. "Yes. Elder Marlow managed to escape the palace and is currently in hiding. He performed the ceremony himself. Kaitlin is now our Queen."

They both cast cautious glances around them, ensuring they were not being overheard before continuing their conversation. The Commander's voice was barely above a whisper as he ventured, "Where is she?"

Keltor, keeping his hands busy as he shovelled another load of granite into the cart, replied quietly, "It's best I don't tell you, for now."

The Commander's expression tightened, a hint of hurt in his tone as he said, "You don't trust me?"

Keltor shook his head gently, his voice barely above a whisper. "No, it's not that," he said, seeking to reassure the Commander. "The less you know for now, the safer she stays. I've seen what that bastard is capable of—what he can do to people. If you were ever captured and tortured for information, you might not have a choice but to give her up."

Talbot's reaction was immediate, his tone fierce with loyalty. "Keltor, I would never," he insisted, his eyes blazing with conviction. "I would die first."

Keltor clenched his jaw as he let out a deep breath, the weight of responsibility pressing heavily on his shoulders. The dim light flickered across his tense features, and for a moment, he listened to the distant clatter of granite echoing through the underground chamber, grounding himself in the present. He fixed Talbot with a steady gaze, his voice low and laced with quiet resolve. "Listen, I understand how you feel, and believe me—when the time is right, I promise I'll let you know. For now, though, keeping everyone in the dark is the only way to keep her safe."

The Commander took a moment to reflect, considering Keltor's words carefully. At length, he gave a slow, affirming nod. "You're right, of course," he conceded, though there was a trace of reluctance in his tone. The gravity of their situation was clear, but beneath it, a profound relief shone in his eyes. "I'm just so relieved that she's alive. Now, we have something to fight for."

Keltor regarded the Commander intently, his voice steady as he asked, "That's what I was hoping you would say. Will your men still fight for her?"

The Commander did not hesitate, his response immediate and unwavering. "Without question, they are all still loyal to Elvendon. Many have lost loved ones to King Iwein, and they all want revenge."

Keltor's gaze sharpened as he leaned closer to the Commander, lowering his voice to ensure their conversation remained private. "Commander, revenge can be dangerous, it makes a man do stupid things. Will they follow orders?" he pressed, the question hanging heavily in the air.

He watched the Commander carefully, searching for any sign of hesitation or uncertainty. Keltor's concern was clear: the intense desire for revenge against King Iwein could easily cloud judgement, leading even the most loyal soldiers to act recklessly and jeopardise their mission. The need for discipline and unwavering obedience was paramount if they were to succeed and keep Queen Kaitlin safe.

The Commander, recognising the seriousness of Keltor's concerns, took a moment to weigh his reply. He was acutely aware of the dangers that came with the desire for vengeance and the vital need to uphold discipline within the ranks—particularly now, with the new queen of Elvendon depending on them for protection.

As both men glanced about to ensure their conversation remained private, Keltor resumed his work, shovelling granite into the cart while the Commander kept a steady grip on the reins, maintaining control of the cart horse.

The Commander finally responded with quiet assurance. "Yes, they will," he affirmed. "Since the fall of Elvendon, it's been the only topic among us. We were uncertain how we would reclaim our home, or who would lead, given that the King and all his heirs are gone."

Keltor hesitated, admitting, "Well, I haven't exactly got a plan as such, that's what I was hoping you can help with."

The Commander gave a firm nod, signalling his willingness to assist. Sensing they needed to be precise, Keltor pressed further. "Commander, do you know if there are some men here—they would be tall, seven feet or thereabouts, and heavily built. Not elves, nor human."

The Commander paused, considering the description. After a thoughtful moment, he replied, "Yes, I think I know who you're talking about. They call them the giants. They're working on the other side of the camp, on the actual build itself. The Aranstream are making the most of their size and strength. I don't know much else about them. Why, do you know who they are?"

Keltor nodded, confirming his familiarity with the group the Commander had mentioned. "Yes," he began, "Kaitlin and I helped them when we were on the quest to find the Star. We travelled to their castle in the mountains about a week ago and discovered they had been captured. We were going to ask them for their help."

The Commander's interest was piqued. "So, you think we can count them in?" he asked, keen to know whether these giants might join their cause.

"Yes, I do," Keltor replied with confidence. "Somehow, I need to get over there and see them."

"If you can't, all prisoners return here to the camp at the end of the day. They will be over in G section." The Commander gestured to his right, prompting Keltor to follow his gaze. "It's the furthest tent, nearest to the tower." He was referring to the lookout towers, which stood at intervals along the camp's walls. Each tower was manned by soldiers armed with bows and arrows, their vigilant eyes sweeping the camp to ensure no one attempted to escape or cause trouble.

Keltor's focus shifted back to his task as he gripped the shovel and dug it into the pile of granite. With measured effort, he lifted another load and tossed it into the back of the cart, the stones clattering as they landed amongst the others.

Without meeting the Commander's eye, Keltor acknowledged the instruction. "Okay, thanks, I'll find them," he said, his attention remaining fixed on the job at hand, determined to follow through on the plan they had discussed.

"Hold," the Commander instructed, drawing the horse to a halt by pulling gently on the bridle. His tone was cautious, aware of the need for subtlety. "I should get this load back before the guard gets suspicious. When will we meet to discuss options?"

Keltor followed the Commander's gaze, noting the guard who had turned and was now watching them with narrowed eyes. With deliberate nonchalance, Keltor shovelled one last load of granite into the back of the cart, careful not to attract further attention.

Maintaining a low profile, Keltor replied softly, his words intended only for the Commander. "We'll catch up tomorrow," he murmured, stepping away from the cart to resume his work and avoid arousing suspicion.

The commander gave a slight dip of his head in agreement, signalling his understanding of the plan. Taking hold of the bridle, he began to lead the horse forward. The waggon groaned beneath the considerable weight of its load, its wooden frame creaking as the cargo shifted. After a few determined pulls, the wheels finally rolled into motion, crunching over the uneven ground of the camp.

Without delay, the commander climbed up and settled himself onto the bench seat at the front of the waggon. With a quick click of his tongue, he urged the horse onwards, and the pair set off, the waggon trailing steadily behind. Hardly had the commander departed when another horse and waggon appeared, making their way into the busy camp and adding to the constant flow of activity.

Keltor drew in a deep breath, a wave of relief washing over him at the thought that he had finally located the Commander and that their plan was progressing at last. This crucial step brought him that much nearer to rescuing Kaitlin from the clutches of Prince Keion. Reassured that matters were moving forward, he set to work once more, methodically shovelling granite into the back of the cart, each movement fuelled by the hope of success.

As the day faded and dusk settled over the camp, the prisoners were gathered and marched off to the wash house. Keltor found himself standing beneath the icy stream of the communal shower, feeling the cold-water cascade down his body and wash away the sweat and grime of hours spent labouring. The chill made him shudder, but he lingered, letting the water run over his face and body. He gave a heavy sigh, then parted his lips to drink a little of the water, hoping it might soothe him, even just for a moment.

Yet, his mind would not rest. Worry gnawed at him relentlessly—Kaitlin was never far from his thoughts. He questioned whether he should have confided her whereabouts to the Commander, but the risk of the prince learning her identity filled him with dread. Repeatedly, he wondered if he should have insisted that she stay behind with the others at the woodsman's cottage. Despite this, Keltor knew deep down that it was not his place to make such demands of her. She was her own remarkable person, independent and strong-willed. It was precisely this spirit that made him love her so deeply.

Keltor's moment of reflection was interrupted by a voice beside him, pulling him from his thoughts as another prisoner moved beneath the neighbouring shower head. Zeb's arrival was unassuming but direct, his tone betraying a sense of urgency.

"Did you find him?" Zeb asked, not bothering to conceal his curiosity.

Keltor, keeping his gaze averted, responded simply. "Yes." His answer was brief, offering no detail and maintaining the air of discretion that had become second nature.

Zeb's eyes wandered over Keltor's physique, taking in the tapestry of tattoos, scars, and the heavy muscles that spoke of a life lived in conflict. After a moment's hesitation, Zeb voiced his observation. "You've been in a lot of fights?"

Meeting Zeb's gaze only briefly, Keltor nodded with a casual air. "A few." His response was understated, designed to close the topic without inviting further questions.

Undeterred, Zeb pressed on, his eagerness unable to be masked. "So, is there a plan?"

The exchange hung in the air, loaded with unspoken tension and the weight of shared hope, as both men quietly measured one another before the conversation moved forward.

"Not yet," Keltor responded as he grabbed his towel and tied it around his waist. His answer was measured, betraying nothing of his true intentions or the uncertainty that lingered in his mind.

"I'll let you know when I know more," he added, making it clear that he would share information only when it was safe to do so. With that, Keltor stepped out of the shower cubicle, distancing himself from further questioning. Trust was a precious commodity in the camp, and he wasn't ready to place it in anyone else's hands—not entirely, at least.

He slipped on a clean pair of trousers. The prisoners had been issued three sets of trousers and tunics, a sparse allowance that required constant care if one wished to maintain any semblance of comfort. After dressing, Keltor made his way over to a nearby sink. He turned on the tap and filled the basin with cold water, rolling up his sleeves before submerging the dirty work clothes he had just removed. The camp demanded that everyone wash their own garments; anyone who neglected this simple routine was left with no choice but to wear their clothes soiled and unwashed.

Keltor scrubbed the fabric methodically, working the grime out of the worn seams until at last he was satisfied. He rinsed his tunic thoroughly, wringing out the excess water with practised hands. Just as he finished this task, Zeb appeared beside him. Keltor cast a cautious glance over his shoulder, instinctively checking that no one was within earshot who might overhear their conversation.

"You can trust me, you know," Zeb said quietly, his tone earnest as he sought Keltor's reassurance. Keltor met his gaze, weighing the sincerity in Zeb's words.

"Yeah, I know, Zeb, but like I said, there is nothing to say yet. We need to be careful. I know you want to get out and rescue your wife, but if we make a mistake now, it could all be over."

Keltor spoke quietly, his voice low and measured as he lifted his hand and placed it reassuringly on Zeb's bare arm. The gesture was meant to convey both caution and support, a subtle reminder of the gravity of their situation.

"I promise, when the time comes, you will know," Keltor continued, offering Zeb the reassurance he desperately needed, while maintaining the boundaries of trust and secrecy that the camp demanded.

Zeb nodded his head, accepting Keltor's words and the silent pact they now shared.

"Okay, but just so you know, I will do anything to get us out of here, and to put the Queen of Elvendon back on the throne." Zeb's voice was quiet but determined, his conviction clear as he spoke of his unwavering loyalty and desperation for freedom. The prospect of restoring the Queen offered him a glimmer of hope amid the darkness of their captivity.

Keltor immediately raised a finger to his lips, scanning the room with caution. His eyes darted about, searching for any sign of eavesdroppers who might overhear their dangerous conversation. He responded in a firm, measured tone, "Never mention her, the risk is too high. If the King even suspects she is alive, he will wipe through Elvendon looking for her and more of our people will die. Do you understand?" His words carried a weight of authority and fear, making his meaning unmistakably clear to Zeb.

Zeb's shoulders drooped as he listened, the gravity of Keltor's warning settling heavily upon him. "Of course, I'm sorry, it's just, well you know. The thought there could be an end to all this." He spoke with quiet regret, his hope for escape and restoration nearly overshadowed by the danger their dreams entailed.

Keltor nodded, his expression softening just slightly. "I understand, but Zeb keep it quiet, okay," he pressed in a low voice, underscoring the critical need for secrecy. The exchange left both men with a silent understanding: hope could not come at the cost of greater peril, and even whispered ambitions must be guarded closely in the camp.

Zeb nodded in understanding, acknowledging Keltor's caution. Keltor gathered his clothes, the tension still lingering between them after their hushed conversation.

"I'll see you back in the tent, Zeb," Keltor said quietly, making his way out of the shower block. As he walked back towards the tent, his mind was troubled by thoughts of Zeb. Although Keltor

441

was confident that Zeb was not a traitor, he could not ignore the risk that, in a moment of carelessness, Zeb might let something slip. The stakes were simply too high for any mistakes.

Determined to prevent any accidental disclosure, Keltor resolved to keep Zeb close. The very idea of having to take drastic action—breaking Zeb's neck to protect Kaitlin—was abhorrent to him, yet if it came to a choice between Zeb's life and Kaitlin's safety, Keltor knew what he would do. The burden of secrecy weighed heavily, and the necessity of vigilance was clearer than ever.

As he hung his wet clothes up on the wooden rack behind his bed, Keltor's eyes drifted over to Mikelle, who lay on his side with the cover pulled up and over his head. The stillness of Mikelle's form struck Keltor as odd, prompting a sense of unease. Determined to check on his companion, Keltor walked over and called out, "Hey," while giving Mikelle a gentle nudge. Despite the attempt to rouse him, Mikelle did not stir. Concerned by this lack of response, Keltor leaned in and asked, "Mikelle, are you okay?" His voice carried an edge of worry, as the silence from Mikelle deepened Keltor's apprehension.

As Zeb made his way up the aisle between the beds towards his own, he paused and called out, "What's up?" sensing that something was amiss.

"Something's wrong," Keltor replied, and his hand cautiously took hold of Mikelle's blanket and slowly he pulled it back.

"Oh, shit," Keltor cursed as his eyes took in the gruesome sight. The sharp metallic tang of blood filled the air, the vivid crimson seeping across the sheet. He dropped the blanket as though it had burned him. His breath hitched painfully in his throat, as he realised the poor man had taken his own life.

Sensing the urgency in Keltor's actions, Zeb hurried over, concern etched across his face. "What is it?" Zeb asked, his voice tight with worry as he moved quickly to Keltor's side.

Keltor's voice was grim as he confirmed, "He's dead," his tone heavy with sorrow. The weight of the statement hung in the air, echoing through the tense silence of the tent.

442

Zeb stared at him in disbelief, his shock evident. "Dead? What do you mean he's dead? I saw him in the shower block earlier," he protested. Zeb shook his head, still struggling to process what he was seeing.

"Yeah, I know—so did I," Keltor said, his voice edged with grim certainty, "but believe me, he is as dead as a doornail."

Confused and alarmed, Zeb stammered, "A door what?"

"Nothing, it doesn't matter," Keltor replied, dismissing the question as unimportant given the gravity of the situation.

Zeb's distress deepened as he pressed for an explanation, "How, I mean, what killed him?"

Keltor answered sombrely, "I would say he slit his own throat."

Zeb stared at the scene in disbelief; his face drained of colour as the reality set in. He muttered, almost as if speaking to himself, "By the spirits, the poor man." The shock of Mikelle's death seemed to hit him all at once, and for a moment Zeb looked as though he might faint. His hands shook as he tried to process what he was seeing, the magnitude of it overwhelming. He struggled to understand, his voice trembling with emotion as he continued, "Why would he do that? I mean, I know it's bad here, but hell, to kill yourself?" Zeb's words hung in the air, echoing the despair and confusion that gripped everyone in the tent. His sorrow and incredulity were palpable, reflecting the deep sense of loss that Mikelle's death had brought upon them all.

Keltor's voice was low and sombre as he explained, "Aranstream soldiers killed his wife, I guess he felt he had nothing left to live for. I'll go and get someone." With those words, he turned towards the exit of the tent, his steps heavy with grief. As he left, a deep sigh escaped him, laden with empathy for the man's suffering. The image of Mikelle—utterly broken by the loss of his wife—haunted Keltor. He understood only too well the depth of sorrow that could drive someone to such despair, for if anything ever happened to Kaitlin, he doubted he would fare any better.

Half an hour later, Zeb and Keltor stood silently, watching as Mikelle's body was carried out of the tent. His form was shrouded in his blankets, the finality of his death made even starker by the

443

quiet efficiency of the men who bore him away. The atmosphere in the tent was oppressive, a heavy silence settling over the group as the other prisoners observed the scene unfolding before them. Each man struggled with his own thoughts, the loss weighing on them all. Though no words were spoken, their faces reflected the shared shock and confusion, a silent understanding passing between them—a collective grief that was almost palpable. Unasked questions hung thick in the air, as everyone tried to comprehend the tragedy that had just occurred in their midst.

Keltor placed a reassuring hand on Zeb's upper arm. "Come on," he urged quietly. "We'd better go and get something to eat before we get locked up for the night." There was a sense of practicality in Keltor's tone, an understanding that, despite the sorrow, life must continue—at least for now.

Zeb hesitated, his face drawn and pale. "I don't know that I feel much like eating," he admitted, the weight of the evening's events clearly pressing heavily upon him. Nevertheless, he fell into step beside Keltor, following him out of the tent and into the dimming light.

"Yeah, me neither," Keltor replied, his voice low but firm. "But we need to keep our strength up. There's nothing we can do for Mikelle, but we need to be ready to fight when the time comes." He spoke with quiet conviction, a reminder that their trials were far from over, and that survival now depended on their resilience and preparation.

After they had finished their meal, Keltor and Zeb made their way back to their tent. By this time, the tent was crowded with men, each one settling in for the night. As Keltor and Zeb walked between the rows of beds, they nodded curtly in acknowledgement to the others around them, quietly greeting those they passed. The atmosphere was thick with tension—subdued conversations and low whispers floated through the air, most of them concerning the tragic fate of Mikelle.

Keltor kept himself apart from the discussions, choosing not to become involved in the speculation and rumours circulating among the men. Zeb, however, found himself at the centre of attention, taking great satisfaction in retelling the evening's grim events to anyone who would listen. While Zeb recounted the story, Keltor watched him carefully, his expression unreadable. He felt a tentative reassurance growing inside him; despite Zeb's enthusiasm for sharing details, he was careful never to mention anything that might expose Keltor, their escape plan, or Kaitlin. This discretion eased Keltor's concerns about Zeb, and he began to feel a measure of trust toward him.

As Keltor glanced down the line of beds, his thoughts shifted to the task at hand. He knew he needed to find a way to touch one of the guards without arousing suspicion. He sat in quiet contemplation, considering how best to achieve this, when a new distraction emerged. One of the men, visibly irritated by the ongoing noise and conversation, sat scowling at the others. After repeatedly shouting at everyone to be quiet, his patience finally wore thin.

On his third outburst, the tent flap was suddenly thrown open and a guard entered, abruptly ending the commotion.

"Shut up, the lot of you!" the guard yelled, his sword in his hand, banging it angrily against the wooden bed frames as he marched down between the rows of beds. Each man immediately fell silent. The tension in the tent mounted as the guard approached the area where Keltor and Zeb—who had quickly returned to his bed—were situated. Keltor, careful not to draw attention to himself, murmured a quiet incantation under his breath.

As the atmosphere in the tent grew even more strained, a subtle surge of magical energy pulsed through the air. The disturbance, though minor, was enough to affect the objects nearby. A broom, propped up beside Mikelle's bed, suddenly wobbled and toppled over with a clatter. The unexpected noise startled the guard, who spun round in alarm.

In his confusion, the guard lost his grip on his sword—the weapon slipped from his hands, skittering noisily across the floor. Unsteady, he stumbled and fell to the ground. The sword slid to a halt directly in front of Keltor's bed, instantly drawing the eyes of everyone present and intensifying the suspense within the tent.

Keltor rose quietly from his bed and made his way over to retrieve the sword, which had slid to a stop in front of him. As he picked it up, the guard—who had just scrambled to his feet after his earlier blunder—fixed him with a wary stare, his expression shifting the moment he saw Keltor holding the weapon.

"Now?" Zeb whispered, the tension in his voice barely contained.

"No," Keltor replied softly, his tone calm and deliberate. He held the point of the sword downwards, making sure there was no misunderstanding, and offered it to the guard. Purposefully, Keltor kept his grip on the pommel so that, as the guard snatched the sword from him, his hand brushed against Keltor's knuckles in the exchange.

The guard shot Keltor a suspicious look but said nothing. "Go to sleep, now," he barked, his voice laced with irritation as he strode back towards the entrance of the tent. "Any more nonsense and you'll all go in the pit," he threatened before disappearing outside, letting the tent flap fall shut with a heavy thud behind him.

The men remained silent, thoroughly cowed by the guard's warning. None of them wished to be sent to the pit—a place infamous among the prisoners for its impenetrable darkness, crawling with spiders and littered with things long dead. The mere mention of it was enough to quell any further disturbance.

Suppressing a smile, Keltor allowed himself a fleeting moment of satisfaction. The brief contact with the guard's pommel had been all he required. With his objective discreetly achieved, he made his way back to his bed.

"I suppose we'd better hit the hay," Keltor remarked, climbing into his bed with deliberate casualness.

Zeb, still a little bewildered by the unfamiliar phrase, looked over at him. "Hit what?" he asked, confusion clear in his voice as he too settled into his bed.

"Nothing," Keltor replied, turning away from Zeb to face the now empty bed beside him. As he did, a quiet smile played on his lips, hidden from the others by the dimness of the tent.

Once the camp had quietened and the steady rhythm of breathing signalled that everyone was asleep, Keltor set his plan in motion. He carefully arranged several pieces of clothing beneath his blanket, shaping them to mimic the outline of a sleeping body. This makeshift decoy would, at a glance, convince any passerby that he remained in his bed.

Moving with deliberate silence, Keltor crept towards the entrance of the tent. Rather than attempting to evade the guards stationed outside, he prepared himself to use magic. Drawing upon his abilities, he summoned a shimmering enchantment that rippled across his form as he slipped through the tent flap. In an instant, his appearance transformed—he now mirrored the guard who had earlier tripped and fallen, down to the smallest detail.

As Keltor emerged from the tent, he was immediately confronted by a guard stationed on the opposite side. The guard's eyes narrowed with suspicion as he demanded, "Hey, when did you go in there?"

Keltor, maintaining the guise of the guard who had previously tripped and fallen, responded in a firm and authoritative manner. "Exactly, you're supposed to be watching this tent. Get your head out your arse and keep watch properly. I swear if any of them escape it's going to be your head and not mine!" His voice perfectly mimicked that of the other man, leaving no room for doubt.

The guard, visibly startled and alarmed by Keltor's reprimand, quickly nodded in panic. "Yes, sir, I'm sorry," he stammered, his tone betraying his anxiety as he hurriedly apologised.

Without hesitation, Keltor made his way directly to his brother's tent. Standing outside was a solitary guard. Keltor gathered his composure, drew a deep breath, and approached the guard with confident strides.

"You're on break," Keltor announced boldly.

The guard looked up, surprised by the statement. "What, already? I thought I still had another hour," he responded with confusion.

447

Maintaining the authoritative tone, Keltor replied, "Look, I don't make the orders; I just follow them. Do you want a break tonight or not?"

The guard hesitated for a moment before admitting, "Yeah, actually, I'm busting for a piss."

"Well, go then," Keltor insisted, fixing the guard with a stern look. "Half an hour, that's it. I need to be back at another tent to relieve them."

The guard nodded quickly, not wanting to test Keltor's patience, and scurried off into the darkness, eager to seize his unexpected break.

Keltor slipped into the tent with practiced silence. He carefully navigated around the beds, mindful not to disturb any of the other occupants. Finally, he located his sleeping brother. Keltor knelt beside him, then gently but firmly placed a hand over his brother's mouth. As Esendil awoke, panic seized him—he struggled fiercely against the hand pressed to his mouth. For a split second, fear gripped his heart as he remembered the rumours whispered among the men: some guards had been known to prey on the younger ones. The thought that the guard had come for him sent a cold wave of terror through his body. Sensing his brother's alarm, Keltor quickly whispered in his own voice, "Shush, it's me, Keltor." His familiar tone aimed to soothe Ese, but the fear persisted and the struggle continued, panic rising within Esendil as he tried to make sense of the situation.

"Ese, stop!" Keltor hissed, still careful to maintain his disguise and not reveal his true appearance. The urgency in his voice was unmistakable, and at last, Esendil recognised the voice of his brother. He ceased his resistance, his body relaxing as the realisation dawned.

Slowly, Keltor withdrew his hand from Esendil's mouth, but raised a warning finger to his lips, signalling for silence. Their eyes met in the dim light, and Esendil, still shaken, whispered in a panicked breath, "Who the hell are you?"

Keltor responded quietly but with his usual brotherly affection, "It's me, Keltor, you numbskull." To reassure him further, he reached out and ruffled Esendil's hair in the familiar, teasing way he always had, a simple gesture that brought a measure of comfort to the tense reunion.

"What the hell, Keltor, you look like a guard," Ese whispered, his eyes wide with disbelief and his body still trembling from the unexpected fright. He could scarcely process the sight before him, his brother standing there in the uniform of the very men Ese feared most.

Keltor, remaining calm yet alert, quickly glanced around the tent to ensure none of the other occupants had stirred or were eavesdropping on their conversation. Satisfied they were not being overheard, he leaned in closer and spoke in a low, urgent tone. "Ese, there's no time to explain at the moment, but I'm a wizard, and I can shapeshift—but only for a while, so you need to listen." His words were hurried but carried a weight of authority that Ese recognised.

Ese's confusion only deepened, his brow furrowing as he tried to comprehend what Keltor was saying. "What?" he replied in a whisper, his voice tinged with incredulity. "You're a wizard? What, like magic and stuff?" The revelation seemed impossible, but the seriousness in Keltor's eyes forced him to consider it. Instinctively, Ese began to sit up, desperate for answers, but Keltor placed a firm hand on his chest, gently yet insistently pressing him back down onto the makeshift bed.

Keltor quickly pressed his brother back down onto the bed. "No, stay down—it's less obvious," he whispered urgently. "Yes, I am a wizard, and I promise I'll explain everything later. But right now, you must listen to me. After I've made plans with the commander, you and I are getting out of here first. Before we do anything else, we need to get Dad out of Aranstream dungeon. I can't risk anyone discovering my real identity and putting his life at risk."

Ese, glancing anxiously down the row of beds to check that no one was listening, whispered back, "How the hell do we get out? There are armed guards everywhere."

449

Keltor leaned in, his voice low and urgent. "Leave that to me, but we must move quickly, Ese. The queen could be in danger, so we can't afford to wait around. Tomorrow, if all goes according to plan, we'll leave the following night." His eyes were intent, impressing upon Esendil the gravity and haste of their situation.

A surge of excitement coursed through Esendil as he realised his escape might finally be at hand. The prospect of leaving behind the nightmare of captivity filled him with hope, and he nodded in eager agreement.

Keltor continued, lowering his voice even further. "I'll try to give you a signal if I see you before then. Watch for me to nod and place my hand over my heart—that'll be your cue." Esendil nodded, committing the gesture to memory.

Before slipping away, Keltor fixed his brother with a serious look. "Take care of yourself, Ese, and keep your head down. Don't do anything to draw attention. We'll get through this together."

"I will," Esendil agreed, and his hand lifted to his. Keltor grasped it, they both squeezed and then released hands.

"Stay safe, and keep out of trouble," Keltor whispered one more time, and Esendil watched his brother as he slipped quietly away, and out of the tent.

Keltor lingered for a short while, waiting for the guard to return to his post. Once the man appeared, he nodded his thanks towards Keltor, resuming his vigilant watch outside the tent. Seizing the moment, Keltor moved swiftly back towards his own tent, conscious of the need to avoid drawing attention. The guard, now on high alert after having previously been caught off guard by the head guard, was determined not to make the same mistake again. His posture was rigid, eyes scanning the area with renewed focus, making Keltor's task of slipping inside undetected even more challenging.

Keltor glanced over at a cluster of barrels stacked outside one of the nearby tents. Another guard was stationed at that post, standing watch. With a subtle movement, Keltor raised his hand and muttered a quick incantation under his breath. A faint pulse of magic rippled through the air, directed at the barrels. They shifted

450

slightly, rocking back and forth, but did not cause enough commotion to distract the guards.

Determined to create a more convincing diversion, Keltor gave a slight, more forceful lift of his hand, channelling extra power into the spell. This time, the barrels toppled over with a loud crash, clattering noisily across the ground and drawing immediate attention.

The guard outside Keltor's tent reacted at once, drawing his sword and rushing towards the source of the disturbance. The second guard, equally alert, joined him as both hurried to investigate the unexpected commotion. While the two guards were distracted and occupied with the fallen barrels, Keltor seized the opportunity to slip quietly back inside the tent, unnoticed.

He paused briefly in the darkness, his senses alert to every sound outside the tent. With utmost care, he quietly recited an incantation, feeling the subtle shift as he resumed his original form. Moving cautiously between the beds so as not to disturb anyone, he returned to his own place. There, he removed the garments he had used as a decoy, folding them neatly, before slipping beneath his blanket. The tension that had gripped him finally began to ease; he drew a relieved breath, trying to steady his nerves. Eyes closed, he let exhaustion wash over him. Tomorrow would mark the beginning of the plan to reclaim Elvendon, a prospect which filled him with equal parts excitement and terror.

Chapter Twenty
Aranstream Encampment

Kaitlin was awake at the break of dawn, compelled to don the same ghastly pink dress she had worn the previous day. She moved quietly through the chambers, her every step a reminder of her role as she prepared to serve the prince his breakfast. The atmosphere in the room was tense and formal; no one else was seated at the table, and the other servants lingered at the edges, their eyes averted, feigning indifference yet clearly alert to every word and gesture.

As Kaitlin poured more wine into the prince's goblet, he regarded her intently. "Are you sure we've never met before?" he queried, his gaze fixed on her as if searching for a familiar memory. Kaitlin's heart raced and she hastily composed herself, offering a curtsey as she replied, "No, my Lord." Despite her attempt at composure, she could not help but swallow nervously, troubled by the thought that she might be reminding him of her sister—the very sister whose execution he had ordered.

The prince continued to observe her, his tone thoughtful. "Hmm," he murmured, not taking his eyes off her for a moment. After a long pause, he pushed his plate away, a silent indication that he had finished his meal. As he rose from his chair, the servants in the room, including Kaitlin, all dropped to their knees in a gesture of deference.

With deliberate authority, Prince Keion moved around his chair and placed his hand firmly atop Kaitlin's head. His gesture was neither gentle nor affectionate—rather, it underscored his expectation of obedience.

452

With a tone that brooked no argument, Prince Keion issued his directive. "You will come with me today," he instructed, his words carrying the weight of royal authority as he turned and strode away, expecting immediate compliance.

Kaitlin's response was swift and deferential. "Yes, my Lord," she replied, her voice steady despite the nerves fluttering beneath the surface. She held a deep, submissive curtsey, ensuring her posture conveyed the utmost respect and obedience required in the prince's presence.

Kaitlin glanced up and watched as Prince Keion left the room. The pressing need to obtain the amulet weighed heavily on her mind; it was so tantalisingly close, practically within reach. All she needed was a swift, decisive action to snatch it from his neck. Yet, uncertainty held her back—she had no idea how sturdy the chain was, nor whether she would be able to break it free in a single motion. Frustration and anger surged within her, and she clenched her fists, struggling to maintain her composure as the opportunity slipped away, at least for now.

A while later, Kaitlin sat quietly within the open horse-drawn carriage, surrounded by four other women who made up Prince Keion's entourage. Kaitlin's gaze settled on Prince Keion riding ahead. His posture was impeccable; his head held high in a manner that radiated royal pride. She could not help but think how arrogant he appeared, his every movement exuding self-importance.

Clutched in Kaitlin's hands were a jug of wine and the prince's silver goblet—her role was clear: she was there solely to serve him, ready at a moment's notice should he desire a drink. But as the carriage rolled on, she suddenly drew in a sharp breath, realising their destination. They were heading straight for the encampment. A surge of hope fluttered in her chest; perhaps, just perhaps, she would catch a glimpse of Keltor among those within the camp.

The group came to a stop in front of the bridge. At this point, Prince Keion and his entourage dismounted from their horses, their movements coordinated and deliberate. Kaitlin exited the waggon with the other women, moving swiftly to join the prince as protocol dictated.

As Kaitlin surveyed her surroundings, she took in the scale of the encampment. Tall wooden fences encircled the area, providing a formidable barrier. Guards were stationed atop each tower, their vigilant eyes scanning the camp and monitoring every activity beyond the perimeter.

A wave of nervousness swept over Kaitlin. The prospect of encountering someone from the palace on the other side filled her with unease. She questioned whether, if recognised, they would have the discretion to remain silent. This uncertainty left her feeling exposed and vulnerable as she continued toward the prince.

Escorted by a formidable contingent of twenty armed soldiers, the group moved purposefully through the imposing gates and into the heart of the encampment. Kaitlin's eyes darted about, taking in every detail of her surroundings. The area was scattered with makeshift camps, each one marked by rows of tents that appeared to serve as temporary lodgings for the soldiers stationed there.

Directly ahead, the quarry came into view, its workers labouring tirelessly to extract rock and stone. These materials were destined for the construction of King Iwein's new castle, a project that loomed large over all those present. As Kaitlin surveyed the scene, a wave of unease washed over her. The question lingered in her mind: was he here?

Kaitlin watched the Elvendon men as they toiled, their arms swinging pickaxes and sledgehammers to break apart the unforgiving stone. Her eyes lingered over each figure, searching intently for any sign of her husband amongst the labourers. As she and the prince's procession passed by, the workers halted their efforts and, with visible reluctance, dropped to their knees in a gesture of respect. The sight ignited a surge of anger within Kaitlin; it was unbearable to witness her own people compelled to kneel before a ruler she regarded as a tyrant.

The prince came to a halt and turned his attention to a man clad in an Aranstream uniform. After a brief exchange, the man bowed respectfully and motioned for the prince to follow him. Without hesitation, Prince Keion walked deeper into the heart of the camp, accompanied by his guide.

The heat of the day pressed down relentlessly, the sunlight beating upon the backs of the men who toiled in the open quarry. Not a single tree remained—every scrap of shade had been stripped away, leaving only bare, sun-baked earth littered with rubble and jagged stones.

As they made their way further, the prince halted once more. He issued a concise instruction to one of his guards, who listened intently before nodding in acknowledgement. Without delay, the guard turned and began to make his way in Kaitlin's direction, carrying out the prince's command.

As the guard approached, he spoke with authority, "His Highness requests a drink." Without hesitation, Kaitlin acknowledged the request. "Okay," she replied, and promptly followed the guard as he led her back towards Prince Keion.

Upon reaching the prince, Kaitlin carefully poured wine into the silver goblet. Prince Keion observed her with a frown, unsettled by her presence for reasons he could not quite explain. Maintaining her composure, Kaitlin handed the goblet to him, her head bowed in deference. The prince considered her in silence for a moment before accepting the drink. He took a sip, then turned his attention back to his ongoing conversation with the soldier, leaving Kaitlin to retreat quietly to her place.

The prince and his entourage paused to review the progress at the quarry. Together, they methodically assessed the volume of stone that had been extracted for the castle construction, ensuring that the output met the stringent requirements and that all work was proceeding according to the schedule before the prince would relay his findings to the King.

As Kaitlin lingered nearby, her gaze drifted past the ongoing evaluation. Suddenly, her attention was seized by a figure amongst the workers, and she experienced a profound shock of recognition.

Keltor stood out starkly in the harsh sunlight, his bare torso revealing well-defined muscles that flexed with each forceful swing of his sledgehammer. He had discarded his shirt, knotting it at his waist, and even from her vantage point, Kaitlin could see the sweat streaming down his body as he laboured. Her pulse quickened uncontrollably, a wave of emotion overtaking her as she silently implored him to glance her way.

Keltor brought his sledgehammer down for what felt like the hundredth time that morning, exhaustion and heat pressing upon him with each swing. Sweat dripped down his brow as he toiled alongside the other workers, the relentless labour taking its toll. Suddenly, one of the men nudged him, drawing his attention away from his task.

"Look," the man whispered, nodding behind Keltor. His eyes hinted at something—or someone—significant. Keltor turned to see for himself.

There, unmistakable in his regal attire and flanked by soldiers, stood Prince Keion. The prince's presence commanded attention, his bearing setting him apart from the men who worked the quarry. But it wasn't simply the prince that caught Keltor's eye; amidst the royal entourage, he caught sight of Kaitlin. The sight of her made his heart leap, relief flooding through him at the knowledge that she was safe. A genuine smile broke across his face, his earlier fatigue momentarily forgotten as he gazed at her from across the worksite.

As Prince Keion continued his conversation with the soldier, a flicker of curiosity prompted him to glance back at Kaitlin. He expected to find her attention fixed upon him, awaiting further instruction or acknowledgement. To his surprise, her gaze was not directed at the prince at all. Instead, she looked beyond him, her eyes searching the crowd with unwavering focus.

Intrigued, Keion followed the trajectory of her gaze and soon discovered its destination. Amidst the labourers, he saw the man she was looking at—her brother, unmistakable even at a distance. Yet, as Keion studied Kaitlin's expression, a pang of unease struck him. The look in her eyes was not the simple affection one might reserve for a sibling. Rather, her gaze was suffused with love and longing, a depth of emotion that could not be easily explained away.

Keion bit his lip, silently pondering the meaning behind the exchange. The intensity of Kaitlin's feelings was clear, and the prince found himself unsettled by the realisation, uncertain of the true nature of the bond between the two.

Commander Talbot stormed over to Keltor, his expression thunderous with disbelief and frustration.

"You've got to be kidding me!" Talbot growled, his voice low but fierce as he glanced towards Kaitlin. "That's your idea of keeping her safe? For heaven's sake, Keltor, the Prince has her!"

Keltor met the commander's glare, his own voice tense with regret and defensiveness. "Yes, all right, I should have mentioned it, but I had no idea she would end up here," he muttered under his breath, the weight of the situation evident in his tone.

Talbot shook his head in exasperation. "You let her get captured! What on earth were you thinking, Keltor? She should be miles away from this place, not in the hands of the prince!"

"Commander, you don't know her. If Kaitlin decides to act, she will do so—nothing can stop her," Keltor stated, his voice laced with conviction. He hesitated for a moment, then continued, "That's precisely why she's my wife, and why I bonded with her. Her spirit and will is so different from other Elvendon women, and I love her for that reason. I will not take that from her." The admission slipped out almost unintentionally.

Commander Talbot's reaction was instant and dramatic; his eyes widened in shock; disbelief etched across his face. "You've bonded with the Queen?" he exclaimed, unable to fully process the revelation as he spoke.

Keltor nodded. "Yes," he confirmed, a smile tugging at his lips as he watched the Commander struggle to comprehend the gravity of the situation.

Still reeling, Commander Talbot stared at Keltor, astonishment evident in his tone. "Are you telling me you're our fricking King?"

"Yes, Commander Talbot, I am your king," Keltor stated, his voice calm and resolute. He met the commander's gaze directly, his expression unwavering as he confirmed the truth. "Do you have a problem with that?"

Commander Talbot's brow furrowed as he searched Keltor's face, his eyes flickering briefly to Kaitlin before returning to Keltor. The weight of the revelation was evident in his tense posture. Finally, he shook his head and replied, "No, if the queen has chosen you, then so be it." His words were steady, but a hint of uncertainty lingered in his tone.

Keltor watched the commander's reaction closely, noting the hesitation in his manner. "Commander, I know I am not a prince," Keltor continued, his voice earnest, "but trust me, we were bonded legally. I have concealed our bonding and hidden our royal marks to protect us." His words hung in the air, carrying both reassurance and an unspoken request for loyalty.

The commander eyed Keltor intently, his curiosity piqued. "By whom were you bonded?" he asked, his tone quiet but serious.

"Elder Marlow," Keltor replied, meeting the commander's gaze directly.

A faint smile crept across the commander's face. "That old man is still alive," he remarked, a hint of fondness in his voice.

Keltor nodded. "Yes, he is hiding on the other side of the bridge."

"Hmm," the commander mused thoughtfully, his eyes searching Keltor's for answers. After a moment, he added, "I always knew there was something different about you, Keltor. I didn't know what it was, but just something."

Keltor responded with a gentle smile, sensing the commander's gradual acceptance of his new role. He could see the shift in the commander's attitude as he began to come to terms with the revelation that Keltor was indeed the king.

"Okay," the commander said at last. He glanced around, ensuring that no one was watching them, and then bowed his head in a gesture of respect. "My king," he said solemnly. "We will follow your command."

A broad grin spread across Keltor's face. He reached out, tapping the commander's arm lightly in gratitude. "Thank you," he said sincerely, his relief and appreciation unmistakable.

Xxx

"Refill my goblet," the prince said suddenly, his tone sharp and unexpected. For a moment, Kaitlin did not register his words, her mind elsewhere until he repeated the order, his voice louder and more commanding. "Woman, I said refill my goblet!" The abruptness of his demand jolted her, and she snapped to attention.

"My Lord, I'm sorry," Kaitlin murmured, her voice trembling as she hurried to refill his goblet. She kept her gaze downcast, but beneath her lowered lashes, her mind raced. The cool metal of the wine jug felt oddly heavy in her hand, matching the weight pressing on her chest. As she leaned forward to pour, her eyes flickered to the prince's neck—and there it was: the amulet, glinting in the sunlight. Her heart hammered against her ribs and for a moment she struggled to steady her breathing. Fear and hope collided inside her, tightening her throat. If she could just reach out, snatch the amulet away, perhaps—just perhaps—she could end all of this tonight. Would Keltor be ready? Could she risk everything in this single, desperate moment? Her mind whirled with uncertainty and dread, but the possibility of freedom blazed sharp and bright. Every muscle in her body tensed as she weighed her next move, knowing that one wrong step could mean disaster—for her and for everyone depending on her.

Keltor observed Kaitlin closely as she attended to the prince, refilling his goblet. Anger surged within him at the prince's lingering, possessive gaze, a silent fury that tightened his grip. Then, Kaitlin made a move that caught Keltor entirely off guard— she lifted her hand and contacted the prince's arm. The gesture was shocking; in the world they inhabited, it was an unspoken law that no one should ever touch a member of the royal family unless expressly invited. Keltor's heart pounded as he watched, fully aware of the gravity and potential consequences of her bold action.

459

Prince Keion's gaze bore down on her as Kaitlin's hand lifted and made contact with his arm. His initial reaction was a surge of anger—an urge to strike her for the brazen act of touching him without permission, a grave breach of royal protocol. Yet, to his surprise, rather than recoiling in outrage, he found himself oddly drawn to the sensation. The unexpected intimacy of her touch unsettled him, stirring a conflicting mix of indignation and intrigue within. For a fleeting moment, the usual instinct to punish her was tempered by a curious appreciation, leaving him uncertain how to proceed.

"My Lord," Kaitlin murmured, her words soft yet deliberate as she raised her eyes to meet the prince's. Her features shifted into a provocative smile, the kind that held both invitation and challenge. She wished desperately that she could use her magic to charm him, bend his will to hers just for a fleeting moment. It had been enough with Aragon, briefly, before he had realised her intent—but all she needed now was a second or two. If she could distract the prince, just long enough, she might be able to snatch the amulet from around his neck and change everything.

Keltor watched in horror as the scene unfolded before him. His instincts screamed at him to intervene, but he forced himself to remain rooted to the spot. He took an involuntary step forward, unable to tear his eyes from Kaitlin.

'No,' he whispered under his breath, his voice barely audible. "Kaitlin, no, don't do it." He could see the amulet glinting around the prince's neck and instantly understood her intentions—she was going to try to take it. Keltor's hand tightened around the sledgehammer, his knuckles whitening with the force of his grip. He stood poised, every muscle taut with anticipation, ready to act the moment Kaitlin showed any sign of distress. The prince's unpredictable behaviour, coupled with Kaitlin's risky attempt to reach for the amulet, left Keltor on edge. He struggled to remain still, fighting the urge to intervene and defend her, knowing that any rash action now could jeopardise everything. Yet his resolve was unwavering; should Kaitlin need him, he would not hesitate to step in and shield her, regardless of the danger.

Kaitlin summoned her courage and sent a surge of magic into the prince's arm, fully aware of the risk she was taking. She hoped desperately that her gamble would pay off and that she might seize the amulet now, ending the tyranny in a single, daring act. For a moment, there was a tense pause as the prince's hand rose and cupped her cheek, his expression unreadable as he seemed to weigh his response. Suddenly, the prince felt a searing heat radiate from the amulet pressed against his chest—a sharp, unmistakable warning that Kaitlin's magic had been detected and immediately suppressed. Reacting instinctively and with anger, he lashed out, striking Kaitlin harshly across the face and shoving her away from him. The force of his blow caused Kaitlin to stumble backwards; she barely managed to keep her footing, almost collapsing under the sudden assault.

Keltor's instincts screamed at him to protect Kaitlin. He took a step towards her, unable to stand by as the prince's cruelty unfolded before his eyes. However, before he could act, a firm hand landed on his shoulder, halting him in his tracks. Commander Talbot's voice was low and resolute as he warned, "No, you must not give yourself away yet."

Fury burned in Keltor's eyes as he glanced at the Commander, his voice trembling with anger. "I won't let him hurt her," he whispered, unable to mask the depth of his concern.

Commander Talbot's words were quietly urgent as he placed a restraining hand on Keltor's shoulder. "Kaitlin will be alright, but if you intervene now, she won't. As soon as he realises who she is, she's dead." The warning echoed in Keltor's mind, stark and unyielding. He understood the gravity of the situation all too well. One wrong move, and Kaitlin's life would be forfeit the moment her true identity was revealed.

Keltor bit down so hard on his lower lip he made it bleed as he fought his need to rush and protect her. The pain was sharp, but it helped ground him, forcing him to remain where he was despite the overwhelming urge to intervene. His body tensed with the struggle, every instinct screaming for him to move, yet he held himself back, knowing that any action now could endanger them

461

both. The taste of blood was a reminder of the consequences, and he clung to it as he battled his desperation to shield Kaitlin from harm.

Kaitlin fought to regain her composure, forcing herself to remain upright even as fear sent tremors through her limbs. After a shaky breath, she knelt before the prince in a gesture of submission, hoping to appease his unpredictable temper. Her voice was barely audible as she murmured, "My Lord, forgive me." She kept her eyes fixed on the ground, unable to meet his gaze, every muscle tense with anxiety. Uncertainty gnawed at her—she could not tell whether the prince had sensed her attempt at magic or if his anger was simply provoked by her daring to touch him. Afraid to betray any further sign of guilt, Kaitlin remained perfectly still, her heart pounding as she awaited his next move.

The prince regarded Kaitlin intently, his thoughts swirling as he tried to make sense of what had just transpired. A lingering discomfort nagged at him—the curious burning sensation that had seared into him from the amulet as she reached for it. His mind drifted back to the moment they had taken her into custody, recalling the hushed warning from one of his soldiers about her being a witch. Suspicion and unease warred within him.

Turning to one of the guards, the prince's voice was sharp and commanding. "Take her back to the castle," he ordered, his tone brooking no argument, "and lock her in her room. I will deal with her on my return."

"Yes, my Lord," the soldier replied, stepping forward promptly. He seized Kaitlin by the arm, his grip unyielding as he began to escort her away under the prince's watchful gaze.

Kaitlin risked a backward glance, her gaze locking with Keltor's for a brief instant before he vanished from sight. In that silent moment, a world of unspoken emotion passed between them—frustration and helplessness clearly written across Keltor's features. He stood rooted to the spot, unable to intervene as Kaitlin was led away, his fists clenched tightly at his sides in a visible struggle to restrain his anger. The sense of powerlessness gnawed at him, his fury simmering just beneath the surface as he watched events unfold without the means to alter them.

Noticing the heightened tension, Commander Talbot quickly leaned in, his voice reduced to a sharp whisper. "Stop staring, you're getting too much attention," he cautioned, having observed the prince's persistent gaze lingering in their direction. The warning was clear—any further display of emotion could draw unwanted scrutiny and put them all at even greater risk.

Keltor dropped his gaze and returned to his work, the tension evident in every movement. He gripped the sledgehammer tightly and brought it down with such force that the large piece of rock beneath it shattered instantly, fragments scattering in every direction.

Commander Talbot watched, his tone sharp with irritation as he remarked, "Well, that really helped!" His words were laced with frustration, but Keltor was unmoved by the Commander's criticism. At that moment, his anger was so intense that all he could think about was the prince—the granite he had just destroyed felt like a stand-in for the prince's head, and the act of smashing it provided a fleeting outlet for his pent-up fury.

The prince studied Keltor with narrowed eyes, recalling their previous encounter earlier in the week. His gaze flicked briefly to Kaitlin as she was marched away by the guards, before settling once more on Keltor. The way Kaitlin had looked at Keltor as she was escorted off did not strike the prince as a gesture between siblings; rather, it hinted at a more complex connection between them. This observation piqued the prince's curiosity, and he made a mental note to investigate the true nature of their relationship further.

Turning towards the soldier in charge, the prince issued a sharp instruction. "Keep an eye on that one with the sledgehammer," he commanded, gesturing pointedly towards Keltor.

"Yes, my Lord," the soldier replied, nodding in acknowledgement and immediately taking heed of the prince's order.

Chapter Twenty-One

Escape

Keltor's voice was low but urgent as he brought the sledgehammer down against another rock. "We need to make a move now," he insisted, his frustration evident. "She's made herself a target for the prince now."

Commander Talbot cast a wary glance towards the prince's party, who were already making their way out through the gates. "Yes, I agree," he replied quietly, acknowledging the seriousness of the situation.

Determined, Keltor continued, "Tomorrow I'm going with Ese to get my father out of the dungeon, and then I'll go back for Kaitlin." His plan was clear—he would not leave anyone behind.

"I'll ready the men," the Commander said, nodding in support. "Are you sure you'll be able to get the keys?"

Keltor's eyes followed the soldier walking beside the prince as they headed back towards the gate. "Yes, I'll do it this evening," he confirmed. His gaze lingered on the head guard, noting the keys to the gate and the armoury clipped securely inside the guard's jacket.

Keltor turned to Commander Talbot, his voice steady with resolve. "Give me two days, and I'll send a signal," he said, outlining the next step in their escape plan.

Commander Talbot looked at him, uncertainty flickering in his eyes. "What signal?" he asked quietly.

Keltor's gaze shifted towards the distant castle. He gestured subtly, drawing the Commander's attention to the tall structure

464

silhouetted against the horizon. "See the tower?" Keltor murmured, and the Commander nodded in understanding.

"I'll blow it up. It will cause a distraction as well and will hopefully give you more chance of getting into the castle. By all accounts the castle is not well guarded as most of the King's men are at Elvendon. They will not be expecting a rebellion."

Commander Talbot glanced over his shoulder, his voice steady and controlled, as he kept a watchful eye on the bustling quarry around them. "How the hell are you going to blow up a tower?" he asked, scepticism evident in his tone. Clearly, he was unsure of Keltor's plan and needed reassurance.

Keltor hesitated for a moment, twitching his nose as he weighed whether to confide in the commander. After a brief pause, he took a deep breath and made his decision. "Commander, I'm a wizard," he revealed quietly.

The commander stared at him, his expression one of disbelief, as if he thought Keltor had lost his senses. "Are you serious?" he replied, frowning deeply, struggling to process what he had just heard.

"Yes, Commander, I am," Keltor insisted. "Trust me, okay? Between me and Kaitlin, we're a strong force of magic. Her aunt is also a witch. The only problem we have is that the prince possesses a magical device—a medallion he wears around his neck that amplifies his magic. But I will get it from him."

The commander shook his head, still struggling to process the revelation. "Okay," he conceded, though the uncertainty in his voice was unmistakable.

Glancing around to ensure no one was watching, Keltor turned his back to the prince's entourage. "Commander, look at me," he instructed, his tone commanding and urgent. The commander, though unsettled by Keltor's sudden assertiveness, complied with the request.

In a brief but unmistakable display of magic, Keltor's eyes flashed a brilliant white before quickly reverting to their usual blue. The commander's response was a whispered exclamation,

"Holy stars," his gaze darting anxiously as he checked to see if anyone else had witnessed the event.

With quiet conviction, Keltor affirmed, "I told you, I am a wizard, and I am your king, and we will take back Elvendon." The commander, now witnessing Keltor's authority firsthand, nodded in acknowledgement, accepting both the truth and the leadership Keltor offered.

"I'll come to you after lights out to go over the specifics," Keltor said, his voice low and determined, signalling his commitment to the plan.

"How will you get over to me?" the commander asked, still wary of the risks involved.

"Leave that for me to worry about, okay," Keltor replied, reassuring him that he had a solution in mind.

As Keltor and Commander Talbot conversed in low voices, their secretive discussion was suddenly cut short. Commander Talbot, ever alert to their surroundings, spotted a guard approaching at speed. He tried to warn Keltor, calling out, "Watch out!" but his warning was just a second too late.

The guard backhanded Keltor. The blow knocked him off balance, sending him sprawling onto his back. Wiping the blood from his lip, Keltor took a firm grip on his anger. In any other circumstance he would have been on his feet in an instance and breaking the man's damn neck. Instead, he stayed where he was.

The guard loomed over him, voice sharper than before. 'Enough talking! Back to work—unless you want another lesson."

Keltor shook his head, steadying himself after the blow. Forcing his aching body upright, he rose slowly, affecting a stagger as he made his way back to his assigned post. Each step was deliberate, designed to appear unsteady, masking his true composure from prying eyes.

The head guard observed Keltor intently, maintaining his focus on him until Keltor resumed his position and continued operating the sledgehammer.

Keltor knew time was slipping away, and the urgency of his mission pressed heavily upon him—he still had to locate Belrack before it was too late. Casting a furtive glance towards the far side of the quarry, he weighed his options. He understood that waiting until nightfall, when they would all be back in the main camp, was no longer feasible; the risk was necessary. However, one obstacle remained: the persistent guard. Keltor shot a sidelong look in the man's direction, noticing how the guard's gaze never wavered. Commander Talbot's warning echoed in his mind—by drawing attention to himself, he had become a target and now found himself under constant surveillance. If he hoped to slip away unnoticed, he would first have to deal with the guard standing in his way.

As the waggon pulled up alongside Keltor, Jack hopped down and approached him, keeping his voice low and discreet. "All set?" he asked, his tone casual but laced with purpose.

Keltor shook his head, casting a wary glance in the direction of the watchful guard. "Not entirely," he admitted, shovelling another load of granite into the back of the waggon. "I need to get over to the other side of the camp, but that damn guard is watching me like a hawk." The frustration in his voice was clear; every move he made seemed to draw unwanted attention.

Jack considered the situation for a moment, then leaned in, offering a practical solution. "You need a distraction?" he asked, raising an eyebrow. Keltor nodded in agreement, grateful for any help that would allow him to slip away unnoticed.

"Okay, leave it to me," Jack replied confidently, a mischievous grin spreading across his face. He was clearly already formulating a plan. Sensing the risk, Keltor offered a word of caution. "Don't go getting yourself killed," he warned, concerned for his friend's safety despite his own pressing need.

Jack waved off the concern with a reassuring smile. "I won't, don't worry; these old waggons are always breaking down, and the old horses are so temperamental. If it happens to tip over right on him, that's not my fault. Just be ready to go when the chaos starts." His words held a promise of calculated chaos, and Keltor knew that the moment the distraction began, he would have his chance to move.

Keltor gave Jack a nod, suppressing a smile as he shovelled another load of granite into the back of the waggon. While Keltor kept up appearances, Jack busied himself with one of the waggon's wheels, carefully examining it for any signs of wear. He then plucked a thistle from a bush growing nearby, preparing for the next stage of his plan.

Jack stood beside the horse, his tone gentle and apologetic. "Sorry, Angus," he murmured, addressing the old workhorse with genuine concern. "But it will only be uncomfortable for a short while." As he spoke, Jack carefully tucked the thistle into the bridle near the horse's mouth, knowing the plan relied on the animal's reaction. He finished by giving Angus an affectionate pat, a silent promise that the discomfort would soon be over, and that no lasting harm was intended. With gentle reassurance, Jack moved to the leather straps that secured the waggon bars to the horse, his actions calm and deliberate as he began preparing for the next phase of his plan.

He glanced around cautiously, ensuring no one was paying him undue attention, then crouched down, giving the appearance of simply tying his boot laces. Taking advantage of this moment, Jack discreetly withdrew a small knife concealed within his boot. With deft, practised movements, he set to work on the leather straps securing the waggon, carefully slicing through them until they were barely holding the waggon together. Jack took great care to make his handiwork appear accidental, as if the leather had naturally frayed over time, leaving no obvious evidence of sabotage.

Keltor finished loading the cart, pausing to wipe the sweat from his brow with the back of his hand. He leaned heavily on the handle of his shovel, the exertion evident in his posture and expression.

"Thanks, Jack," he said, gratitude clear in his voice as Jack jumped up onto the seat of the waggon.

Jack glanced back over his shoulder, a broad grin spreading across his face, sharing a moment of camaraderie with Keltor before setting off to put their plan into motion.

Jack, always thinking ahead, made sure to leave something useful behind for Keltor. As he prepared to set off, he called out, "I've left something under the wheel for you. Get on, Angus." There was no need for reins; Angus, the old workhorse, knew the routine and responded to Jack's familiar voice, pulling the waggon forward at a slow and steady pace.

Observing Jack's movements, Keltor's attention was drawn to the spot where the wheel had been. There, nestled discreetly in the dirt, was Jack's knife—left for him as planned. A small smile crept onto Keltor's face as he recognised the subtle gesture. Maintaining the guise of tying his bootlaces, he knelt, quickly retrieved the knife, and slipped it into his own boot. The exchange was silent and unnoticed, a mark of trust and cooperation between the two friends.

Jack drove the waggon steadily towards the guard, his expression one of feigned focus. As the waggon drew closer, the guard eyed him warily, a scowl deepening across his face. Clearly mistrustful, the guard took a cautious step backwards just as the old horse, Angus, nearly reached him.

At that precise moment, Jack gave a sharp tug on the reins, causing the thistle he had placed earlier to press uncomfortably against Angus's mouth. Startled by the sudden pain, Angus reared up in alarm, his hooves pawing at the air as panic set in. The old horse skittled sideways, eyes rolling with fear, and Jack, anticipating the reaction, quickly pulled the reins to the left. This manoeuvre caused the waggon to veer sharply to the right.

As Jack executed his plan, the waggon's back right wheel suddenly snapped in half, causing the entire vehicle to tip sharply to the right. The incident unfolded with alarming speed, leaving the guard no opportunity to react or escape. In an instant, the waggon—laden with a heavy load of granite—toppled over, burying the guard beneath its massive weight.

The force of the collapse caused the leather straps securing Angus, the workhorse, to the waggon to break apart. Startled and freed from his restraints, Angus reared up once again before bolting away from the scene, galloping into the camp in a frenzy.

469

Reacting quickly, Jack leapt from the waggon to the left, landing with a heavy thud on the ground. He allowed himself a brief smile as he watched Angus escape, knowing the chaos unfolding was all part of the plan.

Within moments of the accident, a wave of anxious workers surged towards the scene of the toppled waggon. Cries of alarm echoed through the air as they pressed forward, each one eager to catch a glimpse of the chaos that had unfolded. Some workers craned their necks, trying to see over the heads of others, while many exchanged worried looks, their voices low as they muttered questions and speculated about what had happened. The sharp scent of dust and sweat lingered, heightening the tension as apprehension spread among the crowd. Each person seemed desperate to discover whether anyone had been hurt or whether help was needed.

As the grim reality of the accident became apparent, a wave of shock and confusion swept through the gathering. Guards stationed nearby exchanged uneasy glances, some frozen by the sudden tragedy, while others shifted uncertainly, hesitating as they tried to decide how to respond. The uproar and mounting alarm quickly drew the full attention of the camp, engulfing all present in the calamity. Amidst the distraction, Jack glanced around searching for Keltor, but he had already vanished into the confusion. A satisfied grin played across Jack's face—his plan had worked perfectly.

As soon as the cart tipped over, Keltor wasted no time. He sprang into action, sprinting away from the scene whilst the confusion still held the attention of the guards in the tower. Their focus remained fixed on the commotion that had erupted behind him, ensuring his escape went unnoticed.

Keltor navigated swiftly between the rows of tents, taking care to keep himself out of sight as he made his way towards the newly constructed building. Upon reaching the relative safety of a storage shed, he paused and crouched behind it for cover. Keeping himself concealed, he quietly muttered an incantation under his breath. At once, a wave of magical energy shimmered across his form, and Keltor's appearance shifted, assuming the exact likeness of the guard whose image he had memorised the previous night.

Boldly emerging from his concealment behind the shed, Keltor strode purposefully onto the bustling build site. He scanned the area, and it did not take him long to spot Belrack and his men; their towering stature made them stand out unmistakably amidst the rest of the workers.

Without hesitation, Keltor approached the guard assigned to watch over Belrack's group. Adopting a tone of urgent authority, he called out to the guard, "Hey, they need you over in the main camp?"

The guard regarded Keltor sceptically, a single eyebrow arching in suspicion. "Why, what are you doing over this side?" he queried, clearly not expecting to see him there.

Keltor kept his composure, replying quickly, "There's been an accident, one of the guards has been killed, a waggon full of granite tipped onto him. I've been asked to get help, apparently, I'm not good enough to go on the tower watch. So, they sent for you."

The guard's surprise was evident. "They want me to go in the watch tower?" he asked, unable to hide his astonishment.

"Yeah, but you'd better hurry, all hell's broken loose over there," Keltor urged, injecting urgency into his words.

"Oh, okay, right, thanks," the guard replied, a grin spreading across his face as he processed the news. At last, he thought, he was being promoted from his tedious post. Without a second thought, he dashed off towards the chaos erupting in the main camp, eager to seize what he believed was a long-awaited opportunity.

Keltor made his way swiftly towards the man he was certain could only be Belrack. The figure stood out easily, towering over the other workers at more than seven feet tall. His long, fair hair cascaded down past his shoulders, framing a face marked by a pronounced, chiselled chin and a stern, unyielding expression. Approaching cautiously, Keltor called out to him, "Belrack?"

The imposing figure halted his labour, pausing to turn his attention towards the guard who had called out. Belrack's face darkened with a scowl, and for a fleeting moment, Keltor feared that the giant might bring the hefty granite slab in his grasp crashing down upon him. Instinctively, Keltor stepped back to maintain a safe distance.

Belrack then let go of the granite, allowing it to fall heavily to the ground with a resounding thud that echoed across the construction site.

"Yes, I am Belrack," he answered gruffly, his tone wary and guarded.

Keltor pressed on, his voice low but earnest. "Belrack, it's me—Keltor. You remember, don't you? Kaitlin and I helped you, when you were trolls?"

Belrack's features tightened, deep lines forming across his brow as he searched his mind for the memory Keltor referenced. His tone was gruff, tinged with suspicion. "You look nothing like him," he said, his voice low and wary.

Keltor met Belrack's gaze and nodded in acknowledgement. "I know, I've shapeshifted," he replied quietly. His eyes darted about, scanning the area for any sign of approaching guards. Satisfied that they were alone, Keltor allowed his disguise to fade, his appearance shifting seamlessly back to his true form.

Belrack recoiled, his voice ringing out in alarm. "Holy spirits!" he cried, stepping backwards as fear momentarily overtook him. Keltor, noticing the sudden terror on Belrack's face, immediately attempted to soothe him.

"It's okay, Belrack, it's just a magic trick," Keltor reassured, striving to calm the giant man, who now appeared genuinely frightened by what he had witnessed. Hoping to restore a sense of normality, Keltor swiftly shifted his appearance back to that of the guard.

Stunned by the transformation, Belrack stammered, his words faltering as he tried to comprehend what had just occurred. "How, how, did you do that?" he asked, disbelief evident in his tone.

Keltor steadied himself and met Belrack's gaze, his voice low but urgent. "I recently discovered that I am a wizard, so I can perform magic," he explained, hoping to provide some context for his earlier transformation. He cast another anxious glance around the site, ever wary of prying eyes or eavesdroppers. "Look, we don't have much time," he continued. "I'm here because we're planning to break out in two days, and I need your help."

Belrack's expression hardened, his scepticism clear. "Break out, how? We've tried three times, and each time we have lost our brothers. Why should we try again?"

Keltor leaned in, his whisper fierce and sincere. "Because Ila needs you, that's why."

The mention of his wife's name caught Belrack off guard. He repeated it quietly, "Ila," and for a moment, the sternness in his face gave way to a deep, personal longing. "How do you know about Ila?"

"I've been to see her, a week or so ago. Kaitlin and I came looking for you, to ask for your help to fight against Aranstream."

Belrack's brow furrowed in concern as he pressed Keltor for news. "Ila, the children, they are all okay?" he asked, his voice betraying his deep worry for his family's safety.

Keltor nodded reassuringly. "Yes, Belrack, they were all fine when we left them, but I can't say if anything has happened since. King Iwein is insane, Belrack. He is taking and killing children and women. He needs to be stopped."

Belrack's posture stiffened as the gravity of the situation settled over him. "Yes, I know that," he admitted, his voice tinged with frustration. "But how, how do we get out of here?"

Keltor leaned in closer, his tone earnest as he shared a critical piece of information. "Belrack, what we didn't tell you when you were trolls was that Kaitlin was not only the Keeper of the Star, but also a Princess of Elvendon. Because King Iwein killed her father and her sister, Kaitlin is now the rightful queen, and ruler of Elvendon."

For a moment, Belrack was silent, clearly weighing the gravity of Keltor's request. Eventually, he spoke, his voice thoughtful yet resolute.

"So, what are you saying, that you want us to help you get the throne of Elvendon back for Kaitlin?" he asked, seeking clarity and confirmation.

"Yes, that's exactly what I am saying. If you want your children to grow up in a safe, free world, we must take down King Iwein and Aranstream." Keltor replied, his conviction unwavering as he articulated the necessity of their mission.

Belrack rubbed his hand back and forth against his mouth, the gesture betraying his internal struggle. There was a long silence as he considered the implications for himself and his people.

Finally, Belrack made his decision. "We'll do it, we will help you and Kaitlin. If it were not for the Keeper of the Star my children would not be alive now, and I, and my tribe would still be those sick, vicious trolls. We owe her our lives." His words carried the weight of gratitude and a promise of loyalty.

"Thank you, Belrack," Keltor said gratefully, acknowledging the significance of Belrack's commitment.

Belrack regarded Keltor with an intense gaze, seeking clarity on what lay ahead. "What's your plan?" he asked, his voice low and urgent.

Keltor looked carefully around, ensuring they would not be overheard. He then began to explain the plan in detail. First, he intended to rescue his father from captivity, a daring objective that would require stealth and coordination. Following that, the next phase would see him and his allies setting fire to the tower atop Aranstream castle—an unmistakable signal for the next stage of their operation.

"When you see the tower ablaze," Keltor explained, "that will be the sign for you and your men. That is the moment to move against the guards." The plan was that, at this signal, Commander Talbot and the rest of their allied army would launch their attack, swiftly overtaking the camp. With the guards subdued and the camp in their control, the force would then march on the city, determined to storm the castle and reclaim it from King Iwein's rule.

Belrack listened closely, his attention unwavering as Keltor outlined the daring strategy. The seriousness of the situation was evident in Belrack's expression; he took a moment to reflect, fully comprehending what was at stake.

"And you are sure this will work?" Belrack asked, his voice laced with uncertainty and concern. The enormity of the plan and its potential consequences weighed heavily upon him.

Keltor met Belrack's gaze with determination. "Belrack, I believe if we all work together, we can take back Elvendon," he replied earnestly. "It's not going to be easy, and, sadly, people will die—perhaps even us—but if we don't strike now, this is how life will be for all Elvendons. Families will remain separated, and loved ones will continue to be killed or tortured."

Understanding the necessity of action, Belrack gave a resolute nod, silently affirming his commitment to the cause and acknowledging the risks they all faced.

Belrack's voice was tinged with regret as he spoke. "We lost good men when they attacked us," he said, reflecting on the cost of past battles. The pain was evident in his words, and it was clear that the memories weighed heavily upon him. "I have feared the worst for my wife and children in these past months. You say they're okay, this has given me new hope, and I know the others will agree with me." With this, Belrack acknowledged the renewed sense of purpose he now felt, reassured by the news of his family's safety and hopeful for the future.

Keltor responded with quiet gratitude. "Thank you, Belrack. Look, I should be getting back before I'm missed." His words conveyed both appreciation and the urgency of the moment.

"Okay," Belrack replied, understanding the need for caution. As Keltor turned to depart, Belrack called after him, his tone resolute. "Keltor." Keltor paused, glancing back over his shoulder. "We will be ready."

Keltor acknowledged Belrack's commitment with a firm nod, then made his way back to camp, carrying with him the weight of their agreement and the hope it inspired.

As Keltor approached the encampment, he discreetly reverted to his own appearance, careful not to draw attention. He made his way swiftly back to his assigned post, noting that he had only been absent for half an hour. The area surrounding the waggon was still in disarray, evidence of the recent turmoil. The body of the deceased man had already been removed, and the soldiers were now issuing orders to the Elvendons, directing them to transfer the cargo onto a different waggon. Without attracting notice, Keltor blended seamlessly in with the group of men loading the new waggon, resuming his role amongst them.

Zeb was present among the men, and as soon as he caught sight of Keltor, he quietly moved to join him. Keeping his voice low, Zeb bent down beside Keltor and picked up a hefty slab of granite.

"Where did you go?" Zeb inquired quietly, his eyes fixed on Keltor as they worked side by side.

Keltor, lifting a large piece of granite and heaving it into the back of the waggon, responded in a similarly hushed tone, "Sorting out plans."

A knowing grin spread across Zeb's face. He leaned in closer and, as he lifted the granite, muttered under his breath, "I've got something for you."

Keltor paused, curiosity piqued. He cast a cautious glance around to ensure no one was watching, then asked quietly, "What?"

Zeb gave him a sly wink and replied mysteriously, "I'll give it to you later, it's too risky here."

Keltor's eyebrow arched, his curiosity piqued by Zeb's cryptic assurance. What could Zeb possibly have that required such secrecy?

After the waggon had been reloaded, the men were dismissed to return to their respective posts. Keltor resumed his arduous labour, methodically smashing granite as the routine demanded.

The repetitive clang of stone echoed through the camp, each strike underscoring the monotony of the task.

As a new waggon rolled to a halt beside him, Keltor seized the moment to pause. He dropped his shovel, drawing in a deep, steadying breath, allowing himself the briefest respite before the next stage of work began.

As Commander Talbot leapt down from the waggon, Keltor approached him purposefully. "Commander," he called out, drawing the officer's attention.

Commander Talbot approached Keltor, his voice carrying a note of authority and curiosity. "Keltor," he began, then with a hint of accusation added, "I take it that accident with the waggon earlier was down to you?"

Keltor responded calmly, bending down to retrieve his shovel. He scooped up a load of granite and, as he tipped it into the back of the waggon, clarified, "Indirectly, but yes, I needed to get over to Belrack."

Commander Talbot pressed further, wanting to confirm the outcome of Keltor's efforts. "And will he and his men join us?" the Commander asked.

Keltor gave an assured nod. "Yes, they will," he confirmed, signalling that Belrack and his men had agreed to support their cause.

"Good," Commander Talbot said with a decisive nod, his tone firm and resolute. "I have been organising the plans with the lads. We will divide our defences. King Iwein will expect us to be vulnerable; he believes we have little chance of success. Yet, he is unaware of what you and the Queen are capable of."

Keltor halted, considering the Commander's words. The gravity of their situation weighed on him, but he remained focused on the necessity of secrecy. "Commander, none of the men must know what Kaitlin and I can do," he cautioned, his voice low and earnest. "If even one of them is captured and tortured, any knowledge of our abilities could be exploited. We must maintain the advantage if we are to defeat them."

From the corner of his eye, Keltor noticed his brother Ese. He offered him a subtle nod and placed his hand over his heart—a silent signal, laden with meaning between the two siblings.

Ese gave a nod in return and turned his back to him. The exchange was brief, but laden with significance. Keltor had just delivered the signal: tonight was the night. As the realisation settled, Ese's heart began to race. The prospect of finally escaping the confines of this grim place was overwhelming, but another thought took precedence in his mind—he was going to find his father.

Though the passage of time had blurred his memories, fragments of his father lingered. Ese could recall certain moments, fleeting and half-remembered, kept alive by stories his mother had told him over the years. She often remarked on the resemblance between father and son, a comparison that made those faded recollections all the more precious.

Amongst all the memories, one stood out above the rest: an adventure shared with his father and Keltor, when they had gone hunting together. Ese had only been a small child at the time, but the memory had anchored itself firmly in his mind, a source of comfort and strength that he had clung to through the years of hardship.

"Once you have the Queen," the Commander continued, his tone grave and deliberate, "send that signal. At that moment, we will move to eliminate the guards stationed here. We know precisely where the weapons are kept within the camp, so our first action will be to raid that location." He fixed Keltor with a steady gaze, underscoring the importance of the task. "Your priority must be to get the Queen away from the castle. Ensure her safety above all else."

Keltor interrupted the Commander, his tone firm and insistent. "Commander, you're going to need our help to take Aranstream," he stated as he dropped another load of granite into the waggon. His words underscored the critical importance of collaboration in the face of the daunting task ahead.

However, Commander Talbot responded with quiet confidence. "No, we can do it," he asserted. "So long as we can get into the armoury, you need to keep Kaitlin safe. We're going to need her when the King finds out what we have done. He will assemble his men for battle, and that's when we are going to need both of you." The Commander's strategy was clear: while the main force would focus on securing the armoury, the safety of Kaitlin remained paramount. Her presence would be vital once the King became aware of their actions, as both she and Keltor would be essential in the confrontation that would inevitably follow.

Keltor gave a nod, though a deep furrow appeared on his brow, betraying the anxiety that gnawed at him beneath his calm exterior. The burden of responsibility pressed heavily on his shoulders—a weight not easily shrugged off, even as others looked to him for reassurance and direction.

Commander Talbot, ever perceptive, sought to bolster the young man's resolve. "Keltor, we can do this," he declared with conviction. "There are more than three thousand men in this encampment. All they needed was hope and a leader to inspire them, and you and the Queen have provided exactly that. Nearly all of King Iwein's men are currently stationed in Elvendon. That gives us a real chance." The Commander's words were intended to instil courage, emphasising the strength in unity and the significance of the hope Keltor and the Queen had rekindled among their people.

Taking a steadying breath, Keltor nodded in agreement. "Okay. I'll get Kaitlin to safety and then return to you," he promised, committing to his role in the plan and acknowledging the importance of prioritising the Queen's security before rejoining the broader effort.

With their agreement firmly in place, Commander Talbot offered Keltor a final nod of approval, signalling his trust in the young man's commitment and capability. Without further delay, the Commander climbed back up onto the waggon, a clear indication that the time had come for their plan to unfold.

Before setting off, Commander Talbot asked in a low, urgent voice, "Have you got the key yet?" His question cut to the heart of their preparations, acknowledging the crucial role the key would play in their escape.

Keltor replied with determination, shaking his head. "No, not yet, but I will get it tonight, somehow." His response was resolute, a promise that even in the face of uncertainty, he would not let their hopes falter.

With no time to lose, the Commander called out to the horse and flicked the reins. The horse strained against its harness, pulling the waggon forward with a jolt. As the vehicle began to move, the sense of anticipation in the air grew, marking the beginning of the operation that would decide their fate.

Keltor leaned on the shovel, his thoughts heavy with uncertainty. The challenge before him seemed insurmountable— how was he supposed to obtain the key when the head guard, its previous keeper, was now dead? The absence of any clear information about who held the key left him feeling lost and troubled.

After another three arduous hours of relentless labour, Keltor finally made his way to the shower block. He stripped off his clothes and stepped beneath the cold stream, letting the water cascade over his tired body. As he stood there, he released a hefty sigh, the weight of responsibility pressing down on him. Everything hinged upon his ability to secure that elusive key; without it, their plans would come to nothing.

As Keltor stood beneath the cold stream, lost in thought and weighed down by the enormity of his task, a voice broke through his reverie. "You alright?" someone said, standing beside him. Keltor turned to his right and saw Zeb, his familiar face offering a measure of comfort amidst the uncertainty.

"Kind of," Keltor replied, wiping the water from his face and running a hand through his wet hair. Zeb's presence was reassuring, and Keltor could sense there was more to the encounter than a simple exchange of concern.

With a mysterious grin stretching across his face, Zeb leaned in slightly. "When you're finished, I've got something for you. I've hidden them in your boot," he said, his tone laced with excitement and secrecy.

Keltor's curiosity was instantly piqued, a flicker of hope igniting within him as he realised Zeb might hold the answer to their most pressing problem. Without hesitation, he grabbed his towel and wrapped it securely around his waist, turning to face Zeb with an eager expression.

"Zeb, what is it?" Keltor asked, his voice low but urgent, betraying his anticipation for whatever revelation Zeb was about to share.

Rather than responding with words, Zeb simply met Keltor's gaze and gave a subtle nod, his eyes flicking meaningfully towards the area where he had hidden something. The seriousness in Zeb's expression made it clear that whatever he had concealed carried significant importance, urging Keltor to investigate without delay.

Keltor raised an eyebrow at Zeb, then turned and exited the shower cubicle. As he walked past the other men in the showers, they acknowledged him with subtle nods. Keltor knew each of them was steadfastly loyal to Elvendon and involved in the upcoming plan for battle.

Before continuing, Keltor glanced over his shoulder to ensure no guards were nearby. Satisfied that the coast was clear, he bent down and picked up his boot. Upon lifting it, he heard a faint sound coming from inside. He reached his hand into the boot, pausing momentarily to check his surroundings once more. At that moment, he noticed Zeb emerging from the shower cubicle.

"Are these what I think they are?" Keltor asked, his heart pounding with hope as he peered at the object Zeb had indicated. The prospect that Zeb might have brought him the key sent a surge of anticipation through him.

"Yep," Zeb replied, barely able to suppress a grin. His attempt to remain composed betrayed the excitement that flickered in his eyes.

Keltor, lowering his voice to a whisper, pressed, "How the hell did you get them?" The urgency in his tone reflected the gravity of the situation. Zeb, moving closer so they would not be overheard, reached up for his clean shirt that hung on a peg. He cast a cautious glance over his shoulder, ensuring their exchange remained private, before turning back to Keltor. The air was thick with secrecy, and the unspoken understanding of the risk Zeb had taken.

"When I helped move the body. I realised who he was, and they were just there, hanging off his belt," Zeb explained, his voice quiet but resolute as he recounted the discovery.

Keltor could not contain his gratitude as he turned to Zeb, his voice brimming with emotion. "Zeb, I could hug you!" he exclaimed, struggling to suppress a broad grin. The relief and hope that surged within him were undeniable, and for a moment the tension between them eased, replaced by a sense of camaraderie forged in adversity.

Zeb met Keltor's enthusiasm with a steady resolve. "I told you; you can trust me. I want nothing more than to kill these sons of bitches for what they did to me and my family," he declared, his words carrying the weight of personal loss and determination. His gaze hardened with resolve, then softened as he continued, "Keltor, I want to find my wife, and I know she's in that castle somewhere." The enormity of Zeb's longing was evident as he paused, lifting a trembling hand to wipe away a solitary tear that had slipped down his cheek.

Keltor, noticing the abrupt shift in Zeb's demeanour, leaned in with concern etched across his brow. "Are you okay?" he asked quietly, his tone gentle yet urgent as he sought to understand the cause of Zeb's distress.

With a tremor in his voice, Zeb finally confided, "Keltor, my wife is three months with child. I'm terrified of what may happen to her and the baby. I need to get out of here." The weight of his fear and desperation was unmistakable, his words revealing both a deep vulnerability and an urgent need to escape for the sake of his family.

Keltor studied Zeb, reading the raw honesty etched into every line of his face. There was no mistaking it—Zeb's fear and desperation were genuine, and Keltor felt the weight of his friend's trust settle heavily on his shoulders.

"Hey, don't worry," Keltor said quietly, his tone steady and reassuring despite the tumult of uncertainty that surrounded them. "In a few days you'll be out, and we will find her, okay?" He held Zeb's gaze, determined to offer hope where so little existed.

Zeb nodded in response, a flicker of gratitude softening his weary features. His hand rose and, in a rare gesture of camaraderie, he patted Keltor's arm, the silent gesture conveying more than words could manage.

"Thank you," Zeb murmured, his voice barely above a whisper, yet filled with sincerity.

After darkness had fallen and the camp was silent, Keltor quietly slipped out of bed. He cast a brief glance towards Zeb, who was fast asleep, completely unaware of Keltor's true intentions. A pang of guilt tugged at Keltor—he regretted not having told Zeb the full truth about his identity or his decision to escape that very night, along with his brother. Keltor knew that, come morning, Zeb would wake to find him gone and would likely be left questioning his sudden disappearance. The thought troubled him, as he hoped the guards would not place the blame on Zeb for his absence. Yet, Keltor recognised he had no other option; the plan was already set in motion, and the urgency of the situation left no room for hesitation. He needed to act now to rescue his father and Kaitlin, before it was too late.

He moved like a shadow towards the farthest corner of the tent; each step deliberate and silent. At this point, it no longer mattered if anyone discovered a rip in the canvas—by morning, he would be far from here and well beyond their reach. With the knife Jack had discreetly given him earlier, Keltor carefully sliced through the tent's heavy fabric, creating an opening just large enough for him to slip out.

Once outside, Keltor quickly adjusted his posture and movements, mimicking the mannerisms of the guards to avoid suspicion. Confident in his disguise, he strode boldly through the camp, making his way towards Commander Talbot's tent with purpose.

The man stationed outside the tent eyed Keltor warily as he approached, his grip tightening on the hilt of his sword. Sizing up Keltor, he hesitated for a moment before recognising the familiar uniform. With a subtle sigh of relief, the guard lowered his weapon, though his posture remained tense and vigilant.

"I need to go inside," Keltor said, adopting the authoritative tone expected of the guards.

The guard shook his head, clearly uncomfortable with the request. "No one can go in at night; those are the rules," he replied, standing firm in his duty.

Keltor pressed his case, maintaining an air of impatience. "Yeah, but I only need a few minutes."

Suspicion flickered across the guard's face as he demanded, "What for?"

With a raised eyebrow, Keltor responded coolly, "Does it matter?" His words carried just enough authority to sway the guard's resolve.

The guard relented, muttering, "Oh, right, hell. Go on then, you've got ten minutes." He stepped aside, pulling open the flap of the tent for Keltor to enter. Before Keltor could step through, the guard lifted a cautioning hand, his voice low and insistent. "Don't wake them all up," he warned.

Keltor offered a slight smirk in response. "I only want one," he replied, slipping inside the tent with deliberate silence.

Keltor moved swiftly along the row of beds, scanning each one until he located Commander Talbot. Just as he had done with his brother earlier, Keltor knelt quietly beside the Commander and pressed a firm hand over his mouth to keep him from crying out.

The Commander, jolted from sleep, reacted with alarm. Despite his efforts to remain awake, the fatigue from a long day's work had overcome him, leaving him vulnerable and startled as he awoke.

Keltor knelt beside Commander Talbot, ensuring the startled man remained silent by pressing a firm hand over his mouth. Leaning in close, Keltor whispered reassuringly, "Shh, it's me, Keltor." The Commander's eyes widened, disbelief etched on his face as he recognised Keltor. "Trust me, Commander, I've brought you the key to the armoury." Sensing the Commander's understanding, Keltor gradually eased his grip and allowed him to speak.

The Commander, still unnerved, mumbled in a low, fearful voice, "How the hell can you do that?" His eyes darted between Keltor and the dim shapes of the sleeping men around them, as if uncertain whether he was caught in a dream or witnessing something extraordinary.

Keltor, maintaining his composure and speaking in a calm, measured tone, replied, "Look, I told you, I'm a wizard, and being able to shape-shift is one of my many abilities." His words hung in the air, the significance of his revelation settling slowly over the Commander.

As the reality of Keltor's confession began to sink in, the Commander gasped, "By the spirits." Still processing the information, he pressed further, voice barely above a whisper, "And the Queen, can she do this?"

Keltor offered a gentle smile and shook his head. "No, her magic is very different." Without further hesitation, he placed the keys decisively into the Commander's hand, sealing his promise and ensuring the Commander understood the gravity of the trust he had placed in him.

With excitement evident in his voice, the Commander asked, "The armoury keys?"

"Yes. Look, I need to go," Keltor responded hastily as he rose to his feet, eager to make his departure.

The Commander, now sitting upright, glanced anxiously along the line of sleeping men in the tent, his concern for their safety and the seriousness of the situation clear on his face. After a moment's pause, he offered a sincere wish, "I hope you find your father."

485

"Thanks, and I'll see you in a few days. Oh, before I go, could you do me a favour?" Keltor asked, pausing for a moment as he glanced back at the Commander.

"Yes, what is it?" the Commander replied, his voice quieter now, laced with concern.

"My friend Zeb—could you keep an eye on him for me? I'm worried that the guards might punish him when they realise I've gone. If they end up throwing him in the hell hole, please, make sure you get him out. I'd never forgive myself if something happened to him because of me."

The Commander nodded solemnly, fully comprehending the seriousness of Keltor's request. "You have my word, my Lord. I'll watch over Zeb and do everything I can to protect him." His voice carried a quiet determination, the pledge holding the weight of a solemn oath.

Keltor paused, his eyes lingering on the Commander. A warm smile touched his lips, moved by the way the Commander now addressed him—not just as an ally, but as his king. The Commander's acceptance was a source of relief for Keltor, and his gratitude was clear. "Thank you. Good luck, Commander."

The Commander, acknowledging both the weight of their exchange and the respect between them, replied in a quieter, more formal tone, "And you, my King." With that, he dipped his head in a gesture of deference and respect.

Keltor grinned, a brief flash of camaraderie and relief passing between the two men, before he slipped quietly away into the night, leaving the Commander to his thoughts and duties.

Chapter Twenty-Two

Forde

Keltor moved silently through the camp, making his way towards Esendil's tent. This time, rather than approaching openly, he circled round to the rear of the tent, careful not to disturb anyone nearby. With deliberate precision, he took out his knife and carefully sliced through the canvas, creating a discreet opening. Once the gap was wide enough, Keltor shifted back into his usual form and slipped quietly inside, squeezing through the makeshift entrance with practiced ease.

Esendil lay awake, nerves stretched taut with anxiety. Every sound made him flinch, and he was acutely aware of how little he owned—just three sets of clothing, the same as the others. There was nothing for him to prepare or gather; he was ready, if only in the most basic sense.

Keltor approached silently from behind, his presence announced only by a hushed whisper. "Ese," he said softly.

Startled, Esendil spun round, his tension dissolving into a wide, relieved grin when he saw his brother.

"Come on," Keltor urged, his voice low as he kept his body close to the ground and his eyes alert for any movement from the others who still slept. "We need to go, now."

Esendil nodded and swiftly followed Keltor to the rear of the tent, slipping through the hole Keltor had created in the canvas. Outside, the air was cool and hushed, amplifying the urgency of their escape. As soon as they were clear, Keltor turned to his brother, his voice barely audible as he whispered, "It's so good to see you, brother." Unable to contain his relief, Keltor pulled Esendil into a tight embrace.

For a moment, the tension of the night faded as Esendil clung to him, his voice thick with emotion. "I thought you were dead, K," he whispered, squeezing his brother tightly. The two stood together for a heartbeat longer, their bond reaffirmed in the darkness before necessity urged them onward.

"I know, and I'm sorry I put you all through that," Keltor murmured, his voice tinged with genuine regret. "Honestly, we had no idea what had happened. For Kaitlin and me, it felt like we'd only been gone from Elvendon for a couple of weeks. He paused, glancing around the shadowed camp, his expression serious. "Look, I promise I'll tell you more once we're out of here. Right now, we need to keep low and stay in the shadows."

With that, Keltor gently released Esendil from their embrace. The brothers exchanged a silent understanding, their bond strengthened by the urgency of their situation. Without a single spoken word, they moved in perfect synchrony, slipping quietly through the shadows that lay between the sleeping tents. Their movements were cautious and deliberate, each step taken with care to avoid attracting attention. Ducking low and weaving between the rows of canvas, they kept themselves hidden from view, making certain to avoid the circles of torchlight that illuminated the camp. Every so often, their eyes flicked upwards to the watchtowers, where vigilant men paced, ever alert for signs of trouble. Together, Keltor and Esendil pressed on, invisible in the darkness, united in purpose as they made their way towards freedom.

It took them twenty minutes to reach the edge of the river. Keeping to the shadows, Keltor led the way, moving with purpose and caution until they arrived at the perimeter fence. Once there, Keltor crouched low by the wire, signalling for Esendil to come closer. Esendil did so, his eyes fixed on his brother's careful movements as Keltor produced a knife and began to cut through the wire with deliberate precision.

Esendil, his voice barely above a whisper, leaned in and asked, "Why don't you use your magic to deal with this?"

Keltor paused for a moment, glancing at his brother before returning his attention to the fence. "I don't want to attract attention," he replied quietly. "Sometimes, when I use magic, there's this odd light that appears. It could give us away."

As soon as Keltor had cut through enough of the wire, he braced himself and delivered a forceful kick to the fence. The section gave way, creating an opening just large enough for them to slip through. Without hesitation, Esendil followed his brother, and together they hurried towards the riverbank, their movements swift and silent in the darkness.

Hidden by the cloak of night, the brothers located a small boat waiting at the water's edge. Fortune favoured them—for the sky was overcast, and thick clouds masked the moon, shrouding the world in deep shadow. Clambering into the boat, they kept low, mindful of every sound. Keltor took hold of the oars and, with great care, pushed the boat away from the bank. Letting the current guide their escape, he used the oars only enough to keep them steady, making as little noise as possible so as not to alert any nearby sentries or patrols.

The most perilous part of their escape loomed ahead as Keltor and Esendil rounded a bend in the river. Sensing imminent danger, Keltor quickly pulled his brother down, and together they lay motionless at the bottom of the boat, hardly daring to breathe. Above them, the glow of torches traced the outline of the lookout towers, their flames casting flickering shadows on the stone. The brothers watched in tense silence as soldiers paced back and forth, their figures outlined against the firelight.

As the boat drifted with the current, they passed another bend and gradually moved away from the encampment, tension easing only slightly. Keltor, ever cautious, inched forward to the prow of the boat, eyes narrowing at the obstacle ahead. The tunnel beneath the castle offered their only route to freedom, but its entrance was blocked by a heavy metal grate. Leaning over the boat's edge, Keltor stretched out his hands, steadying the vessel and preventing it from banging loudly against the barrier. The current pushed stubbornly, causing the boat to turn sideways, but Keltor's careful manoeuvring kept them from making any noise that might betray their presence. The risk was heightened; every movement had to be slow, controlled, and silent as they faced this critical moment in their escape.

Keltor murmured a quiet chant under his breath, *"Ego invocabo fons, augendae viribus meis,"* focusing his energies as his hands gripped the metal grate firmly. He repeated the incantation, feeling a surge of magic ripple through the iron bars. Drawing upon this newfound strength, Keltor pulled with determination, and the grate yielded, coming away in his grasp.

Esendil, witnessing the feat, was visibly impressed. "Woah, that's so cool," he whispered, awestruck by his brother's magical ability. With the passage now open, the boat slipped through the opening, carrying them onward into the darkness beneath the castle.

"Esendil, grab the arch, now," Keltor instructed in a hushed tone. Responding immediately, Esendil shot up and reached for the side of the archway. His muscles tensed as he clung tightly to the stone, preventing the boat from drifting forward and holding it steady beneath the tunnel's entrance.

Keltor groaned with effort as he hefted the heavy metal grate. With careful manoeuvring, he lifted it over the boat and guided it to the opposite side, making sure not to let it drop or clatter against the stone. "Mind," he warned, prompting Esendil to duck out of the way just in time.

Once the path was clear, Keltor pushed the grate back into the opening, ensuring it was firmly secured in place behind them.

With a final murmured incantation, *"Sicut erat,"* Keltor carefully secured the grate back into its original position, ensuring they left no trace of their passage behind. "Okay, let's go," he said quietly, settling himself in the boat.

Esendil released his grip on the stone archway, and the boat began to drift gently along the river. They found themselves deep beneath the castle, enveloped in complete darkness. The boat floated silently as they moved further away from the entrance, the world above now out of reach.

Once they had put a safe distance between themselves and the tunnel's opening, Esendil reached for the oil lamp. With a careful motion, he lit it, casting a warm, flickering glow that illuminated the immediate space around them, allowing the brothers to see as they continued their journey through the shadowy undercroft.

As the boat drifted quietly beneath the castle, Esendil broke the silence with a question that had clearly been weighing on his mind. "How is it you can do magic, and I can't?" he asked, gazing at his brother with a mixture of curiosity and mild frustration.

Keltor met his brother's eyes and replied simply, "It was to do with a prophecy, and I'm the first born."

Esendil frowned, his disappointment evident as he muttered, "Oh, that's so unfair."

In response, Keltor offered a reassuring grin. "Never mind bro, I'm sure there are many things you can do that I can't."

Still dissatisfied, Esendil pressed on. "Yeah, like what?" he moaned.

Keltor chuckled and teased, "I don't know, get on your sister's nerves for a start."

"You're such a jerk," Esendil said, but this time his words were laced with affection. He let out a laugh and thumped Keltor's arm, a small burst of relief bubbling up inside him at the normalcy of the gesture—after everything, his brother was still here. Keltor, grinning, seized the opportunity and wrapped Esendil in a headlock, his hands rough as he ruffled the top of Esendil's hair.

"Get off!" Esendil protested, struggling half-heartedly as Keltor laughed and finally let go. Esendil ran his hands through his hair, trying to smooth it back down—not just out of habit, but to steady himself, to remind himself that this was real and his brother was alive.

"I'm glad you're not dead," Esendil said, running his hands through his hair to flatten it back down. Despite the underlying seriousness of his words, he couldn't resist a grin. "Even though you're annoying," he added, his tone lightening the moment.

"Yeah, me too," Keltor replied, sharing in the relief that lingered between them. He dipped the paddle into the water, gently steering the boat away from the castle wall, his actions signalling a return to normalcy after all they had been through.

Esendil leaned forward, curiosity etched on his face. "So, are you going to bond with her then?" he asked.

Keltor glanced over, slightly amused. "What, Kaitlin?"

Esendil rolled his eyes and replied with dry sarcasm, "No, her bloody maid, of course Kaitlin."

With a grin, Keltor revealed, "Actually, we're already bonded."

Esendil's eyes widened in disbelief. "What, seriously!" he exclaimed, struggling to process the news.

Keltor nodded, his expression smug. "Yes, a few days ago we had a ceremony in the forest."

Contemplating the implications, Esendil frowned thoughtfully before meeting his brother's gaze. "Hang on, does that make you the King then?"

Keltor's smirk lingered as he confirmed, "Yes, it does."

Esendil paused for a moment, a grin slowly spreading across his face as a thought occurred to him. "So, as I'm your brother, does that make me a prince?" he asked, his tone filled with hope and excitement at the prospect.

Keltor couldn't help but laugh at his brother's question, shaking his head as he replied, "No, it doesn't."

Disappointment flickered across Esendil's features as he protested, "Oh, why not?"

Keltor explained with a wry smile, "Because I'm not royalty. I'm only King by bonding; Kaitlin is still the boss."

Esendil let out a dramatic sigh. "That sucks," he moaned, clearly unimpressed by the technicalities.

Keltor, however, tried to offer some consolation. "It will make you a Lord though, and you can come and live in the castle if you want, if mum says it's okay that is."

Esendil's mood brightened at the new possibility. "Really." He paused, considering his prospects. "Girls still like Lords, right?" he asked, looking hopeful.

Keltor gave him a knowing look. "Ese, is that what this is about, whether or not you get the girls?"

Esendil didn't hesitate with his reply. "Yeah. It's okay for you, you've got yourself a Queen. Keltor, I've seen those girls at the palace, and they're fine."

"Ese," Keltor said, laughing. Their playful banter revealed a close bond and mutual understanding, each brother amused by the other's hopes and optimism.

Esendil immediately responded, his tone defensive yet earnest, "What, I'm sixteen, what do you expect?"

Keltor simply shook his head, a smile playing on his lips as he regarded Esendil with fondness. "Nothing," he replied, clearly amused by his brother's enthusiasm.

Just then, the beam from Keltor's lamp revealed something lurking in the darkness ahead. Sharpening his focus, he instructed his brother urgently, "It looks like the landing point, quick, Ese, get the rope ready." With swift determination, Keltor grasped the oar and expertly guided the boat towards the landing point, preparing for their arrival.

Esendil stood, holding the guide rope in his hand. The cold, damp air clung to their skin as the boat scraped against unseen rocks beneath the surface, sending shivers up their spines.

"Don't miss," Keltor said, his tone serious as he glanced at Esendil.

"I won't," Esendil replied, determined to prove himself. Keeping true to his word, he expertly threw the rope and managed to hook it securely over the pole at the small docking area.

Keltor watched with approval and offered praise. "Well done," he said, as Esendil pulled the boat in towards the shore. The brothers wasted no time, jumping off the boat together. Keltor raised the lamp, its light illuminating the surroundings as he looked up.

With a sense of relief, Keltor remarked, "Well, there it is, just as Logan said." His tone conveyed both confidence and reassurance. Turning to Esendil, he outlined their plan once more.

"Right, as we discussed, you stay here, and if I am not back in a few hours you take yourself down the river and find mum, okay."

Esendil acknowledged his brother with a nod, signalling his readiness. At Keltor's instruction, Esendil cupped his hands together, forming a platform. Keltor carefully placed his foot in the centre of Esendil's palms, preparing to be lifted.

"Don't drop me," Keltor said, flashing a grin to lighten the moment.

"Just get your butt up there and find Dad," Esendil retorted, his voice full of determination and encouragement.

Summoning every ounce of his strength, Esendil braced himself and heaved Keltor upwards with all his might. Keltor reached up, his fingers wrapping around the cold, iron bars overhead. As he tried to push them open, he could feel how stiff and unyielding they were, resisting his efforts at every turn.

"Hurry up," Esendil urged, his arms beginning to shake from the strain. "You weigh like a horse!" Despite his best efforts to stay steady, the effort of holding Keltor aloft was quickly taking its toll.

"Okay, I've nearly got it," Keltor said, determination evident in his voice. Below, Esendil gritted his teeth, his arms shaking from the effort yet refusing to yield. The air was filled with the sound of their strained breathing, and the gentle lapping of the river against the boat echoing in the background.

Esendil, his arms trembling with fatigue, let out an exasperated groan. "Use your magic, why don't you!" he muttered, his voice betraying both frustration and exhaustion. Keltor couldn't help but laugh quietly at his brother's outburst. "I am, Ese," he replied with a reassuring grin, though the truth was he hadn't been using magic at all. Keltor's awkward expression betrayed the lie—a moment of realisation flashing across his face. Only then, did he channel his magic through the grate, sending a surge of energy that instantly loosened it from its stubborn place. Keltor shoved it aside with an almighty push, the old metal scraping harshly against the stone. Without wasting a moment, he grabbed the edge of the

494

opening, hauled himself up, and climbed through, emerging into the darkness above.

Before moving on, Keltor glanced back down at Esendil, his voice filled with concern and encouragement. "Keep your eyes peeled, okay? Just because you're down there doesn't mean you can relax."

Esendil looked up at his brother, his voice steady but tinged with concern as he assured him, "I won't, be careful." The seriousness of the moment was clear in the way he spoke, and after a brief pause, he added quietly, "And please, find our dad."

"I will," Keltor promised, offering his brother a reassuring smile. With a final glance down, he reached out and pulled the heavy iron grate back over the hole, making sure it was securely in place to protect Esendil below.

It was dark in the chamber, but Keltor's eyes quickly adapted to the gloom. Shapes gradually took form, revealing a room cluttered with old barrels stacked haphazardly against the walls. Thinking only of his brother's safety, Keltor dragged one of the heavy barrels over the open grate, concealing the entry point and providing some protection for Esendil below.

Turning away from the grate, Keltor made his way to a sturdy wooden door. He reached out, grasped the cold iron handle, and turned it. The latch gave with a soft click, and the door eased open. He stepped through, pausing momentarily to take stock of his surroundings. The corridor beyond stretched out in both directions, bathed in the flickering glow of torches held in iron sconces along the stone walls. The presence of these torches told him that this passage was regularly patrolled by guards, a fact that made him proceed with greater caution.

To the right, the corridor faded into darkness. Keltor reckoned that the lack of light meant there were probably no prisoners kept that way, so he decided against venturing further into the gloom. Instead, he turned to his left, moving slowly and cautiously down the more illuminated passage. Every step was measured, his senses heightened as he crept along, ever mindful of the risk of discovery.

Soon, he found himself at a T-junction, where the corridor split in two directions, both equally lit by the flickering torches mounted in iron sconces. He paused, uncertainty gripping him—there was no clear indication of which path might lead to his father. Standing still, Keltor closed his eyes and drew in a deep, calming breath, silently pleading, "Dad, where are you?" He tried to sense his father's presence, hoping for any sign or intuition to guide him. When he opened his eyes, a strange pull directed him to the left, so he followed it, trusting his instincts.

As he proceeded along this corridor, he passed by a series of cell doors. At each one, he paused, peering through the small peepholes in hopes of spotting his father. Each time, however, the cells were empty, and with each disappointment, his spirits sank further. Doubt gnawed at him, yet he clung to the hope that his father had to be here somewhere—he had glimpsed him in a vision, and his father had described the Aranstream cells to him. The conviction that he was in the right place kept him moving forward, determined not to give up the search.

Keltor moved quietly, his senses on high alert. He pressed himself close to the chill of the stone wall, careful not to make a sound as he edged towards another heavy cell door. Leaning in, he placed his ear against the rough timber, straining to catch any sign of life from within. The silence was thick, broken only by the steady thud of his own heartbeat. Despite the lack of response, a strange sensation surged through him—a mixture of nerves, fear, and a flicker of hope. Something deep inside told him he was close, that a connection existed between himself and whatever lay behind that door. The possibility that his father might be just a few feet away filled him with both trepidation and excitement, urging him not to give up.

Keltor moved quietly towards the next cell door, anxiety tightening in his chest. He pressed himself against the wall, ensuring he remained concealed from any passing guards. With a soft voice, barely louder than a whisper, he called out, "Dad, are you in here?"

Reaching up, he found the small latch that secured the peephole and gently slid it open. Peering through, his eyes strained to adjust to the gloom inside the cell. The interior was shrouded in darkness, but as Keltor focused, he thought he could just make out a figure seated at the back of the cell, perched on the edge of a narrow bed. A frown creased his brow—he couldn't be certain it was his father, and yet he knew he had to take the risk. There was always the chance that the person inside was not Forde, but another unfortunate soul, and he had no idea how a stranger might react to his presence.

Drawing a steadying breath, Keltor tried again, this time keeping his voice low and urgent as he whispered through the peephole, "Dad, Forde?" He waited, hope and trepidation warring within him, for any sign that his father was truly inside.

The shadow in the darkness shifted, catching Keltor's attention. His heart pounding, he called out once more, his voice trembling with hope, "Dad, is that you?"

From the gloom came a reply—a man's voice, low and incredulous, whispering, "Keltor?" The recognition was unmistakable, and the shock in the tone sent a jolt through Keltor.

A surge of emotion overwhelmed him, making his whole body tremble. Tears welled in his eyes as he struggled to compose himself. "Dad," he repeated, his voice thick with feeling.

Quickly, Keltor's hand darted to the lock on the cell door. He hesitated for a moment, his gaze flickering anxiously up and down the corridor to check for any sign of approaching guards. Satisfied that he was alone, he proceeded with desperate urgency.

Softly, he chanted, "*Aperta clauditis,*" while tracing a circular motion with his hand. A surge of magic flowed into the lock, and with a quiet click, it sprang open. Without wasting another moment, Keltor swung the cell door open and slipped quietly into the darkness beyond. He pulled the door closed behind him, then paused, allowing his eyes to adjust to the dimness. Inside the cell, the only light came from a slender strip of sunlight streaming through a narrow arrow slit high up on the wall.

The man sprang up from the bed, his movements abrupt and filled with disbelief as he peered through the gloom. "Keltor, son, is that really you?" Forde's voice was hushed and trembling, unable to conceal the hope and fear mingling within him. For a moment, it seemed as though he scarcely dared to believe his own eyes, worried that this might be nothing more than a cruel hallucination.

"Yes, it's me, Dad," Keltor replied softly, his voice thick with emotion as he struggled to contain his tears and remain composed.

Forde attempted to rush to his son but was abruptly halted by the chain fastened securely around his ankle, preventing him from closing the distance between them. The restraint clinked dully in the silence, and the frustration was evident on his face as he reached out towards Keltor, yearning for the embrace that the chain now denied them both.

Keltor took a tentative step towards his father, his heart pounding in his chest. Forde's eyes, bright with unshed tears, met his son's gaze, and a weary but genuine smile broke through the tangled beard that covered much of his gaunt face.

"I knew one day you would find me, my boy," Forde whispered, his voice trembling with emotion as he spoke. Though worn down by hardship, his expression was illuminated by a flicker of hope and pride at the sight of Keltor standing before him.

Keltor gazed intently at his father's face, noticing how gaunt and drawn it had become. Though his memories of his father were hazy, there was no mistaking those eyes—gentle, kind, and full of love. Overcome with emotion, Keltor uttered a broken, "Dad," before collapsing into his father's arms. The embrace revealed just how frail his father had grown; beneath the threadbare rags, he was little more than skin and bones, a far cry from the strong, broad-shouldered man Keltor remembered. The sour scent of captivity clung to him, but Keltor didn't care. He held his father tightly, refusing to let go, cherishing the reunion despite the hardships time and imprisonment had inflicted.

Forde's voice quivered with emotion as he clung to his son, unable to contain the overwhelming relief and joy that surged through him at their long-awaited reunion. Tears streamed down his face as he sobbed, "I can't believe you're here," the words escaping in a broken whisper that spoke of years of longing and hope.

Keltor, equally overcome by the moment, wept openly in his father's embrace. "I can't believe it's you," he managed between sobs, the reality of their reunion washing over them both. They held each other tightly, neither willing to let go, as if afraid the other might vanish if they loosened their grasp.

After a long, silent moment, Forde rested his head on Keltor's shoulder, his mind reeling at how much his son had grown. "By the spirits, you've grown, son," he murmured, his voice thick with wonder and pride at the young man before him.

Letting out a shaky laugh and wiping at his tears, Keltor replied, "Yeah, just a bit." The disbelief lingered in his voice as he continued, "Oh my god, Dad, I can't believe I've found you. We all thought you were dead." His words tumbled out, heavy with guilt and relief. "I'm so sorry we didn't look for you before, but the King, he said you were killed on that last mission, and we all believed him."

Forde slowly released his grip on his son, his hands trembling as he looked Keltor over, shaking his head in disbelief. He managed a rueful smile, trying to reassure his son. "Hey, it's all right. The King probably truly believed I was dead. We were caught off guard in an ambush, and before I even realised what was happening, I was taken prisoner." Forde's voice faltered for a moment as he recalled the ordeal. "The other night, I thought I caught a glimpse of you, but I convinced myself I was imagining things, that perhaps I was finally losing my mind."

Keltor reached for his father's hand, his voice gentle but earnest. "It really was me, Dad. Mum gave me your book, and somehow, I was able to connect with it. It sounds strange, but that's how I found you. I saw you sitting here, on this very bed. That's how we knew you were still alive."

Forde's eyes glimmered with longing as he allowed himself a fleeting smile, his thoughts turning to Sharelle. The question that

499

had haunted him through endless days and nights in the suffocating darkness of his cell finally escaped in a hesitant, almost apologetic tone. "How is your mother? I mean, has she… you know, moved on?" he asked, a nervous shrug belying the depth of his fear that Sharelle might have found solace in another's arms during his long absence.

Keltor, moved by his father's vulnerability, reached up and gently touched his father's bearded cheek, shaking his head with quiet certainty. "No, Dad, there has never been anyone else," he replied softly. "Mum misses you so much. Her heart never healed enough for her to move on."

Forde's smile was bittersweet, his heart soaring at the knowledge that Sharelle had never moved on, yet aching for the suffering she must have endured after being told of his death. The thought of her raising their children alone brought a deep sadness.

Turning his thoughts to his children, Forde asked with concern, "And Anna and Esendil, are they both okay?"

Keltor offered reassurance, his tone gentle. "Anna is fine as far as I know. Esendil was captured, but," he said, his expression brightening as he dropped his hand and smiled, "I've found him, and he's safe. He's waiting back at the boat."

Worry crept into Forde's voice as he sought clarity. "Captured, by who, what's happened?" he pressed, anxious to understand the dangers his family had faced in his absence.

Keltor's voice trembled as he began to explain the turmoil that had unfolded in their homeland. "So much has happened, Dad, but we need to get out of here," he urged, urgency pressing into every word. "Aranstream launched an attack on Elvendon. It was swift and brutal."

His eyes darkened as he continued, "King Severon is dead—executed by King Iwein. And they killed his daughter, Elouise." The enormity of the loss weighed heavy in the air.

"With King Severon gone, King Iwein has seized control of the throne of Elvendon. All our soldiers, every able-bodied man, and even boys over fourteen have been taken by Aranstream. King

Iwein is building a new castle and city, and he is using them as his workforce."

Forde's expression twisted in horror as the gravity of their situation settled over him. "By the spirits," he exclaimed, his voice tinged with desperation. "How are we going to get these chains undone?" The urgency in his words betrayed his eagerness to leave the confines of his prison.

Keltor, undeterred and calm, knelt beside his father. "Leave that to me," he assured, placing a steady hand on the cold metal lock. Concentrating, he uttered the incantation, *"Aperta Claudities."* A sharp click echoed as the lock sprang open, the chains falling away.

Forde stared at Keltor, astonished by the sudden and unexpected display of magic that had just freed him from his shackles. "Keltor?" he uttered, his voice thick with surprise as he cast aside the chains and stood, finally liberated from his confinement.

Keltor offered a reassuring grin, sensing his father's disbelief. "Dad, I'll explain everything when we're out of here," he promised, his tone both earnest and light. "Just know that I'm a wizard, and although I'm still learning, I have a few tricks up my sleeve."

Forde, still trying to grasp the reality of his son's abilities, asked, "You have my amulet?"

Keltor shook his head, replying simply, "No, Dad, I'm naturally gifted."

"By the stars, son," Forde murmured, his eyes alight with a proud smile as he looked at Keltor.

Keltor's resolve was clear as he continued, "Look, I'll tell you everything, I promise, but we need to get out of here."

With a supportive pat on Keltor's back and a nod, Forde responded with a grin, ready to trust his son's abilities as they prepared for escape.

Keltor approached the cell door with deliberate caution. He eased it open just enough to peer into the corridor, scanning his surroundings for any signs of movement. The muffled sound of voices and the heavy thud of approaching boots echoed down the passageway, making him tense with anticipation. Acting quickly, Keltor closed the door once more, ensuring it was securely shut.

"Someone's coming," Keltor announced, his voice raised just enough to warn his father of the approaching presence.

"It's a guard check," his father replied, and he hurried back to the bed and sat down. Then he remembered, and he reached down and grabbed the chain and put the shackles loosely around his ankles.

Keltor moved swiftly to the side of the cell door, pressing his back against the cold stone wall. He hoped desperately that the guards would not open it. A sudden thought struck him, and with a determined glance towards his father, he raised his hand in preparation.

"*Closerua,*" Keltor chanted softly, his voice barely above a whisper. Instantly, the cell door responded to his magic, the lock sliding shut with a quiet but resolute click.

The steady murmur of conversation and the rhythmic sound of footsteps reverberated down the corridor, each moment growing louder and more distinct. Keltor felt his muscles tighten as the noise drew nearer, every sense on high alert. The footsteps came to an abrupt stop just outside their cell, leaving a tense silence in their wake.

The sharp voice of a man rang out through the cell door, demanding, "Are you still alive?"

Forde responded calmly, "Yes."

A mocking laugh followed from the other side. "Hmm, not for long," the man taunted, his amusement clear in his tone.

Forde pressed for answers, asking, "What do you mean by that?"

"You'll find out soon enough," the man replied cryptically. With that, the peep hole slammed shut and Keltor distinctly heard a key turning in the lock.

"Hell," Keltor muttered, casting a quick glance at his father, who returned the look with anxious eyes as the heavy door creaked open, swinging inward into the dimly lit cell. Keltor moved silently with the motion of the door, positioning himself so he remained concealed behind it. Two men entered the cell; one of them, who had spoken earlier, was idly swinging a bunch of keys attached to a chain at his waist, their metallic clinking echoing in the confined space.

Forde broke the silence first. "So, what's going on?" he asked, his voice measured but clearly seeking answers

The guard regarded Forde with a snarly grin. "Well, it seems our Prince wishes to execute you," he announced, his tone laden with cruel satisfaction.

Forde, unshaken by the threat, looked directly at the guard and responded, "Oh, really, and why is that after all these years?" His voice was calm but demanded an explanation, determined to uncover the truth behind their sudden peril.

The guard's expression grew colder as he fixed his gaze on Forde. "It would appear that your son, whom we all thought dead, is causing a significant amount of trouble for our Prince. So, he has decided to show him what he does to troublemakers."

Forde regarded him with a measured look, unfazed by the threat. "Hmm," he murmured, rising slowly to his feet. "And what has my son been doing that has upset your Prince?"

The guard leaned forward, his tone heavy with implication. "Well, the rumours are that he and the Princess of Elvendon, whom we also thought was dead, are not. They are building a resistance to take back Elvendon." His words hung in the air, causing Forde to pause and process the gravity of the situation.

"Take back Elvendon?" Forde echoed, his voice tinged with disbelief, even though he was aware, from Keltor's brief explanations, that the circumstances were dire. He sought confirmation, hoping for more clarity about the unfolding events.

The second guard smirked, the sarcasm unmistakable in his voice. "Oh dear, has no one told you?" he mocked, clearly enjoying Forde's confusion.

"Told me what?" Forde pressed, his gaze fixed on the guard. Out of the corner of his eye, he noticed Keltor beginning to move out from behind the door, prepared for whatever might come next.

The guard's sneer deepened as he launched into his explanation. "Our King has killed the King of Elvendon and the other princess. We have taken over Elvendon and their army."

Forde's eyes widened in surprise. "There were two princesses?" he asked, his tone indicating his disbelief at this sudden revelation.

The guard nodded, his voice laced with a hint of triumph. "Yes, apparently King Severon sent one of them to Earth. Well, we thought she was dead, but rumours have emerged that she's still alive."

A determined look settled on Forde's face as he absorbed the implications of the guard's words. "Well, then I believe my son and the princess have every right to form a resistance. In fact, I think I will join them."

"Oh really, and how do you suppose you're going to do that without your head!" the first guard said with a laugh.

Without warning, Keltor moved with remarkable speed and precision. Silently positioning himself behind the first guard, he acted decisively—his hands rose and, before the man could react or even comprehend the danger, Keltor snapped his neck. The guard collapsed lifelessly to the floor.

The second guard's mouth opened to shout, but Keltor's fist shot out, driving into the man's throat with a dull, sickening thud. The guard staggered, gasping and clutching at his neck as air refused to come. Without hesitation, Keltor gripped the guard's chin and twisted hard. There was a brittle snap, echoing in the tiny cell, and the guard crumpled silently beside his fallen companion. The hallway fell into an eerie hush, broken only by the faint scuffle of Keltor steadying himself, the chill of danger lingering in the air.

"I see the protection training went well," his father said as he stepped over their bodies and stood in front of his son.

"Yes, well, I've had a lot of practice over the years. Come on, clearly, they know about me and Kaitlin," he said, and he turned to walk to the door. His father grabbed his arm.

Forde felt his father's grip tighten as concern etched itself clearly across his face. He looked at Keltor, confusion evident. "Who is Kaitlin?" he asked, voice low but urgent.

Keltor stopped in his tracks and glanced over his shoulder. "The other Princess," he replied calmly, "or should I say, our new Queen—and my wife." Without waiting for a response, he continued towards the door.

Forde paused, raising his eyebrow in disbelief. "Your wife," he echoed, the shock settling in as the implications of Keltor's words registered. "Wait, that means you're…"

Keltor nodded, his expression resolute. "The King, yes, Dad."

"By the spirits," Forde muttered, his hand lifting to scratch his shaggy beard, clearly taken aback by the revelation. The shock was evident in his posture as he tried to process the unexpected news.

Noticing his father's reaction, Keltor glanced over his shoulder and reassured him, "Dad, I will tell you everything, when we get out of here and get to mum."

Forde responded with a slight raise of an eyebrow, accepting his son's promise for answers despite the whirlwind of questions surely running through his mind.

Keltor grinned knowingly, understanding that his father must be wrestling with a hundred thoughts but was willing to wait until they were safe to hear the whole story.

Forde's voice trembled slightly as he admitted, "My body is weak, son." He extended his arm towards Keltor, the effects of years spent in neglect and malnutrition now painfully obvious in his frail movements.

Noticing his father's condition, Keltor rushed to his side. "Sorry, dad. Put your arm around my shoulder," Keltor encouraged, positioning himself to offer support. Forde complied, draping his arm over Keltor's shoulder, while Keltor gently wrapped his own arm around his father's waist to steady him.

"Okay?" Keltor asked, concern evident in his tone.

Forde gave a small nod of gratitude. "Yes, son, thank you."

With that reassurance, Keltor readied himself to move. "Right, let's go."

Keltor closed the cell door quietly behind him, determined to ensure their escape remained unnoticed. Raising his hand, he murmured the incantation, "Aperta," sealing the door securely. Both men paused for a moment, their eyes scanning the corridor to confirm the coast was clear. Satisfied that no one was nearby, Keltor gently supported his father as they began to make their way down the dimly lit passage.

"It's not far, dad," Keltor whispered, reassuring his father as they pressed forward.

Forde managed a faint smile despite his weakness, his pride evident in his gaze. "I'm okay, just a little weak, that's all," he replied, casting a loving look at his son. As they walked together, Forde marvelled not only at Keltor's abilities as a wizard, but also at the knowledge that his son was now the King of Elvendon.

They stopped at the oak door to the wine cellar.

As Keltor opened the door to the cellars, the atmosphere was eerily silent. Forde's voice broke the stillness, his tone soft but troubled. "It's very quiet," he observed, glancing around the dimly lit space. The absence of sound only heightened their sense of unease, every echo seeming to carry a warning.

Keltor nodded in agreement, his brow furrowed with concern. "Yeah, I know, something's happening, and I'm worried about Kaitlin." The weight of apprehension was clear in his voice, every word betraying the deep unease gnawing at him. The silence that filled the cellar only served to magnify Keltor's fears for Kaitlin's safety, each second of stillness carrying the possibility of hidden threats.

Understanding his son's turmoil, Forde squeezed Keltor's shoulder gently in a silent gesture of reassurance. He sensed the tension but placed his faith in Keltor's judgement. Together, they pressed on, moving past dusty barrels and beneath the flicker of lanterns. The air felt dense with anticipation, every footstep echoing their urgency through the empty corridors. Forde, though weary and leaning heavily on his son, remained resolute, keeping his attention fixed on Keltor.

As they wound their way past the ageing barrels of wine, Forde cast a worried glance at his son. "Where is she, your wife?" he asked quietly, unable to hide the concern in his voice.

Keltor hesitated, then replied in a low tone, "I think she's somewhere here in the castle. We were both captured by Prince Keion and his men. It was too soon for us to reveal our identities, and I had to make a split-second decision to give us a chance to fight back later and reclaim the Kingdom." He paused, anxiety flickering across his expression. "Dad, Kaitlin is half witch and half elf. She has magic too, but just like me, we've only recently discovered our powers and are still figuring out what we're capable of. I only hope I made the right choice."

Forde stopped, turning to face his son, his gaze gentle but searching. "You love her very much, don't you?" he asked, seeing the pain and worry etched deeply in Keltor's eyes.

Keltor looked at his father and nodded, his voice steady but full of emotion. "With all of my heart, Dad."

Forde placed a reassuring hand on his son's shoulder. "Do you want to go now and look for her?" he asked softly, understanding the turmoil Keltor was experiencing.

Keltor shook his head, determination evident despite the longing in his eyes. Though his heart ached to search for Kaitlin right away, he knew he had to get his father out first. The thought of leaving his father vulnerable during the chaos that would surely erupt when he went after Kaitlin weighed heavily on him. Keltor understood that once he set out to find her, the confrontation would begin, and in his father's weakened condition, it was too great a risk.

"No, it's okay, I'll come straight back for her," Keltor replied quietly, reassuring his father with a steady voice.

In response, Forde reached out, wrapping his arm around Keltor in a heartfelt embrace. His voice trembled with emotion as he spoke. "You've grown into an amazing man, Keltor. I am so proud of you, and I'm so sorry I missed you growing up. It broke my heart, you know. Every day, knowing you and your brother and sister were growing up without me there. I don't suppose they even remember me much; they were so little the last time they saw me."

Keltor met his father's gaze, offering comfort. "Hey, they do remember, dad. Mum made sure of that."

Forde managed a smile, though tears streamed quietly down his cheeks, the weight of memories and emotion threatening to overwhelm him. The journey through the castle had stirred feelings he had long tried to suppress, and now, on the brink of escape, those emotions became almost too much to bear.

"We're almost out, Dad," Keltor said softly, doing his best to keep hope alive in his father's heart. He guided Forde to sit on an old wooden box, ensuring he was comfortable and safe for what came next. "Just wait here," Keltor reassured, determined to protect his father in any way he could.

Turning his attention to the hidden exit, Keltor moved the huge barrel he had previously used to conceal the grate. He bent down, gripping the cold iron bars with determination, and heaved with all his strength. The grate lifted, and with a final effort, Keltor swung it to the left and let it drop, opening their path to freedom.

"Esendil, are you there?" Keltor called down, his voice echoing through the passage below.

Relief was evident in Esendil's reply as he called back, "Keltor!" The sound of his brother's voice, after what had felt like an age since Keltor had left, brought comfort to both of them.

Keltor grinned down as Esendil's face came into view, illuminated by the faint light filtering through the opening.

"Have you got him?" Esendil asked, looking up with anticipation.

"Yes," Keltor replied, reassuring his brother. Esendil's smile broadened, radiating joy and relief at the success of their daring rescue.

"Dad, let's go," Keltor said softly, extending his hand towards his father. Forde took his son's hand, allowing Keltor to help him up from the old wooden box. Leaning heavily on Keltor for support, Forde shuffled towards the edge of the opening, his movements slow but determined, spurred on by the urgency of their escape and the comfort of his son's presence.

"Okay," Keltor said gently as he helped his father towards the opening, offering steady support. Forde nodded, his voice soft as he replied, "Yes, son." With deliberate care, he eased himself down, settling on the edge of the passage. As Forde glanced below, his gaze found Esendil waiting for him, looking up with anticipation. In that moment, Forde's heart melted; the sight of his son, who had been just four years old the last time they were together, overwhelmed him with emotion and longing.

"Come on, Dad, I'll catch you," Esendil urged, stepping forward with his arms outstretched in readiness to support his father. The care and anticipation were clear in his voice, a mixture of hope and concern as he waited for Forde to descend.

Keltor, steady and strong, took hold of his father's arms. Gently but firmly, he began to lower Forde down towards Esendil. It was no struggle—Keltor's strength and Forde's frailty, the result of years spent in hardship, made the task easier than it ought to have been. Carefully, he guided his father until Esendil could reach him.

"I've got him!" Esendil called out as his father came safely into his waiting arms. Relief and pride mingled in his tone as he embraced Forde, holding him close for the first time in years.

"Ese, son," Forde said, his voice thick with affection as he returned the embrace. The moment was heavy with emotion, a long-awaited reunion that neither had truly believed would happen.

"Hi, Dad," Esendil replied softly, his eyes brimming with tears. The bond between father and son, stretched but unbroken by their long separation, was reaffirmed in that quiet moment of connection.

Keltor carefully edged his way over to the hole, his movements deliberate and cautious. Reaching out, he grasped the heavy grate, pulling it aside to clear the way. With a swift motion, he dropped down through the opening, landing securely below.

"Come on, in the boat both of you, let's get out of here," Keltor instructed, urgency in his voice as he beckoned Esendil and Forde to follow. The boat rocked gently as Esendil assisted his father, helping him aboard with careful hands and steady support.

Keltor unhooked the boat from the dock, then reached down to retrieve the oars from where they lay at the bottom of the vessel. Once his father and brother had settled themselves, he pressed off from the side of the wall, allowing the craft to merge once more with the current of the river.

Forde, overwhelmed by the reunion, looked at his sons and said, "My boys, I can't believe you're here." The muscles in his jaw ached from grinning, a sensation unfamiliar after so many years. For what felt like an eternity, he had not smiled, let alone grinned. The past eleven years had been a torment, not only in body but also in mind and spirit. Through all those hardships, the hope of seeing his family again had been his sole source of strength and perseverance.

Keltor reached into the boat and extinguished the lantern, plunging them into darkness. "Hang on, you two, it's going to get a little bumpy as we join the main river," he warned, his tone steady despite the uncertainty ahead. As their small craft emerged from beneath the castle, they found the world outside still shrouded in night. For a short distance, the river channel narrowed, hemmed in on both sides by the formidable stone walls that formed the castle's foundations. The close, echoing space amplified every splash of the water as they moved cautiously forward, bracing themselves for the shifting current beyond.

"Here we go," Keltor warned, as he drew the oars into the boat, bracing himself for the imminent challenge. The sound of rushing water grew louder as they approached, and he shouted above the thunder, "It drops three times!" His voice barely carried through the roar, but the urgency was unmistakable.

The trio gripped the sides of the boat tightly, holding on as they were swept over the edge of the first waterfall. The vessel plunged sharply, crashing down onto the lower level with a heavy jolt. Without pause, they were carried onward, dropping over the second and third falls in quick succession. Each descent tested their resolve, forcing them to fight to keep the boat upright as the tumultuous water threatened to overturn them.

In total, they descended nearly two hundred feet, the relentless cascade leaving their nerves raw. At last, the boat levelled out, gliding smoothly as Keltor replaced the oars in the water. The river took command, guiding them away from the chaos and into the tranquil embrace of the forest that awaited beyond.

"By the spirits," Forde exclaimed, his gaze lingering on the waterfalls they had just navigated. The adrenaline of their descent still pulsed through him as he turned to Keltor, awe and curiosity mingling in his voice. "That was one hell of a ride."

Pausing for a moment, Forde regarded his son with renewed interest. "How did you know about this way out?" he asked, clearly impressed by the daring and ingenuity behind their escape.

Keltor replied, "A good friend of mine's father was from Aranstream. He knew about the cellar trap, and thankfully, his father used to share stories of the old castle and the secret passageways beneath it. When Aranstream took control of the castle, they redirected the waterways under the foundations, using what was once a delivery route for wine. He believed the access to the old cellar remained intact."

"So, you just took the chance that he was right?" Forde pressed, his tone a mixture of admiration and disbelief.

Keltor nodded, his expression resolute, confirming the risk he had taken to secure their escape.

Keltor explained, "It was the only way in, and it was worth the risk. It didn't go quite to plan as Kaitlin and I were captured by Prince Keion, and I was taken to the encampment." His voice carried the strain of the ordeal, but also a note of determination.

Turning to his brother, Keltor continued, "That's where I found Esendil and most of King Severon's elite guards, and thankfully Commander Talbot. I don't know what I would have done if he hadn't been there. He's rallied the men ready to fight to take back Elvendon."

"Once I have Kaitlin, we're going to take Aranstream Castle. When I get you back to Mum, I'm going straight back. Kaitlin's in there still and Prince Keion knows the Princess of Elvendon is back, or should I say Queen of Elvendon, but he doesn't know it's Kaitlin, at least I hope he doesn't."

Ahead of them, the river split into two branches. Keltor carefully steered the boat to the right, guiding them further into the depths of the forest. As the dense trees closed in around them and the waterway narrowed, Keltor announced, "Okay, we're going to pull over here." He expertly directed the boat towards the bank, then leapt onto the shore. Moving quickly, he grabbed the rope and tied the boat securely to a nearby log to ensure it would not drift away.

With the boat safely moored, Keltor's brother stepped forward to help their father. Together, they gently lifted Forde out of the boat. "I've got him, Ese," Keltor reassured, supporting their father by wrapping his arm around Forde's waist. Forde, grateful for the help, placed his arm around Keltor's neck as they prepared to continue their journey on foot.

Esendil carefully re-lit the lamp, casting a warm glow over the group as they prepared to continue their journey. Forde, feeling the effects of their recent ordeal, offered a quiet apology. "Sorry to be such a burden," he murmured as they began to walk.

Esendil immediately dismissed his father's concern, rubbing Forde's arm affectionately. "Dad, don't be ridiculous," he said, his tone gentle but firm. "We're just so glad to have found you. Mum is going to go insane when she sees you," he added, grinning broadly.

Forde couldn't help but smile at his son's words. "You think so?" he asked, a hint of hopefulness in his voice.

"Oh yes," Esendil and Keltor replied in perfect unison, sharing a grin that spoke of relief and camaraderie.

Forde glanced down at himself, noting the state of his clothes and appearance after their narrow escape. "I am rather bedraggled," he remarked, attempting to lighten the mood with a touch of humour.

Keltor stepped in with reassurance, his voice full of conviction. "She won't care, believe me dad, she is going to be so happy to see you."

Forde nodded, a glimmer of hope in his eyes. "I hope so," he replied, comforted by his sons' words as they pressed on together.

As they continued their journey, Keltor suddenly turned to his father, curiosity evident in his expression. "Do you remember your bonding day, dad?" he asked, raising an eyebrow. Forde came to an abrupt stop, momentarily halting their progress. He looked at Keltor, clearly puzzled by the unexpected question.

"My bonding day?" Forde echoed, his head tilting slightly as he tried to discern why his son would bring this up now.

Keltor clarified, "Yes, your real one, not the one you told us about in the village. The one where you and mum were dragon riders, and you were bonded by the King of Malgar."

Forde couldn't help but chuckle at this. "She told you?" he asked, a smile tugging at the corners of his mouth.

At this, Esendil, still confused by the conversation, interjected. "Told you what, who's a dragon rider?" he asked, his brow furrowing as he glanced between his father and brother.

Keltor nodded, confirming, "Yes, she did, last night." He then turned to Esendil, explaining, "Our mum and dad, believe it or not, used to be dragon riders for a King from another realm."

Esendil looked back and forth between his father and Keltor, searching their faces for any sign they were joking. After a moment, he shook his head in disbelief at his brother. "Have you gone nuts while you've been away?" he asked, struggling to process what he was hearing.

Forde couldn't help but laugh, placing a reassuring hand on Esendil's upper arm. "No, he hasn't lost his mind, son. It's true—your mum and I were exceptional dragon riders. We made a remarkable team together."

Esendil stared at them both in disbelief, struggling to take in what he was hearing. "Wait, are you serious? That's my mum you're talking about—the most sensible person in all of Elvendon!

And now you're both telling me that you and mum used to ride dragons?"

"Yes, son, we did," Forde affirmed, a note of pride in his voice. "And she fought in battles—your mum was truly formidable." He paused, a heavy sigh escaping him as he was swept up by a vivid memory. "She really could handle herself—she was incredible on the battlefield."

Forde's eyes softened as he continued, "And, I can't deny it, she looked absolutely stunning in her uniform…"

"Dad!" Esendil protested, interrupting with a groan and a shake of his head, clearly embarrassed by his father's admission.

Keltor glanced over at his brother, his eyebrows raised in amusement. "She's wearing it now," he remarked, a fond smile on his lips.

Esendil's confusion was evident. "Wearing what?" he asked, unsure what Keltor meant.

"Her dragon rider outfit, with her sword," Keltor clarified, nodding towards their father. "And I have to agree with Dad—she does look amazing."

Forde returned Keltor's smile, and for a moment, he was lost in the memory of when he had first met his wife, both of them young and in training to become dragon riders.

"This is too much," Esendil said, shaking his head in disbelief. "So, when do I get a special skill?" he asked, his tone revealing how earnestly he yearned for his own unique abilities.

Forde smiled gently and placed his arm around Esendil's shoulder, offering comfort and reassurance. "Your time will come, Ese," he promised.

Esendil grumbled in response, "It had better," unable to hide his impatience.

As they walked on, Keltor teased his brother, "What, being a Lord isn't enough for you?"

Esendil replied, "No, not if my mum and dad are dragon riders, and my brother's a King and a wizard. Where are they now, your dragons?" His curiosity was piqued by the family's extraordinary history.

Forde explained, "Oh, back on the world of Malgar. Erandril, my dragon, was given a new rider when we left to come back here to Elvendon. I haven't heard from him since."

Esendil reflected, "Why did you come back here? If I had a dragon, I wouldn't leave it."

Keltor glanced over to his father, offering the answer. "It was because of me and Kaitlin."

Forde's eyes narrowed as he looked at Keltor. "It was about you, yes. Has your mother told you about the prophecy then?" There was a note of uncertainty in his voice, as if he were searching for confirmation.

Keltor met his father's gaze. "Dad, we're living it now." The statement hung in the air, heavy with meaning, as if the very fate of their family was unfolding before them.

Forde shook his head, still not fully comprehending. "I don't understand?" he admitted, the confusion clear in his tone.

Keltor's voice took on a solemn tone as he began to explain the events that had transpired. "Kaitlin and I – we've already saved Earth. That was eight months ago, and the repercussions of our actions left Elvendon in a war with Aranstream." He paused, glancing at his brother and father to ensure they understood the weight of what he was about to say.

Keltor's voice took on a reflective tone as he addressed his family. "It turns out, it was never Princess Elouise I was destined to protect. All along, it was Kaitlin. She was the Keeper of the Star, the true chosen one."

His expression became sombre as he continued, "We had to stop Prince Aragon. He was determined to prevent us from saving Earth, and there was no other choice but to fight him. In the end, we were forced to kill him to ensure Earth's survival."

His father listened intently, the gravity of Keltor's words settling in. "Aranstream declared war on Elvendon. But Kaitlin and I were powerless to intervene – we were held in stasis for eight months. During that time, we were completely unaware of what was happening. It wasn't until just a few weeks ago, when we

515

finally awoke, that returned to Elvendon and found it was destroyed."

Keltor's voice softened, tinged with regret as he shared the painful truth with his family. "Mum thought we were dead. In fact, everyone did. Our disappearance left a void, and the world carried on, believing we had been lost forever." The weight of his words hung in the air, the enormity of what had transpired settling over them all.

Forde shook his head in disbelief, struggling to comprehend the magnitude of what he had missed. The weight of sorrow pressed heavily upon him as he murmured, "By the stars," his voice thick with emotion. He grappled with the reality that he had missed every crucial moment, unable to fulfil his role as a father when his children needed him most.

"I was supposed to be there for you," he admitted, the disappointment clear in his tone. "Instead, I ended up captured, leaving your poor mother alone to face it all." Forde's words were laced with regret, the pain of his absence evident as he considered the hardship his wife endured, believing she had lost not just him but their children as well.

The atmosphere was thick with a shared sense of regret, as father and son were forced to face the painful truth of their separation. Forde's sorrow was palpable, casting a gloomy pall over their reunion as each tried to come to terms with everything that had happened whilst they were apart.

Despite the weight of their emotions, Keltor spoke with gentle resolve. "She was, but Dad, things have unfolded as they have. We can't change what's already happened, but Kaitlin and I can try to reclaim our Kingdom." His words carried a quiet determination, suggesting that, while the past was unalterable, their future remained within their grasp.

Forde shook his head, the disbelief clear in his voice. "I still can't believe it's already happened, and I missed it." The sense of loss lingered, his mind struggling to accept that so much had occurred beyond his reach.

With a note of sarcasm, Esendil broke the tension. "I still can't believe I knew nothing about any of this."

Keltor offered a reassuring glance. "You're not the only one, Ese. I didn't know any of this either – at least, not until recently." He turned to Forde, his tone turning serious. "Dad, Prince Keion has got your amulet."

Forde's expression shifted instantly to one of shock as he fixed his gaze on Keltor. "My amulet—you know what I was, then?" he asked, his voice tinged with disbelief.

Keltor nodded. "Yes, Mum told me."

Esendil, still piecing together the snippets of conversation, interjected with confusion. "Mum told you what? What were you, Dad?" he asked, clearly out of his depth as he tried to keep up with the revelations unfolding around him.

Turning to his brother, Keltor attempted to clarify. "Ese, you know I said I'm a wizard?"

Esendil replied, drawing out the word with uncertainty, "Yeah…"

"Well, Dad's one too," Keltor revealed, casting a glance at their father.

Esendil's eyes widened in astonishment. "You're kidding—you're a wizard as well as a dragon rider?" he exclaimed, struggling to process this new facet of their father's identity.

Forde confirmed his own magical heritage with a sense of resignation. "Yes, son, I am—well, I was. Unlike your brother, who seems to have a natural talent, I needed the amulet in order to wield that power."

Esendil, still reeling from the cascade of revelations, scratched his head in confusion. "I have totally lost the plot; it's like I belong to a completely different family. Was I adopted?"

Forde let out a heartfelt laugh at his son's bewilderment. "No, Ese, you were not adopted, and neither was your sister. I'm sorry I never had the chance to explain everything to you." He glanced between his sons, seeking to reassure them. Shifting the conversation, he pressed Keltor for more information. "Does the prince know how to use the amulet?"

Keltor nodded thoughtfully. "Yes, well, a little. I don't think he realises how powerful it is."

Forde's concern deepened as he pressed the issue. "Son, you must get that back. It's far too powerful to be in the hands of Aranstream. If he were to figure out its power, then there would be nothing you or Kaitlin could do to stop him."

"I know, Dad, we have a plan in motion," Keltor reassured him.

Esendil, still struggling to keep up with the conversation, interjected, "What amulet?"

Forde turned to his younger son to explain, "It's an amulet that contains great magical power. It was given to me, along with training, by an old wizard back on Malgar. Malgar is my homeland, son. It's where I was born."

Esendil looked at his father in surprise. "Malgar? I always thought you were human. So, what does that make us? I thought we were half elf, half human."

Forde offered a gentle smile as he clarified, "It is kind of the same thing. Our race came from Earth originally, like five hundred or so years ago."

Esendil nodded slowly, his gaze dropping in confusion. "Oh, okay."

Keltor reached out, placing a reassuring hand on his brother's shoulder. "It's okay, Ese, we're still the same mad, crazy family we used to be," he said, hoping to comfort him.

Esendil let out a small chuckle, nudging his head against Keltor's arm in a gesture of affection. "Yeah, I guess. It's great to have you home, Dad, even though my mind is blown by all of this."

"Thanks, son," Forde replied warmly, offering Esendil a gentle smile. "I promise, I will tell you all about it later."

The family continued their walk, sharing conversation and laughter as they made their way through the forest. After about an hour, the dense trees began to thin, and they finally caught sight of a welcoming cottage. Warm light glowed from its windows and smoke curled from the chimney, signalling the end of their journey and the comfort of home.

Forde paused, anxiety flickering across his face as he gazed at the cottage just a few hundred yards away. The thought of seeing his wife, Sharelle, again brought a rush of nerves. He voiced his fears, admitting, "Oh, my goodness, I'm suddenly so nervous." The idea of reuniting with Sharelle, his beautiful wife, filled him with both anticipation and uncertainty.

He turned to his sons, voicing his concern, "What if she doesn't like me anymore, when she sees this old, skinny, weak man?" The vulnerability in his question hung in the air for a moment.

Keltor responded immediately, his tone reassuring. "Dad, seriously. She loves you, for you, not what you look like. Besides, a couple of months with mum's cooking and you'll be as plump as a pig." His words were meant to comfort, reminding Forde that Sharelle's affection was deeper than appearances, and gently teasing him about the hearty meals awaiting him.

Forde couldn't help but laugh at his son's remark. The tension eased slightly as he agreed, "Yeah, you're right, son. Boy, have I missed her cooking!" The exchange brought a sense of warmth and reassurance, highlighting the bond between father and son as they prepared to cross the threshold.

Keltor was the first to notice the men standing watch outside the cottage, their presence hidden from the others. As they drew closer to the front door, he acknowledged them with a subtle nod. The men, recognising Keltor from the description provided by the old forester, responded in kind, returning his nod and sheathing their weapons in a sign of trust.

Turning to his father, Keltor asked quietly, "Ready?" Forde nodded in response, though inside he was battling a swirl of nervous anticipation.

Esendil stepped forward and gently opened the cottage door. Instantly, a welcoming wave of heat washed over their faces, a stark contrast to the cool air outside. The warmth within promised comfort and safety—the embrace of home after a long and uncertain journey.

With a courteous gesture, Esendil motioned for Keltor and their father to enter first. "After you," he said, his voice soft but inviting. Keltor and Forde accepted the invitation and walked into the cottage together.

As Keltor entered, his gaze immediately landed to his left, where Esimae stood waiting. Relief spread across her face as she recognised Keltor and then she gave a slight frown at the bedraggled man who clung so tightly to him. Her expression softened and she glanced behind at the young boy, whose dark hair and brown eyes mirrored Forde's, a striking resemblance that did not go unnoticed.

Unable to contain his emotion, Keltor called out, "Mum," his voice carrying a mixture of joy and disbelief.

At the sound, Sharelle looked up from where she sat. Her eyes widened in utter astonishment, struggling to comprehend the sight before her. "Forde!" she cried, her voice trembling as her heart surged with a powerful wave of love. Tears welled in her eyes, threatening to spill over.

Desperate to reach him, Sharelle pressed her hands on the table and pushed herself to her feet. "Forde," she whispered again, barely able to speak as emotion overwhelmed her.

Hearing Sharelle's voice, Forde responded, his emotions evident as he straightened himself and released his supportive hold on Keltor's shoulder. His gaze immediately found her, the sight of her filling him with a surge of longing and disbelief.

"Dad," Keltor said, concern etched in his voice as he watched his father step forward, worried that Forde might falter in his eagerness.

"I'm okay, son," Forde reassured him softly, steadying himself and moving towards Sharelle.

Overcome by emotion, Sharelle called out to him, tears streaming down her cheeks. "Forde," she wept, unable to believe her eyes. Rushing to him, she reached out, her trembling hand gently touching his bearded face as she searched for reassurance that this was truly happening.

"Yes, my love, it is," Forde replied, his voice filled with warmth and certainty.

Sharelle's gaze locked with Forde's, her heart overflowing. "Oh, my love, my heart cannot believe it's you," she whispered, her words trembling with joy and disbelief.

They embraced tightly, arms wrapping around each other in a long-awaited reunion, the world momentarily fading as they simply held one another, lost in the relief and ecstasy of being together again.

"You are so beautiful," Forde murmured to her, his words a tender affirmation of his love.

Sharelle gazed up at Forde, a teasing glint in her eyes despite the tears on her cheeks. Smiling affectionately, she brushed her fingers through his long, tangled beard and said, "And you are very hairy, stinky and skinny." Her tone was gentle, filled with both relief and playful affection as she continued to stroke his matted beard, revelling in the tangible proof that he was truly there.

Forde let out a shy laugh, his cheeks colouring slightly. "Yeah, I may have lost a bit of weight," he replied, managing a joke about his gaunt appearance. Though his frame was thin and marked by hardship, the warmth in his eyes showed how grateful he was for this moment.

Sharelle's composure wavered as overwhelming emotion took hold. "I can't believe you're here, you're alive, I love you so much," she sobbed, her voice thick with relief and love. Without hesitation, she pulled him back into her arms, clinging to him tightly as if fearful he might slip away again. "I don't ever want to let you go," she whispered, holding him close and refusing to loosen her embrace, her heart finally at peace after so much longing and uncertainty.

Overcome with emotion, Keltor could no longer contain himself. Tears streamed freely down his cheeks as he turned away from the scene inside, his heart both rejoicing at the reunion of his parents and aching with concern for Kaitlin. Unable to remain in the room, he stepped outside, seeking solace in the quiet of the evening.

Leaning back against the wall of the cottage, Keltor sniffled, struggling to compose himself. He glanced up towards the trees, suddenly reminded of the unseen eyes that watched him. With urgency, he brushed away his tears with his sleeve, trying to regain his composure amidst the swirl of emotions and the lingering worry for Kaitlin.

"Mum." The word broke the spell of the embrace between Sharelle and Forde. Sharelle pulled back, her gaze shifting beyond Forde to the source of the voice.

"Esendil!" she cried, relief and love swelling in her voice. With one arm supporting Forde, she extended the other towards her son. Esendil hurried to her, falling into her welcoming embrace.

Overwhelmed by emotion, Sharelle reached out to her son, her voice trembling with relief and affection. "My son, I can't believe it, are you okay?" she wept, holding Esendil in a tight embrace as though she might never let go, her tears betraying the multitude of feelings flooding through her.

Esendil returned her hug, offering her reassurance. "I'm fine, Mum," he murmured, his words muffled by her arms as she smothered him in her embrace.

After a moment, Sharelle's gaze swept the room, realisation dawning that someone was missing. "Where's Keltor?" she asked, looking around anxiously when she could not see him.

"He went outside," Esimae explained, assuming Keltor had returned to Kaitlin. She then offered, "Here, come and sit down."

"Thank you, Esimae," Sharelle replied warmly, assisting Forde as he settled himself. Esendil took a seat beside his father. With a gentle smile, Sharelle reached up and touched Forde's beard, a gesture filled with affection and relief.

"I'm so happy," she said sincerely, leaning forward to kiss him. "I just can't believe after all this time you were in that castle."

Forde met her gaze, his voice soft with emotion. "Yes, so near yet so far from you, my love."

Sharelle's voice trembled as she finally found the words she had been holding back for so long. "I'm so sorry," she said, unable to contain a sob that escaped her lips. "We thought you were dead.

I haven't changed a thing at home—all your clothes are still hanging in the wardrobe, just as you left them. Your trinkets and potions are still locked away safely in the cellar. I just couldn't bear to clear them out. It would have made everything feel too final, and I never wanted to accept that you were truly gone."

She reached up, her hand gently stroking the side of Forde's face. Her touch was filled with all the love and longing she had carried through the years. "There's been no one else. You will always be my only love," she whispered, her gaze unwavering and full of devotion.

Forde gazed at Sharelle, emotion thickening his voice. "Oh, Sharelle, I have missed you so much, the thought of seeing you and the kids has been the only thing that has kept me going," he said gently, his words filled with heartfelt longing. "And I love you so much." Leaning in, he kissed her, the affection between them palpable.

He pulled back slightly, a sheepish smile crossing his face. "Sorry," he apologised, "my dental hygiene hasn't been that great, although I tried my best."

Sharelle shook her head, her reply barely more than a whisper, but her eyes sparkled as she looked at him. "I don't care," she said, her gaze unwavering and full of love.

Esimae moved quietly around the room, placing steaming mugs on the table for everyone to enjoy. "There you go," she said, her voice gentle as she set the hot drinks down in front of the others.

Forde looked up with appreciation. "Thank you," he replied, reaching for his mug. He wrapped his hands around it, savouring the warmth, and took a grateful sip. The comforting heat of the drink spread through him, prompting a satisfied gasp as he settled back in his seat.

Esimae straightened up, glancing towards the door. "I'm going to pop outside," she announced to the room, letting them know she would return shortly. With a nod of understanding from Forde, Esimae stepped out, leaving the others to enjoy the quiet comfort of their drinks.

Forde's eyes widened in amazement as he lifted the mug to inspect its contents. "My goodness, this is incredible, what is it?" he asked, turning to Sharelle with genuine curiosity.

Sharelle smiled warmly, her eyes twinkling. "It's just coffee," she replied, her tone light and affectionate.

Forde inhaled deeply, the familiar aroma stirring distant memories. "Coffee. I'd forgotten what it tasted like." Without hesitation, he drank the entire mug in one swift motion, clearly relishing every drop.

Seeing his enjoyment, Sharelle reached for the coffee pot and offered him a refill. "Would you like another?" she asked, her gesture filled with care.

Forde nodded eagerly, his gratitude evident. "Oh, yes please, thank you," he replied, ready to savour the comforting warmth once more.

Esimae stepped outside, pulling the door to the cottage closed behind her. She called out, her voice echoing in the quiet air, "Keltor, Kaitlin?" as she searched for their presence.

Hearing her voice, Keltor looked up from where he stood at the side of the cottage. As Esimae approached, she took in his appearance, noting the tension in his posture and the absence of Kaitlin at his side.

"Hey, are you okay?" Esimae asked gently, concern evident in her tone as she drew nearer. Her gaze quickly swept the area, searching for her niece. When she realised Kaitlin was not with him, her worry intensified. "Where's Kaitlin?" she pressed, her voice rising with anxiety.

Keltor shifted his weight, pushing himself away from the wall and taking a hesitant step towards her. "Esimae," he managed, his voice strained with emotion.

Esimae's eyes narrowed as she studied him more closely. "Have you been crying?" she asked softly, her concern deepening. She then demanded more insistently, "Keltor, where's my niece?" Her voice was sharp with fear as she looked around, desperate for any sign of Kaitlin.

Keltor's eyes were bloodshot, evidence of the emotional strain he had endured. He released a heavy sigh before addressing Esimae, his voice laced with regret and exhaustion. "Esimae, we were captured by Prince Keion. I was taken to the encampment, and Prince Keion took Kaitlin to Aranstream castle."

Esimae's reaction was immediate and fierce. "What!" she shouted, disbelief and alarm flooding her expression. "Are you kidding me, he has Kaitlin!"

"Yes," Keltor replied, his determination clear. "Look, I'm going back to get her."

Esimae scowled, her frustration boiling over. She raised her hand, wagging her finger at him in anger. "You rescued your father but left her there!"

Keltor's brow furrowed deeply, remorse etched across his face. It was clear that he was already struggling with his decision, even before Esimae's reprimand.

"Esimae, it's complicated," Keltor said, his voice heavy with the burden of his actions. "Plans have been set in motion with the commander of our army, and I must time it right, otherwise they won't be able to escape. If I didn't get my father out before Kaitlin, they would have killed him."

Esimae's face contorted with anguish and anger as she shot back, "I don't care, you left her with that evil man, to do goodness only knows what to her. She's my niece, my blood!"

Keltor's voice rose in frustration and pain as he defended his actions. "I would never have left her if I didn't think she could defend herself. You have no idea what she is capable of," he shouted, gesturing emphatically towards the cottage. His desperation was clear, the anguish in his words betraying how much the situation weighed on him. "He's, my father; I couldn't just let him rot and die in that cell when I had the chance to save him. Kaitlin is not just my wife—she's, my world. My heart is breaking with the decision I made, but I'm going back for her now, and I will tear down that fucking castle to get her out if I have to!"

Esimae's hand slowly dropped to her side as she caught sight of Keltor's eyes, which had begun to glow a brilliant white—a clear sign of his unchecked anger. The intensity of his gaze made her pause, and she swallowed hard, suddenly uncertain and wary of what he might do next.

Keltor's frustration spilled over as he addressed Esimae, his voice trembling with both anger and the force of magic coursing through him. "You don't know half of what's been going on, of what we've been through," he insisted, desperate to convey the gravity of the situation. "The prince has an amulet that holds a great magical power; if he figures out how to use it, he will wipe us all out."

He gestured emphatically towards the cottage, his hands visibly shaking. "It used to belong to my dad, in there. I need to know everything about that amulet; I need to know if I can get it off that prince and if I can use it to save Elvendon. I need his help."

Keltor's anxiety was unmistakable as he continued, "Kaitlin knew this, she knew I was going to get my father out first, and she agreed it was the right thing to do." The words hung in the air, underscored by the intensity of his emotions and the flicker of uncontrollable magic threatening to erupt.

Esimae's apprehension grew as she instinctively took a step back from Keltor, sensing the intensity of his emotions. Her voice trembled as she pleaded with him, her hands rising and falling in a defensive gesture. "I'm sorry, Keltor, please just calm down," she begged, hoping to diffuse the situation and ease his distress.

Keltor's response was heartfelt, his words laced with anguish. "I love her, Esimae, the last thing I wanted was for her to be captured." His sincerity was unmistakable, revealing the depth of his feelings and the pain he was experiencing over Kaitlin's predicament.

Esimae quickly sought to reassure him, her earlier frustration replaced by understanding. "I know, and I'm sorry I had a go, it was just such a shock," she hurried, eager to mend the rift between them. Keltor glanced upwards, noticing the men on watch observing the exchange from a distance. He drew in several deep, steadying breaths, determined to regain control of his emotions and composure.

"Look, Keltor, let's go back in and discuss this, on how we can help you. Ben has been briefing the men here, and he has sent out word to those still free and in hiding. Come and talk with him, I am sure he, or Mick, or some of the other guys can help you, and your dad can tell you about the amulet, maybe he does know a way to stop its power. I'm sorry I shouted at you; I'm just scared for her."

"I know, and I'm sorry I yelled back, I'm scared too, Esimae," Keltor admitted, his voice cracking with emotion. He drew a shaky breath, struggling to maintain his composure. "I have spent my whole life protecting her and not being with her or knowing what's happening to her is killing me. I saw her yesterday and she was okay then." The memory clearly weighed heavily on him, and the pain in his words underscored just how much Kaitlin's safety meant to him.

Esimae felt a wave of relief as she noticed Keltor's eyes returning to their usual colour, signalling that he was regaining control over his emotions and the power that had surged within him moments earlier. Despite this, a lingering worry gnawed at her—she was concerned that the magic now evident in Keltor might one day prove too strong for him to contain.

Seeking to reassure him and offer support, Esimae spoke gently. "You don't have to go in alone, Keltor. Come on, let's get back inside and discuss this with the others." Her invitation was clear: the burden of rescuing Kaitlin and facing the dangers ahead did not have to rest on Keltor's shoulders alone. Together, with the help of their friends, they would try to find a way forward.

Keltor knew what he had to do, and it was clear that going alone was his best option. Alone, he could move quickly and blend into his surroundings without having to worry about others slowing him down or putting themselves at risk. If he took anyone with him, he would constantly be concerned for their safety and the potential for mistakes that could jeopardise the plan.

He offered Esimae a silent nod, signalling his agreement with her suggestion for now, but with the firm intention of slipping away later that night, once everyone else was asleep. The thought

527

of staying weighed heavily on him—his anxiety was not simply about the prince discovering Kaitlin's true identity. He was deeply troubled by the knowledge that Kaitlin's beauty would inevitably attract the prince's attention, and he feared that her magic would only keep the prince at bay for so long. Eventually, the prince would realise what she was doing, and then the danger would only grow.

Chapter Twenty-Three
Kaitlin and Prince Keion

Kaitlin slowly pushed herself up onto her elbows, feeling the weight of exhaustion pressing down on her. Her long blonde hair, now tangled and dishevelled, fell about her face as she frowned in discomfort. A sharp, throbbing pain pulsed through her head, making it ache intensely. She realised she was lying on a bed, the soft furs beneath her providing little comfort amid her confusion.

Attempting to make sense of her situation, Kaitlin lifted her head to take in her surroundings. However, the effort proved too much—the room spun wildly, leaving her feeling dizzy and nauseous. Unable to steady herself, she let her head fall back onto the covers, overwhelmed by the disorientating sensation and growing unease. Questions raced through her mind: Where was she? What had happened to her?

As she tried to piece together her memories, fragments returned to her. She remembered being taken away from the encampment and then locked in the room she shared with the other girls. The hours spent pacing within those confines had only served to heighten her anxiety and deepen her worries about Keltor. Now, regret gnawed at her—she felt foolish for her actions, convinced that her behaviour had likely blown her cover and drawn unwanted attention to Keltor.

As evening descended, Kaitlin had been instructed to resume her duties. Throughout the night, she was acutely aware of the prince's watchful gaze fixed upon her as she dutifully poured his wine. His expression was tinged with both suspicion and curiosity, making her increasingly uneasy. The last clear memory she could recall was the prince offering her a drink—one she could not refuse, regardless of her apprehension.

Sometime later, a faint noise reached her ears, pulling her from the haze clouding her mind. Summoning her remaining strength, she forced herself to lift her head and look towards the source of the sound. The room was shrouded in darkness, save for the outline of a shadowy figure rising from a nearby chair and approaching her. The world spun violently around her, the sensation leaving her nauseous. Desperate to steady herself, she closed her eyes and drew a deep breath, attempting to regain control over her senses.

"Finally, you're awake," Prince Keion remarked, his gaze unwavering as he studied Kaitlin. The familiarity in his voice pierced through the fog enveloping her mind, prompting her to fight to regain full consciousness. Despite her effort, she could only manage a faint moan, her body still weighed down by the effects of the drug and exhaustion. Helpless, she remained at the mercy of the prince, struggling to orient herself in the oppressive atmosphere of the dimly lit room.

Kaitlin felt the bed dip as the prince settled beside her, the subtle movement sending a ripple of unease through her tense body.

"I know who you are," Prince Keion murmured as he leaned over, his hand gently brushing the tangled strands from her face. She felt the warmth of his breath against her ear; every sensation magnified in the heavy hush of the room. His finger traced slowly down the side of Kaitlin's face, moving opposite to her hairline—a deliberate gesture that made her shudder and instinctively shrink deeper into the furs, wanting to disappear. "Princess," Prince Keion said quietly, his voice laced with a chilling certainty that unsettled her further.

"I'm not," Kaitlin replied, maintaining composure despite the storm swirling within her.

The prince let out a short, calculated laugh, then rose and made his way over to the window. "Yes, you are," he declared, his tone steady and unyielding. He turned his gaze towards Kaitlin, a faint glint of satisfaction in his eyes. "You see, I was bonded to your sister." He paused deliberately, as if weighing his next words for effect, before adding with chilling casualness, "Well, before I killed her."

Anger surged within Kaitlin at his admission, threatening to overwhelm her. She drew a slow, measured breath, forcing herself to remain calm. Determined not to betray any sign of the fury roiling inside, she kept her expression carefully neutral, refusing to give the prince the satisfaction of seeing her upset.

"There, that's better," the prince remarked, drawing back the heavy brown velvet curtains that had concealed the room from the world outside. The early morning sunlight streamed in, flooding the chamber and causing Kaitlin to instinctively shut her eyes, shielding herself from the sudden glare.

He observed her with a calculating gaze; his tone edged with a quiet satisfaction. "Did you truly believe you could escape detection? Hide from me as though you were nothing more than a common villager?" His words lingered in the air, heavy with meaning. "The longer I watched you, the more certain I became of your identity. You could never convincingly pass as one of the ordinary peasants."

The prince's scrutiny was unwavering. "You may never have met your sister, and it's true she bore little resemblance to you in appearance, but there is something about you—a quality, an undeniable air of noble lineage. It's unmistakable." His voice softened yet retained its edge. "And, by all accounts, you are the very image of your father."

Kaitlin's voice was barely more than a whisper, laced with a mixture of defiance and dread as she addressed the prince. "What will you do with me—kill me like my sister and father?" The question hung heavily in the air, her words trembling with the weight of grief and accusation. She met his gaze, searching for any sign of mercy or remorse, though she expected none. In that moment, her vulnerability was laid bare, but so too was her courage—Kaitlin refused to cower, even as the threat of death loomed over her once more.

He approached and sat on the bed beside her, his presence commanding and uncomfortably close. Reaching towards her face, he hesitated for a moment, as if considering his next move. "I haven't made up my mind yet," he admitted, his tone measured. "I will probably keep you here, in the tower."

He regarded Kaitlin with a lingering gaze, his eyes roaming over her features. "You know, Kaitlin, you're far more beautiful than your sister ever was. She was attractive, certainly, but you…" His hand moved to stroke the side of her face, the touch sending a wave of revulsion through her. "You are something else entirely. You would make an excellent choice for me—someone to father a child with."

He paused, inhaling deeply as if savouring the moment, then fixed her with an intense stare. "Can you imagine what a child between us would look like? What he would be capable of achieving?"

"I'd rather die," she said sharply, flinching back from his fingers. The prince responded with a slight laugh, his hand briefly touching her shoulder, his tone both dismissive and mocking. "Well, that can be arranged," he remarked, clearly relishing her defiance. "It would be a shame—you have more spark than your sister." He met her gaze, a smile playing at his lips, and continued, "I like a bit of feistiness." His words were laced with twisted admiration, hinting at the perverse satisfaction he found in Kaitlin's resistance.

His voice grew more confident as he shifted the conversation to his future, his ambitions laid bare. "My father won't rule much longer; soon, I'll take the crown and lead both kingdoms." The prince's eyes gleamed with the anticipation of power, and his posture straightened, reflecting his growing self-assurance.

He paused, considering his recent gains with thinly veiled pride. "You did me a favour killing Aragon, although I wish I could have done it myself. My father idolised him, compared to him I was nothing, but now." He stood, smiling at her, clearly revelling in the shift of power. "Now I'm the next in line, and I finally have my father's respect." The weight of his words hung in the air, his satisfaction at the change in his fortunes unmistakable.

Turning his attention back to Kaitlin, the prince's tone became inquisitive yet remained edged with suspicion. "Oh, I'm assuming that man you were with was not your brother, seeing as you don't have one. Your protector perhaps?" His question lingered, the prince clearly eager to uncover more about Kaitlin's connections and vulnerabilities.

Her eyes lifted to meet his, a silent challenge passing between them, defiance gleaming in her gaze.

The prince grinned slyly, his tone taunting. "I can tell he matters to you." The words hung in the air, weighted with implication and a hint of satisfaction at having uncovered another vulnerability.

Kaitlin looked away, refusing to give him the satisfaction of a response, but her silence spoke volumes. The prince pressed on, his voice cold and assured. "Forget him, Princess. My men are already retrieving him from the camp." His words were a deliberate provocation, designed to unsettle her and demonstrate his control over the situation.

Kaitlin turned back to the prince. Her glare burning with distain. "You think you can kill my protector? He's going to tear you to pieces; that's if I don't kill you first," Kaitlin threatened.

Prince Keion knelt beside the bed, deliberately invading Kaitlin's personal space as he leaned in closer to her face. His expression was one of predatory amusement, clearly delighted by her show of defiance.

"There's that feistiness I think I'm going to like," he remarked, his tone laced with a twisted sense of admiration. "But Princess, I really don't think you are in any position to be telling me what to do." His words dripped with condescension, highlighting the imbalance of power between them and reminding her of her vulnerability.

Keion's gaze hardened, and his voice grew colder. "In fact, if it wasn't for the fact I have somewhere to be, you and I would be having a little play time, if you get my meaning." The threat within his words was unmistakable, as he made it clear that her resistance would only serve to entertain him when he was ready, and that her fate lay entirely in his hands.

In a surge of raw emotion, Kaitlin channelled her anger and summoned what little strength she could muster. Fuelled by adrenaline, her hand lifted off the bed, and, with a swift and defiant motion, she slapped the prince hard across his face. The prince's face turned away from her with the impact. For a moment he remained quiet and still. His posture remained rigid, the flush of anger slowly spreading across his cheek as he fought to maintain his composure. The air in the room felt charged, both parties acutely aware of the boundaries that had just been crossed, and the consequences that might follow.

His cheek reddened from the blow, Prince Keion slowly turned his gaze back to her, fury simmering beneath the surface of his polished composure. For a fleeting heartbeat, the air crackled with tension, neither willing to look away. Then, the mask of amusement melted away, baring a flash of unrestrained wrath as he lashed out, seizing her cheeks in a bruising grip.

Kaitlin met his glare with unwavering defiance, sparking a visible blaze of anger within him. He slapped her sharply, and Kaitlin cried out in pain. He then took a deep breath and looked at her. The anger that was in his eyes sent a sudden wave of fear through her, she was still defenceless, the drug rendering her almost immobile.

Prince Keion's voice dropped to a chilling whisper as he fixed Kaitlin with a piercing stare. "Don't do that again," he commanded, his words carrying a weight of menace as he held her gaze unflinchingly. The intensity in his eyes left no room for misunderstanding—he was not accustomed to being defied.

Leaning even closer, his tone darkened. "I want you, Kaitlin, but don't doubt for a moment that I wouldn't kill you if necessary. Understand?" The threat was clear and unequivocal, making it evident that, despite his apparent desire, her life hung in the balance should she continue to challenge him.

Kaitlin remained silent, swallowing the urge to cry as she forced herself to hold back tears. She channelled the sting of pain radiating from her cheek into a growing ember of anger, refusing to grant Prince Keion the satisfaction of seeing her break. Deep within, she could sense the faint stirrings of her magic—an awakening power responding to her distress. Yet, despite this flicker of hope, her body was still sluggish and unresponsive, the effects of the drug rendering her unable to move as she wished.

The prince slowly rose to his feet; his movements deliberate as he strode towards the door. He paused with his hand resting on the handle, turning his head to look back at Kaitlin. As their eyes met, he offered her a smile, but it was devoid of warmth; instead, it was laced with a cold, calculated malice that sent a chill through the room.

"I'll see you later," he remarked, his words carrying a pointed edge. His lips curled into a smirk, and he added, "When I have more time to get to know you." The threat in his voice was clear, his intentions unmistakable as he lingered for a moment longer, ensuring she understood that their encounter was far from over.

Prince Keion slammed the door shut with such force that the sudden noise made Kaitlin flinch. The sharp click of a key turning in the lock followed immediately, sealing her inside. Through the thick wood, she could hear his muffled voice as he spoke to someone outside—likely giving instructions to the guard stationed at her door. After a brief exchange, the sound of his heavy boots gradually faded as he strode away down the corridor, leaving her alone in the oppressive silence of the room.

Kaitlin's head dropped back onto the pillow, a quiet whimper escaping her lips. She gingerly lifted her hand to her cheek and flinched at the sharp sting as her fingers brushed the tender skin. The pain was a grim reminder of how close she'd come to serious injury—she was fortunate her cheekbone hadn't been broken.

Tears welled in Kaitlin's eyes as she thought of Keltor, the dreadful certainty pressing upon her that the prince would likely execute him first. She refused to let her emotions overcome her, forcing herself to focus—she had to escape and do whatever she could to help Keltor.

For a while, she stayed on the bed, waiting for the dizzying sensation to fade. Her vision remained somewhat blurred, but eventually, she managed to sit up. Drawing several steadying breaths, Kaitlin swung her legs over the side of the bed. The sunlight poured into the room through the tall, arched windows, making the space exceptionally bright. She kept her gaze lowered to the floor, waiting until her eyes gradually adjusted to the light.

With considerable effort, Kaitlin pushed herself upright and clung to the sturdy oak post of the four-poster bed for support. Her gaze shifted towards the door, fully aware that a guard stood vigilant on the other side. She knew she would need her strength—and perhaps her magic—to overcome him should the opportunity arise. At least, she consoled herself, Prince Keion seemed oblivious to the true extent of her magical abilities. Men like him, she reflected bitterly, still clung to the belief that women were somehow inferior—a notion her own father had once held. Yet, this arrogance played to her advantage, for Keion had drastically underestimated her. He probably thought that a simple locked door would be enough to confine her, but she was determined to prove otherwise.

Feeling her strength returning, Kaitlin raised her hand and whispered, "*Illumanartry!*" Instantly, a shimmering orb of light materialised in her palm. For a moment, the glow cast gentle patterns across the stone walls, filling her with a brief sense of hope. She allowed herself a quiet, relieved breath before closing her hand, snuffing out the light as swiftly as it had appeared.

Kaitlin found herself with no plan and no clear sense of what she should do next, nor any idea of her precise location within the sprawling Aranstream castle. The prince had mentioned that she was being kept in the tower, but beyond that, she was uncertain. Releasing her grip on the bedpost, Kaitlin glanced down at the garish pink dress she still wore. She hitched up the hem, feeling self-conscious yet determined, and cautiously took a step forward.

To her relief, her body felt steady enough, so she made her way towards the window.

Peering out, Kaitlin quickly realised she was indeed high above the ground, confirming the prince's claim that she was in one of the castle's towers. Far below, the main courtyard sprawled out, just as she remembered it from her arrival. Groups of guards were gathered in front of the imposing main gates, their presence making it clear that escape by the obvious route was impossible. Sighing, Kaitlin leaned back against the cold stone wall, deep in thought. It was all too evident that slipping out through the front entrance was not an option.

Keltor's plan, set in motion before their capture, was straightforward but daring. He intended to reach the encampment, locate his brother and Commander Talbot, and then access the dungeons through the underground river to rescue his father. Recent events had forced Kaitlin to consider that, after her reckless encounter with Prince Keion the previous day, any strategy Keltor had devised would now be progressing at an accelerated pace.

The likelihood that Keltor might already be inside the castle, actively working to free his father, weighed heavily on Kaitlin's mind. She recalled his promise to come for her but also knew he trusted her abilities and believed she could manage on her own if necessary. Kaitlin was certain that Keltor's priority would be to secure his father's rescue before chaos erupted within the castle walls.

"God damn it," she muttered under her breath, frustration mounting as she struggled to piece together her next move. The sequence of events had unravelled so quickly that there had been no opportunity to formulate a backup plan before their capture. She was left with no choice but to trust that Keltor would adhere to the original strategy they had devised. If she could manage to escape on her own, she would need to make her way to the forest and seek out the cottage where his mother was hiding. That was where they had agreed to regroup should they be separated, and Kaitlin clung to the hope that Keltor would be waiting for her there.

Kaitlin approached the door, hesitating as a surge of uncertainty washed over her. She carefully considered her options, torn between the urge to investigate the dungeons and the pressing need to escape while she still had the chance. If she ventured down to the dungeon, there was a possibility she could discover whether Keltor's father was still being held prisoner. Should the cells prove empty, it would serve as confirmation that Keltor had been successful in his daring rescue and had likely already returned to the safety of the cottage.

However, Kaitlin recognised the considerable risk this course of action posed. Being discovered in the dungeon could jeopardise everything they had worked for, placing not only her own safety but also Keltor's plans in jeopardy. Weighing up the dangers, she took a deep, steadying breath and resolved to trust in their original strategy. It was imperative that she escape now, before the prince had a chance to return and find her.

Despite her longing for Keltor to be proud of her for having managed to obtain the amulet—Kaitlin knew she could not risk acting alone. She needed Keltor's magic; only by combining their powers could they hope to seize the amulet from the prince. With this in mind, she steeled herself for what lay ahead, determined to see their plan through together.

Kaitlin pressed her index finger to the lock and whispered, "*Operana.*" Instantly, she heard the distinct click of the mechanism as the lock sprang open. The guard stationed outside turned abruptly at the unexpected sound, his frown deepening as he realised it was unmistakably the noise of the door unlocking. Cautiously, he reached for the iron handle, his expression wary, and slowly turned it. As the door swung open, confusion flickered across his face. He peered warily up and down the barren stone corridor, clearly uncertain. The guard knew the prince had drugged Kaitlin and had personally helped lay her on the bed— there was no reason for her to be anywhere but inside, still incapacitated. Yet, the lock had unlocked itself, and he could not fathom how.

Kaitlin took a measured step back as she heard the handle begin to turn. Her body tensed, every sense alert, as she prepared herself for whatever might come next. The door creaked open, and the guard cautiously peered inside. He was a burly man, his features obscured in part by a thick black beard. A metal helmet, complete with a visor that extended over his nose, gave him an imposing appearance.

Kaitlin instinctively retreated further, positioning herself behind the door where she could remain out of immediate sight. The guard hesitated at the threshold, his voice uncertain as he called out, "Hello?" Receiving no reply, he stepped fully into the room. His eyes swept the space, searching for any sign of movement, before he began to move purposefully towards the bed, evidently expecting to find her still lying there.

Kaitlin darted through the doorway, her heart pounding, and quickly slammed the door shut behind her. She raised her hand and pointed at the lock, uttering, "Closure." Instantly, the mechanism snapped shut with a definitive click. The guard, realising what had happened, began to shout and hammered his fists against the heavy door, the sound echoing along the corridor. Kaitlin braced herself to make a run for it, but she was halted by the unmistakable sound of a key turning in the lock from the other side.

Kaitlin's heart lurched as she realised, too late, that the guard still possessed the key. Panic flashed through her mind. She quickly raised her hand and aimed at the lock, reacting just as he began to turn the key in the mechanism.

Kaitlin acted swiftly, whispering, "*Belcara*," as she channelled a surge of magic directly into the lock. The enchantment worked immediately, melting the metal of the key as it turned in the mechanism. On the far side of the door, the guard gave a startled yelp of pain; the wave of magic had travelled through the keyhole, searing his hand where he gripped the key. The acrid scent of charred metal filled the air, mingling with the guard's cries as he recoiled from the door, dropping the ruined key to the floor.

Kaitlin exhaled in relief, her breath steadying as the immediate danger passed. Without wasting a moment, she slipped from the room and made her way towards the stairwell, pressing herself close to the cold stone wall for cover. Each step down the spiral staircase was taken with deliberate care, her movements slow and measured to avoid detection by any patrolling guards.

At the foot of the stairs, Kaitlin paused, glancing cautiously around the edge of the wall before venturing into the corridor beyond. The unfamiliar surroundings heightened her sense of vulnerability. She moved swiftly, doing her utmost to silence the clatter of her wooden clogs against the hard floor, every sound a possible betrayal of her presence.

As Kaitlin lingered in the unfamiliar corridor, anxiety coiled within her, every nerve taut with apprehension. The cold, unyielding surface of the stone wall pressed against her back as she hesitated, torn between the desire to dart towards the distant exit and the need to remain hidden. All at once, Kaitlin's progress was halted by the unmistakable sound of footsteps echoing steadily from the passage ahead. The rhythmic tread grew louder, each step reverberating off the cold stone, sending a jolt of panic through her. She froze, heart pounding, as the dim outline of a figure appeared in the corridor's gloom—a shadow stretching long and ominous across the flagstones before her. Kaitlin's breath caught in her throat as she realised, with mounting dread, that she had nowhere to conceal herself; the bare corridor offered no alcoves or doors behind which to hide. Exposed and vulnerable, she pressed herself as close to the wall as possible, desperately hoping to remain unnoticed as the footsteps drew nearer.

Prince Keion emerged, his bearing resolute and commanding. He strode forward with deliberate confidence, his gaze fixed on Kaitlin, a faint, knowing smile curving his lips. Six bodyguards accompanied him, their presence alert and imposing as they flanked him protectively. Coming to a halt just metres away, Prince Keion regarded her intently, his voice laced with mockery as he remarked, "Well, I see you're feeling better."

Kaitlin instinctively retreated, every muscle tensed as she assessed her slim chances of escape. Her eyes flickered briefly to the amulet at the prince's throat—a gleaming symbol of power she was determined to seize. The air was thick with tension, every movement observed by the prince's retinue. With each moment that passed, the possibility of fleeing diminished as Prince Keion issued a cold warning: "Do not attempt it. You will not succeed in escaping. I was actually on my way to visit you again. My prior engagement was cancelled, as it appears the individual in question was dead."

Six bodyguards stood behind Prince Keion, each one watching Kaitlin intently, their expressions unyielding and alert. She risked a quick glance over her shoulder, mind racing as she weighed the possibility of making a desperate run for freedom. At the far end of the corridor, she noted a door; through a narrow arrow-slit window to her left, she could just make out the hints of the outside world beyond. The possibility of escape hovered tantalisingly, but the presence of the prince and his guards made it perilous.

Kaitlin's gaze shifted back to Prince Keion, her attention irresistibly drawn to the amulet that hung prominently around his neck. The weight of the ornament seemed almost symbolic, a tangible reminder of the immense power he wielded—power she was desperate to claim for her husband. As her eyes lingered on the amulet, a wave of doubt washed over her. What chance did she truly have of defending herself against him? Her magical abilities, though growing, were not yet strong enough to challenge him directly. The realisation gnawed at her resolve, underscoring her vulnerability in the face of the prince's authority and magical defences. Despite her determination, Kaitlin was painfully aware of her limitations; for now, the amulet remained out of reach, its promise of protection and strength tantalising but unattainable.

Suddenly, a guard stationed behind the prince cleared his throat in a subtle attempt to draw attention. The prince's immediate reaction was sharp; he shot the guard a sour glare, causing the man to lower his head in silent apology. Kaitlin caught the guard's eyes fixed on her, but she quickly averted her gaze as Prince Keion began to speak, forcing herself to appear unfazed despite the tension coiling in her chest.

Prince Keion regarded Kaitlin with smug confidence, his tone dripping with patronising intent as he addressed her. "I think princess," he began, "that it's time you and I get to know each other properly."

Kaitlin bristled at the title, refusing to be cowed. She squared her shoulders and met his gaze, her composure unwavering. "Never," she replied, her voice ringing with unyielding defiance. She stood tall, chin raised, proud and resolute, refusing to let him undermine her authority. "And I am the Queen, not a princess."

Prince Keion paused, deliberately feigning confusion. He stepped closer, his eyes narrowing in a calculated attempt to intimidate her. "Sorry?" he asked, his tone laced with mockery.

Kaitlin held her ground, her words crisp and unwavering. "I said, I'm the Queen of Elvendon, you son of a bitch."

A mocking smile flickered across the prince's face. "Really," he drawled. "Well, Kaitlin, Queen of Elvendon," he continued, dipping into an exaggerated, sarcastic bow, "you don't have a choice." With a dismissive gesture, he turned to his guards and gave the order: "Take her back to the tower."

"No! Get off me!" Kaitlin shouted as two guards seized her arms. She struggled fiercely, twisting and pulling to break free from their grasp. Every fibre of Kaitlin's being urged her to unleash her magic. The urge was almost overwhelming, her power simmering just beneath the surface, begging to be set free. Yet, she forced herself to hold back, resolutely determined not to expose the full extent of her abilities to Prince Keion—not until it was absolutely necessary. The peril of her predicament was unmistakable; she was hopelessly outnumbered, the circle of danger closing in on her from all directions. The gravity of the moment weighed heavily upon her as her thoughts raced, calculating every possible avenue of escape. Kaitlin understood, with chilling clarity, that her only chance of survival was to break free now—no matter what it took.

Suddenly, the guard standing just behind Prince Keion cleared his throat, the deliberate cough cutting through the tension in the corridor. The prince's reaction was immediate and sharp; he spun around to face the guard, his irritation palpable.

"Are you serious?" Prince Keion shouted, his voice echoing off the stone walls, making it clear he would tolerate no interruptions.

Dropping to one knee, the guard shifted his cloak aside, revealing a gesture of respect as he pleaded earnestly, "My Lord, I apologise."

Kaitlin's attention was drawn to the guard as he lifted his head—not towards Prince Keion, but directly at her. His gaze was intense, piercing through the charged air, and she felt her heart begin to race beneath his scrutiny.

For a moment, their eyes locked, and an unspoken surge of emotion passed between Kaitlin and the guard. Moving with careful deliberation, the guard raised his open hand to his chest and held it there, he then clenched it into a fist. After pausing for a single heartbeat, he extended one finger, the gesture subtle but undeniably intentional.

Kaitlin's eyes widened as sudden realisation struck her. Her heart pounded in her chest, knowing in an instant what the gesture meant—the guard had just confessed his love for her, a silent declaration that spoke volumes amidst the tension and uncertainty of the corridor.

"Don't you look at her!" Prince Keion shouted furiously, his voice echoing with authority as he lifted his hand, pointing menacingly at the guard. The amulet hanging around his neck began to glow ominously, casting shifting patterns of magical light that swirled in the air above his palm. Without hesitation, the prince summoned his power, shaping it into a crackling orb of energy. He flung the spell towards the guard with lethal intent.

At that critical moment, Kaitlin acted. With swift decisiveness, she delivered a sharp kick to the back of the prince's leg, catching him off guard. The sudden blow sent Prince Keion stumbling, his balance lost, and he crashed heavily to the floor, the magical attack thrown off course.

The prince's aim lost direction as he fell, and the ball of energy, shot across the space between them at the wrong angle, and it hit another guard in the chest. The man shrieked as he was enveloped in light, and in an instant, exploded into dust.

Before the prince registered what was happening, the guard was on his feet. His movements were quick and purposeful, betraying no hesitation. In one fluid motion, he positioned himself defensively between Kaitlin and the prince, his stance radiating both defiance and determination. He seized one of Kaitlin's captors by the throat, lifted him in the air and snapped his neck. Dropping his dead body to the ground. The corridor, moments before charged with tension, now crackled with an added layer of urgency as the guard prepared to face whatever would come next.

Kaitlin's heart thundered in her chest as the shock of the moment gripped her. Her eyes went wide, locking onto the guard as the full weight of understanding dawned upon her. Without hesitation, she seized the fleeting opportunity before her, acting decisively to shift the balance in their favour. Kaitlin seized her captor's hand. *"Belcara,"* she chanted, as she spoke the word, heat surged from her core and raced down her arm, igniting her palm with unnatural fire. Her captor immediately released her. He screamed in agony, grasping at his burning hand with his other as his flesh began to disintegrate from it.

Two of the remaining guards, spurred on by Prince Keion's furious command, lunged towards the traitorous guard with intent to subdue him. Their movements were swift and aggressive, but the traitor was faster. He drove his fist hard into the face of the nearest attacker, the force of the blow sending the man sprawling to the ground. The guard landed awkwardly, his head hitting the stone floor, and lay there, semi-conscious, unable to rise or defend himself further.

The remaining guard hesitated for a second. That was long enough for the traitor guard to high kick him in the throat. The guard dropped his sword, and his hands pulled to his throat. He stumbled backwards struggling to breathe.

Kaitlin's breath caught as she recognised the familiar presence beside her. "Keltor?" she asked, her voice trembling, uncertain yet hopeful, as she allowed the stranger to take her hand.

Keltor nodded, his tone hushed and apologetic. "Yes, Kitcat, it's me, I'm sorry I'm late," he replied in a low whisper. His other hand lifted gently to her face, his eyes tracing the bruises marring her cheek. Anger flickered across his features as he bit down on his lower lip, struggling to contain his frustration at the sight of her injuries. With urgency, he urged her forward. "Come on," he said, pulling her towards the door, intent on leading her to safety.

Prince Keion, furious and desperate, sprang to his feet and unleashed a lightning bolt towards Kaitlin and Keltor. The crackling energy surged through the air, aimed with lethal precision.

Reacting swiftly, Keltor raised his hand mid-stride. "*Shield,*" he pronounced with authority. A shimmering magical barrier materialised instantly, absorbing the brunt of the prince's attack. The lightning sizzled against the shield's surface before dissipating harmlessly into the air, leaving Keltor and Kaitlin unharmed.

With the immediate threat neutralised, Keltor dropped the shield and cast a sharp, defiant glare at the prince, wordlessly challenging his authority. Without delaying further, he seized Kaitlin's hand and propelled her towards the door, determined to secure their escape.

Prince Keion's face twisted with rage as he spat out a curse, "You son of a bitch!" His fury intensified as he watched Keltor force the door open and usher Kaitlin through it, the act defying both his authority and expectations. A deep frown settled on the prince's brow, a mixture of anger and confusion clouding his expression. He could not comprehend how one of his own guards had managed to wield magic without his knowledge, especially since he had not sensed any magical presence himself.

Prince Keion's anger boiled over as he surveyed the chaos that had just unfolded. His voice rang out through the corridor, sharp and commanding, leaving no room for hesitation among the remaining guards. "Don't just stand there, you idiots, get after them!" he yelled at them. The order was unmistakable, his tone laden with fury and desperation as he sought to regain control of the situation. The guards, momentarily stunned by the rapid turn of events, snapped into action, driven by the prince's urgent command. Their movements betrayed a mix of fear and obedience as they prepared to pursue Keltor and Kaitlin, their resolve hardened by the intensity of Keion's words. "And you," the prince bellowed, addressing the man who was holding his burned hand, clearly in pain. "Get more men. If Kaitlin gets away, I'll have your heads!"

Clutching his injured hand, the guard gave a shaky nod, his face etched with pain and fear. Without daring to look back, he turned and hurried away down the corridor, desperate to escape the prince's wrath. The urgency in his movements was unmistakable, driven by the knowledge that his failure had placed him in mortal danger. He quickened his pace, determined to summon reinforcements before Prince Keion's fury could claim him as its next victim.

Gnashing his teeth in frustration, Prince Keion strode after the guards, his footsteps echoing down the corridor as he fought to reassert his authority and rein in the chaos. The tension among his men was palpable, and he could sense their unease as they prepared to carry out his orders. With every hurried step, Keion's mind raced, determined not to let Kaitlin and her mysterious ally slip through his grasp. As the group reached the heavy door, the prince's scowl deepened; he could already hear the muffled sounds of their quarry making their escape on the other side, the sting of betrayal burning in his chest. Undeterred, he gestured sharply for his men to force the door, unwilling to let anything impede his pursuit.

Keltor swiftly led Kaitlin into a secluded walled courtyard garden, where vibrant summer flowers and perfectly trimmed shrubbery lined the edges. The air was thick with the scent of blossoms, and the sunlight poured down with such intensity that

Kaitlin was forced to squint as her eyes struggled to adjust to the sudden brightness.

They paused just inside the courtyard, taking in the scene. A solid stone wall rose before them, marking the boundary between the garden and the dense forest that lay beyond. Acting quickly, Keltor turned towards the door through which they had entered. He raised his hand, his voice steady as he uttered a precise incantation. Instantly, a white light radiated from his palm, enveloping the lock. The light shimmered and fused the mechanism, ensuring that the door would remain firmly sealed behind them and barring any immediate pursuit.

As the last traces of white light faded from the fused door lock, a wave of magical luminescence surged through Keltor. The energy rippled over his body, momentarily illuminating his features with an ethereal glow. In that instant, the spell work that had disguised him as an Aranstream guard unravelled, revealing his true identity beneath. The transformation was seamless yet unmistakable; his true form, no longer hidden by enchantment, emerged in the dappled sunlight of the courtyard.

Keltor," she said, breathless and overwhelmed at seeing him.

Without hesitation, Keltor pulled her close, enveloping her in a protective embrace. For a moment, the chaos faded as he held her tightly, offering reassurance through his presence.

He gently lifted his hand to her face, his fingers brushing softly against her cheek. Concern etched in his voice, he asked, "Are you okay?" His gaze lingered on the bruise marring her skin, and his tone grew sharper as he pressed, "Did he do this?" Keltor's fury was barely contained as he realised the full extent of Kaitlin's injury—the bruise a stark reminder that Prince Keion had harmed her. His jaw clenched with anger, but there was no time to dwell on it.

"Yes, but I'm okay. Keltor, I can't believe you're here," Kaitlin replied, her voice trembling with emotion as tears of relief welled in her eyes. The overwhelming shock and exhaustion of the ordeal finally caught up with her, and she struggled to compose herself in Keltor's reassuring presence. Her breath hitched as she added,

"Thank God, we made that sign for when you change. I never would have recognised you otherwise." The secret signal they had agreed upon for moments like this had been their lifeline, and its success filled her with gratitude even as she clung to Keltor, drawing comfort from knowing he was truly by her side.

Keltor's hand moved with a gentle tenderness as he brushed Kaitlin's face, his bright blue eyes locking with hers. The overwhelming relief he felt at finding her unharmed steadied the frantic beat of his heart. The events of the previous night replayed in his mind: he had managed to snatch only a few hours of restless sleep before slipping quietly out of the Woodsman's cottage at around three in the morning. Driven by urgency, he had run through the dense forest with a speed and determination he had never known before, desperate to reach Aranstream in time.

Upon arriving, Keltor had found it relatively straightforward to ambush a lone guard and assume his appearance, his skills in disguise serving him well. However, gaining access to Prince Keion had proved more complicated. It soon became apparent that the prince's personal guards wore distinctive uniforms, forcing Keltor to incapacitate another guard in order to get close to the prince. He was certain that wherever the prince was, Kaitlin would not be far away, and he was prepared to do whatever it took to reach her side.

Suddenly, the sound of forceful rattling at the door drew his attention; the prince's guards were already trying to break through from inside, desperate to pursue them.

Turning to Kaitlin, Keltor's tone was urgent and commanding. "There's no time, you need to go, over there," he instructed, releasing his hold on her and gesturing firmly towards the section of the wall where her escape lay. Every second counted, and his protective instincts drove him to prioritise her safety above all else.

Kaitlin's voice trembled with concern as she focused on the danger still looming. "What about the amulet? He has it around his neck," she stated, worry etched in every word.

Keltor's response was immediate and firm, his protective instincts overriding all else. "It will have to wait, you need to go, now!" he insisted, urgency rising in his tone.

Panic flickered in Kaitlin's eyes. "I'm not leaving you," she protested, her voice thick with fear and desperation.

"Kaitlin, go," Keltor commanded, his voice growing louder as he grasped her shoulders, turning her body towards the escape route. "There's a hole in the wall; I will catch you up. There's something I must do first."

She lingered for a split second, uncertainty holding her in place—until the tension shattered as the door burst open. Two guards charged out from the doorway, their arrival forcing Keltor to make a swift decision.

Keltor glanced quickly at the guards, then turned his intense gaze to Kaitlin. "Go!" he shouted, his voice sharp with urgency as he pushed her away from the immediate danger. His determination was unmistakable; he needed her to get to safety so he could focus on the fight ahead without distraction.

Hearing the firmness in his command, Kaitlin didn't hesitate. Instead, acknowledging his authority and understanding the gravity of the situation. With swift resolve, she gathered up her dress to avoid tripping and sprinted towards the escape route. As she reached the gap in the wall, her concern for Keltor compelled her to look back over her shoulder, casting one last anxious glance before moving through to safety.

The two guards hesitated for a moment as they unexpectedly found themselves confronting Keltor, rather than the traitor from their own ranks who had abducted the woman. Their eyes darted anxiously around, searching for the rogue guard, but he was nowhere in sight.

"Oh god, Keltor," Kaitlin mumbled under her breath, her heart trembling as the guards closed in on him. She peered back through the hole, her heart nearly stopping as she watched the guards attack Keltor. She knew she had responsibilities—she needed to survive—but leaving him to fight alone felt unbearably cowardly.

For a moment, she hovered in indecision, torn between escape and the urge to go back.

Having no weapon to defend himself, Keltor was forced to act swiftly. His eyes flickered to the wall on his left, searching for any advantage. Without hesitation, he sprinted directly at the two guards. At the final moment, he veered sharply to the left, propelling himself up the wall. With remarkable agility, he flipped backwards, landing nimbly behind one of the guards.

Wasting no time, Keltor lashed out with a powerful kick, sending the guard tumbling forward and crashing to the ground. The force of the impact caused the guard's sword to fly from his grasp. Seizing the opportunity, Keltor ran up the prone man's body, his booted foot coming down hard on the guard's head just as he tried to rise, forcing his face back into the earth.

As Kaitlin watched with bated breath, a familiar figure emerged in the doorway—it was Prince Keion. Instinct took over. Without hesitation, she darted back through the hole in the wall, her heart thundering in her chest. She raised her hands, the air around her crackling with anticipation, and she whispered fiercely, "*Belcara destructor!*"

Instantly, her palms tingled with a surge of electric energy, heat swirling up her arms as the magic built within her. With an audible hum, a dazzling beam of brilliant white light exploded from her hands, filling the air with a sharp, almost metallic scent. The beam arced across the courtyard in a blinding flash, cutting over Keltor as he battled below. The magical energy struck the lintel above the doorframe with a thunderous crack, sending shards of stone raining down and causing Prince Keion to stumble back inside as the entrance became blocked with falling rubble.

Keltor startled by the rush of magic, and the tremendous crash, jumped back in alarm. He spun to see Kaitlin; her eyes fixed on him. He gave her a brief smile, before being alerted to the second guard as he charged at him, swinging his blade with determination. Keltor bent down in a fluid motion, scooping up the fallen guard's sword. The sound of clashing steel rang out as their swords met. Despite the guard's efforts, he was simply no match for Keltor's skill. Within moments, Keltor had disarmed him, leaving the guard staring helplessly at Keltor, then down at his own sword lying at Keltor's feet.

Without taking his eyes off the guard before him, Keltor nudged the sword with his foot, flipping it into the air. With swift precision, he snatched it in his left hand, his grip tightening instinctively around the hilt. The guard standing opposite hesitated, expecting Keltor to return the weapon and resume a fair fight—but Keltor had no intention of giving him a chance.

The guard in front of him turned to run. Keltor darted forwards, lifted his blade and swung it wide, before bringing it back around and taking off the man's head.

Without a moment's hesitation, Keltor hurled the second sword with unwavering precision. His actions were swift and deliberate, driven by the urgency of the battle and the need to ensure his own survival. The blade spun through the air and found its mark, plunging deeply into the back of the first guard, who was still sprawled face down in the grass. Keltor was taking no chances— he could not risk the possibility of the man recovering and rising to his feet to join the fight again.

Keltor slid the remaining guard's blade into the sheath at his belt, securing it with a practiced motion. Blood, spattered across his cheek during the chaos, was swiftly wiped away with the back of his hand, leaving a reddish smear upon his skin. Drawing in a deep, steadying breath, Keltor began to summon his magic. His arms dropped to his sides, fists tightening and loosening rhythmically as he focused his concentration and prepared to unleash the power within him.

The tower loomed just beyond, its formidable silhouette dominating the scene. Keltor's jaw clenched, his teeth pressing firmly against his lower lip as he studied the structure, calculating his next move with unyielding determination. He understood the significance of setting the tower ablaze—it was not simply an act of destruction, but a crucial signal to Commander Talbot, a message that could alter the course of events.

Taking a moment to steady his racing heart, Keltor drew a deep breath, focusing every ounce of his willpower. He concentrated intensely, reaching deep within himself to gather his reserves of magical energy, summoning the strength required to unleash enough power to bring the tower crashing down. The weight of responsibility pressed upon him, but Keltor was resolute, prepared to do whatever it took to accomplish his mission.

With a low, resolute voice, he began to chant, "*Etoo destructor, belcara.*" He spread his arms wide, channelling the magic from every fibre of his being. The sheer force of the power made his hands tremble. He stepped forward, planting one foot ahead and bending his knee slightly to brace himself.

Raising his voice, he repeated the incantation with greater intensity, "*Etoo destructor, belcara!*" Pouring every ounce of strength into the spell, Keltor unleashed a colossal bolt of lightning that shot skywards and struck the very top of the tower.

Kaitlin instinctively ducked as the deafening sound of an explosion echoed across the courtyard. Her eyes darted upwards, widening in alarm as she witnessed flames and dense smoke billowing from the tower, spiralling high into the sky. The very structure of the tower began to tremble, sending ominous vibrations through the ground beneath her feet. Stonework cracked and splintered, with large sections breaking loose and crashing violently to the earth below.

"Holy shit!" Kaitlin exclaimed, her shock rendering her momentarily frozen. Panic surged through her as the tower continued to collapse, and she cried out, desperate for reassurance. "Keltor!"

Through the swirling smoke and falling debris, Keltor appeared, emerging at a run as he made his way towards her.

Kaitlin, breathing heavily and urgency clear in her voice, reached out for Keltor's outstretched hand. He caught her hand firmly, his expression stern yet protective as he addressed her. "I told you to stay back, Kitkat," he admonished gently, gripping her hand tightly. "I would have taken out the door after I killed the guards."

Kaitlin shook her head, her words tumbling out in a rush. "I know, but I saw the prince coming through the door, and you were distracted," she explained, her concern evident.

At her words, Keltor's eyes widened, a flicker of alarm crossing his face as he realised that he had missed the prince's entrance entirely. He paused, the gravity of the moment settling between them.

"I'm sorry," Keltor admitted, his voice sincere. "Thank you. You're right—I didn't see him." With a relieved exhale, he drew Kaitlin into a close embrace, gratitude and relief mingling as he held her tight.

Kaitlin pulled back from Keltor, her gaze fixed on the inferno consuming the shattered tower. The flames raged unchecked, casting a fiery glow across the ruined building. Her voice was edged with disbelief as she asked, "The tower?"

Keltor followed her eyes to the burning structure, his tone urgent and resolute. "It's a signal to Commander Talbot. The battle is about to start, Kaitlin, and I need to get you out of here." His words carried a sense of immediate danger, underscoring the necessity for haste.

Kaitlin hesitated, torn, her glance shifting back towards the castle. "But the amulet," she protested, the importance of the object clear in her voice.

Keltor reached for her hand, determination tightening his grip. "I will get it, but for now I need to get you out of here." His expression left no room for argument, making it clear that her safety was his top priority.

Kaitlin nodded in silent agreement, gathering the hem of her dress and climbing carefully through the opening Keltor had created earlier. Despite her aversion to thinking of herself as important, she was acutely aware of her position—she was the Queen of Elvendon. The weight of responsibility pressed upon her; she understood that the fate of thousands depended on her survival. Her recent experiences with Prince Keion had given her a new perspective, helping her to appreciate his determination to keep her safe.

553

They entered the forest, moving swiftly as they pushed deeper into the dense undergrowth. Kaitlin found it increasingly difficult to keep pace, her clogs hampering her progress. More than once, she considered abandoning them and running barefoot, but the ground was strewn with sticks, thorns, and old acorns left from the previous autumn, making such a choice perilous. The continuous run began to take its toll; after nearly an hour, Kaitlin's muscles ached with fatigue, and each step grew heavier. At last, struggling to continue, she reached out and pulled at Keltor's arm, wordlessly signalling her need for a pause.

Chapter Twenty-Four
The Awakening of Kaitlin's Power

Kaitlin, exhausted and struggling to catch her breath, pleaded, "Can we rest, just for a minute?" Her voice was strained, the fatigue from their journey evident. Keltor slowed to a stop, his own breathing heavy as he nodded in agreement. His hands settled on his thighs while he paused to recuperate, momentarily allowing the tension of their escape to ease.

Looking at Keltor, Kaitlin asked gently, "Your dad, did you find him?" seeking reassurance and hoping for good news. Keltor stood upright, a smile spreading across his face as he replied, "Yes, and Ese as well. They're with mum," he confirmed, relief and happiness colouring his words.

"That's amazing, Keltor," Kaitlin responded warmly, her joy for him evident. "I'm so happy for you."

Keltor cast a careful glance back into the forest they had traversed, his eyes scanning the undergrowth for any signs of danger. Kaitlin, sensing his concern, continued her inquiry. "Is he alright?"

Turning back to her, Keltor answered, "Yes, weak, and thin, but he's alive, and mum is overjoyed. It's great to see them back together."

"And your brother?" she asked, her tone betraying a hint of anxiety.

Keltor reached out, drawing her gently closer as he reassured her. "I found him in the encampment, and he's fine. He's with mum and dad." He paused, then added with quiet regret, "Look, Kaitlin, I'm sorry I took so long to get to you, it took longer than I thought to sort out the plans with the commander."

Kaitlin smiled warmly, her relief evident, as she asked, "He was okay, then?"

With a gentle nod, Keltor replied, "Yes, a little beaten about, but he was okay. I found Belrack and his men as well."

Letting out a breath she hadn't realised she was holding, Kaitlin said, "Oh, thank god." The concern for Ila had weighed heavily on her, and now she felt a wave of relief wash over her. "I was so worried for Ila."

Keltor nodded in understanding, his expression softening as he met her gaze. "Kaitlin," he said, his eyes locking with hers, "I can't emphasise how overjoyed they are to find you are still alive. You mean everything to them—the people of Elvendon, you know that, right?"

Kaitlin gave a thoughtful nod, her voice quiet but sincere. "I'm beginning to understand." She moved closer to Keltor, her movements gentle and full of affection, as she wrapped her arms softly around his neck. Keltor averted his gaze for a moment, his eyes dropping in concern, before he looked back up at her, worry etched on his face.

"Keion hurt you?" he asked, his voice thick with regret and anxiety at the mark on her cheek.

Kaitlin lifted her hand to her bruised cheek, brushing it lightly. "This?" she replied, her tone calm and reassuring. "It's nothing, honestly. I had it under control." She offered him a warm smile, hoping to ease his worry, her confidence and composure clear in her expression.

Keltor let out a heavy breath, his voice tinged with remorse. "I'm sorry we got captured, it shouldn't have happened," he admitted, the weight of responsibility evident in his words. "Esimae went mad when I returned with Dad and you weren't with me."

A gentle smile played on Kaitlin's lips as she responded, "Did she?" Keltor nodded in confirmation.

"I think I might have frightened her," he confessed.

"Frightened her? How?" Kaitlin asked, her brow furrowing in concern as she looked at him.

He hesitated before continuing, "When she started shouting at me, my magic surged through my veins—I was just so angry."

"Keltor," she said softly, her tone gentle and inviting, encouraging him to go on.

He hesitated, then admitted, "I wasn't angry with Esimae, but with myself. I desperately wanted to come straight to you, but I had to get my dad out first—for my mum's sake. If I'd chosen to save you before him, everything would have descended into chaos, and the prince would have killed him without a second thought."

Kaitlin reached out, placing a reassuring hand on his arm. "Keltor, it's okay," she soothed. "We agreed before we left that you would rescue your dad first. That was always the plan."

He looked at her, his expression torn with guilt and longing. "I know, but it still didn't feel right. My heart wanted to save you first, because you are my life, Kitcat. I love my dad, but you mean more to me than anything."

Kaitlin offered Keltor a gentle reassurance, her voice calm and steady. "Keltor, it's fine, really, I had it under control. Yes, the prince has the amulet, but I don't think he knows how to use it properly. I wasn't worried that I couldn't defend myself from him." Her words were meant to soothe him, dismissing any fears about her safety and showing her unwavering confidence. Yet, she omitted telling him about Keion drugging her, unwilling to burden him further with guilt and pain.

As she spoke, her luminous eyes radiated a deep love for Keltor, capturing his heart in that moment. The emotion between them was electrified—when Kaitlin closed her eyes, Keltor responded instinctively, his heart almost bursting with affection. They shared a tender kiss, surrounded by the familiar comfort of her scent and touch. For Keltor, nothing else in the world mattered but her, and he allowed himself to be completely lost in the embrace they shared.

Keltor's eyes flew open in shock as Kaitlin was abruptly torn from his arms. His horror intensified as Kaitlin screamed as tendrils of snake-like energy coiled around her, hoisting her helplessly into the air. The magical force gripped her tightly and crackled with lethal electricity.

"Kaitlin!" Keltor cried, his heart pounding furiously. Whipping around to face Prince Keion, rage surged through him as he caught sight of his father's amulet glowing ominously at the prince's throat, its energy being channelled directly at Kaitlin. White-hot power flashed in Keltor's eyes. With a swift, instinctive movement, he unleashed a bolt of crackling energy from his hand, aiming it straight at Prince Keion. As Keltor's magic collided with the electrical tendrils streaming from the prince's hands, a massive explosion reverberated around the clearing, shaking the very ground beneath them.

Kaitlin dropped and slammed hard onto the ground. Her lungs contracted so hard she couldn't even think about taking a breath. She curled into a ball. Panic clawed at her mind as she fought for air, terror mixing with the pain still sparking through her body.

Prince Keion fixed his gaze on Keltor, his words dripping with contempt. "You," he spat, fury evident in his voice, "a mere Protector would dare to defile a Queen of the elves!" The accusation hung in the air, sharp and deliberate, intended to belittle Keltor and cast aspersions on his worthiness. Keion's scornful tone underscored his disdain for Keltor's position and his outrage at the perceived transgression against royal elven lineage.

"I'm no mere Protector," Keltor spat back, his words sharp and defiant. Fury surged within him as his gaze flickered to Kaitlin, who lay curled on the ground, wracked with pain. The sight of her suffering ignited a deeper rage in Keltor, his anger burning so fiercely it seemed to radiate from him. He stood tall, refusing to be diminished by the prince's scorn or the title meant to belittle him. In that moment, Keltor's resolve was unshakeable—he would not allow anyone, least of all Prince Keion, to question his worth or threaten the woman he loved.

The crunch of boots on twigs echoed as two soldiers flanked him on either side—two to his left, two to his right. Keltor's fingers tightened around the hilt, the steel's chill biting into his skin. His sword flashed free in an instant, the metallic rasp ringing through the tense air as adrenaline surged and the world narrowed to the pounding of his heart and the threat closing in. Without pause Keltor spun to his left, his sword whipping around and beheading the two soldiers in one fluid sweep before they even saw him coming.

He flipped, spun and twisted over, his move fast, yet graceful.

One of the soldiers met his blade with his own and the sound of clashing metal rang out loudly. Keltor's muscles flexed hard, he could feel the anger igniting the magic within him, sending the power straight down and into his sword. His other hand grasped the hilt, and with two hands he lunged forward hard. His blade met his opponent's blade side on and cut it clean in half. Keltor's move continued and he plunge his sword deep into the man's stomach, he then pulled the blade upwards splitting him almost in half.

Keltor whipped his sword out of the dead man, the lifeless body collapsing heavily to the ground. A violent spray of red blood burst outward as the soldier fell, painting the forest floor with the aftermath of battle.

Prince Keion, his composure shaken, barked a desperate order to the lone surviving soldier. "Get him!" he commanded, his voice sharp and urgent, betraying the worry etched across his face. The scene was tense—Keltor had dispatched nearly all of the prince's guards with alarming ease, demonstrating skill and strength far beyond their expectations. The prince's concern was evident as he watched Keltor stand defiant, a formidable adversary who had reduced his escort to just one soldier with barely any effort.

The final soldier's face was etched with fear, caught between two terrifying choices. Defying Prince Keion meant certain death at the hands of his ruthless leader, yet facing Keltor—whose lethal prowess had just been demonstrated—was equally risky. The fear and uncertainty warred within him, torn between the dread of being branded a coward and the peril of going against a formidable opponent.

Despite the overwhelming sense of danger, the soldier steeled himself, making the difficult decision to meet his fate head-on. Resolving to die as a soldier rather than live as a coward, he took a bold step forward and advanced towards Keltor, ready to face whatever would come.

Keltor observed the soldier's approach with sharp focus, his reflexes primed by the tension of the moment. As the soldier advanced, there was no hesitation in his movements—he was intent on carrying out Prince Keion's desperate command. The soldier's blade sliced through the air in a swift, deadly arc, aiming straight for Keltor's neck. Instinctively, Keltor leaned back with force, narrowly avoiding the attack; the blade passed so close that it missed his throat by scarcely an inch. The proximity of the strike underscored the peril of the encounter, and Keltor's quick reaction was all that kept him from a fatal wound. He twisted around almost full circle and threw his sword directly at the soldier. The man stopped in his tracks, with Keltor's sword embedded in his chest he collapsed to his knees and keeled over.

Keltor turned to face Prince Keion, his eyes blazing with unrestrained fury. The intensity of his anger seemed almost tangible, radiating from him in waves. As he lifted his hands, arcs of magic began to swirl and dance around his fingers, crackling with raw energy and anticipation.

His voice rang out, powerful and unwavering, as he proclaimed his true identity. "I am the Queen of Elvendon's husband, and a wizard of the elves!" Keltor shouted, his words echoing through the tense air. Every syllable was charged with the weight of his authority and the depth of his resolve.

Fixing his defiant gaze on the prince, Keltor made a chilling promise. "And I will destroy you and your father," he vowed, his tone leaving no doubt as to his determination. The threat lingered between them, underscoring the gravity of the moment and the formidable power Keltor now wielded.

The prince hesitated, every muscle in his body taut with apprehension as he watched the magic swirling and twisting around Keltor's hands. His gaze flickered to the bodies of his fallen soldiers—men who had been cut down in mere minutes. The words Keltor had spoken took him by surprise, and as he looked over at Kaitlin, still curled on the ground, a deep furrow of confusion and anger creased his brow. The risk of keeping her now seemed far too great.

In a split second he turned his attention back to Keltor, weighing his chances of emerging victorious from this confrontation. Although he possessed the amulet, doubts gnawed at him; Keltor's prowess with a blade had already proven exceptional, and the extent of his magical power was still unknown. The prince's uncertainty was unmistakable, but before he could make his decision, Keltor's magic surged forward, charging at him with full force.

The prince's left hand lifted instantly, a flash of power blocking Keltor's magic. The prince's right hand moved deliberately to grasp the amulet hanging around his neck, its power tangible in the charged atmosphere. With swift determination, he turned, his left-hand extended outwards, directing its intent towards Kaitlin, who remained vulnerable amid the chaos.

Reacting without a moment's hesitation, Keltor threw himself in front of his wife, determined to shield her from harm. With unwavering resolve, he positioned himself as her protector, placing his own body between Kaitlin and the prince's impending attack.

Keltor's right hand shot up instinctively, his movements sharp and purposeful. Channelling his magical energy, he unleashed a powerful bolt of magic, aiming it directly at the prince's assault. The spell was not only a defensive manoeuvre but also a fierce act of retaliation, meant to counter the prince's offensive and safeguard Kaitlin from the danger that threatened her.

The collision of their magical forces was instantaneous and overwhelming. As the beams of energy met in mid-air, the intensity of the clash electrified the entire area, filling the air with a palpable sense of power. The magnitude of their combined magic was immense, neither man willing to yield or falter; they were evenly matched, each pushing against the other with equal strength and determination.

As the confrontation reached its breaking point, the prince suddenly uttered a spell, his voice sharp and commanding: *"Itoor charnor,"* he chanted. In that very moment, an intense burst of radiant white light erupted, enveloping him completely. Instinctively, Keltor raised the back of his hand to shield his eyes from the blinding brilliance. When the glare faded, the prince had vanished—gone without a trace, leaving only the charged air and the echoes of his magic behind.

"You son of a bitch!" Keltor bellowed, his voice thick with rage and disbelief. The realisation hit him hard—the prince had used the potent magic of his father's amulet to escape, slipping from Keltor's grasp in a blinding flash of light. The bitterness of the prince's sudden disappearance fuelled Keltor's anger, his fists clenching as he grappled with the injustice of the moment. The charged air still crackled with residual energy, a stark reminder of the power that had just been wielded against him.

Kaitlin drew in a much-needed breath, the air searing as it filled her lungs, but gradually, the tension in her muscles began to subside as oxygen spread through her body. She felt herself slowly relaxing, unwinding from the shock of the electrical charge—just as Keltor, without warning, collapsed to his knees before her.

"Keltor!" Kaitlin gasped, her voice trembling with desperation as it sliced through the charged air. The acrid tang of magic lingered, mingling with the metallic scent of blood rising from the scorched earth. She staggered upright, her legs shaking beneath her as she pushed through the lingering ache in her muscles and the sting of fear that prickled her skin. Each breath felt sharp and hot.

Keltor's hands pressed into the cool, damp earth, the chill seeping through his palms and grounding him against the wave of weakness flooding his body. As his strength ebbed away, a crushing pain tore through his left side, sharp and relentless. The forest around him seemed to pulse with his agony—the distant rustle of leaves, the faint calls of birds, each sound magnified by his distress. His brow furrowed, not only from the physical torment but from the dread that gnawed at the edges of his mind. Keltor's right hand pressed desperately to his side, blood seeping between his trembling fingers, the sticky warmth a stark contrast

562

to the cold earth below. With every heartbeat, the stakes of his injury became clearer, and the enormity of what he might lose weighed heavily on him.

"Keltor, what's wrong?" Kaitlin begged as she reached him, her voice tight with panic. Desperation etched her features as she searched his face for reassurance, but his pain was evident. Her hands hovered uncertainly over him, torn between comfort and alarm, as she tried to make sense of his sudden weakness and the danger that surrounded them both.

"It was Keion's magic. I don't know what happened, I didn't feel it," Keltor said, his voice trembling with fear and confusion, unsure if he would survive whatever magic had struck him. He started coughing relentless. Suddenly, the crushing pain in Keltor's stomach forced him to keel over.

"Keltor!" Kaitlin screamed as she dropped to her knees beside him, her hands shaking as she clutched his shoulders. His body trembled beneath her touch, cold sweat slick on his skin. Their eyes locked for an instant—panic and fear mirrored in both their gazes—just as Keltor doubled over, a violent cough wracking his chest. Blood spattered across his lips.

"Keltor," she choked out, her voice cracking as her heart shattered at the sight of his pain. A cold dread flooded her stomach, icy and paralysing, as the truth hit her—he might not survive this.

Kaitlin pulled up Keltor's blood-soaked shirt, her breath coming in ragged gasps as she took in the sight before her: a deep, penetrating wound in his stomach, the flesh around it scorched by magic

Keltor whispered, his breath becoming laboured, "Kitcat, I don't think I'm going to make it."

"Keltor, don't you go dying on me, don't you bloody dare!" Kaitlin screamed at him, her hand pawing at his face.

"Kaitlin, you have to get that amulet," Keltor mumbled, his voice barely more than a rasp, the words trembling on his blood-stained lips.

"Keltor, shut up, stop talking," Kaitlin cried out. Her body shook with fear as she pressed down on his stomach, trying desperately to stem the bleeding. She couldn't lose him—not after everything they'd been through together. He was her life.

She looked around urgently for help, but there was no one there. Kaitlin glanced to his face, she could see he was wracked with pain, A sob escaped her lips as her hands trembled uncontrollably, terror tightening her chest when she saw the veins in his neck start to turn dark.

Keltor's voice was barely audible as he gazed at Kaitlin, his words heavy with urgency and love. "You must stop Keion. I love you so much, you know that right," he mumbled, the depth of his feelings plain in the trembling of his breath. "More than life itself."

Kaitlin's eyes filled with tears, her heart aching at his confession. She clung to hope, refusing to accept the possibility of losing him. "Please, stop talking like that, you're going to be fine," she wept, desperation and helplessness sharp in her voice as she tried to comfort him, even as the gravity of the situation weighed on them both.

"Kitcat, I'm not," he said, his sodden eyes locked on hers as he shook his head, a faint shiver running through his battered frame. His breath came in ragged, shallow gasps, each one an effort. "There's no magic potion for this," he whispered, his voice trembling with apology and regret. "I'm so sorry, you're going to have to do this without me." As the words left his lips, his hand reached for hers, fingers cold and trembling, seeking comfort.

Kaitlin's shoulders shook as she clung to him, feeling the clammy chill of his skin beneath her touch. Tears streamed down her cheeks, catching on her lips, her sobs barely contained. "No, no, I can't," she choked out, her voice raw and desperate. "Keltor, you're my world—there is no point to any of it if you're not with me." Her words broke around the edges, thick with grief. "I don't want to live without you, Keltor." She pressed her forehead against his, their breath mingling in the cold air, as the world around them seemed to fade, leaving only their shared pain and longing.

Keltor lay sprawled on a bed of damp moss, his body half-curled against the gnarled roots of an ancient oak, the chill of the forest floor pressing through his blood-soaked shirt. Shadows from the tangled branches above flickered across his pain-lined face as he forced his eyes to stay open. Kaitlin knelt beside him, her knees sinking into the soft earth. Her trembling hand gripped his, desperate to anchor him to the world.

"You have to be their Queen now, you have to be strong," he murmured, his voice faltering. "He hit me with magic; there's nothing you can do. The people need their Queen." As the darkness of the spell crept through his veins, Keltor could feel each organ struggling within him. He squeezed Kaitlin's fingers weakly before his words trailed off, barely audible. "Find the commander…"

"No, no, no, not again!" she cried, her voice breaking as she cupped his face in her trembling hands. The desperation in her eyes was unmistakable as she pleaded, her words tumbling out in ragged breaths. "Keltor, please, you can't do this to me! You can't leave me," she begged, her tears spilling freely onto his cheeks. Frantically, she cast her gaze around the forest, searching for any sign of help, but there was nothing—only the endless trees enclosing them in their solitude. The harsh reality pressed in on her: Esimae was not here, and with her absence went any hope of medicinal magic that might have saved him. Kaitlin felt utterly alone, powerless to stop the life slipping from the man she loved.

"Oh my god, don't you dare do this to me, don't you fucking dare!" Kaitlin screamed, her voice cracking as she looked skywards. The icy wind lashed at her cheeks, making her skin sting, while her trembling hands clung desperately to Keltor's fading warmth. All around her, the forest pressed in with suffocating silence, broken only by the rasp of his shallow breaths. "Don't you take him from me, not after everything we have done for you!" she cried out to the heavens, her words swallowed by the stillness. "Star, please, you've got to help me!" she pleaded, her heart pounding as tears blurred her vision.

Kaitlin's desperation was overwhelming. She clung to a faint hope, uncertain whether Star could even hear her cries, yet her need for help was stronger than ever. In that moment, it no longer mattered to her what force governed the worlds—be it a God, the Source, or something else entirely. All Kaitlin wanted was their intervention, their assistance, anything that could save Keltor. Her faith was rooted not in the identity of the power, but in the hope that someone, somewhere, would answer her plea in her darkest hour.

Kaitlin's grief-stricken pleas were suddenly interrupted by a voice—ethereal and unmistakably female, yet without any visible source. "It's time," the voice declared, its words floating through the air like a gentle whisper imbued with magic and urgency.

Startled, Kaitlin whipped her head around, searching desperately for the speaker. "Who's there?" she cried out, her eyes darting through the shadows, but all around her was emptiness. No one appeared.

Again, the voice repeated, "It's time." The words seemed to drift from everywhere and nowhere, enveloping Kaitlin like a breeze carrying a secret. She realised with growing unease that the voice was not coming from any physical direction. It was reaching her from somewhere beyond the realm of sight, echoing in her mind and soul. Shaken, Kaitlin shook her head furiously, unwilling to accept the impossible, yet unable to deny the reality of what she had heard.

Kaitlin's voice rang out, defiant and desperate. "No, no, you're not taking him," she cried, clutching Keltor protectively to her chest. Her grip tightened, as though her touch alone could shield him from whatever unseen force threatened to steal him away. "If you take him, you take me too!" she screamed, her eyes wild as they darted around, searching for any glimpse of the mysterious voice that had filled the air, terrified of whatever presence dared to claim Keltor. The terror that gripped her was overwhelming; the idea of losing Keltor after all they had endured together was simply unimaginable. The mere thought of being left to face the world alone filled her with anguish—she could not, would not, bear such a loss.

As Kaitlin clung desperately to Keltor, her grief and terror threatening to overwhelm her, the ethereal, feminine voice returned—this time softer yet filled with a sense of urgency. The voice whispered, "Use the power from the earth, Kaitlin. It's time for you to unlock your power."

Kaitlin's heart thundered in her chest, panic mixing with a cold sweat that slicked her brow. Her eyes darted wildly through the encroaching shadows, searching for the source of the voice. "What? Who are you?" she cried out, her voice trembling as she turned in every direction, struggling to comprehend the impossibility of what she was hearing. The weight of the unseen presence pressed in on her, urging her towards a destiny she had never wished for and a power she did not yet understand.

Suddenly, an overwhelming force surged through Kaitlin's body. It was so intense that she gasped for breath, her whole frame trembling as the energy took hold. Her eyes blazed with an unearthly glow, radiant with the purest magic as the power flooded every fibre of her being. The sensation was both terrifying and exhilarating—energy pouring into her, drawn directly from the Source, rising from the very earth beneath her and suffusing her from root to crown.

Kaitlin's voice broke with desperation as she cried, "*Spiritus exaudi me*," tears streaming down her cheeks. She pleaded for aid, her words raw with emotion, while she struggled to maintain control over the immense magical energy now coursing through her from the earth. The power was almost overwhelming— surging through her veins, filling her with both fear and hope as she battled to harness it, determined not to let Keltor slip away.

Keltor couldn't speak, he couldn't get out any more than a gasping moan which made him cough out the blood collecting in his mouth. A chill seeped into his bones, making his limbs numb and heavy. He couldn't focus his mind. Her voice was distant, like she was far away in the depths of a tunnel. Each breath rattled in his chest, sharp and shallow. His eyes filled with tears as try as he might, he couldn't open them to look at her.

Kaitlin took a steadying breath, her eyes wide and shining as magical energy pulsed through her. With gentle care, she cupped Keltor's face in her hand, determined not to let him slip away. "I'm not going to let you go, Keltor. You're not leaving me here to do this all alone. If it was magic that injured you, then I shall use magic to heal you."

Slowly, Kaitlin withdrew her hand from his face and drew in a deep breath, clarity flooding her mind with the knowledge of what had to be done. She gripped the earth firmly with one hand, grounding herself in its strength, while she pressed her other hand against his wound, ready to channel the power within her to heal him. Her voice trembled with determination as she chanted, "*Spiritus, adiuva me, da mihi potestatem sanandi.*" In response, a surge of pure white magic poured from her fingertips into his wounded body, its radiance illuminating the darkness around them.

Keltor groaned in agony as the force of Kaitlin's magic surged through him, his entire body arching off the ground as though struck by a bolt of lightning. Each breath was ragged, and his face contorted with pain as the energy coursed through him. Kaitlin's hand continued to press down on him, her fingers trembling with both fear and hope as she watched his body react to the power she channelled.

As a surge of powerful magic coursed through his body, Keltor trembled violently, unable to resist the overwhelming force that now flowed within him. The magic, relentless and purposeful, sought out every wound and affliction, weaving its way through his veins and organs. Each thread of energy moved with intent, repairing damaged tissues and flushing out the remnants of pain and injury that lingered within him. It was as if the magic itself possessed an innate understanding of what needed healing, sparing nothing as it continued its relentless pursuit of restoration.

The sensations were overwhelming—an intense battle of agony and bliss waged within him, leaving Keltor scarcely aware of

Kaitlin's presence at his side. The pain threatened to consume him, yet within it, a strange euphoria flickered, as though hope itself was woven into the magic that worked to restore him.

Beside him, Kaitlin reached deep within herself, instinctively tapping into the earth's energy to heal him. Although she did not fully comprehend the source of her strength, she recognised that this power had always resided within her, waiting for her to truly believe in herself. Her voice wavered with emotion as she chanted, "*Spiritus, adiuva me, da mihi potestatem sanandi.*" Through tears she fought to hold back, she watched his still, pale face, her heart pounding with anxiety and resolve. Desperate to draw even more strength, Kaitlin pressed her hand further into the soil, willing the earth to grant her all it could offer. "*Spiritus, adiuva me, da mihi potestatem sanandi,*" she repeated, her words heavy with hope and determination, as she watched intently as the magic flowed through Keltor's body, following the intricate lines of his veins, which had been tainted by Keion's dark influence. Her eyes widened in awe as her own magic gradually dispelled the darkness, transforming the veins back to their natural blue. She studied his face for any sign of change; although he remained motionless, she noticed that his breathing had eased, becoming less laboured and steadier.

After about thirty minutes, Kaitlin carefully lifted her hand away and turned her attention to the wound. With a deep, relieved breath, she saw that it was completely healed. The magical glow that had surrounded her faded, and her eyes returned to their usual appearance. She wiped the blood and dirt from her hands onto her dress, then leaned towards Keltor, her concern and hope visible in every movement.

Kaitlin leaned in close, her voice barely more than a whisper as she pleaded, "Keltor?" The silence that followed made her heart ache with fear. Desperation edged her words as she begged, "Please, Keltor, wake up." Overwhelmed by emotion, she lowered her head to his chest, gripping him tightly, as if her touch alone could anchor him to the world. Her voice trembled, "Please wake up, I need you."

For what felt like an eternity, only the sound of her quiet sobs filled the air. Then, from the stillness, a faint murmur finally broke through—"Kitcat," Keltor mumbled in a low, weak voice.

Startled, Kaitlin sat up abruptly, hope flickering in her tear-filled eyes. "Keltor!" she cried, relief and disbelief mingling in her voice.

As Keltor slowly opened his eyes and looked at her, the dam of Kaitlin's emotions broke. Tears streamed down her face as she collapsed onto him, overcome with relief and joy, her sobs wracking her body as she clung to him. For a moment, all the fear and anxiety that had built up within her spilled forth, her arms tightening around him as though she might lose him again at any second.

Gently, Keltor moved his hand from his side and wrapped his arm around her. His touch was tender as he rubbed her back, offering comfort and reassurance in the aftermath of their ordeal. In that embrace, the anguish and uncertainty of the past moments were replaced with a sense of safety, as both found solace in the presence of one another.

Keltor drew in a shaky breath, his voice barely above a whisper as he sought to reassure Kaitlin. "I'm okay, Kitcat," he murmured, yet the tears streaming down his cheeks belied the strength of the emotions churning within him. The ordeal he had just survived weighed heavily upon him, and the memory of how narrowly he had escaped death brought a sorrow that was nearly impossible to bear. The thought of losing Kaitlin, of them being parted forever, pierced him with a pain so sharp it threatened to consume him entirely. Despite this turmoil, he found solace in Kaitlin's presence, clinging to the comfort she gave him and feeling an overwhelming gratitude for the second chance they had been granted to remain together.

Her head lifted, revealing tear-soaked eyes that searched his face for reassurance. Seeing her distress, Keltor offered her a gentle smile, his own emotions barely concealed beneath the surface. In a soft whisper, he asked, "How did you do that?"

570

Kaitlin reached out, her hand cradling his face tenderly. Her thumb traced a gentle path across his cheek, grounding him in the present moment. "I don't know," she admitted, her voice thick with emotion. "It was Star, I think, and the earth, and the universe." Her words hung in the air, filled with wonder and uncertainty. Turning her gaze to him, she added, "Keltor, I don't want to do this anymore, I thought I'd lost you."

Keltor's voice was gentle, yet firm as he spoke, "I know, Kitcat, I'm so sorry. Believe me, I don't want to do this either, but we must. I promise you, when this is over, we can be together, forever."

Emotions overwhelmed Kaitlin as she snivelled, her eyes searching his for any hint of doubt. "You promise me?" she asked, her vulnerability laid bare.

He nodded with conviction, his hand rising to tenderly brush away the tears on her cheek with the back of his finger. "Yes, I promise you," he reassured her, his touch a silent comfort.

Unable to contain the flood of feeling, Kaitlin struggled to speak through her tears. "It's just all too much now. A few weeks ago, or months, or whatever the hell it was, I'd never even heard of this place. People just keep dying, and you, oh god Keltor, if I'd lost you... I can't live… without you."

Keltor's expression grew earnest, his voice imbued with quiet determination as he cradled Kaitlin's face between his hands. "Kaitlin, please, don't say that, you must," he pleaded gently, his eyes searching hers. "Regardless of what happens to me, you must carry on. You must bring the people back together." His words were laced with both hope and the weight of responsibility, urging her to find strength even in the shadow of uncertainty.

Kaitlin's resolve faltered, her voice trembling as she replied, "I can't—I can't do it without you." The raw pain in her voice made it clear how deeply she relied on Keltor's presence, her fear of loss almost overwhelming her hope for the future.

Keltor gazed deeply into Kaitlin's eyes, his voice filled with conviction. "Yes, you can. You are so much stronger than you know, you must believe in yourself Kitcat. And your magic—by the stars, Kaitlin, how the hell did you do that? You healed me, you saved me." He paused, his words trembling with emotion. "And what about little Logie? He needs to be cared for. I don't know anyone who could love him like his mother would, except for you."

Moved by the weight of his words, Keltor pulled Kaitlin into his arms and held her close. The warmth of his embrace offered comfort and strength, a silent promise that they would face the challenges ahead together. "We can do this, Kitcat," he assured her, determination ringing in his tone. "I just need to get the amulet from Prince Keion. Without that power, we can defeat him. I underestimated him, and I won't be doing that again."

Kaitlin's hands tightened their grip around him, reluctant to let go. Despite her fears, she knew he was right—there was no other way forward. Together, they would have to summon every ounce of courage and determination to overcome the obstacles that lay ahead.

"Keltor, I feel different," Kaitlin said, her voice unsteady as he released her from his embrace. She watched him carefully as he reached into his pack and retrieved a bottle of water.

Keltor, ever attentive, paused and offered her the water first, his concern written plainly across his face. "What do you mean, different?" he asked gently, encouraging her to share what was troubling her. Kaitlin hesitated, shaking her head at the offer of water, indicating she didn't need a drink. Keltor took a swig himself.

Kaitlin was about to continue speaking, her words lingering on her lips, when Keltor signalled her to pause by raising a finger. The gesture was abrupt and silent, immediately catching her attention and halting her mid-sentence. Without offering any explanation, Keltor rose swiftly to his feet and walked a short distance away from her, his steps purposeful and tense.

Once apart from her, he leaned forward and spat out the water he had just drunk. The action, sudden and unexpected, filled Kaitlin with concern. Watching him closely, she couldn't help but call out, her worry clear in her voice. "Are you okay?" she asked, unable to mask the anxiety that gripped her as she waited for his reply, her eyes following his every movement.

"Yes," he replied, quickly glancing at her. "There's a lot of blood, that's all." Keltor wiped away the blood at the corner of his mouth with a trembling finger, then rinsed his mouth again, trying to erase the metallic taste.

"Sorry about that," he said, kneeling back down beside her, his concern for her still evident despite his own discomfort.

She reached for him, relief softening her expression. "As long as you're okay," Kaitlin replied, her fingers brushing his arm in reassurance, her worry lingering but her trust in him unwavering.

Keltor reassured her, his tone gentle and steady. "I'm fine," he said, pulling her into a comforting embrace. He held her close, offering a sense of safety amidst the uncertainty. As they parted slightly, Keltor prompted her to continue. "You were saying?" he asked, his eyes searching hers with genuine concern, looking for any sign that he might still be in pain.

Kaitlin hesitated, her worry for him still evident. She met his gaze, uncertainty flickering in her eyes, before finally speaking. "I heard a voice," she confessed quietly. "At first, I thought it was Star, but it wasn't in my head, it was all around me. So now I'm not so sure. Anyway, the voice said it was time—and at first, I thought she meant it was your time, but she clarified it was time to unlock my power." She looked to Keltor, seeking understanding.

She continued, her voice tinged with both awe and confusion. "I thought I'd already done that, when I went back to being an elf. But Keltor, I feel so much stronger now. Magically, I mean. Mentally, I'm an emotional wreck," she admitted, running her hands through her hair in a gesture of frustration and disbelief. Despite her confession, a faint smile touched her lips as she glanced at him.

"I can take power from the earth and use it to wield magic," she explained. The words hung between them, a testament to the profound transformation she was experiencing, and the unknown potential that now lay within her.

Keltor regarded her with curiosity, his brow furrowing as he asked, "Is that a normal thing, for a syronic witch to do?"

Kaitlin shook her head, uncertainty colouring her response. "Not that I know of," she replied thoughtfully. "I mean, witches have always used the power of the earth, sort of—in medicine and potions, at least—but I don't really know if they can do this."

As she spoke, Keltor watched her intently. Kaitlin reached down and placed her hand upon the ground, murmuring softly under her breath. In response, the vines and brambles nearby began to stir. They twisted and coiled upwards into the air, winding around one another in a mesmerising dance, as though animated by her very will.

Keltor stared in disbelief, his shock evident as he exclaimed, "Holy shit."

Kaitlin immediately admonished him, her tone sharp. "Keltor!" She looked at him pointedly, causing him to laugh, the tension between them momentarily diffused.

He gestured towards the display of magic she had just performed. "Well, seriously," he said, nodding at the writhing vines and brambles she had summoned. Kaitlin chuckled softly, then lifted her hand away from the earth, causing the plants to fall limply to the ground.

Curiosity got the better of Keltor, and he asked, "How do you even know how to do that?"

Kaitlin shrugged, her uncertainty clear. "No idea, I just do. It's like I've been reprogrammed, or upgraded, or something. I know that sounds stupid, but I don't know how else to explain it."

"Well, whatever it is, I'm glad you were able to use it to save me, and I'm so sorry you had to go through that, Kitcat – again." He gently raised his hand to her face and leaned in to kiss her. Kaitlin closed her eyes, experiencing a deep sense of connection that resonated throughout her.

He released her, their gazes meeting for a moment as his hand softly brushed her cheek. With a calm, measured voice, he chanted, "*Velum tuum revela*," allowing his fingertips to linger gently on her forehead. Instantly, the symbol that proclaimed her as Queen shimmered back into view upon her brow.

She lifted her hand, touching the reappeared mark with a thoughtful expression. "Is it safe to do that?" she asked quietly, her concern evident.

He gave her a reassuring nod and pressed his own fingertips to his forehead. "Yes, it's time people knew who we were, and that we are taking back Elvendon." Echoing the same chant for himself, he revealed his own kingly mark, prompting a smile from her as his royal symbol appeared once more.

"Come on," Keltor urged, casting a wary glance over his shoulder. "We should get out of here in case he comes back with his men. We need to re-think how we're going to get that amulet."

Keltor rose to his feet, brushing debris from his knees. He took a moment to examine himself, noticing that his clothes were stained with his own blood. As he glanced over to Kaitlin, he realised she too bore the marks of his wounds, her clothing similarly streaked with his blood.

Keltor knew he would not have survived without Kaitlin's ability to wield the Source magic. The gravity of his earlier carelessness weighed on him, and he silently acknowledged how close he had come to disaster. He resolved to remain vigilant, determined not to be caught off guard again.

"Let's go," he said, offering his hand to Kaitlin. She accepted, and together they moved quietly into the shelter of the trees.

As they hurried through the trees, Kaitlin's anxious voice cut through the quiet. "What did you arrange with the commander?" she asked, her tone both urgent and searching.

Keltor kept his pace steady, glancing briefly at her. "Blowing up the tower was to let the Commander know you were safe," he explained, "and to draw attention away so the Commander and his men could overpower the guards at the encampment. By now, they should be breaking free and making their move towards the castle."

Kaitlin suddenly pulled him to a stop, her concern plain. "Why are we still walking away from Aranstream? We should be there, helping them," she insisted, frustration evident in her voice.

He shook his head, resolute in his decision, signalling that he had his reasons for keeping them on their current path.

"No, the commander told me to get you as far away as possible, at least until they have taken over the castle."

Kaitlin's anxiety deepened as she pressed Keltor for reassurance. "But what if they need our help, what if they can't take the castle down?" she asked, her voice tense with worry. "Keltor, there were still a lot of soldiers in the city, and what about the people? Most of them are terrified of King Iwein. We can't kill them; they're innocent in all of this."

Keltor reached out, his hand resting gently on Kaitlin's arm in a gesture of reassurance. "It's okay," he said, his voice calm but resolute. "The Commander knows exactly what he's doing. Unless anyone in the city resists, the Commander and our army will not harm the civilians. You have my word."

He paused, his gaze meeting Kaitlin's to convey the gravity—and the hope—of their situation. "There are more than three thousand men assembled in the encampment. Every one of them is ready to fight for you, Kaitlin. Even Belrack, who has sworn that he owes you his life, stands with us. Together, they are determined to help us reclaim Elvendon."

He continued, outlining their next steps with conviction. "We'll return to gather Mum and the others. By the time we're ready, we should have the castle under our control. The Commander has the armoury key, so once our forces are inside, the castle will be ours. Especially since we know Prince Keion is not there to oppose us."

The pair moved swiftly through the forest, their urgency clear in every step.

"So, what then?" Kaitlin asked, her voice sharp with anticipation.

Keltor's reply was unwavering. "We arm ourselves and march to Elvendon castle."

Kaitlin's eyes widened in disbelief. "What, just like that? Don't you think the King will send his men once he hears what's happening at Aranstream?"

Keltor shook his head, conviction in his tone. "No, I don't think he will. He'll stand his ground in Elvendon and use our people against us."

Kaitlin stopped abruptly, her hand pressing firmly against his chest to halt him. "What do you mean, use our people? Keltor, we can't risk our people being killed."

Keltor met Kaitlin's worried gaze, his voice steady yet tinged with regret. "I know, Kaitlin, but he will use our people as a shield. We must find a way to work around it."

Kaitlin's brow furrowed as she pressed for answers. "But how?"

"We draw them out into the plains, away from the city," Keltor explained, outlining the strategy that might spare the innocents.

Still uncertain, Kaitlin asked with concern, "And how do we do that?"

Keltor hesitated, clearly troubled by the risk his plan required. He looked at her with a mixture of determination and reluctance. "We use you as bait," he admitted, his words weighted with worry.

The implication of his plan became clear. Kaitlin's eyes drifted away from him as she absorbed the gravity of what he was asking. "Oh, I see," she replied softly, her voice reflecting both understanding and fear.

Keltor's voice was filled with reluctance as he spoke. "Kitcat, I don't want to do this. If I could send you miles away until all of this was over, I would. But the King needs to see you are real."

Gently, he lifted his hand to her chin, guiding her gaze to meet his. "We can do this, Kitcat," he said, his words meant to reassure her as her green eyes met the deep blue of his own. "I won't let anything happen to you." He brushed his hand by her cheek and into her hair, holding her face tenderly. With compassion, he acknowledged her fears. "I know this is frightening, and you have already been through so much and lost so many. But it's the only way I can think of to draw him and his men away from Elvendon and the city."

Kaitlin's voice trembled as she tried to reassure him. "It's okay, I'm not worried about me," she insisted, her eyes lifting to meet his gaze with sincerity. She hesitated for a moment, her concern evident. "Keltor, I'm worried about you, and the men, and all the families in Elvendon." Her words were laced with a deep sense of responsibility and anxiety for those around her. "I still can't help thinking if we hadn't killed Aragon, none of this would have happened. I wouldn't have the blood of all those people and children who have already died on my hands." Her chest tightened with every word, and her vision blurred as she struggled to steady her breath. Aragon had been more than just an enemy—his fall had unleashed chaos none of them could have foreseen.

"No, no," he said, shaking his head at her. "Kaitlin, you know King Iwein was going to attack Elvendon regardless of us killing his son. The plan was in motion long before you came back to Elvendon. When I think back to the last few months, and the arguments your father had with the elders about Aranstream, it starts to make sense. Your father was scared, that's why he was marring his daughters off to the princes of Aranstream. He didn't think we could win a battle against them."

Kaitlin's uncertainty lingered as she challenged Keltor's confidence. "Then what makes you think we can do it now, if my father, with all the army behind him, thought he couldn't do it?"

Keltor drew her close, a gentle resolve in his embrace. "Because, my love," he murmured, holding her tightly, "we have you, and me, and our magic. King Iwein will not be expecting us to use magic against him." His conviction was clear; together, their unique bond and powers offered hope where conventional strength had failed.

Yet Kaitlin's concern sharpened. "But Keion knows now that you can perform magic, he knows you are a wizard." Her words carried a new layer of anxiety, a reminder that their advantage might not be as secret as Keltor believed.

Keltor paused, considering the options before him, then gave a small nod of agreement. "Okay, maybe you're right," he conceded, his tone thoughtful. "We need to return to Aranstream, back to the castle, and find Commander Talbot. You should stay with him, where it's safe, and I'll go after the prince." His plan carried a sense of urgency and resolve, yet also a heavy burden of responsibility.

"No, Keltor, that's too dangerous. We should stick together," Kaitlin pleaded, her voice filled with desperation as she gripped his upper arms tightly. The thought of letting him go once more was almost unbearable, and her fear for his safety was clear in her trembling words.

He met her gaze with determination, though sorrow flickered in his eyes. "No, I have to," he replied, the finality in his voice signalling that his mind was made up, despite the pain it caused them both.

"Keltor, he could be anywhere. If he's using a portal to move, he could already be at Elvendon." Kaitlin's voice was urgent, her concern clear as she voiced the possibility that their enemy might have already escaped.

Keltor paused, his mind racing as he tried to piece together the events that had unfolded. The aftermath of what had happened still clouded his thoughts, but as he forced himself to recall the details, a deep frown settled on his brow. He was beginning to see things more clearly.

Noticing the intensity in his expression, Kaitlin anxiously asked, "What is it?"

He met her worried gaze, finally able to voice his realisation. "He's still here."

Kaitlin's alarm was immediate; she glanced around, searching the shadows for any sign of movement. "What do you mean he's still here?"

Keltor explained, his tone steady but urgent. "Kaitlin, he can't possibly open a portal. If he didn't sense you using magic when we were captured, there's no way he knows how to open a portal.

579

That was all a misdirection, an illusion. To open a portal, you'd need to be a really, powerful wizard."

Kaitlin glanced anxiously back towards the trees, her voice tense as she asked, "What do we do?" The uncertainty in her words hung in the air, underscoring the urgency of their situation.

Keltor's response was immediate and decisive. "Shit, I need to go after him, we've already wasted too much time, but I don't want you to come with me." His words conveyed his resolve to pursue the prince, yet also his deep concern for Kaitlin's safety. He was torn between the need for swift action and the desire to protect her from further danger.

"Seriously, you're not leaving me here while you go off on your own, Keltor. You've already nearly died because of him—what if he tries again, and I'm not there to save you?" Kaitlin's voice rose in frustration and fear, her hands balled into fists at her sides as she glared at him. "You know we're stronger when we're together."

Keltor bit down hard on his lower lip, torn by indecision. The thought of Kaitlin accompanying him filled him with dread—it was simply too dangerous, and he was unwilling to put her at further risk.

He met her eyes, trying to convey both his resolve and his care. "I know we're stronger together, Kaitlin, but you must trust me on this. Please," he said, his voice gentle but firm.

Kaitlin's frustration flared, her voice rising as she gestured angrily. "No, it's not okay! You're just going to leave me here, in the forest?" Her distress was unmistakable as she waved her arms, the idea of being left behind clearly unbearable.

Keltor shook his head, his tone urgent yet reassuring. "No, I'm not leaving you here. I need you to go back to Aranstream and find Commander Talbot. Tell him what's happened—ask him to send someone to fetch my parents and Ese, and any of the other men willing to fight alongside us."

He searched her gaze, wanting her to understand the urgency. "Commander Talbot will know where to find the cottage if you tell him, it's Ben's place. That's all you need to say—he'll understand, I promise."

"Keltor," she implored, her voice trembling as her hand reached out to grip his arm. "Please, I don't want to leave you." Her words were soft but desperate, the fear of separation clear in her eyes.

Keltor's resolve wavered for a moment as he looked at her, but he forced himself to remain steady. "Kitcat, you have to," he insisted gently, using the nickname that always softened her heart. "I must stop the prince from getting to Elvendon. As soon as the King finds out what's happened at Aranstream, all hell's going to break loose, and what we don't want is the prince telling him about my magic."

He squeezed her hand, trying to reassure her despite his own anxiety. "You need to lead the army to the plains at first light tomorrow. If I can't get back in time, I'll meet you there. Promise me you'll do this."

Kaitlin shook her head, tears streaming down her cheeks as she faced Keltor. Her voice trembled with desperation, "Keltor, please, I don't want to leave you. What if you can't beat him? What if he kills you?" The anguish in her voice was unmistakable, her fear not born from the looming battle itself, but from the terrifying thought of losing Keltor. Her heart ached, overwhelmed by dread at the possibility of his death, and the love she felt for him made the prospect of separation unbearable.

Keltor tried to reassure her, his voice gentle yet resolute. "I'll be okay, I promise, and so will you. Kaitlin, you'll need to be careful—there are Aranstream soldiers nearby, so if you must use your magic to protect yourself, do it."

Overwhelmed by emotion, Kaitlin broke down. "Oh god, Keltor," she sobbed, flinging her arms around him and clinging on tightly. Keltor held her close, feeling the weight of the moment. He breathed in the scent of her hair and closed his eyes, wishing he could freeze time, just for a second.

He pressed his lips close to her ear, his words barely more than a whisper. "I love you more than life itself, Kitcat. Remember that always—you are my Queen, my wife, my everything."

She pulled back from him, her resolve wavering even as she tried to put on a brave face. With a shaky voice, she managed, "You'd better come back to me."

Keltor gently placed his hand against the side of Kaitlin's face. His touch was both tender and reassuring as he looked into her eyes and gave his solemn promise. "I will, I promise," he said, his voice soft but filled with conviction.

Kaitlin closed her eyes, surrendering herself to the moment. As their lips met in a kiss, a surge of energy coursed through her body, the sensation tangible and powerful, binding them together in emotion and purpose.

As they parted from their kiss, Keltor looked deeply into Kaitlin's eyes, his voice soft but charged with conviction. "Did you feel that?" he asked, searching her face for understanding. Kaitlin nodded, sensing the same surge of energy that had passed between them.

"That's our power, Kaitlin," Keltor continued, his words deliberate and filled with meaning. "We are destined to be together, or I would have died today. The spirits have a greater purpose for us." He urged her gently, reinforcing his faith in their bond. "Trust in me, and trust in yourself, okay?" His gaze was unwavering, inviting her to believe not only in him but in the shared strength that bound them together.

"Okay," she sniffled, her voice trembling as she tried to steady herself. With tears still glistening in her eyes, Kaitlin reached for Keltor and pulled him into her arms for one final embrace. She pressed herself close, breathing in his familiar scent, seeking comfort in the warmth and reassurance it brought. For a moment, time seemed to stand still; she could feel the depth of his love radiating from him, a silent promise that lingered between them. Eventually, with great reluctance, she loosened her hold and let him go, her hands lingering for just a heartbeat longer before she stepped back, her heart aching with the weight of their impending separation.

Keltor's eyes lingered on Kaitlin, his expression torn with worry and love. "Keep safe, Kitcat," he pleaded, his voice trembling as he began to step away from her. As he retreated, he paused for a moment, raising his hands to signal 'I love you' in their silent language. Without waiting for her reply, Keltor turned and ran off into the trees, his figure quickly swallowed by the forest's shadows.

Kaitlin stared after him, her heart pounding and her fists clenched at her sides. "Shit, Keltor," she muttered under her breath, frustration and fear mingling in her tone as she watched him vanish from sight. Raising her voice, she called out after him, her words laced with desperation, "You'd better come back to me!" The silence of the woods was her only answer.

With a heavy sigh, her shoulders slumped and sadness etched across her face, Kaitlin turned towards the looming outline of the trees. Taking a steadying breath, she set off in the direction of Aranstream castle, determination carrying her forward despite the ache of separation that weighed on her heart.

Leaving Kaitlin behind was, without question, the hardest thing Keltor had ever had to do—made all the more painful by the promise he had only just made to her that he would never leave. Yet, circumstances had forced his hand; he simply could not be in two places at once, and time was slipping away far too quickly. He tried to reassure himself with the knowledge that Kaitlin had her own magic to protect her, convinced that she would be safe in his absence.

His thoughts quickly shifted to the king, who was stationed at Elvendon, leaving only the prince unaccounted for. Keltor could tell the prince was just ahead; he'd already picked up Keion's trail, and the evidence lay in the streaks of blood smeared across the bracken and forest floor. It was clear that the prince was injured, most likely dragging his left leg—Keltor recalled the blast of magic he'd landed before the prince made his abrupt disappearance.

Despite the tension, Keltor drew some reassurance from his surroundings. The familiar scents of rich soil, wildflowers, and the forest's trees filled the air—but there was another, more personal scent as well. Intermingled with the woodland aromas was the lingering trace of the prince's cologne, letting Keltor know his adversary was not far ahead.

Keltor moved swiftly through the dense woodland, weaving beneath low-hanging branches as his boots crushed cones and leaves underfoot, sending up the earthy scent of the forest floor. Every sense was heightened as he pressed on, the urgency of his mission driving him forward.

Amidst the ferns and low-lying scrub, Keltor's sharp eyes caught sight of a figure attempting to conceal themselves. Instinctively, he slowed his pace, approaching with caution as he became aware of the nearby ravine, its edge obscured by the thick undergrowth.

Suddenly, Prince Keion rose to his feet, emerging from his hiding place and fixing Keltor with a piercing stare. Keltor halted at once, his gaze sweeping over the prince. He immediately noticed the blood staining Keion's left trouser leg and the way the prince leaned to his right, favouring his injured side. It was clear that the wound had slowed Keion, explaining how Keltor had managed to catch up to him so quickly.

Keltor's hand drifted automatically towards the hilt of his sword, readying himself for a confrontation. Yet, as he observed the prince's hand move towards the amulet hanging at his neck, Keltor realised that a blade would be of little use in this encounter. This would not be a battle of steel, but a clash of magic.

Prince Keion's eyes flashed with determination as he uttered a single command. "Light destroy," he declared, thrusting his hand forward. Instantly, a searing bolt of lightning surged from his fingertips, crackling through the air and heading straight for Keltor.

Reacting swiftly, Keltor brought his hands up before him and called out, "*Reflectar.*" A shimmering forcefield materialised, enveloping him in a protective barrier. The lightning strike collided with the shield, energy arcing across its surface. For a moment, the forcefield glimmered under the intensity of the assault, but then the bolt lost its strength and faded away, leaving Keltor unharmed but acutely aware of the prince's magical prowess.

As the searing bolt of lightning shot from Prince Keion's hands, he did not remain stationary. Instead, he sprinted after the magical attack, pushing himself to move at full speed towards Keltor despite the pain radiating from his wounded left leg. His face contorted in agony with each step, yet his determination did not waver. Keltor, having underestimated the prince due to his injury, was caught off guard by this aggressive advance. He had assumed the prince would be hindered and unable to mount such a swift assault. However, as the energy from the lightning dissipated, Keion crashed into Keltor with the full force of his body, driving his shoulder hard into Keltor's chest. The unexpected impact sent Keltor staggering backwards. Instinctively, Keltor's hand shot up and, summoning his own power, he unleashed a potent ball of energy directly at the prince, refusing to yield to the sudden onslaught.

Keion lifted his hand, his expression resolute, and with a deft motion deflected the ball of energy away from himself. Without hesitation, he strode purposefully towards Keltor, every step radiating confidence and intent. As he advanced, Keion called upon the formidable magic contained within the amulet around his neck. Raising both hands, he unleashed its power, seizing Keltor in an invisible grip and lifting him clean off the ground. With a surge of force, Keion hurled Keltor backwards, sending him reeling through the air.

Keltor crashed to the ground with force, the impact sending him skidding ever closer to the precipitous edge of the ravine. Disoriented and with adrenaline surging, he had scarcely a moment to formulate a spell before Prince Keion seized the advantage. With a swift, commanding gesture, the prince used his magic to yank Keltor upright, holding him aloft in an unyielding grip conjured from sheer force of will and arcane power.

Keltor's boots scraped at the loose earth, teetering on the brink as dust and pebbles tumbled down into the abyss below. Try as he might, Keltor found himself utterly immobilised. The prince's mastery of the amulet's magic far surpassed Keltor's own abilities, and the overwhelming strength of the artefact's enchantment left him powerless to resist its hold.

Through the shimmering haze of the magical veil, Keltor's eyes locked onto the amulet that was the source of his adversary's dominance. The chain had worked its way loose during their fierce struggle, and the amulet now dangled visibly outside of the prince's tunic—tantalisingly close, yet still out of reach. Desperation welled up within Keltor; if only he could break free, if only he could stretch out his hand to grasp the amulet, he might stand a chance of turning the tide.

Prince Keion's voice rang out, saturated with triumph and scorn. "Without you, your Queen will have to surrender to my father. You have failed her," he gloated, his words carrying the weight of impending defeat. With a measured motion, Keion drew back his hands and unleashed a powerful, invisible force that slammed into Keltor, sending him staggering precariously close to the edge of the ravine.

For an instant, the magical energy surrounding them shimmered, betraying a fleeting change as Prince Keion shifted his focus and altered his spell. Sensing this brief lapse, Keltor seized the opportunity. His hand shot forward, reaching desperately towards the prince, intent on grasping him and perhaps wresting control of the situation in a final attempt to turn the tide of their confrontation.

Prince Keion's laughter echoed across the chasm as Keltor lost his footing and tumbled over the edge of the ravine. Keion rushed to the precipice, arriving just in time to catch a final glimpse of Keltor as he disappeared into the swirling clouds below.

Chapter Twenty-Five
Malgar

As Keltor plummeted, the world transformed into a blur of white mist, the clouds enveloping him in their chill embrace. He barely had a moment to gather his thoughts before he emerged from the other side of the cloudbank, the ground looming far below but rushing up towards him with terrifying speed. Realising the peril he was in, Keltor seized the amulet and forced it over his neck, desperate for any hope of survival as he continued his rapid descent. In those harrowing seconds, his thoughts turned to Kaitlin—haunted by the prospect of never seeing her again and the sorrow his loss would bring her.

Suddenly, a portal began to open beneath him. Keltor's heartbeat quickened as he caught sight of it; without hesitation, he angled his body and dived towards the mysterious gateway. He had no idea where the portal would lead, but with the ground rushing up to meet him, he was willing to risk the unknown rather than face certain destruction.

Keltor plunged headlong into the portal, which closed instantly behind him. As he spun and twisted through the gateway, disorientation set in. When he finally emerged, he found himself utterly confused by his surroundings. No longer falling, Keltor realised he was now simply floating in a strange, white mist, disoriented and uncertain whether he was even still alive, a man's voice rang out, clear and commanding, "Keltor Dracon." Startled, Keltor's eyes widened. He struggled to orient himself, but in this peculiar void, there was no sense of direction—he could not even tell which way was up.

With nothing left to lose, Keltor replied, "Yes." He waited, his heart pounding as he clung to the hope that answering might provide some clarity to his predicament.

The mysterious voice responded with a single word, "Gravitas." Instantly, the mist that had enveloped Keltor vanished. Without warning, he plummeted downwards, hitting the ground hard and landing in a patch of grass.

"Ouch!" Keltor groaned involuntarily, feeling the sting of the impact. As he looked up, he saw an old, bearded man standing before him, watching him with a curious expression.

"Keltor, it is good to finally meet you," the old man said with a smile, though the only sign of warmth Keltor noticed was a slight twitch in the man's long white beard. Disoriented but alert, Keltor pushed himself up from the ground, scanning his new surroundings. He found himself standing in a field beneath a brilliant blue sky, where vibrant red poppies swayed gently in the breeze.

Still processing the shock of his abrupt journey, Keltor asked, "Am I dead?"

The old man responded with a laugh, his eyes crinkling at the corners. He then placed a reassuring hand on Keltor's back. "No, you're not dead," he assured him. "Now, walk with me," he said, giving Keltor a gentle, encouraging push forward. "We do not have long."

"Where am I, who are you?" Keltor asked, his relief at not being dead quickly giving way to confusion as he tried to comprehend his new surroundings. Despite his bewilderment, he complied with the old man's gentle request to walk alongside him.

The old man introduced himself, his tone calm and reassuring. "My name is Marton," he said, removing his hand from Keltor's back as they walked together.

Hearing the name, Keltor murmured it to himself. "Marton..." The name ignited a flicker of recognition in Keltor's mind, though he could not immediately place it. There was something about it that felt oddly familiar.

As they continued, Marton's gaze fell upon the amulet now resting around Keltor's neck. A look of relief passed over the old man's face, and he offered a small, knowing smile. "I knew your father, Forde," Marton revealed, his voice touched with the warmth of old memories.

Keltor halted, his eyes widening as he turned to face the old man more directly. The pieces began to fall into place. "Wizard Marton?" he asked, raising an eyebrow as the realisation dawned on him.

The old man nodded in affirmation. "Yes, that was how I was known. Your father, Forde, was my apprentice."

"What, I don't understand, where am I?" Keltor asked again, his voice tinged with confusion as he looked all around him. All he could see was an endless stretch of poppy fields, the vibrant flowers swaying gently in the breeze, offering no clues or answers.

The old man turned to face him, his gaze steady. "You are in the world beyond worlds," he replied, his tone calm yet carrying an air of mystery.

Panic began to rise in Keltor, and he blurted out, "So, I am dead?" The prospect sent a chill through him, his mind racing with uncertainty.

"No, no, young man," the old man responded quickly, his movements deliberate as his old, gnarled hand reached out to touch Keltor's arm with a reassuring gesture. "I can assure you; you are not dead. I have brought you here to help you."

Still gripped by confusion, Keltor struggled to make sense of what was happening. "Help me, how? I don't understand what's going on," he admitted, searching for clarity in the old man's words and actions.

Marton glanced at Keltor, his expression thoughtful. "You know of the spirit world, Keltor?" he asked quietly.

Keltor nodded, remembering tales from his childhood. "Yes, we were told about it as kids, but I wasn't sure it was real," he admitted, his eyes shifting restlessly as he surveyed the fields around him.

Marton offered a gentle smile. "Well, it is real, my boy. You are here now amongst the great elders—like myself—whose duty it is to guide those chosen to help keep our worlds in balance."

Perplexed yet intrigued, Keltor searched Marton's face. "You mean, the Source?" he asked.

The old man nodded solemnly. "Yes, the Source is the power of everything."

Keltor frowned, slowing his pace as he processed Marton's words. He stopped walking, turning to face the old man more directly. "Is it just our world you watch?" he asked, the question lingering in the air as they stood among the swaying poppies.

Marton's eyes softened as he responded, his steps unhurried. "No, it is all worlds within the universe," he explained, making it clear that their responsibilities extended far beyond a single realm.

Still grappling with the enormity of what was unfolding, Keltor pressed on, trying to make sense of his own presence here. "Why am I here? Did you open the portal that I fell into?" he asked, hurrying to match Marton's pace.

Marton turned to him with a measured look. "Yes, Keltor, I did. In times of great need, we are permitted to interfere and guide such people as yourself, and Kaitlin." His words carried both gravity and reassurance, revealing the importance of their roles.

At the mention of Kaitlin, urgency returned to Keltor's voice. "Kaitlin," he exclaimed, the memory of her plight suddenly at the forefront of his mind. "I need to get back to her," he insisted, anxiety tightening his tone.

Marton nodded with understanding but held up a hand to pause him. "Yes, I know, but first there is something I must do," he said, his tone firm yet gentle, signalling that their encounter was not yet finished and there was more for Keltor to learn before he could return.

Keltor hesitated, his thoughts racing as he recalled the events of earlier that day. "Did you help her, save me earlier today? Kaitlin said someone spoke to her and gave her magic which connected her to the earth."

Marton offered him a reassuring smile. "She was given power directly from the Source."

Confused, Keltor shook his head. "I don't understand?"

With a gentle patience, Marton explained, "Kaitlin has a deep-rooted connection to the Source. The Source is many things, including what we call mother nature. She is the one who is guiding Kaitlin."

Keltor paused, reflecting on Marton's explanation. After a moment's thought, he asked quietly, "Is She a person?"

Marton shook his head, a gentle smile flickering across his face. "Oh no, She is much more than that. She is the giver of life."

"Like a god?" Keltor ventured, his voice tinged with uncertainty.

Marton nodded slightly. "If you like," he replied, his tone accepting of Keltor's comparison. Then, shifting the conversation, Marton continued, "Keltor, give me your father's amulet."

Keltor's hand instinctively moved to the amulet hanging around his neck. "Why?" he asked, gripping it protectively.

"Because it's too dangerous to have in its current form," Marton explained, his voice calm but firm.

"But I was going to give it back to my father," Keltor said, his voice tinged with reluctance as he held the amulet close.

Marton shook his head, his expression gentle yet resolute. "No, Keltor. His time as a wizard has passed. He has fulfilled everything that was required of him. Now, it is your turn."

With a deep breath, Keltor slowly removed the amulet from around his neck and handed it to the old man, acknowledging the shift in destiny. "I don't need it," he said quietly. "I already have wizard's power."

"Yes, I know, but it's not enough, and you have no time to learn how to use it," the wizard said with a sombre gravity. His gaze was unwavering. "It is yours and Kaitlin's destiny to bring the world of elves back together. You are the Destroyer, Keltor, and she is the Protector."

591

A flicker of confusion crossed Keltor's face. "But I thought I was the Protector," he interrupted, unable to hide the uncertainty in his voice.

The wizard shook his head gently, offering a small, understanding smile. "Yes, you are her protector, but not the Protector. That is Kaitlin's role. She is a protector of worlds. You must hold all the cards of power, Keltor."

The old man's tone shifted, becoming more serious. "Now, this may hurt a little," he warned, his eyes meeting Keltor's with a look of concern.

Keltor's apprehension grew. "What will?" he asked, bracing himself for what was to come.

Marton regarded Keltor with a steady gaze. "Open your shirt," the wizard requested, his tone gentle but insistent.

Casting a wary look at the old man, Keltor slowly began to unbutton his blood-stained shirt, each movement betraying his unease. He hesitated for a moment, but then allowed the garment to fall open, exposing his chest.

Without delay, the wizard brought the amulet forward and pressed it firmly against Keltor's bare skin, holding it in place with both hands. The ancient jewellery seemed to pulse with a hidden energy between them.

"Keltor, all the magic within the amulet is about to transfer into your soul," Marton explained, his voice calm but charged with significance. "It is the safest place to store the power it possesses."

"My soul?" Keltor echoed, his eyes widening in uncertainty and his eyebrow arching as he tried to grasp the gravity of what was about to happen.

"Yes," the old man replied with a gentle nod, offering reassurance even as the atmosphere grew heavier with anticipation.

A beat of silence passed before Keltor found his voice again. "Will it help us defeat King Iwein?" he asked, the question hanging between them, heavy with hope and fear.

Keltor looked at Marton, confusion flickering across his face. "Yes, but you are going to need a little help. You are a Dragon

Lord, Keltor. Call upon Kailan as you return—it is imperative that you do this as soon as you leave here. Do you understand?" Marton's voice was steady, his words carrying a weight of urgency.

Keltor hesitated, searching Marton's eyes for reassurance. "You mean, that dragon Kaitlin and I met back in the world of Malgar?" he asked, his mind racing as he recalled the powerful creature and the strange bond they shared.

Marton nodded, his expression earnest. "Yes. You and he are bonded; he will come when you call. Now, brace yourself," he warned, signalling that what was coming next would test Keltor's courage and resolve.

Keltor paused, drawing in a deep breath as confusion clouded his thoughts. The notion of calling upon a dragon, especially one residing in another world, left him bewildered. The question gnawed at him: how could a dragon so far away possibly hear his summons?

Marton noticed Keltor's apprehension and addressed him directly, his tone calm and reassuring. "Keltor," he said softly, prompting Keltor to lift his gaze and meet the old wizard's eyes.

With unwavering confidence, Marton explained, "Your mind is linked with the dragon; he will hear you."

Keltor was taken aback, surprised not only by Marton's insight into his private doubts but also by the wizard's ability to read his thoughts so precisely. Still, he managed only a silent nod in response, accepting the truth of Marton's words as best he could.

"*Ego invocabo fons. Traduxisset potentiae. Consensu,*" Marton chanted, and he pushed the amulet hard into Keltor's chest.

The amulet burned, hot and painfully, and Keltor yelped as his fleshed sizzled.

"I'm sorry boy, but it is the only way. Remember, call for Kailan," Marton said.

The words crackled with ancient power; their meaning lost to Keltor but heavy with intent. Or: "*Ego invocabo fons. Traduxisset potentiae. Consensu,*" Marton chanted—a call to summon the source, transfer power, and bind agreement.

As Keltor lifted his head to meet Marton's gaze, he suddenly felt his feet leave the ground. A sensation of weightlessness overtook him, and, almost without warning, he began to float upwards into the sky. Below him, the old man's face grew smaller, but Marton's voice carried clearly through the mist that was rapidly enveloping Keltor. As he vanished into the billowing white cloud above, Marton's urgent cry echoed after him: "Call the dragon!"

Keltor's body began to spin uncontrollably, the world around him blurring into streaks of colour as he felt himself being drawn back through the portal. For a moment, he struggled to catch his breath, squeezing his eyes shut in anticipation of what was to come. He was sure, with a sinking certainty, that the portal was sending him back to where he had come from.

As Keltor shot out of the portal, his eyes snapped open, and he found himself once more hurtling through the air, plummeting towards the earth below. The terror of falling gripped him, but he knew what he had to do. Desperately, Keltor hollered, *"Draco, Draco, vocavi te, Kailan,"* his voice carried by the rush of wind as he tumbled through the sky. Time was running out and panic set in; still, he refused to give up. With a final, frantic burst of energy, he screamed again, *"Draco, Draco, vocavi te, Kailan!"* His plea was urgent, raw with the fear that any second could be his last.

A tremendous gust of wind surged around Keltor, the force so intense that he had to clamp his eyes shut, bracing himself against the overwhelming speed. In the blink of an eye, his rapid descent ceased as he struck something with a resounding thud. The landing was jarring, sending a shock through his body and expelling the air from his lungs. Keltor gasped, struggling to regain his breath, a rough grunt escaping him as he fought to recover from the powerful impact.

Inside his mind, a voice echoed powerfully: *"Etor, Dragonar Elmeran."* The words rang out, filling his consciousness and resonating with unmistakable authority.

Finding himself atop the dragon, Keltor's hands instinctively sought out the scales beneath him. He held on tightly to Kailan's

594

back, clinging for stability and reassurance amidst the chaos of his arrival.

Keltor gasped with relief, finally finding his voice. Turning to the dragon, he expressed his gratitude, his disbelief clear in his tone. "*Kailan,*" he breathed, overwhelmed by the realisation that his desperate plea had been heard, and relieved that the powerful bond between them endured.

The enormous dragon turned his head mid-flight, his eyes meeting Keltor's. "*I've got you, young dragon lord,*" he rumbled reassuringly. "*Hang tight, I'm going to land.*"

Keltor gripped Kailan tightly between his thighs, ensuring he had a firm hold on the dragon's back. He wedged his feet securely behind the dragon's scales, anchoring himself as the massive creature soared through the sky. The wind rushed past, whipping against Keltor's face with tremendous force. His hair streamed backwards, and his cheeks quivered from the sheer velocity, the sensation both terrifying and exhilarating all at once. Each moment in the sky balanced the edge between fear and the thrill of flight, leaving Keltor awestruck by the power and majesty of his dragon companion.

As Kailan touched down with a resounding thud, Keltor felt a wave of relief wash over him. The impact of the landing jolted him, causing his head to drop down against the dragon's sturdy back. Grateful for his survival, he silently offered thanks to the spirits and to Marton, whose intervention had helped him escape disaster.

Once he had caught his breath, Keltor pushed himself upright, steadied his nerves, and swung his leg over Kailan's side. He slid down the dragon's massive form, the ground seeming a long way below. When he finally reached the earth, he landed heavily, feeling the impact echo up through his legs. Keltor took a moment to gather himself before making his way to the front of the dragon. He came to a halt, pausing for a brief second, and then lifted his gaze, ready to face his loyal companion.

Keltor turned to Kailan, gratitude shining in his eyes. "*Thank you,*" he said, his voice thick with relief. "*I didn't know if you would hear me or be able to get to me so fast.*" The weight of his near escape lingered in his words, and he exhaled shakily, still coming to terms with the ordeal.

Kailan's gaze was steady and reassuring. "*You are a dragon lord, and I am your dragon,*" he replied, his deep voice resonating with unwavering confidence. "*We are connected. When you call, I hear you, and I will find you.*"

Keltor gazed up at Kailan, awe and disbelief mingling on his face as the reality of their situation dawned on him. The enormity of what he had just heard left him momentarily speechless. Struggling to comprehend, he asked, "Even from another world?" His tone betrayed his astonishment, his eyes searching Kailan's for reassurance.

Kailan's deep rumble was gentle and patient. "*My Lord, you are in Malgar, not your Elvendon,*" he explained, his gaze kind as he sought to ease Keltor's confusion.

The name struck Keltor with sudden clarity. "*Malgar!*" he exclaimed, immediately scanning the unfamiliar landscape around him. He was desperate to understand how he had come to be in this strange place, his mind racing to piece together the events that had led him here. "*How, I don't understand?*" he pressed, his bewilderment evident.

Kailan replied with quiet certainty, offering the explanation Keltor needed. "*It was Marton, he opened the portal so you would fall onto my back.*" The simplicity of the answer stood in stark contrast to the extraordinary nature of what had just occurred, yet it was enough to confirm the involvement of the wizard and the miraculous escape Keltor had experienced.

Keltor shook his head in disbelief. Unable to contain his admiration, Keltor smiled warmly at the great dragon, he said with genuine awe. "*I forgot how stunning you are, Kailan.*"

Kailan ducked his head with exaggerated shyness, his tone playful. "*Aw, now come my Lord, you embarrass me,*" he said, lowering his face comically as if feigning bashfulness.

Keltor couldn't help but laugh, the tension of their ordeal easing for a moment in the shared lightness. The dragon's playful demeanour brought welcome relief, allowing Keltor to briefly forget the peril he had just escaped.

However, as the laughter faded, Kailan's expression grew more serious. With a hint of concern in his deep, resonant voice, he asked, *"So, how is it that you were falling to your death?"* The shift in the dragon's tone reminded Keltor of the gravity of the situation that had brought him here, the air between them now charged with curiosity and genuine worry.

Keltor's expression darkened as he recalled the recent ordeal. *"I was pushed over the ravine by a prince,"* he confessed, his voice tight with the strain of reliving the event.

Kailan regarded Keltor thoughtfully, his massive form settling onto the ground with a measured grace. The dragon's voice was low and contemplative as he spoke. *"Hmm,"* he mused, his eyes never leaving Keltor. After a moment, Kailan shifted his weight, lowering himself down and sitting more comfortably, signalling that he was ready to listen. *"Tell me what has happened to put you in such a predicament that you needed to summon my help."* The concern in his tone was unmistakable, and his posture showed he was fully attentive to Keltor's plight, inviting him to share the events that had led to this desperate situation.

Keltor settled himself on a nearby boulder, gathering his thoughts before speaking. He began to recount to Kailan, in detail, the events that had transpired since he and Kaitlin parted ways with the dragon all those months ago. His words painted a vivid picture of the trials and challenges they had faced during their journey.

After taking a steadying breath, Keltor continued his account. *"So,"* he said, *"I went over the edge, having managed to snatch my father's amulet from around Prince Keion's neck. As I fell, the ground rushed up towards me at a terrifying pace. In that moment, a portal suddenly opened in the air. I had only a split second to react, and I dived towards it, hoping for escape."*

He glanced at Kailan, searching his face for recognition. "*You know this wizard, called Marton, then?*" Keltor asked, his voice tinged with uncertainty as he sought to connect the fragments of his ordeal with Kailan's own knowledge and experiences.

Kailan nodded in response to Keltor's mention of the wizard, his manner thoughtful and assured. "*I do indeed, Keltor,*" he replied, his voice resonant with memory. "*He was a fine wizard. In fact, he was the very one who taught your father.*"

Understanding dawned in Keltor's eyes, and he returned the nod, a sense of connection growing between them. "*Yes, I know that now,*" he said quietly. He paused, recalling Kailan's earlier words from months before, and offered a rueful smile. "*You were right, what you said all those months ago about me possessing magic. I am a wizard.*" Keltor's tone carried both apology and newfound conviction. "*I'm sorry I didn't believe you then.*"

Kailan drew in a long, steady breath, letting it out in a warm, gentle stream that washed over Keltor. The dragon's exhalation was comforting, carrying with it a sense of reassurance. He paused, his gaze steady upon Keltor, before finally speaking.

"*I did not realise the full extent of your magical abilities,*" Kailan admitted, his tone measured and thoughtful. The dragon's gaze lingered on Keltor, reflecting both curiosity and a newfound respect at this revelation. Kailan's words acknowledged not just the surprise at Keltor's talents, but also the gravity of discovering that the young wizard's powers ran deeper than previously known. "*It was only after you left that I discovered something important— your father is Ford Dracon. Once, he was a renowned dragon rider who served our King with great distinction.*" The dragon's words held a mixture of respect and wonder, underscoring the significance of Keltor's lineage and the legacy he carried.

Keltor nodded in agreement, his voice steady as he revealed more about his heritage. "*Yes, that's right, and my mum is Sharelle. She was a dragon rider too. I've only just found that out as well.*" The weight of this discovery lingered in his words, underscoring the significance of his parents' legacy and the recent revelations that had come to light.

598

Upon hearing this, the dragon offered a warm smile and gently lowered his head, a gesture of both respect and affection. His manner grew softer as he recounted the events that had brought them together. "*They both helped rescue me, from my torturous prison where I was being held by Gemini the dark Lord.*" The dragon's acknowledgement not only highlighted the courage of Keltor's parents but also the deep bonds that tied their histories together, marking this moment as one of profound understanding and shared experience.

Keltor's eyes widened with astonishment as he processed the dragon's words. "*Mum and Dad rescued you—wow, that's incredible,*" he murmured, his voice filled with awe. The revelation left him momentarily speechless, the reality of his parents' bravery slowly sinking in.

He glanced down, a thoughtful frown crossing his face as he considered the unexpected depth of their histories. "*There are so many questions I must ask them when we get back home,*" Keltor admitted, his tone tinged with both curiosity and longing. The weight of all he had just discovered pressed upon him, the truth about his parents' identities and origins reshaping his understanding of his own past.

"*I had no idea about any of this, of who they were, or where they came from,*" he added quietly, the words hanging in the air as he struggled to reconcile these new truths with the life he had always known.

Kailan looked at Keltor, his expression earnest as he spoke. "*Perhaps, Keltor, you need my help in solving your issue with King Iwein,*" he suggested, offering his assistance with a gentle sense of purpose.

Keltor's eyes widened, hope flickering across his face at the possibility of such powerful support. "*You would help us?*" he asked, the prospect of a dragon's aid filling him with renewed confidence.

Kailan considered the question carefully. "*Hmm, I would need to discuss this with our king first. We are not always permitted to interfere in the action of other realms if it does not directly affect us. However, we have always had a link with Elvendon, and you are a dragon lord.*" Kailan's words hinted at the deep-rooted bonds between their peoples, as well as the protocols and traditions that governed their involvement in conflicts beyond their own realm.

Curiosity and concern mingled in Keltor's next question as he looked intently at Kailan. "*Your king is back?*" he inquired, recalling the last time he had seen Kailan and remembering that the King of Malgar had then been away on a crucial quest to find his daughter and niece.

Kailan nodded in confirmation, a subtle warmth infusing his tone. "*He is indeed,*" he replied, his words carrying a sense of relief and pride at the King's return.

Eager to understand what had unfolded, Keltor pressed further, keen to learn the outcome of the King's journey. "*Did he find his daughter and niece?*" he asked, hope flickering in his voice.

With a touch of pride, Kailan recounted the tale. "*He did, it was quite an epic adventure by all accounts. Our King had to fight a tyrant and regain a throne for the true King of that realm.*" The scope of the King's trials and triumphs was evident in the way Kailan spoke, hinting at the magnitude of the journey recently completed.

Keltor's eyes widened at the story, an eagerness kindling within him. "*Wow, I would love to hear all about it some other time,*" he said, the prospect of hearing the details clearly appealing to him. However, the urgency of his own situation pressed upon him. "*How long will it take, I mean to ask him?*" he continued, anxiety creeping into his voice. "*Do you have to go back? I'm really worried about Kaitlin; I need to find her before the battle starts, and it will, probably by first light in the morning. How do we even get back to Elvendon?*"

His words hung in the air, a slight panic rippling through his core. The memory of how Kaitlin had used her magic to bring them to Malgar before, and how now it was the Wizard Marton who had facilitated their journey, only heightened his anxiety. Without either of them, he was left uncertain and apprehensive about how he might return home—and, more importantly, how he could get back to Kaitlin. The gravity of his predicament was unmistakable, underscoring not only the pressing nature of the challenges ahead but also the desperate need for timely help. The path forward was unclear, and the weight of these uncertainties pressed upon him, urging him to find a solution before it was too late.

Kailan gave a warm, amused chuckle, the sound lightening the tension in the air. "*You will take us back, of course,*" he said with confidence, his eyes glinting with a touch of mischief.

Startled, Keltor pressed a hand to his chest, his expression a mixture of disbelief and uncertainty. "*Me?*" he questioned, hardly able to believe that he might possess such an ability.

Kailan simply nodded, his tone both reassuring and matter-of-fact. "*Yes, you're a wizard, are you not?*" he reminded, his statement suggesting a quiet confidence in Keltor's untapped potential.

Keltor hesitated, still grappling with self-doubt and the enormity of the task before him. "*Well, yes, but…*" he began, his voice trailing off as uncertainty clouded his thoughts, leaving the possibility of what he might accomplish hanging in the air.

"*Let me contact my King, and we will work that out later. Like you, dragon lord, I am able to communicate directly with my King through thought alone. It will only take a moment or two. If you'll wait here, I'll reach out to him now,*" he explained, his voice steady with assurance.

Relief and gratitude washed over Keltor at Kailan's words. "*Okay, of course. Thank you, Kailan,*" he replied, his tone hopeful and sincere, trusting that the King would permit Kailan to offer his invaluable support.

Keltor stepped away from Kailan, his mind racing with worry. Thoughts of Kaitlin weighed heavily on him—her safety and the unknown dangers she might face. He could not help but think of his brother and sister, his mother and father, and even baby Logie. The fate of his loved ones was intertwined with the outcome of the looming conflict, and the wellbeing of the whole of Elvendon depended on what would happen next.

He considered the odds they faced. If he could secure the help of a dragon and combine that power with his own magic and Kitcat's, their chances of victory would be much improved. For a moment, hope flickered within him at the thought of such formidable allies standing by his side.

Then, a sudden memory surfaced, drawing his attention downward. He glanced at his chest. "Bloody hell," Keltor muttered under his breath, running his hand over the raised welts marking his chest. The pattern was unmistakable: it matched the shape of the amulet. He inhaled deeply, watching the rise and fall of his chest, uncertain of the significance of this transformation.

Questions surged through his mind. Did these marks mean he could wield the amulet's magic even without physically possessing it? Or was it possible that the amulet itself had become part of him, embedded within his flesh? Would he be able to open a portal back to Elvendon?

As he grappled with these possibilities, Keltor recalled Marton's words: the magic of the amulet was now buried within his soul. The phrase echoed ominously, leaving him to wonder what that truly meant—and how, or even if, he would ever learn to harness its power.

"*Keltor,*" Kailan's voice interrupted his thoughts, drawing him back from his inner turmoil.

"*Yes, Kailan,*" Keltor responded, making his way over to where Kailan stood.

Kailan's expression was reassuring as he delivered his message. *"My King has agreed I may help you, and he has agreed to send one more dragon through the portal to help us."*

Keltor's relief was clear. The idea of having another dragon at their side, in addition to Kailan's assistance, sparked a newfound hope within him. "*Another dragon, thank you Kailan. With two dragons and mine and Kaitlin's magic, I'm sure we can succeed and defeat King Iwein,*" he said, and for the first time in what felt like ages, a genuine grin spread across his face. The odds were shifting, and the path ahead no longer seemed quite so impossible.

Kailan nodded, his voice measured. "*Yes. However, it never pays to be too overconfident.*"

As daylight began to find its way through the shadows, Keltor's impatience grew. "*How long before the other dragon gets here?*" he asked, longing to return to Elvendon.

Kailan, settling down and resting his head on his forearms, answered with gentle practicality. "I would suggest you get some rest," he advised. "It will be a few hours." The words struck Keltor—waiting for hours was not the answer he had hoped for.

Seeking distraction, Keltor questioned, "*How comes you came to me so quickly?*"

Kailan opened his eyes, meeting Keltor's gaze. "You summoned me with your magic and Marton opened the portal right near me. The other dragon would have been on patrol, further out on the other side of our realm," he explained. Keltor frowned, he hadn't realised the words he used to Kailan were magical.

With quiet authority, Kailan offered final encouragement. "Now, get some sleep, dragon lord. You have a big day ahead of you tomorrow."

Chapter Twenty-Six
Belrack

Kaitlin pressed onwards through the forest, a wave of nausea rising as she approached Aranstream castle. Fear gripped her—fear for Keltor's safety and dread of the looming battle she was expected to lead. The weight of responsibility was overwhelming, and she questioned her own readiness. What did she truly know of warfare or the art of command? The uncertainty gnawed at her, threatening to consume her confidence.

Yet, amidst her inner turmoil, a spark of strength flickered within. Ever since she had saved Keltor by harnessing the power of the earth, she felt a newfound resilience. It was as if an unseen force was guiding her, lending her courage and direction when she needed it most.

Stopping for a moment to catch her breath, Kaitlin paused beneath the dense canopy, her chest heaving. She wiped away the last lingering tears from her cheeks, willing herself to push aside the wave of emotion threatening to overwhelm her. Drawing in a deep breath, she steeled herself, determined to find strength—even if she had to pretend. With a frustrated tug, she adjusted the hideous dress she wore, pulling the fabric back over her bust. The garment felt cumbersome and uncomfortable, and she longed for the moment she could finally be rid of it. For now, though, she forced herself to focus, knowing she had to carry on despite her discomfort and fear.

Kaitlin was abruptly startled by the sharp sound of men yelling, their voices echoing through the forest and sending a chill down her spine. She tensed, her senses straining to determine the origin of the commotion. The shouts grew louder, quickly escalating into screams of terror that reverberated ominously through the trees.

"What the hell," she muttered under her breath, feeling her pulse quicken as a surge of adrenaline coursed through her. Instinctively, Kaitlin retreated, lowering herself into the dense undergrowth. She crouched low, hidden by the thick shrubbery, her body motionless and her breath held, determined to remain as inconspicuous as a shadow while she watched and waited for whatever was unfolding nearby.

Four Aranstream soldiers shot out of the trees heading straight towards her direction. From behind them came the sound of men yelling, and right on their heels she saw them. They were like giants, men easily over seven feet tall, some almost eight, all of them wearing grey tunics and trousers, with black cloaks, the hoods of which were pulled up hiding their faces.

Kaitlin's eyes widened in alarm as the Aranstream soldiers, having ceased their frantic flight, abruptly turned to face their pursuers. It was clear that they had resolved to make a stand, choosing to confront their adversaries rather than continue running. With grim determination, the soldiers drew their swords, steel scraping against leather as the blades were pulled from their sheaths. Gripping the hilts tightly, they levelled their weapons, brandishing them menacingly at the approaching giants in a desperate attempt to ward them off.

In stark contrast, the giant men carried no swords. Instead, they wielded long, sturdy sticks, each fitted with a crudely fashioned spike at one end. The improvised weapons, though primitive, looked no less threatening in the hands of men of such imposing stature. As the two groups squared off in the forest clearing, Kaitlin's thoughts raced, her mind whirling as she tried to comprehend the standoff unfolding before her eyes. She remained concealed, compelled to watch as the tension between the opposing forces crackled in the air, unsure of what would happen next.

Without hesitation, the giant men surged forward, launching their attack against the Aranstream soldiers. The forest rang with shouts of fury as the soldiers swung their swords, desperately trying to fend off the spiked sticks wielded by their towering adversaries. The clash was brutal and swift; one soldier fell almost immediately, the sharpened spike driven straight through his heart. The giant who struck him hoisted the lifeless body aloft on the pole, then cast it aside with chilling indifference, marking the deadly strength and resolve of the attackers.

Kaitlin's eyebrow arched with recognition; the tactic used by the 'giant' men struck her as oddly familiar, stirring memories she couldn't quite place. Before she could dwell on this, the confrontation reached its grim conclusion—the remaining three Aranstream soldiers were dispatched with ruthless efficiency by the towering attackers. The clearing fell into an uneasy lull as the victorious 'giants' exchanged words of self-congratulation, seemingly oblivious to further danger.

As the men basked in their triumph, Kaitlin's attention was drawn to movement at the forest's edge. Her eyes narrowed, quickly picking out the shapes of more Aranstream soldiers creeping through the undergrowth. She counted six archers, bows drawn and ready, accompanied by seven more armed with swords. The archers moved into position, silently raising their weapons, while the 'giant' men, engrossed in their conversation, remained blissfully unaware of the imminent threat gathering behind them.

Kaitlin pressed her hands firmly against the rich forest floor, channelling the energy that surged from the earth beneath her fingertips. The recent actions of the 'giant' men—having slain Aranstream soldiers—suggested that they might be allies of Elvendon, though she had no time to dwell on the implications. Her attention was abruptly drawn to the archers, who had already notched their arrows and were preparing to let loose.

Without hesitation, Kaitlin sprang to her feet, abandoning her hiding place in the undergrowth. She thrust her hands towards the approaching threat, her voice ringing out in a desperate warning.

"Get down!" Kaitlin screamed, her command echoing through the clearing as she tried to alert those around her to the imminent danger.

One of the giant men hefted his spiked stick, his arm drawing back as he prepared to hurl it directly at her. In that tense moment, the tallest among the group stepped forward, intercepting the impending attack with a swift, authoritative gesture. The raised weapon was immediately lowered as the tall man's attention fixed on the woman before them—he had recognised her instantly.

Kaitlin did not hesitate. Although her heart hammered furiously within her chest, she transformed her fear into unwavering focus, determined to act amid the confusion around her. With purposeful movement, she thrust her hands forward and shouted, *"Belcara!"* Instantly, a searing sphere of crackling blue-white energy burst from her outstretched hands, accompanied by a deafening hum as it tore through the air towards the line of archers. The sudden explosion of light illuminated the forest in a harsh, strobing glare, throwing jagged shadows across the surrounding trees.

As the energy sphere struck the soldiers, brilliant sparks erupted outward, and the sharp, acrid scent of scorched earth filled the clearing. The archers were hurled backwards by the force of the blast, their bows scattering across the ground as the overwhelming energy dissipated, leaving only a profound silence and a faint, shimmering glow marking its path.

Drawing a steady breath, Kaitlin pressed her palms firmly to the earth, allowing the cool, earthy aroma of the forest to ground her. She sensed the latent energy pulsing just beneath her fingertips—ancient, warm and alive—threading through her veins like liquid fire. Fear and resolve flickered through her thoughts as she became fully aware of the magnitude of her actions, but she steadied herself and released the energy, letting it surge upwards and crackle through her body. The sensation was overpowering, an intoxicating blend of exhilaration and terror that filled her entirely.

Rising to her feet, Kaitlin felt the gathered power coalesce in her hands, which shimmered with an intense light as she raised them high. With a blinding flash, she directed the energy at the remaining soldiers. The raw force erupted from her, striking with unerring accuracy. Each adversary fell instantly, their bodies marked by the devastating scorch of her magic, while the echoes of her spell reverberated through the forest, leaving the air thick with the aftermath of her power.

The largest of the 'giants' turned to face Kaitlin. For a moment, an uncanny silence settled over the clearing as they stared at each other, both seemingly searching for recognition in the other's eyes.

It was the leader who broke the hush, his voice steady but laced with curiosity as he asked, "Keeper of the Star?"

At that instant, Kaitlin understood who stood before her. "Belrack?" she responded, her tone uncertain but hopeful.

Belrack nodded in confirmation, and Kaitlin nearly laughed, overwhelmed with relief at the reunion.

Belrack's command rang out, crisp and unwavering—"Check they are dead." He cast a hard look over his shoulder, the tension etched into his features. His men exchanged brief, silent nods, the weight of the moment evident in their hurried movements as they dashed across the clearing. The air was thick with the lingering scent of scorched earth and the sharp tang of fear; each footfall stirred dust and leaves, echoing the urgency of their task. As they neared the fallen Aranstream soldiers, the grim purpose in their eyes betrayed a flicker of unease, their breaths shallow as they prepared to confirm the aftermath of Kaitlin's powerful magic.

Belrack approached Kaitlin, his movements respectful. He bent down on one knee before her, his cloak falling in elegant folds across his back. With a measured gesture, he pushed back the hood that had shadowed his features and ran a hand through his hair, clearing it from his face as he prepared to address her.

Belrack rose from his kneeling position, his cloak settling back into place as he addressed Kaitlin with reverence. "Thank you, my Queen," he said, his voice carrying both relief and gratitude for the reunion. Straightening, Belrack's expression shifted from gratitude to concern as he asked, "Is Keltor here?" The question lingered in the charged air, reflecting the urgency and uncertainty that still gripped the group in the aftermath of the confrontation.

Kaitlin shook her head; her expression clouded with anguish. "No," she replied softly, the weight of the situation evident in her voice. She hesitated before continuing, her tone heavy with concern. "He's gone after Prince Keion, hoping to stop him from reaching King Iwein."

Gathering herself, Kaitlin explained her current intentions with determination, despite her anxiety. "I'm making my way back to Aranstream castle," she said, outlining her immediate plan. "I need to meet with Commander Talbot and arrange the attack on King Iwein."

Belrack responded with unwavering resolve. "Then, my Queen, we shall take you to him. The castle was almost in our control when we chased after these men. For the same reason as Keltor chases the prince, to stop them getting word to King Iwein for as long as possible."

Kaitlin let out a breath she hadn't realised she was holding, gratitude evident in her voice. "Thank you, Belrack," she said, her relief apparent. She confessed that she had been frightened making her way back through the forest on her own, uncertain of what she would have done if she had encountered more Aranstream soldiers. Yet, after what had just occurred, she realised she was more capable than she had thought.

Belrack's voice rang with authority as he issued his orders. "Men, we're going back to the castle. Two of you scout on ahead, we are escorting the Queen." His command was met with a series of respectful nods from his followers. Without hesitation, two of the men moved forward, slipping silently through the trees to ensure the path ahead was clear. Another pair fell back, keeping a careful watch on the group's rear, alert for any sign of danger that might follow them from the forest.

The remaining members of Belrack's party closed in around Kaitlin, their formation tightening as they prepared to accompany her back to Aranstream castle. Each person aware of the gravity of their mission and the importance of protecting their Queen. As they began their journey, Kaitlin walked at Belrack's side, shielded on all sides by her loyal escort.

As they made their way through the forest towards Aranstream castle, Kaitlin glanced up at Belrack and spoke quietly. "I met your wife, Belrack. Did Keltor tell you?" she asked, her tone gentle and sincere.

Belrack looked down at Kaitlin, his expression solemn, and gave a single nod. "Yes, he did," he replied. He paused for a moment, gathering his thoughts. "And this is why we fight, so we may get home to our families and get you back the throne of Elvendon. Only then can we live in peace, and ensure our children have a better future." His voice carried a quiet determination, his loyalty to both his family and to Kaitlin evident in every word.

He regarded her with gratitude, adding, "Again, you and Keltor have saved us. We owe you so much." Belrack stopped walking, prompting Kaitlin to halt as well and turn to face him, the weight of their shared struggles and hopes lingering in the air between them. As the group paused amidst the quiet of the forest, Kaitlin noticed a sudden flicker of pain cross Belrack's face. Concerned, she asked gently, "Is everything okay?"

Belrack took a moment, then spoke with genuine regret. "I am truly sorry, for what I did to you, and to Keltor when we were trolls."

Kaitlin's reply was warm and reassuring. "Hey, it's okay, you were not yourselves, Keltor and I understand that Belrack."

He nodded in acknowledgement, his remorse still evident. "Even so, we are sorry."

With a comforting gesture, Kaitlin placed her hand on his lower arm. "It's okay," she repeated softly, her words offering forgiveness and understanding.

Belrack's head dipped slightly in gratitude, and, with the moment passed, they continued their way through the woods towards Aranstream castle.

It took about another hour or so before Kaitlin finally saw Aranstream castle come into view. Smoke was billowing from the towers, a sign of the recent conflict or ongoing unrest within its walls. Outside the gates, groups of men could be seen, all dressed in the same grey tunics and trousers that Belrack and his men wore. The uniformity of their attire marked them as allies, signalling that the party was nearing friendly territory as they drew closer to the castle.

As they drew nearer to the castle gates, Kaitlin hesitated for a moment, eyeing the group of men stationed outside. Seeking confirmation, she turned to Belrack. "Are those our men?" she asked quietly, her voice tinged with uncertainty.

Belrack followed her gaze, then nodded in affirmation. "Indeed, those are the garments provided to us upon arrival to the camp. However, ours required custom tailoring due to our size," he explained, a hint of amusement flickering in his eyes as he recalled the memory. Offering her a reassuring smile, he added a touch of levity to the tense moment. Kaitlin, comforted by his response, managed a small smile in return.

Belrack's men maintained their protective circle around Kaitlin as they proceeded towards the imposing entrance of the castle. The scene ahead was grim; her stomach churned at the sight of piles of fallen soldiers lying just beyond the threshold. Nearby, Elvendon men tasked with clearing away the bodies paused in their work. They turned to watch the approaching group, their expressions wary and uncertain. While the soldiers recognised Belrack and his men from earlier battles, they were unfamiliar with the woman being guarded so closely at the centre of the party.

Halting at the gates, Belrack raised his voice so all could hear. "This is your Queen," he declared with authority. "Spread the word, we are taking back Elvendon!" His proclamation echoed across the courtyard, marking the beginning of their reclaiming of the stronghold.

Kaitlin raked trembling fingers through her tangled, sweat-matted hair, wincing as she caught knots and strands caked with dirt. The acrid scent of smoke from the castle mingled with coppery, dried blood—Keltor's blood—staining the tattered remains of her dress. She became acutely aware of the men's eyes on her: their gazes flickered with uncertainty, some filled with pity, others with discomfort, as if they could not quite reconcile the battered figure before them with the Queen Belrack had just introduced. Feeling exposed beneath their scrutiny, Kaitlin hastily tugged the ragged top of her gown higher over her bloodstained chest, trying to reclaim a fragment of dignity amidst the ruin. Her cheeks burned as she met the men's uncertain stares, sensing both their confusion and their reluctance to look away.

Belrack leaned down and spoke softly, his voice filled with both respect and urgency. "My Queen," he whispered, catching Kaitlin's attention. She looked up at him, uncertainty flickering in her eyes. "Show them a little of your magic," Belrack continued, his tone gentle yet firm, "I think they need to learn some manners."

Kaitlin hesitated, momentarily unsure of herself and the situation. She searched Belrack's face for reassurance. With a steady, encouraging nod, he signalled his trust and belief in her abilities.

Drawing a deep breath, Kaitlin lifted her gaze to meet the eyes of the assembled men. The crowd, now much larger, watched her intently. Despite Belrack's declaration of her status, scepticism still lingered in their expressions; the men remained unconvinced that she was truly the Queen, he claimed her to be.

Kaitlin nodded, her voice barely more than a whisper as she murmured, "Okay." Focusing her intent, she quietly uttered the words, *"Etorma, regaranta,"* summoning the ancient magic.

A sharp breath escaped her as, in response to her incantation, sparks of power erupted from the ground and leapt into her hands. The energy gathered there, pulsing vibrant and real, as Kaitlin drew strength from the earth itself, preparing to reveal a glimpse of her abilities to those assembled before her.

Belrack heard the crackle of magical energy next to him and felt a tingling warmth radiate through the air as Kaitlin stepped forward out of his protection. Belrack watched intently as she began to move her hands in slow, deliberate circles, the glowing energy swirling around her fingers. Sparks leapt and danced across her skin, the scent of ozone mingling with the smoky air. The men gazed in awe, some with mouths agape, utterly mesmerised by the luminous display and the subtle hum of power that seemed to vibrate in the very ground beneath their feet.

Kaitlin's eyes darted around the courtyard as she weighed her options, careful not to cause harm to anyone sheltering nearby. She was determined not to bring down a building; in case there were innocents inside. Her gaze finally settled on an empty waggon standing a little distance away.

With quiet determination, she raised her voice and uttered a single word of power, "*Bretora.*" A surge of magic radiated from her, not in a destructive blast, but in a controlled wave. She stretched out her hands, and the heavy waggon began to rise from the ground, lifted effortlessly by her magic. Gasps rippled through the crowd of soldiers and even Belrack himself, all taken aback by the display of her abilities. Kaitlin glanced briefly at Belrack, catching his astonished expression. Then, with a decisive gesture, she flipped the waggon over in midair. It crashed back down to earth with a resounding thud, further emphasising the strength and control she commanded over her power.

Cries of shock rippled through the assembled men as Kaitlin's display of magical prowess settled over the courtyard. She turned to face them, her gaze steady, and in response, a wave of homage swept through the crowd. One by one, the men dropped to their knees, bowing their heads in reverence before her, finally recognising her authority and power.

Belrack's voice thundered above the murmurs of awe, his tone both commanding and approving. "That is better," he boomed, ensuring that the gesture of respect was acknowledged by all present. Turning to Kaitlin, he offered his arm, inviting her to step forward and continue, now fully embraced as their Queen.

Kaitlin held her head high, her recent display of magical power lending her the confidence she had so desperately needed only moments before. Drawing strength from the energy still coursing through her, she looked to Belrack and offered a sincere, "Thank you, Belrack," as she held onto his arm, acknowledging both his unwavering support and the critical role he had played in helping her accept her new identity. With that, their party pressed forward, making their way towards the imposing doors of the castle.

As they walked, Kaitlin paused for a steadying breath, the enormity of her situation finally settling upon her shoulders. She realised, in that instant, that she was no longer the frightened teenager who had once lived in Guildford. Instead, she had become something much greater—a powerful elf witch, and, more importantly, the Queen of the elves.

Determined to embrace her new role, Kaitlin straightened her posture and walked with renewed purpose. As the men around her looked up, she responded with a regal nod, meeting their eyes confidently. Gone were the expressions of fear and uncertainty. In their place, she saw hope—hope for freedom, for the chance to be reunited with their families, and for a better future under her reign.

Kaitlin's entourage guided her steadily through the castle gates. Flanked on either side, Belrack's men advanced with spears poised, ever vigilant for any sign of threat. Yet, rather than opposition, they encountered only the loyal Elvendon men— warriors who had fought valiantly to restore her to the throne. As she passed, these men dropped to one knee, their hands pressed over their hearts in a gesture of unwavering allegiance and respect.

The weight of their loyalty pressed heavily upon Kaitlin. Tears pricked at the corners of her eyes, threatening to fall as she witnessed the depth of faith these men placed in her. She knew that so many depended on her now; she needed to embody strength and fearlessness for their sake. However, without Keltor by her side, she could not help but feel adrift and uncertain. Swallowing her emotions, Kaitlin blinked back her tears, inhaled deeply, and composed herself, determined to stand resolute for those who looked to her for guidance.

"Where are the people of Aranstream?" Kaitlin asked, her voice quiet but steady as she looked up at Belrack for reassurance.

Belrack responded with a measured tone, "Inside their homes. Most of the townsfolk had no desire to engage in a fight with us. In fact, as we advanced, some even cheered us on before retreating behind their doors and locking themselves in." He paused, his face reflecting the weight of what he had witnessed. "The people here have suffered greatly. They were almost as repressed and abused under King Iwein's rule as Elvendons themselves. Living in constant fear, they dared not live freely, always wary of what punishment or cruelty might befall them at the king's whim."

Belrack led Kaitlin into the castle, his presence both protective and commanding. The familiar surroundings sent a shiver down her spine; it was hard to believe that only hours earlier, she had walked these same halls under such different circumstances. Everything was moving at a relentless pace, and Kaitlin knew deep down that this was just the beginning—the challenges ahead would only grow more daunting.

As they progressed further, it became clear that news of her return had travelled swiftly. Each Elvendon man they passed dropped to one knee, placing a hand across his heart in a formal gesture of respect. The murmurs that followed her echoed through the corridors. Kaitlin caught fragments of their whispered conversations and sensed a mixture of scepticism and curiosity—some still doubted her abilities, uncertain if she truly possessed the strength required of a queen. She could not blame them; in the ill-fitting, stained dress she still wore, she hardly looked the part. To them, she must have seemed ordinary and unremarkable, rather than the powerful leader they hoped for.

Chapter Twenty-Seven
Preparing for Battle

As they entered the banqueting chamber, Commander Talbot looked up from the table where he had been meticulously planning their next move. Upon seeing Kaitlin and her entourage, his eyes widened in surprise and recognition. Rising promptly from his seat, he greeted her with a respectful, "Your highness," a genuine smile spreading across his face.

The men gathered around the table followed his lead, standing and then dropping to one knee in a show of deep loyalty and respect. Each man bowed his head, acknowledging Kaitlin's authority and presence as their queen.

Kaitlin steadied herself, gripping the folds of her dress while she drew in a deep breath. Though she did not entirely feel like a queen, she understood the importance of embodying the role for her people. Summoning her composure, she crossed the chamber and addressed the commander directly, her voice clear and steady. "Commander Talbot, it's a relief to see you again," she said, reaffirming both her connection to her allies and her position as their leader.

The men rose respectfully to their feet upon Kaitlin's approach. Commander Talbot's concern was immediately evident as his gaze fell upon the bloodstains covering her dress. "You are unharmed?" he asked, his voice edged with worry.

Kaitlin offered a quick reassurance, nodding. "Yes, thank you. This is not my blood, it's Keltor's," she replied, noticing the commander's face blanch with horror at her words.

Seeing his alarm, Kaitlin hurried to clarify, raising her hand to halt any further concern. "No, he's okay. I was able to heal him."

Commander Talbot, still processing this revelation, looked beyond her and asked, "Where is the king?"

Kaitlin hesitated for a moment. "Oh, he told you?" she asked, referring to Keltor.

Commander Talbot nodded. "Yes, your highness, he told me everything that has happened to you both these past months."

Kaitlin breathed a sigh of relief; grateful she would not have to recount every detail of the recent ordeal. She addressed Commander Talbot, her concern evident. "Keltor went after the prince after he attacked us. He wanted to stop him reaching King Iwein, but I don't know if he made it." Her voice faltered, betraying her worry for Keltor's safety. "He told me to come back to you, and I found Belrack and his men on the way. They escorted me here."

Belrack, unable to contain his admiration, stepped forward and addressed the assembly. "The Queen saved us," he declared, his voice ringing with pride. "We were under attack and believed we had the situation under control, but another group of Aranstream soldiers had been stalking us. Our Queen killed them all—at least thirteen men, by herself." His words carried a sense of awe, as he looked around at the gathered men, eager for them to recognise the true extent of Kaitlin's courage and strength.

The Commander regarded Kaitlin carefully. In his eyes, she still appeared fragile, her slight frame and delicate demeanour at odds with the title she bore. Despite her status as his Queen, he had long harboured doubts about her strength and ability to lead. Even after hearing Keltor's accounts of her bravery, he could not help but see her as more of a figurehead—a symbol of hope for their people, rather than a true sovereign capable of defending her realm. Yet, as he listened to the testimony of Belrack and witnessed the respect she commanded from the men around the table, a realisation began to dawn on him. Perhaps his assumptions had been misplaced. Perhaps, he had underestimated the woman

617

before him, and she was far more than the mere symbol he had believed her to be.

Kaitlin felt a wave of unease as Belrack's words echoed in her mind. She had not truly considered the gravity of her actions until now. The fact that she had killed thirteen men weighed heavily on her conscience. In the heat of the moment, her focus had been solely on survival—her own and that of Belrack and his men. The enemy had left her with no choice; it had been a matter of life or death, with no room for hesitation or regret.

"I am deeply relieved you are safe, your highness. We have been making plans," Commander Talbot informed her, extending his hand towards the table as he encouraged her to join him. His expression conveyed both his concern for her wellbeing and the seriousness of the matters at hand.

Kaitlin could not help but notice the way the Commander had looked at her. His eyes seemed to betray his doubts about her capabilities, suggesting he did not truly believe she was fit for the responsibilities she bore. Glancing down at her attire, Kaitlin realised that, with the state of her dress, she probably appeared more like a common woman than the queen of the Elves. Gathering her composure, she adjusted her dress and followed Commander Talbot to the banqueting table. There, spread out before them, were a collection of maps and various important documents, signalling the gravity of the discussions that awaited her.

The door to the room opened, drawing Kaitlin's gaze. She could not help but hope, in her heart, that it might be Keltor returning. Instead, a woman entered, balancing a tray of refreshments. The tension eased from Kaitlin's expression as she recognised the newcomer.

"Elizabeth!" the woman exclaimed with joyful relief on seeing Kaitlin.

Kaitlin's smile widened at the sight of her. "Maria," she replied warmly, acknowledging the familiar face. Maria set the tray down gently on the banqueting table, then crossed the room swiftly to embrace her.

"You made it; I'm so relieved," Maria said, her voice betraying the worry she had carried. "When the commander and his men arrived and I couldn't find you, I feared the prince had taken you with him." Without hesitation, she wrapped Kaitlin in an impromptu hug, gratitude and relief evident in her gesture.

"Maria," a man's voice called out, firm and authoritative. Maria immediately let go of Kaitlin, offering an apologetic, "Oh, sorry," as she stepped back. Composing herself, Maria turned to Kaitlin with a broad grin and made the introduction, "Elizabeth, this is my husband, Zeb."

Zeb approached from the table, his movements respectful and deliberate. He came to stand before Kaitlin and bowed his head in deference. Maria, observing this unexpected gesture, appeared momentarily puzzled by her husband's formality.

With a gentle smile, Zeb beckoned Maria into his open arms, reassuring her as she moved in for a brief embrace. Holding her close, he explained softly, "This is Kaitlin, the Queen of Elvendon." The significance of his words took a moment to sink in, and Maria's confusion deepened as she glanced between Zeb and Kaitlin. "What?" she stammered, astonishment clear in her expression as she looked at Kaitlin for confirmation.

Kaitlin met Maria's gaze with an apologetic look. "I'm sorry, Maria," Kaitlin said, her tone earnest. "I had to lie so that I wasn't found out. That's why I knew help was coming." Her words clarified the secrecy she had maintained, and the reason behind her earlier actions.

Maria's voice trembled as she recalled, "But you saved me from that old hag." Her words came out in a rush; her gratitude mingled with embarrassment.

Zeb regarded Maria with a raised eyebrow, his curiosity piqued by her sudden outpouring. Maria, recalling the recent events, spoke hesitantly, "The old hag was going to strike me with her stick, but Eliza—her highness," she corrected herself, glancing at Kaitlin with a mixture of awe and embarrassment, "stepped in and took the blow on her arm for me." The memory seemed to overwhelm her, and she turned towards Kaitlin, her voice full of remorse. "Oh my gosh, I am so sorry," Maria pleaded, breaking away from her husband's embrace. Overcome by guilt and respect, she dropped to her knees before Kaitlin. "If I had known who you were, I would never have—" Her words faltered as she struggled to express the depth of her regret.

"Maria, get up, please," Kaitlin gently interrupted, crossing the space between them to offer her hand and help Maria to her feet. Her voice was soft yet firm, conveying both kindness and authority. "It doesn't matter that I'm your queen, I would have done it even if I were not." Kaitlin's words were accompanied by a warm, reassuring smile. Leaning in close, she added in a quiet whisper, "Besides, you've got this little one to think of."

Maria, visibly moved, drew in a steadying breath, her features relaxing into a grateful smile as she looked up at the Queen. "Thank you," she replied sincerely, her relief and appreciation plain in her tone.

"Your highness," the commander addressed Kaitlin respectfully, "may I show you, our plans?" He gestured towards the table, indicating the documents awaiting her attention.

Kaitlin nodded in agreement and started to make her way back to the table. However, Maria, ever attentive had noticed Kaitlin's discomfort, interjected gently, "Commander, do you not think the Queen would like to change first?" Her concern was evident; she had noticed that Kaitlin's dress was torn, stained with blood, and no longer provided the modesty befitting her station, despite Kaitlin's efforts to cover herself with her long hair.

The commander glanced at Kaitlin, realising his oversight. "Oh yes, of course, I'm sorry. I should have asked if you needed to rest," he apologised sincerely, acknowledging the Queen's condition and the need for her comfort before proceeding with official matters.

"Commander, I don't need to rest, we don't have the time, but if you could spare me for half an hour, I would like to change into something more appropriate," Kaitlin replied, offering Maria a grateful look for her consideration.

The commander responded with immediate respect and understanding. "Of course, I will organise everything here, so it is all ready for when you return." As he spoke, he gave a formal bow, pressing his fisted hand to his heart in a gesture of loyalty and respect.

"Thank you," Kaitlin replied warmly. As she turned to leave the room, her presence commanded such respect that everyone present instinctively followed suit, bowing in unison.

"Come with me, your highness," Maria said, and she began to walk towards the door.

As Kaitlin followed Maria down the corridor, Belrack and three of his men accompanied them, their footsteps echoing through the stone passages of the castle. Kaitlin glanced at Belrack, a trace of concern in her expression, and spoke quietly, "Belrack, is this really necessary?"

Belrack responded with unwavering resolve, his deep voice carrying a note of reassurance. "Yes, my Queen, it is. We cannot be certain that everyone within these walls is loyal to you, and with the King absent, the responsibility of your safety falls to me and my men." His words were firm, underscoring both the seriousness of the situation and his dedication to her protection.

Kaitlin looked up at Belrack, the weight of recent events clear in her eyes. She gave him a grateful nod, silently acknowledging both his loyalty and the gravity of their circumstances. The small procession continued along the corridor, the tension in the air a reminder of the uncertain times that lay ahead.

Kaitlin fell silent as they continued down the corridor, her thoughts consumed by worries for her king. Where was Keltor? Prince Keion could not have gained much ground ahead of them, so surely Keltor should have returned by now. Anxious concern surged within her, and she could not help but fear the worst. If he had recklessly put himself in danger and was lost to her, she knew she would never be able to forgive him. Trying to steady her nerves, she ran her hands through her long hair, brushing it back behind her shoulders. She chastised herself for such dark thoughts—of course he was not dead. He had given her his word that he would return, and she clung to that promise, willing herself to believe in his safety.

As Maria approached an arched oak door, she paused as Belrack spoke, her hand hovering uncertainly over the handle.

"Let me check the room first," Belrack insisted, his tone leaving no room for argument. Maria nodded in acknowledgement and stepped aside, pressing herself against the cool stone wall to make way for him.

Belrack, gripping his spear so tightly his knuckles whitened, moved to the door. With careful deliberation, he pushed it open and stepped inside, his senses alert to any potential threat lurking within. Kaitlin, close behind, instinctively began to follow him into the room. However, Belrack swiftly raised his hand, palm outward in a silent command to halt.

"Wait, please, my Queen," he ordered, his voice low but firm. At his words, Kaitlin stopped in her tracks, her body tensing with the urge to press forward but yielding to his command. She stepped aside, allowing another of Belrack's men—also armed and vigilant—to slip past her and enter the chamber alongside their captain.

Suddenly, a piercing scream shattered the tense silence. Instinctively, Kaitlin rushed towards the source of the sound, alarmed and desperate to intervene. "What the hell is that!" she cried out, her anxiety clear as she attempted to enter the room. However, one of Belrack's men quickly intercepted her, blocking her way.

"No, your highness, we wait for Belrack," he insisted firmly, his hand outstretched to prevent her from moving forward. Reluctantly, Kaitlin stepped back, positioning herself beside Maria, who was visibly nervous and unsettled by the unfolding events.

Moments later, the door swung open and Belrack emerged. His imposing figure dominated the doorway, his large hand gripping the arm of a struggling woman. As she was brought into the corridor, Kaitlin recognised her instantly.

"Ava," Kaitlin spat, her voice laced with scorn and accusation.

The suspicion Eva had long harboured was finally confirmed. "You, I knew it, I knew you were up to no good," she hissed, her anger barely contained.

Belrack wasted no time, addressing the captive with authority. "Get on your knees to our Queen," he commanded, pushing Ava down forcefully so she knelt before Kaitlin.

"Your Queen..." Ava stuttered, her voice quivering as Belrack's grip held her in place.

"Yes, Ava," Kaitlin replied, standing tall and resolute over the woman. "I am the Queen of Elvendon, and you will pay for what you did to these poor women." Her gaze shifted to Maria, who remained paralysed with fear, further underscoring the gravity of Ava's actions.

Ava's voice trembled, her eyes darting desperately between Kaitlin and Belrack as she pleaded, "Please, I didn't have a choice. You know what the prince is like—if I'd refused, he would have killed me!" Her whole body shook under the grip of Belrack's hand, fear written plainly on her face.

Kaitlin frowned at Ava, her expression conveying a mixture of disappointment and understanding. She was well aware of the fear Ava harboured towards King Iwein and Prince Keion, yet she could not excuse the cruelty Ava had displayed towards the other women. "Maybe, but you didn't have to be so cruel to those women. Where are the other ladies who work for you?" Kaitlin pressed, seeking answers.

With tears streaming down her face, Ava's voice was thick with emotion as she replied, "They were taken, by the Elvendon soldiers when they attacked. I hid in the wardrobe," she sobbed, her guilt and fear evident in every word.

Kaitlin glanced up to Belrack. "Where are they?" she asked.

"The women are all being held in the tower rooms," Belrack replied, "they are unharmed my lady," he added.

Kaitlin's resolve was unwavering as she made her decision. "Good, I will deal with them all once we have taken back Elvendon. Belrack, please can one of your men take her up there?" she requested, her tone stern and decisive.

"Rictar," Belrack said, turning to one of his men. "Take her to the tower and put her with the other women." He handed her over to him. Rictar bowed his head respectfully to both Kaitlin and Belrack before stepping forward to fulfil his orders. Without hesitation, he grasped Ava firmly by the arm and began to lead her away down the corridor, guiding her towards the tower where the other women were being held.

Ava's heart pounded in her chest, and the cold grip on her arm sent a wave of panic through her body I'm sorry! Please! I didn't want to..." Ava cried repeatedly as she disappeared around the corner.

"Now, you may go inside," Belrack said, pushing the door back open for her and dipping his head in respect.

"Thank you, Belrack," Kaitlin replied. She and Maria entered the room together, both casting quick glances around at their surroundings. The room was softly lit by the pale evening light filtering through the tall windows, casting a gentle glow across the polished floorboards.

Kaitlin strode directly over to a large wardrobe—one of two standing against the wall—intent on finding something suitable to wear. Maria moved to the other wardrobe and, after a moment of searching, pulled out a blue dress.

"What about this one, my lady?" Maria asked, holding up the dress for Kaitlin to see.

Kaitlin glanced at it and shook her head, clearly uninterested in wearing a dress. She began sorting through the contents of the wardrobe herself, passing over one grey gown after another, followed by pink, blue, and red dresses, none of which appealed to her.

Then, at the very back of the wardrobe, something caught her eye. She reached in and pulled out a pair of brown leather trousers, holding them up against herself to judge the fit—they appeared just right. She continued searching and soon found a blue smock dress, noticeably shorter than the other dresses.

"These might do," Kaitlin said, gathering the trousers and smock dress and placing them over the back of a nearby chair, satisfied with her selections.

Maria eyed the trousers in Kaitlin's hands with clear disapproval. "My lady, those are trousers," she remarked, her tone betraying her unease at the unconventional choice.

Kaitlin met Maria's gaze, her expression defiant. "Yes, I know that, Maria," Kaitlin replied calmly, unwilling to be swayed by tradition. Maria looked at Kaitlin with concern, voicing her disapproval. "Trousers are for men," she added.

Kaitlin stood her ground; her voice tinged with annoyance. "No, Maria, they are not. Where I grew up women wore trousers all the time. In fact, they wore what the hell they wanted." She began to untie the pink dress, slipping it off with a sense of relief at finally being rid of the ghastly dress she had been forced to wear.

"Can I help you?" Maria asked, her tone gentle but edged with concern.

"No, thanks, I can dress myself," Kaitlin replied.

Maria dipped her head and stepped back from her.

Kaitlin pulled on the trousers, the supple brown leather feeling cool and smooth against her legs. The waistband, finished with a braided tie, allowed her to cinch it snugly around her waist, the pressure oddly comforting. Next, she lifted the blue smock dress, the coarse linen brushing her fingertips as she slipped it over her head. The fabric settled softly against her skin, a gentle contrast to the stifling, scratchy pink dress she had just shed. She carefully fastened the ties at the front of the dress, making sure it was snugly secured across her bust. The fabric's loose folds draped over her body, successfully concealing her shape and granting her a sense of security she realised she had been lacking. She paused for a brief moment, allowing herself to absorb the reassuring sensation—any lingering embarrassment from earlier quickly melted away, replaced by a soothing wave of relief. The dress's modest cut and subdued blue hue made her feel less visible and exposed. Gradually, the awkwardness she had felt gave way, and she was left with a quiet gratitude for the simple comfort and protection the smock provided.

As Kaitlin considered her appearance, she realised one thing was missing. "I need some boots," she muttered, turning back to the wardrobe and searching through the remaining items. Her hands moved quickly, pushing aside old shoes and slippers, until Maria appeared at her side, holding out a pair of knee-high leather boots.

"My Lady, what about these?" Maria offered quietly, presenting the boots with both hands.

Kaitlin's eyes widened in disbelief as she recognised them. "I don't believe it, those are mine!" she exclaimed, a surge of delight in her voice. "Ava must have kept them for herself. Thank you, Maria."

She wasted no time in pulling on the boots, relishing the familiar, comfortable fit. As she tugged them up over her calves, she let out a contented sigh. Finding them again brought a sense of comfort and reassurance that she sorely needed.

Maria approached quietly, holding out a blue cloak. "My Lady," she said, her voice soft.

"Perfect, thank you," Kaitlin replied, accepting the cloak from Maria and slipping it over her shoulders. The thick blue fabric draped around her, settling comfortably and providing a final layer of reassurance to her chosen ensemble.

Kaitlin picked up a hairbrush from the dressing table and began to carefully work through the tangles in her hair. She kept her gaze fixed on her reflection in the mirror, watching each stroke as she smoothed her locks. As she turned her head to one side, she leaned in, noticing a streak of blood on her skin—Keltor's blood. The sight gave her pause, a visible reminder of recent events. Maria, observing from nearby and noticing the blood as well, spoke up with gentle concern. "My Lady, do you want me to fill the wash bowl for you?" she offered softly, ready to assist if needed.

Kaitlin thought for a moment, her hand lifting and touching the blood on the side of her face. It was part of Keltor. She would wear it like a warrior would paint their face before a battle.

"No, thank you," Kaitlin replied, her tone gentle yet firm as she declined Maria's offer. Without further explanation, she turned her attention to her hair, deftly gathering the strands and weaving them into a single, long braid that fell over one shoulder. Each movement was deliberate, her fingers working with practised precision as she styled her hair into a neat sideways plait.

Once finished, Kaitlin straightened, a new sense of resolve in her posture. "Right, let's go," she declared, turning decisively towards the door and setting off with purposeful steps.

Belrack and his men stood patiently outside the chamber, awaiting Kaitlin's arrival. With renewed confidence, Kaitlin strode towards them, her steps firm and resolute. "Let's go, Belrack," she announced, her voice clear and authoritative. Without hesitation, she began making her way down the corridor, her head held high.

As she walked, Kaitlin was acutely aware of the transformation in herself. No longer burdened by the impractical, uncomfortable pink dress, she now felt every inch the Queen her people needed. The boots, cloak, and her carefully braided hair gave her a sense of purpose and assurance, allowing her to embody the leader she was determined to become.

As Belrack strode alongside her, he cast a sideways glance and remarked, "That is an interesting outfit, my Queen."

Kaitlin met his gaze, her voice steady. "Yes, I know it's not what is expected of me, but I cannot go into a battle wearing a long dress, it's not practical."

Belrack raised an eyebrow, a faint note of surprise in his tone. "Into battle, my Queen? I don't think the commander intends to let you join in the battle."

Kaitlin stopped abruptly, prompting Belrack to halt as well. She turned to face him, her expression questioning. "Let me?" she repeated, her eyes narrowing slightly as she held his gaze.

He hesitated, his eyebrow remaining arched. Belrack had seen the battle plans and knew there was no role assigned for her on the field—her purpose was to serve as the symbol for which the men would fight.

Kaitlin's lips pressed into a determined line. "Really, well, we'll see about that," she muttered, then continued down the corridor, her resolve undiminished.

As Kaitlin entered the banqueting room, the men gathered around the table immediately stood and bowed in her presence. She was acutely aware of their eyes following her, silently questioning her choice of attire as she approached the table with measured confidence.

The commander greeted her respectfully, dipping his head. His gaze lingered over her, but Kaitlin chose to ignore it, focusing instead on the matter at hand.

"Right, show me what your plan is," she demanded, resting her hands firmly on the table as she scrutinised the maps laid before her.

"Okay," the commander replied, shifting his attention from Kaitlin to the plans on the table, ready to explain the strategy.

The commander cleared his throat, preparing to explain the strategy in more detail. "In simple terms," he began, his tone measured and direct. Kaitlin shot him a frown at the use of the word 'simple', though he appeared not to notice and pressed on.

He leaned over the map spread across the table, indicating key positions with the tip of his finger. "We will split our forces," he explained. "The main army will march from this point"—he gestured decisively—"while a second force will approach from the rear, here." Again, he jabbed at another location on the map, outlining the intended manoeuvres.

Kaitlin listened intently, then interrupted with a pointed question. "And where will I be?" she asked, her voice carrying a note of challenge.

Without hesitating, the commander responded, pressing his finger on the map well away from the front lines. "Here," he said, "far back from the battlefield, with the other women. We shall establish a camp there, ready to tend to those who are injured."

Kaitlin was openly taken aback by the commander's words, her surprise evident as she fixed him with an intense glare. "No," she declared, her tone resolute and unwavering.

The commander paused in his explanation, meeting her gaze as she continued. "I want to be here," Kaitlin insisted, tapping the map firmly to indicate the front lines. "And I also require some of your men to head immediately to the woodman's cottage to collect my aunt and Keltor's family. The cottage belongs to Ben—Keltor said you would know its location."

The commander nodded stiffly. "Yes, I do, but my Queen, the battlefield is no place for a woman," he replied, his irritation clear as he dismissed her request with a careless wave of his hand.

Kaitlin's patience snapped. "Excuse me," she retorted sharply, turning on him. "If I were a King, would I not be here?" she challenged, jabbing once more at the map's front line.

The commander responded, "Well, yes. If Keltor were here, he would take up the front-line position."

"Commander, I am the Queen of Elvendon. These are my people and my lands, and I will take up the front-line position," Kaitlin declared, her voice unwavering and full of conviction.

The commander hesitated, bowing his head respectfully before replying, "Your highness, with all due respect, you're not experienced in the art of war—especially an elven war. We need you to be safe." He pointed again to the rear of the battlefield on the map, emphasising the location where he believed she should remain for her security.

Kaitlin met his gaze, her tone low and firm. "Commander, I know I did not grow up here in Elvendon, although I did spend a lot of my childhood here, with Keltor in secret." Her words carried the weight of personal experience and an unspoken understanding of both worlds.

The commander frowned deeply at Kaitlin, clearly unsettled by her determination. She met his gaze unflinchingly and began to speak, her voice steady and resolute. "I first came through a portal to Elvendon when I was only five years old," she revealed. "No one knew who I was then—not even Keltor. But that is not the crux of my point." She paused for emphasis, her expression unwavering. "I grew up in a world where women are treated as equals to men, and you should know, Commander, once I have reclaimed Elvendon, that will become the way of the elves as well."

As she finished speaking, a surge of anger coursed through her, manifesting visibly—her eyes glowed an intense, startling white as she fixed her gaze upon the commander. "I will not place the lives of these men above my own," she declared, her tone fierce and unyielding.

The commander, momentarily taken aback by her display of power, attempted to reason with her. "But my Queen, without you, we will have no Elvendon. Your survival is essential to us all." Despite his words, he instinctively took a cautious step away from her, clearly aware of the force of her resolve.

Kaitlin slammed her hands down onto the table, a surge of magic pulsing through the wood and causing it to rise and tremble beneath her touch. Her eyes flashed a fierce white, the physical manifestation of her anger radiating through the room.

"Listen to me!" she demanded, her voice carrying authority that commanded the attention of everyone present. The room fell silent; all eyes fixed on her. "I am your Queen."

She paused, her expression hardening as she continued. "My father made the greatest mistake of his life. He did not believe that a woman could rule Elvendon. He thought that by forcing me to bond with Prince Aragon, without my consent, he would unite Elvendon and Aranstream, creating one Elven Kingdom." Kaitlin let out a cold laugh, shaking her head at the memory. "He was a fool."

Her gaze grew even more intense. "Yes, I rejected Aragon, and yes, Keltor and I killed him, because he attacked us both. Aragon wanted a submissive woman, someone to parade on his arm like a trophy. Let me assure you, I am not that woman."

Her voice carried both sorrow and conviction. "Yet, the truth is that King Iwein never intended to bring peace to the elven realm. His aim was always for Aranstream to conquer and destroy Elvendon, and to subjugate our people—regardless of whether I accepted his son."

Her eyes swept the room, making certain that her message was understood. "Even when King Iwein believed I was dead and that Elvendon had no heir, he continued his assault. He persisted in killing our people and razing our home. The cruelty of his campaign is evident—he brutally murders our kin or enslaves them, and he will not stop until we are either destroyed or completely subjugated by Aranstream. I'm sorry I will not stand back and let that happen," Kaitlin said, shaking her head. "This evil man is even killing our children! I have lost my mother, father and my sister to Aranstream and if you think I am going to stand back in a safe place you are clearly mistaken.

If you thought you could defeat King Iwein on your own you would have done it by now, but you didn't. Yes, I understand Keltor is my King, and you want a man upfront leading your army. Keltor is the most amazing, brave and powerful man who I love deeply, but he is not here, and I don't know where he is or if he will even get to us in time before the battle commences. I am your Queen, albeit young and inexperienced in war, and I will be standing here, on the front line commanding my army. Magic is our first line of defence, and King Iwein will not be expecting it."

The room fell silent, every eye fixed on Kaitlin as the commander considered her words. The atmosphere was charged, the palpable energy she exuded making her resolve impossible to ignore. Her unwavering determination had left a clear impression on all present, and even the commander could not deny the authority radiating from her presence.

After a tense pause, the commander finally spoke. "Okay, it's against my better judgement, but you are our Queen, and if this is where you want to be, then let it be so." His words were measured, a reluctant but respectful acknowledgement of her decision and their bond of loyalty.

Kaitlin responded with calm gratitude. "Thank you, commander," she said, her tone steady. She then turned her attention to the matter at hand, signalling a shift from confrontation to collaboration. "Now, shall we sit, and go over these plans?"

The commander nodded in agreement, but before they could proceed, he added, "Yes, my Queen, but first let me make the arrangements to collect Keltor's family, and your aunt." His response demonstrated both strategic foresight and care for her loved ones, ensuring that those dearest to her would be protected as they prepared for the challenges ahead.

"Thank you," she replied gratefully, her tone gentle yet resolute. She watched as the commander turned away, moving purposefully towards one of the other men in the room. His actions spoke of the responsibility he felt, and the care he was taking to ensure the arrangements for Keltor's family, and her aunt would be carried out swiftly and with due consideration. Kaitlin remained where she stood, quietly observing, her mind already shifting towards the next steps in their preparations. The atmosphere in the room was tense yet hopeful, underscored by her determination and the commander's loyalty. With this small but significant exchange, the transition from confrontation to collaboration was made, and the weight of leadership settled more firmly upon her shoulders as the planning continued.

As the evening wore on and the final plans were drawn, Commander Talbot remained vigilant, his gaze never far from the Queen. The weight of responsibility pressed upon him, and the shift in leadership was clear; Kaitlin's resolve had surprised him, challenging his previous doubts about her capabilities. When the council ended, Commander Talbot found himself reflecting on the transformation he'd witnessed. Her unwavering determination in the face of adversity, coupled with her unexpected mastery of magic, had earned his respect. Although he still harboured concerns about her safety at the front lines, he could not help but acknowledge the authority she brought to the role. The transition from guarded scepticism to genuine loyalty had taken root, and as preparations continued, Commander Talbot was determined to honour the trust she had placed in him, ensuring every measure was taken to protect her and those dearest to her, even as the dawn of battle approached.

Chapter Twenty-Eight
Forester's Cottage

As the door burst open, Ben, the Forester, instinctively reached for his sword, prepared for anything. However, the tension eased slightly when he recognised the two scouts accompanying the newcomer—John and Carl, both trusted men from his own ranks.

John, visibly exhilarated, wasted no time sharing the news. "Ben, he said Commander Talbot sent him. They've escaped the encampment and have taken Aranstream castle," John announced, his eyes wide with excitement, struggling to contain his disbelief at the turn of events.

Ben, taken aback by the announcement, stepped forward in disbelief. "What?" he exclaimed, unable to process the gravity of the situation straight away.

The stranger, sensing the urgency and confusion, stepped forward and introduced himself. "It's true," he confirmed, "My name is Michael." His voice carried both relief and pride as he continued, "We've taken control of Aranstream. And...," he added with a broad grin, "our Queen, Kaitlin, is still alive and she is at the castle."

Esimae abruptly stood, her hands pressing firmly onto the oak table. "Kaitlin is safe?" she demanded, her voice tight with urgency. Michael turned to face her and gave a reassuring nod. "Yes, ma'am, she arrived a few hours ago."

Sharelle, equally concerned, also rose to her feet. Her attention fixed on Michael, she asked, "And my son, Keltor?" Forde made to stand as well, but Sharelle placed a gentle hand on his shoulder, indicating for him to remain seated as she awaited Michael's response.

"No, ma'am," Michael said, "the King wasn't with her. He went after Prince Iwein, from what I've been told."

"Hell," Forde muttered, shaking his head. The weight of his worries was plain for all to see; he remembered only too well that Keltor had confided in him about the prince possessing his amulet. The unease on Forde's face deepened, unable to mask the apprehension that gnawed at him.

Breaking the silence, Michael stepped forward, his expression earnest. "I've come to ask you to come back to Aranstream Castle, by request of the Queen and Commander Talbot. We are going to attack King Iwein at first light." His words hung in the air, the gravity of the situation settling over the group.

Ben wasted no time, his mind already turning over preparations. "Okay," he replied with a firm nod. He immediately began organising the next steps, knowing every moment was precious. "Carl, get the word out to the men that we're leaving for Aranstream Castle."

"Yes, Ben," Carl responded without hesitation, giving a sharp nod before slipping quietly out through the cottage door to relay the urgent message.

Ben took charge of the preparations, his tone both practical and encouraging. "Ladies, I suggest you get yourselves ready—we have a long walk ahead of us," he announced, addressing the group as everyone began to gather their belongings. Without missing a beat, Ben turned his attention back to Michael, noting the man's weary state and the unmistakable scent of horse that clung to him—a clear sign of his urgent journey. Sensing Michael's exhaustion, Ben offered a gesture of hospitality. "Do you want a coffee?" he asked, his voice warm and genuine.

Michael responded with visible relief, his gratitude evident. "That would be great," he replied, nodding appreciatively as he followed Ben over to the coffee pot, eager for a moment of rest before the journey continued.

Sharelle turned towards Forde, her gaze lingering as she took in his appearance. Now freshly shaven, having showered and changed into clean clothes provided by Ben, Forde bore a striking resemblance to the man he once was. Despite the noticeable loss of weight that marked his figure, the familiar features of his old self had returned, bringing a sense of comfort to those around him. Sharelle eased herself back into her seat beside Forde, her worry evident. Turning to him, she spoke quietly, "Forde, I'm worried about Keltor," her concern clear in her voice.

Forde reached over, taking her hand in his, an expression of shared anxiety etched across his face. "I know, my love. I'm worried too," he replied softly. He glanced away, his thoughts clearly weighed down. "Prince Keion has my amulet, and if he knows how to use it, Keltor could be in serious danger." Forde's voice faltered as he tried to steady his nerves. "I know Keltor insists he's a wizard, but in the wrong hands, that amulet…" He let the sentence hang unfinished, shaking his head, the gravity of the situation settling between them.

As the preparations for departure continued, Esimae busied herself with Magic's basket, ensuring everything was in order. Mick, noticing her preoccupation, offered a helping hand. "Do you want me to carry the cat?" he asked, cutting through Esimae's thoughts. She looked up at him, her heart pounding as she met the depth of his gaze. There was something undeniably gentle about Mick that made her feel at ease, yet at the same time, she was troubled by a sense of guilt—Jaike had only been gone a few months, and the idea of feeling anything for someone else unsettled her.

Shaking off the feeling, Esimae replied, "No, thank you, I can manage," as she opened the lid of the basket. Turning her attention to her pet, she called out, "Magic, we're leaving." The cat, lounging lazily by the fire, stood and stretched, taking his time as he flexed his claws with no sense of urgency. Growing impatient as she saw the others slipping on their jackets and cloaks in readiness to leave, Esimae urged, "Magic, now!"

Mick let out a laugh. "He is a character," he remarked, watching the cat's leisurely pace. Esimae managed a small smile in return, nodding in agreement. "Yes, he is a pain in the neck sometimes," she admitted. Magic, clearly unimpressed by this comment, meowed his protest in response.

"Oh, be quiet and get in the basket," Esimae muttered, her tone both fond and exasperated as she coaxed Magic to comply.

Sharelle cast a worried glance at Forde as he rose to his feet, concern evident in her voice. "Forde, are you strong enough for this walk? I can see if I can get a horse for you," she offered, clearly anxious about his wellbeing.

Forde gave a reassuring smile, lifting her hand to his lips in a tender gesture. "No, I'm fine," he replied warmly. "Honestly, I have a full belly of food and coffee to keep me going." His confidence was apparent as he turned to Esendil, his son, seeking further support. "And Ese can give me a hand if I need it."

Esendil stepped forward without hesitation, patting his father's arm in solidarity. "Of course, dad," he said, ready to help in any way needed.

Accepting Forde's decision, Sharelle nodded and wrapped her cloak tightly around her shoulders. She made a final check of the sword hanging at her hip, ensuring she was prepared for whatever lay ahead.

"Right, let's move out," Ben instructed, positioning himself near the front door. Equipped with a sword and a bow and arrow, he pulled the hood of his black cloak over his head before stepping outside, leading the way.

The rest of the group followed in his footsteps. Upon exiting, Sharelle paused, her gaze sweeping over the growing numbers of men who seemed to be appearing from every direction. The crowd quickly swelled, and she estimated there were at least a hundred gathered.

Curious and somewhat unsettled, Sharelle turned to Ben as they walked. "Where have they all been hiding?" she asked.

Ben responded with a dismissive shrug. "Oh, here and there. There will probably be a few hundred more once the word gets out."

An urgent cry of "Aranstream!" rang out from the front, sending a ripple of panic through the assembled line. Ben reacted instantly, his voice sharp with authority. "Shit," he exclaimed, turning to the group. "Separate, into the trees – soldiers!"

Panic surged through the men as they began to scatter. The sudden cry had sent shockwaves of fear through the gathered crowd, and many immediately broke formation. Some dashed for the shelter of the surrounding trees, while others hesitated, looking around in confusion for direction. Shouts and hurried movements echoed through the air as the urgency of the situation became overwhelmingly clear. The orderly line dissolved into chaos, with men pushing and weaving past one another in their desperation to find cover and avoid the oncoming threat.

Her voice urgent and edged with anxiety, Sharelle's eyes flickered to Forde. "Ese, quickly—get your dad into the trees," she commanded, her grip tightening on her sword as protectiveness surged through her.

"Mum, no!" Esendil said in a panic as he saw his mother with her sword.

Sharelle reached out to reassure her son, placing her hand gently on his cheek, her tone steady and sincere. "I will be fine. I know you don't know this side of me and I'm just your mum, but trust me, I will be okay," she assured, trying to ease Esendil's fears. Despite the urgency of the moment and the chaos erupting around them, Sharelle's words conveyed a sense of confidence and calm.

"Son, listen to her, she can kick arse, your mum," Forde said, his voice tinged with both pride and regret. He gazed at Sharelle; his expression filled with love and a sense of guilt for being unable to stand and fight at her side. Sharelle returned the gesture, squeezing Forde's hand firmly before leaning in to plant a quick, meaningful kiss. Determination blazed in her eyes as she pulled back, locking her gaze with his.

"I love you," she said softly. Forde lifted his hand to her face, the touch gentle yet urgent. "And I you," he replied. His voice faltered slightly, weighed down by concern. "Please, be careful," he implored, his words hanging in the air as both braced themselves for the uncertainty ahead. Forde's voice trembled with emotion as he leaned closer to Sharelle, his words barely audible amid the chaos. "I don't want to lose you now, not when I've only just got you back," he whispered, the fear evident in his tone. Sharelle caught his gaze, offering him a reassuring smile and a gentle nod, silently conveying her understanding and determination to return safely.

Esimae shifted Magic's basket onto her back, freeing her hands in anticipation of what was about to unfold. The urgency in her voice was unmistakable as she called out, "How many!" Moving quickly to stand beside Sharelle, both women positioned themselves behind a large oak, using its broad trunk as cover while they waited for any sign of the enemy.

Sharelle, her eyes narrowed with concentration, responded, "I don't know, I can't even see them?" Anxiety and uncertainty flickered across her face as she scanned the area, searching for any indication of how many adversaries might be approaching. Looking to the far side of the trail, she spotted Ben flanked by half a dozen men, all with weapons drawn and ready for action. Their tense postures spoke of readiness and resolve.

Her gaze then travelled upwards to the thick canopy of the oak trees above, where more of Ben's men had climbed and now lay in wait. Concealed among the branches, they watched silently, poised to strike at the crucial moment. The scene was tense, with every ally prepared and alert, bracing themselves for the incoming threat.

"There," Esimae whispered, her voice barely audible above the rustling leaves, as a group of Aranstream soldiers came into view along the winding trail. They rode on horseback, their formation tight and disciplined, and were accompanied by half a dozen or so waggons trundling steadily behind them.

Watching the procession draw closer, Sharelle leaned in, her own voice hushed with tension. "Why would they be heading back to Aranstream?" she wondered aloud, the question laden with suspicion and uncertainty.

Esimae considered the situation for a moment, then offered a possible explanation. "Maybe they don't know what's happened? If they are coming back from a scouting mission, they may not know," she suggested, her eyes fixed on the approaching soldiers as she tried to make sense of their movements.

Sharelle nodded in agreement, accepting Esimae's reasoning. It was a plausible explanation—if these soldiers had been out on reconnaissance, they could be completely unaware of the recent events that had unfolded in their absence.

Casting a quick glance across to Ben, Sharelle caught his eye. Their gaze met, a silent understanding passing between them as they prepared for what was to come. Ben lifted his hand, signalling for her to wait. Sharelle gave a subtle nod in response, acknowledging the command and steadying herself behind the cover of the oak tree.

The procession of Aranstream soldiers and waggons continued its approach, drawing ever closer to their concealed positions. The air was thick with anticipation as the enemy neared, the tension fierce amongst the hidden group.

When the soldiers and waggons were finally within striking distance, Ben lifted his sword high and shouted, "Attack!" His battle cry echoed through the trees, a clear signal to his waiting men. In an instant, Ben's men sprang into action, launching themselves from their hiding places within the trees. Some dropped directly onto the waggons from above, while others leapt down to tackle the Aranstream soldiers, toppling them from their horses and driving them forcefully to the ground.

With the battle erupting around her, Esimae unleashed bursts of magical energy, directing each bolt at the Aranstream soldiers. Her attacks struck with precision, felling the enemy one after another. Some were killed outright by her spells, while others were left unconscious, making them easy targets for Ben's men, who swiftly finished them off with their swords.

Amidst the chaos, Esimae kept a watchful eye on Mick. When she noticed an Aranstream soldier moving in to attack him from behind, she reacted instantly, sending out a powerful blast of magic. The force of her spell knocked the soldier to the ground, killing him instantly and allowing Mick to continue fighting unharmed.

The atmosphere was charged with the lingering power of Esimae's spells, the very air seeming to hum in the aftermath of her magical assault. Mick, instantly understanding what had happened, turned sharply and caught Esimae's eye. Gratitude shone in his smile before he quickly returned to the thick of the fighting. Esimae managed a brief smile in return, a fleeting but reassuring moment between the chaos that surrounded them.

Amidst the turmoil, Esimae muttered under her breath, "Oh shush, Magic," addressing the familiar complaint emanating from the basket secured to her back. Magic, unsettled by the jostling, offered a soft protest. Suddenly, Esimae was struck down, completely blindsided by an Aranstream soldier wielding a hefty branch. The blow rendered her unconscious before she even had a chance to react.

As she collapsed, Magic's basket was thrown to the ground and sprung open from the impact. With a furious hiss, Magic leapt out, baring his teeth at the attacking soldier before darting swiftly into the safety of the trees.

The Aranstream soldier who had taken Esimae by surprise crouched beside her limp body, sweat beading on his brow. With trembling hands, he grasped her wrists and dragged her through the tangle of damp undergrowth, every muscle straining as he glanced anxiously over his shoulder at the brutal melee raging behind him.

"It's the witch," the man muttered to two other soldiers waiting anxiously beside the waggon, his voice tinged with both triumph and unease as he eyed Esimae's unmoving, bloodied form. "Get her in quick, we need to get out of here," one urged, his words urgent and breathless, betraying the fear that crackled in the air around them as the sounds of battle grew louder.

The first soldier exchanged a tense glance with his companion, then together they carefully lifted Esimae's limp, unconscious form into the waggon. The cold bite of iron cuffs soon followed, snapping tightly around her wrists and ankles—a harsh reminder of her sudden captivity, and an ominous chill settled over the scene as her fate hung in the balance.

As the waggon lurched forward, bumping over the tangled roots and uneven ground, Magic—hissing with determination—slipped through the undergrowth, tracking the movement of the captors. The little creature darted silently alongside the waggon; his eyes fixed on the narrow gap beneath the canvas. When the two guards, distracted by the commotion outside, turned their backs for a moment, Magic seized his chance: with a nimble leap, he slipped through the opening and landed lightly beside Esimae's still form. He pressed his small body close to hers, purring insistently and pawing at her face as if urging her to wake. Though Esimae remained unconscious, Magic's presence offered a fragile thread of hope—one that might yet grow stronger as the chaos of battle raged on around them.

Mick witnessed the moment Esimae was taken, his heart pounding as he watched the Aranstream soldiers dragging her away. Determined to reach her, he fought his way through the press of enemy soldiers, dodging swinging weapons and pushing aside anyone who tried to block his path. As the waggon carrying Esimae began to move, Mick seized his chance: he sprinted forward and, with a burst of desperate energy, leapt onto the back of the waggon. He slipped beneath the canvas cover, careful not to draw the guards' attention.

As soon as Mick slipped beneath the canvas cover of the waggon, he found himself face to face with Magic. The small cat hissed defensively, positioning himself protectively over Esimae's unconscious body. Mick crouched low beside Esimae, his concern deepening at the sight of the blood streaking her face.

641

"Hey, little guy," Mick said softly, keeping his voice calm and gentle so as not to startle Magic. "It's okay, it's me, Mick. Your mistress, she likes me, remember?" Carefully, he brushed a strand of hair from Esimae's forehead and tenderly stroked her cheek. His voice dropped to a whisper as he called her name, "Esimae." Worry was etched across his features as he tried to wake her, hoping for any sign that she might regain consciousness.

Suddenly, before Mick could do anything more, a sharp blow landed on the back of his head. As darkness overtook him and he slumped beside Esimae, Magic's ears flattened at the sudden threat. In a flash of instinctive agility, Magic darted past the soldier who had struck Mick, squeezing through the nearest gap in the canvas and disappearing outside the flap of the waggon.

Around half an hour later, Mick regained consciousness with a low groan, a sharp ache pulsing at the back of his head. Instinctively, he tried to lift a hand to check the source of the pain, only to discover that his wrists were tightly bound in cold, unyielding shackles. The waggon lurched and jolted beneath him, its wheels rattling harshly over the uneven, rugged ground.

Steeling himself, Mick managed to pull his body upright, shifting onto his knees despite the restraints. His first concern was for Esimae, who lay motionless nearby. Panic edged his voice as he leaned closer to her, whispering her name with urgency. "Esimae," he called, his words trembling with worry. With shackled hands, he gently pushed her shoulder, desperate to rouse her from her unconscious state. "Esimae, wake up," he urged again, his eyes darting anxiously between the back of the waggon and her still form, searching for any sign of response.

Esimae stirred slightly, a soft moan escaping her lips. Relief washed over Mick, and he quietly urged her to wake, gently stroking her face in the hope she might regain consciousness. Suddenly, movement caught his attention on his left. Glancing over, Mick saw Magic, the black cat, poking his head through the back of the canvas. Magic's vivid green eyes surveyed Mick, then shifted to his mistress, Esimae, before he let out a plaintive meow.

Mick whispered the cat's name, surprised and grateful that Magic had managed to stay close. With a determined squeeze, Magic slipped completely through the gap in the canvas flap. Mick's eyes widened as he noticed a bunch of keys clutched in the cat's mouth. The sight filled him with hope and disbelief, prompting him to ask, "Magic, what the hell have you got there, are those the keys to these shackles?"

Magic approached Mick with an unmistakable air of grace, his movements purposeful and composed. With a delicate drop, he released the set of keys directly onto Mick's lap before letting out a soft, insistent meow. Mick, momentarily stunned, could not help but laugh quietly in disbelief, marvelling at the fact that Esimae's clever cat had somehow managed to retrieve the keys from the soldiers seated up front, driving the horses.

"You are an amazing cat, Magic," Mick murmured with heartfelt gratitude, reaching for the keys. He methodically worked through the collection, his hands trembling slightly with urgency, until he located the correct one. With careful precision, he slipped the key into the lock, freeing both his hands and feet from the cold, restrictive shackles.

Esimae let out a groan as her eyelids fluttered, the world slowly coming back into focus. Her gaze landed on Mick, who was hurriedly working the keys into the locks on his shackles, determination etched across his face. Esimae managed to murmur his name, "Mick, is that you?" Her voice was weak but carried a note of relief. Mick's eyes widened in surprise and hope as he looked over at her, his concern for her wellbeing clear in his expression.

"Esimae," Mick said, his voice filled with relief as he let his shackles fall to the floor of the waggon and moved closer to her. The anxiety that had weighed on him was obvious in his gentle tone, his emotions laid bare by the ordeal they had just endured. As Esimae's eyelids fluttered open, Mick knelt beside her, his eyes searching her face for any sign that she was truly awake. He reached out with careful hands, supporting her as she slowly sat up, his concern evident in the way he helped her.

Esimae blinked, her vision gradually sharpening as she saw Magic, her loyal black cat, nearby. Still disoriented, she murmured, "Magic?" before pushing herself to sit up a little more. Her confusion was clear, her brow furrowed as she took in the unfamiliar setting of the waggon and the cold shackles weighing down her wrists. Raising her bound hands, Esimae looked to Mick, bewildered. "Where are we, what happened?" she asked, seeking answers and trying to make sense of their predicament.

Mick, still kneeling beside her, quickly attempted to explain the situation. "You got jumped by an Aranstream soldier," he began, his voice tinged with regret. "I chased after you, but I ended up getting caught as well." He managed a sheepish, apologetic smile before his tone brightened with a touch of disbelief and gratitude. "But your cat, he got the keys!" Mick continued, gesturing towards Magic and lifting the keys for her to see.

Mick, sensing Esimae's discomfort, reached for the set of keys Magic had delivered. "Let me unshackle you," he offered, his voice gentle and filled with concern as he held the keys out towards her.

Esimae, however, shook her head, her brow furrowed as she tried to gather her thoughts and recall the events that led to their capture. "No need," she replied quietly, maintaining her focus. With determined concentration, she raised her bound wrists and spoke a soft incantation under her breath. The shackles around Esimae's wrists snapped open at once, responding instantly to her spell. She let them fall from her arms, the cold metal clattering onto the wooden bench where she had been lying. Without hesitation, Esimae shifted her attention to her ankles. She pointed towards her feet and repeated the spell, her voice steady despite her earlier disorientation. The shackles binding her ankles obeyed, unlocking with a faint metallic click and sliding away, finally granting her complete freedom from her restraints. Mick watched on clearly in awe of her use of magic.

Esimae turned to Mick, her expression marked by surprise as their eyes met. "You came after me?" she asked, her voice soft with disbelief.

"Yes," Mick replied, a gentle smile touching his lips as he extended his hand towards her. His hand came to rest lightly on her arm, offering comfort and reassurance. Esimae gazed at his hand, uncertainty flickering in her eyes. She liked Mick, but the lingering pain of losing Jaike still weighed heavily upon her heart, making it difficult for her to accept comfort so easily.

Noticing Esimae's unease, Mick quietly withdrew his hand, making it clear he respected her boundaries. Wanting to ease the tension between them, he shifted the conversation to a lighter subject. "Your cat, he's pretty amazing. He chased after you too, and he managed to somehow get the keys from the guard up front," Mick remarked, his voice filled with genuine admiration for the clever feline.

As if on cue, Magic leapt gracefully onto Esimae's lap, purring contentedly and nuzzling against her face. The cat's affectionate gesture brought a faint, grateful smile to Esimae's lips, providing her with a moment of comfort amid their uncertain circumstances.

"Thank you, Magic," she said softly, hugging the faithful black cat close. Mick, watching the scene, couldn't help but notice the warmth and affection Esimae showed Magic. He found himself wishing that she might one day feel able to let down her guard with him as well.

Mick broke the silence, his tone practical yet tinged with urgency. "Anyway," he said, "we'd best get off this waggon before they get to Elvendon. I am assuming that's where they are heading with us." His words carried a sense of cautious optimism, as though he was hopeful for a chance at escape but wary of what lay ahead.

Esimae nodded in agreement. She lifted Magic gently into her arms as she rose to her feet, determination shining in her eyes. "Yes, I would think so," she replied, confirming Mick's suspicion. For a moment, she considered their next move, then offered a suggestion with quiet resolve. "I guess we just jump for it?"

Mick met her gaze, a small smile crossing his lips as he acknowledged her plan. "I guess," he agreed, accepting the risk with a touch of camaraderie.

As Esimae moved towards the back of the waggon, she paused and turned to Mick, her expression softening. "Mick," she said, her voice gentle and sincere.

He responded simply, "Yes?"

Esimae offered him a grateful smile, her words heartfelt. "Thank you, for coming after me."

Mick gave her a knowing nod, his eyes reflecting understanding and quiet reassurance as they prepared to make their escape together.

Mick carefully pulled back the flap of the waggon, peering out to assess their surroundings. The vehicle was rattling along a rough track, deep within the dense forest. He noted that, once they disembarked, it would not be difficult to lose themselves amongst the towering trees that surrounded them.

Turning to Esimae, Mick spoke in a low, urgent tone, "Okay, you and Magic go first. Head straight for the left, into the trees. The forest looks darker and deeper that way. I'll be right behind you, all right?" His instructions were clear, underscored by a determination to ensure their escape went smoothly.

Esimae gave a resolute nod in response. She swiftly took her cloak and wrapped it securely around Magic, tucking the cat safely inside. "Stay still," she whispered, giving the animal a reassuring glance. Magic meowed softly in understanding, ready to trust Esimae's guidance as they prepared to make their move.

The waggon lurched and jolted as it travelled across the uneven ground, the clatter of wheels masked by the dense cover of the forest. On the count of three, Esimae launched herself from the back, determination etched across her face. She hugged Magic tightly to her chest, ensuring the cat's safety as she landed in a low crouch upon the leaf-strewn earth. Without hesitation, she sprinted towards the shadowy cover of the trees, her senses heightened and heart thundering in her chest.

Glancing back, Esimae caught sight of Mick following suit, leaping from the moving waggon and landing just behind her. He wasted no time, hurrying after her through the thick undergrowth. Together, they pressed on into the depths of the forest, neither daring to pause or look back, their flight continuing without respite for at least half an hour as they sought safety beneath the ancient, towering trees.

Amidst the chaos of battle, Sharelle moved with unwavering resolve. Her sword flashed through the air, a blur of motion as she dispatched opponent after opponent, her skill and determination evident with every strike. Not pausing for breath, she pushed forwards, making her way to one of the waggons at the edge of the skirmish.

With a forceful tug, Sharelle pulled open the back of the waggon. The sight that greeted her made her heart lurch—a group of Elvendon women and children huddled inside, their faces etched with fear and uncertainty. Some of the women cried out in alarm as the flap was thrown back, their fear heightened by the chaos outside.

Quickly raising her hand in a calming gesture, Sharelle addressed them in a gentle, reassuring tone. "It's okay!" she called, striving to ease their panic. She offered a warm, encouraging smile. "We're here to help," she assured them, her presence a beacon of hope amid the turmoil.

Frankie hurried to the back of another waggon, his heart pounding as he flung open the canvas flap. Inside, he was met by the sight of Elvendon men, all bound tightly and gagged, their faces marked by exhaustion and despair. Without hesitation, he vaulted up into the waggon, his resolve unwavering. Drawing his knife, Frankie swiftly began to cut through the ropes restraining the prisoners, working as quickly and carefully as he could. As he freed each prisoner, he gently removed their gags, offering them a reassuring nod. One of the men, his voice hoarse yet filled with gratitude, looked up at Frankie and asked, "Who are you?"

"My name's Frankie," he replied, his tone steady and earnest. "We are the Elvendon rebellion, and we're on our way to Aranstream castle. Our Queen is alive and has taken the castle of Aranstream."

A surge of joy swept through the cramped confines of the waggon. The news sparked a round of cheers from the newly freed men, their faces alight with relief and hope for the first time in what felt like an eternity.

Amidst the confusion and turmoil that followed the attack, Sharelle's heart raced as she desperately searched for her friend. "Where's Esimae!" she cried out, her voice edged with panic as she scanned the chaos around her, unable to spot Esimae amongst the fleeing and regrouping figures.

Unable to compose herself, Sharelle rushed over to her husband, Forde, and collapsed into his arms. He held her close, offering reassurance. "You were amazing, my love," he said with heartfelt admiration, his words momentarily grounding her.

Esendil, their son, quickly joined them and wrapped his arms around his mother. "Mum," he said, pulling her into a tight hug, "that was insane, and also really scary." Despite her own anxiety, Sharelle managed a gentle smile, ruffling Esendil's hair in a comforting gesture. "I know, my boy," she replied, her tone both soothing and proud. Esendil, slightly embarrassed by the display, ducked his head away from her hand.

Still gripped by worry, Sharelle turned urgently to Forde. "Forde, did you see where Esimae went? I can't find her," she asked, her concern intensifying. Forde shook his head regretfully. "No, sorry. I was transfixed on watching you," he admitted, his gaze apologetic as he shook his head once more, unable to offer any answers.

"Okay, look, I'm going to have a quick search of the area," Sharelle said, determination evident in her voice. Without waiting for a response, she set off, intent on finding any sign of Esimae. Her eyes scanned the ground and surrounding trees as she moved quickly but methodically through the area, her heart pounding with anxiety.

After a few tense moments, her gaze landed on a familiar object nestled in the undergrowth—Magic's basket. "Oh, my stars," Sharelle breathed, dread spreading through her as she bent to pick it up. Clutching the basket, she called out into the trees, her voice carrying a note of desperation. "Magic," she called, hoping for a response. "Magic!"

The absence of any sound or movement from the cat deepened Sharelle's worry. She knew Esimae would never willingly leave without Magic, and the realisation sent a wave of panic through her. Sharelle pressed on, searching the area as thoroughly as she could, her calls growing more urgent. Despite her determined efforts, there was no answer—no sign of Esimae or her beloved cat. With each fruitless pass, Sharelle's fear grew, the uncertainty gnawing at her as she continued to search in vain.

Hurrying back to Forde and Esendil, Sharelle's panic was evident in her voice. "I can't find her, but Magic's basket is here. I'm terrified something has happened to her," she said, her words tumbling out in distress. The fear for her friend was apparent, underscored by the abandoned basket—a sign Esimae would never leave behind willingly.

At that moment, Ben approached, concern etched on his face. "Hey, have either of you seen Mick? He's missing," he asked, scanning the small group for any sign of the lost companion.

Sharelle shook her head, her worry deepening. "No, I can't find Esimae either, or her cat," she replied, her voice tinged with frustration and dread.

Ben cursed softly, shaking his head in resignation. "Damn. Look, we need to get these people to Aranstream and to safety. If we don't find them enroute, I'll come back," he promised, glancing at Sharelle with understanding.

Although every instinct urged her to keep searching, Sharelle knew Ben was right. She nodded reluctantly, her resolve clear even through her anxiety. "Okay, I will come back with you," she agreed, determined not to abandon her friend, even as they pressed on towards Aranstream.

Ben gave a firm nod of agreement; his mind already set on their next move. Without delay, he returned to one of the waggons, deftly climbing aboard and taking up the reins. With a steady hand, he guided the horse forward, signalling the start of their journey towards Aranstream and the promise of safety.

"Come, we'll ride on one of the waggons," Sharelle urged Forde, offering her support as she helped her husband towards the next waggon. Together with Esendil, they climbed up and settled into their places, ready to follow Ben's lead. Sharelle took control of the reins herself; determination etched on her face. With a sharp, encouraging call of "Yah!" she urged the horse onward, and the waggon rolled into motion behind the first, carrying them and their hopes towards Aranstream.

Mick and Esimae moved swiftly through the forest, their footsteps purposeful and urgent. For more than an hour, they maintained a brisk pace, driven by the need to cover as much ground as possible before nightfall threatened to close in around them. The forest's shadows lengthened, but Mick's familiarity with the landscape offered a reassuring sense of direction. He had spent over six months seeking sanctuary at the Forester's Cottage, and his knowledge of the hidden trails and landmarks ensured they rarely faltered. Esimae kept close by his side, trusting Mick's judgement as they pressed on together, determined to reach their destination safely.

It wasn't long after that when they found the road that led to Aranstream castle. Keeping close to the edge they pressed on. Esimae suddenly paused, her senses alert. "I can hear waggons," she remarked, her voice low but edged with anticipation. The sun had already dipped below the horizon, leaving only the gentle light of the moon to illuminate the winding road ahead.

Mick, ever cautious, glanced quickly at Esimae. "It could be more Aranstream soldiers, not knowing we've taken control of their castle," he warned, his tone urgent. Without hesitation, he reached for Esimae's arm, guiding her swiftly off the road and into the concealment of the trees.

They stood motionless among the shadows for several tense minutes, the sound of distant wheels growing steadily louder. Through the moonlit branches, they watched as waggons drew near, accompanied by men walking on foot. The uncertainty in the air was tense as they waited to see who would emerge from the darkness.

Mick's eyes widened with relief as he recognised the approaching waggons. "It's our men, it's Ben," he declared, a broad grin breaking across his face. Without hesitation, he reached for Esimae's hand, gripping it firmly. The gesture, though unexpected, was met with equal resolve as Esimae held on tightly, seeking reassurance in his touch.

As the first waggon approached, Ben sat alert at the reins, a bow in hand and an arrow nocked, prepared for any danger that might emerge from the shadows at the roadside. His posture was tense, every muscle ready, his gaze fixed on the figures waiting just beyond the moonlit track. For a moment, uncertainty hung in the air.

Then, as the faces of the waiting figures became clear in the soft light, recognition dawned on Ben. Relief washed over his features; his guarded expression melted away, replaced by a welcoming grin. He immediately lowered his bow, setting it aside, the tension leaving his shoulders as he realised they were friends, not foes, waiting in the night.

Eyes wide with relief, Ben called out, "Mick!" as the waggons rolled nearer. Hearing his name, Mick lifted a hand in greeting, acknowledging Ben's presence as he guided his waggon alongside the others, a silent camaraderie passing between them in that moment of reunion.

Ben looked down at Mick and Esimae, concern evident in his voice. "What the hell happened?" he asked, wanting to understand the events that had led to their unexpected reunion on the moonlit road.

"We got caught," Mick admitted, his voice low but steady as he recounted their ordeal. "They knocked us out and dumped us in a waggon," he continued, the memory still fresh in his mind.

Ben, visibly relieved to find Mick and Esimae safe, let out a laugh that eased the tension lingering in the night air. "Well, I'm glad you're both not dead," he remarked, his tone lifting the mood and offering a moment of lightness after their ordeal. Turning his attention to Esimae, Ben's expression softened, the worry that had lined his face replaced by genuine warmth and reassurance.

Glancing over his shoulder, Ben gestured with his thumb towards the other waggons rolling steadily along the moonlit track. "Sharelle has been worried sick about you," he told Esimae, his voice filled with earnest concern. "She's been searching along the route for any sign of you. She's three waggons down." The message conveyed not only Sharelle's dedication but also the strong bonds of friendship that had guided their companions in their search, bringing comfort to Esimae in that uncertain moment.

Esimae's features softened with gratitude as she looked at Ben. "Thank you," she replied sincerely, clearly moved by the concern her friends had shown during her absence.

Ben leaned over from the driver's seat, offering Mick a hand up onto the waggon. "Jump up," he said, his tone friendly and encouraging. Mick hesitated for a moment, glancing at Esimae, his reluctance clear in the way he held her hand a little longer. Esimae caught his expression and offered him a reassuring smile. "I'll be fine," she said quietly, hoping to ease his worry. Seeing the confidence in her eyes, Mick gave a firm nod, then finally let go of her hand. With a swift movement, he climbed up onto Ben's waggon, settling in beside his friend as the convoy prepared to move on.

Esimae lingered by the roadside, watching as the procession of waggons continued along the moonlit track. Her eyes searched each passing face until, at last, she caught sight of Sharelle, Ford, and Esendil approaching amidst the column.

Sharelle's eyes widened in delight as she spotted her friend. "Esimae!" she exclaimed, pulling her horse to an abrupt halt. The waggon shuddered to a stop as Sharelle leaned down, her face breaking into a wide grin at the sight of Esimae.

With a relieved smile, Esimae looked up and called out, "Hey! Do you have room for one more?"

Sharelle responded with a laugh, her voice warm and welcoming. "Of course, we do," she assured her, shifting across to make space. Esendil, seated beside her, obligingly slid over to provide Esimae with room to climb aboard the waggon.

Sharelle pulled Esimae into a tight embrace as she settled beside her on the waggon. Her concern was clear as she exclaimed, "What happened, where have you been? I've been worried sick!"

Esimae, still shaken but grateful, explained, "I was caught by some Aranstream soldiers. One of them attacked me from behind—I just didn't see him coming."

Sharelle gasped, her worry deepening. "Oh, my goodness. Have you seen Mick? He's missing."

A gentle smile crossed Esimae's face as she replied, "Yes, he was with me. He came after me, to rescue me, but he ended up getting caught as well."

Sharelle's eyes widened, "and magic?" she asked hopeful. As if on cue, Magic popped his head out from the shelter of Esimae's cloak and let out a soft meow. Sharelle laughed, the tension easing, and she flicked her reins to encourage the horses to move forward.

"Tell me everything," she begged, eager to hear the full story.

Chapter Twenty-Nine
Advance to Elvendon

As the Queen entered the banqueting room, she immediately moved towards her aunt, Esimae, embracing her warmly. Observing the scene, the commander regarded the Queen with a thoughtful smile, silently acknowledging that he had misjudged her in the past. Now, he could see that Keltor's unwavering faith in her had been justified.

"Esimae," Kaitlin uttered with heartfelt relief as they embraced. Her gaze then shifted to the man standing just behind Esimae: an elf, roughly Esimae's age and notably handsome.

Her aunt's voice trembled with emotion as she responded, "Honey, are you okay? I've been so worried."

"Yes, I'm fine," Kaitlin replied. She instinctively reached up to brush away some blood that had dried on her aunt's face. "What happened? Are you okay?" she asked, her concern evident.

Esimae nodded and glanced over to her right, where Mick stood. "Yes, I'm fine. We had a little run-in with some Aranstream soldiers, but we're all good now."

Relief washed over Kaitlin, but worry quickly returned as she blurted out, "Oh, thank God. Esimae, Keltor is missing. He went after the prince and hasn't come back. I'm so worried about him."

Esimae gently let go of Kaitlin, offering a reassuring smile. "He will be okay. You know what he's like—he can take care of himself. He's probably out there right now, gathering support and rallying troops for our cause."

Kaitlin shook her head, her worry undiminished. "No, Esimae, he would have come back to me. He promised." As she spoke, her words faltered and she fell silent, noticing Sharelle and Forde as they entered the room.

Sharelle greeted her formally, dipping her head in respect. "My Queen," she said.

Unable to maintain her composure, Kaitlin stepped forward and embraced Sharelle tightly. "I'm so relieved you are all safe," she murmured, her voice trembling as she struggled to contain her emotions.

"Hey," Sharelle said softly, offering reassurance. "It's okay, we're all okay."

Forde entered the room, walking carefully with the aid of a wooden staff. He was visibly still weak and fatigued from the arduous journey. Despite this, he greeted Kaitlin with a gentle smile and dipped his head respectfully. "I'm Forde, Keltor's father," he introduced himself.

Kaitlin, moved by his presence, released Sharelle and stepped towards Forde. Without hesitation, she embraced him. Forde, though surprised, responded warmly, his free hand coming up to rest on her back as he returned the hug.

As they parted, Kaitlin whispered quietly, "He has missed you so much," her voice filled with emotion. Forde's eyes glistened, and a single tear rolled down his cheek. He quickly brushed it away with the back of his hand.

Turning to the others, Forde continued, "This is Esendil, Keltor's brother." He shifted aside, allowing Esendil to approach.

The young man stepped forward and bowed his head politely. "Hi," he greeted her.

Kaitlin returned his smile warmly. "Hi." She couldn't help but notice how much Esendil resembled his father, sharing the same dark hair and eyes.

Sharelle's anxiety was clear as she voiced the question that weighed heavily on everyone's mind. "Where is Keltor, isn't he back yet?" she asked, her concern evident. Although she was aware that her son had pursued the prince, she had held a quiet hope that he would be waiting for them upon their arrival.

Kaitlin responded with a worried shake of her head. "No, I don't know where he is," she admitted. "He went after the prince earlier this morning and no one has seen or heard from him." The uncertainty in her voice only heightened the tension in the room.

At this, Sharelle lifted her hand to her mouth, her complexion growing noticeably paler as the reality of Keltor's absence began to sink in. Anxious thoughts flickered across her features, the weight of uncertainty pressing down on her as she tried to come to terms with what it might mean.

To provide comfort, Kaitlin spoke up, her words gentle but lacking in confidence. "I'm sure he is fine. The commander thinks he may have gone to get extra help." Despite her efforts, the tremor in her voice betrayed her own anxieties, and the reassurance she offered felt tenuous and uncertain, doing little to dispel the growing sense of worry in the room.

The commander stepped forward with a sense of urgency, addressing those gathered in the room. "We should go over the plans quickly and bring you up to speed. We're going to strike at first light. We can't assume that Keltor stopped the prince. King Iwein will be getting his army ready to strike back," he explained, moving towards the table where maps and documents were laid out.

As Kaitlin observed the group, her attention was drawn to the elf standing quietly behind Esimae. She noticed him lift his hand, guiding Esimae gently towards the table before stepping back to give her space.

Curiosity getting the better of her, Kaitlin leaned in and asked, "Esimae, who is the elf?" She gestured subtly towards the man in question.

Esimae glanced over her shoulder and, catching the elf's eye, received a friendly smile from him. "Oh, no one, that's just Mick. He and Frankie over there," she replied, nodding towards another man standing by the door, "they jumped us when we arrived at the Forester's cottage. Sharelle pinned Frankie down, and I kind of electrocuted Mick with my magic."

656

Kaitlin's eyes widened in amusement as she turned to Esimae, a playful grin lighting up her face. "You did what?" she asked, glancing back over at the elf, whose hair was sticking up in all directions. "Is that why his hair is sticking up?"

Esimae tried to stifle her laughter, her shoulders trembling with the effort. She gave a quick nod, unable to keep the smile from her lips.

"Oh my god, Esimae," Kaitlin exclaimed, letting out a quiet snigger that she tried, unsuccessfully, to hide.

Leaning closer, Esimae whispered conspiratorially, "He's kind of cute though, don't you think?" She risked a brief glance over her shoulder towards the elf, her expression softening ever so slightly.

Kaitlin's eyebrows shot up in surprise. "You've got feelings for him?" she asked, her voice a mixture of shock and teasing curiosity.

Esimae immediately shook her head, though the hesitation in her voice betrayed her uncertainty. "No, no, well, maybe. I don't know," she admitted. Her gaze dropped as she recounted what had happened. "I got captured when we were attacked earlier, and he came after me, to rescue me. Although, he managed to get caught as well. But we escaped, and he got me back here."

Noticing Kaitlin's lingering look, Esimae nudged her niece firmly and insisted, "Stop looking at him."

"Okay, oh my god, Esimae, he's an elf, and an Aranstream at that," Kaitlin remarked, a smile spreading across her face as she teased her aunt, her tone light but affectionate.

Esimae's expression shifted, warmth mingling with a trace of wistfulness. "I know," she replied, her words thoughtful. "Well, Keltor's turned out okay, and so was Jaike, so why not give him a chance? Besides, humans are rather lacking in this world." She paused, reflecting on everything she had experienced. "If I've learnt anything these last few months, it's that life is too short, and we need to embrace every moment of happiness we can find."

Kaitlin's eyes softened, clearly moved by Esimae's honesty. "Esimae, that's beautiful," she said quietly, and without hesitation, she stepped forward and wrapped her arms around her aunt in a gentle hug.

Esimae let out a quiet laugh, her affection evident. "Yeah, well, you're rubbing off on me, I guess," she admitted with a smile. Pulling back, she gave Kaitlin a playful nudge. "Now come on, tell me what these plans are then."

The banqueting hall, once a place of celebration and festivity, now served as a hub for strategy and resolve. Esimae and Kaitlin assembled with Commander Talbot, Sharelle, Forde, and the principal officers of the Elvendon army around a long, polished table. The golden glow of chandeliers shimmered above, casting shifting patterns across the maps and tactical notes strewn before them. The weight of the coming battle pressed in, yet there was comfort in the camaraderie of familiar faces and seasoned leaders.

Talbot led the session, outlining defensive strategies and anticipated enemy movements. The lead soldier of Elvendon, had raided the Aranstream armoury. They'd found a store deep underneath the castle where King Iwein had clearly been preparing his army for war. Countless swords, shields and chainmail were found. Enough to supply the first thousand soldiers who were to take up the front line.

Esimae and Kaitlin listened attentively, sometimes pausing the flow with sharp questions or alternative perspectives, with Kaitlin still instant that she and her aunt would be up front and that their magic would be their primary weapon.

The deliberations, which stretched for hours within the grandeur of the hall, fostered a sense of unity among all present. Every discussion and strategy session worked to solidify a shared vision for the defence that lay ahead, ensuring that each participant understood their role and the collective goal.

As the final plans were settled, the group took a moment to pause, allowing themselves to exchange words of encouragement amidst the vast, echoing chamber. It was in these brief, but meaningful exchanges that they drew renewed strength, their resolve bolstered by a powerful sense of shared purpose and camaraderie. Finally, the Commander announced that it was time to rest; only five hours remained until dawn.

Chapter Thirty

Dragons

Keltor paced anxiously, his mind racing with worry. If he had a watch, he would have been checking it relentlessly; the time since he parted from Kaitlin felt interminable. He could not help but imagine her fretting over his absence, perhaps overwhelmed with concern or thinking he was dead.

Unable to contain his apprehension any longer, Keltor finally addressed Kailan. *"How much longer?"* he asked, his voice edged with frustration.

Kailan, the dragon, slowly opened his eyes, having been basking in the moon's gentle glow and relishing its cool comfort. He gazed down at Keltor, attentive to the urgency in his companion's tone.

Keltor's concern continued to escalate. *"We need to go,"* he insisted, the thought of Kaitlin alone gnawing at him. The prince would have informed King Iwein by now, and the threat of an attack upon Kaitlin loomed heavily over his thoughts. They could already be striking at her, and every moment that passed felt perilous.

Kailan paused, his enormous form momentarily still. *"One moment, I will see,"* he murmured. The great dragon closed his eyes, surrendering himself to the silent depths of his mind. Through a connection that transcended spoken language, Kailan reached out mentally to his fellow dragons and to the King himself, stretching his senses across the distance that separated them.

Keltor watched, restless and impatient, as Kailan seemed to slip into a trance-like state. Time stretched uncomfortably, his nerves frayed by the urgency of their situation. He understood how crucial it was to have another dragon fighting on their side; their presence could decisively shift the balance of power. Yet, the wait felt interminable, every heartbeat echoing his anxiety.

Finally, Kailan stirred, opening his golden eyes. Unable to contain himself any longer, Keltor pressed, *"Well?"* His voice carried the weight of his worry and anticipation, as he looked to Kailan for an answer.

The dragon remained silent, his gaze fixed upon the heavens. Sensing his companion's intent, Keltor lifted his eyes to the sky as well. Suddenly, out of the soft silver wash of moonlight, another dragon descended from above. Keltor's breath caught and his eyes grew wide with astonishment as the newcomer approached, its vivid green wings shimmering brilliantly in the light as it banked gracefully and turned toward them.

Kailan turned to Keltor and informed him, *"It's Ayver."*

Keltor instinctively moved closer to Kailan as the dragoness descended. Compared to Kailan, Ayver was colossal—her size was imposing, her presence overwhelming. As she touched down, the earth trembled beneath her massive feet, each step resonating with power. Keltor felt his heart pounding rapidly in his chest, caught between awe and fear. Ayver was a magnificent sight to behold, her beauty matched only by the formidable aura she exuded.

Kailan stepped forward and greeted Ayver, their snouts meeting in a gesture of mutual respect and recognition.

Keltor felt utterly dwarfed beside Ayver, as if he were a mere child standing before a giant. The dragoness turned her attention to him, inhaled deeply, and a warm, knowing smile appeared on her lips.

"Son of Sharelle," she greeted him. Keltor nodded in response, acknowledging her recognition. *"You have the same scent. I am Ayver,"* she introduced herself.

Gathering his composure, Keltor replied in dragona, the ancient tongue of dragons, *"Ayver, I'm Keltor. Thank you for coming to help me."*

Ayver's eyes softened as she responded, *"You are the son of my rider. There is nothing I would not do for you, or for Sharelle."*

The realisation struck Keltor with a wave of astonishment. *"You were my mother's dragon?"* he asked, his voice tinged with disbelief. Although his mother had told him she had been a dragon rider, the true significance had never quite taken hold until this moment. As he gazed at Ayver, pride for his mother swelled within him. She had ridden this magnificent dragon, fought fearsome battles by her side, and soared across the skies with her. The bond between his mother and Ayver was suddenly vivid and profound in his mind.

Ayver's voice was tinged with uncertainty as she asked, *"Sharelle, how is she?"* Though hesitant, the dragoness could sense that Sharelle was still alive; their bond, forged for life, remained unbroken despite their separation.

"Mum is fine," Keltor reassured her, but urgency coloured his words. *"But we really need to go. Do you know what the situation is?"*

Ayver nodded. *"Yes, I've been briefed. We just need to wait a little longer. Erandril is coming."*

Keltor's brow furrowed in confusion. *"Erandril?"*

A gentle smile spread across Ayver's lips as she lowered her head, her yellow eyes meeting his gaze. *"He is your father's dragon. When he heard, I was going to Elvendon, he insisted to our King that he must come."*

A smile broke across Keltor's face, and before he realised, his hand reached out to touch Ayver's snout. She leant into his touch, and as their connection deepened, Keltor felt something more than mere friendship—a profound bond linking them through heritage and shared purpose. Keltor turned to Ayver. *"I can hardly believe my parents were dragon riders,"* he admitted, still coming to terms with the magnitude of what he had learned.

Ayver's eyes glimmered with fond remembrance as she replied, "*They were the best—masterful and elegant. Forde and Sharelle are greatly missed, even now, by us and by our King and Queen.*" Her words carried the weight of cherished memories and the respect both dragons and royalty held for his parents.

Suddenly, a thunderous sound echoed overhead, drawing everyone's attention skywards. A dragon of breathtaking size soared towards them. Keltor's mouth fell open in astonishment; the dragon was even larger than Ayver, and easily twice the size of Kailan.

In awe, Keltor whispered, "*My dad rode him?*" His eyes widened as Erandril banked gracefully, turning downwards towards the waiting group. The dragon's sheer enormity would have sent Keltor running, had he not known Erandril was an ally. Erandril's bright green wings glittered in the rising sunlight, his red, fiery underbelly serving as a vivid warning of his power—a truly massive, fire-breathing dragon.

Keltor felt the gentle touch of Ayver's snout on his shoulder, prompting him to look up at her. The reassuring look in her eyes conveyed a silent message of friendship and trust, bringing a small, grateful smile to his lips.

Suddenly, the ground trembled underfoot as Erandril landed nearby, his immense presence impossible to ignore. He strode towards the group with purpose, the earth thudding with each step.

As Erandril drew closer, he addressed them directly, "*Ayver, Kailan.*"

Ayver greeted him in return, and the two dragons exchanged a traditional gesture of respect and camaraderie, touching snout to snout in acknowledgement of their shared bond.

Erandril's enormous head lowered towards Keltor, casting a deep shadow over him. The dragon's hot breath washed over Keltor's face, and as Erandril inhaled, the resulting updraft caused Keltor's hair to lift and flutter. Even though Keltor knew Erandril was a friend, his body trembled involuntarily—aware that this mighty dragon could devour him with a single, effortless bite.

Noting Keltor's unease, Erandril spoke in a deep, reassuring voice. "*Son of Forde, fear me not.*" The dragon's words were calm and understanding, having sensed the fear radiating from Keltor. Keltor managed a nod in response, even though his voice remained trapped in his throat. His gaze lingered on the dragon's thick, armoured scales, marvelling at their imposing strength and the power they represented.

Ayver glanced at Keltor and explained, "*He is also a dragon Lord, as he understands Kailan too.*"

Erandril nodded in agreement, his voice thoughtful. "*Just like your father.*"

Keltor, finally finding his voice amidst the awe and tension, replied, "*Yes, I understand that now.*" He hesitated for a moment before continuing, "*I haven't really had the chance to ask him about you and the other dragons. Thank you for coming to help us.*" His words were filled with genuine gratitude.

Erandril's massive snout lowered slightly, a note of sadness in his tone. "*I cannot wait to see that old devil, I've missed him greatly.*"

Keltor's lips curled into a smile as he heard the warmth in Erandril's voice when speaking of his father. However, his expression soon darkened, the weight of recent events settling on his features.

"*My father is unwell,*" Keltor confided, his tone tinged with sadness. "*He was held captive for many years, and his body has grown weak. For a long time, we believed he was dead, but I found him only a couple of days ago. I have missed him too.*"

Erandril regarded him with understanding and reassurance. "*Do not worry, young king. When we are reunited, I will help him recover,*" he promised, his voice steady and full of conviction.

Keltor looked up, hope flickering in his eyes. "*You can do that? How?*" he asked, eager yet uncertain.

"*Even though your father is no longer my rider, our bond endures for life,*" Erandril explained. "*I am able to share my lifeforce with him. You will see—he will soon be back to his old self.*"

Keltor could scarcely believe what he was hearing. He managed another smile at the mighty dragon, the entire experience feeling almost unreal.

"*Now, young King, can you make a portal directly to your Queen?*" Erandril asked, his eyes fixed expectantly on Keltor.

Keltor hesitated, uncertainty clouding his features. "*I don't know,*" he replied, frowning as he considered the possibility. Could he truly manage such a feat? His hand instinctively went to his chest, fingers pressing against the amulet embedded in his flesh. He remembered the old man's words: the magic was now a part of him.

"*I will give it a go,*" Keltor said with determination. He pulled back the sleeves of his shirt and began to swirl his hands together, palms close but not touching, as he concentrated on building up his power.

He chanted, "*Etora, mistooma, portala, et Kaitlin,*" focusing intently as he tried to find her presence within his mind. He repeated the incantation: "*Etora, mistooma, portala, et Kaitlin.*"

Suddenly, Keltor's heart nearly stopped. In his mind's eye, he caught a glimpse of what was happening from afar—the battle for Elvendon had already begun. Time was slipping away; they had none left to spare.

"*We need to hurry!*" Keltor shouted, his voice ringing with urgency as a surge of anger, dread, and newfound power coursed through him. Channelling his energy, he drew his hands back and then thrust them skywards. The air reverberated with a massive, explosive boom, echoing across the landscape. In that very instant, a swirling portal began to materialise above them, its edges crackling with magic.

"*Hurry, young king, on my back,*" Kailan commanded without hesitation.

Obeying the dragon's words, Keltor reached out and grasped the tough scales before him. He climbed up Kailan's leg, pulling himself higher, and then swung onto the dragon's broad back.

"*Hold tight,*" the dragon warned, his deep voice resolute as they prepared to plunge through the portal together.

Keltor gripped his thighs tightly around Kailan's scaly body, bracing himself for the flight to come. He dug his feet in behind some of the dragon's sturdy scales, his hands grasping firmly for support as Kailan bent back on his powerful hind legs in preparation for take-off. With a sudden, mighty surge, the dragon launched them both into the air.

At first, fear overwhelmed Keltor. He squeezed his eyes shut, not daring to look as the wind whipped around him. The sensation of soaring so rapidly skyward was almost too much to bear. Gradually, curiosity got the better of him, and he risked opening one eye. To his relief, he saw Ayver flying right beside them, keeping pace with Kailan in the ascent.

Summoning his courage, Keltor opened his other eye just as they reached the swirling portal above. He drew in a deep breath, steadying himself as he glanced down to the ground far below. Behind them, Erandril followed, bringing up the rear in their airborne procession.

As they plunged into the darkness of the portal, Keltor's vision was swallowed by shadow. He closed his eyes tightly once more, his thoughts turning to prayer. Inwardly, he pleaded with the elders to guide them safely, hoping with all his strength that he was leading them towards Kaitlin—and not into some unknown, perilous realm.

Chapter Thirty-One
The Battle for Elvendon

Kaitlin rode alongside the commander atop a black stallion, carefully observing the landscape as they approached the summit of the hill. The weight of the chainmail across her chest pressed down upon her, feeling especially burdensome given her slight build. Shifting in the saddle to relieve some discomfort, she turned to glance behind her.

Following in her wake were Esimae and Sharelle, each mounted on elegant white mares. Despite Kaitlin's earlier plea for Forde to remain behind due to his fragile health, he had been resolute in his decision to accompany them. Both Kaitlin and Forde's wife had voiced their objections, but Forde's determination would not be swayed. Riding together with him were their son, Esendil—Keltor's brother—who provided support and assistance to his father as they shared the same horse.

More than two thousand individuals marched together in disciplined ranks. The majority of these were people who had previously been held captive in detention camps, only recently liberated and now eager to reclaim their homeland. Others among them had chosen to emerge from hiding when they heard of the impending attempt to recapture Elvendon, determined to play their part in the struggle.

In preparation for the confrontation, a contingent of five hundred men had already broken away from the main body of the force. Their mission was to make their way westward, with the intention of manoeuvring behind King Iwein's army and gaining a strategic advantage over their adversaries.

Kaitlin quietly murmured, "Keltor, where the hell are you?" Her reluctance to face the impending battle without him weighed heavily on her, yet she recognised that there might be no other choice. Deep down, she hoped that if word of the conflict had reached those in hiding, Keltor would have returned to her, provided he was able. The thought that something might have happened to him was almost unbearable, and she tried not to dwell on it.

Turning her gaze to the army assembled behind her, Kaitlin felt a deep sense of responsibility for their lives. She was determined to avoid unnecessary loss and was not willing to sacrifice her people in a traditional battle. Instead, her plan was to confront King Iwein using her magic. Only if her magical assault failed would she instruct her men to take up arms and engage in combat.

As the group reached the crest of the hill, Kaitlin gazed out towards Elvendon, her eyes settling on the distant turrets of her castle. The sight filled her with a mixture of longing and apprehension. The commander, alert and focused, raised his hand to signal a halt. Spread out below them in the meadow, King Iwein's army stood in formation, effectively blocking the route to the city and making any further progress on horseback impossible.

"We go on foot," the commander declared with quiet authority, swinging himself down from his horse. Kaitlin, along with the others in her party, followed his lead and dismounted, bracing themselves for the encounter ahead.

Concerned for the welfare of those closest to her, Kaitlin turned to Forde, who, despite his frail health, had insisted on joining the advance. "Forde, please stay here," she urged, as both he and Sharelle stepped up beside her.

Forde, steadfast in his resolve, replied respectfully, "No, your highness, I'm okay. My place is here fighting for my Queen." He bowed his head, determined not to be left behind.

At his side, Esendil—Forde's son and Keltor's brother— offered reassurance. "I will look after him," he said, standing protectively alongside his father.

668

Kaitlin relented, though her concern remained evident. "Fine," she said with reluctance, "but not on the frontline, okay? Keltor would never forgive me if something happens to you all." Her words emphasised the gravity of the situation, and Forde nodded, accepting her conditions.

Kaitlin advanced to the front of the formation, moving in step with the commander as their troops arranged themselves to mirror the disciplined lines of King Iwein's army. Directly behind Kaitlin, her archers took up their positions at the very forefront, ready to respond at a moment's notice. Esimae, following the plan, made her way further down the line, ensuring the advance was coordinated and deliberate. Together, Kaitlin and her officers led their force forward, gradually closing the gap between their own ranks and those of King Iwein, all the while maintaining discipline and cohesion among their troops.

A few rows back, Sharelle's anxious voice carried forward. "Who is he holding?" she called, her concern evident as she tried to discern the identity of the captive in the enemy's grasp.

Kaitlin's expression became increasingly sombre as her eyes fixed on a man restrained by one of King Iwein's soldiers. The sight caused her to falter, her composure wavering for just a moment. Resolute, she lifted her hand and issued a clear signal for her forces to come to a halt. Instantly, a profound silence descended upon the meadow, the tension palpable in the air as all eyes turned towards the Queen.

With measured steps, the Queen of Elvendon advanced several paces forward, breaking away from her formation. She paused, standing between her assembled forces and the enemy lines, her focus shifting between King Iwein and the soldier holding Keltor captive. In that moment, a tumult of emotions surged within her— fear for Keltor's safety, anger at the king's cruelty, and a deep, abiding love for the man in peril. These feelings mingled and threatened to overwhelm her, yet Kaitlin held her ground, preparing to address both her adversary and the captor.

King Iwein's voice rang out across the tense divide, his threat chilling the assembled forces. "Surrender now, or I'll kill him—

and then all of you!" he shouted, his authority and ruthlessness evident to all.

"Kaitlin, please, he's our son," Sharelle cried out, her voice trembling with desperation as she forced her way to the front of the line, panic etched across her face. The urgency in her tone was unmistakable, driven by a mother's fear for her child's life.

Kaitlin glanced over at Sharelle, her concern mirrored in Sharelle's anxious gaze. Turning her attention back to Keltor, she observed that his hands were bound in front of him. Despite the restraints, Kaitlin knew they posed little obstacle for Keltor; he possessed the strength to break free if needed, just as he could easily answer her if given the chance.

With deliberate subtlety, Kaitlin raised her hand. She placed her palm flat against her heart, then curled her fingers into a fist before opening her hand and pointing across her chest with her index finger. It was their secret signal—an unspoken message shared only between them, to communicate without alerting their adversaries.

The figure, appearing to be Keltor and restrained by the Aranstream soldier, remained silent in response to Kaitlin's silent signal. As the soldier's sword pressed menacingly against his neck, he broke his silence, his voice raw with terror. "Kaitlin. Please, I don't want to die!" he shouted, his plea echoing across the tense gap between the two armies. The desperation in his voice sent a jolt through those who heard him, intensifying the already charged atmosphere on the battlefield.

Kaitlin's heart lurched painfully as she listened to the desperate pleas of the man before her. His voice, so full of terror, seemed to pierce through the tense air, but Kaitlin could not ignore the certainty settling within her. Closing her eyes, she allowed silent tears to roll down her cheeks, her grief deepening with each passing second. The truth was undeniable—this was not her husband, not her King. The realisation hit her with brutal clarity, and every word uttered by the imposter only served to intensify her anguish.

In that suspended moment, Kaitlin's mind was flooded with memories of Keltor: his warm laughter, the comforting embrace that had always made her feel safe, and the subtle details that marked him as hers. These recollections sharpened her sorrow, making the imposter's frantic appeals all the more unbearable. Even as her heart ached, Kaitlin steeled herself for what had to come next.

The chilling realisation that someone could replicate Keltor with such precision sent a wave of dread through Kaitlin. For the imposter to imitate Keltor so flawlessly, he must have been able to touch Keltor. Achieving this level of mimicry would require powerful magic—magic that immediately brought Aragon to the forefront of Kaitlin's mind, recalling how he had once impersonated Keltor almost perfectly.

As Kaitlin grappled with this unsettling truth, her jaw tightened in response to her growing anger and anguish. The evidence pointed inexorably towards one conclusion: the man before her was most likely Prince Keion. With this, a devastating possibility took shape within Kaitlin's heart—if Prince Keion was able to take Keltor's place so effectively, it could only mean one devastating possibility: Keltor was dead. The weight of this thought pressed upon her, threatening to overwhelm her, but she forced herself to swallow her grief. Instead, she allowed anger to surge within her, transforming her pain into determination.

Kaitlin recognised the gravity of her next actions. She understood that what she was about to do could result in great loss, possibly costing many lives. Yet, in her mind, there was no other choice. King Iwein's cruelty and malice were laid bare before her; his wickedness could not go unchallenged, and Kaitlin knew she must act, whatever the cost.

"Power of Source, please give me the energy of the earth," she said. As she began to chant, her hands moved at her sides and her power accumulated.

Sharelle's voice quivered with uncertainty as she watched Kaitlin's every move. "Kaitlin, my Queen, what are you doing?" she asked, her eyes fixed on the swirling magic beginning to form in Kaitlin's hands. Despite the anxious plea, Kaitlin remained silent, her focus unwavering. She kept her hands poised by her sides, carefully shaping and guiding the energy she had summoned, waiting until she could feel the surge of the earth's power channelling upwards into her fingertips.

Realisation dawned painfully on Sharelle, and tears streamed down her face as she struggled to accept what was unfolding before her. "No," she whispered, her voice thick with emotion, fully comprehending the Queen's intentions. "How could you? He loves you." The anguish in Sharelle's words echoed her heartbreak, her grief and disbelief mingling with the tension that gripped the entire assembly.

King Iwein's voice rang out over the battlefield, cutting through the tense silence that had settled over the opposing forces. His tone was resolute and unyielding as he delivered his ultimatum, "This is your final warning," he declared, his words carrying unmistakable authority and menace across the distance that separated the two armies. The threat in his proclamation was clear, leaving no room for negotiation or mercy, and its impact was felt keenly by all who listened—a stark reminder of the perilous stakes and the gravity of the moment.

Kaitlin drew deeply upon the energy she had summoned, fusing the raw elemental force with her innate magical abilities. Composed and resolute, she advanced steadily towards the imposter, her presence strengthened by the unwavering support of her soldiers and the archers at her side. Each step she took was grounded in the very essence of nature, as if the earth itself was lending her its power.

Without warning, Kaitlin halted and dropped to one knee, her movement both deliberate and commanding. The suddenness of her action left her soldiers momentarily perplexed, uncertainty flickering across their faces. Yet, when she glanced back at them and gave a subtle, decisive nod, her intent was clear. Trusting in her leadership, the soldiers mimicked her actions, lowering themselves to one knee despite their confusion, unified in their obedience and faith in their Queen.

As confusion rippled through the ranks, Forde's uncertainty mirrored that of many around him. "What's she doing?" he asked, unable to hide his bewilderment at the Queen's sudden actions.

Commander Talbot, however, exuded quiet confidence. He glanced away from Kaitlin just long enough to meet Forde's gaze and then looked towards Forde's wife, who was overcome with emotion. "Trust her," the Commander said firmly, his voice carrying an assurance that brooked no argument.

Taking decisive action, the Commander dropped to one knee, setting a clear example. Without hesitation, he issued a command to those around him. "Kneel," he ordered, his tone resolute and unwavering.

Forde responded immediately, taking his wife's trembling hand and gently guiding her down beside him. Together, they lowered themselves to the ground in a show of obedience and faith.

In that pivotal moment, inspired by the Commander's conviction and leadership, the entire army followed suit. In a unified movement, every soldier knelt, a silent but powerful display of loyalty and trust in their Queen and her cause.

Sharelle's voice trembled with anguish as she cried out, "What's she doing, is she going to kill our son?" The weight of her fear was evident, her words cutting through the tense silence that had settled over the assembled soldiers.

Commander Talbot, recognising her distress, placed a steady, reassuring hand upon her arm. His presence was calm and unwavering, a silent support amid the chaos and confusion. "He would give his life for her; Keltor would never ask for mercy," he said firmly, his tone resolute and filled with respect for Keltor's courage and loyalty.

Without another word, Commander Talbot turned his attention back to the scene unfolding before them, his focus fixed on the Queen. The fate of all hung in the balance as he, along with the others, awaited Kaitlin's next move.

King Iwein interpreted the sudden kneeling of Kaitlin and her soldiers as a clear act of surrender. His confidence grew, and his men, emboldened by what they perceived as a sign of victory, exchanged triumphant glances and began to smile amongst themselves.

However, Kaitlin had no intention of yielding. Her resolve hardened as she looked from Keltor to King Iwein, her anger mounting at the King's smug expression. Determined to put an end to his arrogance, she let her emotions show—her nose wrinkled and her brow furrowed, intent on wiping the self-satisfied smile from his face.

With sudden purpose, Kaitlin sprang to her feet. Her voice rang out, strong and commanding: "Power of the source, seek and destroy!" Instantly, electricity and raw energy crackled all around her, filling the air with a tangible charge. In one sweeping motion, she directed her hands forward, unleashing a massive beam of white magic straight towards Keltor.

The beam struck Keltor squarely in the chest. The force of Kaitlin's magic lifted his body high above the others, suspending him in mid-air and enveloping him in a dazzling display of electric energy.

Sharelle's scream pierced the tense atmosphere, her anguish echoing across the field. Forde, unable to contain his terror, immediately wrapped his arms around her, his entire body trembling. He held her close, desperately hoping that the Queen was right, that the horror unfolding before them would not end with the destruction of their son. The weight of fear was almost unbearable as he clung to Sharelle, silently praying for mercy.

Amid the chaos, the Queen's eyes suddenly blazed with an unnatural white light. Her voice rose above the noise, clear and commanding as she shouted, "Reveal yourself!" Though uncertainty warred within her, deep down she knew the truth—this was not her husband, nor her King. The conviction in her heart was unmistakable, guiding her actions even as she fought to accept what she saw.

A subtle smile played at the corners of her lips as the illusion faded before her eyes. The form that had appeared to be Keltor shimmered, and then vanished, revealing the true identity concealed beneath the disguise—Prince Keion was exposed, his deception finally uncovered for all to see.

"No!" King Iwein exclaimed in distress, his eyes widening as he witnessed his son cry out in agony, his body contorting as he resisted the force of Kaitlin's magical control. Panic overtook the King as he turned towards Kaitlin, desperate to save his son from her grasp. Drawing upon his own elven magic, King Iwein lifted his hands and unleashed a sizzling, searing bolt of lightning, hurling it towards Kaitlin in an attempt to shatter her hold.

As the King's beam of magic collided with Kaitlin's, the air crackled with energy, white lightning sparking violently where the two forces met. King Iwein fought with all his might to break Kaitlin's control, pouring his power into the attack. Yet, despite his efforts, Kaitlin's strength proved overwhelming. The King's attempt faltered—her grip on his son remained unbroken, and his magic could not overpower hers.

Kaitlin's voice dropped to a whisper, her words laden with grief and determination: "This is for Logan and Alarna." Her resolve unwavering, she swept her arms outward in a powerful gesture. Magic surged at her command, focused entirely on Prince Keion. The force of her spell was devastating—Keion's body was wrenched apart, the explosive burst of energy tearing him asunder in a violent conclusion to his deception and betrayal.

"Stay down!" Kaitlin's voice cut through the tumult, sharp and unwavering as she addressed her soldiers. As some of her troops began to rise from their knees amid the chaos, her order rang with unmistakable urgency, leaving no room for hesitation or doubt. The tone and clarity of her command made it clear that this was not simply a suggestion, but an imperative born from necessity and tactical awareness.

The soldiers, recognising both the wisdom and necessity in her directive, obeyed at once. Without hesitation, they pressed themselves even closer to the ground, understanding that Kaitlin's command was not to be questioned in the midst of such magical chaos. Each one remained motionless, bracing themselves against the unpredictable onslaught of energy that still lingered in the air.

United by their trust in Kaitlin's leadership and their shared will to survive, they waited in tense silence for her next move, eyes fixed on her as she prepared to confront the danger ahead.

King Iwein, his mind consumed by a fury that teetered on the edge of madness, gave voice to his rage in a scream that was more primal than any battle cry that had ever echoed across the battlefield. The sound reverberated over the field, carrying with it the raw essence of his unrestrained anger and desperation.

His grip tightened around the hilt of his sword as he brandished the weapon, eyes ablaze with the full force of his wrath. With a violent thrust of his blade pointed directly at Kaitlin, he unleashed a thunderous command that left no doubt as to his intent: "Kill them, kill them all!" The words, carried on the wind, drove into the hearts of his soldiers, igniting an overwhelming and savage determination amongst the ranks.

The force of King Iwein's command sent a palpable ripple of dread through the ranks of his troops. Instantly, the atmosphere shifted—his soldiers, stirred by the raw intensity of their monarch's emotions, found themselves gripped by a savage determination. The King's unrestrained fury became a driving force, sharpening their focus and galvanising them to act without hesitation.

Fuelled by the violence of King Iwein's order, the army surged forward with renewed aggression, each soldier propelled by a mix of fear and loyalty. The battlefield, already fraught with chaos and swirling magic, seemed to teeter on the very brink of total carnage. King Iwein's rage, echoing in every corner of the field, pushed his forces into relentless action, threatening to overwhelm all opposition in their path.

Regardless of Keltor's fate, Kaitlin understood that her duty remained unchanged. She had to persevere and continue the fight for the people of Elvendon; she was their final and sole hope. With unwavering resolve, she lifted her chin, determination etched across her face and started to advance towards the approaching elven forces.

She drew in a deep breath, steadying herself, and released it slowly. Gathering strength from the earth beneath her feet, Kaitlin focused, allowing herself to absorb its energy. Once more, she channelled the power of the land, ready to confront the challenge ahead.

With unwavering resolve, Kaitlin raised her voice in a powerful incantation: "Light within me, by the grace of the earth, and the universe protect and destroy." As she uttered these words, her hands swept forward in a wide, commanding gesture, channelling all the strength she could muster into a single, devastating attack.

As Kaitlin's magic collided with the first line of Aranstream soldiers, the results were immediate and catastrophic. The force of her spell lifted their bodies into the air, violently hurling them backwards where they landed atop the ranks of elves positioned behind them. The brutal impact of this magical assault led to numerous fatalities amongst the Aranstream troops, with many others rendered unconscious or otherwise incapacitated. The sheer magnitude and unfamiliar nature of Kaitlin's power left the surviving soldiers momentarily stunned, plunging their ranks into a brief but significant state of disorder.

King Iwein's command rang out over the chaotic battlefield, cutting through the lingering confusion and fear. At his order, the soldiers who had survived the initial magical onslaught struggled to their feet, their movements betraying both exhaustion and apprehension. Despite their battered state, these Aranstream troops quickly gathered themselves and fell in with the ranks of the second line, eager to avoid incurring their king's wrath.

A palpable tension lingered amongst the soldiers. Their fear of King Iwein was as great—if not greater—than their dread of facing the witch queen herself. Driven onward by the memory of his furious command and the threat it carried, the Aranstream forces advanced once more, their resolve steeled by necessity rather than hope.

Kaitlin's voice rang out with unwavering authority as she called out, "Archers," her tone brooking no hesitation. Without sparing a glance behind her, she placed her trust in the discipline and readiness of her own men, confident that they would heed her summons at once. Each step she took towards the advancing enemy was deliberate and resolute, her presence growing more luminous with each stride. As her body began to shimmer with an ethereal glow, she drew in another deep, steadying breath, preparing herself for the immense task ahead.

Centring her will and drawing on the ancient powers around her, Kaitlin invoked a chant, her words carrying both hope and strength: "With the power of the earth, the stars, the universe, hold and protect." Raising her hands and sweeping them in a wide arc behind her, she cast a protective wave that surged over the entire Elvendon army. The powerful magic required such focus and energy that it forced her down to one knee, the sheer force of the protective spell momentarily overwhelming, yet she remained steadfast, determined to shield her people at all costs.

Esimae lifted her hands, focusing her energy with unwavering determination. She sent out a concentrated beam of power, directing it towards Kaitlin's magical barrier. The sheer intensity of the connection nearly knocked Esimae off her feet, the force of magic threatening to overwhelm her. However, she managed to steady herself, refusing to yield to the pressure.

Drawing upon her own magical reserves, Esimae joined her power seamlessly with Kaitlin's. Together, their combined strength fortified the barrier, making it more resilient against the relentless assault. Esimae's support was crucial, helping Kaitlin maintain the protective shield that stood between them and the advancing Aranstream forces.

Kaitlin's voice rang out with unwavering authority as she called out, "Archers, forward and protect me." She knew that in order to maintain the magical barrier shielding her forces, she would need to focus all her strength and concentration. Her survival—and that of her people—depended on her ability to sustain the protective spell for as long as possible.

As the archers responded to her command, surging ahead to form a protective ring around her, Kaitlin braced herself for the inevitable onslaught. The act of holding the barrier drained her, but she forced herself to endure, drawing on every reserve of energy. She desperately needed every precious moment to recover and prepare for the next wave of attack, aware that the safety of the Elvendon army rested on her shoulders.

The next wave of King Iwein's soldiers pressed forward, undeterred by the bodies of their fallen comrades scattered across the battlefield. Driven by duty and the fear of their king's wrath, they advanced with grim determination, forging a relentless path directly towards Kaitlin. Within moments, a tight formation of archers moved swiftly to her side, forming a protective barrier around her. Their presence provided a crucial shield, readying themselves to defend their queen against the renewed threat bearing down upon her.

Kaitlin, breathless and straining beneath the weight of her magic, looked up at the loyal archers who had formed a protective ring around her. Her eyes glowed an intense white, a sign of the immense power surging through her as she struggled to maintain the barrier shielding her forces.

"I'm sorry, I can't protect you as well," she said, her voice heavy with regret and exhaustion.

One of the archers met her gaze without hesitation. "We know, my Queen," he replied steadfastly, his tone resolute and unwavering in the face of danger.

Another archer stepped forward, his voice steady and filled with devotion. "My Queen, we are prepared to die for you," he declared. His words resonated with the unshakeable loyalty of the archers, their dedication shining through even in the face of overwhelming danger. Each archer's commitment was clear— they stood ready to make the ultimate sacrifice to protect their queen and their people, their resolve unwavering as the threat loomed ever closer.

"Please, don't," Kaitlin urged softly, her words heavy with emotion. The archer, understanding the gravity of the moment, simply nodded in acknowledgment of her plea.

The archers moved swiftly, positioning themselves in a protective ring around Kaitlin while also stretching out along the front line of her soldiers. Their formation was disciplined, each archer standing shoulder to shoulder, ready to defend their queen and comrades against the advancing enemy. With bows raised and arrows notched, they awaited the crucial command.

At the signal from their lead soldier—his voice ringing clear and decisive—every archer released their arrow in perfect unison. The missiles soared high across the battlefield, their flight a testament to the archers' unwavering skill and coordination. As the arrows descended, they rained down upon the front ranks of the Aranstream soldiers, striking with deadly precision and disrupting their advance.

As the first line of Aranstream soldiers advanced, they dropped to one knee and raised their shields in perfect synchrony. The hail of arrows loosed by Kaitlin's archers struck with force—some found their mark, but many glanced off the polished metal, deflecting harmlessly aside. The disciplined shield wall blunted much of the initial assault, creating a formidable barrier against the Elvendon archers' deadly volley.

Without missing a beat, the second rank of Aranstream Elves responded. Rising from behind their shielded comrades, they drew their bows and unleashed a fierce barrage of arrows. The missiles soared through the air in a relentless wave, raining down upon Kaitlin's soldiers and those she had sworn to protect. The counterattack was swift and merciless, testing the resolve and defensive preparations of Kaitlin's forces as they braced against the incoming storm of arrows.

At the decisive cry of their leader—"Protect"—the archers sprang into action. Without hesitation, they formed a solid barrier around Kaitlin, using their own bodies and sturdy shields to shield her from harm. The archers' unwavering loyalty manifested in their readiness to face danger head-on, each one prioritising the safety of their queen above all else.

As the enemy arrows began to fall, Kaitlin watched in anguish as some of her protectors were struck. Nevertheless, she maintained her magical force field, ensuring that the majority of the arrows were deflected. The barrier shimmered with power, rebounding the deadly missiles and saving the lives of those within its reach. Kaitlin's inner turmoil was unmistakable—she wept silently for those who had been wounded, but her resolve remained unbroken as she continued to shield the others with every ounce of strength she could muster.

Consumed by rage following the tragic death of his sons at the hands of the witch, King Iwein surged forward through the ranks of his elves, driven by a singular purpose. His anger was marked for Kaitlin. His eyes burning with vengeance as he pressed towards her, undeterred by the chaos erupting on the battlefield.

Determined to counter the witch's dark sorcery, King Iwein resolved to meet her magic with his own. The intensity of his resolve was unmistakable; he would not be satisfied until retribution was exacted for his lost heirs. With a chilling promise, King Iwein declared his intent to leave no survivors, vowing to bring ruin upon every last member of the Elvendon clan. His threat hung in the air, a dire warning of the devastation he intended to unleash.

Kaitlin peered through the ranks of her archers and caught sight of King Iwein striding inexorably towards her. The shimmering barrier she had conjured quivered, its strength waning as exhaustion began to take its toll. With mounting urgency, Kaitlin steeled herself, mentally preparing to muster another surge of magic towards the Aranstream army.

In the meantime, her archers responded with disciplined precision. As one, they stepped back, swiftly nocking fresh arrows to their bows. With practised coordination, they loosed another volley at the advancing king. The arrows sailed through the air towards King Iwein, only to be met by the swift reaction of his loyal elves. In perfect formation, they raised their shields, creating an impenetrable bulwark that sheltered their sovereign. Undeterred, King Iwein pressed on, his determination undiminished as he continued his relentless approach towards Kaitlin.

"Shit," Kaitlin swore, her eyes widening as she noticed the surge of magic gathering in King Iwein's hands. The imminent threat forced her into a critical decision. She could lower her protective shield to focus on safeguarding herself and the archers closest to her, but doing so would expose her remaining army to the full force of his magic. The risk was clear: by protecting those at her side, she might inadvertently allow the vengeful king to redirect his attack towards her vulnerable soldiers. Torn between her own safety and the welfare of her troops, Kaitlin hesitated, fully aware of the potential consequences her choice might bring.

Chapter Thirty-Two
Keltor and the Dragons

Suddenly, a thunderous boom reverberated across the battlefield, drawing every eye skyward. The clouds above churned violently before parting to reveal a swirling portal, crackling with energy. From this rift in the sky, a colossal dragon erupted, its enormous green wings slicing through the air as it swooped down towards the assembled Aranstream soldiers. The beast's fiery red underbelly glowed ominously, casting a menacing light upon the stunned ranks below. Its arrival struck terror into the hearts of the enemy, as the sheer scale and power of the creature became unmistakably clear. As the colossal beast soared above, ominous flames flickering from its powerful jaws, panic gripped the enemy soldiers. Overcome by fear, they faltered and began to withdraw, stumbling back through their own lines in a desperate attempt to escape the creature's menacing presence.

Kaitlin stood transfixed, her heart pounding in her chest as she gazed skyward. Relief and disbelief mingled within her as she recognised the figure seated atop the mighty dragon—it was her King. In that moment, hope surged through her, even as the chaos of the battlefield raged on around them. Kaitlin's voice rang out, trembling with disbelief as she called, "Keltor!" Overcome with emotion at the sight of him alive and astride the mighty dragon, tears welled up in her eyes. The sense of hope and reassurance that his arrival brought was almost too much to bear after the chaos and peril she had just endured.

With renewed courage, Kaitlin allowed the magical shield protecting her people to dissipate, lowering it so she could step forward from behind the protective line of her archers. Eager for a clear view of Keltor, she moved out into the open, her gaze fixed on him as the dragon swooped closer.

The great beast responded to its rider's guidance, banking sharply to the right as it drew nearer to Kaitlin's position, its massive wings stirring the air and casting a formidable shadow across the battlefield.

The Elvendon soldiers, momentarily overcome by the awe and uncertainty brought by the dragon's dramatic arrival, began to hesitate and step back, their previous discipline wavering. In that charged instant, a voice sounded within Kaitlin's mind—a voice that resonated with warmth and familiarity, addressing her with profound respect: "*My Queen.*"

Kaitlin paused mid-step, her heart catching as she recognised the presence reaching out to her. She moved forward purposefully, scanning the horizon. "*Kailan?*" she called out, her brow furrowing as she glanced towards the sun, searching for the source of the voice. When the reply came, Kaitlin's expression softened into a small, relieved smile.

"*Yes, my Queen, we are here. Apologies we are late,*" the dragon's voice assured her, carrying both strength and humility in its tone.

As panic rippled through the ranks and her soldiers began to fall back, Kaitlin's voice rang out, clear and commanding above the chaos. "No, stand your ground! The dragon is with us!" she shouted, her words halting the retreat as the soldiers hesitated, casting anxious glances at one another in search of reassurance. Sensing their uncertainty, Kaitlin pressed on, determination burning in her eyes. "Your King rides this dragon!" she called, her gaze lifting with pride towards Keltor, whose presence atop the mighty beast was both a beacon of hope and a rallying point for her beleaguered army.

"Get back in line!" Commander Talbot commanded, his voice ringing out sharply across the chaos of the battlefield as he struggled to maintain order among his troops. His gaze was irresistibly drawn skyward, heart thundering in his chest as he tried to comprehend the spectacle unfolding above. Awe and disbelief swept through him—never in his life had he imagined that dragons truly existed, let alone witnessed one soaring overhead. The sight of Keltor astride the mighty dragon was almost too extraordinary to fathom.

Galvanised by their commander's urgent call, the Elvendon soldiers hurriedly returned to formation. Their long, slender swords were drawn and held at the ready, the metal gleaming in the shifting light as they stood to attention, prepared to face whatever might come next.

Keltor gazed down at Kaitlin, his chest swelling with pride and emotion. The sight of her standing boldly at the forefront, leading her people against the formidable King of Aranstream, was almost overwhelming. Surrounding her, a dazzling array of magic shimmered—an aura of rainbows that seemed to pulse with her strength and determination. To Keltor, it was the most captivating and enchanting vision he had ever witnessed, a testament to Kaitlin's courage and the indomitable spirit she inspired in those around her.

Another magnificent dragon burst through the opening. This striking creature possessed vibrant green wings and a belly that glowed with a fiery orange hue, its scales shimmering as it descended gracefully towards the battlefield. Sharelle, caught off guard by the sight, slowly rose to her feet, her astonishment evident in her wide-eyed gaze. "Ayver?" she uttered, her voice trembling as she struggled to comprehend the vision before her— her loyal dragon, who she hadn't seen since returning to Elvendon before Keltor was even born, now soaring down to her side. The familiar warmth of Ayver's presence filled her mind as the dragon's gentle, affectionate voice resonated within her thoughts: "*Sharelle, I have missed you.*"

Overcome by emotion, Sharelle's disbelief gave way to tears. "*By the stars, Ayver,*" she wept, barely able to contain her joy and relief at being reunited with her beloved companion.

Suddenly, another dragon burst through the clouds above. This one was even larger than the others, its mighty wings shimmering with the same vibrant green as Ayver's, but its belly burned with

685

a fiery red glow. The sight was breathtaking, and the air seemed to tremble with the power of its arrival.

At the appearance of the magnificent creature, Sharelle's emotions surged. She clutched her husband's arm, her eyes wide with a mixture of shock and delight. "Forde!" she exclaimed, her voice ringing with surprise and joy as she recognised the dragon.

Forde, too, was caught off guard. He stared upwards, disbelief mingling with excitement as the dragon descended. "Erandril?" he murmured, barely daring to trust his eyes as his heart raced. In that instant, a powerful wave of emotion swept through him—a shock that seemed to resonate in every part of his being as the deep, long-lost connection to his dragon was suddenly restored.

Within his mind, Forde heard the familiar, affectionate voice of Erandril. "*Forde, my friend, I have missed you,*" the dragon said, his thoughts warm and unwavering.

Overcome with emotion, Forde responded in kind, unable to tear his eyes from the majestic form settling on the ground before him. "*And I you, my friend,*" he replied, watching as Erandril landed gracefully, their bond rekindled in that extraordinary moment.

As the three dragons descended from the sky, their enormous forms touched down with such force that the earth itself seemed to tremble beneath their weight. The ground thundered with the impact, echoing across the battlefield and drawing the attention of all present. Each dragon came to a halt directly before the assembled Aranstream soldiers, their imposing figures forming a formidable barrier between the hostile force and the King of Aranstream.

As Keltor slid off Kailan's back, Kaitlin rushed towards him, unable to contain her relief and joy. Tears streamed down her face as she embraced him tightly. "My god, Keltor, I thought I had lost you," she sobbed, clinging to him as if afraid he might disappear once more. In response, Keltor kissed her deeply, his gesture filled with passion, love and the overwhelming relief of their reunion.

He gently pulled away, his eyes meeting hers. "No, I made you a promise," he assured her, his voice steady and reassuring. "I'm so sorry I took so long," Keltor continued, a warm smile crossing his face, "but I had to get the help of a few friends."

Kaitlin's breath caught as she looked at him in disbelief. "I can't believe you brought the dragons here," she said, her voice filled with wonder and astonishment at the sight of the mighty creatures now gathered on the battlefield.

Keltor gazed at her with pride, recognising her strength and courage. "You did all this, you held them back?" he asked, admiration clear in his tone. Kaitlin nodded, her determination evident, as she stood firm in the face of adversity.

"Yes, my magic, it's so powerful now," Kaitlin declared, her voice brimming with newfound confidence. She reached out, drawing Keltor into her embrace once more, holding him tightly as if to reassure herself he was truly there. The shock of the moment lingered, and she gazed at him with wonder. "How on earth did you get Kailan, and these dragons?" she exclaimed, still struggling to comprehend the sight of him accompanied by such mighty creatures.

Keltor turned his attention towards the dragons, his eyes reflecting both pride and gratitude for the allies now at their side.

"I'll tell you later," he said, offering her a reassuring smile. Relief washed over him, knowing she was safe and that he was there, ready to protect her—as he always had been and always would be.

King Iwein stood motionless, his gaze locked on the dragons before him. Then, his eyes shifted to Keltor and Kaitlin as they embraced. Fury twisted his features, and he cursed them quietly under his breath.

Keltor gently released Kaitlin from his embrace. "I think it's time we ended this and take back our Queendom," he declared.

She laughed, a lightness breaking the tension. "What?" he asked, smiling in response to her laughter.

"You said Queendom, and not Kingdom," she replied, amusement and pride mingling in her voice.

His hand lifted to her face, cradling her gently. "Well, it is yours, Kitcat, and you are our Queen," he said with conviction.

687

She drew in a deep breath and gave him a determined nod, their resolve now united.

He turned, Kaitlin steadfastly at his side, and together they advanced towards the frontline. A hush fell over the field as all eyes fixed on their steady approach. The gathered armies watched in suspense, united briefly by uncertainty as the pair advanced. Every movement seemed amplified in the quiet, broken only by the faint clink of armour and the measured tread across the earth. Even the dragons remained still, their powerful forms alert and observant, taking in every detail. For a moment, the battle itself seemed suspended, the outcome hanging in the silence as everyone waited to see what would unfold next.

Keltor's voice rang out, clear and commanding, as he addressed King Iwein directly. "King Iwein," he called, ensuring all assembled could hear. The King's attention snapped to him.

"There is no need for any more bloodshed," Keltor declared, his tone resolute and unwavering. "You cannot win against us. I am a wizard, and our Queen—as you have seen—is powerful in magic. We have three dragons at our command." As he spoke, he extended his left hand, gesturing pointedly towards the mighty creatures that now stood in solidarity with them, a visible testament to their formidable strength and unity.

Kaitlin stepped forward, leaving the safety of Keltor's protective embrace, her voice carrying clear across the battlefield. "Please," she implored, her tone earnest and filled with emotion. "We only want peace between our lands; there is no need for this. There is no need for anyone else to die."

Turning her attention to the assembled soldiers, Kaitlin raised her voice so all could hear. "Soldiers, I implore you, lay down your arms and join us in Elvendon. Let us unite and live together in peace, as we once did. I know many of you have family and friends in Elvendon—do you truly want them all to die?"

She paused, her gaze sweeping over the anxious faces before her. "Do you wish to live in a kingdom ruled by fear?" Kaitlin pressed on, determined to reach their hearts. "I am Kaitlin, Queen of Elvendon, and my husband, Keltor, is the King of Elvendon.

Together, we offer you a Queendom—" she glanced at Keltor, who gave her an encouraging smile, "—where you can live in peace, united together."

Kaitlin took a measured step forward, her gaze unwavering as she addressed the assembled soldiers. Her voice rang out, clear and compelling, as she confronted the reality of their allegiance. "How many of you are standing here today out of genuine love and respect for your King?" she called, her words resonating across the tense silence. "And how many of you are here out of fear—because your King threatens you and your families if you refuse to obey?"

A heavy silence settled over the field as her question lingered in the air. Kaitlin's words challenged each soldier to reflect on their true motivations and the future they wished to secure. Gradually, uncertainty began to ripple through the ranks. The soldiers exchanged uneasy glances, their confidence visibly shaken as they looked between one another and towards their King. It was clear that for many, loyalty was born not of devotion, but of apprehension—especially faced with the looming threat of the dragons, whose presence made the cost of continued conflict all too real.

Keltor's attention was drawn to an unexpected disturbance from behind the ranks of Aranstream soldiers. He watched closely as a hooded figure astride a horse pushed their way through the mass of troops, steadily advancing towards King Iwein.

"Keltor, what's going on?" Kaitlin whispered urgently, her eyes fixed on the mysterious rider. "What's he carrying?"

Before Keltor could answer, a piercing cry rang out—a baby's wail, unmistakeable and chilling. The sound cut through the tension, and Kaitlin's face twisted in horror as realisation dawned. "Oh god, no," she cried, her voice trembling as she instinctively stepped forward, desperate to see more clearly.

"Kaitlin, it can't be," Keltor whispered, moving to stand beside her, his own disbelief evident. "How, how did they get him? Who would do this, who would betray us like this?"

Desperation edged Kaitlin's reply. "I don't know, Keltor," she said, her voice fraught with anguish and uncertainty.

King Iwein approached, the bundle in his arms taken from the mysterious rider who had pushed through the Aranstream ranks. Even at a distance, the malicious satisfaction was evident on his face, his smirk betraying a sense of triumph and cruelty as he advanced towards Kaitlin and Keltor. The sight of the King, so brazen and unfeeling, stirred a deep and uncontrollable fury within Keltor. He struggled to master his emotions, clenching his hands tightly in an attempt to contain the surge of energy and anger threatening to overwhelm him.

King Iwein's voice thundered across the field, his words heavy with accusation and malice. "So, tell me Queen of Elvendon, Queen of the people, would you sacrifice this child for the greater good of your people!" he shouted, making his challenge clear to all assembled.

He proceeded to unwrap the swaddling from the infant, exposing the baby to the gathered crowd. Holding the child aloft, King Iwein paraded him before his army. The reaction was mixed—while some soldiers cheered, swept up by the spectacle, many others gazed on in shock and dismay, deeply unsettled by the King's ruthless display.

Kaitlin, torn between her duty to her people and her compassion for the innocent, leaned towards Keltor and whispered desperately, "Keltor, what do I do?" The dilemma weighed heavily upon her: she could not allow the baby to die, yet surrendering to King Iwein's demands was equally unthinkable.

Erandril unleashed a deafening roar, the sheer force of it driving the Aranstream soldiers to their knees, their faces contorted with terror. The sound reverberated across the battlefield, underscoring the dragons' overwhelming power and presence. Yet, even as fear rippled through his ranks, King Iwein stood his ground, clutching the infant defiantly in his arms. Raising his voice to be heard above the chaos, he shouted, "Your dragons cannot harm me, or they will kill this baby!" His words

690

rang out as both a threat and a challenge, making it clear that any action against him would place the child in mortal danger.

As the tension mounted among the Aranstream ranks, the soldiers looked on in disbelief at the unfolding scene. A voice rang out from within their midst, a soldier daring to question the King's sanity: "He's gone mad," the man uttered, his words cutting through the charged atmosphere.

Without hesitation, King Iwein reacted to the dissident voice among his ranks. In a swift, chilling motion, he removed one hand from the baby and unleashed a bolt of magic that crackled through the air. The arc of power struck the soldier who had dared to question him, the force of the spell so potent that the man's body disintegrated instantly before the stunned onlookers. Shock rippled through the surrounding soldiers, who recoiled in horror at the ruthless display of the King's power, their faces betraying fear and disbelief at the fate that had befallen their comrade.

"I too am powerful in magic; I may not have dragons, but I am the King of Aranstream, and I will not surrender to a half breed!"

Kaitlin's rage was unmistakable as King Iwein openly derided her before all those gathered, his taunts sharp and dripping with scorn. The insult to her dignity was wounding, but it was the sight of Alana's infant child, held hostage and threatened in his grasp, that truly pushed her to breaking point. Her anger, already simmering, flared within her, awakening the dormant magic she bore. With each steady breath, Kaitlin sensed the energy of the land—the very grass beneath her feet—rising up, flowing into her and fuelling the gathering tempest of magic within. The strength of her emotion became tangible; her eyes blazed with a brilliant white light, a clear sign of the formidable power she was ready to release.

Turning to Keltor at her side, she spoke quietly but firmly, "Keltor, I've had enough of this king."

"Me too," Keltor replied, reaching out to take her hand. She gripped his hand tightly, drawing strength from his presence.

"Destroy," her husband said, meeting her gaze.

"Protect," Kaitlin responded with a nod of affirmation. In that silent exchange, they both understood what was required of them.

Together, they faced King Iwein, lifting their free hands in unison. They began to chant, their eyes both aflame with magical intensity—Kaitlin's shining white as the energy surged up from the earth, Keltor's turning the deepest black as the amulet's magic ignited within him. In perfect synchrony, they unleashed a colossal beam of swirling, crackling energy towards King Iwein.

"*Praesidio,*" Kaitlin intoned, her voice resonant with command.

With unwavering determination, Keltor intoned, "*Perdere,*" his voice ringing clear and resolute through the air. The power in his words seemed to reverberate, amplifying the intensity of the moment.

In perfect accord, Keltor and Kaitlin advanced together, their movements synchronised as they pressed forward against King Iwein. United in purpose and resolve, they embodied the strength and unity that the dire circumstances demanded.

Sharelle's voice trembled with disbelief as she cried out, "What the hell is going on?" Her eyes darted between her son and the Queen, unable to comprehend the spectacle before her.

Standing nearby, Forde tried to offer some explanation. "It's the magic from the amulet," he said, his tone filled with uncertainty. "He must be wearing it."

But Sharelle's confusion only deepened. "And Kaitlin, the Queen, how is she doing this? Where does her magic come from?" she demanded, seeking answers that seemed just beyond reach.

Keltor's mother, her voice barely above a whisper, looked to Forde for reassurance. He met her gaze, but his reply was laced with awe and apprehension. "I don't know, Sharelle. I truly don't know. It's more than elder magic, that I do know."

The soldiers surrounding King Iwein recoiled in haste, stepping back as he was enveloped by swirling currents of white and black energy. The spectacle was both terrifying and awe-inspiring, as the very air seemed to crackle with raw magical power. Slowly, King Iwein's body began to rise from the ground, suspended helplessly in the grasp of the opposing forces. The King and Queen of Elvendon, united in purpose, held him in stasis, their combined magic manifesting in the shifting vortex that imprisoned him.

With unwavering resolve, Kaitlin intoned, *"Praesidio,"* her voice carrying the force of her protective magic through the stillness. Simultaneously, Keltor called out, *"Perdere,"* his tone firm and resolute, channelling the destructive power of the amulet. Together, their voices resonated in harmony, amplifying the intensity of the magic that bound the king, marking a pivotal moment in the confrontation.

King Iwein held the baby aloft, his arm trembling with desperation as he attempted to summon his magic. He strained to utter an incantation, but no words escaped his lips; his power faltered at the crucial moment, leaving him vulnerable and exposed.

Sensing the pivotal instant, Kaitlin turned to Keltor, catching his gaze. For a fleeting moment, their eyes met, a silent understanding passing between them. Kaitlin offered a determined nod, and Keltor returned it, their resolve mutual and unwavering.

In perfect unison, they unleashed their magic. Kaitlin's voice rang out, strong and commanding, *"Praesidio, protect!"* At that exact moment, Keltor's voice echoed hers, equally forceful, *"Perdere, destroy!"* Their incantations intertwined, a harmonious blend of protection and destruction, as their combined power surged forth towards the King and the helpless child suspended above.

A deafening explosion suddenly erupted, sending shockwaves across the battlefield. Instinctively, both the Aranstream and Elvendon armies ducked for cover, shielding themselves from the blast. When the dust and echoes subsided, all eyes turned to the centre of the chaos, only to find that King Iwein had vanished without a trace.

Suspended high above the stunned soldiers, the baby could be seen enclosed in a shimmering protective bubble, floating serenely amidst the lingering tension. The magical sphere held the child safely out of harm's reach, a clear testament to the powerful enchantments at play.

Kaitlin, her composure unwavering, extended her hand and uttered, "*Praesidio.*" A gentle smile touched her lips as she guided the bubble closer, drawing the baby safely towards herself and Keltor.

Silence settled across the battlefield, a profound hush falling over both armies as they witnessed the miraculous sight before them. Every eye was fixed on the child, whose small form floated gently through the air towards Keltor and Kaitlin, encased in a shimmering magical bubble. The collective disbelief was overwhelming; no one dared to speak, each person transfixed by the extraordinary moment unfolding before them. The scene was charged with tension and awe, as every witness struggled to comprehend the magnitude of what had just occurred. Soldiers, commanders, and onlookers alike found themselves unable to break the silence, their eyes fixed on the magical events at the heart of the battlefield. In that suspended instant, the air seemed to hold its breath, the weight of astonishment pressing down on all present and binding them together in shared wonder.

With steady composure, Kaitlin carefully lowered the baby, guiding him towards her husband's open arms. A grateful smile passed between them, their relief and triumph unspoken but deeply felt.

Keltor gazed down at the baby, his features softening with affection. "Hey, little man, how are you doing?" he whispered, his voice tender as he pressed a gentle kiss to the baby's forehead. To his immense relief, the baby—Logie—appeared unharmed by the ordeal. Keltor tucked Logie securely inside his shirt, ensuring he was warm and safe, holding him close as the tension of the battle slowly began to ebb away.

Kaitlin turned her attention to the Aranstream army, her posture straightening as she faced the defeated ranks. Gradually, a wave of submission spread through the soldiers; one by one, they fell to their knees, the gesture rippling outward until nearly all had bowed before her. Drawing in a steadying breath, Kaitlin strode purposefully towards King Iwein's second-in-command, the weight of the moment pressing upon her shoulders.

As she advanced, Kaitlin sensed movement behind her. Glancing over her shoulder, she saw Belrack accompanied by his loyal troops, standing as silent support at her back. The sight brought a smile to her lips, which Belrack acknowledged with a respectful nod.

When Kaitlin reached the man kneeling before her, she addressed him with a calm yet unwavering tone, her voice resonating across the quieted battlefield. "Do you surrender to Elvendon?" she asked, ensuring that every soldier present could hear her words.

The Aranstream commander looked up at her, his gaze shifting momentarily to Belrack and his men, whose spears were now pointed downwards in a gesture of readiness. He then glanced at the soldiers on either side of him, clearly weighing his decision with great reluctance. As his eyes lingered on the dragons poised nearby, their presence a silent but formidable warning, he finally nodded in acceptance.

"Yes, we surrender to Elvendon," the commander replied, his voice heavy with resignation. With deliberate care, he laid his sword at Kaitlin's feet, a symbolic gesture of defeat and submission.

As Kaitlin surveyed the defeated Aranstream army, a cold knot twisted in her stomach. The knowledge that some of these men had committed unspeakable acts against her people—especially those responsible for the innocent children found hanging just days before—filled her with a raw, aching grief that simmered beneath her collected exterior. Rage and sorrow warred within her, mingling with a desperate longing for justice. She could feel the weight of every loss, every cry for mercy unheard, pressing upon her heart. Though her face remained composed, inside she battled with the enormity of what had been done, and what she must now do. Kaitlin knew she could not allow such heinous crimes to go unanswered; the thought of letting the murderers walk free was intolerable. The demand for justice—both for her people and her own conscience—burned fiercely within her, steeling her resolve as she prepared to face those responsible.

"I want all the high-ranking commanders to stand," Kaitlin ordered, her voice steady but commanding, echoing across the tense field. Her gaze then narrowed as she pointed to the man partially hidden behind a horse. "And you," she said sharply, "step forward and remove your hood."

The battlefield was silent except for the distant whinny of horses and the low moan of the wind stirring through the grass, every eye fixed on the figure emerging from the shadows. The man hesitated, a flicker of fear crossing his features. His hands trembled uncontrollably as he moved into the open, each step heavy with reluctance. Slowly, he reached up, fingers quivering, and pushed back his hood, revealing a face etched with anxiety, his eyes darting nervously towards Kaitlin and the assembled soldiers.

As the hood fell away, Kaitlin's eyes widened in shock. "Shona?" she cried in disbelief, realising that the figure before her was not a man at all, but Esimae's friend. Her voice trembled with anger and hurt as she confronted her. "How could you betray us like this?" Kaitlin demanded, her words cutting through the tense silence on the battlefield.

Shona stared at Kaitlin defiantly, her voice ringing out with bitter resolve. "I honour my King, not a half breed!" she declared, her words heavy with contempt and unwavering loyalty to King Iwein.

Kaitlin's anger surged, her voice rising as she faced Shona. "You honour a man that kills children!" she screamed, the pain and fury of recent losses evident in her words. The accusation hung heavy in the air, drawing the gaze of both Aranstream and Elvendon soldiers alike. She fixed Shona with a piercing stare, seeking any sign of remorse or shame.

Undeterred, Kaitlin pressed further, her tone sharp and unyielding. "Did you tell them where we were when they ambushed us?" she demanded, the memory of betrayal and its consequences fresh in her mind.

696

Shona's response was immediate and defiant, her eyes flashing with unrepentant conviction. "Yes, and I would do it again!" she snapped back, her loyalty to King Iwein unwavering despite the horrors committed. The admission sent another ripple of shock and outrage through the ranks, deepening the sense of division and betrayal that now threatened to fracture the fragile peace on the field.

Kaitlin's gaze locked onto Shona, a storm of emotion churning behind her eyes. Stepping forward, she spoke with a voice that quivered with both grief and righteous fury. "Shona, I trusted you. Esimae trusted you. After everything we've suffered, after all the pain King Iwein's soldiers have inflicted—how could you stand among those who murder children and call it loyalty?" Her words cut through the murmurs on the field, her heartbreak and anger laid bare for all to witness.

Shona straightened, chin raised in defiance. "I did what I believed was right. My loyalty is to my king—always."

Kaitlin shook her head, her disappointment and sorrow etching deep lines in her face. "There is no honour in following a king who murders innocent people for the price for power." She gestured sharply, her voice now unyielding. "Go join the others. You will answer for your betrayal—and for every life lost at your king's command."

A hush fell over the battlefield, the magnitude of Kaitlin's words reverberating through soldiers and traitors alike as Shona moved to stand with the condemned, her defiance flickering uncertainly in the shadow of the Queen's wrath.

Kaitlin stood firm as Keltor approached, his concern evident in his voice as he questioned her actions. "Kaitlin, what are you doing?" he asked, joining her side.

She met his gaze, her expression set with determination. "They need to be punished, Keltor," she replied. "They cannot be trusted to live."

Keltor reached out, his hand gently resting on Kaitlin's arm as he spoke with quiet insistence. "Kaitlin, this is not for you to do," he said, his concern for her evident in both gesture and tone.

Kaitlin's response was resolute, her voice firm and unwavering as she met his gaze. "Keltor, I must. If I do not show my strength now, they will see me as a weak Queen. It will only be a matter of time before they seek a new leader and rise against us. I cannot, and I will not allow people like this to do such things to anyone else."

Keltor nodded, acknowledging her reasoning. "No, I know, and I agree," he replied, "but let me do it." His tone was earnest, offering to take on the burden himself.

Refusing to yield, Kaitlin stood her ground. "Keltor, no, I can do this," she replied firmly, conviction clear in her voice.

Keltor met Kaitlin's gaze, his voice steady and resolved. "I know you can, but I am the destroyer, Kaitlin. You are the protector. I can open a portal and send them to your equivalent of hell."

Surprise flickered across Kaitlin's face as she questioned him, "A portal, but how?" She paused, then added, "Is that what you and the dragons came through?"

He nodded. "Yes, I opened a portal from where we were, to you. Look, something strange happened to me—I met Marton. Do you remember? Mum told us about him, the wizard who trained Dad," he explained, his words measured and serious.

Kaitlin's brow furrowed as she recalled the stories. "Yes, I remember, but surely he would have passed on by now?"

"He has... sort of. It was surreal, really. He was in a place he called the world between worlds, and he did this to me." Keltor opened his shirt, revealing a mark on his chest. "It's my father's amulet. The wizard put it inside my soul, so its magic and power are now part of me."

With gentle concern, Kaitlin lifted her hand to his chest, her fingers brushing lightly against the mark left by the amulet. "Oh my god, Keltor, did it hurt?" she asked, her eyes searching his for the truth.

He gave a shrug. "A little, but it was worth it. I will tell you everything that happened later," he said, glancing to the Aranstream men, and then back to her, "but in the short, I can

698

harness its power at my will. I can open a portal Kaitlin and send them all through it."

"To where?" she asked, her voice low with both curiosity and apprehension.

Keltor's expression darkened as he replied, "There is a place, an unspeakable place full of darkness and horror. It will be their punishment, and to be honest, they will probably wish they were dead."

Kaitlin's eyes narrowed slightly as she pressed further, her curiosity piqued by Keltor's mysterious understanding. "How do you know of this place?" she asked, her tone both probing and cautious.

Keltor paused, taking a moment to find the right words. There was a subtle uncertainty in his expression as he searched for an explanation that eluded him. "I really don't know, I just do," he confessed, honesty resonating in his voice. Recalling a shared experience, he added, "You remember what you said yesterday, when you healed me, that you just know instinctively?"

Kaitlin nodded in recognition, her understanding unmistakable. In that instant, she fully comprehended the very sensation Keltor had described—a deep, inexplicable certainty that seemed to arise from nowhere. The experience was not just one of similarity, but of shared perspective, forging a silent yet powerful connection between them. Without the need for words, both acknowledged that some truths simply appeared unbidden, carrying with them a sense of inevitability and assurance that defied explanation. This unspoken bond united them, grounding their relationship in a profound mutual understanding. In the midst of the surrounding turmoil and uncertainty, their extraordinary abilities set them apart, but it was this moment of realisation and acceptance that truly deepened their connection, offering a sense of solidarity and purpose as they faced the challenges unfolding around them.

"Well, it's the same for me," Keltor continued, his tone earnest. "The knowledge is just there." There was a gentle shift in his demeanour as he turned towards Kaitlin, the intensity of their previous exchange giving way to a softer moment. Carefully, he cradled the baby in his arms before holding him out to her. "Here, take Logie for me," he requested softly, his words carrying both trust and tenderness.

Kaitlin accepted the child, pulling him gently to her chest. With her hand, she lifted and supported the baby's head, cradling him securely. As she rocked him softly, her actions were instinctive, providing comfort and protection to Logie. The tenderness in her movements served as a quiet counterpoint to the gravity of the events unfolding around them, offering solace and safety to the infant even as uncertainty and apprehension lingered in the air.

The wind whipped around Keltor, lifting his cloak and tousling his hair as he strode with purpose towards the assembled men. His determination was evident in every step, the resolute set of his shoulders signalling his intent. Despite the swirling gusts, Keltor pressed forward unfalteringly, his gaze locked on the group before him. The intensity of the moment was heightened by the elemental force, as if the very air itself responded to his resolve. As he approached, a voice echoed in his mind—Kailan, his dragon, communicating with him telepathically. "*My Lord, what are you doing, do you wish me to burn them?*" Kailan inquired, his tone edged with readiness for action. Keltor glanced towards his loyal companion and gave a slight shake of his head.

"*No, instant death is too good for them, Kailan,*" Keltor replied in his thoughts, his gaze hardening. "*I'm going to send them somewhere where they will be punished for a very long time.*"

Turning his attention to the crowd, Keltor's eyes searched the assembled faces until he spotted his brother. Raising his hand, he beckoned for Esendil to join him. Without hesitation, Esendil moved purposefully through the gathered onlookers, weaving between them until he stood firmly at Keltor's side.

Keltor then turned to his brother, his voice low but filled with determination. "Brother, do you see the men that took Marcus amongst these?" he asked, gesturing towards the cluster of men before them. The gravity of the moment was clear in his tone, signalling the seriousness with which Keltor approached the task of identifying those responsible.

700

Esendil carefully scanned the group before him, his gaze settling on several individuals as he tried to recall the faces of those responsible. The weight of the situation was evident in the silence that fell between the two brothers, each understanding the significance of this moment.

After a tense pause, Esendil nodded, his expression solemn. "Yes, it was those four who took Markus and the others," he declared with certainty. He extended his hand and pointed unambiguously to four of the men standing in the line before them, ensuring there was no mistake in his identification.

With this confirmation, Esendil then shifted his attention towards the larger crowd of Aranstream soldiers, many of whom remained kneeling in submission. His actions underscored the gravity of the accusation and the seriousness with which the brother's approached justice for Markus and the others.

Esendil's eyes narrowed as he scanned the faces before him. With a firm gesture, he pointed out another individual among the soldiers. "And him," he added, directing Keltor's attention to a specific figure within the group.

Keltor followed his brother's indication, his gaze settling on the man in question. "You are sure?" he asked, seeking confirmation before proceeding.

Esendil nodded with certainty. "Yes, check him if you like. He has a tattoo on his left arm—a skull," he explained, providing a distinctive detail to ensure there could be no mistake in identifying the culprit.

Keltor accepted this information with a nod. "Okay," he replied, his resolve unwavering.

Esendil's concern broke through the tension, his voice tinged with urgency. "Keltor, can you ask him where Marcus is? He wasn't in the dungeons or in the encampment, before you, well, you know, kill him or whatever you're going to do."

Keltor's heart grew heavy at his brother's request, the weight of what he had to reveal pressing upon him. With a sorrowful glance, he turned to Esendil, his resolve faltering momentarily.

Keltor drew a steadying breath and spoke softly, his eyes locking with those of his brother. "Ese," he said, his voice barely above a whisper. The sorrow clouding Keltor's gaze was unmistakable, conveying a truth that needed no words. Esendil, sensing the gravity of the moment, asked the question he dreaded, his voice unsteady with emotion. "He's dead, isn't he?"

With a slow, mournful nod, Keltor confirmed Esendil's worst fears. His words were laden with grief. "Ese, I'm so sorry. We found him on our way to the encampment. I didn't want to tell you like this—I was hoping to find a gentler way."

Esendil fought back his sudden tears, as he fixed his gaze upon the man standing before them, his expression twisting with fury. The weight of grief bore down upon him, mingling with a surge of anger that contorted his features. Though sorrow threatened to overwhelm him, Esendil refused to let it show, channelling the intensity of his emotions into a glare that left no doubt of his pain and rage. He stood resolute, refusing to look away, his eyes locked on the culprit as he struggled to contain the torrent of feelings within. "Kill him," he demanded of his brother, his voice low and edged with anger.

Keltor's expression hardened, and his voice took on a chilling edge. "I'm going to do worse than that," he responded flatly.

Esendil's anger flared, his tone sharp as he challenged his brother's words. "Worse? What's worse than killing someone?"

Without replying straightaway, Keltor extended his hand, resting it gently on Esendil's arm. The gesture, though simple, spoke volumes in the charged silence between them. His touch was steady and reassuring—a silent offer of solace amid the tumult of anger and grief swirling around them. In that moment, Keltor's intent was unmistakable: he sought to anchor his brother, to provide a brief island of comfort despite the heaviness of what lay ahead.

Keltor's jaw tightened as he gazed over the gathered Aranstream soldiers, the haunting memory of their fallen comrades stirring a cold fury within him. The loss, still raw and unyielding, fuelled the determination in his stance. His tone, grim

702

and resolute, was directed not only at his brother but at himself—a reminder of the duty he felt compelled to uphold.

"Believe me, where I'm sending these people, they'll wish they were dead." The words, laden with sorrow and vengeance, reflected the complex blend of emotions twisting within him. Each syllable carried the weight of their shared tragedy, a longing for justice that had become inseparable from their grief.

Esendil's eyes burned with anguish and fury, his knuckles whitening as he struggled to keep his composure. "Will they suffer there?" he asked, his tone brittle, desperate for some sense of retribution for Marcus and the others.

"Oh yes," Keltor replied, a bitterness underscoring his promise. The pain in his voice was matched only by the resolve in his eyes; this was not mere cruelty, but a punishment he believed their enemies deserved.

"Good," Esendil sneered, but the edge in his voice could not quite mask the sorrow behind it. He wanted those responsible for the atrocities at Elvendon to feel a fraction of the pain they had inflicted – perhaps it was the only way he could keep from breaking.

Keltor then turned his attention to one of the prisoners, his tone sharp with command. "You, stand and come here."

The man hesitated, his reluctance plain in every trembling movement. Fear flickered in his eyes as he slowly got to his feet. As he drew closer, he shot a glare at Esendil –defiance tightening his features. Keltor's voice cut through the tense air as he snapped, "Take your eyes off him!" sensing his brother nervously shifting behind him. Without hesitation, Keltor seized the man's left arm and yanked up his sleeve. As soon as the fabric slid back, the mark became visible—a skull tattoo, just as Esendil had described.

Leaning in close to his brother's ear, Esendil whispered, "They all have them." Keltor, momentarily puzzled, shot a questioning look over his shoulder. "Have what?" he asked quietly.

Esendil replied in a low voice, "The skull tattoos. Every one of those who beat and killed our soldiers at Aranstream bore this mark. They're part of a clan the prince calls his Death Walkers.

Essentially, they're assassins—men who carried out killings for the King and Prince, even targeting women and children."

Determined to uncover the true extent of their enemy, Keltor spoke with urgency. "We have to check every one of these men," he said, directing his attention to Kaitlin as she approached him purposefully.

Kaitlin, assessing the daunting task of examining each soldier individually, shook her head. "That will take too long," she replied, her gaze sweeping over the ranks of Aranstream soldiers arrayed before them. A glimmer of resolve appeared in her eyes as she added, "I have a faster way."

"Esendil, please can you hold Logie for a minute?" Kaitlin requested, her tone gentle but urgent as she turned to him. Esendil nodded in silent agreement, reaching out to take the baby from her arms. As Logie settled against his chest, Esendil's stern expression softened slightly, a faint smile tugging at the corners of his mouth despite the anger that still lingered in his eyes.

Without hesitation, Kaitlin drew back the sleeves of her cloak, preparing herself for what needed to be done. Facing the man before her, she spoke firmly, "Hold out your arm." The man, however, responded only with a dark scowl, his reluctance and defiance clear for all to see.

"The Queen said, hold out your arm," Keltor growled, seizing the man's arm and stretching it out. Kaitlin glanced at Keltor, a small smile tugging at her lips at how he addressed her. She pulled up his sleeve; the fabric rasped against his skin, and the tattoo's dark lines seemed to pulse under her touch. She placed her hand over the tattoo and closed her eyes.

With her hand still firmly pressed against the man's tattoo, Kaitlin began to chant, "*Quaerere hoc marcam.*" The words hung in the air, and the man flinched as a wave of heat from her magic radiated through the mark on his arm, causing him visible discomfort.

After a moment, Kaitlin opened her eyes, her attention shifting to Keltor. He watched her closely, curiosity etched on his face as he asked, "Okay?"

"Yes," Kaitlin confirmed, her voice calm yet assured. At her reply, Keltor released his grip on the man's arm, allowing the inspection to end. Instantly, the man yanked his arm back to his chest, cradling the angry-red tattoo as if to shield it from further scrutiny. His eyes narrowed, and he shot a glare of deep resentment directly at Kaitlin, his pride wounded and his hostility plain to see.

Keltor caught the man's offensive glare. In an instant, fury surged through him; his fist clenched tight and then snapped forward, striking the man squarely in the jaw. The force of the blow sent the soldier sprawling to the ground, his defiance abruptly silenced as he lay stunned and defeated at Keltor's feet. The man looked back up at him in shock, his mouth bleeding from where he'd been struck.

You young King's voice cut through the tense silence, his warning unmistakable. "Don't look at the Queen again," he growled, his eyes flashing with an intense, unwavering black. The effect was immediate—the man on the ground, cowed by the authority and menace in Keltor's tone, swiftly turned his face away, fear etched plainly in his features. The display of power left no doubt as to who commanded respect and obedience among the assembled ranks.

A moment lingered as Kaitlin's gaze rested on the man sprawled on the ground, then drifted to Keltor. A faint smile played on her lips, gratitude welling for his steadfast support— Keltor, always vigilant, ever her protector. Drawing strength from his presence, she composed herself and turned her focus to the daunting ranks of the Aranstream army stretched before her. No fewer than two thousand soldiers knelt upon the field, their posture rigid and backs straight, discipline radiating through their unmoving forms. A strange hush blanketed the troops, tension thick in the air, as every soldier held fast, faces carefully impassive, waiting for Kaitlin's next move.

Behind the ranks of the Aranstream army, a formidable force of five hundred Elvendon soldiers stood apart, having earlier split from their main contingent. This disciplined rearguard formed an unyielding barrier, their presence impossible to ignore. Standing shoulder to shoulder in an unwavering line, the Elvendon warriors remained alert, their eyes scanning the battlefield for any sign of movement or subterfuge.

Each soldier held their weapon at the ready, prepared to intercept any Aranstream troops who might attempt to escape amidst the confusion. Their strict formation was a clear deterrent, sending a silent but resolute message: no one would pass unnoticed. The vigilance with which the Elvendon rearguard maintained their station ensured that the Aranstream forces were contained, leaving no opportunity for evasion or retreat.

Kaitlin extended her hands towards the ground, her fingers brushing the earth as she prepared to wield her magic. Slowly, she lifted her arms, channelling power through her body as she began the incantation. "*Ostende mihi*," she intoned, her voice resonating with authority. With a deliberate, sweeping motion, Kaitlin cast her magic across the assembled ranks of the Aranstream army.

The effect was immediate and unmistakable. Across the field, soldiers began to rise to their feet, compelled by Kaitlin's spell. Involuntarily, each man raised one arm above his head. As Kaitlin watched closely, it became clear that every standing soldier bore the same distinctive skull tattoo on their arm. One after another, the marked men revealed themselves, the dark symbol stark against their skin. After several minutes had passed, it was evident that no one else would rise—those without the tattoo remained where they were, exposed by Kaitlin's magic for all to see.

Kaitlin surveyed the assembled soldiers, her gaze unwavering and filled with determination. With the tension in the air unmistakable, she took a steadying breath, allowing herself a moment to gather her strength and composure before addressing the marked men now revealed before her.

Standing tall and resolute, Kaitlin projected her voice, so it rang out clearly across the silent ranks. "All of you, that are standing up," she commanded, her words resonating with unmistakable authority. The marked soldiers reacted at once, compelled by the force in her tone. Kaitlin then gestured decisively towards the front line, ensuring there could be no confusion about her instructions. "Go join the others," she continued, her directive leaving no room for dissent or hesitation among the men. The clarity and strength of her command reinforced her leadership, setting the next actions firmly in motion.

Although reluctant, the marked soldiers obeyed. With hesitation evident in their movements, they began to step forward, filtering through the lines of the Aranstream troops as they made their way towards the front, just as Kaitlin had instructed. A heavy silence hung over the group, each man keenly aware of the scrutiny and consequences that awaited them. Despite their visible discomfort and unease, not one among them dared to challenge or resist her command.

As the scene unfolded, Keltor observed with genuine respect. Watching the marked soldiers comply under Kaitlin's authoritative presence, he spoke with sincere admiration, "My Queen." His words were a clear acknowledgement of her leadership and the strength she had displayed. Turning to meet his gaze, Kaitlin allowed a smile to form on her lips, her expression reflecting both gratitude and confidence in response to his praise.

Keltor turned his attention to the man sprawled on the ground before him. With a firm tone, he issued a command: "You as well," instructing the man to stand and join the others. The man hesitated only briefly, casting a wary glance in their direction before slowly rising to his feet. As he walked forward, his movements suggested compliance, but in an instant, he broke free, attempting a desperate escape across the field.

Reacting with remarkable speed, Kaitlin spun around and raised her hand, clearly intending to halt the escaping man with her magic. Before she could act, however, Keltor intervened. With a gentle but firm gesture, he reached out and drew her arm back, silently communicating his intention. Shaking his head, he indicated his decision to let the man attempt his escape. "No, wait," Keltor murmured softly to Kaitlin, his quiet words making it clear that he wished to see how the situation would resolve itself without immediate intervention.

707

In the tense moment that followed, two additional men suddenly broke away from the group. Driven by fear and desperation, they dashed frantically towards the trees at the edge of the battlefield. Their hurried movements betrayed the panic that had taken hold in the aftermath of Kaitlin's powerful display of magic and the unmasking of the marked soldiers. The urgency of their flight underscored the atmosphere of confusion and dread now gripping those who remained.

As the Elvendon troops readied themselves to pursue the fleeing men, Keltor stepped forward, his presence commanding immediate attention. His voice rang out across the field, firm and resolute: "Soldiers, let them go." The effect was instantaneous; the disciplined warriors halted in their tracks, abandoning the chase without hesitation. All eyes turned to Keltor as he raised his hand, a clear signal for them to stand down and await further instruction.

With the Elvendon forces now withdrawn, Keltor shifted his focus to Kailan, the mighty dragon waiting expectantly nearby. Reaching out telepathically, he conveyed his decision: "*Kailan, they're yours.*" The words were both a relinquishment of responsibility and an act of trust, transferring the fate of the fugitives into the dragon's formidable hands. Kailan's response carried a touch of humour and anticipation: "*Finally, a snack.*" With this, the dragon prepared to fulfil his role, while the men continued their desperate sprint for freedom.

A smirk spread across Keltor's lips as he watched the majestic dragon, Kailan, ascend into the sky. The moment was striking—wielding influence over such a formidable beast was an experience that continued to feel almost surreal. As Kailan's powerful wings beat against the air, a forceful downdraft swept through the ranks of soldiers below, causing all present to raise their eyes and fix their gaze on the dragon's awe-inspiring silhouette overhead.

In a matter of seconds, Kailan was airborne, soaring high above the men who were desperately attempting to escape across the open terrain. The fugitives, sensing the ominous presence above, glanced upwards. Their faces were contorted in terror as they saw the enormous shadow cast by the dragon, looming over them with undeniable menace.

The two fleeing men, their faces etched with terror, made a desperate attempt to save themselves. In a last, hopeless act, they flung their arms over their heads, trying in vain to ward off what was to come. Above them, Kailan loomed, his massive wings casting a shadow across the field. With a single, decisive motion, the dragon unleashed a torrent of fire. The blazing flames engulfed the men instantly, consuming them utterly until all that remained was a scatter of ash blowing across the grass. The display left no doubt as to the futility of their escape and the absolute power held by the mighty dragon.

Kailan, having already dealt with the first two fugitives, now turned his attention to the third man—the one previously struck by Keltor. With precision and ferocity, the dragon swooped down, seizing the man effortlessly in his powerful jaws. In a fluid motion, Kailan banked to the left, tossing the remainder of the man's body further into his mouth before biting down with a decisive crunch. In moments, the deed was done; the man was swallowed whole by the dragon, leaving no trace behind.

Keltor took in the scene before him, watching as the Aranstream army reacted to the events unfolding on the battlefield. The grim atmosphere on the field was unmistakable. Among the enemy soldiers, faces revealed a palpable blend of fear and anxiety. Their eyes darted nervously from Kaitlin to Keltor, acutely aware of the power and authority now arrayed against them. Shoulders tensed and jaws clenched, they stood rooted to the spot, unable to mask the dread that had overtaken them in the wake of the dragon's devastating attack and the unrelenting display of magical prowess. The sense of impending judgement weighed heavily, leaving many unable to disguise the turmoil raging within. The display of power had clearly shaken their resolve, leaving them subdued and cautious. Observing the palpable fear now gripping the remaining prisoners, Keltor recognised the powerful impact such terror could have. He understood that this deep-seated dread, brought about by the swift and merciless fate of the fleeing men, could serve as a deterrent against further acts of defiance or violence. Reassured by this, Keltor allowed himself a measure of relief, hoping that the severity of their actions would be enough to prevent future bloodshed and spare innocent lives from needless loss.

As the aftermath of the dragon's devastating assault lingered on the battlefield, a sudden intrusion into Keltor's thoughts brought an unexpected shift in mood. The familiar, comical voice of Erandril echoed telepathically in Keltor's mind. *"Wow, how come he gets all the fun!"* Erandril quipped, his tone light and teasing despite the grimness surrounding them. The remark drew a genuine chuckle from Keltor, momentarily lifting the tension that had gripped him.

Glancing over his shoulder, Keltor found his dragon companion standing vigil behind the Elvendon lines—majestic and imposing, ever ready to defend their forces. Responding with a quiet amusement that only Erandril could hear, Keltor replied mentally, *"Maybe next time, Erandril."*

Out loud, Erandril released a deep, resonant sound that to Keltor was unmistakably laughter. However, to the already terrified Aranstream soldiers, it was interpreted as a fearsome roar. The thunderous, guttural noise rolled across the field, sending a renewed wave of dread rippling through the enemy ranks. Soldiers flinched and shrank back, their fear magnified by what they believed to be the dragon's anger, while only Keltor and Erandril shared the secret of the jest. Not far off, Forde chuckled as he heard Erandril's laughter ripple across the field—a sound that sent even their own soldiers recoiling in alarm at the presumed wrath of the dragon. Alongside him, Sharelle, ever perceptive, turned with a curious glance. "Why are you laughing?" she asked, her voice low, for as a dragon rider she could understand her own Ayver but not the others. Forde turned, amusement lightening his features. "Erandril is laughing. Clearly, he found Kailan's meal of that soldier highly entertaining." Sharelle responded with a gentle smile, her hand finding Forde's arm.

"He obviously hasn't lost his sense of humour," he said, his mind reaching back to memories of Erandril's playful nature during their days together in Malgar. Forde leaned into her touch, offering her a grateful nod as his fatigue from standing so long began to take its toll. "We'll see them both soon," Sharelle offered with quiet reassurance, "when Keltor and Kaitlin have finished whatever this is." Drawn close by uncertainty, they found reassurance in each other while watching their son and his Queen prepare for what would come next.

Meanwhile, the tension lingered, threading through every rank, until a sudden burst of laughter shattered the hush—Keltor turned towards the source, his gaze landing on Esendil, who stood close by. Cradled securely in Esendil's arms was baby Logie, the infant's small form held with gentle but unwavering care. Catching his brother's eye, Esendil offered a wry observation on the fate of the man who had been devoured by Kailan. "He got his comeuppance," he remarked, his tone tinged with satisfaction at the justice that had been served.

Keltor, sharing in the sentiment, met Esendil's gaze and responded with a broad grin of his own. "He sure did," Keltor replied, their brief exchange an unspoken acknowledgement of shared understanding. Amidst the chaos and gravity of the battlefield, this moment between the brothers stood out—a small but meaningful instance of camaraderie and mutual reassurance.

Kaitlin stood transfixed, her unwavering gaze fixed upon Kailan, the formidable dragon. The awe she experienced in the presence of such power was balanced by a determined sense of purpose. Witnessing Kailan devour the fugitive, Kaitlin felt no pang of pity; her resolve held firm, fully aware of the atrocities those men had perpetrated against the innocent. In her eyes, their demise was nothing more than justice—swift and deserved.

Her thoughts momentarily wandered to her earliest days in Elvendon, recalling a time when she was vastly different: young, innocent, and fearful of all that was unknown. The memory caused her to pause, taking a steady breath as she anchored herself in the strength she had since cultivated.

With composure restored, Kaitlin redirected her attention to the remaining prisoners. The atmosphere was tense, fraught with anticipation, but she confronted it not as the once frightened newcomer, but as a steadfast witness to retribution. Prepared for whatever would follow, Kaitlin stood ready, embodying the fortitude demanded by the moment.

Kaitlin took a resolute step forward, her voice unwavering as she addressed the assembled prisoners. "Your King murdered my father and my sister, and you are all guilty of violent, sickening atrocities against the people of Elvendon," she declared, her words ringing out over the silent field. Her anger was clear; every syllable laced with the weight of injustice suffered by her people.

"We show you the same mercy you showed our people. None," she continued, spitting the words with contempt. With her statement made, she turned sharply to face Keltor, her king, signalling that she had said all that needed to be said and awaited his judgement on the fate of those before them.

Keltor stepped forward, his posture commanding as he addressed the assembled prisoners. His presence alone demanded attention, and the field grew silent as all eyes turned towards him.

His voice, cold and resolute, carried across the silent ranks. "Death is too good for you," he declared, every word deliberate and laden with judgement. The air seemed to thicken as the weight of his pronouncement settled over the prisoners, who stood motionless, gripped by dread. "Instead, you will be punished for an eternity." Keltor drew in a deep breath and spread his arms wide, summoning the deepest reserves of his formidable magic.

"*Ego invocabo fons. Aperi portal ad Etendor,*" Keltor chanted, his hands moving in a swirling motion. Light crackled and spat as powerful magic erupted from his hands, sending sharp bursts of illumination through the thick, heavy air. The acrid scent of ozone filled the field, prickling nostrils and heightening the sense of imminent danger. As Keltor repeated the incantation louder, the magic intensified and a chilling wind swept through the ranks, making the prisoners shiver in fear.

Dark mist began to coil from Keltor's hands, snaking around his body and spilling outwards, its tendrils twisting and reaching hungrily towards the ground and the frightened onlookers. The energy pulsed with a sinister rhythm, casting shadows that seemed to writhe, threatening to engulf anyone who stood too close. The air was thick with tension and the unmistakable scent of magic, as the mist enveloped Keltor, lending him an almost otherworldly, terrifying presence that sent a shudder through all who watched.

Sharelle clung tightly to Forde's arm, her voice barely above a whisper. "Forde, what's happening to him?" she asked, her eyes wide with fear and confusion as she observed the unfolding display of raw magical energy.

Forde's expression was grave as he watched Keltor. "He's using the amulet. Sharelle, I have never seen anything like it, his power is intense. I couldn't do this," he admitted quietly, the worry evident in his tone. "And I had years of training."

Still seeking understanding, Sharelle pressed him further. "What do you mean, what's he doing?"

Forde's gaze remained fixed on Keltor, awe and concern mingling in his features. "I think he is opening a portal," he replied, the words hanging heavily in the charged air.

"*Ego invocabo fons. Aperi portal ad Etendor.*" Keltor continued, his voice echoing with authority as the spell intensified. Suddenly, a massive booming sound swept across the field, reverberating through the tense silence and signalling the unleashing of powerful magic. Above them, a large, ominous black portal began to materialise, its swirling darkness casting a foreboding shadow over everyone present.

Keltor's eyes glowed an unsettling black as his hands moved decisively forward, channelling the potent energies required for the ritual. He drew upon the raw power of the portal, harnessing its force like a raging tornado until the swirling vortex descended and touched down at ground level. With unwavering control, Keltor held the portal open, its terrifying energy spiralling and crackling in the air, a stark manifestation of his formidable magical abilities.

Kaitlin watched Keltor intently, unable to contain her astonishment at the extraordinary display of magic before her eyes. The sheer strength and magnitude of his power left her utterly speechless, her heart racing wildly with adrenaline. It was, without question, the most remarkable and awe-inspiring spectacle she had ever witnessed in her life.

What made the moment even more profound was the realisation that this immense power emanated from Keltor, the man she cherished above all else. As he glanced in her direction, their eyes met in a brief, meaningful exchange. Keltor gave her a reassuring nod, and she returned the gesture, silently acknowledging the significance of the moment and the deep connection they shared.

Kaitlin stepped forward, her voice ringing out across the field as she addressed the gathered crowd of roughly two hundred people. She pointed with authority towards the ominous, swirling mass of darkness that marked the portal's entrance.

"All of you," Kaitlin commanded, her tone leaving no room for argument. "Into the portal, now!"

The assembled group hesitated, fear evident in their eyes. Many instinctively shook their heads, unwilling to approach the terrifying spectacle before them. The air was thick with apprehension, and uncertainty rippled through the crowd as they grappled with the prospect of stepping into the unknown.

Kaitlin turned to Commander Talbot, her voice steady and composed despite the chaos surrounding them. "Commander Talbot, would you mind?" she asked, addressing him with authority and calm assurance. Her request was clear, signalling for his assistance in managing the crowd and enforcing her command.

The Commander bowed respectfully to Kaitlin, acknowledging her authority and the gravity of the situation. Straightening with renewed determination, he withdrew his sword, its blade gleaming in the dim light cast by the swirling portal. Turning to face his men, he issued a clear, commanding order: "With me."

Without hesitation, the Commander began to shepherd the selected Aranstream soldiers towards the ominous vortex. His presence and unwavering resolve left no room for dissent, as he ensured each soldier moved steadily forward, guiding them towards the darkness of the portal and the uncertain fate that awaited beyond.

"You'll pay for this!" one of the men yelled at Kaitlin.

Kailan let out a fierce roar, causing the man to stumble backward in fear before he hurried toward the porta

"I doubt it," Kaitlin replied, standing firm, and with her head held high as she watched all the men, and lastly Shona, step into the portal.

Keltor raised his voice, calling out, "*Prope in porta!*" as he brought his hands together with a resounding clap. In that instant, the swirling mass of darkness that formed the portal abruptly vanished, the black vortex sealing shut and leaving nothing but empty space where it had once loomed.

Silence settled over the battlefield as Keltor paused to draw a deep, steadying breath. He turned towards Kaitlin, offering her one of his signature, heart-melting smiles. The look alone sent Kaitlin's heart fluttering, a wave of emotion washing over her as he approached.

"We did it, Kitcat," Keltor said, his gaze locking with hers, holding her eyes in a moment that seemed to stretch on forever.

"We did," Kaitlin whispered in reply, her voice barely audible. She let her eyes flutter closed as Keltor's hand gently lifted to her cheek. Then, with a tenderness that spoke of shared triumph and deep affection, he leaned in and kissed her.

They both jumped, startled, as the Elvendon army suddenly erupted into a chorus of cheers, the triumphant noise echoing powerfully across the battlefield. Keltor and Kaitlin could not help but laugh at the sight, turning to watch their soldiers. The army, overjoyed by the victory, leapt and celebrated, their spirits visibly lifted as they rejoiced together in the aftermath of the struggle.

Esendil approached the group, a wide grin spreading across his face as he stepped forward. In his arms, he carefully cradled little Logie, whom he now offered to Kaitlin with a flourish. Bowing respectfully, he said, "I believe this belongs to you, my Queen."

Kaitlin accepted the child with gratitude, gently taking Logie from Esendil and holding the baby close to her chest. "Yes, he does," she replied warmly, her voice filled with relief and affection. "Thank you."

As she cuddled Logie, Kaitlin looked to Esendil and added, "And Esendil."

Esendil responded with a respectful dip of his head, "Yes, my Queen."

Seeing the continued formality, Kaitlin offered him a gentle smile and said, "You don't have to keep bowing to me. We're family."

Esendil laughed softly, his quiet amusement matching the joy that filled the air around them. He nodded in wholehearted agreement, his features relaxing into an easy expression of camaraderie. The warmth of victory and relief was evident in his posture as he turned towards Keltor, his eyes shining with excitement and admiration.

"Brother," Esendil exclaimed, his voice brimming with enthusiasm, "that was fricking awesome!"

Keltor's grin widened, his eyebrows lifting in playful acknowledgement of their shared triumph. "It was, wasn't it?" he replied, his voice brimming with pride. Without hesitation, Keltor reached out, pulled Esendil into a hearty embrace, and affectionately ruffled his brother's hair.

For once, Esendil did not protest the gesture. Instead, he simply basked in the warmth of Keltor's embrace, overwhelmed with gratitude and relief that they had both survived. In that moment, the bond between the brothers felt stronger than ever, forged anew by the trials they had faced and the victory they now celebrated together.

Keltor turned abruptly as a tremor rippled through the ground beneath him, prompting him to release his hold on Esendil. The source of the disturbance soon became clear—Erandril was striding purposefully towards the line of Elvendon soldiers. Although the troops were aware that the dragon was an ally, their earlier cheering came to an immediate halt. Uncertainty spread through the ranks, causing many of the soldiers to instinctively retreat from the dragon's imposing presence.

Esendil, observing the scene and noticing his father leaning on Sharelle for support as he moved towards Erandril, turned to Keltor in bewilderment. "Keltor, where the hell did you get dragons from?" he asked, his tone marked by astonishment.

Keltor, his gaze fixed on the dragon and his father, replied without looking away. "I'll tell you later," he said, clearly intent on witnessing the unfolding moment.

Kaitlin, curiosity etched on her face, gently placed her hand on Keltor's arm. "What's he doing?" she asked quietly.

Keltor replied, "That's Erandril. He was—well, still is, I guess—my father's dragon. Come on." He took her hand in his, and together they made their way towards his parents.

Kaitlin's eyes widened in disbelief as she turned to Keltor, her brow arching in surprise. "Your father's dragon?" she asked, the incredulity clear in her voice. Keltor met her gaze, a broad grin spreading across his face as he nodded, the pride and excitement evident in his expression.

As they approached, Forde greeted the dragon warmly, saying, "*Erandril, my dear friend.*" The genuine smile that spread across Forde's face brought tears to Keltor's eyes, for he knew that only he and his father could truly understand the dragon's words. To everyone else, Erandril's deep voice sounded like little more than low, rumbling growls.

Erandril halted in front of Forde, his gaze warm and affectionate as he looked upon his old friend. The dragon's deep voice, tinged with fondness, rumbled, "*My, you are a skinny wretch.*"

Forde responded with a gentle nod, a soft smile touching his lips. "*That I am, my friend,*" he replied, his tone filled with gratitude and familiarity.

With a sense of reverence, Forde released his hold on Sharelle. Slowly, he lifted his hands to Erandril's great head. Together, man and dragon pressed their foreheads together, closing their eyes as

717

they reconnected in a silent, powerful exchange—an ancient bond rekindled, their energies flowing between them once more.

Watching this intimate moment from nearby, Keltor turned to Kaitlin, awe clear on his face. "Kaitlin, I can't believe this is happening. My parents were dragon riders. Isn't that insane?"

Kaitlin, equally moved, leaned in close and whispered, "No more than mine being a King and a Syronic Witch." Her words brought a broad grin to Keltor's face, and with a surge of affection, he drew his arm around her and the baby, holding his family close as they witnessed the extraordinary reunion.

Erandril lowered his head, his eyes full of compassion as he addressed Forde. "*Let me heal you, my friend,*" the dragon offered, his voice resonating with warmth and concern. Forde, understanding the gravity of the moment, took a hesitant step back from Erandril. With a weary nod, and leaning heavily on his staff for support, he slowly lowered himself to his knees, showing both trust and vulnerability in front of his old companion.

Watching the scene unfold, Kaitlin's brow furrowed with worry. She leaned in towards Keltor, her voice laced with concern. "Hey, what's he doing?" she asked, unable to hide her anxiety for Forde's wellbeing.

Keltor turned to her, trying to reassure her though he could not conceal his own uncertainty. "He said, he's going to heal him," Keltor translated, relaying Erandril's intent.

Kaitlin, still uneasy, lowered her voice to a whisper. "How?" she pressed, seeking clarity.

Keltor shook his head, admitting quietly, "I don't know." Despite his attempt at reassurance, it was clear that he too was anxious about what was to come.

Suddenly, a voice echoed in Keltor's mind, addressing him with respect, "*My King.*" Both he and Kaitlin turned, searching for the source, and saw Kailan approaching. Kailan, calm and reassuring, explained, "*Do not fear, they share a bond. Erandril will restore your father's strength and heal his wounds, drawing upon his own life force.*"

718

Concerned, Keltor turned to his dragon and asked, *"Will it hurt either of them?"*

Kailan responded with gentle confidence, *"No, no, they will be fine, you'll see."*

Trusting in the ancient connection that existed between dragon and rider, Forde committed himself fully to the process, lowering his body to the ground in preparation. Erandril, moving with remarkable gentleness despite his immense size, carefully lifted his enormous foot and placed it delicately over Forde. This was the beginning of the healing ritual, a sacred act that spoke of deep trust and centuries-old tradition between them.

The dragon let out a thunderous roar, so deafening that everyone instinctively clamped their hands over their ears— everyone except Keltor. While others were overwhelmed by the sheer volume, Keltor alone could discern that the roar was not merely a display of power, but a chant, ancient and purposeful. He listened intently, recognising the significance of the moment.

As the chant continued, Keltor watched in awe as a surge of energy radiated from the dragon, channelling through his massive foot and flowing directly into Forde. Instantly, Forde's entire body was enveloped in a bluish white glow. The magical light wrapped around him completely, illuminating the scene with an ethereal brilliance. For several minutes, the spectacle continued, the glow unwavering, until finally the magic subsided and the radiant light gently faded away.

Erandril gently withdrew his foot from above Forde, marking the end of the healing ritual. For several minutes, Keltor observed anxiously, his concern evident as he watched for any sign of recovery. Then, at last, Forde's eyes fluttered open and he sat up, alert and revitalised.

As Forde rose to his feet unaided—without needing support from his wife or his trusty staff—Keltor let out a relieved sigh. It was clear that the restoration had worked; Forde's muscles appeared robust once more, and the weariness that had lined his face was gone. Though he remained the same age, he had regained his former vitality. He stood tall, strong and muscular, a broad grin spreading across his face, fully himself again.

"*Thank you, my friend*," Forde said, his voice thick with emotion as he wrapped his arms around his dragon's massive neck. Erandril responded with gentle affection, nuzzling his broad snout against Forde, the two sharing a moment of deep connection and gratitude after the profound healing ritual they had just experienced.

"*You are welcome, Forde. It's been a long time*," Erandril replied, his tone warm and full of relief, the words resonating with the weight of years spent apart.

Forde smiled, his eyes glistening as he held onto his dragon. "*It has, my friend, it has. I have missed you so much.*" The bond between them was unmistakable, their reunion a testament to the loyalty and friendship that had endured through hardship and separation.

Sharelle's heart swelled with emotion as she watched her husband, Forde, reunited with his dragon, Erandril. Witnessing the embrace between Forde and Erandril—their bond renewed and strengthened after the healing ritual—filled Sharelle with a profound sense of joy and gratitude.

Suddenly, Sharelle heard a familiar female voice call her name, drawing her attention away from the touching scene between her husband and his dragon. Turning, she found herself face to face with her own beloved dragon, Ayver. Overcome with feeling and barely able to contain her tears, Sharelle approached Ayver, moved by the reunion and the strength of their enduring connection.

Ayver lowered her massive head, bringing her forehead gently down to meet Sharelle's. The two shared a tender moment, pressing their foreheads together in a gesture of reconnection and mutual affection. The air between them was charged with the deep bond that had always existed between dragon and rider.

"*I can't believe you're here; I have missed you so much,*" Sharelle whispered, wrapping her arms around Ayver's neck in a heartfelt embrace.

Ayver responded softly, her words full of warmth and reassurance. "*And I you*," she replied, reaffirming the unbreakable connection they shared.

Kaitlin called out, her voice clear and authoritative, "Commander Talbot." She addressed the head of the army with purpose, capturing the attention of those nearby.

Commander Talbot responded promptly, striding over to Kaitlin. Upon reaching her, he bent the knee in a gesture of respect and placed his hand across his heart. "Your highness," he greeted her solemnly as he rose to stand before her.

Without hesitation, Kaitlin gave her command. "Commander, please can you divide your army, and bring half with us. We're going to take back our castle," she announced, determination ringing in her voice as she set forth her intentions for the next stage of their campaign.

Keltor turned to the commander, her tone steady and resolute. "Commander, Erandril and my father will remain here with the other half of the army. If you could please organise and disarm the Aranstream army, I would be most grateful," she instructed, her authority clear in her words.

The commander bowed his head respectfully in response. "Yes, my Lady, my Lord," he replied, acknowledging both Kaitlin and Keltor before moving swiftly to carry out her orders.

"I won't be a minute, I just need a quick word with mum and dad," Keltor said softly, gently releasing Kaitlin's hand before turning away. He walked over to where his parents stood waiting, and they welcomed him into their embrace. Watching this tender reunion, Kaitlin felt her heart swell with affection for Keltor and his family. Yet, beneath the warmth, she could not help but feel a pang of sorrow for herself, mourning the loss of her own loved ones and the emptiness their absence had left behind.

"Hey," a voice called from behind Kaitlin, prompting her to turn swiftly on her heel. Relief and warmth washed over her as she recognised Esimae. Despite everything that had happened, Kaitlin realised she hadn't lost everyone—her wonderful aunt was still by her side.

Esimae glanced at the baby in Kaitlin's arms and offered, "Shall I take him?"

"Oh, yes, please. Probably shouldn't take him with us, just yet," Kaitlin replied gratefully, carefully handing little Logie over to her aunt's waiting arms.

Once Logie was settled, Esimae looked at Kaitlin with pride and affection. "Kaitlin," she said softly.

"Yes?" Kaitlin responded, sensing something important in her aunt's tone.

"Well done, that really was bloody amazing, what you both did. Especially saving this little one. But I don't understand where all this power is coming from—I have never known a witch, even a Syronic, to have so much power?" Esimae admitted, her voice tinged with both awe and curiosity.

Esimae's question hung in the air, her eyes filled with a mixture of pride and curiosity. Kaitlin met her gaze, her expression earnest as she explained, "Esimae, it comes from the earth. I can draw on earth's power. Something happened to me yesterday. Keltor was fatally wounded, and I begged the spirits for help, and they did. They gave me more magic."

Hearing this, Esimae reached out and placed a comforting hand on Kaitlin's arm, gently rubbing it in support. She offered a warm, reassuring smile. "Your mother and Richard would be so proud of you, as am I," she said softly, her words filled with affection and encouragement.

At the mention of her parents, Kaitlin felt a wave of emotion. She pressed her lips together, fighting back tears, and nodded in gratitude to her aunt, silently acknowledging the strength she drew from her family's love and legacy.

Chapter Thirty-Three
Taking Back Elvendon Castle

Keltor hurried over to Kaitlin, his expression determined yet hopeful. "Okay, ready to go?" he asked, searching her face for any sign of hesitation. Kaitlin met his gaze and nodded confidently.

"Yes, let's go and take back our Queendom," she replied, her eyes sparkling with resolve and excitement.

Keltor then explained their next step. "We're going to ride on Kailan, are you okay with that?" he asked, wanting to ensure she was comfortable with the plan.

Although the idea of riding atop a dragon made Kaitlin both excited and nervous, she nodded in agreement, embracing the adventure that lay ahead. Keltor reached out, taking her hand in his, and gave it a gentle, reassuring squeeze. Together, they walked towards Kailan, ready to face whatever awaited them.

The battlefield that sprawled before Elvendon castle bore the marks of both conflict and transformation. Where chaos might once have reigned, there was now an uneasy calm: remnants of the Aranstream army stood in scattered clusters, their armour dulled by exhaustion and surrender. Broken banners lay tangled among discarded swords, and the hush of anticipation rippled through the air as dragons—majestic and imposing—cast long shadows across the trampled grass.

Kailan lowered himself gracefully to his knees, allowing Kaitlin and Keltor to approach. Together, they climbed up onto the dragon's broad back, settling themselves securely as they straddled him. As they prepared for the journey ahead, Kaitlin gently tugged on her husband's arm to get his attention. Keltor turned to look over his shoulder at her, curiosity written on his face.

"Look," she said quietly, directing his gaze by pointing towards Ayver.

Sharelle sat tall upon Ayver, her sword jutting up behind her, a striking figure amidst the gathering. Keltor's gaze drifted to Erandril; his father was already mounted on Erandril's back, with his brother seated securely behind him. In that moment, as he took in the sight of his family—each member poised and ready, united in purpose—Keltor was filled with a deep sense of pride. It was a pride that encompassed not only his parents and brother but also his new wife, whose courage and resolve stood equal with them all.

Keltor turned towards Kaitlin, the tension of the moment softened by a gentler emotion. "I love you," he said quietly, his voice steady but full of feeling.

Kaitlin responded with equal warmth, her own feelings shining in her eyes. "I love you too," she replied, her words a comfort amidst the uncertainty surrounding them. She reached up, her hand cupping his cheek tenderly. For a lingering moment, Keltor leaned into her touch, drawing strength and reassurance from her presence before finally facing forward, ready to meet whatever awaited them.

The dragon rose to his feet, his powerful muscles rippling beneath shimmering scales as he moved forward with measured confidence. Behind him, Sharelle followed astride Ayver, the pair presenting an awe-inspiring spectacle against the backdrop of the battered battlefield. Seated tall and proud, Sharelle's presence atop the dragon radiated authority and grace.

As Keltor watched his mother, he was struck by how naturally she fitted the role of a dragon rider. In that moment, his perspective shifted—Sharelle was no longer just his mother in his eyes. She stood before him as an individual, courageous and strong, her own person deserving of respect. Now, she rode not only as his mother but as a champion for the Queen and King of

Elvendon, embodying the spirit and unity that bound their family and their people together.

Rows of disciplined soldiers advanced across the fields towards Elvendon castle, joined by civilians who had been prepared to stand beside their Queen and King should the need arise. The procession, led by Belrack and his men, displayed unity and resolve—a testament to the strength and spirit of those who had endured hardship and now pressed forward together toward their home and the castle that awaited them.

Word of the attack on Aranstream, along with the deaths of both its prince and king, travelled quickly, reaching the people of Elvendon even before their army returned. The news cast a heavy shadow across the village, leaving many filled with apprehension, especially with the dragons' approach. At first, fear kept the villagers at bay, uncertainty writ large on their faces as the formidable creatures drew closer.

However, as Kaitlin and Keltor, came into view, the mood shifted. Drawn by the sight of the mysterious new Queen and King of Elvendon, the villagers—mainly women, children, and a handful of elders—ventured out from their homes, curiosity and awe mingling on their faces. Relief mingled with anxiety as they hurried to greet the returning soldiers, each person's gaze scanning the ranks for loved ones whom many hadn't seen for months or even known if they were still alive. The crowd pressed forward along the castle approach, their faces etched with hope and worry, hearts pounding as they searched for familiar figures among the weary troops. Tears threatened at the sight of a husband, a brother, or a child, while for others, the absence of a beloved face brought a fresh wave of dread. The air was filled with whispered names and the soft, desperate calls of families hoping for joyful reunions, all underscored by the uncertainty of what news the soldiers might bear.

Yet, in those precious moments, the promise of reunion and the relief of survival carried the villagers through, even as anxiety lingered on the edge of every smile and embrace. Brief, heartfelt reunions took place in the growing throng, though the moment for celebration was fleeting. The men, resolute and purposeful, quickly prepared to follow their Queen and King, their focus set firmly on the path that still lay ahead.

Keltor and Kaitlin approached the castle gates with caution, their senses heightened by the tense atmosphere. Inside the courtyard, they were met with a striking sight: Aranstream soldiers knelt in orderly rows, heads bowed low, their weapons carefully stacked in a pile before them—a clear signal of surrender.

Keltor brought Kailan to a halt, taking in the scene. He exchanged a glance with Kaitlin, his voice tinged with hope as he spoke. "They've surrendered."

Despite the apparent submission of the enemy, Kaitlin's instincts urged vigilance. "Be careful—it could be a trap," she warned quietly. Keltor acknowledged her concern with a nod, his expression serious.

He slid down from Kailan's back and extended a steadying hand to Kaitlin as she dismounted. As her feet touched the ground, he caught her securely in his arms. "Ready?" he asked, searching her eyes for confirmation. Kaitlin nodded, determination set on her face, and together they prepared to face whatever awaited them within the castle walls.

As they continued forward, Belrack and his men moved purposefully, forming a protective circle around Kaitlin and Keltor. Their presence was reassuring, a visible shield against any sudden threat. When the group reached the assembled soldiers, they came to a halt, tension hanging in the air despite the apparent surrender.

Kaitlin took a step forward, her voice steady as she addressed the group. "Who is in charge here?" she demanded, her keen eyes scanning the faces before her. Though the soldiers appeared to have submitted, she could sense an underlying uncertainty among them.

After a brief pause, a man stepped out from the centre of the group, his posture erect and confident. Yet, as his eyes wandered to the dragon, Kailan, standing behind Keltor, a flicker of doubt betrayed his composure. He swallowed fearfully; the tales of dragons having reached him before—though he hadn't truly believed them. He'd dismissed them as the Elvendon's attempt to frighten and intimidate his men with wild rumours. Nor was he convinced that his king had truly fallen.

He met Kaitlin's gaze directly as he answered, "I am."

Keltor, adopting a tone of quiet authority, followed up with a question of his own. "And your name?"

"My name is Ezra. I'm head guard," the man replied without hesitation, his voice clear and unwavering.

Kaitlin stepped forward from behind Belrack, her presence commanding the group's attention as she addressed the man before her. "Ezra, are you surrendering? Your king and prince have both fallen." Her words hung heavily in the air; the weight of recent events clear in her tone.

The assembled men tensed, uncertainty and apprehension written across their faces. Sensing the rising tension, Keltor remained vigilant, his gaze sweeping over the castle walls and peering into the shadowed windows for any sign of danger. He moved closer to Kaitlin, adopting a protective stance beside her.

"Exercise caution," he murmured quietly, his voice a warning meant only for her ears.

Refusing to be deterred, Kaitlin pressed her question with greater authority, her tone sharpening. "Well, answer me?" she demanded, her eyes locked on Ezra, awaiting his response.

"Never!" the man exclaimed abruptly. At this signal, he and his companions swiftly stood, drawing their swords and raising their bows as they advanced toward Kaitlin and Keltor.

Keltor, sensing the imminent threat, urgently projected his command in his mind. "*Burn them!*" he ordered Kailan, the great dragon who stood loyally at his side. At the same moment, he shouted to Kaitlin and Belrack, "Get down!"

Kaitlin, Belrack, and their men reacted instantly, dropping to the ground as instructed. Keltor moved swiftly, throwing himself over Kaitlin to shield her from the impending danger. Kailan, scales glinting in the daylight and wings partially unfurled, let out a deafening roar that echoed off the castle walls. As the advancing

Aranstream guards surged forward, Kailan unleashed a torrent of fire, the intense heat and blinding flames engulfing their foes completely. The roar of the dragon and the crackle of fire filled the courtyard, heightening the chaos and tension of the moment.

The heat radiating from Kailan's fiery breath was overwhelming, threatening to scorch everything in its path. Reacting swiftly, Kaitlin raised her voice in a steady incantation. *"Ensura protect,"* she chanted, her words weaving a shimmering barrier of magic that enveloped herself, Keltor, Belrack, and the surrounding men. The protective wave settled over them, instantly dispelling the searing heat and replacing it with a welcome coolness. Kaitlin exhaled slowly, relief washing over her as the oppressive warmth faded away, securing their safety as the fire burned.

Within moments, the Aranstream men were reduced to nothing but ash, the devastating power of Kailan's flames leaving no trace of their defiance. As the last echoes of the dragon's roar faded, Kaitlin allowed the shimmering shield of protection to dissipate. The magical barrier faded away, leaving Kaitlin, Keltor, and their companions to slowly rise from where they had taken shelter. They cautiously surveyed the aftermath, taking in the devastation left by the dragon's flames. The air was thick with the heavy scent of smoke and ash, swirling around them and mingling with the fading echoes of the battle. All around, the scorched remains of the courtyard bore silent witness to the ferocity of the encounter, and the group stood together in the uneasy stillness that followed.

Keltor broke the heavy silence that had settled over the courtyard. "Well, I guess that's it then," he remarked quietly, his voice carrying a sense of finality.

Kaitlin offered a subdued response, her gaze drifting over the destruction that now marked the place where their foes had stood. "Yeah, I guess," she replied, the shock and sorrow evident in her voice. "Why the hell would they do that, didn't they see we had a dragon?" Her words captured her disbelief at the senseless choice made by their enemies.

Keltor met her eyes, his expression steady but tinged with regret. "I guess they preferred to die, rather than surrender, and that was their choice, Kaitlin," he answered solemnly. "There was nothing more we could have done."

With a resigned sigh and a gentle nod, Kaitlin accepted his words, the reality of what had transpired settling over her and the group.

Suddenly, the quiet that had settled over the courtyard was broken by a wave of exuberant cheering from behind. Kaitlin and Keltor turned to witness the people and soldiers of Elvendon erupting in celebration, their voices rising in joyful relief at the end of the conflict. The sombre mood began to shift as women and children, previously hidden away in fear, emerged cautiously from their shelters, their faces lighting up with hope and happiness.

Families rushed together, arms outstretched, embracing one another with tearful joy. The bonds of love and friendship that had been strained by the battle were rekindled amidst the jubilant crowd. Kaitlin, moved by the sight, smiled through her tears, her heart swelling with emotion as she watched the people of Elvendon reunited with their loved ones. The sense of victory and togetherness filled the air, offering a stark contrast to the devastation that had just unfolded.

Keltor, his mind still focused on the safety of his people, turned towards Belrack with a clear directive. "Belrack, can you get some of the men to search the castle? I don't want anyone left in there who is from Aranstream," he commanded, his tone resolute amidst the aftermath of the battle.

Belrack inclined his head in acknowledgement, demonstrating his characteristic discipline and loyalty. Without hesitation, he moved to confer with his men and several of the soldiers nearby. After a brief exchange of words, Belrack gathered a small group and, with purposeful strides, led them towards the castle entrance, intent on carrying out Keltor's orders and ensuring that no Aranstream enemies remained hidden within its walls.

Tears streamed down Kaitlin's face as she looked at Keltor, barely able to speak through her emotion. "Is it really over?" she asked, her voice trembling with a mix of disbelief and hope.

Keltor turned to her, his features softening as the tension of the battle faded away. A gentle smile broke across his face, and he drew her close. "Yes, Kitcat, it's over," he replied, his tone tender and reassuring. He pressed a gentle, loving kiss to her lips, sealing his promise and offering comfort amidst the lingering sorrow.

As the atmosphere shifted from sorrow to celebration, a sudden voice pierced through the commotion. "Keltor!" called a young woman, her tone filled with urgency and emotion.

At the sound of his name, Keltor broke away from the moment, opening his eyes and instantly recognising the familiar voice. "Anna!" he exclaimed, turning quickly to see his little sister sprinting towards him. "Anna!" he cried again, overwhelmed with relief and happiness at the sight of her.

However, Anna came to an abrupt halt, her run interrupted by a startled scream. Keltor quickly realised the cause of her alarm— she had spotted Kailan, the dragon, looming behind him. With an amused chuckle, Keltor reassured her, "It's okay, Anna, the dragon is my friend."

Anna eyed Kailan warily, uncertainty clear on her face. Noticing her apprehension, Keltor spoke again, his voice gentle but confident. "It's okay, I promise, he won't hurt you," he insisted, hoping to soothe her fears.

As he approached, Keltor reached out and, upon reaching Anna, swept her up into his arms. He embraced her tightly, relief and love radiating from both siblings as they reunited amid the jubilant crowd.

"Thank the stars, are you okay?" Keltor asked, concern etched deeply in his voice as he gently set Anna back down onto the ground. Relief washed over him at seeing her unharmed.

"Yes, yes, I'm okay." Anna's voice broke as she buried her face in his shoulder. "Keltor, I thought you were dead. Mum said you were dead." Tears streamed down Anna's cheeks as she clung to Keltor, her body trembling with relief and disbelief. Keltor stroked her hair gently as he spoke. "I know, it's not her fault, she thought I was. I will tell you all about it later," he said pulling her tight against his chest.

Kaitlin gently placed her hand on Keltor's arm, prompting him to turn towards her. She greeted him with a warm smile, the affection between them evident.

Keltor then introduced Kaitlin to Anna, releasing his sister from their embrace. "Hey, Anna, this is Kaitlin, our new Queen," he announced, making the introduction official.

Anna responded with respect, dipping into a curtsy. "Your highness," she said, acknowledging Kaitlin's new role.

With a playful expression, Keltor raised his eyebrows at Anna. "Hey Anna, guess what?" he teased, keeping her in suspense.

Anna frowned, curious about what he would say next. Keltor slipped his arm around Kaitlin and declared proudly, "Kaitlin is also my wife—and your new sister-in-law." His grin reflected his happiness at sharing the news.

Anna stared at them in confusion. "What, for real? You got bonded?" she asked, trying to comprehend the revelation.

Kaitlin smiled and confirmed, "Yes, we did," as she leaned in to hug Keltor, visibly moved by the moment.

Anna's mind raced to connect the dots. "That's amazing, so, hang on, if she's the queen, then…"

Keltor finished the thought for her with a proud nod, "I'm the king."

Anna paused, processing the information before asking, "Does that mean I'm a princess, and I don't have to clean anymore?"

Keltor laughed, teasing her gently. "Anna, you're as bad as Ese. No, it means you will be a Lady of the realm, but yes, I guess you won't have to clean anymore."

Kaitlin joined in the laughter, enjoying the family's light-hearted banter and the sense of togetherness that filled the air.

Anna looked at Keltor, her eyes filled with concern. "Is Ese okay?" she asked, her voice quiet but urgent.

Keltor offered a reassuring smile. "Yeah, he's fine. He's with Mum and..." His words trailed off as he realised Anna was unaware of what had happened. He took a steadying breath, preparing to reveal the truth he had uncovered.

"Anna, there's something I have to tell you," he began, his tone serious. "It's about our dad."

Anna's brow furrowed in confusion. "Our dad?" she repeated, searching his face for answers.

Keltor nodded, a smile appearing on his lips as he delivered the news. "Yes. Anna, Dad is alive. He was being held all these years in a dungeon in Aranstream. I found him. He's with Ese."

Anna fell silent, taking a minute or two to let the revelation sink in. She struggled to recall her father, having been so young when he vanished, yet she cherished the few memories she had, always determined to keep them alive. Her mother often told her that Ese was the image of their father.

"For real, Keltor?" Anna's voice wavered between disbelief and hope.

"For real, Anna," he replied, nodding again in reassurance.

Overcome with emotion, Anna flung her arms around Kaitlin and Keltor, holding them both tightly.

Kaitlin struggled to hold back her tears, the intensity of her emotions almost too much to bear. Despite the pain of losing her own family, she found comfort in the new family she had gained with Keltor and his loved ones. The sense of belonging was strong, and she realised that she already cared deeply for each of them.

Chapter Thirty-Four
Three Months Later

"Where are we going?" Kaitlin asked, slipping her arm through his.

"It's a surprise," Keltor replied, a mischievous glint in his eyes as he guided the horse and cart along the winding path through the castle grounds. The atmosphere was thick with anticipation as they travelled down a long drive that Kaitlin had never explored before.

Unable to contain her curiosity, she pressed him again. "So, where are we going?"

He laughed at her impatience. "You'll see, in a minute."

With a sigh, Kaitlin let go of his arm and sat upright, her gaze fixed ahead. A set of towering gates soon came into view, their imposing size making them seem almost impenetrable. On either side, the high walls stretched far into the distance, fading from sight as they merged with the horizon. The trees beyond the wall concealed whatever lay inside, only adding to the intrigue and excitement of the moment.

"Keltor, what on earth is it?" Kaitlin begged, sitting forwards with curiosity. Her anticipation was clear as she tried to uncover the nature of Keltor's secret. "Is this where you kept sneaking off to?"

Keltor affirmed her suspicion with a simple, "Yep," though he still refused to give anything away, maintaining an air of mystery that both frustrated and excited her.

As their carriage approached the towering gates, Kaitlin noticed something unusual. "Why are there guards?" she inquired, observing the guard huts stationed on both sides of the gates within the castle grounds. Her curiosity grew as, in perfect synchronisation, a guard from each hut emerged, bowed respectfully, and opened the gates, allowing them to continue their journey.

Kaitlin glanced at the gates as they passed through, taking in their striking appearance—painted black and trimmed with gold, with her family's coat of arms proudly displayed at the centre of each one. The sight only deepened her confusion and anticipation.

"Seriously, what's going on?" she pleaded, spinning round to face Keltor. Her growing impatience was met with nothing but a broad grin from him, which did little to soothe her curiosity.

The drive continued, winding its way through the dense forest. Finally, through the trees ahead, Kaitlin spotted a cottage in the distance.

"Keltor, what the hell is that?" she burst out, unable to contain herself any longer. But Keltor remained silent, his refusal to answer only heightening her frustration and curiosity.

"Oh my god, it's beautiful," Kaitlin exclaimed as their carriage drew to a halt. Set before them was a charming, thatched cottage, its whitewashed walls gleaming softly in the dappled light. Four neat windows framed the facade, and a central door beckoned invitingly. The garden that surrounded the cottage was vibrant with flowers of every colour, their blooms spilling over the carefully tended beds and lending the air a sweet, lively fragrance. Encircling the entire property stood a pristine white picket fence, which gave the place the unmistakable air of an idyllic English countryside home.

Keltor brought the buggy to a stop and placed the reins down. "Wait," he said with a conspiratorial smile, quickly jumping down from his seat. He hurried round to Kaitlin's side and offered his hand to help her down. As she slipped gently into his arms, her eyes met his, filled with surprise and wonder.

"Welcome to our new home," Keltor said warmly, his heart swelling as he took in the astonishment written all over her face.

Still bewildered, Kaitlin echoed his words. "Our new home, I don't understand." Keltor smiled, taking her hand in his and gently guiding her towards the cottage's welcoming front door.

He turned the handle and opened the door.

"Wait," he said, and she squealed as he lifted her up into his arms and carried her through the door. Kaitlin burst into laughter, exclaiming, "Keltor, you're crazy!" Once inside, he gently set her back down, and she stood in awe, taking in the interior of the cottage. The room before them was stunning. Sturdy oak beams stretched across the ceiling, adding a rustic charm to the space. A roaring fireplace cast a warm glow, its crackling flames reflecting off the polished stone hearth. At the centre of the room lay a soft fur rug, inviting them to sink their toes into its plush surface. Comfortable sofas were arranged around the fire, creating a welcoming and cosy atmosphere that instantly felt like home.

"This is ours. I built it for you," Keltor explained, his voice gentle but full of pride. "You said you hated living in the palace, so I thought we could live here. We are still technically living in the castle, albeit the grounds. Or even if it's just at the weekends, or whenever. It's only on a couple of acres, but it's completely safe as I have placed a protection wall of magic all around it. There's a small lake as well, where we can swim."

Kaitlin's eyes widened in disbelief as she looked around the cottage. "Oh my god, Keltor, are you serious? This place is incredible," she gasped, her excitement evident. She quickly took in the spacious kitchen off to the side, admiring the large pine table surrounded by sturdy chairs, and her gaze swept to a room filled to the brim with books, each detail making the cottage feel more like a true home.

As Kaitlin wandered through the cottage, her emotions threatened to overwhelm her once more. "You've even put up some of my paintings," she murmured, her voice trembling with emotion as she took in the familiar artwork adorning the walls. Each piece was a reminder of her passions and dreams, lovingly showcased in this new home.

Keltor's eyes sparkled with delight as he nodded. "Yes, and out the back there is a workshop for you. I've set it up with all your arty stuff," he said, grinning at her reaction.

"For real?" Kaitlin gasped, tears trickling down her cheeks as she realised just how much thought he had put into every detail.

"Yep, and look—there's even a room for little Logie, for when he comes and stays with us," Keltor continued, opening a door to reveal a small, cosy bedroom. The room was thoughtfully decorated with playful animals, vibrant flowers, and fluttering butterflies, and in the corner stood a tiny cot, ready for their young guest.

He glanced at Kaitlin, mischief in his eyes. "Or, maybe one day, one of our own," he added with a wink. Kaitlin's eyes widened in surprise and a gentle smile played across her lips as she returned his look, feeling the promise and possibility of their future together.

Keltor noticed Kaitlin's sudden tears and gently asked, "Are you okay?" Overwhelmed by emotion, Kaitlin managed to reply, "Yes, I mean. Keltor, I love you so much, I just can't believe you have done this for me."

Keltor offered a comforting smile, understanding the depth of her feelings. "Hey, I know how much you miss that little fellow now he's living with his great aunt." At this, Kaitlin gave him a small nod, recalling the bittersweet decision they had made. It had been difficult when Seline requested to raise Logie on her farm, just outside the city. Though it was hard to let him go, they both recognised that Seline was Logie's blood family and had every right to ask for him.

Despite the change, Kaitlin and Keltor remained Logie's guardians and saw him every week. Often, Logie would stay with them, giving Seline a well-deserved break and allowing them to maintain their cherished bond with him.

"Come and see the bedroom," he said with a grin, eagerly grabbing her hand. "It's my favourite room."

Kaitlin stepped inside and gasped in delight. "Keltor, it's beautiful," she cried, her eyes immediately drawn to the elegant four-poster bed at the centre of the room. Above them, the roof was crafted from shimmering glass, allowing sunlight to stream through and scatter rainbows across the plush furs draped over the bed. She couldn't help but laugh with joy, spinning around in wonder as she gazed up at the dazzling glass dome overhead. "This is insane," she exclaimed, her laughter echoing softly through the magical space.

"Do you like it?" Keltor asked, bouncing onto the bed and reclining comfortably. He gestured upwards, a playful light in his eyes. "Look, when it's dark, we can lie here together and watch the stars. Or, if you like, during the day we can cloud watch and make up animals in the sky." He pointed excitedly towards the heavens visible through the glass dome. "Look, there's a satyr!"

Kaitlin's laughter filled the room, her delight echoing Keltor's enthusiasm. "Like it, I love it!" she exclaimed, flinging herself down beside him on the bed. As she gazed up, her hand shot out to point at a passing cloud. "A dragon!" she declared, her imagination sparked by the shifting shapes above them.

Keltor laughed, reaching across the bed until his hand found Kaitlin's. He took her hand in his own, holding it firmly, a gesture full of affection and reassurance. "I know it has been one hell of a year," he admitted, his voice warm yet tinged with the weight of their shared experiences. "These past few months—integrating Aranstream into Elvendon—have been incredibly stressful. I just wanted somewhere for us, away from all the rules and the restraints of being King and Queen. Somewhere we could simply be ourselves, like we were before all of this happened. We have been through so much together, Kitcat, and to be honest—" He paused, turning to look at her, the sincerity clear in his eyes.

Kaitlin's gaze drifted away from the glass dome above and came to rest on Keltor, her attention fully captured by the depth of feeling in his words and the strength of his presence beside her.

"I didn't think we would make it," Keltor confessed, his voice barely above a whisper. As he looked at Kaitlin, emotion threatened to overwhelm him, his love for her filling his heart to the brim.

Kaitlin met his gaze, her own feelings laid bare. "Neither did I, Keltor, and I'm not going to lie, it has been awful. Sometimes I thought I was going to go mad, but you make it all possible. You give me such strength to do things I would never have imagined I could, and I love you so much, my King."

A warmth spread across Keltor's features as he listened to her, moved by her honesty and devotion. "And I you, my Queen," he replied softly, lifting his hand to gently touch her face. Then, tenderly, he kissed her, sealing their shared understanding and love.

"Talking of dragons," Keltor said, his tone shifting slightly as he introduced a new subject. "I've been speaking with Kailan, and he and his King have agreed that he can come and live here and help protect the city."

At this, Kaitlin turned onto her side, moving closer to Keltor. Her hand rose gently and settled on his chest, a silent gesture of connection and support as she took in the significance of his words.

"That's amazing, but won't he be lonely without his other dragon clan?" Kaitlin asked, her brow creased with concern for her dragon friend's wellbeing.

Keltor nodded, understanding her worry. "I did ask that, so he's bringing a friend," he replied, offering reassurance.

Kaitlin's eyes widened in surprise, her initial concern shifting to curiosity and amusement. Then, with a laugh, she asked, "He's bringing a friend—who?"

Keltor shrugged. "I don't know, it's another young dragon though."

"Wow, that's so cool," Kaitlin breathed, her eyes lifting to the magnificent glass dome stretching above them. For a moment, she let herself be captivated by the shimmering patterns of light and the expanse of the sky beyond.

Keltor, sensing her wonder, leaned closer and whispered, "This is also cool." He gave her a quick, conspiratorial glance, a mischievous glint in his eye as he raised his hand towards the glass overhead.

With calm assurance, he began to chant, "*Estora, ilantra iluminara.*" As the ancient words left his lips, magic surged through the room. Kaitlin's eyes widened in astonishment as the glass above them gradually darkened, veiling the dome in a gentle shadow. Amid the darkness, a cascade of twinkling stars suddenly burst into view, illuminating the chamber with a soft and enchanting glow. The effect was breathtaking—transforming the space around them into a private universe, filled with the quiet brilliance of a thousand tiny lights.

"It's beautiful," she whispered. As she spoke, his bright blue eyes met hers, and in that gaze, she felt her heart swell with the love she held for him.

"Just like you, Kitcat," he replied tenderly. Gently, he pulled her into his arms—a place where she knew she would always be held and protected, now and forever.

The end

Thank you for reading my story!

If you want to read more of my fantasy adventures!

Please have a look at my website!

www.rosie-lynch.co.uk

rosellynch14@gmail.com

www.ingramcontent.com/pod-product-compliance
Lightning Source LLC
Chambersburg PA
CBHW072340030726

47505CB00013B/30

9 781739 570644